The Dark Dance

Lightning speared through the sky. Despite the closeness of the atmosphere, Gundersen felt a chill. He saw himself as a wanderer on a prehistoric Earth, spying on some grotesque conclave of mastodons. All the things of man seemed infinitely far away now. The drama was reaching some sort of climax. The nildoror were bellowing, stamping, calling to one another with tremendous snorts. They were taking up formations, assembling in aisled rows. Gundersen could no longer hear individual words, only rich deep chords of massed grunts, ah ah *ah* ah, ah ah *ah* ah, and the whole jungle seemed to echo with it.

And the nildoror were dancing.

The universe trembled. Gundersen saw the sulidoror entranced, hairy heads switching back and forth in the rhythm of the dance; but not one of the bipeds has risen from the cross-legged posture. They were content to rock and nod, and now and then to pound their elbows on the ground.

Gundersen was cut off from his own past, even from a sense of his own kinship to his species. Again he was at the serpent station, a prisoner of the hallucinatory venom, feeling himself transformed into a nildor and capering thickly in the grove. Tonight he felt little allegiance to mankind. He found himself longing to join that black and incomprehensible frenzy at the lakeshore. Something monstrous was running free within him. His feet hesitantly traced out the four-step as he continued down the slope toward the lake.

Did he dare?

THREE NOVELS:

THORNS

·

DOWNWARD TO THE EARTH

·

THE WORLD INSIDE

Robert Silverberg

BANTAM BOOKS

TORONTO · NEW YORK · LONDON · SYDNEY · AUCKLAND

THREE NOVELS

A Bantam Spectra Book / May 1988

PRINTING HISTORY

THORNS *copyright © 1967 by Robert Silverberg*

DOWNWARD TO THE EARTH *copyright © 1969 by Universal Publishing and Distributing Corporation. Copyright © 1971 by Robert Silverberg.*

THE WORLD INSIDE *copyright © 1971 by Robert Silverberg. Copyright © 1970, 1971 by UPD Publishing Corporation. Copyright © 1970 by Harrison Harrison. Copyright © 1970 by Avon Books.*

ISBN 0-553-27287-X

Published simultaneously in the United States and Canada

Bantam Books are published by Bantam Books, a division of Bantam Doubleday Dell Publishing Group, Inc. Its trademark, consisting of the words "Bantam Books" and the portrayal of a rooster, is Registered in U.S. Patent and Trademark Office and in other countries. Marca Registrada, Bantam Books, 666 Fifth Avenue, New York, New York 10103.

PRINTED IN THE UNITED STATES OF AMERICA

O   0 9 8 7 6 5 4 3 2 1

Introduction

Working out a private definition of science fiction is one of those nasty but inescapable tasks that every science fiction writer must do—even those who deny that they're doing it. Some will tell you that they hate defining science fiction, because science fiction is by its very nature indefinable and illimitable and they don't want to be constricted within a definition. (That is in itself a definition, but let it pass.) Others will say that the process of abstract thinking that the making of definitions requires is boring. (Anyone who genuinely finds thinking boring is not going to last long as a science fiction writer.) Still others will say that they don't need a working definition for science fiction, because science fiction is whatever they want it to be in relation to whatever they happen to be working on. I feel some sympathy for that position, but I remain convinced that some kind of map of the territory is necessary, if only for the sake of finding out where the territory *isn't*, and that everyone who works with the materials of science fiction, be he Robert A. Heinlein or Harlan Ellison, be he Larry Niven or Ray Bradbury, is functioning with a mental set of boundaries and descriptions which is, if not a full-scale definition, at the very least a catalog of operating equipment which implicitly defines the nature of the operations to be performed.

My own working definition of science fiction is a relatively vague and flexible one: those are easier to stretch than the rigid kind. I used to offer the glib and not particularly original one that science fiction concerns the interactions of human beings and technology. But while that is perfect for such stories as Heinlein's "The Roads Must Roll" or Asimov's *I, Robot* or C. L. Moore's "No Woman Born" or even Bradbury's *Martian Chronicles*, it applies less readily to works like Sturgeon's *More Than Human*, Heinlein's *Stranger in a*

Strange Land, Philip K. Dick's *The Man in the High Castle*, and my own *Dying Inside*, all of which are nevertheless universally considered to be science fiction. Still, the definition is not entirely useless. With some juggling, one can make things fit. (Miller's *A Canticle for Leibowitz* and Pangborn's *Davy*, though they are set in post-technological societies, are science fiction because they deal with the *consequences* of man's interaction with technology. Jean Auel's *Clan of the Cave Bear* qualifies because it depicts, among other things, the *birth* of technology. And so forth.)

All the same, I have come to prefer something looser, a rough sort of definition which says simply that science fiction attempts to portray that which does not exist, a speculative reality, but endeavors to explore the consequences of such a speculation in a rigorous, systematic, and scientifically plausible way. Under that definition, the writer can use any sort of fanciful notion—that certain people turn into wolves when the moon is full, that a man can be his own mother, that Pluto is a huge ball of Camembert—so long as the idea can be made to seem believable within the context of the story and the consequences of so strange a departure from known reality are developed in an intelligent and logical way.

The three novels making up this collection—all of them written between 1966 and 1970, a fertile and exciting time for science fiction and a particularly creative period for me— fulfill this definition each in a different fashion.

Thorns, the earliest of them, attempts all sorts of things, but basically it tries to demonstrate the impersonal capriciousness of the universe by focusing on two characters who have been oddly victimized by future high-technology societies. *Suppose*, I say, a spaceman far from home falls into alien hands, and they do alien (and therefore incomprehensible to us) things to him. And *suppose*, I say, that a young woman on Earth is used in a fertility experiment that makes her, while still a virgin, the mother of a hundred simultaneous children. And *then*, I say, let us turn these two loose on an Earth hungry for novelty and sensation, and see what happens to them. Allow one speculative assumption—two of them, actually, but of the same underlying sort—and then develop the consequences, one bizarre and mysterious event after another, all flowing from the initial departure from conventional reality.

In *Downward to the Earth*, written a few years later after a visit to post-Colonial Africa, I offered the hypothesis that the supposedly beast-like inhabitants of an alien world might, in fact, have mental capabilities far beyond those of human beings, though to us they seemed to be nothing more than odd green elephants. If that is the case—if the indigenous dwellers on Belzagor are not merely "animals," any more than the indigenous dwellers in the colonialized parts of Earth were not merely "natives"—then what emotions would a former colonial official experience when he returned to Belzagor and found himself being initiated into the deep mysteries of the creatures he had so underestimated? Once again, everything follows logically from the initial speculation.

The third of the books, *The World Inside*, is more obviously technological science fiction. I propose a civilization a few hundred years hence that lives in thousand-story-high skyscrapers that house close to a million people each: whole cities within a single building. It is not, to me, a particularly likely possibility, but it is a reasonable if extreme extrapolation from the actuality of twentieth-century New York City, and it has some ecological and economic merits to recommend it. But what would life be like in such an urban monad? What social structures would develop among people who spent all their days within a single gigantic high-rise? What conflicts would exist in such close quarters, and how would they be resolved? How would the building itself work? Where would its food come from? How would waste products be disposed of? What about maintenance? Light? Heat? Power? *The World Inside* is as close as I have ever come, I think, to pure science fiction: the methodical and unswerving realization of a basically fantastic idea. Grant me my one improbable premise of a civilization living in mile-high buildings and everything else follows logically. And, I think, once you have allowed me my premise and spent a few chapters in the world of Urbmon 116 you will find that that fantastic place seems very real indeed to you.

Which is a prime goal of science fiction: to make the unreal real, to provide the reader with an alternate reality that, for the moment, seems at least as solid and authentic as the one he inhabits daily. That is what I set out to achieve in these three novels of twenty years ago. The writer is never a very trustworthy judge of his own achievement; but, all the same, these books seem to me very close to the best work I have managed to do, and I hope they will provide for you that special science fictional sense of the unreal made real that they provided for me as I transferred my initial visions to the written page.

Robert Silverberg
September, 1987

THORNS

For Jim and Judy Blish

CAMILLA: You, sir, should unmask.

STRANGER: Indeed?

CASSILDA: Indeed it's time. We have all laid aside disguise but you.

STRANGER: I wear no mask.

CAMILLA: (Terrified, aside to Cassilda.) No mask? No mask?

The King in Yellow: Act 1—Scene 2.

One

The Song the Neurons Sang

"Pain is instructive," Duncan Chalk wheezed.

On crystal rungs he ascended the east wall of his office. Far on high was the burnished desk, the inlaid communicator box from which he controlled his empire. It would have been nothing for Chalk to sail up the wall on the staff of a gravitron. Yet each morning he imposed this climb on himself.

A variety of hangers-on accompanied him. Leontes d'Amore, of the mobile chimpanzee lips; Bart Aoudad; Tom Nikolaides, notable for shoulders. And others. Yet Chalk, learning the lesson of pain once more, was the focus of the group.

Flesh rippled and billowed on him. Within that great bulk were the white underpinnings of bone, yearning for release. Six hundred pounds of meat comprised Duncan Chalk. The vast leathery heart pumped desperately, flooding the massive limbs with life. Chalk climbed. The route zigged and backswitched up forty feet of wall to the throne at the top. Along the way blotches of thermoluminescent fungus glowed eagerly, yellow asters tipped with red, sending forth pulsations of warmth and brightness.

Outside it was winter. Thin strands of new snow coiled in the streets. The leaden sky was just begining to respond to the morning ionization poured into it by the great pylons of day. Chalk grunted. Chalk climbed.

Aoudad said, "The idiot will be here in eleven minutes, sir. He'll perform."

"Bores me now," Chalk said. "I'll see him anyway."

"We could try torturing him," suggested the sly d'Amore in a feathery voice. "Perhaps then his gift of numbers would shine more brightly."

Chalk spat. Leontes d'Amore shrank back as though a stream of acid had come at him. The climb continued. Pale fleshy hands reached out to grasp gleaming rods. Muscles

5

snarled and throbbed beneath the slabs of fat. Chalk flowed up the wall, barely pausing to rest.

The inner messages of pain dizzied and delighted him. Ordinarily he preferred to take his suffering the vicarious way, but this was morning, and the wall was his challenge. Up. Up. Toward the seat of power. He climbed, rung by rung by rung, heart protesting, intestines shifting position inside the sheath of meat, loins quivering, the very bones of him flexing and sagging with their burden.

About him the bright-eyed jackals waited. What if he fell? It would take ten of them to lift him to the walkway again. What if the spasming heart ran away in wild fibrillation? What if his eyes glazed as they watched?

Would they rejoice as his power bled away into the air?

Would they know glee as his grip slipped and his iron grasp over their lives weakened?

Of course. Of course. Chalk's thin lips curved in a cool smile. He had the lips of a slender man, the lips of a bedouin burned down to bone by the sun. Why were his lips not thick and liquid?

The sixteenth rung loomed. Chalk seized it. Sweat boiled from his pores. He hovered a moment, painstakingly shifting his weight from the ball of the left foot to the heel of the right. There was no reward and less delight in being a foot of Duncan Chalk. For an instant nearly incalculable stresses were exerted across Chalk's right ankle. Then he eased forward, bringing his hand down across the last rung in a savage chopping motion, and his throne opened gladly to him.

Chalk sank into the waiting seat and felt it minister to him. In the depths of the fabric the micropile hands stirred and squeezed, soothing him. Ghostly ropes of spongy wire slid into his clothes to sponge the perspiration from the valleys and mounds of his flesh. Hidden needles glided through epithelium, squirting beneficial fluids. The thunder of the overtaxed heart subsided to a steady murmur. Muscles that had been bunched and knotted with exertion went slack. Chalk smiled. The day had begun; all was well.

Leontes d'Amore said, "It amazes me, sir, how easily you make that climb."

"You think I'm too fat to move?"

"Sir, I—"

"The fascination of what's difficult," said Chalk. "It spins the world on its bearings."

"I'll bring the idiot," d'Amore said.

"The idiot-savant," Chalk corrected him. "I have no interest in idiots."

"Of course. The idiot-savant. Of course."

D'Amore slipped away through an irising slot in the rear wall. Chalk leaned back, folding his arms over the seamless expanse of chest and belly. He looked out across the great gulf of the room. It was high and deep, an open space of large extent through which glowworms floated. Chalk had an old fondness for luminous organisms. Let there be light, be light, be light; if he had had the time, he might have arranged to glow himself.

Far below on the floor of the room, where Chalk had been at the commencement of the daily climb, figures moved in busy patterns, doing Chalk's work. Beyond the walls of the room were other offices, honeycombing the octagonal building whose core this was. Chalk had built a superb organization. In a large and indifferent universe he had carved out a sizable private pocket, for the world still took its pleasure in pain. If the deliciously morbid thrills of mulling over details of mass murders, war casualties, air accidents, and the like were largely things of the past, Chalk was well able to provide stronger, more extreme, and more direct substitutes. He worked hard, even now, to bring pleasure to many, pain to a few, pleasure and pain at once to himself.

He was uniquely designed by the accident of genes for his task: a pain-responsive, pain-fed eater of emotion, depending on his intake of raw anguish as others did on their intake of bread and meat. He was the ultimate representative of his audience's tastes and so was perfectly able to supply that vast audience's inner needs. But though his capacity had dwindled with the years, he still was not satiated. Now he picked his way through the emotional feasts he staged, a fresh gobbet here, a bloody pudding of senses there, saving his own appetite for the more grotesque permutations of cruelty, searching always for the new, and terribly old, sensations.

Turning to Aoudad, he said, "I don't think the idiot-savant will be worth much. Are you still watching over the starman Burris?"

"Daily, sir." Aoudad was a crisp man with dead gray eyes

and a trustworthy look. His ears were nearly pointed. "I keep watch over Burris."

"And you, Nick? The girl?"

"She's dull," said Nikolaides. "But I watch her."

"Burris and the girl..." Chalk mused. "The sum of two grudges. We need a new project. Perhaps... perhaps..."

D'Amore reappeared, sliding from the opposite wall atop a jutting shelf. The idiot-savant stood placidly beside him. Chalk leaned forward, doubling fold of belly over fold of belly. He feighed interest.

"This is David Melangio," D'Amore said.

Melangio was forty years old, but his high forehead was unfurrowed and his eyes were as trusting as a child's. He looked pale and moist, like something out of the earth. D'Amore had dressed him stylishly in a glittering robe shot through with iron threads, but the effect was grotesque on him; the grace and dignity of the expensive garment were lost, and it served only to highlight Melangio's blank, boyish innocence.

Innocence was not a commodity the public would pay any great price to buy. That was Chalk's business: supplying the public with what it demanded. Yet innocence coupled with something else might fill the current need.

Chalk played with the computer node at his left hand and said, "Good morning, David. How do you feel today?"

"It snowed last night. I like the snow."

"The snow will be gone soon. Machines are melting it."

"I wish I could play in the snow." Wistfully.

"You'd chill your bones," said Chalk. "David, what day was February 15, 2002?"

"Friday."

"April 20, 1968?"

"Saturday."

"How do you know?"

"It has to be like that," said Melangio simply.

"The thirteenth President of the United States?"

"Fillmore."

"What does the President do?"

"He lives in the White House."

"Yes, I know," said Chalk mildly, "but what are his duties?"

"To live in the White House. Sometimes they let him out."

"What day of the week was November 20, 1891?"

"Friday." Instantly.

"In the year 1811, in which months did the fifth day fall on a Monday?"

"Only August."

"When will February 29 next fall on a Saturday?"

Melangio giggled. "That's too easy. We only get a February 29 once very four years, so—"

"All right. Explain Leap Year to me," said Chalk.

Blankness.

"Don't you know why it happens, David?"

D'Amore said, "He can give you any date over nine thousand years, sir, starting from the year 1. But he can't explain anything. Try him on weather reports."

Chalk's thin lips quirked. "Tell me about August 14, 2031, David."

The high, piping voice responded: "Cool temperatures in the morning, rising to a hundred and three along the eastern seaboard by two in the afternoon when the overload coils cut in. At seven P.M. the temperature was down to eighty-two, where it remained past midnight. Then it started to rain."

"Where were you that day?" Chalk asked.

"At home with my brother and my sister and my mother and my father."

"Were you happy that day?"

"?"

"Did anyone hurt you that day?" Chalk said.

Melangio nodded. "My brother kicked me here, in my shin. My sister pulled my hair. My mother made me eat chemifix for breakfast. Afterward I went out to play. A boy threw a rock at my dog. Then—"

The voice was free of emotion. Melangio repeated his boyhood agonies as blandly as though he were giving the date of the third Tuesday in September, 1794. Yet beneath the glassy surface of prolonged childishness lay real pain. Chalk sensed it. He let Melangio drone on, occasionally prompting him with a guiding question.

Chalk's eyelids slipped together. It was easier to throw forth the receptors that way, to reach out and drain the substratum of sorrow that had its existence beneath David Melangio's trick brain. Old tiny griefs flowed like arcing currents across the room: a dead goldfish, a shouting father, a naked girl turning with heaving rosy-tipped breasts to utter words that killed. Everything was there, everything was accessible: the raw, maimed soul of David Melangio, forty

years old, a human island well walled off from the stormy sea
about him.

At length the recitation subsided. Chalk had had enough
nourishment for now; he wearied of pushing Melangio's buttons. He tapered off by returning to the idiot-savant's strange
powers of recall.

"David, catch these numbers: 96748759."

"Yes."

"And these: 32807887."

"Yes."

"Also: 333141187698."

Melangio waited. Chalk said, "Now, David."

Numbers gushed in a smooth stream. "9674875932807887-
333141187698."

"David, how much is seven times twelve?"

A pause. "Sixty-four?"

"No. Take nine from sixteen."

"Ten?"

"If you can memorize the whole calendar upside down and
backward, why can't you do arithmetic?"

Melangio smiled pleasantly. He said nothing.

"David, do you ever wonder why you are as you are?"

"As what?" Melangio asked.

Chalk was satisfied. The only pleasures to be extracted
from David Melangio were low-level ones. Chalk had had his
mind jolt of pleasure for the morning, and the faceless public
would find a flicker of amusement in Melangio's freakish
abilities to reel off dates, numbers, weather reports. But no
one would draw real nourishment from David Melangio.

"Thank you, David," Chalk said in easy dismissal.

D'Amore looked ruffled. His prodigy had failed to awe the
big man, and d'Amore's continued prosperity depended on
making frequent impacts here. Those who did not generally
did not long remain in Chalk's service. The shelf in the wall
retracted, taking d'Amore and Melangio away.

Chalk contemplated the gleaming rings imprisoned in ridges
of fat on his short, thick fingers. He sat back then, closing his
eyes. The image came to him of his body made up of
concentric inner cores, like an onion, only with each discrete
layer insulated from its neighbors by a sheet of quicksilver.
The separate strata of Duncan Chalk slipping and sliding
across one another, well lubricated, moving slowly as the

quicksilver yielded to pressures and squirted down dark channels . . .

To Bart Aoudad he said, "We must investigate the starman a little further."

Aoudad nodded. "I'll monitor the tracers, sir."

To Tom Nikolaides Chalk said, "And the girl. The dreary little girl. We'll try an experiment. Synergy. Catalysis. Bring them together. Who knows? We might generate some pain. Some human feeling. Nick, we can learn lessons from pain. It teaches us that we're alive."

"This Melangio," Aoudad pointed out. "He doesn't seem to feel his pain. He registers it, he engraves it on his brain. But he doesn't feel it."

"Exactly," said Chalk. "My entire point. He can't feel anything, only record and replay. The pain's there, enough of it. But he can't reach it."

"What if we liberated it for him?" suggested Aoudad. He smiled, not pleasantly.

"Too late. He'd burn up in an instant if he could ever really reach that pain now. No, leave him to his calendars, Bart. Let's not destroy him. He'll do his trick, and everyone will applaud, and then we'll drop him back into his puddle. The starman, though—that's something else again."

"And the girl," Nikolaides reminded him.

"Yes. The starman and the girl. It should be interesting. We should learn a great deal."

Two
On Earth as in Heaven

Long afterward, when fresh blood would stain his hands and his heart would pound with the surge of renewed life, it might all begin to seem like no more than an ugly, nasty dream to him. But he'd have to cross Heimdall's shining bridge to get there. Just now he still lived in pain, and he felt now as he had felt while it was happening. Many terrors enfolded Minner Burris.

He was not a man normally vulnerable to terror. But this had been too much: the great greasy shapes moving about his ship, the golden manacles, the case of surgical instruments open and ready.

"———," the pockmarked monster to his left had said.

"— ——— ———," the creature on the other side had replied in what sounded like unctuous terms.

Then they had begun the work of destroying Minner Burris.

Then was then and now was now, but Burris carried about a load of pain and strangeness that eternally reminded him, waking or sleeping, of the thing that had been done to him behind the cloak of darkness, beyond the unspinning chill of Pluto.

He had returned to Earth three weeks ago. He lived now in a single room of the Martlet Towers, supported by a government pension and propped somehow by his own inner resilience. To be transformed by monsters into a monster was no easy fate to accept, but Burris was doing his best.

If only there were not so much pain—

The doctors who had examined him had been confident at first that they could do something about the pain. All it took was the application of modern medical technology.

"—damp down the sensory intake—"

"—minimal dosage of drugs to block the afferent channels, and then—"

"—minor corrective surgery—"

But the lines of communication within Burris's body were hopelessly scrambled. Whatever the alien surgeons had done to him, they had certainly transformed him into something that was beyond the comprehension, let alone the capabilities, of modern medical technology. Ordinary pain-killing drugs merely intensified Burris' sensations. His patterns of neural flow were bizarre; sensation was shunted, baffled, deflected. They could not repair the damage the aliens had done. And finally Burris crept away from them, throbbing, mutilated, aggrieved, to hide himself in a dark room of this moldering residential colossus.

Seventy years before, the Martlet Towers had been the last word in dwelling-places: sleek mile-high edifices arrayed in serried ranks along the formerly green slopes of the Adirondacks, within easy commuting distance of New York. Seventy years is a long time in the lifetime of contemporary buildings. Now the Towers were corroded, pitted by time, transfixed by the arrows of decay. Suites of earlier resplendence were subdivided into single-room warrens. An ideal place to hide, Burris thought. One nestled into one's cell here like a polyp within its limestone cave. One rested; one thought; one worked at the strenuous task of coming to terms with what had been committed upon one's helpless form.

Burris heard scrabbling sounds in the corridors. He did not investigate. Whelks and prawns, mysteriously mutated for land life, infiltrating the crawl spaces of the building? Millipedes seeking the sweet warmth of leaf mold? Toys of the dull-eyed children? Burris stayed in the room. He often thought of going out at night, prowling the passages of the building like his own ghost, striding through darkness to strike terror into chance beholders. But he had not left the four walls since the day he had rented—by proxy—this zone of calm in tempest.

He lay in bed. Pale green light filtered through the walls. The mirror could not be removed, for it was part of the structure of the building, but it could at least be neutralized; Burris had switched it off, and it was nothing now but a dull brown oblong on the wall. From time to time he activated it and confronted himself, as discipline. Perhaps, he thought, he would do that today.

When I rise from bed.

If I rise from bed.

Why should I rise from bed?

There was an inner spike embedded in his brain, clamps gripping his viscera, invisible nails riveting his ankles. His eyelids sandpapered his eyes. Pain was a constant, even growing now to become an old friend.

What was it the poet said? The *withness* of the body . . .

Burris opened his eyes. They no longer opened up and down, as human eyes did. Now the membranes that served as lids slid outward from the center toward the corners. Why? Why had the alien surgeons done any of it? But this in particular seemed to serve no valid purpose. Top-and-bottom eyelids were good enough. These did not improve the function of the eyes; they served only to act as intrusive wardens against any sort of meaningful communication between Burris and the human race. At each blink he shouted his weirdness.

The eyes moved. A human eye moves in a series of tiny jerking motions, which the mind melds together into an abstraction of unity. Burris's eyes moved as the panning eye of a camera would move if cameras were perfectly mounted:

smoothly, continuously, unflickeringly. What Burris saw lacked glamour. Walls, low ceiling, neutralized mirror, vibrator sink, food conduit hatch, all the drab appurtenances of a simple low-cost room designed for self-sufficiency. The window had been kept opaqued since he had moved in. He had no idea of time of day, of weather, even of season, though it had been winter when he came here and he suspected that it was winter still. The lighting in the room was poor. Squibs of indirect illumination emerged on a random pattern. This was Burris's period of low receptivity to light. For days at a time the world at its brightest seemed a murky darkness to him, as though he were at the bottom of a muddy pond. Then the cycle would reverse itself with an unpredictable flip, and a few photons would be sufficient to light up his brain in a wild blaze.

Out of the murk came the image of his vanished self. The obliterated Minner Burris stood in a blunted corner of the room, studying him.

Dialogue of self and soul.

"You're back, you filthy hallucination!"

"I won't ever leave you."

"All I have, is that it? Well, make yourself welcome. A bit of cognac? Accept my humble hospitality. Sit down, sit down!"

"I'll stand. How are you coming along, Minner?"

"Poorly. A lot you care."

"Is that a note of self-pity I detect in your voice?"

"What if it is? What if it is?"

"A terrible voice, and one that I never taught you."

Burris could not sweat any longer, but a cloud of vapor gathered over each of his new exhalator pores. He stared fixedly at his former self. In a low voice he said, "Do you know what I wish? That they'd get hold of you and do to you what they did to me. Then you'd understand."

"Minner, Minner, it's already been done to me! *Ecce homo!* There you lie to prove that I've been through it!"

"No. There you stand to prove that you haven't. Your face. Your pancreas. Your liver and lights. Your skin. It hurts, it hurts—it hurts me, not you!"

The apparition smiled gently. "When did you begin feeling so sorry for yourself? This is a new development, Minner."

Burris scowled. "Perhaps you're right." The eyes smoothly scanned the room from wall to wall again. He muttered, "They're watching me, that's the trouble."

"Who is?"

"How would I know? Eyes. Telelenses in the walls. I've searched for them, but it's no use. Two molecules in diameter— how am I ever going to find them? And they see me."

"Let them look, then. You have nothing to be ashamed of. You're neither pretty nor ugly. There's no point of reference for you. I think it's time you went outside again."

"It's easy for you to say that," Burris snapped. "No one stares at *you*."

"You're staring at me right now."

"So I am," Burris admitted. "But you know why."

With a conscious effort he induced the phase-shift to begin. His eyes dealt with the light in the room. He no longer had retinas, but the focus-plates embedded against his brain served well enough. He looked at his former self.

A tall man, broad-shouldered and blocky, with heavy muscles and thick sandy hair. So he had been. So he was now. The alien surgeons had left the underlying structure intact. But all else was different.

The vision of self before him had a face nearly as wide as it was high, with generous cheekbones, small ears, and dark eyes set far apart. The lips were the sort that compress themselves easily into a rather fussy line. A light powdering of freckles covered the skin; there was fine golden hair almost everywhere on him. The effect was routinely virile: a man of some strength, some intelligence, some skill, who would stand out in a group not by virtue of any conspicuous positive trait but by grace of a whole constellation of inconspicuous positive traits. Success with women, success with other men, success in his profession—all those things accompanied such triumphant unspectacular attractiveness.

All that was gone now.

Burris said quietly, "I don't mean to sound self-pitying now. Kick me if I whine. But do you remember when we would see hunchbacks? A man with no nose? A girl folded into herself with no neck and half an arm? Freaks? Victims? And we'd wonder what it was like to be hideous."

"You're not hideous, Minner. Just different."

"Choke on your stinking semantics! I'm something that everyone would stare at now. I'm a monster. Suddenly I'm out of your world and into the world of the hunchbacks. They know damned well that they can't escape all those eyes. They cease to have independent existences and blur into the fact of their own deformities."

"You're projecting, Minner. How can you know?"

"Because it's happening to me. My whole life now is built around what the Things did to me. I don't have any other existence. It's the central fact, the only fact. How can we know the dancer from the dance? I can't. If I ever went outside, I'd be on constant display."

"A hunchback has a lifetime to get used to himself. He forgets his back. You're still new at this. Be patient, Minner. You'll come to terms. You'll forgive the staring eyes."

"How soon? *How soon?*"

But the apparition was gone. Prodding himself through several shifts of vision, Burris searched the room and found himself again alone. He sat up, feeling the needles pricking his nerves. There was no motion without its cluster of discomforts. His body was ever with him.

He stood up, rising in a single fluid motion. This new body gives me pain, he told himself, but it is efficient. I must come to love it.

He braced himself in the middle of the floor.

Self-pity is fatal, Burris thought. I must not wallow. I must come to terms. I must adjust.

I must go out into the world.

I was a strong man, not just physically. Is all my strength— *that* strength—gone now?

Within him coiling tubes meshed and unmeshed. Tiny stopcocks released mysterious hormones. The chambers of his heart performed an intricate dance.

They're watching me, Burris thought. Let them watch! Let them get a good eyeful!

Within a savage swipe of his hand he switched on the mirror and beheld his naked self.

Three

Subterranean Rumbles

Aoudad said, "What if we traded? You monitor Burris, I'll watch the girl. Eh?"

"Nix." Nikolaides drew the final consonant out luxuriously. "Chalk gave her to me, him to you. She's a bore, anyway. Why switch?"

"I'm tired of him."

"Put up with him," Nikolaides advised. "Unpleasantness is upbuilding to character."

"You've been listening to Chalk too long."

"Haven't we all?"

They smiled. There would be no trade of responsibilities. Aoudad jabbed at the switch, and the car in which they were riding cut sharply from one mastercom network to the other. It began rocketing northward at a hundred and fifty miles an hour.

Aoudad had designed the car himself, for Chalk's own use. It was a womb, more or less, lined with soft warm pink spongy fibers and equipped with every sort of comfort short of gravitrons. Chalk had wearied of it lately and was willing to let underlings make use of it. Aoudad and Nikolaides rode it often. Each man considered himself Chalk's closest associate; each quietly considered the other a flunky. It was a useful mutual delusion.

The trick was to establish some sort of existence for yourself independent of Duncan Chalk. Chalk demanded most of your waking hours and was not above using you in your sleep when he could. Yet there was always some fragment of your life in which you stood apart from the fat man and regarded yourself as a rounded, self-guiding human being. For Nikolaides the answer lay in physical exertion: skimming lakes, hiking to the rim of a boiling sulfurous volcano, sky-paddling, desert-drilling. Aoudad had chosen exertion, too, but of a softer kind; legs spread and toe touching toe, his women would form a trestle stretching across several continents. D'Amore and the others had their own individual escapes. Chalk devoured those who did not.

Snow was falling again. The delicate flakes perished almost as soon as they landed, but the car-track was slippery. Servo-mechanisms quickly adjusted the tracking equipment to keep the car upright. Its occupants reacted in different ways; Nikolaides quickened at the thought of the potential danger, minute though it was, while Aoudad thought gloomily of the eager thighs that awaited him if he survived the journey.

Nikolaides said, "About this trade—"

"Forget it. If the answer's no, the answer's no."

"I just want to find out. Tell me this, Bart: are you interested in the girl's body?"

Aoudad recoiled in excessive innocence. "What the hell do you think I am?"

"I know what you are, and so does everyone else. But I'm just fishing around. Do you have some odd idea that if we switch assignments and you get Lona, you'll be able to have her?"

Sputtering, Aoudad said, "I draw the line at some women. I'd never meddle with her. For Christ's sake, Nick! The girl is too dangerous. A seventeen-year-old virgin with a hundred kids—I wouldn't touch her! Did you really think I would?"

"Not really."

"Why'd you ask, then?"

Nikolaides shrugged and stared at the snow.

Aoudad said, "Chalk asked you to find out, is that it? He's afraid I'll molest her, is that it? Is it? Is it?" Nikolaides did not answer, and suddenly Aoudad began to tremble. If Chalk could suspect him of such desires, Chalk must have lost all faith in him. The compartments were separate: work here, women there. Aoudad had never straddled those compartments yet, and Chalk knew it. What was wrong? Where had he failed the fat man? Why had faith been withdrawn this way?

Aoudad said hollowly, "Nick, I swear to you I had no such intentions in proposing a switch. The girl doesn't interest me sexually at all. Not at *all*. You think I want a goddam grotesque kid like that? All I had in mind was I was tired of looking at Burris's mixed-up body. I wanted variety in my assignment. And you—"

"Cut it out, Bart."

"—read all sorts of sinister and perverse—"

"I didn't."

"Chalk did, then. And you went along with him. Is this a plot? Who's out to get me?"

Nikolaides nudged his left thumb into the dispenser button, and a tray of relaxers popped out. Quietly he handed one to Aoudad, who took the slender ivory-colored tube and pressed it to his forearm. An instant later the tension ebbed. Aoudad tugged at the pointed tip of his left ear. That had been a bad one, that surge of tension and suspicion. They were coming more frequently now. He feared that something nasty was happening to him and that Duncan Chalk was tapping in on his emotions, drinking in the sensations as he passed on a predestined course through paranoia and schizophrenia to catatonic suspension.

I will not let it happen to me, Aoudad resolved. He can have his pleasures, but he won't get his fangs into *my* throat.

"We'll remain on our assignments until Chalk says otherwise, yes?" he said aloud.

"Yes," Nikolaides replied.

"Shall we monitor them as we ride along?"

"No objections."

The car was passing the Appalachia Tunnel now. High blank walls hemmed them in. The highway was steeply banked here, and as the car barreled along at a high-G acceleration, a gleam of sensual appreciation came into Nikolaides's eyes. He sat back in the huge seat meant for Chalk. Aoudad, beside him, opened the communication channels. The screens lit.

"Yours," he said. "Mine."

He looked at his. Aoudad no longer shivered when he saw Minner Burris, but the sight was a spooky one even now. Burris stood before his mirror, thereby providing Aoudad with the sight of two of him.

"There but for the grace of something-or-other go we," Aoudad murmured. "How'd you like to have that done to you?"

"I'd kill myself instantly," said Nikolaides. "But somehow I think the girls in a worse mess. Can you see her from where you're sitting?"

"What is she doing? She's naked?"

"Bathing," said Nikolaides. "A hundred children! Never been had by a man! The things we take for granted, Bart. Look."

Aoudad looked. The squat bright screen showed him a nude girl standing under a vibraspray. He hoped that Chalk was fastened to his emotional stream right now, for as he looked at Lona Kelvin's bare body he felt nothing. Not a thing. No shred of sensuality.

She could not have weighed more than a hundred pounds. Her shoulders sloped, her face was wan, her eyes lacked sparkle. She had small breasts, a slender waist, narrow boyish hips. As Aoudad watched, she turned around, showing him flat, scarcely feminine buttocks, and switched off the vibraspray. She began to dress. Her motions were slow, her expression sullen.

"Maybe I'm prejudiced because I've been working with Burris," Aoudad said, "but it seems to me that he's very much more complicated than she is. She's just a dumb kid who's had a hard time. What will he see in her?"

"He'll see a human being," said Nikolaides. "That may be enough. Perhaps. Perhaps. It's worth a try, bringing them together."

"You sound like a humanitarian," Aoudad said in wonder.

"I don't like to see people hurting."

"Who does, aside from Chalk? But how can you possibly get involved with these two? Where's the handle? They're too remote from us. They're grotesques. They're baroques. I don't see how Chalk can sell them to the public."

Nikolaides said patiently, "Individually they're baroques. Put them together and they're Romeo and Juliet. Chalk has a certain genius for things like that."

Aoudad eyed the girl's empty face and then the eerie, distorted mask that was the face of Minner Burris. He shook his head. The car rocketed forward, a needle penetrating the black fabric of the night. He switched off the screens and shut his eyes. Women danced through his brain: real women, adults, with soft, rounded bodies.

The snow came thicker in the air about them. Even in the shielded snout of the womb-like car, Bart Aoudad felt a certain chill.

Four
Child of Storm

Lona Kelvin donned her clothes. Two undergarments, two overgarments, gray on gray, and she was dressed. She walked to the window of her little room and looked out. Snowfall. White swirls in the night. They could get rid of the snow fast enough once it hit ground, but they couldn't keep it from falling. Not yet.

A walk in the Arcade, Lona decided. Then sleep and another day put to rest.

She drew her jacket on. Shivered in anticipation. Looked about her.

Pasted neatly to the walls of the room were photographs of babies. Not a hundred babies; more like sixty or seventy. And not her babies. But sixty baby photographs might just as well be a hundred. And to a mother like Lona, any babies might be her babies.

They looked as babies look. Rounded, unshaped faces with button noses and glossy, drooling lips and unseeing eyes. Tiny ears, painfully perfect. Clutching little hands with improbably splendid fingernails. Soft skin. Lona reached out and touched the photograph nearest the door and imagined that she was touching baby-velvet. Then she put her hand to her own body. Touched the flat belly. Touched a small, hard breast. Touched the loins from which a legion of infants had and had not sprung. She shook her head in what might have been thought a self-pitying gesture, but most of the self-pity had been drained away by now, leaving only a gritty residual sediment of confusion and emptiness.

Lona went out. The door quietly sealed itself behind her.

The dropshaft took her swiftly to ground level. Wind whipped down the narrow passage between the tall buildings. Overhead, the artificial glow of night pressed back the darkness; colored globes moved silently to and fro. Snowflakes danced against them. The pavement was warm. The buildings that flanked her were brightly lit. To the Arcade, Lona's feet told her. To the Arcade to walk awhile in the brightness and the warmth of this snowy night.

Nobody recognized her.

Only a girl out by herself for the evening. Mouse-colored hair flipping about her ears. A thin-naped neck, slumping shoulders, an insufficient body. How old? Seventeen. Could be fourteen, though. No one asked. A mousy girl.

Mousy.

Dr. Teh Ping Lin, San Francisco, 1966:

"At the scheduled time of hormonally induced ovulation, female mice of the black-agouti C3H/HeJ strain were caged with fertile males of an albino strain, either BALB/c or Cal A (originally A/Crgl/2). Nine to twelve hours after the expected

mating, eggs were flushed from the oviducts, and fertilized
eggs were identified by the presence of the second polar
body or by observation of pronuclei."

It was a taxing experiment for the doctor. Microinjection of
living cells was nothing new even then, but work with
mammalian cells had been flawed. The experimenters had
not been able to safeguard the structural or functional integri-
ty of the whole ovum.

No one had ever informed Lona Kelvin that:

"The mammalian egg is apparently more difficult to inject
than other cells because of the thick zona pellucida and the
vitelline membrane, both of which are highly elastic and
resistant to the penetration of a microinstrument, especially
at the unfertilized stage."

Crowds of boys were gathered, as usual, in the vestibule
that led to the Arcade. With some of them were girls. Lona
eyed them shyly. Winter did not extend to this vestibule; the
girls had shucked their thermal wraps and stood proudly on
display. This one had given her nipples a phosphorescence.
That one had shaved her skull to exhibit the fine bony
structure. There, voluptuous in the final weeks of pregnancy,
a redhead linked her arms with two tall young men and
laughingly roared obscenities.

Lona viewed her, edge-on. Big belly, bulky burden. Can
she see her toes? Her breasts were swollen. Do they hurt?
The child was conceived in the old way. Lona blinked. Gasp
and thrust and shudder in the loins and a baby made. *One*
baby. Possibly two. Lona drew her narrow shoulders back,
filled her pinched lungs with air. The gesture raised her
breasts and thrust them outward, and color came to her
angular cheeks.

"Going to the Arcade? Go with me."

"Hey, robin! Let's chirp!"

"Need a friend, friend?"

Eddies of talk. Buzzing basso invitations. Not for her.
Never for her.

I am a mother.

I am *the* mother.

"These fertilized eggs were then placed in a medium
consisting of three parts modified Locke's solution, one part
2.9 percent sodium citrate dihydrate, and 25 mg of bovine
gamma globulin (BGG, Armour) per milliliter of the citrate-
Locke's solution. Penicillin (100 unit/ml) and streptomycin (50

μg/ml) were added to the medium. Viscosity of the medium at 22° C was 1.1591 cp and its pH 7.2. Eggs were retained for micromanipulation and injection within a drop of the bovine gamma globuline-citrate-Locke's solution (GCL) which was covering with mineral oil in a vaseline well on a microscope slide."

Tonight there was a small surprise for Lona. One of the loungers at the vestibule approached her. Was he drunk? So sexually deprived that she was attractive to him? Moved by pity for the waif? Or did he know who she was and wish to share her glory? That was the least probable of all. He did not know, would not wish. Of glory there was none.

He was no beauty, but not conspicuously repulsive. Of medium height; black hair slicked straight forward almost to his eyebrows; eyebrows themselves slightly distorted surgically to arch in a skeptical inverted V; eyes gray, and bright with shallow craftiness; chin weak; nose sharp, prominent. About nineteen years old. Sallow skin marked with underlying striations, sun-sensitive patterns that would blaze in glory at noon. He looked hungry. On his breath a mixture of things: cheap wine, spiced bread, a hint of (splurge!) filtered rum.

"Hello, lovely. Let's match. I'm Tom Piper, Tom Piper's son. You?"

"Please—no," Lona murmured. She tried to move away. He blocked her, exhaling.

"Matched already? Meeting someone inside?"

"No."

"Why not me, then? You could do worse."

"Let me be." A faint whimper.

He leered. Small eyes boring into her own. "Starman," he said. "Just in from the outer worlds. We'll get a table and I'll tell you all about them. Mustn't turn a starman down."

Lona's forehead furrowed. Starman? Outer worlds? Saturn dancing within its rings, green suns beyond the night, pale creatures with many arms? He was no starman. Space marks the soul. Tom Piper's son was unmarked. Even Lona could tell that. Even Lona.

"You aren't," she said.

"Am. I'll tell you the stars. Ophiuchus. Rigel. Aldebaran. I've been out there. Come on, flower. Come with Tom."

He was lying. Glamorizing himself to enhance his magnetism. Lona shivered. Past his thick shoulder she saw the lights of the Arcade. He leaned close. His hand descended, found her hip, curled lasciviously over the flat haunch, the lean flank.

"Who knows?" he whispered huskily. "The night could go anywhere. Maybe I'll give you a baby. I bet you'd like that. You ever had a baby?"

Her nails raked his cheek. He reeled back, surprised, bloodied, and for a moment the banded ornaments beneath his skin glowed brightly even in the artificial light. His eyes were wild. Lona swung around and sidestepped him, losing herself in the throng surging through the vestibule.

Elbows busy, she sliced a path into the Arcade.

Tom, Tom, the piper's son, give you a baby before he's done....

"Three hundred and one newly fertilized eggs were maintained in vaseline well preparations and each received one of the following experimental treatments: (i) no pipette puncture and no injection; (ii) puncture of egg but no injection; (iii) injection of $180\mu^8$ of the solution containing about 5 pg of BGG; (iv) injection of $770\mu^8$ of the solution containing 20 pg of BGG; or (v) injection of $2730\mu^8$ of the solution containing 68 pg of BGG."

The Arcade glittered. Here were all the cheaper pleasures, gathered under one glassy roof. As Lona passed the gate, she thrust her thumb against the toller to register her presence and be billed for her visit. It was not costly to enter. But she had money, she had money. They had seen to that.

She planted her feet squarely and looked up at tier after tier, reaching toward the roof two hundred feet above. Up there snow was falling but not landing; efficient blowers kept it from touching the arching roof, and the flakes fell to a sticky death on the heated pavement.

She saw the gambling tiers where a man could play any game for any stake. The stakes were generally not high. This was a place for the young, for the purse-poor. For the grubby. But with a will a man could lose thickly here, and some had. Up there wheels turned, lights flashed, buttons clicked. Lona did not understand the gambling games.

Farther up, in mazy networks of corridors, flesh could be purchased by those with the need or the inclination. Women for men, men for women, boys for girls, girls for boys, and any conceivable combination. Why not? A human being was free to make disposition of his body in any way that did not directly interfere with the well-being of another. Those who sold were not forced to sell. They could become shopkeepers instead. Lona did not go to the houses of flesh.

Here on the main level of the Arcade were the booths of small merchants. A handful of coins would buy a pocketful of surprises. What about a tiny rope of living light to brighten the dull days? Or a pet from another world, so they said, though in truth the jewel-eyed toads were cultured in the laboratories of Brazil? What of a poetry box to sing you to sleep? Photographs of the great ones, cunningly designed to smile and speak? Lona wandered. Lona stared. Lona did not touch, did not buy.

"Viability of eggs was tested by transplantation into mated inbred albino BALB/c or Cal A recipients which were under anesthesia. The recipients had been induced by hormone injection to ovulate simultaneously with the agouti C3H donors and had been mated with fertile males of their own albino strain."

Someday my children will come here, Lona told herself. They'll buy toys. They'll enjoy themselves. They'll run through the crowds—

—a crowd all by themselves—

She sensed breath on her nape. A hand caressed her rump. Tom Piper? She turned in panic. No, no, not Tom Piper, just some giraffe of a boy who studiously stared upward at the distant tiers of the fleshmongers. Lona moved away.

"The entire procedure from the time experimental eggs were flushed from the donor oviduct to the time of their transplantation into the recipient infundibulum required 30 to 40 minutes. During this period of maintenance in vitro at room temperature many eggs shrank within their zonae pellucidae."

Here was the zoo exhibit. Caged things pacing, peering, imploring. Lona went in. The last beasts, here? A world swept free of animals? Here was the giant anteater. Which was the snout, which the tail? A tree sloth lavishly hooked its claws into dead wood. Nervous coati-mundis paced their quarters. The stink of beasts was flogged from the room by whirring pumps beneath the flagstone floor.

". . . the shrunken eggs usually survived and were regarded as essentially normal. . . ."

The animals frightened Lona. She moved away, out of the zoo, circling the main gallery of the Arcade once again. She thought she saw Tom Piper pursuing her. She brushed lightly against the rigid belly of the pregnant girl.

". . . the number of degenerating embryos and resorption sites was also examined in the autopsied recipients . . ."

She realized that she did not want to be here at all. Home, safe, warm, alone. She did not know which was more frightening: people in great herds, or one person, singly.

". . . a fair number of eggs survive micromanipulation and injection of a foreign substance. : . ."

I want to leave, Lona decided.

Exit. Exit. Where was the exit? Exits were not featured here. They wanted you to stay. Suppose fire broke out? Robots sliding from concealed panels quenching the blaze. But I want to leave.

". . . a useful method is thus provided. . . ."

". . . the survival of pronuclear eggs after the various treatments is shown in Table 1. . . ."

". . . the fetuses which developed from the microinjected eggs were smaller more frequently than their native littermates, although no other external abnormality was observed. . . ."

Thank you, Dr. Teh Ping Lin of San Francisco.

Lona fled.

She rushed in a frenzied circle around the belly of the bright Arcade. Tom Piper found her again, shouted to her, reached forth his hands. He's friendly. He means no harm. He's lonely. Maybe he really is a starman.

Lona fled.

She discovered an exfundibulum and rushed to the street. The sounds of the Arcade dwindled. Out here in the darkness she felt calmer, and the sweat of panic dried on her skin, cooling her. Lona shivered. Looking over her shoulder many times, she hurried toward her building. Clasped to her thigh were anti-molestation weapons that would thwart any rapist: a siren, a screen of smoke, a laser to flash pulsations of blinding light. Yet one never could be certain. That Tom Piper; he could be anywhere and capable of anything.

She reached home. My babies, she thought. I want my babies.

The door closed. The light went on. Sixty or seventy soft

images clung to the walls. Lona touched them. Did their diapers need changing? Diapers were an eternal verity. Had they gurgled milk over their rosy cheeks? Should she brush their curly hair? Tender skulls, not yet knit; flexible bones; snub noses. My babies. Lona's hands caressed the walls. She shed her clothes. A time came when sleep seized her.

Five
Enter Chalk; To Him, Aoudad

Duncan Chalk had been studying the tapes on the pair for three days, giving the project nearly his undivided attention. It seemed to him now that he knew Minner Burris and Lona Kelvin as thoroughly as anyone had ever known them. It seemed to him, also, that the idea of bringing them together had merit.

Intuitively, Chalk had known that from the beginning. But, though he trusted his intuitive judgments, he rarely acted on them until he had had time to make a more rational reconnaissance. Now he had done that. Aoudad and Nikolaides, to whom he had delegated the preliminary plases of this enterprise, had submitted their selections of the monitor tapes. Chalk did not rely on their judgment alone; he had arranged for others to scan the tapes as well and prepare their own anthologies of revealing episodes. It was gratifying to see how well the choices coincided. It justified his faith in Aoudad and Nikolaides. They were good men.

Chalk rocked back and forth in his pneumatic chair and considered the situation while all about him the organization he had built hummed and throbbed with life.

A project. An enterprise. A joining of two suffering human beings. But were they human? They had been, once. The raw material had been human. A sperm, an ovum, a set of genetic codons. A whimpering child. So far, so good. A small boy, a small girl, blank planchets ready for life's imprint. Life had come down hard on these two.

Minner Burris. Starman. Intelligent, vigorous, educated.

Seized on an alien world and transformed against his will into something monstrous. Burris was distressed by what had become of himself, naturally. A lesser man would have shattered. Burris had merely bent. That was interesting and praiseworthy, Chalk knew, in terms of what the public could gain from the story of Minner Burris. But Burris also suffered. That was interesting in Chalk's own terms.

Lona Kelvin. Girl. Orphaned early, a ward of the state. Not pretty, but of course her years of maturity were still ahead of her and she might ripen. Insecure, badly oriented toward men, and not very bright. (Or was she brighter than she dared let herself seem to be, Chalk wondered?) She had a thing in common with Burris. Scientists had seized upon her, too: not grisly alien Things, but kindly, benevolent, impartial high-order abstractions in white lab smocks, who without injuring Lona in any way had merely borrowed some unnecessary objects stored within her body and had used them in an experiment. That was all. And now Lona's hundred babies were sprouting in their gleaming plastic wombs. Had sprouted? Yes. Born already. Leaving a certain vacuum within Lona. She suffered.

It would be an act of charity, Duncan Chalk decided, to bring this suffering pair together.

"Send Bart in here," he said to his chair.

Aoudad entered at once, as though rolling in on wheels, as though he had waited tensely in an anteroom for just this summons. He was gratifyingly tense. Long ago Aoudad had been self-sufficient and emotionally agile, but he had broken down, Chalk knew, under the lengthy strain. His compulsive womanizing was a clue to that. Yet to look at him, one saw the pretense of strength. The cool eyes, the firm lips. Chalk felt the subsurface emanations of fear and edginess. Aoudad waited.

Chalk said, "Bart, can you bring Burris to see me right away?"

"He hasn't left his room in weeks."

"I know that. But it's futile if I go to him. He's got to be coaxed back into public. I've decided to go ahead with the project."

Aoudad radiated a kind of terror. "I'll visit him, sir. I've been planning techniques of contact for some while. I'll offer incentives. He'll come."

"Don't mention the girl to him just yet."

"No. Certainly not."

"You'll handle this well, Bart. I can rely on you. You know that. There's a great deal at stake, but you'll do your usually fine job."

Chalk smiled. Aoudad smiled. On one, the smile was a weapon. On the other a defense. Chalk sensed the emanations. Deep within him, ductless glands were triggered, and he responded to Aoudad's uneasiness with a jolt of pleasure. Behind Aoudad's cool gray eyes uncertainties revolved. Yet Chalk had spoken the truth: he *did* have faith in Aoudad's skill in this matter. Only Aoudad himself did not have faith; and so Chalk's reassurances twisted the blade a trifle. Chalk had learned such tactics early.

Chalk said, "Where's Nick?"

"Out. I think he's tracking that girl."

"He nearly blundered last night. The girl was in the Arcade and wasn't properly protected. Some fool fingered her. Nick was lucky the girl resisted. I'm saving her."

"Yes. Of course."

"Naturally, no one recognized her. She's forgotten. Her year was last year, and today she's nothing. Still," Chalk said, "there's a good story in her, properly handled. And if some ignorant grease gets his hands on her and stains her, it ruins the story. Nick should watch her more closely. I'll tell him that. You see about Burris."

Aoudad quickly left the room. Chalk sat humming idly, enjoying himself. This thing would work. The public would love it when the romance flowered. There'd be money to reap. Of course, Chalk had little need for further money. It had motivated him once, but not now. Nor did the acquisition of greater power please him much. Despite the customary theories, Chalk had attained sufficient power so that he was willing to stop expanding if only he could be sure of holding what he had. No, it was something else, something inner, that governed his decisions now. When the love of money and the love of power are both sated, the love of love remains. Chalk did not find his love where others might find it, but he had his needs. Minner Burris and Lona Kelvin could fill those needs, perhaps. Catalysis. Synergy. Then he would see.

He closed his eyes.

He saw himself naked, afloat, gliding through the blue-green sea. Lofty waves buffeted his sleek white sides. His vast bulk moved easily, for it was weightless here, supported by the bosom of ocean, the bones for once not bowed by gravity's pull. Chalk was swift here. He wheeled to and fro, displaying his agility in the water. About him played dolphins, squid, marlin. Alongside him moved the solemn, stupid upright mass of a sunfish, no midget itself but dwarfed by his shining immensity.

Chalk saw boats on the horizon. Men coming toward him, upraised, grim-faced. He was quarry now. He laughed a thundering laugh. As the boats approached, he turned and swam toward them, teasing them, inviting them to do their worst. He was near the surface, gleaming whitely in the midday light. Sheets of water cascaded from his back.

Now the boats were near. Chalk pivoted. Mighty flukes lashed the water; a boat sprang high, became matchsticks, dumped its flailing cargo of men in the brine. A surge of muscle carried him away from his pursuers. He blew a great spouting geyser to celebrate his triumph. Then he plunged, sounding joyously, seeking the depths, and in moments his whiteness vanished into a realm where light was not free to enter.

Six

Moder, Merci; Let Me Deye

"You should go out of your room," the visitation suggested gently. "Show yourself to the world. Meet it head on. There's nothing to fear."

Burris groaned. "You again! Won't you leave me alone?"

"How can I ever leave you?" his other self asked.

Burris stared through layers of gathering darkness. He had fed himself three times this day, so perhaps it was night, though he did not know and did not care. A gleaming slot provided him with any food he requested. The rearrangers of his body had improved his digestive system but had not made any fundamental changes in it. A small enough blessing, he felt; yet he still could cope with Earthside food. God knew where his enzymes now came from, but they were the same enzymes. Rennin, pepsin, the lipases, pancreatic amylase, trypsin, ptyalin, the whole diligent crew. What of the small intestine? What the fate of duodenum, jejunum, and ileum? What had replaced the mesentery and the peritoneum? Gone, gone, all gone, but rennin and pepsin somehow did their work. So the Earthside doctors who had examined him had said. Burris sensed that they would gladly dissect him to learn his secrets in more detail.

But not yet. Not just yet. He was coming toward that pass, but it would be a while.

And the apparition of former felicity would not absent itself.

"Look at your face," Burris said. "Your eyelids move so stupidly, up, down, blink, blink. The eyes are so crude. Your nose admits garbage to your throat. I must admit I'm a considerable improvement over you."

"Of course. That's why I say go out, let yourself be admired by humanity."

"When did humanity ever admire improved models of itself? Did Pithecanthropus fawn on the first Neanderthals? Did Neanderthal applaud the Aurignacians?"

"The analogy isn't proper. You didn't evolve past them, Minner. You were changed by external means. They have no reason to hate you for what you are."

"They don't need to hate. Only to stare. Besides, I'm in pain. It's easier to remain here."

"Is the pain really so hard to bear?"

"I grow accustomed to it," Burris said. "Yet every motion stabs me. The Things were only experimenting. They made their little mistakes. This extra chamber of my heart: whenever it contracts, I feel it in my throat. This shiny and permeable gut of mine: it passes food and I ache. I should kill myself. It's the best release."

"Seek your comfort in literature," the apparition counseled. "Read. You once did. You were quite a well-read man, Minner. Three thousand years of literature at your command. Several languages. Homer. Chaucer. Shakespeare."

Burris looked at the serene face of the man he had been. He recited: *"Moder, merci; let me deye."*

"Finish it."

"The rest's not applicable."

"Finish it anyway."

Burris said:

"For Adam ut of helle beye
And manken that if forloren."

"Die, then," the visitation said mildly. "To buy Adam out of hell and mankind that is lost. Otherwise remain alive. Minner, do you think you're Jesus?"

"He suffered at the hands of strangers."

"To redeem them. Will you redeem the Things if you go back to Manipool and die on their doorstep?"

Burris shrugged. "I'm no redeemer. I need redeeming myself. I'm in a bad way."

"Whining again!"

"Sune, I se thi bodi swungin,
thi brest, thin hond, thi fot thurch-stungen."

Burris scowled. His new face was well designed for scowling; the lips rippled outward, like a sphincter door irising, baring the subdivided palisade of imperishable teeth. "What do you want of me?" he asked.

"What do *you* want, Minner?"

"To put off this flesh. To have my old body back."

"A miracle, that is. And you want the miracle to happen to you within these four walls."

"As good a place as any. As likely as any."

"No. Go outside. Seek help."

"I've been outside. I've been prodded and poked. Not helped. What shall I do—sell myself to a museum? Go away, you damned ghost. Out! Out!"

"Your redeemer liveth," said the apparition.

"Tell me his address."

No answer came. Burris found himself staring at cobwebbed shadows. The room purred with silence. Restlessness throbbed at him. His body now was designed to maintain tonus despite all idleness; it was a perfect spacefarer's body, equipped to drift from star to star, enduring all the long silence.

So had he drifted to Manipool. It lay on his route. Man was a newcomer among the stars, hardly having left his own planets behind. There was no telling what one would meet out there and what would happen to one. Burris had been the unlucky one. He had survived. The others lay in cheerful graves under a speckled sun. The Italians, Malcondotto and Prolisse—they had not come out of surgery. They were trial runs for Manipool's masterpiece, himself. Burris had seen Malcondotto, dead, after they had finished with him. He was at peace. He had looked so tranquil, if a monster can seem tranquil even in death. Prolisse had preceded him. Burris had not seen what they had done to Prolisse, and it had been just as well.

He had gone to the stars as a civilized man, alert, flexible of mind. No tubemonkey, no deckswabber. An officer, the highest product of mankind, armed with the higher mathematics and the highest topology. Mind stuffed with literary nuggets. A man who had loved, who had learned. Burris was glad now that he had never married. It is awkward for a starman to take a wife, but it is far more awkward to return from the stars transformed and embrace a former darling.

The ghost was back. "Consult Aoudad," it advised. "He'll lead you to help. He'll make you a whole man again."

"Aoudad?"

"Aoudad."

"I will not see him."

Burris was in solitude once more.

He looked at his hands. Delicate, tapering fingers, essentially unchanged except for the prehensile tentacle they had grafted to the outer phalanx on each side. Another of their little amusements. They might have put a pair of such tentacles below his arms, for that would have been useful. Or given him a prehensile tail, making him at least as efficient a brachiator as a Brazilian monkey. But these two muscular ropy things, pencil-thick and three inches long, what good were they? They had broadened his hand, he noticed for the first time, so that it would accommodate the new digit without disturbing the proportions. Considerate of them. Burris discovered some new facet of his newness every day. He thought of the dead Malcondotto. He thought of the dead Prolisse. He thought of Aoudad. Aoudad? How could Aoudad help him in any conceivable way?

They had stretched him on a table, or the Manipool equivalent of a table, something dipping and uncertain. They had measured him. What had they checked? Temperature, pulse rate, blood pressure, peristalsis, pupil dilation, iodine uptake, capillary function, and how much else? They had put calipers to the salty film over his eyeballs. They had computed the volume of cell content in the seminal duct. They had searched out the pathways of neural excitation, so that they could be blocked.

Anesthesia. Successful!

Surgery.

Peel back the rind. Seek for pituitary, hypothalamus, thyroid. Calm the fluttering ventricles. Descend with tiny intangible scalpels to enter the passages. The body, Galen had suspected, was merely a bag of blood. Was there a circulatory system? Was there a circulation? On Manipool they had discovered the secrets of human construction in three easy lessons. Malcondotto, Prolisse, Burris. Two they had wasted. The third endured.

They had tied off blood vessels. They had exposed the gray silkiness of the brain. Here was the node of Chaucer. Here Piers Plowman. Aggression here. Vindictiveness. Sensory perception. Charity. Faith. In this shining bulge dwelled Proust, Hemingway, Mozart, Beethoven. Rembrandt here.

See, see where Christ's blood streams in the firmament!

He had waited for it to begin, knowing that Malcondotto had perished under their ministrations and that Prolisse, flayed and diced, was gone. *Stand still, you ever-moving spheres of heaven, that time may cease and midnight never come.* Midnight came. The slithering knives dug at his brain. It would not hurt, he was sure of that, and yet he feared the pain. His only body, his irreplaceable self. He had not harmed them. He had come in innocence.

Once, in boyhood, he had cut his leg while playing, a deep cut, gaping wide to reveal raw meat within. *A gash,* he thought, *I have a gash.* Blood had spouted over his feet. They had healed it, not so swiftly as such things were done today, but as he watched the red slash knit, he had meditated on the change that had worked. His leg would never be the same again, for now it bore the cicatrix of injury. That had moved him profoundly, at twelve—so fundamental a change in his body, so permanent. He thought of that in the final moments before the Things began work on him. *Mountains and hills, come, come and fall on me, and hide me from the heavy wrath of God! No, no! Then will I headlong run into the earth: earth, gape!*

An idle command.

O, no, it will not harbour me!

The silent knives whirled. The nuclei of the medulla, receiving impulses from the vestibular mechanism of the ear—gone. The basal ganglia. The sulci and the gyri. The bronchi with their cartilaginous rings. The alveoli, the wondrous sponges. Epiglottis. Vas deferens. Lymphatic vessels.

Dendrites and axons. The doctors were quite curious: how does this marvelous creature work? What composes him?

They unstrung him until he was spread out etherized on a table, extending an infinite distance. Was he still alive at that point? Bundles of nerves, bushels of intestine. *Now, body, turn to air, or Lucifer will bear thee quick to hell! O soul, be chang'd into little water-drops, and fall into the ocean, ne'er be found!*

Patiently they had restored him. Tediously did they reconstruct him, improving where minded on the original model. And then, no doubt in great pride, they of Manipool had returned him to his people.

Come not, Lucifer!

"Consult Aoudad," the apparition advised.

Aoudad? *Aoudad?*

Seven

Here's Death, Twitching My Ear

The room stank. Its stink was vile. Wondering if the man ever troubled to ventilate, Bart Aoudad subtly introduced an olfactory depressant into his system. The brain would function as keenly as ever; it had better. But the nostrils would cease for the moment to report all that they might.

He was lucky to be in here, stink or not. He had won the privilege through diligent courtship.

Burris said, "Can you look at me?"

"Easily. You fascinate me, honestly. Did you expect me to be repelled?"

"Most people so far have been."

"Most people are fools," said Aoudad.

He did not reveal that he had monitored Burris for many weeks now, long enough to steel himself against the strangeness of the man. Strange he was, and repellent enough; yet the configurations grew on one. Aoudad was not yet ready to

apply for the same sort of beauty treatment, but he was numb
to Burris's deformities.

"Can you help me?" Burris asked.

"I believe I can."

"Provided I want help."

"I assume that you do."

Burris shrugged. "I'm not certain of that. You might say I'm
growing accustomed to my present appearance. In another
few days I might start going outdoors again."

It was a lie, Aoudad knew. Which one of them Burris was
trying to delude, Aoudad could not positively say. But,
however blandly Burris had his bitterness at the moment, the
visitor had ample knowledge that it still festered within him.
Burris wanted out of this body.

Aoudad said, "I am in the employ of Duncan Chalk. Do
you know the name?"

"No."

"But—" Aoudad swallowed his surprise. "Of course. You
haven't spent much time on Earth. Chalk brings amusement
to the world. Perhaps you've visited the Arcade, or maybe
you've been to Luna Tivoli."

"I know of them."

"They are Chalk's enterprises. Among many others. He
keeps billions of people happy in this system. He is even
planning to expand to other systems shortly." That was a bit
of imaginative hyperbole on Aoudad's part, but Burris did not
need to know it.

Burris said, "So?"

"Chalk is wealthy, you see. Chalk is humanitarian. The
combination is a good one. It hold possibilities that may
benefit you."

"I see them already," said Burris smoothly, leaning forward
and entwining the outer tentacles that squirmed on his
hands. "You hire me as an exhibit in Chalk's circuses. You pay
me eight million a year. Every curiosity-seeker in the system
comes to have his look. Chalk gets richer, I become a million-
aire and die happy, and the petty curiosities of the multitudes
are gratified. Yes?"

"No," Aoudad said, alarmed by the nearness of Burris's
guess. "I'm sure you're merely joking. You must realize that
Mr. Chalk could not conceivably exploit your—ah—misfortune
in such a way."

"Do you think it's such a misfortune?" asked Burris. "I'm

quite efficient this way. Of course, there's pain, but I can stay underwater for fifteen minutes. Can you do that? Do you feel so sorry for me?"

I must not let him lead me astray, Aoudad resolved. He's devilish. He'd get along well with Chalk.

Aoudad said, "Certainly I'm happy to know that you find your present situation reasonably satisfactory. Yet—let me be frank—I suspect you'd be glad to return to normal human form."

"You think so, do you?"

"Yes."

"You're a remarkably perceptive man, Mr. Aoudad. Have you brought your magic wand?"

"There's no magic involved. But if you're willing to supply a quid for our quo, it's possible that Chalk can arrange to have you transferred to a more conventional body."

The effect on Burris was immediate and electric.

He dropped the pose of casual indifference. He cast aside the mocking detachment behind which, Aoudad realized, he hid his agony. His body trembled like a glass flower strummed by the breeze. There was momentary loss of muscular control: the mouth convulsively flashed sidewise smiles, a flapping gate, and the shuttered eyes clicked a dozen times.

"How can this be done?" Burris demanded.

"Let Chalk explain it to you."

Burris's hand dug into Aoudad's thigh. Aoudad did not shrink at the metallic touch.

Burris said hoarsely: "Is it possible?"

"It may be. The technique is not perfected yet."

"Am I to be the guinea pig this time, too?"

"Please. Chalk would not expose you to further distress. There will be additional research before the process can be applied to you. Will you talk to him?"

Hesitation. Once more eyes and mouth acted seemingly without Burris's volition. Then the starman regained command of himself. He straightened, twining his hands together, crossing his legs. How many kneejoints does he have, Aoudad wondered? Burris was silent. Calculating. Electrons surging down the pathways of that tormented brain.

Burris said, "If Chalk can place me in another body—"

"Yes?"

"What will he gain from it?"

"I told you. Chalk's a humanitarian. He knows you're in

pain. He wants to do something about it. See him, Burris.
Let him help you."

"Who are you, Aoudad?"

"No one. A limb of Duncan Chalk."

"Is this a trap?"

"You're too suspicious," Aoudad said. "We mean the best
for you."

Silence. Burris rose, pacing the room in a peculiarly liquid
gliding step. Aoudad was taut.

"To Chalk," Burris murmured finally. "Yes. Take me to
Chalk!"

Eight
Stabat Mater Dolorosa

In the dark it was easy for Lona to pretend that she was dead.
She often mourned at her own grave. She saw herself on a
hillside, on a grassy breast of earth with a tiny plaque set in
the ground at her feet. HERE LIES.

VICTIM.

MURDERED BY SCIENTISTS.

She drew the coverlets up over her thin body. Her eyes,
tightly closed, held back the tears. BLESSED REPOSE.
HOPE OF REDEMPTION. What did they do with dead
bodies nowadays? Pop them in the oven! A bright hot flash.
Light, like the sun. And then dust. Dust to dust. A long
sleep.

I was nearly dead once, Lona reminded herself. But they
stopped me. They brought me back.

Six months ago, in the full blaze of summer. A good season
for dying, Lona thought. Her babies had been born. It didn't
take nine months, the way they did it, bringing them along in
bottles. More like six months. The experiment had taken
place exactly a year back. Six months for the babies to hatch.
Then the unbearable publicity—and the brush with deliberate death.

Why had they chosen her?

Because she was there. Because she was available. Because she could not object. Because she carried a bellyful of fertile eggs that she wasn't likely ever to need.

"A woman's ovaries contain several hundred thousand ova, Miss Kelvin. During your normal lifetime about four hundred of these will reach maturity. The rest are superfluous. These are the ones we wish to use. We need only a few hundred. . . ."

"In the name of science . . ."

"A crucial experiment . . ."

"The ova are superfluous. You can dispense with them and feel no loss. . . ."

"Medical history . . . your name . . . forever. . . ."

"No effect on your future fertility. You can marry and have a dozen normal children. . . ."

It was an intricate experiment with many facets. They had had a century or so to perfect the techniques, and now they were bringing them all together in a single project. Natural oögenesis coupled with synthetic ripening of the ova. Embryonic induction. External fertilization. Extramaternal incubation after reimplanting of fertilized ova. Words. Sounds. Synthetic capacitation. *Ex utero* fetal development. Simultaneity of genetic material. My babies! My babies!

Lona did not know who the "father" was, only that a single donor would contribute all of the sperm, just as a single donor would contribute all of the ova. She understood that much. The doctors were very good about explaining the project to her, step by step, speaking to her as they would to a child. She followed most of it. They patronized her because she had had no education to speak of and because she was timid of embracing tough ideas, but the raw intelligence was there.

Her part in the project was simple and ended at the first phase. They flushed from her ovaries several hundred fertile but immature eggs. So far as they were concerned, Lona could then drop into outer darkness. But she had to know. She followed the subsequent steps.

The eggs were coddled along in artificial ovaries until they were ripe. A woman could ripen only two or three ova at a time in the hidden greenhouse of her middle; the machines could and did handle hundreds. Came then the taxing but not essentially new process of microinjection of the eggs to strengthen them. And then fertilization. The swimming sperms wriggled toward their goal. A single donor, a single explosive burst at harvest-time. Many ova had been lost in the earlier stages. Many were not fertile or not fertilized. But a hundred were. The tiny wriggler reached its harbor.

Reimplantation of the fertilized ova now. There had been talk of finding a hundred other women to carry the hundred sprouting zygotes. Cuckoo fetuses, swelling the wrong bellies. In the end, though, that was considered excessive. A dozen women volunteered to carry to term; the rest of the fertilized ova went to the artifical wombs. A dozen pale bellies bare under the bright lights. A dozen pairs of smooth thighs opening not to a lover but to dull gray aluminum sheathing. The slow thrust, the squirting entry, the completion of implantation. Some attempts were failures. Eight of the sleek bellies soon were bulging.

"Let me volunteer," Lona had said. Touching her flat belly: "Let me carry one of the babies."

"No."

They were gentler than that. They explained that it was unnecessary within the framework of the experiment for her to go through the bother of pregnancy. It had been shown long ago that an ovum could be taken from the woman's body, fertilized elsewhere, and reimplanted to her for the usual term of nurture. Why repeat? That had been verified, confirmed. She could be spared the nuisance. They wished to know how well a human mother carried an intrusive embryo, and for that they did not need Lona.

Did anyone need Lona now?

No one needed Lona now.

No one. Lona paid heed to what was happening.

The eight volunteer mothers did well. In them pregnancy was artifically accelerated. Their bodies accepted the intruders, fed blood to them, folded them warmly in placentas. A medical miracle, yes. But how much more exciting to dispense with maternity altogether!

A row of gleaming boxes. In each a dividing zygote. The pace of cell-splitting was breathtaking. Lona's head reeled. Growth was induced in the cortical cytoplasm of the zygotes as they cleaved, then in the main axial organs. "As gastrulation proceeds, the mesodermal mantle extends forward from the blastopore, and its anterior edge comes to lie just posterior to the future lens ectoderm. This edge is the future heart, and it, too, is an inductor of the lens. At the open-neuralplate state of development, the future lens cells are located in two areas of the epidermis that lie just lateral to the anterior brain plate. As the neural plate rolls up into a tube, the future retinal cells evaginate from the prospective brain as part of the optic vesicle."

In six months a hundred bouncing babies.

A word never before used in a human context now on the lips of all: *centuplets*.

Why not? One mother, one father! The rest was incidental. The carrier women, the metal wombs—they had lent warmth and sustenance, but they were not mothers to the children.

Who was the mother?

The father did not matter. Artificial insemination was a matter for yawns. Statistically, at least, one male could fertilize every woman in the world in two afternoons. If a man's sperm had spawned a hundred babies at once, what of it?

But the *mother* . . .

Her name was not supposed to be released. "Anonymous donor"—that was her place in medical history. The story was too good, though. Especially that she was not quite seventeen. Especially that she was single. Especially that (so the physicians swore) she was technically virgin.

Two days after the simultaneous centuplet delivery, Lona's name and achievement were matters of public record.

She stood slim and frightened before the flashing lights.

"Will you name the babies yourself?"

"What did it feel like when the eggs were taken from you?"

"What does it feel like to know that you're the mother of the biggest family in human history?"

"Will you marry me?"

"Come live with me and be my love."

"Half a million for the exclusive rights to the story!"

"*Never* with a man?"

"How did you react when they told you what the experiment was going to be?"

"Have you met the father?"

"   "

A month like that. Fair skin reddened by camera-glow. Eyes wide, strained, bloodshot. Questions. Doctors beside her to guide her answers. Her moment of glory, dazzling, bewildering. The doctors hated it nearly as much as she did. They would never have released her name: except that one of them had, for a price, and the floodgates had opened. Now they tried to ward off more blunders by coaching her in what to say. Lona said quite little, actually. Part of her silence rose from fright, part from ignorance. What could she tell the world? What did the world want from her?

Briefly she was a wonder of the world. They sang a song about her on the song machines. Deep thrumming of chords; sad lament of the mother of centuplets. It was played everywhere. She could not bear to listen. Come make a baby with me, sweetie. Come make a hundred more. Her friends, not many of them to begin with, sensed that it embarrassed her to talk of It, so they talked deliberately of other things, anything else at all, and finally they simply stopped talking. She kept to herself. Strangers wanted to know what it was like, with all those babies. How could she say? She scarcely knew! Why had they made a song about her? Why did they gossip and pry? What did they *want*?

To some, it was all blasphemy. There was thunder from the pulpits. Lona felt the tang of brimstone at her nostrils. The babies cried and stretched and gurgled. She visited them once, and wept, and picked one up to hug it. The child was taken from her and restored to its aseptic environment. She was not permitted to visit them again.

Centuplets. A hundred siblings sharing the same group of codons. What would they be like? How would they grow? Could a man live in a world shared by fifty brothers and fifty sisters? That was part of the experiment. This experiment was to be a lifetime long. The psychologists had moved in. Much was known of quintuplets: sextuplets had been studied somewhat, and there had briefly been a set of septuplets thirty years before. But centuplets? An infinity of new research!

Without Lona. Her part had ended on the first day. Something cool and tingly swabbed across her thighs by a smiling nurse. Then men, staring without interest at her body. A drug. A dreamy haze through which she was aware of penetration. No other sensation. The end. "Thank you, Miss Kelvin. Your fee." Cool linens against her body. Elsewhere they were beginning to do things to the borrowed ova.

My babies. My babies.

Lights in my eyes!

When the time came to kill herself, Lona did not quite succeed at it. Doctors who could give life to a speck of matter could also sustain life in the source of that speck. They put her back together, and then they forgot about her.

A nine days' wonder is granted obscurity on the tenth day.

Obscurity, but not peace. Peace was never granted; it had to be won, the hard way, from within. Living again in darkness, Lona yet could never be the same, for somewhere else a hundred babies thrived and fattened. They had reached not only into her ovaries but into the fabric of her life itself to draw forth those babies, and she reverberated still with the recoil.

She shivered in the darkness.

Someday soon, she promised herself, I'll try again. And this time no one will notice me. This time they'll let me go. I'll sleep a long time.

Nine

In the Beginning Was the Word

For Burris it was something like being born. He had not left his room in so many weeks that it had come to seem a permanent shelter.

Aoudad thoughtfully made the delivery as painless as possible for him, though. They left at dead of night, when the city slept. Burris was cloaked and hooded. It gave him such a conspiratorial look that he was forced to smile at the effect; yet he regarded it as necessary. The hood hid him well, and so long as he kept his head down, he was safe from the glances of the casual. As they left the building, Burris remained in the far corner of the dropshaft, praying that no one else would summon it as he descended. No one did. But on the way through the entrance, a drifting blob of glowing light illuminated him for a moment just when a homecoming resident appeared. The man paused, staring beneath the hood. Burris remained expressionless. The man blinked, seeing the unexpected. Burris's harsh, distorted face regarded him coldly, and the man moved on. His sleep would be tinctured with nightmare that night. But that was better, thought Burris, than having the nightmare steal into the texture of your life itself, as had happened to him.

A car waited just beyond the lip of the building.

"Chalk doesn't ordinarily hold interviews at this hour," Aoudad chattered. "But you must understand that this is something special. He means to give you every consideration."

"Splendid," Burris said darkly.

They entered the car. It was like exchanging one womb for another less spacious but more inviting. Burris settled against a couch-seat big enough for several people, but evidently modeled to fit a single pair of enormous buttocks. Aoudad sat beside him in a more normal accomodation. The car started, gliding quietly away in a thrum of turbines. Its transponders picked up the emanations of the nearest highway, and shortly they left city streets behind and were hurtling along a restricted-access route.

The windows of the car were comfortingly opaque. Burris threw back the hood. He was accustoming himself in short stages to showing himself to other people. Aoudad, who did not appear to mind his mutilations, was a good subject on whom to practice.

"Drink?" Aoudad asked. "Smoke? Any kind of stimulant?"

"Thank you, no."

"Are you able to touch such things—the way you are?"

Burris smiled grimly. "My metabolism is basically the same as yours, even now. The plumbing's different. I eat your food. I drink your drinks. But not right this moment."

"I wondered. You'll pardon my curiosity."

"Of course."

"And bodily functions—"

"They've improved excretion. I don't know what they've done to reproduction. The organs are still there, but do they function? It's not a test I've cared to make."

The muscles of Aoudad's left cheek pulled back as though in a spasm. The response was not lost on Burris. *Why is he so interested in my sex life? Normal prurience? Something more?*

"You'll pardon my curiosity," Aoudad said again.

"I already have." Burris leaned back and felt his seat doing odd things to him. A massage, perhaps. No doubt he was tense and the poor chair was trying to fix things. But the chair was programmed for a bigger man. It seemed to be humming as if with an overloaded circuit. Was it troubled just by the size differential, Burris wondered? Or did the restructured contours of his anatomy cause it some distress?

He mentioned the chair to Aoudad, who cut it off. Smiling, Burris complimented himself on his state of mellowed relaxation. He had not said a bitter thing since Aoudad's arrival. He was calm, tempest-free, hovering at dead center. Good. Good. He had spent too much time alone, letting his miseries corrode him. This fool Aoudad was an angel of mercy come to lift him out of himself. I am grateful, said Burris pleasantly to himself.

"This is it. Chalk's office is here."

The building was relatively low, no more than three or four storeys, but it was well set off from the towers that flanked it. Its sprawling horizontal bulk compensated for its lack of height. Wide-legged angles stretched off to right and left; Burris, making useful use of his added peripheral vision, peered as far as he could around the sides of the building and calculated that it was probably eight-sided. The outer wall was of a dull brown metal, neatly finished, pebbled in an ornamental way. No light was visible within; but, then, there were no windows.

One wall abruptly gaped at them as a hidden portcullis silently lifted. The car rocketed through and came to a halt in the bowels of the building. Its hatch sprang off. Burris became aware that a short bright-eyed man was peering into the car at him.

He experienced a moment of shock at finding himself so unexpectedly being viewed by a stranger. Then he recovered and reversed the flow of the sensation, staring back. The short man was worth staring at, too. Without the benefit of malevolent surgeons, he was nonetheless strikingly ugly. Virtually neckless; thick matted dark hair descending into his collar; large jug ears; a narrow-bridged nose; incredible long, thin lips that just now were puckered in a repellent pout of fascination. No beauty.

Aoudad said: "Minner Burris. Leontes d'Amore. Of the Chalk staff."

"Chalk's awake. He's waiting," said d'Amore. Even his voice was ugly.

Yet he faces the world every day, Burris reflected.

Hooded once more, he let himself be swept along a network of pneumatic tubes until he found himself gliding into an immense cavernous room studded with various levels of activity-points. Just now there was little activity; the desks were empty, the screens were silent. A gentle glow of thermoluminescent fungi lit the place. Turning slowly, Burris panned his gaze across the room and up a series of crystal rungs until he observed, seated thronewise near the ceiling on the far side, a vast individual.

Chalk. Obviously.

Burris stood absorbed in the sight, forgetting for a moment the million tiny pricking pains that were his constant companions. So big? So enfleshed? The man had devoured a legion of cattle to gain that bulk.

Beside him, Aoudad gently urged him forward, not quite daring to touch Burris's elbow.

"Let me see you," Chalk said. His voice was light, amiable. "Up here. Up to me, Burris."

A moment more. Face to face.

Burris shrugged off the hood and then the cloak. Let him have his look. Before this mound of flesh I need feel no shame.

Chalk's placid expression did not change.

He studied Burris carefully, with deep interest and no hint of revulsion. At a wave of his pudgy hand, Aoudad and d'Amore vanished. Burris and Chalk remained alone in the huge, dim room.

"They did quite a job on you," Chalk remarked. "Do you have any idea why they did it?"

"Sheer curiosity. Also the desire to improve. In their inhuman way, they're quite human."

"What do they look like?"

"Pockmarked. Leathery. I'd rather not say."

"All right." Chalk had not risen. Burris stood before him, hands folded, the little outer tentacles twining and untwining. He sensed a seat behind him and took it unbidden.

"You have quite a place here," he said.

Chalk smiled and let the statement roll away. He said, "Does it hurt?"

"What?"

"Your changes."

"There's considerable discomfort. Terran painkillers don't help much. They did things to the neural channels, and no one here knows quite where to apply the blocks. But it's bearable. They say the limbs of amputees throb for years after they've been removed. Same sensation, I guess."

"Were any of your limbs removed?"

"All of them," Burris said. "And put back on again a new way. The medics who examined me were very pleased by my joints. Also my tendons and ligaments. These are my own original hands, a little altered. My feet. I'm not really sure how much else of me is mine and how much theirs."

"And internally?"

"All different. Chaos. A report is being prepared. I haven't been back on Earth long. They studied me awhile, and then I rebelled."

"Why?"

"I was becoming a thing. Not only to them but to myself. I'm not a thing. I'm a human being who's been rearranged. Inside, I'm still human. Prick me and I'll bleed. What can you do for me, Chalk?"

A meaty hand waved. "Patience. Patience. I want to know more about you. You were a space officer?"

"Yes."

"Academy and all?"

"Naturally."

"Your rating must have been good. You were given a tough assignment. First landing on a world of intelligent beings—never a cinch. How many in your team?"

"Three. We all went through surgery. Prolisse died first, then Malcondotto. Lucky for them."

"You dislike your present body?"

"It has its advantages. The doctors say I'm likely to live five hundred years. But it's painful, and it's also embarrassing. I was never cut out to be a monster."

"You're not as ugly as you may think you are," Chalk observed. "Oh, yes, children run screaming from you, that sort of thing. But children are conservatives. They loathe anything new. I find that face of yours quite attractive in its way. I daresay a lot of women would fling themselves at your feet."

"I don't know. I haven't tried."

"Grotesqueness has its appeal, Burris. I weighed over twenty pounds at birth. My weight has never hampered me. I think of it as an asset."

"You've had a lifetime to get used to your size," said Burris. "You accommodate to it in a thousand ways. Also, you chose to be this way. I was the victim of an incomprehensible whim. It's a violation. I've been raped, Chalk."

"You want it all undone?"

"What do you think?"

Chalk nodded. His eyelids slid down, and it appeared that he had dropped instantly into a sound sleep. Burris waited, baffled, and more than a minute passed. Without stirring, Chalk said, "Surgeons here on Earth can transplant brains successfully from one body to another."

Burris started, seized by a *grand mal* of fevered excitement. A new organ within his body injected spurts of some unknown hormone into the bowl of strangenesses beside his heart. He dizzied. He scrabbled in the roiling surf, dashed again and again onto the abrasive sand by relentless waves.

Chalk went on calmly, "Does the technology of the thing interest you at all?"

The tentacles of Burris's hands writhed uncontrollably.

The smooth words came: "The brain must be surgically isolated within the skull by paring away of all contiguous tissues. The cranium itself is preserved for support and protection. Naturally, absolute hemostasis must be maintained during the long period of anticoagulation, and there are techniques for sealing the base of the skull and the frontal bone to prevent loss of blood. Brain functions are monitored by electrodes and thermoprobes. Circulation is maintained by linking the internal maxillary and internal carotid arteries. Vascular loops, you understand. I'll spare you the details by which the body is shaved away, leaving only the living brain. At length the spinal cord is severed and the brain is totally isolated, fed by its own carotid system. Meanwhile the recipient has been prepared. The carotid and jugular are dissected away and the major strap muscles in the cervical area are resected. The brain graft is put in place after submergence in an antibiotic solution. The carotid arteries of the isolated brain are connected by a siliconized cannula to the proximal carotid artery of the recipient. All this is done in a low freeze to minimize damage. Once the grafted brain's circulation is meshed with that of the recipient body, we bring the temperature toward normal and begin standard post-operative techniques. A prolonged period of re-education is necessary before the grafted brain has assumed control over the recipient body."

"Remarkable."

"Not much of an achievement compared with what was done to you," Chalk conceded. "But it's been carried out successfully with higher mammals. Even with primates."

"With humans?"

"No."

"Then—"

"Terminal patients have been used. Brains grafted into recently deceased. Too much goes against the chance of success there, though. Still, there have been some near misses. Another three years, Burris, and human beings will be swapping brains as easily as they swap arms and legs today."

Burris disliked the sensations of intense anticipation that roared through him. His skin temperature was uncomfortably high. His throat throbbed.

Chalk said, "We build a synthetic for you, duplicating in as many respects as possible your original appearance. We assemble a golem, you see, from the spare-parts bank, but we do not include a brain. We transplant your brain into the assemblage. There will be differences, naturally, but you'll be fundamentally integral. Interested?"

"Don't torture me, Chalk."

"I give you my word I'm serious. Two technological problems stand in the way. We have to master the technique of total assembly of a recipient, and we have to keep it alive until we can successfully carry out the transplant. I've already said it would take three years to achieve the second. Say two more to build the golem. Five years, Burris, and you'll be fully human again."

"What will this cost?"

"Perhaps a hundred million. Perhaps more."

Burris laughed harshly. His tongue—how like a serpent's now!—flickered into view.

Chalk: "I'm prepared to underwrite the entire cost of your rehabilitation."

"You're dealing in fantasy now."

"I ask you to have faith in my resources. Are you willing to part with your present body if I can supply something closer to the human norm?"

It was a question that Burris had never expected anyone to ask him. He was startled by the extent of his own vacillation. He detested this body and was bowed beneath the weight of the thing that had been perpetrated on him. And yet, was he coming to love his alienness?

He said after a brief pause, "The sooner I could shed this thing, the better."

"Good. Now, there's the problem of your getting through the five years or so that this will take. I propose that we attempt to modify your facial appearance, at least, so that you'll be able to get along in society until we can make the switch. Does that interest you?"

"It can't be done. I've already explored the idea with the doctors who examined me after my return. I'm a mess of strange antibodies, and I'll reject any graft."

"Do you think that's so? Or were they merely telling you a convenient lie?"

"I think it's so."

"Let me send you to a hospital," Chalk suggested. "We'll run a few tests to confirm the earlier verdict. If it's so, so. If not, we can make life a little easier for you. Yes?"

"Why are you doing this, Chalk? What's the quid pro quo?"

The fat man pivoted and swung ponderously forward until his eyes were only inches from Burris's face. Burris surveyed the oddly delicate lips, the fine nose, the immense cheeks and puffy eyelids. In a low voice Chalk murmured, "The price is a steep one. It'll sicken you to the core. You'll turn down the whole deal."

"What is it?"

"I'm a purveyor of popular amusement. I can't remotely get my investment back out of you, but I want to recover what I can."

"The price?"

"Full rights to commercial exploitation of your story," said Chalk. "Beginning with your seizure by the aliens, carrying through your return to Earth and your difficult adjustment to your altered condition, and continuing on through your forth-coming period of re-adaptation. The world already knows that three men came to a planet called Manipool, two were killed, and a third came back the victim of surgical experiments. That much was announced, and then you dropped from sight. I want to put you back in sight. I want to show you rediscovering your humanity, relating to other people again, groping up-ward out of hell, eventually triumphing over your catastroph-ic experience and coming out of it purged. It'll mean a frequent intrusion on your privacy, and I'm prepared to hear you refuse. After all, one would expect—"

"It's a new form of torture, is it?"

"Something of an ordeal, perhaps," Chalk admitted. His wide forehead was stippled with sweat. He looked flushed and strained, as though approaching some sort of inner emotional climax.

"Purged," Burris whispered. "You offer me purgatory."

"Call it that."

"I hide for weeks. Then I stand naked before the universe for five years. Eh?"

"Expenses paid."

"Expenses paid," said Burris. "Yes. Yes. I accept the torture. I'm your toy, Chalk. Only a human being would refuse the offer. But I accept. I accept!"

Ten
A Pound of Flesh

"He's at the hospital," Aoudad said. "They've begun to study him." He plucked at the woman's clothes. "Take them off, Elise."

Elise Prolisse brushed the questing hand away. "Will Chalk really put him back in a human body?"

"I don't doubt it."

"Then if Marco had returned alive, he might have been put back, too."

Aoudad was noncommittal. "You're dealing in too many ifs now. Marco's dead. Open your robe, dear."

"Wait. Can I visit Burris in the hospital?"

"I suppose. What do you want with him?"

"Just to talk. He was the last man to see my husband alive, remember? He can tell me how Marco died."

"You would not want to know," said Aoudad softly. "Marco died as they tried to make him into the kind of creature Burris now is. If you saw Burris, you would realize that Marco is better off dead."

"All the same—"

"You would not want to know."

"I asked to see him," Elise said dreamily, "as soon as he returned. I wanted to talk to him about Marco. And the other, Malcondotto—he had a widow, too. But they would not let us near him. And afterward Burris disappeared. You could take me to him!"

"It's for your own good that you keep away," Aoudad told her. His hands crept up her body, lingering, seeking out the magnetic snaps and depolarizing them. The garment opened. The heavy breasts came into view, deathly white, tipped with circlets of deep red. He felt the inward stab of desire. She caught his hands as he reached for them.

"You will help me see Burris?" she asked.

"I—"

"You will help me see Burris." Not a question this time.

"Yes. Yes."

The hands blocking his path dropped away. Trembling, Aoudad peeled back the garments. She was a handsome woman, past her first youth, meaty, yet handsome. These Italians! White skin, dark hair. *Sensualissima!* Let her see Burris if she wished. Would Chalk object? Chalk had already indicated the kind of matchmaking he expected. Burris and the Kelvin girl. But perhaps Burris and the widow Prolisse first? Aoudad's mind churned.

Elise looked up at him in adoration as his lean, tough body poised above her.

Her last garment surrendered. He stared at acres of whiteness, islands of black and red.

"Tomorrow you will arrange it," she said.

"Yes. Tomorrow."

He fell upon her nakedness. Around the fleshy part of her left thigh she wore a black velvet band. A mourning band for Marco Prolisse, done to death imcomprehensibly by incomprehensible beings on an incomprehensible world. *Pover'uomo!* Her flesh blazed. She was incandescent. A tropical valley beckoned to him. Aoudad entered. Almost at once came a strangled cry of ecstasy.

Eleven
Two If by Night

The hospital lay at the very edge of the desert. It was a U-shaped building, long and low, whose limbs pointed toward the east. Early sunlight, rising, crept along them until it splashed against the long horizontal bar linking the parallel vertical wings. The construction was of gray sandstone tinged with red. Just to the west of the building—that is, behind its main section—was a narrow garden strip, and beyond the garden began the zone of dry brownish desert.

The desert was not without life of its own. Somber tufts of sagebrush were common. Beneath the parched surface were the tunnels of rodents. Kangaroo mice could be seen by the lucky at night, grasshoppers during the day. Cacti and euphorbias and other succulents studded the earth.

Some of the desert's abundant life had invaded the hospital grounds themselves. The garden in the rear was a desert garden, thick with the thorned things of dryness. The courtyard between the two limbs of the U had been planted with cacti also. Here stood a saguaro six times the height of a man, with rugged central trunk and five skyward arms. There, framing it, were two specimens of the bizarre variant form, the cancer cactus, solid trunk, two small arms crying help, and a cluster of gnarled, twisted growths at the summit. Down the path, tree-high, the grotesque white cholla. Facing it, squat, sturdy, the thorn-girdled barrel of a water cactus. Spiny canes of an opuntia; flat grayish pads of the prickly pear; looping loveliness of a cereus. At other times of the year these formidable, bristling, stolid gargoyles bore tender blossoms, yellow and violet and pink, pale and delicate. But this was winter. The air was dry, the sky blue in a hard way and cloudless, though snow never fell here. This was a timeless place, the humidity close to zero. The winds could be chilling, free of weather, going through a fifty-degree shift of temperature from summer to winter but otherwise remaining unaltered.

This was the place to which Lona Kelvin had been brought in summer, six months ago, after her attempt at suicide. Most of the cacti had already flowered by then. Now she was back, and she had missed the flowering season once more, coming three months too soon instead of three months too late. It would have been better for her to time her self-destruction impulses more precisely.

The doctors stood above her bed, speaking of her as though she were elsewhere.

"It'll be easier to repair her this time. No need to heal bones. Just a lung graft or so and she'll be all right."

"Until she tries again."

"That's not for me to worry about. Let them send her for psychotherapy. All I do is repair the shattered body."

"Not shattered just now, though. Just badly used."

"She'll get herself sooner or later. A really determined self-destroyer always suceeds. Let them step into nuclear converters, or something permanent like that. Jump from ninety floors up. We can't paste a smear of molecules together."

"Aren't you afraid you'll give her ideas?"

"If she's listening. But she could have thought of that herself if she wanted to."

"You've got something there. Maybe she's not a really determined self-destroyer. Maybe she's just a self-advertiser."

"I think I agree. Two suicide attempts in six months, both of them botched—when all she needed to do was open the window and jump—"

"What's the alveolar count?"

"Not bad."

"Her blood pressure?"

"Rising. Adrenocortical flow's down. Respiration up two points. She's coming along."

"We'll have her walking in the desert in three days."

"She'll need rest. Someone to talk to her. Why the hell does she want to be dead, anyway?"

"Who knows? I wouldn't think she was bright enough to want to kill herself."

"Fear and trembling. The sickness unto death."

"Anomie is supposedly reserved for more complex . . ."

They moved away from her bed, still talking. Lona did not open her eyes. She had not even been able to decide how many of them had been over her. Three, she guessed. More than two, less than four—so it had seemed. But their voices were so similar. And they didn't really argue with each other; they simply placed one slab of statement atop the next, gluing them carefully in place. Why had they saved her if they thought so little of her?

This time she had been certain she was going to die.

There are ways and ways of getting killed. Lona was shrewd enough to conceive of the most reliable ones, yet somehow had not permitted herself to try them, not out of fear of meeting death but out of fear of what she might encounter on the road. That other time she had hurled herself in front of a truck. Not on a highway, where vehicles hurtling toward her at a hundred and fifty miles an hour would swiftly and effectively mince her, but on a city street, where she was caught and tossed and slammed down, broken but not totally shattered, against the side of a building. So they had rebuilt her bones, and she had walked again in a month, and she was without outer scars.

And yesterday—it had seemed so simple to go down the hall to the dissolver room, and carefully disregard the rules by opening the disposal sac, and thrust her head in, and take a deep breath of the acrid fumes—

Throat and lungs and throbbing heart should have dissolved away. Given an hour's time, as she lay twitching on the cold floor, and they would have. But within minutes Lona was in helpful hands. Forcing down her throat some neutralizing substance. Thrusting her into a car. The first-aid station. Then the hospital, a thousand miles from home.

She was alive.

She was injured, of course. She had burned her nasal passages, had damaged her throat, had lost a considerable chunk of lung tissue. They had repaired the minor damage last night, and already nose and throat were healing. In a few days her lungs would be whole again. Death had no dominion in this land any longer.

Pale sunlight caressed her cheeks. It was late afternoon; the sun was behind the hospital, sinking toward the Pacific. Lona's eyes fluttered open. White robes, white sheets, green walls. A few books, a few tapes. An array of medical equipment thoughtfully sealed behind a locked sheet of clear sprayon. A private room! Who was paying for that? The last time the government scientists had paid. But now?

From her window she could see the twisted, thorny shapes of the cacti in the rear garden. Frowning, she made out two figures moving between the rows of rigid plants. One, quite a tall man, wore a buff-colored hospital gown. His shoulders were unusually broad. His hands and face were bandaged. He's been in a fire, Lona thought. The poor man. Beside him was a shorter man in business clothes, lean, restless. The tall one was pointing out a cactus to the other. Telling him something, perhaps lecturing him on cactus botany. And now reaching out with a bandaged hand. Touching the long, sharp spines. Watch out! You'll hurt yourself! He's sticking his hand right on the spines! Turning to the little one now. Pointing. The little one shaking his head—no, he doesn't want to stick himself on the spines.

The big one must be a little crazy, Lona decided.

She watched as they came nearer her window. She saw the smaller man's pointed ears and beady grey eyes. She could see nothing of the bigger man's face at all. Only the tiniest of slits broke the white wall of his bandage. Lona's mind quickly supplied the details of his multilation: the corrugated skin, the flesh runneled and puddled by the flames, the lips drawn aside in a fixed sneer. But they could fix that. Surely they could give him a new face here. He would be all right.

Lona felt a profound envy. Yes, this man had suffered pain, but soon the doctors would repair all that. His pain was only on the outside. They'd send him away, tall and strong and once more handsome, back to his wife, back to his . . .
. . . children.

The door opened. A nurse entered, a human one, not a robot. Though she might just as well have been. The smile was blank, impersonal.

"So you're up, dear? Did you sleep well? Don't try to talk, just nod. That's so good! I've come to get you ready. We're going to fix your lungs up a bit. It won't be any trouble at all for you—you'll just close your eyes, and when you wake up, you'll be breathing good as new!"

It was merely the truth, as usual.

When they brought her back to her room, it was morning, so Lona knew that they had worked her over for several hours and then stored her in the post-op room. Now she was swathed in bandages herself. They had opened her body, had given her new segments of lung, and had closed her again. She felt no pain, not yet. The throbbing would come later. Would there be a scar? Sometimes there were scars after surgery even now, though generally not. Lona saw a jagged red track running from the hollow of her throat down between her breasts. Please, no, no scar.

She had hoped to die on the operating table. It had seemed like her last chance. Now she would have to go home, alive, unaltered.

The tall man was walking in the garden again. This time he was alone. And now he was without his bandages. Though his back was to her, Lona saw the bare neck, the edge of jaw. Once more he was examining the cacti. What was it about those ugly plants that drew him so? Down on his knees now, prodding at the spines. Now standing up. Turning.

Oh, the poor man!

Lona stared in shock and wonder at his face. He was too far away for the details to be visible, but the wrongness of it was plain to her.

This must have been the way they fixed him up, she thought. After the fire. But why couldn't they have given him an ordinary face? Why did they do that to him?

She could not take her eyes away. The sight of those artificial features fascinated her. He sauntered toward the building, moving slowly, confidently. A powerful man. A man who could suffer and bear it. I feel so sorry for him. I wish I could do something to help him.

She told herself she was being silly. He had a family. He'd get along.

Twelve
Hell Hath No Fury

Burris got the bad news on his fifth day at the hospital.

He was in the garden, as usual. Aoudad came to him.

"There can't be any skin grafts. The doctors say no. You're full of crazy antibodies."

"I knew that already." Calmly.

"Even your own skin rejects your skin."

"I scarcely blame it," Burris said.

They walked past the saguaro. "You could wear some kind of mask. It would be a little uncomfortable, but they do a good job these days. The mask practically breathes. Porous plastic, right over your head. You'd get used to it in a week."

"I'll think about it," Burris promised. He knelt beside a small barrel cactus. Convex rows of spines took a great-circle route toward the pole. Flower buds seemed to be forming. The small glowing label in the earth said *Echinocactus grusonii*. Burris read it aloud.

"These cacti fascinate you so much," said Aoudad. "Why? What do they have for you?"

"Beauty."

"*These?* They're all thorns!"

"I love cacti. I wish I could live forever in a garden of cacti." A fingertip touched a spine. "Do you know, on Manipool they have almost nothing but thorny succulents? I wouldn't call them cacti, of course, but the general effect is the same. It's a dry world. Pluvial belts about the poles, then mounting dryness approaching the Equator. It rains about every billion years at the Equator and somewhat more frequently in the temperate zones."

"Homesick?"

"Hardly. But I learned the beauty of thorns there."

"Thorns? They stick you."

"That's part of their beauty."

"You sound like Chalk now," Aoudad muttered. "Pain is instructive, he says. Pain is gain. And thorns are beautiful. Give me a rose."

"Rose bushes are thorny, too," Burris remarked quietly.

Aoudad looked distressed. "Tulips, then. Tulips!"

Burris said, "The thorn is merely a highly evolved form of leaf. An adaptation to a harsh environment. Cacti can't afford to transpire the way leafy plants do. So they adapt. I'm sorry you regard such an elegant adaptation as ugly."

"I guess I've never thought about it much. Look, Burris, Chalk would like you to stay here another week or two. There are some more tests."

"But if facial surgery is impossible—"

"They want to check you out generally. With an eye toward the eventual body transplant."

"I see." Burris nodded briefly. He turned to the sun, letting the feeble winter beams strike his altered face. "How good it is to stand in the sunlight again! I'm grateful to you, Bart, do you know that? You dragged me out of that room. That dark night of the soul. I feel everything thawing in me now, breaking loose, moving about. Am I mixing my metaphors? You see how less rigid I am already."

"Are you flexible enough to entertain a visitor?"

"Who?" Instantly suspicious.

"Marco Prolisse's widow."

"Elise? I thought she was in Rome!"

"Rome's an hour from here. She wants very badly to see you. She says you've been kept from her by the authorities. I won't force you, but I think you ought to let her see you. You could put the bandages on again, maybe."

"No. No bandages, ever again. When will she be here?"

"She's already here. You just say the word and I'll produce her."

"Bring her down, then. I'll see her in the garden. It's so much like Manipool here."

Aoudad was strangely silent. At length he said, "See her in your room."

Burris shrugged. "As you say." He caressed the spines.

Nurses, orderlies, doctors, technicians, wheel-chaired patients, all stared at him as he entered the building. Even two work-robots scanned him oddly, trying to match him against their programmed knowledge of human bodily configurations. Burris did not mind. His self-consciousness was eroding swiftly, day by day. The bandages he had worn on his first day here now seemed an absurd device. It was like going naked in public, he thought: first it seemed unthinkable, then, in time, it became tolerable, and at length customary. One had to accustom one's self.

Yet he was uneasy as he waited for Elise Prolisse.

He was at the window, watching the courtyard garden, when the knock came. Some last-minute impulse (tact or fear?) caused him to keep his back turned as she entered. The door closed timidly. He had not seen her in five years, but he remembered her as lush, somewhat overblown, a handsome woman. His enhanced hearing told him that she had come in alone, without Aoudad. Her breathing was ragged and hoarse. He heard her lock the door.

"Minner?" she said softly. "Minner, turn around and look at me. It's all right. I can take it."

This was different from showing himself to nameless hospital personnel. To his surprise, Burris found the seemingly solid serenity of the past few days dissolving swiftly. Panic clutched him. He longed to hide. But out of dismay came cruelty, an icy willingness to inflict pain. He pivoted on his heel and swung around to hurl his image into Elise Prolisse's large dark eyes.

Give her credit: she had resilience.

"Oh," she whispered. "Oh, Minner, it's"—a smooth shift of gears—"not so awful. I heard it was much worse."

"Do you think I'm handsome?"

"You don't frighten me. I thought it might be frightening." She came toward him. She was wearing a clinging black tunic that probably had been sprayed on. High breasts were back in vogue, and that was where Elise wore hers, sprouting almost from her collar-bones, and deeply separated. Pectoral surgery was the secret. The deep mounds of flesh were wholly concealed by the tunic, and yet what kind of concealment could a micron of spray provide? Her hips flared; her thighs were pillars. But she had lost some weight. In the recent months of stress, no doubt, sleeplessness had shaved an inch or two from those continental buttocks. She was quite close to him now. Some dizzying perfume assailed him, and with no conscious effort at all Burris desensitized himself to it.

His hand slipped between hers.

His eyes met hers. When she flinched, it was only for the briefest instant.

"Did Marco die bravely?" she asked.

"He died like a man. Like the man he was."

"Did you see?"

"Not the last moments, no. I saw them take him away. While we waited our turns."

"You thought you would die, too?"

"I was sure of it. I said the last words for Malcondotto. He said them for me. But I came back."

"Minner, Minner, Minner, how terrible it must have been!" She still clasped his hand. She was stroking the fingers... stroking even that tiny prehensile worm of flesh next to his littlest finger. Burris felt the wrench of amazement as she touched the loathsome thing. Her eyes were wide, solemn, tearless. She has two children, or is it three? But still young. Still vital. He wished she would release his hand. Her nearness was disturbing. He sensed radiations of warmth from her thighs, low enough on the electromagnetic spectrum, yet detectable. He would have bit his lip to choke back tension if his lip still could fall between his teeth.

"When did you get the news about us?" he asked.

"When it came from the pickup station on Ganymede. They broke it to me very well. But I thought horrible things. I have to confess them to you. I wanted to know from God why it was that Marco had died and you had lived. I'm sorry Minner."

"Don't be. If I had my choice, I'd be the dead one and he'd be alive. Marco and Malcondotto both. Believe me. I'm not simply making words, Elise. I'd trade."

He felt like a hypocrite. Better dead than mutilated, of course! But that was not the way she would understand his words. She'd see only the noble part, the unmarried survivor

wishing he could lay down his life to spare the dead husbands
and fathers. What could he tell her? He had sworn off
whining.

"Tell me how it was," she said, still holding his hand,
tugging him down with her to sit on the edge of the bed.
"How they caught you. How they treated you. What it was
like. I have to know!"

"An ordinary landing," Burris told her. "Standard landing
and contact procedures. Not a bad world; dry; give it time
and it'll be like Mars. Another two million years. Right now
it's Arizona shading into Sonora, with a good solid slash of
Sahara. We met them. They met us."

His eye-shutters clicked shut. He felt the blasting heat of
the wind of Manipool. He saw the cactus shapes, snaky
grayish plants twisting spikily along the sand for hundreds of
yards. The vehicles of the natives came for him again.

"They were polite to us. They had been visited before,
knew the whole contact routine. No spaceflight themselves,
but only because they weren't interested. They spoke a few
languages. Malcondotto could talk with them. The gift of
tongues; he spoke a Sirian dialect, and they followed. They
were cordial, distant . . . alien. They took us away."

A roof over his head with creatures growing in it. Not
simple low-phylum things, either. No thermoluminescent
fungi. These were backboned creatures sprouting from the
arched roof.

Tubs of fermenting mash with other living things growing
in them. Tiny pink bifurcated things with thrashing legs.
Burris said, "Strange place. But not hostile. They poked us a
bit, prodded us. We talked. We carried out observations.
After a while it dawned on us that we were in confinement."

Elise's eyes were very glossy. They pursued his lips as the
words tumbled from him.

"An advanced scientific culture, beyond doubt. Almost
post-scientific. Certainly post-industrial. Malcondotto thought
they were using fusion power, but we were never quite sure.
After the third or fourth day we had no chance to check."

She was not interested at all, he realized suddenly. She was
barely listening. Then why had she come? Why had she
asked? The story that was at the core of his being should be a
concern to her, and yet there she stood, frowning, big-eyeing
him, unlistening. He glowered at her. The door was locked.

She cannot choose but hear. *And thus spake on that ancient man, the bright-eyed Mariner.*

"On the sixth day they came and took Marco away."

A ripple of alertness. A fissure in that sleek surface of sensual blandness.

"We never saw him again alive. But we sensed that they were going to do something bad to him. Marco sensed it first. He always was a bit of a pre-cog."

"Yes. Yes, he was. A little."

"He left. Malcondotto and I speculated. Some days passed, and they came for Malcondotto, too. Marco hadn't returned. Malcondotto talked with them before they took him. He learned that they had performed some sort of . . . experiment on Marco. A failure. They buried him without showing him to us. Then they went to work on Malcondotto."

I've lost her again, he realized. She just doesn't care. A flicker of interest when I told her how Prolisse died. And then . . . *nulla*.

She cannot choose but hear.

"Days. They came for me. They showed me Malcondotto, dead. He looked . . . somewhat as I look now. Different. Worse. I couldn't understand what they were saying to me. A droning buzz, a chattering rasping sound. What sound would cacti make if they could talk? They put me back and let me stew awhile. I suppose they were reviewing their first two experiments, trying to see where they had gone wrong, which organs couldn't be fiddled with. I spent a million years waiting for them to come again. They came. They put me on a table, Elise. The rest you can see."

"I love you," she said.

"?"

"I want you, Minner. I'm burning."

"It was a lonely trip home. They put me in my ship. I could still operate it, after a fashion. They rehabilitated me. I got going toward this system. The voyage was a bad one."

"But you made it to Earth."

How comes it, then, that thou art out of hell?

Why, this is hell, nor am I out of it.

He said, "I made it, yes. I would have seen you when I landed, Elise, but you have to understand I wasn't a free agent. First they had me by the throat. Then they let go and I ran. You must forgive."

"I forgive you. I love you."

"Elise—"

She touched something at her throat. The polymerized chains of her garment gave up the ghost. Black shards of fabric lay at her ankles, and she stood bare before him.

So much flesh. Bursting with vitality. The heat of her was overpowering.

"Elise—"

"Come and touch me. With that strange body of yours. With those hands. I want to feel that curling thing you have on each hand. Stroking me."

Her shoulders were wide. Her breats were well anchored by those strong piers and taut cables. The hips of the Earth-mother, the thighs of a courtesan. She was terribly close to him, and he shivered in the blaze, and then she stood back to let him see her in full.

"This isn't right, Elise."

"But I love you! Don't you feel the force of it?"

"Yes. Yes."

"You're all I have. Marco's gone. You saw him last. You're my link to him. And you're so—"

You are Helen, he thought.

"—beautiful."

"Beautiful? I am beautiful?"

Chalk had said it, Duncan the Corpulent. *I daresay a lot of women would fling themselves at your feet . . . grotesqueness has its appeal.*

"Please, Elise, cover yourself."

Now there was fury in the soft, warm eyes. "You are not sick! You are strong enough!"

"Perhaps."

"But you refuse me?" She pointed at his waist. "These monsters—they did not destroy you. You are still a . . . man."

"Perhaps."

"Then—"

"I've been through so much, Elise."

"And I have not?"

"You've lost your husband. That's as old as time. What's happened to me is brand-new. I don't want—"

"You are afraid?"

"No."

"Then show me your body. Take away the robe. There is the bed!"

He hesitated. Surely she knew his guilty secret; he had

coveted her for years. But one does not trifle with the wives of friends, and she was Marco's. Now Marco was dead. Elise glared at him, half melting with desire, half frigid with anger. Helen. She is Helen.

She flung herself against him.

The fleshy mounds quivering in intimate contact, the firm belly pressing close, the hands clutching at his shoulders. She was a tall woman. He saw the flash of her teeth. Then she was kissing him, devouring his mouth despite its rigidity.

Her lips suck forth my soul: see where it flies!

His hands were on the satiny smoothness of her back. His nails indented the flesh. The little tentacles crawled in constricted circles. She forced him backward, toward the bed, the mantis-wife seizing her mate. *Come, Helen, come, give me my soul again.*

They toppled down together. Her black hair was pasted to her cheeks by sweat. Her breasts heaved wildly; her eyes had the gloss of jade. She clawed at his robe.

There are women who seek hunchbacks, women who seek amputees, women who seek the palsied, the lame, the decaying. Elise sought him. The hot tide of sensuality swept over him. His robe parted, and then he was bare to her.

He let her look upon him as he now was.

It was a test he prayed she would fail, but she did not fail it, for the full sight of him served only to stoke the furnace in her. He saw the flaring nostrils, the flushed skin. He was her captive, her victim.

She wins. But I will salvage something.

Turning to her, he seized her shoulders, forced her against the mattress, and covered her. This was her final triumph, woman-like, to lose in the moment of victory, to surrender at the last instant. Her thighs engulfed him. His too-smooth flesh embraced her silkiness. With a sudden great burst of demonic energy he mastered her and split her to the core.

Thirteen
Rosy-Fingered Dawn

Tom Nikolaides stepped into the room. The girl was awake now and looking out the window at the garden. He carried a small potted cactus, an ugly one, more gray than green and armed with vicious needles.

"Feeling better now, are you?"

"Yes," Lona said. "Much. Am I supposed to go home?"

"Not yet. Do you know who I am?"

"Not really."

"Tom Nikolaides. Call me Nick. I'm in public relations. A response engineer."

She received the information blankly. He put the cactus on the table beside her bed.

"I know all about you, Lona. In a small way I was connected with the baby experiment last year. Probably you've forgotten, but I interviewed you. I work for Duncan Chalk. Do you know who he is, perhaps?"

"Should I?"

"One of the richest men in the world. One of the most powerful. He owns newstapes... vidstations.... He owns the Arcade. He takes a great interest in you."

"Why did you bring me that plant?"

"Later. I—"

"It's very ugly."

Nikolaides smiled. "Lona, how would you like to have a couple of those babies that were born from your seed? Say, two of them, to raise as your own."

"I don't think that's a very funny joke."

Nikolaides watched the color spread over her hollow cheeks and saw the hard flame of desire come into her eyes. He felt like an unutterable bastard.

He said, "Chalk can arrange it for you. You *are* their mother, you know. He could get you a boy and a girl."

"I don't believe you."

Leaning forward, Nikolaides turned on the intense sincerity. "You've got to believe me, Lona. You're an unhappy girl, I know. And I know *why* you're unhappy. Those babies. A hundred children pulled out of your body, taken away from you. And then they threw you aside, forgot you. As though you were just a thing, a robot baby-maker."

She was interested now. But still skeptical.

He picked up the little cactus again and fondled the shiny pot, slipping his finger in and out of the drainage opening at the bottom. "We can get you a couple of those babies," he said to her open mouth, "but not easily. Chalk would have to pull a lot of strings. He'll do it, but he wants you to do something for him in return."

"If he's that rich, what could I do for him?"

"You could help another unhappy human being. As a personal favor to Mr. Chalk. And then he'll help you."

Her face was blank again.

Nikolaides leaned to her. "There's a man right here in this hospital. Maybe you've seen him. Maybe you've heard about him. He's a starman. He went off to a strange planet and was captured by monsters, and they messed him up. They took him apart and put him back together again the wrong way."

"They did that to me," Lona said, "without even taking me apart first."

"All right. He's been walking in the garden. A big man. From a distance perhaps you can't tell there's anything wrong with him, unless you can see his face. He has eyes that open like *this*. Sideways. And a mouth—I can't show you what the mouth does, but it isn't human. Close up, he's pretty scary. But he's still human inside, and he's a wonderful man, only naturally he's very angry over what they did to him. Chalk wants to help him. The way he wants to help him is by having someone be kind to him. You. You know what suffering is, Lona. Meet this man. Be good to him. Show him that he's still people, that someone can love him. Bring him back to himself. And if you do that, Chalk will see that you get your babies."

"Am I supposed to sleep with him?"

"You're supposed to be kind to him. I don't expect to tell you what that means. Do whatever would make him happy. You'll be the judge. Just take your own feelings, turn them around, inside out. You'll know a little of what he's going through."

"Because he's been made a freak. And I was made a freak, too."

Nikolaides saw no tactful way of meeting that statement. He simply acknowledged it.

He said, "This man's name is Minner Burris. His room is right across the hall from yours. He happens to be very much interested in cactus, God knows why. I thought you might send him this cactus as a get-well present. It's a nice gesture. It could lead to bigger things. Yes?"

"What was the name?"

"Nikolaides."

"Not yours. His."

"Minner Burris. And look, you could send a note with it. Don't minitype it, write it out yourself. I'll dictate it, and you make any changes you like." His mouth was dry. "Here. Here's the stylus...."

Fourteen
Happily Ever After

With two of his closest aides off in the West performing a complex balletic *pas de quartre* with Burris and Lona, Duncan Chalk was forced to rely almost entirely on the services of Leontes d'Amore. D'Amore was capable, of course, or he'd never have come as far as he had. Yet he lacked Nikolaides's stability of character and also lacked Aoudad's consuming blend of ambition and insecurity. D'Amore was clever but shifty, a quicksand man.

Chalk was at home, in his lakeside palace. Tickers and newstapes chittered all about him, but he tuned them out with ease. D'Amore behind his left ear, Chalk patiently and speedily dealt with the towering stack of the daily business. The Emperor Ch'in Shih Huang Ti, so they said, had turned over a hundred and twenty pounds of documents a day and still had sufficient spare time to build the Great Wall. Of course, documents were written on bamboo slabs in those

days, much heavier than minislips. But old Shih Huang Ti
had to be admired. He was one of Chalk's heroes.

He said, "What time did Aoudad phone in that report?"

"An hour before you awoke."

"I should have been awakened. You know that. He knows
that."

D'Amore's lips performed an elegant entrechat of distress.
"Since there was no crisis, we felt—"

"You were wrong." Chalk pivoted and nailed D'Amore with
a quick glance. D'Amore's discomfort fed Chalk's needs to
some extent, but not sufficiently. The petty writhings of
underlings were no more nourishing than straw. He needed
red meat. He said, "So Burris and the girl have been
introduced."

"Very successfully."

"I wish I could have seen it. How did they take to each
other?"

"They're both edgy. But basically sympathetic. Aoudad
thinks it'll work out well."

"Have you planned an itinerary for them yet?"

"It's coming along. Luna Tivoli, Titan, the whole interplanetary circuit. Though we'll start them in the Antarctic.
Accommodations, details—everything's under control."

"Good. A cosmic honeymoon. Maybe even a small bundle
of joy to brighten the tale. That would be something, if he
turned out fertile! We know *she* is, by God!"

D'Amore said worriedly, "Concerning that: the Prolisse
woman is undergoing tests even now."

"So you've got her. Splendid, splendid! Did she resist?"

"She was given a valid cover story. She thinks she's being
checked for alien viruses. By the time she wakes up, we'll
have the semen analysis and our answer."

Chalk nodded brusquely. D'Amore left him, and the large
man scooped the tape of Elise's visit to Burris from its socket
and fitted it into the viewer for another scanning. Chalk had
been against the idea of letting her see him, at first, despite
Aoudad's strong recommendation. But in short order Chalk
had come to understand some advantages of it. Burris had not
had a woman since his return to Earth. Signora Prolisse,
according to Aoudad (who was in a position to know!) had a
peppery hunger for the distorted body of her late husband's
shipmate. Let them get together, then; see Burris's response.

A prize bull should not be nudged into a highly publicized mating without some preliminary tests.

The tape was graphic and explicit. Three hidden cameras, only a few molecules in lens diameter, had recorded everything. Chalk had viewed the sequence three times, but there were always new subtleties to derive. Watching unsuspecting couples in the act of love gave him no particular thrill; he obtained his pleasures in more refined manners, and the sight of the beast with two backs was interesting only to adolescents. But it was useful to know something of Burris's performance.

He sped the tape past the preliminary conversation. How bored she seems while he tells of his adventures! How frightened he seems when she exposes her body! What terrifies him? He is no stranger to women. Of course, that was in his old life. Perhaps he fears that she will find his new body hideous and turn away from him at the crucial instant. The moment of truth. Chalk pondered it. The cameras could not reveal Burris's thoughts, nor even his emotional constellation, and Chalk himself had not taken steps to detect his inner feelings. So all had to be by inference.

Certainly Burris was reluctant. Certainly the lady was determined. Chalk studied the naked tigress as she staked out her claim. It seemed for a while as though Burris would spurn her—not interested in sex, or in any event not interested in Elise. Too noble to top his friend's widow? Or still afraid to open himself to her, even in the face of her unquestioned yearning? Well, he was naked now. Elise still undeterred. The doctors who had examined Burris upon his return said that he was still capable of the act—so far as they could tell—and now it was quite clear that they had been right.

Elise's arms and legs waved aloft. Chalk tugged at his dewlaps as the tiny figures on the screen acted out the rite. Yes, Burris could make love even now. Chalk lost interest as the coupling ran to its climax. The tape petered out after a final shot of limp, depleted figures side by side on the rumpled bed. He could make love, but what about babies? Chalk's men had intercepted Elise soon after she had left Burris's room. A few hours ago the lusty wench had lain unconscious on a doctor's table, the heavy legs apart. But Chalk sensed that this time he was bound to be disappointed. Many things were within his control; not all.

D'Amore was back. "The report's in."

"And?"

"No fertile sperm. They can't quite figure out what they've got, but they swear it won't reproduce. The aliens must have done a switch there, too."

"Too bad," Chalk sighed. "That's one line of approach we'll have to scratch. The future Mrs. Burris won't have any children by him."

D'Amore laughed. "She's got enough babies already, hasn't she?"

Fifteen
The Marriage of True Minds

To Burris, the girl had little sensual appeal coming along as she did in the wake of Elise Prolisse. But he liked her. She was a kindly, pathetic, fragile child. She meant well. The potted cactus touched him. It seemed too humble a gesture to be anything but friendliness.

And she was unappalled by his appearance. Moved, yes. A bit queasy, yes. But she looked him right in the eye, concealing any dismay she might feel.

He said, "Are you from around here?"

"No. I'm from back East. Please sit down. Don't stand up on my account."

"It's all right. I'm really quite strong, you know."

"Are they going to do anything for you here in the hospital?"

"Just tests. They have an idea they can take me out of this body and put me into a normal human one."

"How wonderful!"

"Don't tell anyone, but I suspect it isn't going to work. The whole thing's a million miles up right now, and before they bring it down to Earth—" He spun the cactus on the bedside table. "But why are you in the hospital, Lona?"

"They had to fix my lungs some. Also my nose and throat."

"Hayfever?" he asked.

"I put my head in a disposal sac," she said simply.

A crater yawned briefly beneath Burris's feet. He clung to his equilibrium. What rocked him, as much as what she had said, was the toneless way she had said it. As though it were nothing at all to let acid eat your bronchi.

"You tried to kill yourself?" he blurted.

"Yes. They found me fast, though."

"But—why? At your age!" Patronizingly, hating himself for the tone. "You have everything to live for!"

The eyes grew big. Yet they lacked depth; he could not help contrasting them with the smoldering coals in Elise's sockets. "You don't know about me?" she asked, voice still small.

Burris grinned. "I'm afraid not."

"Lona Kelvin. Maybe you didn't catch the name. Or maybe you forgot. I know. You were still out in space when it all happened."

"You've lost me two turns back."

"I was in an experiment. Multiple-embryo ovatransplantation, they called it. They took a few hundred eggs out of me and fertilized them and grew them. Some in the bodies of other women, some in incubator things. About a hundred of the babies were born. It took six months. They experimented on me last year just about this time."

The last ledge of false assumptions crumbled beneath him. Burris had seen a high-school girl, polite, empty-headed, concerned to some mild extent about the strange creature in the room across the hall, but mainly involved with the tastes and fashions, whatever they were, of her chronological peer group. Perhaps she was here to have her appendix dissolved, or for a nose bob. Who could tell? But suddenly the ground had shifted and he started to view her in a more cosmic light. A victim of the universe.

"A hundred babies? I never heard a thing about it, Lona!"

"You must have been away. They made a big fuss."

"*How* old are you?"

"Seventeen now."

"You didn't bear any of the babies yourself, then?"

"No. No. That's the whole thing. They took the eggs away from me, and that was where it all stopped, for me. Of course, I got a lot of publicity. Too much." She peered at him shyly. "I'm boring you, all this talk about myself."

"But I want to know."

"It isn't very interesting. I was on the vid a lot. And in the tapes. They wouldn't leave me alone. I had nothing much to say, because I hadn't *done* anything, you know. Just a donor. But when my name got out, they came around to me. Reporters all the time. Never alone, and yet always alone, do you know? So I couldn't take it any more. All I wanted—a couple of babies out of my own body, not a hundred babies out of machines. So I tried to kill myself."

"By putting your head in a disposal sac."

"No, that was the second time. The first, I jumped under a truck."

"When was that?" Burris asked.

"Last summer. They brought me here and fixed me up. Then they sent me back East again. I lived in a room. I was afraid of everything. It got too scary, and I found myself going down the hall to the dissolver room and opening the disposal sac and—well . . . I didn't make it again. I'm still alive."

"Do you still want to die so badly, Lona?"

"I don't know." The thin hands made clutching motions in mid-air. "If I only had something to hang onto. . . . But look, I'm not supposed to be talking about me. I just wanted you to know a little of why I was here. You're the one who—"

"Not *supposed* to be talking about yourself? Who says?"

Dots of color blazed in the sunken cheeks. "Oh, I don't know. I mean, I'm not really important. Let's talk about space, Colonel Burris!"

"Not Colonel. Minner."

"Out there—"

"Are Things that catch you and change you all around. That's what space is, Lona."

"How terrible!"

"I think so, too. But don't reinforce my convictions."

"I don't follow."

"I feel terribly sorry for myself," Burris said. "If you give me half a chance, I'll pour your shell-like ear full of bad news. I'll tell you just how unfair I think it was for them to have done this to me. I'll gabble about the injustice of the blind universe. I'll talk a lot of foolishness."

"But you've got a *right* to be angry about it! You didn't mean any harm to them. They just took you and—"

"Yes."

"It wasn't decent of them!"

"I know, Lona. But I've already said that at great length,

mostly to myself but also to anyone who'd listen. It's practically the only thing I say or think. And so I've undergone a second transformation. From man to monster; from monster to walking embodiment of injustice."

She looked puzzled. I'm talking over her head, he told himself.

He said, "What I mean is, I've let this thing that happened to me *become* me. I'm a thing, a commodity, a moral event. Other men have ambitions, desires, accomplishments, attainments. I've got my mutilation, and it's devouring me. *Has* devoured me. So I try to escape from it."

"You're saying that you'd rather not talk about what happened to you?" Lona asked.

"Something like that."

She nodded. He saw her nostrils flicker, saw her thin lips curl in animation. A smile burst forth. "You know, Col—Minner—it's a little bit the same way with me. I mean, being a victim and all, and feeling so sorry for yourself. They did something bad to me, too, and since then all I do is go back and think about it and get angry. Or sick. And the thing I really should be doing is forgetting about it and going on to something else."

"Yes."

"But I can't. Instead I keep trying to kill myself because I decide I can't bear it." Her eyes faltered to the floor. "Do you mind if I ask—have you—have you ever tried—"

A halt.

"To kill myself since this happened? No. No, Lona. I just brood. Slow suicide, it's called."

"We ought to make a deal," she said. "Instead of me feeling sorry for me, and you for me, let me feel sorry for you, and you feel sorry for me. And we'll tell each other how terrible the world has been to the other one. But not to ourselves. I'm getting the words all mixed up, but do you know what I mean?"

"A mutual sympathy society. Victims of the universe, unite!" He laughed. "Yes, I understand. Good idea, Lona! It's just what I—what we need. I mean, just what *you* need."

"And what *you* need."

She looked pleased with herself. She was smiling from forehead to chin, and Burris was surprised at the change that came over her appearance when that glow of self-satisfaction appeared. She seemed to grow a year or two older, to pick up strength and poise. And even womanliness. For an instant she was no longer skinny and pathetic. But then the glow faded and she was a little girl again.

"Do you like to play card games?"

"Yes."

"Can you play Ten Planets?"

"If you'll teach me," Burris said.

"I'll go get the cards."

She bounced out of the room, her robe fluttering around her slim figure. Returning a moment later with a deck of waxy-looking cards, she joined him on the bed. Burris's quick eyes were on her when the middle snap of her pajama top lost polarity, and he caught a glimpse of a small, taut white breast within. She brushed her hand over the snap an instant later. She was not quite a woman, Burris told himself, but not a child, either. And then he reminded himself: this slender girl is the mother (?) of a hundred babies.

"Have you ever played the game?" she asked.

"Afraid not."

"It's quite simple. First I deal ten cards apiece—"

Sixteen

The Owl For All His Feathers, Was A-Cold

They stood together by the hospital power plant, looking through the transparent wall. Within, something fibrous lashed and churned as it picked up energy from the nearest pylon and fed it to the transformer bank. Burris was explaining to her about how power was transmitted that way, without wires. Lona tried to listen, but she did not really care enough about finding out. It was hard to concentrate on something like that, so remote from her experience. Especially with *him* beside her.

"Quite a contrast from the old days," he was saying. "I can still recall a time when the million-kv lines were strung across the countryside, and they were talking of stepping the voltage up to a million and a half—"

"You know so many things. How did you have time to learn all that about electricity if you had to be a starman, too?"

"I'm terribly old," he said.

"I bet you aren't even eighty yet."

She was joking, but he didn't seem to realize it. His face quirked in that funny way, the lips (were they still to be called lips?) pulling outward toward his cheeks. "I'm forty years old," he said hollowly. "I suppose to you forty is most of the way to being eighty."

"Not quite."

"Let's go look at the garden."

"All those sharp pointed things!"

"You don't like them," he said.

"Oh, no, no, no," Lona insisted, recovering quickly. *He likes the cacti,* she told herself. *I mustn't criticize the things he likes. He needs someone to like the things he likes. Even if they aren't very pretty.*

They strolled toward the garden. It was noon, and the pale sun cut sharp shadows into the crisp, dry earth. Lona shivered. She had a coat on over her hospital gown, but even so, even here in the desert, it was a cold day. Burris, lightly dressed, didn't seem to mind the chill. Lona wondered whether that new body of his had some way of adjusting to meet the temperature, like a snake's. But she didn't ask. She tried not to talk to him about his body. And the more she thought about it, the more it seemed to her that a snake's way of adjusting to cold weather was to crawl off and go to sleep. She let the point pass.

He told her a great deal about cacti.

They paced the garden, up and down, through the avenues of bristling plants. Not a leaf, not even a bough. Nor a flower. *Here are buds, though,* he told her. *This one will have a fine red apple-like fruit in June. They make candy from this one.* Thorns and all? Oh, no, not the thorns. He laughed. She laughed, too. She wanted to reach out and take him by the hand. What would it be like, feeling that curling extra thing against her fingers?

She had expected to be afraid of him. It surprised her, but she felt no fear.

She wished he would take her inside, though.

He pointed to a blurred shape hovering over one of the nastiest-looking of the cactus plants. "Look there!"

"A big moth?"

"Hummingbird, silly! He must be lost." Burris moved forward, obviously excited. Lona saw the things on his hands wriggle around, as they often did when he wasn't paying attention to them. He was down on one knee, peering at the hummingbird. She looked at him in profile, observing the strong jaw, the flat drumhead of twanging skin where an ear should have been. Then, because he would want her to, she looked at the bird. She saw a tiny body and what could perhaps be a long, straight bill. A dark cloud hung about the bird. "Are those its wings?" she asked.

"Yes. Beating terribly fast. You can't see them, can you?"

"Just a blur."

"I see the individual wings. Lona, it's incredible! I see the wings! With these eyes!"

"That's wonderful, Minner."

"The bird's a stray; probably belongs in Mexico, probably wishes he were there now. He'll die up here before he finds a flower. I wish I could do something."

"Catch him? Have someone take him to Mexico?"

Burris looked at his hands as if weighing the possibility of seizing the hummingbird in a lightning swoop. Then he shook his head. "My hands couldn't be fast enough, even now. Or I'd crush him if I caught him. I—there he goes!"

And there he went. Lona watched the brown blur vanish down the garden. At least he's going south, she thought. She turned to Burris.

"It pleases you some of the time, doesn't it?" she asked. "You like it . . . a little."

"Like what?"

"Your new body."

He quivered a little. She wished she hadn't mentioned it.

He seemed to check a first rush of words. He said, "It has a few advantages, I admit."

"Minner, I'm cold."

"Shall we go inside?"

"If you don't mind."

"Anything you say, Lona."

They moved side by side toward the door. Their shadows dribbled off to their left at a sharp angle. He was much taller than she was, nearly a foot. And very strong. I wish. That he would take me. In his arms.

She was not at all put off by his appearance.

Of course, she had seen only his head and his hands. He might have a huge staring eye set in the middle of his chest. Or a mouth under each arm. A tail. Big purple spots. But as the fantasies welled through her mind, it struck her that even those inventions were not really frightening. If she could get used to his face and his hands, as she had so speedily, what would further differences matter? He had no ears, his nose was not a nose, his eyes and his lips were strange, his tongue and his teeth were like something out of a dream. And each hand had that extra thing. Yet quite rapidly she had stopped noticing. His voice was pleasant and normal, and he was so smart, so interesting. And he seemed to like her. Was he married, she wondered. How could she ask?

The hospital door bellied inward as they approached.

"My room?" he asked. "Or yours?"

"What will we do now?"

"Sit. Talk. Play cards."

"Playing cards bored you."

"Did I ever say it did?" he asked her.

"You were too polite. But I could tell. I could see you were hiding it. It was written all over your . . ." Her voice trailed off. "Face."

It keeps coming back, she thought.

"Here's my room," she said.

Which room they went to hardly mattered. They were identical, one facing the rear garden where they had just been, one facing the courtyard. A bed, a desk, an array of medical equipment. He took the bedside chair. She sat on the bed. She wanted him to come over and touch her body, warm her chilled flesh, but of course she did not dare suggest it.

"Minner, how soon will you be leaving the hospital?"

"Soon. A few days. What about you, Lona?"

"I guess I could go out almost any time now. What will you do when you leave?"

"I'm not sure. I think I'll travel. See the world, let the world see me."

"I've always wanted to travel," she said. Too obvious. "I've never really been anywhere."

"Such as where?"

"Luna Tivoli," she said. "Or the Crystal Planet. Or—well, anywhere. China. The Antarctic."

"It's not hard to get there. You get on the liner and go." For an instant his face sealed itself, and she did not know what to think; the lips slid shut, the eyes clicked their lids into place. She thought of a turtle. Then Burris opened again and said, astonishing her, "What if we went to some of those places together?"

Seventeen
Take Up These Splinters

Somewhat higher than the atmosphere Chalk soared. He looked upon his world and found it good. The seas were green verging on blue, or blue verging on green, and it seemed to him that he could discern icebergs adrift. The land was brown in winter's grip, to the north; summer-green lay below the curving middle.

He spent much of his time in lower space. It was the best way, the most esthetically satisfying way, of shunning gravity. Perhaps his pilot felt distress, for Chalk did not permit the use of reverse gravitrons up here, nor even any centrifuging to provide the illusion of weight. But his pilot was paid well enough to endure such discomforts, if discomforts they were.

For Chalk it was not remotely a discomfort to be weightless. He had his mass, his wonderful brontosaurian mass, and yet he had none of the drawbacks thereof.

"This is one of the few instances," he said to Burris and the girl, "where one can legitimately get something for nothing. Consider: when we blast off, we dissipate the gravity of acceleration through gravitrons, so that the extra Gs are squirted away and we rise in comfort. There's no effort for us in getting where we are, no price to pay in extra weight before we can be weightless. When we land, we treat the deceleration problem the same way. Normal weight, weightless, normal again, and no flattening at any time."

"But is it free?" Lona asked. "I mean, it must cost a lot to run the gravitrons. When you balance everything out, the expense of starting and stopping, you haven't really had anything for nothing, have you?"

Chalk, amused, looked at Burris. "She's very clever, did you realize that?"

"So I've been noticing."

Lona reddened. "You're making fun of me."

"No, we aren't," said Burris. "You've hit quite independently on the notion of conservation of gravity, don't you see? But you're being too strict with our host. He's looking at things from his point of view. If he doesn't have to feel the buildup of Gs himself, it doesn't cost him anything in the realest sense of the word. Not in terms of enduring high G. The gravitrons absorb all that. Look, it's like committing a crime, Lona, and paying someone else to go through rehabilitation. Sure, it costs you cash to find a rehab substitute. But you've had your crime, and he takes the punishment. The cash equivalent—"

"Let it go," Lona said. "It's nice up here, anyway."

"You like weightlessness?" Chalk asked. "Have you ever experienced it before?"

"Not really. A few short trips."

"And you, Burris? Does the lack of gravity help your discomforts any?"

"A little, thanks. There's no drag on the organs that aren't where they really ought to be. I don't feel that damned pulling in my chest. A small mercy, but I'm grateful."

Nevertheless, Burris was still in his bath of pain, Chalk noticed. Perhaps more tepid, but not enough. What was it like to feel constant physical discomfort? Chalk knew a little of that, simply through the effort of hauling his body around in full gravity. But he had been bloated so long. He was accustomed to the steady aching pull. Burris, though? The sensations of nails being hammered into his flesh? He did not protest. Only now and then did the bitter rebellion surge to the surface. Burris was improving, learning to accommodate to what was for him the human condition. Chalk, sensitive as he was, still picked up the emanations of pain. Not merely psychic pain. Physical pain, too. Burris had grown calmer, had risen from the black pit of depression in which Aoudad had first encountered him, but he was far from any beds of roses.

The girl, comparatively, was in better shape, Chalk concluded. She was not quite so intricate a mechanism.

They looked happy side by side, Burris and the girl.

That would change, of course, as time went on.

"You see Hawaii?" Chalk asked. "And there, by the edge of the world: China. The Great Wall. We've had it restored, a good deal of it. See, running inland from the sea just above that gulf. Passing north of Peking, up into those mountains. The middle section is gone, the Ordos desert stretch. But then it was never very much, just a line of mud. And beyond, toward Sinkiang, see it coming up now? We have several party centers along the Wall. A new one opening just on the Mongolian side shortly. Kublai Khan's Pleasure Dome." Chalk laughed. "But not stately. Anything but stately."

They were holding hands, Chalk observed.

He concentrated on picking up their emotions. Nothing useful yet. From the girl came a kind of mild, squashy contentment, a blank maternal sort of thing. Yes, she would. And from Burris? Not much of anything, so far. He was relaxed, more relaxed than Chalk had yet seen him to be. Burris liked the girl. She amused him, obviously. He enjoyed the attention she gave him. But he did not have any strong feeling toward her; he did not really think very much of her as a person. Soon she would be powerfully in love with him. Chalk thought it unlikely that the emotion would be reciprocated. Out of that difference in voltages an interesting current might be generated, Chalk surmised. A thermocouple effect, so to speak. We will see.

The ship hurtled westward over China, past the Kansu Panhandle, orbiting over the Old Silk Road.

Chalk said, "I understand that you two will be leaving on your travels tomorrow. So Nick tells me."

"That's right. The itinerary's arranged," said Burris.

"I can't wait. I'm so awfully excited!" Lona cried.

The schoolgirl blurt of words annoyed Burris. Chalk, well attuned to their shifting moods now, dug his receptors into the flash of irritation that rolled from him and gobbled it down. The burst of emotion was a sudden rent in a seamless velvet veil. A jagged dark streak across pearly gray smoothness. A beginning, Chalk thought. A beginning.

"It should be quite a trip," he said. "Billions of people wish you well."

Eighteen

To the Toy Fair

You covered ground swiftly when you were in the hands of Duncan Chalk. Chalk's minions had conveyed them nonstop from the hospital to Chalk's private spaceport; then, after their flight around the world, they had been sped to the hotel. It was the most magnificent hotel the Western Hemisphere had ever known, a fact that seemed to dazzle Lona and that obscurely bothered Burris.

Entering the lobby, he slipped and began to fall.

That had been happening to him more and more, now that he was out in public. He had never really learned how to use his legs. His knees were elaborate ball-and-socket affairs, evidently designed to be frictionless, and at unpredictable moments they failed to support him. That was what happened now. There was a sensation as of his left leg disintegrating, and he began to slide toward the thick yellow carpet.

Vigilant robot bellhops sprang to his aid. Aoudad, whose reflexes were not quite as good as theirs, belatedly clutched at him. But Lona was closest. She flexed her knees and put her shoulder against his chest, supporting him while he clawed for balance. Burris was surprised at how strong she was. She held him up until the others reached him.

"Are you all right?" she asked breathlessly.

"More or less." He swung his leg back and forth until he was sure the knee was locked in place again. Fiery pains shot as high as his hip. "You were strong. You held me up."

"It all happened so fast. I didn't know what I was doing. I just moved and there you were."

"I'm so heavy, though."

Aoudad had been holding him by the arm. As if slowly realizing it, he let go. "Can you make it by yourself now?" he asked. "What happened?"

"I forgot how my legs worked for a second," Burris said.

The pain was nearly blinding. He swallowed it down and, taking Lona's hand, slowly led the procession toward the gravitron bank. Nikolaides was taking care of the routine job of checking them in. They would be here two days. Aoudad entered the nearest liftshaft with them, and up they went.

"Eighty-two," Aoudad said to the elevator's monitor-plate.

"Is it a big room?" Lona asked.

"It's a suite," said Aoudad. "It's lots of rooms."

There were seven rooms altogether. A cluster of bedrooms, a kitchen, a lounging room, and a large conference room in which the representatives of the press would later gather. At Burris's quiet request, he and Lona had been given adjoining bedrooms. There was nothing physical between them yet. Burris knew that the longer he waited, the more difficult it would be, and yet he held back. He could not judge the depth of her feelings, and at this point he had grave doubts about his own.

Chalk had spared no expense to get them these accommodations. It was a lavish suite, hung with outworld draperies that throbbed and flickered with inner light. The spun-glass ornaments on the table, warmed in the hand, would sing sweet melodies. They were costly. The bed in his room was wide enough to hold a regiment. Hers was round and revolved at the touch of a switch. There were mirrors in the bedroom ceilings. At an adjustment, they contorted into diamond facets; at another, they became splintered shards; at another, they provided a steady reflection, larger and sharper than life. They could also be opaqued. Burris did not doubt that the rooms could play other tricks as well.

"Dinner tonight is in the Galactic Room," Aoudad announced. "You'll hold a press conference at eleven tomorrow morning. You meet with Chalk in the afternoon. The following morning you leave for the Pole."

"Splendid." Burris sat.

"Shall I have a doctor up to look at the leg?"

"It won't be necessary."

"I'll be back in an hour and a half to escort you to dinner. You'll find clothes in the closets."

Aoudad took his leave.

Lona's eyes were shining. She was in wonderland. Burris himself, not easily impressed by luxury, was at least interested in the extent of the comforts. He smiled at her. Her glow deepened. He winked.

"Let's look around again," she murmured.

They toured the suite. Her room, his, the kitchen. She touched the program node of the food bank. "We could eat here tonight," he suggested. "If you prefer, we can get everything we need."

"Let's go out, though."

"Of course."

He did not need to shave, nor even to wash: small mercies of his new skin. But Lona was more nearly human. He left her in her room, staring at the vibraspray mounted in its cubicle. Its control panel was nearly as complex as that of a starship. Well, let her play with it.

He inspected his wardrobe.

They had stocked him as though he were going to be the star of a tridim drama. On one shelf were some twenty sprayon cans, each with its bright portrayal of its contents. In this one, green dinner jacket and lustrous purple-threaded tunic. In this, a single flowing robe decked with self-generating light. Here, a gaudy peacock thing with epaulets and jutting ribs. His own tastes ran to simpler designs, even to more conventional materials. Linen, cotton, the ancient fabrics. But his private tastes did not govern this enterprise. Left to his private tastes, he would be huddling in his flaking room in the Martlet Towers, talking to his own ghost. Here he was, a volunteer puppet dancing on Chalk's strings, and he had to dance the proper paces. This was his purgatory. He chose the epaulets and ribs.

Now, would the sprayon work?

His skin was strange in its porosity and other physical properties. It might reject the garment. Or—a waking nightmare—it might patiently undo the clinging molecules, so that in the twinkling of an eye his clothing shredded at the Galactic Room, leaving him not merely naked in a throng but exposed in all his eerie otherness. He would chance it. Let them look. Let them see everything. The image crossed his mind of Elise Prolisse putting a hand to a secret stud and obliterating her black shroud in an instant, unveiling the white temptations. These clothes were unreliable. So be it. Burris stripped and inserted the sprayon can in the dispenser. He stepped beneath it.

Cunningly the garment shaped itself to his body.

The application took less than five minutes. Surveying his

gaudiness in a mirror, Burris was not displeased. Lona would be proud of him.

He waited for her.

Nearly an hour went by. He heard nothing from her room. Surely she must be ready by now. "Lona?" he called, and got no answer.

Panic speared him. This girl was suicide-prone. The pomp and elegance of this hotel might be just enough to tip her over the brink. They were a thousand feet above the ground here; she would not botch this attempt. I should never have left her alone, Burris told himself fiercely.

"*Lona!*"

He stepped through the widening partition into her room. Instantly he saw her and went numb with relief. She was in her closet, naked, her back to him. Narrow across the shoulders, narrower through the hips, so that the contrast of the narrow waist was lost. The spine rose like a subterranean burrow, steeply, shadowed. The buttocks were boyish. He regretted his intrusion. "I didn't hear you," he said. "I was worried, and so when you didn't answer—"

She turned to him, and Burris saw that she had much more on her mind than her violated modesty. Her eyes were red-rimmed, her cheeks streaked. In a token of pudicity she lifted a thin arm across her small breasts, but the gesture was purely automatic and hid nothing. Her lips trembled. Beneath his outer skin he felt the shock of her body's impact, and he found himself wondering why so underfurnished a nudity should affect him this way. Because, he decided, it had lain beyond a barrier that now was shattered.

"Oh, Minner, Minner, I was ashamed to call you! I've been standing here for half an hour!"

"What's the trouble?"

"There's nothing for me to wear!"

He came closer. She turned aside, backing from the closet, standing by his elbow and lowering the arm over her breasts. He peered into the closet. Dozens of sprayon cans were decked there. Fifty, a hundred of them.

"So?"

"I can't wear *those!*"

He picked one up. From the picture on the label it was a thing of night and fog, elegant, chaste, superb.

"Why can't you?"

"I want something simple. There's nothing simple here."

"Simple? For the Galactic Room?"

"I'm afraid, Minner."

And she was. The bare skin was goosebumped.

"You can be such a child sometimes!" he snapped.

The words fishhooked into her. She shrank back, looking more naked than ever, and fresh tears slipped from her eyes. The cruelty of the words seemed to linger in the room, like a silty deposit, after the words themselves were gone.

"If I'm a child," she said hoarsely, "why am I going to the Galactic Room?"

Take her in your arms? Comfort her? Burris was caught in wild eddies of uncertainty. He geared his voice for something that lay midway between parental anger and phony solicitousness and said, "Don't be foolish, Lona. You're an important person. The whole world is going to look at you tonight and say how beautiful, how lucky you are. Put on something Cleopatra would have loved. And then tell yourself you're Cleopatra."

"Do I look like Cleopatra?"

His eyes traveled her body. That was, he sensed, exactly what she wanted them to do. And he had to concede that she was less than voluptuous. Which perhaps she also sought to engineer from him. Yet, in her slight way, she was attractive. Even womanly. She shuttled between impish girlhood and neurotic womanhood.

"Pick one of these and put it on," he said. "You'll blossom to match. Don't be uneasy about it. Here I am in this insane costume, and I think it's wildly funny. You've got to match me. Go ahead."

"That's the other trouble. There are so many. I can't pick!"

She had a point there. Burris stared into the closet. The choice was overwhelming. Cleopatra herself would have been dizzied, and this poor waif was stunned. He fished about uncomfortably, hoping to land on something that would instantly proclaim its suitability for Lona. But none of these garments had been designed for waifs, and so long as he persisted in thinking of her as one, he could make no selection. At last he came back to the one he had grabbed at random, the elegant and chaste one. "This," he said. "I think this is just right."

She looked doubtfully at the label. "I'd feel embarrassed in anything so fancy."

"We've dealt with that theme already, Lona. Put it on."

"I can't use the machine. I don't know how."

"It's the simplest thing in the world!" he burst out, and cursed himself for the ease with which he slipped into hectoring inflections with her. "The instructions are right on the can. You put the can in the slot—"

"Do it for me."

He did it for her. She stood in the dispenser zone, slim and pale and naked, while the garment issued forth in a fine mist and wrapped itself about her. Burris began to suspect that he had been manipulated, and rather adroitly at that. In one giant bound they had crossed the barrier of nudity, and now she showed herself to him as casually as though she were his wife of decades. Seeking his advice on clothing. Forcing him to stand by while she pirouetted beneath the dispenser, cloaking herself in elegance. The little witch! He admired the technique. The tears, the huddled bare body, the poor-little-girl approach. Or was he reading into her panic far more than was to be found there? Perhaps. Probably.

"How do I look?" she asked, stepping forth.

"Magnificent." He meant it. "There's the mirror. Decide for yourself."

Her glow of pleasure was worth several kilowatts. Burris decided he had been all wrong about her motives; she was less complicated than that, had been genuinely terrified by the prospect of elegance, now was genuinely delighted at the ultimate effect.

Which was superb. The dispenser nozzle had spawned a gown that was not quite diaphanous, not quite skin-tight. It clung to her like a cloud, veiling the slender thighs and sloping shoulders and artfully managing to suggest a voluptuousness that was not there at all. No one wore undergarments with a sprayon outfit, and so the bare body lay just fractionally out of sight; but the designers were cunning, and the loose drape of this gown enhanced and amplified its wearer. The colors, too, were delicious. Through some molecular magic the polymers were not tied strongly to one segment of the spectrum. As Lona moved the gown changed hue readily, sliding from dawn-gray to the blue of a summer sky, and thence to black, iron-brown, pearl, mauve.

Lona took on the semblance of sophistication that the garment provided her. She seemed taller, older, more alert, surer of herself. She held her shoulders up, and her breasts thrust forward in surprising transfiguration.

"Do you like it?" she asked softly.

"It's wonderful, Lona."

"I feel so strange in it. I've never worn anything like this. Suddenly I'm Cinderella going to the ball!"

"With Duncan Chalk as your fairy godmother?"

They laughed. "I hope he turns into a pumpkin at midnight," she said. She moved toward the mirror. "Minner, I'll be ready in another five minutes, all right?"

He returned to his own room. She needed not five minutes but fifteen to cleanse the evidence of tears from her face, but he forgave her. When she finally appeared, he scarcely recognized her. She had prettied her face to a burnished glamour that virtually transformed her. The eyes were rimmed now with shining dust; the lips gleamed in lush phosphorescence; earclips of gold covered her ears. She drifted like a wisp of morning mist into his room. "We can go now," she said throatily.

Burris was pleased and amused. In one sense, she was a little girl dressed up to look like a woman. In another, she was a woman just beginning to discover that she was no longer a girl. Had the chrysalis really opened yet? In any case he enjoyed the sight of her this way. She was certainly lovely. Perhaps fewer people would look at him, more at her.

They headed for the dropshaft together.

Just before he left his room, he notified Aoudad that he and Lona were coming down for dinner. Then they descended. Burris felt a wild surge of fear and grimly quelled it. This would be his most public exposure since his return to Earth. Dinner at the restaurant of restaurants; his strange face perhaps souring the caviar of a thousand fellow diners; eyes turned to him from all sides. He looked at it as a test. Somehow he drew strength from Lona and put on a cloak of courage as she had put on her unfamiliar finery.

When they reached the lobby, Burris heard the quick sighs of the onlookers. Pleasure? Awe? The *frisson* of delighted revulsion? He could not read their motives from their hissing uptake of air. Yet they were looking, and responding, to the strange pair who had emerged from the dropshaft.

Burris, Lona on his arm, kept his face taut. Get a good look at us, he thought sharply. The couple of the century, we are. The mutilated starman and the hundred-baby virgin mother. The show of the epoch.

They were looking, all right. Burris felt the eyetracks crossing his earless jaw, passing over his click-click eyelids

and his rearranged mouth. He astounded himself by his own
lack of response to their vulgar curiosity. They were looking
at Lona, too, but she had less to offer them, since her scars
were inward ones.

Suddenly there was commotion to Burris's left.

An instant later Elise Prolisse burst from the crowd and
hurtled toward him, crying harshly, "Minner! Minner!"

She looked like a she-berserker. Her face was bizarrely
painted in a wild and monstrous parody of adornment: blue
cheekstrips, red flanges over her eyes. She had shunned
sprayon and wore a gown of some rustling, seductive natural
fabric, cut low to reveal the milk-white globes of her breasts.
Hands tipped with shining claws were outstretched.

"I've tried to get to you," she panted. "They wouldn't let
me near you. They—"

Aoudad cut toward them. *"Elise—"*

She slashed his cheek with her nails. Aoudad reeled back,
cursing, and Elise turned to Burris. She looked venom at
Lona. She tugged at Burris's arm and said, "Come away with
me. Now that I've found you again I won't let go."

"Get your hand off him!" From Lona. The syllables tipped
with whirling blades.

The older woman glared at the girl. Burris, baffled, thought
they would fight. Elise weighed at least forty pounds more
than Lona, and, as Burris had good reason to know, she was
fiercely strong. But Lona had unsuspected strengths, too.

A scene in the lobby, he thought with curious clarity.
Nothing will be spared us.

"I love him, you little bitch!" Elise cried hoarsely.

Lona did not answer. But her hand moved out in a quick
chopping gesture toward Elise's outstretched arm. Edge of
hand collided with fleshy forearm in a quick crack. Elise
hissed. She pulled back her arm. The hands formed claws
again. Lona, squaring away, flexed her knees and was ready to
leap.

All this had taken only seconds. Now the startled bystand-
ers moved. Burris himself, after early paralysis, stepped in
the way and shielded Lona from Elise's fury. Aoudad seized
one of Elise's arms. She tried to pull it free, and her bare
breasts quivered in the effort. Nikolaides moved in on the
other side. Elise screamed, kicked, pulled. A circle of robot
bellhops had formed. Burris watched as they dragged Elise
away.

Lona leaned against an onyx pillar. Her face was deeply flushed, but otherwise not even her makeup was disarranged. She looked more startled than frightened.

"Who was that?" she asked.

"Elise Prolisse. The widow of one of my shipmates."

"What did she want?"

"Who knows?" Burris lied.

Lona was not fooled. "She said she loved you."

"It's her privilege. I guess she's been under great stress."

"I saw her in the hospital. She visited you." Green flames of jealousy flickered across Lona's face. "What does she want from you? Why did she make that scene?"

Aoudad came to his rescue. Holding a cloth to his bloodied cheek, he said, "We've given her a sedative. She won't bother you again. I'm terribly sorry about this. A silly, hysterical fool of a woman—"

"Let's go back upstairs," said Lona. "I don't feel like eating in the Galactic Room now."

"Oh, no," Aoudad said. "Don't cancel out. I'll give you a relaxer and you'll feel better in no time. You mustn't let a stupid episode like that spoil a wonderful evening."

"At least let's get out of the lobby," Burris said shortly.

The little group hurried toward a brightly lit inner room. Lona sank to a divan. Burris, crackling now with delayed tension, felt pain shoot through his thighs, his wrists, his chest. Aoudad produced a pocket tray of relaxers, taking one himself and giving one to Lona. Burris shrugged the little tube away, knowing that the drug it contained would have no effect on him. In moments Lona was smiling again.

He knew he had not been mistaken about the jealousy in her eyes. Elise had come up like a typhoon of flesh, threatening to sweep away all that Lona possessed, and Lona had fought back fiercely. Burris was both flattered and troubled. He could not deny that he enjoyed, as any man would, being the object of such a struggle. Yet that instant of revelation had shown him just how deeply Lona already was enmeshed with him. He felt no such depth of involvement himself. He liked the girl, yes, and was grateful to her for her company, but he was a long way from being in love with her. He doubted very much that he would ever love her, or anyone else. But she, without even the virtue of a physical bond linking them, had evidently constructed some inner fantasy of romance. The seeds of trouble lay in that, Burris knew.

Drained of tensions by Aoudad's relaxer, Lona quickly recovered from Elise's attack. They rose, Aoudad beaming again despite his injury.

"Will you go to dinner now?" he asked.

"I'm feeling much better," Lona said. "It was all so sudden—it shook me up."

"Five minutes in the Galactic Room and you'll have forgotten the whole thing," said Burris. He gave her his arm again. Aoudad conducted them toward the special liftshaft that led only to the Galactic Room. They mounted the gravity plate and sped upward. The restaurant was at the summit of the hotel, looking outward toward the heavens from its lofty spot like some private observatory, a sybaritic Uraniborg of food. Still trembling from the unexpected onslaught of Elise, Burris felt new anxiety as they reached the vestibule of the restaurant. He kept a calm front, but would he panic in the supernal glamour of the Galactic Room?

He had been there once before, long ago. But that was in another body, and besides, the wench was dead.

The liftshaft halted, and they stepped out into a bath of living light.

Aoudad said portentously, "The Galactic Room! Your table is waiting. Enjoy yourselves."

He vanished. Burris smiled tensely at Lona, who looked drugged and dazed with happiness and terror. The crystal doors opened for them. They went within.

Nineteen
Le Jardin des Supplices

There had never been such a restaurant this side of Babylon. Tier upon tier of terraces rose toward the starry dome. Refraction was banished here, and the dining room seemed to be open to the heavens, but in fact the elegant diners were shielded from the elements at all times. A screen of black light framing the facade of the hotel cancelled out the effect of the city illumination, so that the stars always gleamed over the Galactic Room as they would above an untenanted forest.

The far worlds of the universe thus lay only a short distance out of reach. The things of those worlds, the harvest of the stars, gave splendor to the room. The texture of its curving walls was due to an array of alien artifacts: bright-hued pebbles, potsherds, paintings, tinkling magic-trees of odd alloys, zigzagging constructions of living light, each embedded in its proper niche in the procession of tiers. The tables seemed to grow from the floor, which was carpeted with a not-quite-sentient organism found on one of the worlds of Aldebaran. The carpet was, to be blunt about it, not too different in structure and function from the Terran slime mold, but the management did not make too much ceremony over identifying it, and the effect it produced was one of extreme richness.

Other things grew in select spots of the Galactic Room: potted shrubs, sweet-smelling blossoming plants, even dwarf trees, all (so it was said) imported from other worlds. The chandelier itself was the product of alien hands: a colossal efflorescence of golden teardrops, crafted from the amber-like secretion of a bulky sea-beast living along the gray shores of a Centaurine planet.

It cost an incalculable sum to have dinner at the Galactic Room. Every table was occupied, every night. One made reservations weeks in advance. Those who had been lucky enough to choose this night were granted the unexpected treat of seeing the starman and the girl who had had the many babies, but the diners, most of them celebrities themselves, had only fleeting interest in the much-publicized pair. A quick look, and then back to the wonders on one's plate.

Lona clung tightly to Burris's arm as they passed between the thick, clear doors. Her small fingers dug so deeply that she knew she must be hurting him. She found herself standing on a narrow raised platform looking out onto an enormous expanse of emptiness, with the starry sky blazing overhead. The core of the restaurant-dome was hollow and many hundreds of feet across; the tiers of tables clung like scales to the outer shell, giving every diner a window seat.

She felt as though she were tipping forward, tumbling into the open well before her.

"Oh!" Sharply. Knees trembling, throat dry, she rocked on her heels and quickly closed and opened her eyes. Terror pierced her in a thousand places. She might fall and be lost in the abyss; or her sprayon gown might deliquesce and leave her naked before this fashionable horde; or that she-witch with the giant udders might reappear and attack them as they ate; or she might commit some horrible blunder at the table; or, suddenly and violently ill, she might spray the carpet with her vomit. Anything might happen. This restaurant had been conceived in a dream, but not necessarily a good dream.

A furry voice out of nowhere murmured, "Mr. Burris, Miss Kelvin, welcome to the Galactic Room. Please step forward."

"We get on that gravity plate," Burris prompted her.

The coppery plate was a disk an inch thick and two yards in diameter, protruding from the rim of their platform. Burris led her onto it, and at once it slipped free of its mooring and glided outward and upward. Lona did not look down. The floating plate took them to the far side of the great room and came to rest beside a vacant table perched precariously on a cantilevered ledge. Dismounting, Burris helped Lona to the edge. Their carrier disk fluttered away, returning to its place. Lona saw it edge-on for a moment, wearing a gaudy corona of reflected light.

The table, on a single leg, appeared to sprout organically from the ledge. Lona gratefully planted herself on her chair, which molded itself instantly to the contours of her back and buttocks. There was something obscene about the confident grip, and yet it was reassuring; the chair, she thought, would not release her if she became dizzy and started to slide toward the steep drop to her left.

"How do you like it?" Burris asked, looking into her eyes.

"It's incredible. I never imagined it was like this." She did not tell him that she was nearly sick from the impact of it.

"We have a choice table. It's probably the one Chalk himself uses when he eats here."

"I never knew there were so many stars!"

They looked up. From where they sat they had an unimpeded view of almost a hundred and fifty degrees of arc. Burris told her the stars and planets.

"Mars," he said. "That's easy: the big orange one. But can you see Saturn? The rings aren't visible, of course, but..." He took her hand, aimed it, and described the lay of the heavens until she thought she saw what he meant. "We'll be out there soon, Lona. Titan's not visible from here, not with naked eye, but we'll be on it ourselves before long. And then

we'll see those rings! Look, look there: Orion. And Pegasus."
He called off the constellations for her. He named stars with a
sensuous pleasure in uttering the sounds of them: Sirius,
Arcturus, Polaris, Bellatrix, Rigel, Algol, Antares, Betelgeuse,
Aldebaran, Procyon, Markab, Deneb, Vega, Alphecca. "Each
of them a sun," he said. "Most have worlds. And there they
all are spread out before us!"

"Have you visited many other suns?"

"Eleven. Nine with planets."

"Including any of the ones you just named? I like those
names."

He shook his head. "The suns I went to had numbers, not
names. At least, not names Earthmen had given. Most of
them had other names. Some I learned." She saw the corners
of his mouth pulling open and rapidly drawing closed again: a
sign of tension in him, Lona had learned. *Should I talk about
the stars to him? Perhaps he doesn't want to be reminded.*
Under this bright canopy, though, she could not leave the
theme alone.

"Will you ever go back out there?" she asked.

"Out of this system? I doubt it. I'm retired from the service
now. And we don't have tourist flights to neighboring stars.
But I'll be off Earth again, of course. With you: the planetary
tour. Not quite the same. But safer."

"Can you—can you—" she debated and rushed onward—
"show me the planet where you were—captured?"

Three quick contortions of his mouth. "It's a bluish sun.
You can't see it from this hemisphere. You can't see it with
naked eye even down below. Six planets. Manipool's the
fourth. When we were orbiting it, coming around ready to go
down, I felt a strange excitement. As though my destiny drew
me to this place. Maybe there's a little tinge of the pre-cog in
me, eh, Lona? Surely Manipool had its large place in my
destiny. But I can tell I'm no pre-cog. From time to time I'm
hit with this powerful conviction that I'm marked for a return
trip. And that's absurd. To go back *there* . . . to confront Them
again . . ." His fist closed suddenly, tightening with a convulsive snap that pulled his entire arm inward. A vase of
thick-petaled blue flowers nearly went flying into the void.
Lona caught it. She noticed that when he closed his hand,
the little outer tentacle neatly wrapped itself across the backs
of his fingers. Putting both of her hands over his, she held

him by the knuckles until the tension ebbed and his fingers
opened.

"Let's not talk of Manipool," she suggested. "The stars are
beautiful, though."

"Yes. I never really thought of them that way until I came
back to Earth after my first voyage. We see them only as dots
of light, from down here. But when you're out there caught
in the crisscross of starlight, bouncing this way and that as the
stars buffet you, it's different. They leave a mark on you. Do
you know, Lona, that you get a view of the stars from this
room that's almost as piercing as what you see from the port
of a starship?"

"How do they do it? I've never seen anything like that."

He tried to explain about the curtain of black light. Lona
was lost after the third sentence, but she stared intently into
his strange eyes, pretending to listen and knowing that she
must not be deceiving him. He knew so much! And yet he
was frightened in this room of delights, just as she was
frightened. So long as they kept talking, it created a barrier
against the fear. But in the silences Lona was awkwardly
aware of the hundreds of rich, sophisticated people all about
her, and of the overwhelming luxury of the room, and of the
abyss beside her, and of her own ignorance and inexperience.
She felt naked beneath that blaze of stars. In the interstices of
the conversation even Burris again became strange to her; his
surgical distortions, which she had nearly ceased to notice,
abruptly took on a fiery conspicuousness.

"Something to drink?" he asked.

"Yes. Yes, please. You order. I don't know what to have."

No waiter, human or robot, was in sight, nor did Lona see
any attending at the other tables. Burris gave the order
simply by uttering it into a golden grillwork at his left elbow.
His cool knowledgeableness awed her, as she half suspected it
was meant to do. She said, "Have you eaten here often? You
seem to know what to do."

"I was here once. More than a decade ago. It's not a place
you forget easily."

"Were you a starman already, then?"

"Oh, yes. I'd made a couple of trips. I was on furlough.
There was this girl I wanted to impress—"

"Oh."

"I didn't impress her. She married someone else. They
were killed when the Wheel collapsed, on their honeymoon."

Ten years and more ago, Lona thought. She had been less than seven years old. She felt shriveled with her youthfulness beside him. She was glad when the drinks arrived.

They came skimming across the abyss on a small gravitron tray. It seemed amazing to Lona that none of the serving trays, which now she noticed were quite numerous, ever collided as they soared to their tables. But, of course, it was no great task to program non-intersecting orbits.

Her drink came in a bowl of polished black stone, thick to the hand but smooth and gracile to the lip. She scooped up the bowl and automatically took it toward her mouth; then, halting an instant before the sip, she realized her error. Burris waited, smiling, his own glass still before him.

He seems so damned schoolmasterish when he smiles like that, she thought. Scolding me without saying a word. I know what he's thinking: that I'm an ignorant little tramp who doesn't know her manners.

She let the anger subside. It was really anger directed at herself, not him, she realized after a moment. Sensing that made it easier to grow calm.

She looked at his drink.

There was something swimming in it.

The glass was translucent quartz. It was three-fifths filled with a richly viscous green fluid. Moving idly back and forth was a tiny animal, teardrop-shaped, whose violet skin left a faint glow behind as it swam.

"Is that supposed to be there?"

Burris laughed. "I have a Deneb martini, so-called. It's a preposterous name. Specialty of the house."

"And in it?"

"A tadpole, essentially. Amphibious life-form from one of the Aldebaran worlds."

"Which you drink?"

"Yes. Live."

"Live," Lona shuddered. "Why? Does it taste that good?"

"It has no taste at all, as a matter of fact. It's pure decoration. Sophistication come full circle, back to barbarism. One gulp, and down it goes."

"But it's alive! How can you kill it?"

"Have you ever eaten an oyster, Lona?"

"No. What's an oyster?"

"A mollusk. Once quite popular, served in its shell. Live. You sprinkle it with lemon juice—citric acid, you know—and

it writhes. Then you eat it. It tastes of the sea. I'm sorry,
Lona. That's how it is. Oysters don't know what's happening
to them. They don't have hopes and fears and dreams.
Neither does this creature here."

"But to kill—"

"We kill to eat. A true morality of food would allow us to
eat only synthetics." Burris smiled kindly. "I'm sorry. I wouldn't
have ordered it if I'd known it would offend you. Shall I have
them take it away?"

"No. Someone else would drink it, I guess. I didn't mean
to say all that. I was just a little upset, Minner. But it's your
drink. Enjoy it."

"I'll send it back."

"Please." She touched the left-hand tentacle. "You know
why I object? Because it's like making yourself a god, to
swallow a live living thing. I mean, here you are, gigantic,
and you just destroy something, and it never knows why. The
way—" She stopped.

"The way alien Things can pick up an inferior organism and
put it through surgery, without troubling to explain themselves?" he asked. "The way doctors can perform an intricate
experiment on a girl's ovaries, without considering later
psychological effects? God, Lona, we've got to sidestep those
thoughts, not keep coming back to them!"

"What did you order for me?" she asked.

"Gaudax. An aperitif from a Centaurine world. It's mild
and sweet. You'll like it. Cheers, Lona."

"Cheers."

He moved his glass in orbit around her black stone bowl,
saluting it and her. Then they drank. The Centaurine aperitif
tickled her tongue; it was faintly oily stuff, yet delicate,
delightful. She shivered with the pleasure. After three quick
sips she put the bowl down.

The small swimming creature was gone from Burris's glass.

"Would you like to taste mine?" he asked.

"Please. No."

He nodded. "Let's order dinner, then. Will you forgive me
for my thoughtlessness?"

Two dark green cubes, four inches on each face, sat side by
side in the middle of the table. Lona had thought they were
purely ornamental, but now, as Burris nudged one toward
her, she realized that they were menus. As she handled it,
warm light flushed through the depths of the cube and

illuminated letters appeared, seemingly an inch below the sleek surface. She turned the cube over and over. Soups, meats, appetizers, sweets. . . .

She recognized nothing on the menu.

"I shouldn't be in here, Minner. I just eat ordinary things. This is so weird I don't know where to begin."

"Shall I order for you?"

"You'd better. Except they won't have the things I really want. Like a chopped protein steak and a glass of milk."

"Forget the chopped protein steak. Sample some of the rarer delicacies."

"It's so false, though. Me pretending to be a gourmet."

"Don't pretend anything. Eat and enjoy. Chopped protein steak isn't the only food in the universe."

His calmness reached forth to her, containing but not quite transferring to her. He ordered for both of them. Lona was proud of his skill. It was a small thing, knowing your way around a menu in such a place; yet he knew so much. He was awesome. She found herself thinking, *if only I had met him before they . . .* and cut the thought off. No imaginable set of circumstances would have brought her into contact with the premutilated Minner Burris. He would not have noticed her; he must have been busy then with women like that jiggly old Elise. Who still coveted him, but now could not have him. He's mine, Lona thought fiercely. He's mine! They tossed me a broken thing, and I'm helping to fix it, and no one will take it from me.

"Would you care for soup as well as an appetizer?" he asked.

"I'm not really terribly hungry."

"Try a little anyway."

"I'd only waste it."

"No one worries about waste here. And we're not paying for this. Try."

Dishes began to appear. Each was a specialty of some distant world, either imported authentically or else duplicated here with the greatest of craft. Swiftly the table was filled with strangeness. Plates, bowls, cups of oddities, served in stunning opulence. Burris called off the names to her and tried to explain the foods to her, but she was dizzied now and scarcely able to comprehend. What was this flaky white meat? These golden berries steeped in honey? This soup, pale and sprinkled with aromatic cheese? Earth alone produced so many cuisines; to have a galaxy to choose from was so dazzling a thought that it numbed the appetite.

Lona nibbled. She grew confused. A bite of this, a sip of that. She kept expecting the next goblet to contain some other little living creature. Long before the main course had arrived, she was full. Two kinds of wine had been brought. Burris mixed them and they changed color, turquoise and ruby blending to form an unexpected opal shade. "Catalytic response," he said. "They calculate the esthetics of sight as well as of taste. Here." But she could drink only a tiny bit.

Were the stars moving in ragged circles now?

She heard the hum of conversation all about her. For more than an hour she had been able to pretend that she and Burris had been isolated within a pocket of privacy, but now the presence of the other diners was breaking through. They were looking. Commenting. Moving about, drifting from table to table on their gravitron plates. Have you seen? What do you think of? How charming! How strange! How grotesque!

"Minner, let's get out of here."

"But we haven't had our dessert yet."

"I know. I don't care."

"Liqueur from the Procyon group. Coffee Galactique."

"Minner, no." She saw his eyes open to the full shutter-width and knew that some expression on her face must have scored him deeply. She was very close to getting ill. Perhaps it was obvious to him.

"We'll go," he told her. "We'll come back for dessert some other time."

"I'm so sorry, Minner," she mumured. "I didn't want to spoil the dinner. But this place . . . I just don't feel right in a place like this. It scares me. All these strange foods. The staring eyes. They're all looking at us, aren't they? If we could go back to the room, it would be so much better."

He was summoning the carrier disk now. Her chair released her from its intimate grip. Her legs were wobbly when she stood up. She did not know how she could take a step without toppling. A strange tunnel-like clarity of vision brought her isolated views as she hesitated. The fat jeweled woman with a host of chins. The gilded girl clad in transparency, not much older than herself but infinitely surer of herself. The garden of little forked trees two levels below. The ropes of living light festooned in the air. A tray slicing across the open space bearing three mugs of dark, shining unknownness. Lona swayed. Burris anchored her and virtually lifted her onto the disk, though to a watcher it would not seem that he held her in so supportive a way.

She stared fixedly forward as they crossed the gulf to the entrance platform.

Her face was flushed and beaded with sweat. Within her stomach, it seemed to her, the alien creatures had come to life and were swimming patiently in the digestive sauces. Somehow she and Burris passed through the crystal doors. Down to the lobby via quick dropshaft; then up again, another shaft, to their suite. She caught sight of Aoudad lurking in the corridor, disappearing quickly behind a broad pilaster.

Burris palmed the door. It opened for them.

"Are you sick?" he asked.

"I don't know. I'm glad to be out of there. It's so much calmer here. Did you lock the door?"

"Of course. Can I do anything for you, Lona?"

"Let me rest. A few minutes, by myself."

He took her to her bedroom and eased her down on the round bed. Then he went out. Lona was surprised how quickly equilibrium returned, away from the restaurant. It had seemed to her, at the very end, that the sky itself had become a huge prying eye.

Calmer now, Lona rose, determined to shed the rest of her false glamour. She stepped under the vibraspray. Instantly her sumptuous gown vanished. She felt smaller, younger, at once. Naked, she made herself ready for bed.

She turned on a dim lamp, deactivated the rest of the room glow, and slipped between the sheets. They were cool and agreeable against her skin. A control console governed the movements and form of the bed, but Lona ignored it. She said softly into an intercom beside her pillow, "Minner, will you come in now?"

He entered at once. He was still wearing his flamboyant dinner costume, cape and all. The flaring rib-like projections were so strange that they nearly canceled out the other strangeness that was his body.

Dinner had been a disaster, she thought. The restaurant, so glittering, had been like a torture chamber for her. But the evening might be salvaged.

"Hold me," she said in a thin voice. "I'm still a little shaky, Minner."

Burris came to her. He sat beside her, and she rose a little, letting the sheet slip down to reveal her breasts. He reached for her, but the ribs of his costume formed an unbending barrier, thwarting contact.

"I'd better get out of this rig," he said.

"The vibraspray's over there."

"Shall I turn off the light?"

"No. No."

Her eyes did not leave him as he crossed the room.

He mounted the platform of the vibraspray and turned it on. It was designed to cleanse the skin of any adhering matter, and a sprayon garment would naturally be the first to go. Burris's outlandish costume disappeared.

Lona had never seen his body before.

Unflinchingly, ready for any catastrophic revelation, she watched the naked man turn to face her. Her face was rigidly set, as was his, for this was a double test, showing if she could bear the shock of facing the unknown, showing if he could bear the shock of facing her response.

She had dreaded this moment for days. But now it was here, and in spreading wonder she discovered that she had lived through and past the dreaded moment without harm.

He was not nearly so terrible to behold as she had anticipated.

Of course, he was strange. His skin, like the skin of his face and arms, was glossy and unreal, a seamless container like none ever worn by man before. He was hairless. He had neither breasts nor navel, a fact that Lona realized slowly after searching for the cause of the wrongness.

His arms and legs were attached to his body in an unfamiliar manner, and by several inches in unfamiliar places. His chest seemed too deep in proportion to the width of his hips. His knees did not stand out from his legs as knees should do. When he moved, the muscles of his body rippled in a curious way.

But these were minor things, and they were not true deformities. He bore no hideous scars, no hidden extra limbs, no unexpected eyes or mouths on his body. The real changes were within, and on his face.

And the one aspect of all that had concerned Lona was anticlimatic. Against probability, he seemed normally male. So far as she could tell, at least.

Burris came toward the bed. She lifted her arms. An instant later and he was beside her, his skin against hers. The texture was strange but not unpleasant. He seemed oddly shy just now. Lona drew him closer. Her eyes closed. She did not want to see his altered face in this moment, and in any case her eyes seemed suddenly sensitive even to the faint light of the lamp. Her hand moved out to him. Her lips met his.

She had not been kissed often. But she had never been kissed like this. Those who had redesigned his lips had not intended them for kissing, and he was forced to make contact in an unwieldly way, mouth to mouth. But, again, it was not unpleasant. And then Lona felt his fingers on her flesh, six digits to each hand. His skin had a sweet, pungent odor. The light went out.

A spring within her body was coiling tighter... tighter... tighter...

A spring that had been coiling ever tighter for seventeen years... and now its force was unleashed in a single moment of tumult.

She pulled her mouth from his. Her jaws wrenched themselves apart, and a sheath of muscle quaked in her throat. A blistering image seared her: herself on an operating table, anesthetized, her body open to the probe of the men in white. She struck the image with a bolt of lightning, and it shattered and tumbled away.

She clutched at him.

At last. At last!

He would not give her babies. She sensed that, and it did not trouble her.

"Lona," he said, his face against her clavicle, his voice coming out smothered and thick. "Lona, Lona, Lona..."

There was brightness, as of an exploding sun. Her hand ran up and down his back, and just before joining the thought came to her that his skin was dry, that he did not sweat at all. Then she gasped, felt pain and pleasure in one convulsive unity, and listened in amazement to the ferocious ringing cries of lust that were fleeing of their own accord from her frenzied throat.

Twenty
After Us, the Savage God

It was a post-apocalyptic era. The doom of which the prophets had chanted had never come; or, if it had, the world had lived through it into a quieter time. They had predicted the worst, a Fimbulwinter of universal discontent. An ax-age, a sword-age, a wind-age, a wolf-age, ere the world totters. But shields were not cloven, and darkness did not fall. What had happened, and why? Duncan Chalk, one of the chief beneficiaries of the new era, often pondered that pleasant question.

The swords now were plowshares.

Hunger was abolished.

Population was controlled.

Man no longer fouled his own environment in every daily act. The skies were relatively pure. The rivers ran clear. There were lakes of blue crystal, parks of bright green. Of course, the millennium had not quite arrived; there was crime, disease, hunger, even now. But that was in the dark places. For most, it was an age of ease. Those who looked for crisis looked for it in that.

Communication in the world was instantaneous. Transportation was measurably slower than that, but still fast. The planets of the local solar system, unpeopled, were being plundered of their metals, their minerals, even their gaseous blankets. The nearer stars had been reached. Earth prospered. The ideologies of poverty wither embarrassingly in a time of plenty.

Yet plenty is relative. Needs and envies remained—the materialistic urges. The deeper, darker hungers were not always gratified by thick paychecks alone, either. An era determines for itself its characteristic forms of entertainment. Chalk had been one of the shapers of those forms.

His empire of amusement stretched halfway across the system. It brought him wealth, power, the satisfaction of the ego, and—to the measure he desired it—fame. It led him indirectly to the fulfillment of his inner needs, which were generated from his own physical and psychological makeup, and which would have pressed upon him had he lived in any other era. Now, conveniently, he was in a position to take the steps that would bring him to the position he required.

He needed to be fed frequently. And his food was only partly flesh and vegetables.

From the center of his empire Chalk followed the doings of his star-crossed pair of lovers. They were en route to Antarctica now. He received regular reports from Aoudad and Nikolaides, those hoverers over the bed of love. But by this time Chalk no longer needed his flunkies to tell him what was happening. He had achieved contact and drew his own species of information from the two splintered ones he had brought together.

Just now what he drew from them was a bland wash of happiness. Useless, for Chalk. But he played his game patiently. Mutual sympathy had drawn them close, but was sympathy the proper foundation for undying love? Chalk thought not. He was willing to gamble a fortune to prove his point. They would change toward each other. And Chalk would turn his profit, so to speak.

Aoudad was on the circuit now. "We're just arriving, sir. They're being taken to the hotel."

"Good. Good. See that they're given every comfort."

"Naturally."

"But don't spend much time near them. They want to be with each other, not chivied about by chaperones. Do you follow me, Aoudad?"

"They'll have the whole Pole to themselves."

Chalk smiled. Their tour would be a lovers' dream. It was an elegant era, and those with the right key could open door after door of pleasures. Burris and Lona would enjoy themselves.

The apocalypse could come later.

Twenty-One
And Southward Aye We Fled

"I don't understand," Lona said. "How can it be summer here? When we left, it was winter!"

"In the Northern Hemisphere, yes." Burris sighed. "But now we're below the Equator. As far below as it's possible to get. The seasons are reversed here. When we get summer, they have winter. And now it's their summer here."

"Yes, but why?"

"It has to do with the way the Earth is tipped on its axis. As it goes around the sun, part of the planet is in a good position to get warmed by sunlight, and part isn't. If I had a globe here, I could show you."

"If it's summer here, though, why is there so much ice?"

The thin, whining tone of her questions annoyed him even more than the questions themselves. Burris whirled suddenly. There was a spasm within his diaphragm as mysterious organs spurted their secretions of anger into his blood.

"Damn it, Lona, didn't you ever go to school?" he blazed at her.

She shrank away from him. "Don't shout at me, Minner. Please don't shout."

"Didn't they teach you anything?"

"I left school early. I wasn't a good student."

"And now I'm your teacher?"

"You don't have to be," Lona said quietly. Her eyes were too bright now. "You don't have to be anything for me if you don't want to be."

He was suddenly on the defensive. "I didn't mean to shout at you."

"But you shouted."

"I lost patience. All those questions—"

"All those *silly* questions—isn't that what you wanted to say?"

"Let's stop it right here, Lona. I'm sorry I blew up at you. I didn't get much sleep last night, and my nerves are frayed. Let's go for a walk. I'll try to explain the seasons to you."

"I'm not all that interested in the seasons, Minner."

"Forget the seasons, then. But let's walk. Let's try to calm ourselves down."

"Do you think *I* got much sleep last night, either?"

He thought it might be time to smile. "I guess you didn't, not really."

"But am I shouting and complaining?"

"As a matter of fact, you are. So let's quit it right here and take a relaxing walk. Yes?"

"All right," she said sullenly. "A summertime stroll."

"A summertime stroll, yes."

They slipped on light thermal wraps, hoods, gloves. The temperature was mild for this part of the world: several degrees above freezing. The Antarctic was having a heat wave. Chalk's polar hotel was only a few dozen miles from the Pole itself, lying "north" of the Pole, as all things must, and placed out toward the direction of the Ross Shelf Ice. It was a sprawling geodesic dome, solid enough to withstand the rigors of the polar night, airy enough to admit the texture of the Antarctic.

A double exit chamber was their gateway to the ice-realm outside. The dome was surrounded by a belt of brown bare soil ten feet wide, laid down by the builders as an insulating zone, and beyond it was the white plateau. Instantly, as Burris and the girl emerged, a burly guide rushed up to them, grinning.

"Power-sled trip, folks? Take you to the Pole in fifteen minutes! Amundsen's camp, reconstructed. The Scott Museum. Or we could go out for a look at the glaciers back the other way. You say the word, and—"

"No."

"I understand. Your first morning here, you'd just like to stroll around a little. Can't blame you at all. Well, you just stroll all you like. And when you decide that you're ready for a longer trip—"

"Please," Burris said. "Can we get by?"

The guide gave him a queer look and stepped aside. Lona slipped her arm through Burris's and they walked out onto the ice. Looking back, Burris saw a figure step from the dome and call the guide aside, Aoudad. They were having an earnest conference.

"It's so beautiful here!" Lona cried.

"In a sterile way, yes. The last frontier. Almost untouched, except for a museum here and there."

"And hotels."

"This is the only one. Chalk has a monopoly."

The sun was high overhead, looking bright but small. This close to the Pole, the summer day would seem never to end; two months of unbroken sunlight lay ahead before the long dip into darkness began. The light glittered brilliantly over the icy plateau. Everything was flat here, a mile-high sheet of whiteness burying mountains and valleys alike. The ice was firm underfoot. In ten minutes they had left the hotel far behind.

"Which way is the South Pole?" Lona asked.

"That way. Straight ahead. We'll go over there later."

"And behind us?"

"The Queen Maud Mountains. They drop off down to the Ross Shelf. It's a big slab of ice, seven hundred feet thick, bigger than California. The early explorers made their camps on it. We'll visit Little America in a couple of days."

"It's so flat here. The reflection of the sun is so bright."
Lona bent, scooped a handful of snow, and scattered it gaily.
"I'd love to see some penguins. Minner, do I ask too many
questions? Do I chatter?"

"Should I be honest or should I be tactful?"

"Never mind. Let's just walk."

They walked. He found the slick footing of ice peculiarly
comfortable. It gave ever so slightly with each step he took,
accommodating itself nicely to the modified joints of his legs.
Concrete pavements were not so friendly. Burris, who had
had a tense and pain-filled night, welcomed the change.

He regretted having snarled at Lona that way.

But his patience had snapped. She was strikingly ignorant,
but he had known that from the start. What he had not
known was how quickly her ignorance would cease to seem
charming and would begin to seem contemptible.

To awake, aching and agonized, and have to submit to that
thin stream of adolescent questioning...

Look at the other side, he told himself. He had awakened
in the middle of the night, too. He had dreamed of Manipool
and naturally had burst from sleep screaming. That had
happened before, but never before had there been someone
beside him, warm and soft, to comfort him. Lona had done
that. She had not scolded him for interfering with her own
sleep. She had stroked him and soothed him until the nightmare receded into unreality again. He was grateful for that.
She was so tender, so loving. And so stupid.

"Have you ever seen Antarctica from space?" Lona asked.

"Many times."

"What does it look like?"

"Just as it does on maps. More or less round, with a thumb
sticking out toward South America. And white. Everywhere
white. You'll see it when we head for Titan."

She nestled into the hollow of his arm as they walked. The
arm-socket was adaptable; he extended it, making a comfortable harbor for her. This body had its merits.

Lona said, "Someday I want to come back here again and
see all the sights—the Pole, the museums of the explorers,
the glaciers. Only I want to come with my children."

An icicle slipped neatly through his throat.

"What children, Lona?"

"There'll be two. A boy and a girl. In about eight years,
that'll be the right time to bring them."

His eyelids flickered uncontrollably within his thermal hood. They gnashed like the ringing walls of the Symplegades. In a low, fiercely controlled voice he said, "You ought to know, Lona, I can't give you any children. The doctors checked that part out. The internal organs simply—"

"Yes, I know. I didn't mean children that we'd have, Minner."

He felt his bowels go spilling out onto the ice.

She went on sweetly, "I mean the babies I have now. The ones that were taken from my body. I'm going to get two of them back—didn't I tell you?"

Burris felt oddly relieved at the knowledge that she wasn't planning to leave him for some biologically whole man. Simultaneously he was surprised at the depth of his own relief. How smugly he had assumed that any children she mentioned would be children she expected to have by him! How stunning it had been to think that she might have children by another!

But she already had a legion of children. He had nearly forgotten that.

He said, "No, you didn't tell me. You mean it's been agreed that you're going to get some of the children to raise yourself?"

"More or less."

"What does that mean?"

"I don't think it's really been agreed yet. But Chalk said he'd arrange it. He promised me, he gave me his word. And I know he's an important enough man to be able to do it. There are so many of the babies—they can spare a couple for the real mother if she wants them. And I do. I do. Chalk said he'd get the children for me if I—if I—"

She was silent. Her mouth was round a moment, then clamped tight.

"If you what, Lona?"

"Nothing."

"You started to say something."

"I said, he'd get the children for me if I wanted them."

He turned on her. "That's not what you were going to say. We already know you want them. What did you promise Chalk in return for getting them for you?"

The spectrum of guilt rippled across her face.

"What are you hiding from me?" he demanded.

She shook her head mutely. He seized her hand, and she

pulled it away. He stood over her, dwarfing her, and as always when his emotions came forth in the new body there were strange poundings and throbbings within him.

"What did you promise him?" he asked.

"Minner, you look so strange. Your face is all blotched. Red, and purple over your cheeks..."

"What was it, Lona?"

"Nothing. Nothing. All I said to him... all I agreed was..."

"Was?"

"That I'd be nice to you." In a small voice. "I promised him I'd make you happy. And he'd get me some of the babies for my own. Was that wrong, Minner?"

He felt air escaping from the gigantic puncture in his chest. Chalk had arranged this? Chalk had bribed her to care for him? Chalk? *Chalk?*

"Minner, what's wrong?"

Stormwinds blew through him. The planet was tilting on its axis, rising up, crushing him, the continents breaking loose and sliding free in a massive cascade upon him.

"Don't look at me like that," she begged.

"If Chalk hadn't offered you the babies, would you ever have come near me?" he asked tightly. "Would you ever have touched me at all, Lona?"

Her eyes were flecked now with tears. "I saw you in the hospital garden. I felt so sorry for you. I didn't even know who you were. I thought you were in a fire or something. Then I met you. I love you, Minner. Chalk couldn't make me love you. He could only get me to be good to you. But that isn't love."

He felt foolish, idiotic, shambling, a heap of animate mud. He gawked at her. She looked mystified. Then she stooped, seized snow, balled it, flung it laughing in his face. "Stop looking so weird," she said. "Chase me, Minner. Chase me!"

She sprinted away from him. In a moment she was unexpectedly far away. She paused, a dark spot on the whiteness, and picked up more snow. He watched her fashion another snowball. She threw it awkwardly, from the elbow, as a girl would, but even so it carried well, landing a dozen yards from his feet.

He broke from the stupor that her careless words had cast him into. "You can't catch me!" Lona shrilled, and he began to run, running for the first time since he had left Manipool, taking long loping strides over the carpet of snow. Lona ran,

too, arms windmilling, elbows jabbing the thin, frosty air.
Burris felt power flooding his limbs. His legs, which had
seemed so impossible to him with their multiple jointing,
now pistoned in perfect coordination, propelling him smoothly
and rapidly. His heart scarcely pounded at all. On impulse,
he threw back his hood and let the near-freezing air stream
across his cheeks.

It took him only a few minutes of hard running to overtake
her. Lona, gasping with laughter and breathlessness, swung
around as he neared her, and flung herself into his arms. His
momentum carried him onward five more steps before they
fell. They rolled over and over, gloved hands beating the
snow, and he pushed back her hood, too, scraped a palm's-
load of ice free and thrust it into her face. The ice trickled
down, past her throat, into her wrap, under her clothing,
along her breasts, her belly. She shrieked in wild pleasure
and indignation.

"Minner! No, Minner! No!"

He thrust more snow at her. And she at him now. Con-
vulsed with laugher, she forced it past his collar. It was so
cold that it seemed to burn. Together they floundered on the
snow. Then she was in his arms, and he held her tight,
nailing her to the floor of the lifeless continent. It was a long
while before they rose.

Twenty-Two
Hence, Loathed Melancholy

He woke screaming again that night.

Lona had been expecting it. For most of the night she had
been awake herself, lying beside him in the dark, waiting for
the inevitable demons to take possession of him. He had
been brooding, on and off, much of the evening.

The day had been pleasant enough—barring that nasty
moment right at the outset. Lona wished she could call back
the admission she had made: that it was Chalk who had put
her up to approaching him in the first place. At least she had

withheld the most damning part of all: that Nikolaides had thought of presenting the cactus, that Nikolaides had even dictated her little note. She knew now what effect such knowledge would have on Burris. But it had been stupid even to mention Chalk's promise of restoring the babies. Lona saw that clearly now. But now was too late to unspeak the words.

He had recovered from that taut moment, and they had gone off to have fun. A snowball fight, a hike in the trackless wilderness of ice. Lona had been scared when suddenly she realized that the hotel was no longer in sight. She saw flat whiteness everywhere. No trees to cast shadows, no movements of the sun to indicate directions, and no compass. They had walked miles through an unchanging landscape. "Can we get back?" she asked, and he nodded. "I'm tired. I'd like to go back now." Acutally she was not all that tired, but it frightened her to think of getting lost here. They turned back, or so Burris said they had done. This new direction looked just the same as the old. There was a darkness several feet long just below the snow in one place. A dead penguin, Burris told her, and she shuddered, but then the hotel miraculously appeared. If the world was flat here, she wondered, why had the hotel vanished? And Burris explained, as he had explained so many things to her (but in a more patient tone now) that the world was not really flat here, but actually nearly as curved as at any other place, so that they need walk only a very few miles for familiar landmarks to drop below the horizon. As the hotel had done.

But the hotel had returned, and their appetites were huge, and they had hearty lunches, washed down with flagon after flagon of beer. Here no one drank green cocktails with live things swimming in them. Beer, cheese, meat—that was fit food for this land of eternal winter.

They took power-sled tours that afternoon. First they went to the South Pole.

"It looks like everything else around," Lona said.

"What did you expect?" he asked. "A striped pole sticking out of the snow?"

So he was being sarcastic again. She saw the sorrow in his eyes that followed his crackling comment, and told herself that he had not meant to hurt her. It was natural to him, that was all. Maybe he was in such pain himself—*real* pain—that he had to keep lashing out that way.

But actually the Pole was different from the surrounding blankness of the polar plateau. There were buildings there. A circular zone around the world's bottom some twenty yards in diameter was sacrosanct, untouched. Near it was the restored or reproduced tent of the Norwegian, Roald Amundsen, who had come by dogsled to this place a century or two ago. A striped flag fluttered over the dark tent. They peered inside: nothing.

Nearby was a small building of logs. "Why logs?" Lona asked. "There aren't any trees in Antarctica?" For once her question was a shrewd one. Burris laughed.

The building was sacred to the memory of Robert Falcon Scott, who had followed Amundsen to the Pole and who, unlike the Norwegian, had died on the way back. Within were diaries, sleeping-bags, the odds and ends of explorers. Lona read the plaque. Scott and his men had not died here, but rather many miles away, trapped by weariness and winter gales as they plodded toward their base. All this was strictly for show. The phoniness of it bothered Lona, and she thought it bothered Burris, too.

But it was impressive to stand right at the South Pole.

"The whole world is north of us right now," Burris told her. "We're hanging off the bottom edge. Everything's above us from here. But we won't fall off."

She laughed. Nevertheless, the world did not look at all unusual to her at that moment. The surrounding land stretched away to the sides, and not up and down. She tried to picture the world as it would look from a space ferry, a ball hanging in the sky, and herself, smaller than an ant, standing at the bottom with her feet toward the center and her head pointed to the stars. Somehow it made no sense to her.

There was a refreshment stand near the Pole. They kept it covered with snow to make it inconspicuous. Burris and Lona had steaming mugs of hot chocolate.

They did not visit the underground scientific base a few hundred yards away. Visitors were welcome; scientists in thick beards lived there the year round, studying magnetism and weather and such. But Lona did not care to enter a laboratory again. She exchanged glances with Burris, and he nodded, and the guide took them back on the power-sled.

It was too late in the day to go all the way to the Ross Ice Shelf. But they traveled for more than an hour northwest from the Pole, toward a chain of mountains that never got any closer, and came to a mysterious warm spot where there was no snow, only bare brown earth stained red by a crust of algae, and rocks covered with a thin coating of yellow-green lichens. Lona asked to see penguins then, and was told that at this time of the year there were no penguins in the interior except strays. "They're water birds," the guide said. "They stay close to the coast and come inland only when it's time to lay their eggs."

"But it's summer here. They ought to be nesting now."

"They make their nests in midwinter. The baby penguins are hatched in June and July. The darkest, coldest time of the year. You want to see penguins, you sign up for the Adélie Land tour. You'll see penguins."

Burris seemed to be in good spirits on the long sled ride back to the hotel. He teased Lona in a lighthearted way, and at one point had the guide stop the sled so they could go sliding down a glassy-smooth embankment of snow. But as they neared the lodge, Lona detected the change coming over him. It was like the onset of twilight, but this was a season of no twilight at the Pole. Burris darkened. His face grew rigid, and he stopped laughing and joking. By the time they were passing through the double doors of the lodge, he seemed like something hewn from ice.

"What's wrong?" she asked.

"Who said anything was wrong?"

"Would you like to have a drink?"

They went to the cocktail lounge. It was a big room, paneled in wood, with a real fireplace to give it that twentieth-century look. Two dozen people, more or less, sat at the heavy oaken tables, talking and drinking. All of them couples, Lona noticed. This was almost entirely a honeymoon resort. Young married people came here to begin their lives in icy Antarctic purity. The skiing was said to be excellent in the mountains of Marie Bryd Land.

Heads turned their way as Burris and Lona entered. And just as quickly turned away again in a quick reflex of aversion. Oh, so sorry. Didn't mean to stare. A man with a face like yours, he probably doesn't like to be stared at. We were just looking to see if our friends the Smiths had come down for drinks.

"The demon at the wedding feast," Burris muttered.

Lona wasn't sure she had heard it correctly. She didn't ask him to repeat.

A robot servitor took their order. She drank beer, he a filtered rum. They sat alone at a table near the edge of the room. Suddenly they had nothing to say to each other. All about them conversation seemed unnaturally loud. Talk of future holidays, of sports, of the many available tours the resort offered.

No one came over to join them.

Burris sat rigidly, his shoulders forced upright in a posture that Lona knew must hurt him. He finished his drink quickly and did not order another. Outside, the pale sun refused to set.

"It would be so pretty here if we got a romantic sunset," Lona said. "Streaks of blue and gold on the ice. But we won't get it, will we?"

Burris smiled. He did not answer.

There was a flow of people in and out of the room constantly. The flow swept wide around their table. They were boulders in the stream. Hands were shaken, kisses exchanged. Lona heard people making introductions. It was the sort of place where one couple could come freely up to another, strangers, and find a warm response.

No one freely came to them.

"They know who we are," Lona said to Burris. "They think we're celebrities, so very important that we don't want to be bothered. So they leave us alone. They don't want to seem to be intruding."

"All right."

"Why don't we go over to someone? Break the ice, show them that we're not stand-offish."

"Let's not. Let's just sit here."

She thought she knew what was eating at him. He was convinced they were avoiding this table because he was ugly, or at least strange. No one wanted to have to look him full in the face. And one could not very well hold a conversation while staring off to one side. So the others stayed away. Was that what was troubling him? His self-consciousness returning? She did not ask. She thought she might be able to do something about that.

An hour or so before dinner they returned to their room. It was a single large enclosure with a false harshness about it. The walls were made of split logs, rough and coarse, but the atmosphere was carefully regulated and there were all the modern conveniences. He sat quietly. After a while he stood up and began to examine his legs, swinging them back and forth. His mood was so dark now that it frightened her.

She said, "Excuse me. I'll be back in five minutes."

"Where are you going?"

"To check on the tours they're offering for tomorrow."

He let her go. She went down the curving corridor toward the main lobby. Midway, a giant screen was producing an aurora australis for a group of the guests. Patterns of green and red and purple shot dramatically across a neutral gray background. It looked like a scene from the end of the world.

In the lobby Lona gathered a fistful of brochures on the tours. Then she returned to the screen-room. She saw a couple who had been in the cocktail lounge. The woman was in her early twenties, blonde, with artful green streaks rising from her hairline. Her eyes were cool. Her husband, if husband he was, was an older man, near forty, wearing a costly looking tunic. A perpetual-motion ring from one of the outworlds writhed on his left hand.

Tensely Lona approached them. She smiled.

"Hello. I'm Lona Kelvin. Perhaps you noticed us in the lounge."

She drew tight smiles, nervous ones. They were thinking, she knew, *what does she want from us?*

They gave their names. Lona did not catch them, but that did not matter.

She said, "I thought perhaps it would be nice if the four of us sat together at dinner tonight. I think you'd find Minner very interesting. He's been to so many planets..."

They looked trapped. Blonde wife was nearly panicky. Suave husband deftly came to rescue.

"We'd love to... other arrangements... friends from back home... perhaps another night..."

The tables were not limited to four or even six. There was always room for a congenial addition. Lona, rebuffed, knew now what Burris had sensed hours before. They were not wanted. He was the man of the evil eye, raining blight on their festivities. Clutching her brochures, Lona hurried back to the room. Burris was by the window, looking out over the snow.

"Come go through these with me, Minner." Her voice was pitched too high, too sharp.

"Do any of them look interesting?"

"They all do. I don't really know what's best. You do the picking."

They sat on the bed and sorted through the glossy sheaf. There was the Adélie Land tour, half a day, to see penguins. A full day tour to the Ross Shelf Ice, including a visit to Little America and to the other explorer bases at McMurdo Sound. Special stop to see the active volcano, Mount Erebus. Or a longer tour up to the Antarctic Peninsula to see seals and sea leopards. The skiing trip to Marie Byrd Land. The coastal mountain trip through Victoria Land to Mertz Glacial Tongue. And a dozen others. They picked the penguin tour, and when they went down for dinner later, they put their names on the list.

At dinner they sat alone.

Burris said, "Tell me about your children, Lona. Have you ever seen them?"

"Not really. Not so I could touch, except only once. Just on screens."

"And Chalk will really get you some to raise?"

"He said he would."

"Do you believe him?"

"What else can I do?" she asked. Her hand covered his. "Do your legs hurt you?"

"Not really."

Neither of them ate much. After dinner films were shown: vivid tridims of an Antarctic winter. The darkness was the darkness of death, and a death-wind scoured across the plateau, lifting the top layer of snow like a million knives. Lona saw the penguins standing on their eggs, warming them. And then she saw ragged penguins driven before the gale, marching overland while a cosmic drum throbbed in the heavens and invisible hellhounds leaped on silent pads from peak to peak. The film ended with sunrise; the ice stained blood-red with the dawn of a six-month night; the frozen ocean breaking up, giant floes clashing and shattering. Most of the hotel guests went from the screening-room to the lounge. Lona and Burris went to bed. They did not make love. Lona sensed the storm building within him, and knew that it would burst forth before morning came.

They lay cradled in darkness; the window had to be opaqued to shut out the tireless sun. Lona rested on her back beside him, breathing slowly, her flank touching his. Somehow she dozed, and a poor, shallow sleep came to her. Her own phantoms visited her after a while. She awoke, sweating, to find herself naked in a strange room with a strange man next to her. Her heart was fluttering. She pressed her hands to her breasts and remembered where she was.

Burris stirred and groaned.

Gusts of wind battered the building. This was summer, Lona reminded herself. The chill seeped to her bones. She heard a distant sound of laughter. But she did not leave his side, nor did she try to sleep again.

Her eyes, dark-adjusted, watched his face. The mouth was expressive in its hinged way, sliding open, shutting, sliding again. Once his eyes did the same, but even when the lids were pulled back he saw nothing. He's back on Manipool, Lona realized. They've just landed, he and . . . and the ones with Italian names. And in a little while the Things will come for him.

Lona tried to see Manipool. The parched and reddened soil, the twisted, thorny plants. What were the cities like? Did they have roads, cars, vid-sets? Burris had never told her. All she knew was that it was a dry world, an old world, a world where the surgeons had great skill.

And now Burris screamed.

The sound began deep in his throat, a gargled, incoherent cry, and moved higher it pitch and volume as it progressed. Turning, Lona clung to him, pressing tight. Was his skin soaked with perspiration? No; impossible; it must be her own. He thrashed and kicked, sending the coverlet to the floor. She felt his muscles coiling and bulging beneath his sleek skin. He could snap me in half with a quick move, she thought.

"It's all right, Minner. I'm here. I'm here. It's all right!"

"The knives . . . Prolisse . . . good God, the knives!"

"Minner!"

She did not let go of him. His left arm was dangling limply now, seemingly bending the wrong way at the elbow. He was calming. His hoarse breath was as loud as hoofbeats. Lona reached across him and turned on the light.

His face was blotched and mottled again. He blinked in that awful sidewise way of his three or four times and put his hand to his lips. Releasing him, she sat back, trembling a little. Tonight's explosion had been more violent than the one the night before.

"A drink of water?" she asked.

He nodded. He was gripping the mattress so hard she thought he would tear it.

He gulped. She said, "Was it that bad tonight? Were they hurting you?"

"I dreamed I was watching them operate. First Prolisse, and he died. Then they carved up Malcondotto. He died. And then . . ."

"Your turn?"

"No," he said in wonder. "No, they put Elise on the table. They carved her open, right between the—the breasts. And lifted up part of her chest, and I saw the ribs and her heart. And they reached inside."

"Poor Minner." She had to interrupt him before he spilled all that filthiness over her. Why had he dreamed of Elise? Was it a good sign, that he should see her being mutilated? Or would it have been better, she thought, if I was the one he dreamed about . . . I, being turned into something like him?

She took his hand and let it rest on the warmth of her body. There was only one method she could think of for easing his pain, and she employed it. He responded, rising, covering her. They moved urgently and harmoniously.

He appeared to sleep after that. Lona, edgier, pulled away from him and waited until a light slumber once more enveloped her. It was stained by sour dreams. It seemed that a returning starman had brought a pestilent creature with him, some kind of plump vampire, and it was affixed to her body, draining her . . . depleting her. It was a nasty dream, though not nasty enough to awaken her, and in time she passed into a deeper repose.

When they woke, there were dark circles under her eyes, and her face looked pinched and hollow. Burris showed no effects of his broken night; his skin was not capable of reacting that graphically to short-range catabolic effects. He seemed almost cheerful as he got himself ready for the new day.

"Looking forward to the penguins?" he asked her.

Had he forgotten his bleak depression of the evening and his screaming terrors of the night? Or was he just trying to sweep them from view?

Just how human is he, anyway, Lona wondered?

"Yes," she said coolly. "We'll have a grand time, Minner. I can't wait to see them."

Twenty-Three
The Music of the Spheres

"They're beginning to hate each other already," Chalk said pleasantly.

He was alone, but to him that was no reason for not voicing his thoughts. He often talked to himself. A doctor once had told him that there were positive neuropsychic benefits to be had from vocalizing, even in solitude.

He floated in a bath of aromatic salts. The tub was ten feet deep, twenty feet long, a dozen feet wide: ample room even for the bulk of a Duncan Chalk. Its marble sides were flanked by alabaster rims and a surrounding tilework of shimmering oxblood porcelain, and the whole bathing enclosure was covered by a thick, clear dome that gave Chalk a full view of the sky. There was no reciprocal view of Chalk for an outsider; an ingenious optical engineer had seen to that. From without, the dome presented a milky surface streaked with whorls of light pink.

Chalk drifted idly, gravity-free, thinking of his suffering *amanti*. Night had fallen, but there were no stars tonight, only the reddish haze of unseen clouds. It was snowing once more. The flakes performed intricate arabesques as they spiraled toward the surface of the dome.

"He is bored with her," Chalk said. "She is afraid of him. She lacks intensity, to his taste. For hers, his voltage is too high. But they travel together. They eat together. They sleep together. And soon they'll quarrel bitterly."

The tapes were very good. Aoudad, Nikolaides, both of them remaining surreptitiously close behind, picking up scattered gay images of the pair to relay to a waiting public. That snowball fight: a masterpiece. And the power-sled trip. Minner and Lona at the South Pole. The public was eating it up.

Chalk, in his own way, ate it up, too.

He closed his eyes and opaqued his dome and drifted

easily in the warm, fragrant tub. To him came splintered, fragmented sensations of disquiet.

... to have joints that did not behave as human joints should...

... to feel despised, rejected of mankind...

... childless motherhood...

... bright flashes of pain, bright as the thermoluminescent fungi casting their yellow glow on his office walls...

... the ache of the body and the ache of the soul...

... alone!

... unclean!

Chalk gasped as though a low current were running through his body. A finger flew up at an angle to his hand and remained there a moment. A hound with slavering jaws bounded through his forebrain. Beneath the sagging flesh of his chest the thick bands of muscle rhythmically contracted and let go.

... demon-visits in the sleep...

... a forest of watching eyes, stalked and shining...

... a world of dryness... thorns... thorns...

... the click and scratch of strange beasts moving in the walls... dry rot of the soul... all poetry turned to ash, all love to rust...

... stony eyes lifted toward the universe... and the universe peering back...

In ecstasy Chalk kicked at the water, sending up spewing cascades. He slapped its surface with the flat of his hand. Flukes! There go flukes! Ahoy, ahoy!

Pleasure engulfed and consumed him.

And this, he told himself cozily some minutes later, was merely the beginning.

Twenty-Four

In Heaven as It Is on Earth

On a day of flaming sunlight they left for Luna Tivoli, entering the next stage of their passage through Chalk's aeries of delight. The day was bright, but it was still winter;

they were fleeing from the true winter of the north and the wintry summer of the south to the weatherless winter of the void. At the spaceport they received the full celebrity treatment: newsreel shots in the terminal, then the snub-snouted little car rushing them across the field while the common folk looked on in wonder, vaguely cheering the notables, whoever they might be.

Burris hated it. Every stray glance at him now seemed fresh surgery on his soul.

"Why did you let yourself in for it, then?" Lona wanted to know. "If you don't want people to see you like this, why did you ever let Chalk send you on this trip?"

"As a penance. As a deliberately chosen atonement for my withdrawal from the world. For the sake of discipline."

The string of abstractions failed to convince her. Perhaps they made no impact at all.

"But didn't you have a *reason*?"

"Those were my reasons."

"Just words."

"Never scoff at words, Lona."

Her nostrils flared momentarily. "You're making fun of me again!"

"Sorry." Genuinely. It was so easy to mock her.

She said, "I know what it's like to be stared at. I'm shy about it. But I had to do this, so Chalk would give me some of my babies."

"He promised me something, too."

"There! I knew you'd admit it!"

"A body transplant," Burris confessed. "He'll put me into a healthy, normal human body. All I have to do is let his cameras dissect me for a few months."

"Can they really do a thing like that?"

"Lona, if they can make a hundred babies from a girl who's never been touched by a man, they can do anything."

"But . . . to switch bodies . . ."

Wearily he said, "They haven't perfected the technique yet. It may be a few more years. I'll have to wait."

"Oh, Minner, that would be wonderful! To put you in a real body!"

"This is my real body."

"*Another* body. That isn't so different. That doesn't hurt you so much. If they only could!"

"If they only could, yes."

She was more excited about it than he was. He had lived with the idea for weeks, long enough to doubt that it would ever be possible. And now he had dangled it before her, a gleaming new toy. But what did she care? They weren't married. She'd get her babies from Chalk as her reward for this antic and would disappear into obscurity once more, fulfilled after her fashion, glad to be rid of that irritating, chafing, sarcastic consort. He'd go his own way, too, perhaps condemned to this grotesque housing forever, perhaps transferred to a sleek standard model body.

The car scooted up a ramp, and they were within the ship. The vehicle's top sprang back. Bart Aoudad peered in at them.

"How are the lovebirds?"

A silent exit, unsmiling. Aoudad, worried, fluttered about them. "Everybody cheerful, relaxed? No spacesickness, eh, Minner? Not you! Hah-hah-hah!"

"Hah," said Burris.

Nikolaides, too, was there, with documents, booklets, expense vouchers. *Dante had needed only Virgil to guide him through the circles of Hell, but I get two. We live in inflationary times.* Burris gave Lona his arm, and they moved toward the innerness of the ship. Her fingers were rigid against his flesh. She was nervous about going to space, he thought, or else the unbroken tension of this grand tour was weighing too heavily on her.

It was a brief trip: eight hours under low but steady acceleration to cover the 240,000 miles. This same ship had once made it in two stops, pausing first at the pleasure-satellite orbiting 50,000 miles from Earth. But the pleasure-satellite had exploded ten years ago, in one of the rare miscalculations of a secure epoch. Thousands of lives lost; debris raining down on Earth for a month; bare girders of the shattered globe orbiting like bones of a giant nearly three years before the salvage operation was complete.

Someone Burris had loved had been aboard the Wheel when it died. She was there with someone else, though, savoring the game tables, the sensory shows, the haute cuisine, the atmosphere of never-come-tomorrow. Tomorrow had come unexpectedly.

He had thought, when she broke with him, that nothing worse could happen to him in the rest of his days. A young man's romantic fantasy, for very shortly she was dead, and that was far worse for him than when she had refused him.

Dead, she was beyond hope of reclaiming, and for a while he was dead, too, though still walking about. And after that, curiously, the pain ebbed until it was all gone. The worst possible thing, to lose a girl to a rival, then to lose her to catastrophe? Hardly. Hardly. Ten years later Burris had lost himself. Now he thought he knew what the real worst might be.

"Ladies and gentlemen, welcome aboard *Aristarchus IV*. On behalf of Captain Villeparisis, I want to offer our best wishes for a pleasant trip. We must ask you to remain in your cradles until the period of maximum acceleration is over. Once we've escaped from Earth, you'll be free to stretch your legs a bit and enjoy a view of space."

The ship held four hundred passengers, freight, mail. There were twenty private cabins along its haunches, and one had been assigned to Burris and Lona. The others sat side by side in a vast congregation, wriggling for a view of the nearest port.

"Here we go," Burris said softly.

He felt the jets flail and kick at the earth, felt the rockets cut in, felt the ship lift effortlessly. A triple bank of gravitrons shielded the pasengers from the worst effects of the blast-off, but it was impossible to delete gravity altogether on so huge a vessel, as Chalk had been able to do on his little pleasure-craft.

The shrinking Earth dangled like a green plum just outside the viewport. Burris realized that Lona was not looking at it, but solicitously was studying him.

"How do you feel?" she asked.

"Fine. Fine."

"You don't look relaxed."

"It's the gravity drag. Do you think I'm nervous about going into space?"

A shrug. "It's your first time up since—since Manipool, isn't it?"

"I took that ride in Chalk's ship, remember?"

"That was different. That was sub-atmospheric."

"You think I'm going to congeal in terror just because I'm taking a space journey?" he asked. "Do you suppose that I imagine this ferry is a nonstop express back to Manipool?"

"You're twisting my words."

"Am I, now? I said I felt fine. And you began to construct a great elaborate fantasy of malaise for me. You—"

"Stop it, Minner."

Her eyes were bleak. Her words were sharply accented, brittle, keen-edged. He forced his shoulders back against the cradle and tried to compel his hand-tentacles to uncoil. Now she had done it: he had been relaxed, but she had made him tense. Why did she have to mother him this way? He was no cripple. He didn't need to be calmed in a blast-off. He had been blasting off years before she was born. Then what frightened him now? How could her words have undermined his confidence so easily?

They halted the quarrel as though slicing a tape, but ragged edges remained. He said, as gently as he could, "Don't miss the view, Lona. You've never seen Earth from up here before, have you?"

The planet was far from them now. Its complete outline could be discerned. The Western Hemisphere faced them in a blaze of sunlight. Of Antarctica, where they had been only hours ago, nothing was visible except the long jutting finger of the Peninsula, thumbing itself at Cape Horn.

With an effort not to sound didactic, Burris showed her how the sunlight struck the planet athwart, warming the south at this time of year, barely brightening the north. He spoke of the ecliptic and its plane, of the rotation and the revolution of the planet, of the procession of the seasons. Lona listened gravely, nodding often, making polite sounds of agreement whenever he paused to await them. He suspected that she still did not understand. But at this point he was willing to settle for the shadow of comprehension, if he could not have the substance, and she gave him the shadow.

They left their cabin and toured the ship. They saw the Earth from various angles. They bought drinks. They were fed. Aoudad, from his seat in the tourist section, smiled at them. They were stared at considerably.

In the cabin once more, they dozed.

They slept through the mystic moment of turnover, when they passed from Earth's grasp at last into Luna's. Burris woke joltingly, staring across the sleeping girl and blinking at the blackness. It seemed to him that he saw the charred girders of the shattered Wheel drifting out there. No, no; impossible. But he *had* seen them, on a journey a decade ago. Some of the bodies that had spilled from the Wheel as it split open were said still to be in orbit, moving in vast parabolas about the sun. To Burris's knowledge, no one had actually seen such a wanderer in years; most of the corpses, perhaps nearly all, had been decently collected by torch-ships and carried off, and the rest, he would like to believe, had by this time made their way to the sun for the finest of all funerals. It was an old private terror of his to see her contorted face come drifting up within view as she passed through this zone.

The ship heeled and pivoted gently, and the beloved white pocked countenance of the Moon came into view.

Burris touched Lona's arm. She stirred, blinked, looked at him, then outward. Watching her, he detected the spreading wonder on her face even with her back to him.

Half a dozen shining domes now could be seen on Luna's surface.

"Tivoli!" she cried.

Burris doubted that any of the domes really was the amusement park. Luna was infested with domed buildings, built over the decades for a variety of warlike, commercial, or scientific reasons, and none of these matched his own mental picture of Tivoli. He did not correct her, though. He was learning.

The ferry, decelerating, spiraled down to its landing pad.

This was an age of domes, many of them the work of Duncan Chalk. On Earth they tended to be trussed geodesic domes, but not always; here, under lessened gravity, they usually were the simpler, less rigid extruded domes of one-piece construction. Chalk's empire of pleasure was bounded and delimited by domes, beginning with the one over his private pool, and then on to the cupola of the Galactic Room, the Antarctic hostelry, the Tivoli dome, and outward, outward to the stars.

The landing was smooth.

"Let's have a good time here, Minner! I've always dreamed of coming here!"

"We'll enjoy ourselves," he promised.

Her eyes glittered. A child—no more than that—she was. Innocent, enthusiastic, simple—he ticked off her qualities. But she was warm. She cherished and nourished and mothered him, to a fault. He knew he was underestimating her. Her life had known so little pleasure that she had not grown jaded with small thrills. She could respond openly and wholeheartedly to Chalk's parks. She was young. But not hollow, Burris tried to persuade himself. She had suffered. She bore scars, even as he did.

The ramp was down. She rushed from the ship into the

waiting dome, and he followed her, having only a little trouble coordinating his legs.

Twenty-Five
Tears of the Moon

Lona watched breathlessly as the cannon recoiled and the cartridge of fireworks went sliding up, up the shaft, through the aperture in the dome, and out into the blackness. She held her breath. The cartridge exploded.

Color stained the night.

There was no air out there, nothing to cushion the particles of powder as they drifted down. They did not drift, even, but remained more or less where they were. The pattern was brilliant. They were doing animals now. The strange figures of extraterrestrial figures. Beside her, Burris stared upward as intently as anyone.

"Have you ever seen one of those?" she asked.

It was a creature with ropy tendrils, an infinite neck, flattened paddles for feet. Some swampy world had spawned it.

"Never."

A second cartridge shot aloft. But this was only the obliterator, cleansing away the paddle-footed one and leaving the heavenly blackboard blank for the next image.

Another shot.

Another.

Another.

"It's so different from fireworks on Earth," she said. "No boom. No blast. And then everything just stays there. If they didn't blot it out, how long would it stay, Minner?"

"A few minutes. There's gravity here, too. The particles would get pulled down. And disarranged by cosmic debris. All sorts of garbage comes peppering in from space."

He was always ready for any question, always had an answer. At first that quality had awed her. Now it was an irritant. She wished she could stump him. She kept on trying. Her questions, she knew, annoyed him just about as much as his answers annoyed her.

A fine pair we are. Not even honeymooners yet, and already setting little traps for each other!

They watched the silent fireworks for half an hour. Then she grew restless, and they moved away.

"Where to now?" he asked.

"Let's just wander."

He was tense and jittery. She felt it, sensed him ready to leap for her throat if she blundered. How he must hate being here in this silly amusement park! They were staring at him a lot. At her, too, but she was interesting for what had been done with her, not for the way she looked, and the eyes did not linger long.

They moved on, down one corridor of booths and up the next.

It was a carnival of the traditional sort, following a pattern set centuries ago. The technology had changed, but not the essence. Here were games of skill and Kewpie dolls; cheap restaurants selling dished-up dross; whirling rides to suit any dervish; sideshows of easy horror; dance halls; gambling pavilions; darkened theaters (adults only!) in which to reveal the sagging mysteries of the flesh; the flea circus and the talking dog; fireworks, however mutated; blaring music; blazing stanchions of light. A thousand acres of damp delight, done up in the latest trickery. The most significant difference between Chalk's Luna Tivoli and a thousand tivolis of the past was its location, in the broad bosom of Copernicus Crater, looking toward the eastern arc of the ringwall. One breathed pure air here, but one danced in fractional gravity. This was Luna.

"Whirlpool?" a sinuous voice asked. "Take the Whirlpool, mister, miss?"

Lona pressed forward, smiling. Burris slapped coins onto the counter and they were admitted. A dozen aluminum shells gaped like the remains of giant clams, floating on a quicksilver lake. A squat, barechested man with coppery skin said, "Shell for two? This way, this way!"

Burris helped her into one of the shells. He sat beside her. The top was seated in place. It was dark, warm, oppressively close inside. There was just room for the two of them.

"Happy womb fantasies," he said.

She took his hand and held it grimly. Through the quicksilver lake came a spark of motivating power. Away they went,
skimming on the unknown. Down what black tunnels, through
what hidden gorges? The shell rocked in a maelstrom, Lona
screamed, again, again, again.

"Are you afraid?" he asked.

"I don't know. It moves so fast!"

"We can't get hurt."

It was like floating, like flying. Virtually no gravity, and no
friction to impede their squirting motion as they slid hither
and yon down the byways and cloacae of the ride. Secret
petcocks opened, and scent filtered in.

"What do you smell?" she asked him.

"The desert. The smell of heat. And you?"

"The woods on a rainy day. Rotting leaves, Minner. How
can that be?"

Maybe his senses don't pick up things the way mine do, the
way a human's do. How can he smell the desert? That ripe,
rich odor of mold and dampness! She could see red toadstools
bursting from the ground. Small things with many legs
scuttering and burrowing. A shining worm. And he: the
desert?

The shell seemed to flip over, strike its supporting medium
flat on, and right itself. The scent had changed by the time
Lona noticed it again.

"Now it's the Arcade at night," she said. "Popcorn...
sweat...laughter. What does laughter smell like, Minner?
What does it seem like to you?"

"The fuel-room of a ship at core-changing time. Something
was burning a few hours ago. Frying fat where the rods
leaked. It hits you like a nail rammed up the nostril."

"How can it be that we don't smell the same things?"

"Olfactory psychovariation. We smell the things that our
minds trigger for us. They aren't giving us any particular
scent, just the raw material. We shape the patterns."

"I don't understand, Minner."

He was silent. More odors came: hospital-smell, moonlight-
smell, steel-smell, snow-smell. She did not ask him about his
own responses to this generalized stimulation. Once he gasped;
once he winced and dug fingertips into her thigh.

The barrage of odors ceased.

Still the sleek shell slipped on, minute after minute. Now

came sounds: tiny pinging bursts, great organ throbs, hammer blows, rhythmic scraping of rasp on rasp. They missed no sense here. The interior of the shell grew cool, and then warm again; the humidity varied in a complex cycle. Now the shell zigged, now it zagged. It whirled dizzyingly, a final frenzy of motion, and abruptly they were safe at harbor. His hand engulfed hers as he pulled her forth.

"Fun?" he asked unsmilingly.

"I'm not sure. Unusual, anyway."

He bought her cotton candy. They passed a booth where one flipped little glass globes at golden targets on a moving screen. Hit the target three out of four, win a prize. Men with Earthside muscles struggled to cope with the low gravity and failed, while pouting girls stood by. Lona pointed at the prizes: subtle alien designs, abstract rippling forms executed in furry cloth. "Win me one, Minner!" she begged.

He paused and watched the men making their hapless looping tosses. Most far overshot the target; some, compensating, flipped feebly and saw their marbles droop slowly short of the goal. The crowd at the booth was closely packed as he moved among them, but the onlookers gave way for him, uneasily edging away. Lona noticed it and hoped he did not. Burris put down money and picked up his marbles. His first shot was off the mark by six inches.

"Nice try, buddy! Give him room! Here's one who's got the range!" The huckster behind the boothfront peered disbelievingly at Burris's face. Lona reddened. Why do they have to stare? Does he look that strange?

He tossed again. *Clang*. Then: *clang. Clang*.

"Three in a row! Give the little lady her prize!"

Lona clutched something warm, furry, almost alive. They moved away from the booth, escaping a buzz of talk. Burris said, "There are things to respect about this hateful body, Lona."

Some time later she put the prize down, and when she turned for it, it had disappeared. He offered to win her another, but she told him not to worry about it.

They did not enter the building of the flesh shows.

When they came to the freak house, Lona hesitated, wanting to go inside but uncertain about suggesting it. The hesitation was fatal. Three beer-blurred faces emerged, looked at Burris, guffawed.

"Hey! There's one that escaped!"

Lona recognized the fiery blotches of fury on his cheeks. She steered him quickly away, but the wound had been made. How many weeks of self-repair undone in a moment?

The night pivoted around that point. Up till then he had been tolerant, faintly amused, only slightly bored. Now he became hostile. She saw his eye-shutters pull back to their full opening, and the cold glare of those revealed eyes would have eaten like acid into this playland if it could. He walked stiffly. He grudged every new moment here.

"I'm tired, Lona. I want to go to the room."

"A little while longer."

"We can come back tomorrow night."

"But it's still early, Minner!"

His lips did odd things. "Stay here by yourself, then."

"No! I'm afraid! I mean—what fun would it be without you?"

"I'm not having fun."

"You seemed to be . . . before."

"That was before. This is now." He plucked at her sleeve. "Lona—"

"No," she said. "You aren't taking me away so fast. There's nothing to do in the room but sleep and have sex and look at the stars. This is Tivoli, Minner. *Tivoli!* I want to drink up every minute of it."

He said something she could not make out, and they moved on to a new section of the park. But his restlessness mastered him. In a few minutes he was asking again that they go.

"Try to enjoy yourself, Minner."

"This place is making me sick. The noise . . . the smell . . . the *eyes.*"

"No one's looking at you."

"Very funny! Did you hear what they said when—"

"They were drunk." He was begging for sympathy, and for once she was tired of giving it to him. "Oh, I know, your feelings are hurt. Your feelings get hurt so easily. Well, for once stop feeling so sorry for yourself! I'm here to have a good time, and you're not going to spoil it!"

"Viciousness!"

"No worse than selfishness!" she snapped at him.

Overhead the fireworks went off. A garish serpent with seven tails sprawled across the heavens.

"How much longer do you want to stay?" Steely now.

"I don't know. Half an hour. An hour."

"Fifteen minutes?"

"Let's not bargain over it. We haven't seen a tenth of what's here yet."

"There are other nights."

"Back to that again. Minner, stop it! I don't want to quarrel with you, but I'm not giving in. I'm just not giving in."

He made a courtly bow, dipping lower than anyone with human skeletal structure could possibly have done. "At your service, milady." The words were venomous. Lona chose to ignore the venom and took him onward down the cluttered path. It was the worst quarrel they had had so far. In past frictions they had been cool, snippy, sarcastic, withdrawn. But never had they stood nose to nose, barking at each other. They had even drawn a small audience: Punch and Judy hollering it up for the benefit of interested onlookers. What was happening? Why were they bickering? Why, she wondered, did it sometimes seem as though he hated her? Why did she feel at those times that it could be quite easy to hate him?

They should be giving each other support. That was how it had been at the beginning. A bond of shared sympathy had linked them, for they both had suffered. What had happened to that? So much bitterness had crept into things now. Accusations, recriminations, tensions.

Before them, three intersecting yellow wheels performed an intricate dance of flame. Pulsating lights bobbed and flickered. High on a pillar a nude girl appeared, draped in living glow. She waved, beckoned, a muezzin calling the faithful to the house of lust. Her body was improbably feminine; her breasts were jutting shelves, her buttocks were giant globes. No one was born like that. She must have been changed by doctors. . . .

A member of our club, thought Lona. Yet she doesn't mind. She's up there in front of everybody and happy to draw her pay. What's it like at four in the morning for her? Does she mind?

Burris was staring fixedly at the girl.

"It's just meat," Lona said. "Why are you so fascinated?"

"That's Elise up there!"

"You're mistaken, Minner. She wouldn't be here. Certainly not up there."

"I tell you it's Elise. My eyes are sharper than yours. You hardly know what she looks like. They've done something to her body, they've padded her somehow, but I know it's Elise!"

"Go to her, then."

He stood frozen. "I didn't say I wanted to."

"You just thought it."

"Now you're jealous of a naked girl on a pillar?"

"You loved her before you ever knew me."

"I never loved her," he shouted, and the lie emblazoned itself on his forehead.

From a thousand loudspeakers came a paean of praise for the girl, for the park, for the visitors. All sound converged toward a single shapeless roar. Burris moved closer to the pillar. Lona followed him. The girl was dancing now, kicking up her heels, capering wildly. Her bare body gleamed. The swollen flesh quivered and shook. She was all carnality in a single vessel.

"It's not Elise," said Burris suddenly, and the spell broke.

He turned away, his face darkening, and halted. All about them, fair-goers were streaming toward the pillar, the focal point of the park now, but Lona and Burris did not move. Their backs were to the dancer. Burris jerked as if struck, and folded his arms across his chest. He sank to a bench, head down.

This was no snobbery of boredom. He was sick, she realized.

"I feel so tired," he said huskily. "Drained of strength. I feel a thousand years old, Lona!"

Reaching for him, she coughed. Quite suddenly tears were streaming from her eyes. She dropped down beside him on the bench, struggling for breath.

"I feel the same way. Worn out."

"What's happening?"

"Something we breathed on that ride? Something we ate, Minner?"

"No. Look at my hands."

They were shaking. The little tentacles were hanging limp. His face was gray.

And she: it was as though she had run a hundred miles tonight. Or been delivered of a hundred babies.

This time, when he suggested that they leave the amusement park, she did not quarrel with him.

Twenty-Six
Frost at Midnight

On Titan she broke away and left him. Burris had seen it coming for days and was not at all surprised. It came as something of a relief.

Tension had been rising since the South Pole. He was not sure why, other than that they were unfit for each other. But they had been at each other's throats steadily, first in a hidden way, then openly but figuratively and at the last literally. So she went away from him.

They spent six days at Luna Tivoli. The pattern of each day was the same. Late rising, a copious breakfast, some viewing of the Moon, and then to the park. The place was so big that there were always new discoveries to be made, yet by the third day Burris found that they were compulsively retracing their steps, and by the fifth he was enduringly sick of Tivoli. He tried to be tolerant, since Lona took such obvious pleasure in the place. But eventually his patience wore thin, and they quarreled. Each night's quarrel exceeded in intensity the one of the night before. Sometimes they resolved the conflict in fierce, sweaty passion, sometimes in sleepless nights of sulking.

And always, during or just after the quarrel, came that feeling of fatigue, that sickening, destructive loss of stamina. Nothing like that had ever happened to Burris before. The fact that the fits came over the girl simultaneously made it doubly strange. They said nothing to Aoudad and Nikolaides, whom they occasionally saw on the fringes of the crowds.

Burris knew that the virulent arguments were driving an ever-wider wedge between them. In less stormy moments he regretted that, for Lona was tender and kind, and he valued her warmth. All that was forgotten in his moments of rage, though. Then she seemed empty and useless and maddening

132

to him, a burden added to all his other burdens, a foolish and
ignorant and hateful child. He told her all that, at first hiding
his meaning behind blunting metaphors, later hurling the
naked words.

A breakup had to come. They were exhausting themselves,
depleting their vital substances in these battles. The moments of love were more widely spaced now. Bitterness broke
in more often.

On the arbitrarily designated morning of their arbitrarily
designated sixth day at Luna Tivoli, Lona said, "Let's cancel
and go on to Titan now."

"We're supposed to spend five more days here."

"Do you really want to?"

"Well, frankly . . . no."

He was afraid it would provoke another fountain of angry
words, and it was too early in the day for them to begin that.
But no, this was her morning for sacrificial gestures. She said,
"I think I've had enough, and it's no secret that you've had
enough. So why should we stay? Titan's probably much more
exciting."

"Probably."

"And we've been so bad to each other here. A change of
scenery ought to help."

It certainly would. Any barbarian with a fat wallet could
afford the price of a ticket to Luna Tivoli, and the place was
full of boors, drunks, rowdies. It drew liberally on a potential
audience that went far deeper than Earth's managerial classes.
But Titan was more select. Only wealthy sophisticates comprised its clientele, those to whom spending twice a working-
man's annual wage on a single short trip was trivial. Such
people, at least, would have the courtesy to deal with him as
though his deformities did not exist. Antarctica's honeymooners,
shutting their eyes to all that troubled them, had simply
treated him as invisible. Luna Tivoli's patrons had guffawed
in his face and mocked his differentness. On Titan, though,
innate good manners would decree a cool indifference to his
appearance. Look upon the strange man, smile, chat gracefully, but never show by word or deed that you are aware he is
strange: that was good breeding. Of the three cruelties,
Burris thought he preferred that kind.

He cornered Aoudad by the glare of fireworks and said,
"We've had enough here. Book us for Titan."

"But you have—"

"—another five days. Well, we don't want them. Get us out of here and to Titan."

"I'll see what I can do," Aoudad promised.

Aoudad had watched them quarrel. Burris felt unhappy about that, for reasons which he despised. Aoudad and Nikolaides had been Cupids to them, and Burris somehow held himself responsible for behaving at all times like an enthralled lover. Obscurely, he failed Aoudad whenever he snarled at Lona. Why do I give a damn about failing Aoudad? Aoudad isn't complaining about the quarrels. He doesn't offer to mediate. He doesn't say a word.

As Burris expected, Aoudad got them tickets to Titan without any difficulty. He called ahead to notify the resort that they would be arriving ahead of schedule. And off they went.

A lunar blast-off was nothing like a departure from Earth. With only a sixth the gravity to deal with, it took just a gentle shove to send the ship into space. This was a bustling spaceport, with departures daily for Mars, Venus, Titan, Ganymede, and Earth, every third day for the outer planets, weekly for Mercury. No interstellar ships left from Luna; by law and custom, starships could depart only from Earth, monitored every step of the way until they made the leap into warp somewhere beyond Pluto's orbit. Most of the Titan-bound ships stopped first at the important mining center on Ganymede, and their original itinerary had called for them to take one of those. But today's ship was nonstop. Lona would miss Ganymede, but it was her own doing. She had suggested the early arrival, not he. Perhaps they could stop at Ganymede on the way back to Earth.

There was a forced cheeriness about Lona's chatter as they slid into the gulf of darkness. She wanted to know all about Titan, just as she had wanted to know all about the South Pole, the change of seasons, the workings of a cactus, and many other things; but those questions she had asked out of naïve curiosity, and these were asked in the hope of rebuilding contact, any contact, between herself and him.

It would not work, Burris knew.

"It's the biggest moon in the system. It's bigger even than Mercury, and Mercury's a planet."

"But Mercury goes around the sun, and Titan goes around Saturn."

"That's right. Titan's much larger than our own moon. It's about seven hundred and fifty thousand miles from Saturn. You'll have a good view of the rings. It has an atmosphere: methane, ammonia, not very good for the lungs. Frozen. They say it's picturesque. I've never been there."

"How come?"

"When I was young, I couldn't afford to go. Later I was too busy in other parts of the universe."

The ship slipped on through space. Lona stared, wide-eyed, as they hopped over the plane of the asteroid belt, got a decent view of Jupiter not too far down its orbit from them, and sped outward, Saturn was in view.

To Titan then they came.

A dome again, of course. A bleak landing pad on a bleak plateau. This was a world of ice, but far different from deathly Antarctica. Every inch of Titan was alien and strange, while in Antarctia everything quickly became grindingly familiar. This was no simple place of cold and wind and whiteness.

There was Saturn to consider. The ringed planet hung low in the heavens, considerably larger than Earth appeared from Luna. There was just enough methaneammonia atmosphere to give Titan's sky a bluish tinge, creating a handsome backdrop for glowing, golden Saturn with his thick, dark atmospheric stripe and his Midgard serpent of tiny stone particles.

"The ring is so thin," Lona complained. "Edge-on like this, I can hardly see it!"

"It's thin because Saturn's so big. We'll have a better view of it tomorrow. You'll see that it isn't one ring but several. The inner rings move faster than the outer ones."

So long as he kept conversation on that sober level, all went well. But he hesitated to deviate from the impersonal, and so did she. Their nerves were too raw. They stood too close to the edge of the abyss after their recent quarrels.

They occupied one of the finest rooms in the glistening hotel. All about them were the moneyed ones, Earth's highest caste, those who had made fortunes in planetary development or warp-transport or power systems. Everyone seemed to know everyone else. The women, whatever their ages, were slim, agile, alert. The men were often beefy, but they moved with strength and vigor. No one made rude remarks about Burris or about Lona. No one stared. They were all friendly, in their distant way.

At dinner, the first night, they were joined at table by an industrialist with large holdings on Mars. He was far into his seventies, with a tanned, seamed face and narrow dark eyes. His wife could not have been more than thirty. They talked mostly of the commercial exploitation of extrasolar planets.

Lona, afterward: "She has her eye on you!"

"She didn't let me know about that."

"It was awfully obvious. I bet she was touching your foot under the table."

He sensed a struggle coming on. Hastily he led Lona to a viewport in the dome. "I tell you what," he said. "If she seduces me, you have my permission to seduce her husband."

"Very amusing."

"What's wrong? He has money."

"I haven't been in this place half a day and I hate it already."

"Stop it, Lona. You're pushing your imagination too hard. That woman wouldn't touch me. The thought would give her the shudders for a month, believe me. Look, look out there."

A storm was blowing up. Harsh winds ripped against the dome. Saturn was nearly in the full phase tonight, and his reflected light made a glittering track across the snow, meeting and melding with the white glare of the dome's illuminated ports. The precise needle-tips of stars were strewn across the vault of sky, looking nearly as hard as they would appear from space itself.

It was starting to snow.

They watched the wind whipping the snow about for a while. Then they heard music and followed it. Most of the guests were moving along the same track.

"Do you want to dance?" Lona asked.

An orchestra in evening clothes had appeared from somewhere. The tinkling, swirling sounds rose in volume. Strings, winds, a bit of percussion, a sprinkling of the alien instruments so popular in big-band music nowadays. The elegant guests moved in graceful rhythms over a shining floor.

Stiffly Burris took Lona in his arms and they joined the dancers.

He had never danced much before, and not at all since his

return to Earth from Manipool. The mere thought of dancing in a place like this would have seemed grotesque to him only a few months ago. But he was surprised how well his redesigned body caught the rhythms of it. He was learning grace in these elaborate new bones. Around, around, around...

Lona's eyes held firm on his. She was not smiling. She seemed afraid of something.

Overhead was another clear dome. The Duncan Chalk school of architecture: show 'em the stars, but keep 'em warm. Gusts of wind sent snowflakes skiding across the top of the dome and drove them just as swiftly away. Lona's hand was cold in his. The tempo of the dance increased. The thermal regulators within him that had replaced his sweat glands were working overtime. Could he keep to such a giddy pace? Would he stumble?

The music stopped.

The dinnertime couple came over. The woman smiled. Lona glared.

The woman said, with the assurance of the very rich, "May we have the next dance?"

He had tried to avoid it. Now there was no tactful way to refuse, and Lona's jealousies would get another helping of fuel. The thin, reedy sound of the oboe summoned the dancers to the floor. Burris took the woman, leaving Lona, frozen-faced, with the aging industrial baron.

The woman was a dancer. She seemed to fly over the floor. She spurred Burris to demonic exertions, and they moved around the outside of the hall, virtually floating. At that speed even his split-perception eyes failed him, and he could not find Lona. The music deafened him. The woman's smile was too bright.

"You make a wonderful partner," she told him. "There's a strength about you... a feeling for the rhythm..."

"I was never much of a dancer before Manipool."

"Manipool?"

"The planet where I... where they..."

She didn't know. He had assumed everyone here was familiar with his story. But perhaps these rich ones paid no heed to current vid-program sensations. They had not followed his misfortunes. Very likely she had taken his appearance so thoroughly for granted that it had not occurred to her to wonder how he had come to look that way. Tact could be overdone; she was less interested in him than he had thought.

"Never mind," he said.

As they made another circuit of the floor, he caught sight of Lona at last: leaving the room. The industrialist stood by himself, seemingly baffled. Instantly Burris came to a halt. His partner looked a question at him.

"Excuse me. Perhaps she's ill."

Not ill: just sulking. He found her in the room, face down on the bed. When he put his hand on her bare back, she shivered and rolled away from him. He could not say anything to her. They slept far apart, and when his dream of Manipool came to him, he managed to choke off his screams before they began, and sat up, rigid, until the terror passed.

Neither of them mentioned the episode in the morning.

They went sight-seeing, via power-sled. Titan's hotel-and-spaceport complex lay near the center of a smallish plateau bordered by immense mountains. Here, as on Luna, peaks that dwarfed Everest were plentiful. It seemed incongruous that such small worlds would have such great ranges, but so it was. A hundred miles or so to the west of the hotel was Martinelli Glacier, a vast creeping river of ice coiling for hundreds of miles down out of the heart of the local Himalayas. The glacier terminated, improbably enough, in the galaxy-famed Frozen Waterfall. Which every visitor to Titan was obliged to visit, and which Burris and Lona visited, too.

There were lesser sights en route that Burris found more deeply stirring. The swirling methane clouds and tufts of frozen ammonia ornamenting the naked mountains, for example, giving them the look of mountains in a Sung scroll. Or the dark lake of methane half an hour's drive from the dome. In its waxen depths dwelled the small, durable living things of Titan, creatures that were more or less mollusks and arthropods, but rather less than more. They were equipped for breathing and drinking methane. With life of any sort as scarce as it was in this solar system, Burris found it fascinating to view these rarities in their native habitat. Around the rim of the lake he saw their food: Titanweeds, ropy greasy plants, dead white in color, capable of enduring this hellish climate in perfect comfort.

The sled rolled on toward the Frozen Waterfall.

There it was: blue-white, glinting in Saturnlight, suspended over an enormous void. The beholders made the obligatory sighs and gasps. No one left the sled, for the winds were savage out there, and the breathing-suits could not be entirely trusted to protect one against the corrosive atmosphere.

They circled the waterfall, viewing the sparkling arch of ice from three sides. Then came the bad news from their cicerone: "Storm coming up. We're heading back."

The storm came, long before they reached the comfort of the dome. First there was rain, a sleety downpour of precipitated ammonia that rattled on the roof of their sled, and then clouds of ammonia-crystal snow, driven by the wind. The sled pushed on with difficulty. Burris had never seen snow come down so heavily or so fast. The wind churned and uprooted it, piling it into cathedrals and forests. Straining a little, the power-sled avoided new dunes and nosed around sudden barricades. Most of the passengers looked imperturbable. They exclaimed on the beauty of the storm. Burris, who knew how close they all were to entombment, sat moodily in silence. Death might bring peace at last, but if he could choose his death he did not mean to choose being buried alive. Already he could taste the acrid foulness as the air began to give out and the whining motors fed their exhaust back into the passenger compartment. Imagination, nothing more. He tried to enjoy the beauty of the storm.

Nevertheless, it was a source of great relief to enter the warmth and safety of the dome once again.

He and Lona quarreled again soon after their return. There was even less reason for this quarrel than for any of the others. But very swiftly it reached a level of real malevolence.

"You didn't look at me the whole trip, Minner!"

"I looked at the scenery. That's why we're here."

"You could take my hand. You could smile."

"I—"

"Am I that boring?"

He was weary of retreating. "As a matter of fact, you are! You're a dull, dreary, ignorant little girl! All this is wasted on you! Everything! You can't appreciate food, clothing, sex, travel..."

"And what are you? Just a hideous freak!"

"That makes two of us."

"Am I a freak?" she shrilled. "It doesn't show. I'm a human being, at least. What are you?"

That was when he sprang at her.

His smooth fingers closed around her throat. She battered at him, pounded him with her fists, clawed his cheeks with

raking nails. But she could not break his skin, and that roused
her to smoldering fury. He gripped her firmly, shaking her,
making her head roll wildly on its mooring, and all the while
she kicked and punched. Through his arteries surged all the
byproducts of rage.

I could kill her so easily, he thought.

But the very act of pausing to let a coherent concept roll
through his mind calmed him. He released her. He stared at
his hands, she at him. There were mottled marks on her
throat that nearly matched the blotches newly sprung out on
his face. Gasping, she stepped away from him. She did not
speak. Her hand, shaking, pointed at him.

Fatigue clubbed him to his knees.

All his strength vanished at once. His joints gave way, and
he slipped, melting, unable even to brace himself with his
hands. He lay prone, calling her name. He had never felt this
weak before, not even while he had been recuperating from
what had been done to him on Manipool.

This is what it's like to be bled white, he told himself. The
leeches have been at me! God, will I ever be able to stand
again? "Help!" he cried soundlessly. "Lona, where are you?"

When he was strong enough to lift his head, he discovered
that she was gone. He did not know how much time had
passed. Weakly he pulled himself up inch by inch and sat on
the edge of the bed until the worst of the feebleness was
over. Was it a judgment upon him for striking her? Each time
they had quarreled he had felt this sickness come upon him.

"Lona?"

He went into the hall, staying close to the side partition.
Probably he looked drunk to the well-groomed women who
sailed past him. They smiled. He tried to return the smiles.

He did not find her.

Somehow, hours later, he discovered Aoudad. The little
man looked apprehensive.

"Have you seen her?" Burris croaked.

"Halfway to Ganymede by now. She left on the dinner
flight."

"*Left?*"

Aoudad nodded. "Nick went with her. They're going back
to Earth. What did you do—slam her around some?"

"You let her go?" Burris muttered. "You permitted her to
walk out? What's Chalk going to say about that?"

"Chalk knows. Don't you think we checked with him first?

He said, sure, if she wants to come home, let her come home. Put her on the next ship out. So we did. Hey, you look pale, Burris. I thought with your skin you couldn't get pale!"

"When does the next ship after hers leave?"

"Tomorrow night. You aren't going to go chasing her, are you?"

"What else?"

Grinning, Aoudad said, "You'll never get anywhere that way. Let her go. This place is full of women who'd be glad to take her place. You'd be amazed how many. Some of them know I'm with you, and they come up to me, wanting me to fix you up with them. It's the face, Minner. The face fascinates them."

Burris turned away from him.

Aoudad said, "You're shaken up. Listen, let's go have a drink!"

Without looking back, Burris replied, "I'm tired. I want to rest."

"Should I send one of the women to you after a while?"

"Is that your idea of rest?"

"Well, matter of fact, yes." He laughed pleasantly. "I don't mind taking care of them myself, you understand, but it's you they want. You."

"Can I call Ganymede? Maybe I can talk to her while her ship's refueling."

Aoudad caught up with him. "She's gone, Burris. You ought to forget her now. What did she have besides problems? Just a skinny little kid! You didn't even get along well with her. I know. I saw. All you did was shout at each other. What do you need her for? Now, let me tell you about—"

"Are you carrying any relaxers?"

"You know they won't do you any good."

Burris held out his hand anyway. Aoudad shrugged and put a relaxer into it. Burris touched the tube to his skin. The illusion of tranquillity might be worth nearly as much as the genuine article now. He thanked Aoudad and walked sharply toward his room, alone.

On the way he passed a woman whose hair was spun pink glass and whose eyes were amethysts. Her costume was chastely immodest. Her voice, feather-soft, brushed his earless cheeks. He rushed past her, trembling, and entered his room.

Twenty-Seven
The Grail's True Warden

"It spoiled a lovely romance," said Tom Nikolaides.

Lona did not smile. "Nothing lovely about it. I was glad to get away."

"Because he tried to choke you?"

"That was only at the very end. It was bad a long time before that. You don't have to get hurt that way in order to get hurt."

Nikolaides peered deep into her eyes. He understood, or pretended he did. "True enough. It's too bad, but we all knew it couldn't last."

"Including Chalk?"

"Especially Chalk. He predicted the breakup. It's remarkable how much mail we've had on it. The whole universe seems to think it's a terrible thing that you two split."

Lona flashed a quick, empty smile. Standing, she paced the long room in choppy strides. The plaques mounted to her heels clicked against the polished floor. "Will Chalk be here soon?" she asked.

"Soon. He's a very busy man. But the moment he reaches the building, we'll take you to him."

"Nick, will he really give me my babies?"

"Let's hope so."

She caught up with him. Fiercely her hand caught his wrist. "Hope so? Hope so? He promised them to me!"

"But you walked out on Burris."

"You said yourself Chalk was expecting it. The romance wasn't supposed to last forever. Now it's over, and I kept my part of the bargain, and Chalk's got to keep his."

She felt muscles quivering in her thighs. These fancy shoes; hard to stand this way. But they made her look taller, older. It was important to look outwardly the way she had come to be inwardly. That trip with Burris had aged her five

142

years in as many weeks. The constant tension...the bickering...

Above all, the terrible exhaustion after each quarrel...

She would look the fat man straight in the eye. If he tried to worm out of his promise, she'd make life difficult for him. No matter how powerful he was, he couldn't cheat her! She'd been nursemaid to that weird refugee from an alien planet long enough to have earned the right to her own babies. She—

That wasn't right, she admonished herself suddenly. *I mustn't make fun of him. He didn't ask for his troubles. And I volunteered to share them.*

Nikolaides stepped into the abrupt silence. "Now that you're back on Earth, Lona, what are your plans?"

"To arrange for the children, first. Then I want to disappear from public life for good. I've had two rounds of publicity now, one when the babies were taken from me, one when I went off with Minner. That's enough."

"Where will you go? Will you leave Earth?"

"I doubt it. I'll stay. Maybe I'll write a book." She smiled. "No, that wouldn't be so good, would it? More publicity. I'll live quietly. How about Patagonia?" She peered forward. "Do you have any idea where *he* is now?"

"Chalk?"

"Minner," she said.

"Still on Titan, so far as I know. Aoudad's with him."

"They've been there three weeks, then. I suppose they're having a good time." Her lips curved fiercely.

"I know Aoudad must be," Nikolaides said. "Give him plenty of available women, and he'd have a good time anywhere. But I couldn't vouch for Burris. All I know is that they haven't made any move to come home yet. Still interested in him, are you?"

"No!"

Nikolaides put his hands to his ears. "All right. All right. I believe you. It's just that—"

The door at the far end of the room rippled inward. A small, ugly man with long, thin lips stepped through. Lona recognized him: he was d'Amore, one of Chalk's men. She said at once, "Has Chalk showed up yet? I've got to talk to him!"

D'Amore's unpleasant mouth produced the broadest smile she had ever seen. "You're really asserting yourself these days, milady! No more wispy shyness, eh? But no; Chalk's not here yet. I'm waiting for him myself." He came farther into the room, and Lona noticed that someone stood behind him: white-faced, mild-eyed, totally at ease, a man of middle years who smiled in a foolish way. D'Amore said, "Lona, this is David Melangio. He knows a few tricks. Give him the date you were born and the year; he'll tell you what day of the week it was."

Lona gave it.

"Wednesday," said Melangio instantly.

"How does he do that?"

"It's his gift. Call off a string of numbers for him, as fast as you can, but clearly."

Lona called off a dozen numbers. Melangio repeated them.

"Right?" d'Amore asked, beaming.

"I'm not sure," she said. "I forgot them myself." She walked over to the idiot-savant, who regarded her without interest. Looking into his eyes, Lona realized that Melangio was another freak, all trick, no soul. She wondered, chilled, if they were hatching a new love affair for her.

Nikolaides said, "Why'd you bring him back? I thought Chalk had let his option go."

"Chalk thought Miss Kelvin would like to talk to him," d'Amore replied. "He asked me to bring Melangio over."

"What am I supposed to say to him?" Lona asked.

D'Amore smiled. "How would I know?"

She drew the long-lipped man aside and whispered, "He's not right in the head, is he?"

"I'd say he's missing something there, yes."

"So Chalk's got another project for me? Am I supposed to hold *his* hand now?"

It was like asking the wall. D'Amore merely said, "Take him inside, sit down, talk. Chalk probably won't be here for another hour yet."

There was an adjoining room, with a floating glass table and several lounge chairs. She and Melangio went in, and the door closed with the finality of a cell door.

Silence. Stares.

He said, "Ask me anything about dates. Anything."

He rocked rhythmically back and forth. His smile did not fade at any moment. He was about seven years old mentally, Lona thought.

"Ask me when George Washington died. Ask me. Or anybody else. Anybody important."

"Abraham Lincoln," she sighed.

"April 15, 1865. Do you know how old he'd be if he were still alive today?" He told her, instantly, down to the day. It sounded right to her. He looked pleased with himself.

"How do you do it?"

"I don't know. I just can. I always have been able to. I can remember the weather and all the dates." He giggled. "Do you envy me?"

"Not very much."

"Some people do. They wish they could learn how. Mr. Chalk would like to know how. He wants you to marry me, you know."

Lona winced. Trying not to be cruel, she said, "Did he tell you that?"

"Oh, no. Not with words. But I know. He wants us to be together. Like you used to be, when you were with the man with the funny face. Chalk enjoyed that. Especially when you had arguments with him. I was with Mr. Chalk once, and he got red in the face and chased me out of the room, and later he called me back. It must have been when you and the other one were having a fight."

Lona groped for an understanding of all this. "Can you read minds, David?"

"No."

"Can Chalk?"

"No. Not *read*. It doesn't come in words. It comes in feelings. He reads feelings. I can tell. And he likes unhappy feelings. He wants us to be unhappy together, because that would make him happy."

Perplexed, Lona leaned toward Melangio and said, "Do you like women, David?"

"I like my mother. I sometimes like my sister. Even though they hurt me a lot when I was young."

"Have you ever wanted to get married?"

"Oh, no! Married is for grown-ups!"

"And how old are you?"

"Forty years, eight months, three weeks, two days. I don't know how many hours. They won't tell me what time I was born."

"You poor bastard."

"You're sorry for me because they won't tell me what time I was born."

"I'm sorry for you," she said. "Period. But I can't do anything for you, David. I've used up all my niceness. Now people have to start being nice to me."

"I'm nice to you."

"Yes, you are. You're very nice." Impulsively she took his hand in hers. His skin was smooth and cool. Not as smooth as Burris's, though, nor as cool. Melangio shivered at the contact, but allowed her to squeeze the hand. After a moment she let go and went to the wall and ran her hands over the side of the room until the door opened. She stepped through and saw Nikolaides and d'Amore murmuring to each other.

"Chalk wants to see you now," d'Amore said. "Did you enjoy your little visit with David?"

"He's charming. Where's Chalk?"

Chalk was in his throne-room, perched on high. Lona clambered up the crystal rungs. As she approached the fat man, she felt odd timidness returning. She had learned how to cope with people lately, but coping with Chalk might be beyond her grasp.

He rocked in his huge chair. His broad face creased in what she took to be a smile.

"So nice to see you again. Did you enjoy your travels?"

"Very interesting. And now, my babies—"

"Please, Lona, don't rush. Have you met David?"

"Yes."

"So pitiful. So much in need of help. What do you think of his gift?"

"We had a deal," Lona said. "I took care of Minner, you got me some of my babies. I don't want to talk about Melangio."

"You broke up with Burris sooner than I had expected," said Chalk. "I haven't completed all the arrangements concerning your children."

"You're going to get them for me?"

"In a short while. But not quite yet. This is a difficult negotiation, even for me. Lona, will you oblige me while you're waiting for the children? Help David, the way you helped Burris. Bring some light into his life. I'd like to see the two of you together. A warm, maternal person like you—"

"This is a trick, isn't it?" she said suddenly. "You'll play with me forever! One zombi after another for me to cuddle! Burris, Melangio, and then who knows what next? No. No. We made a deal. I want my babies. *I want my babies*."

Sonic dampers were whirring to cut down the impact of her shouts. Chalk looked startled. Somehow he appeared both pleased and angered at once by this show of spirit. His body seemed to puff and expand until he weighed a million pounds.

"You cheated me," she said, quieter now. "You never meant to give them back to me!"

She leaped. She would scape gobbets of flesh from the fat face.

From the ceiling, instantly, descended a fine mesh of golden threads. Lona hit it, rebounded, surged forward again. She could not reach Chalk. He was shielded.

Nikolaides, d'Amore. They seized her arms. She lashed out with her weighted shoes.

"She's overwrought," said Chalk. "She needs calming."

Something stung her left thigh. She sagged and was still.

Twenty-Eight
Cry, What Shall I Cry?

He was growing weary of Titan. He had taken to the icy moon as to a drug after Lona's departure. But now he was numb. Nothing Aoudad could say or do . . . or get for him . . . would keep him here any longer.

Elise lay naked beside him. High overhead, the Frozen Waterfall hung in motionless cascade. They had rented their own power-sled and had come out by themselves, to park at the glacier's mouth and make love to the glimmer of Saturnlight on frozen ammonia.

"Are you sorry I came here to you, Minner?" she asked.

"Yes." He could be blunt with her.

"Still miss her? You didn't need her."

"I hurt her. Needlessly."

"And what did she do to you?"

"I don't want to talk about her with you." He sat up and put his hands on the controls of the sled. Elise sat up, too, pressing her flesh against him. In this strange light she looked whiter than ever. Did she have blood in that plump body? She was white as death. He started the sled, and it crawled slowly along the edge of the glacier, heading away from the dome. Pools of methane lay here and there. Burris said, "Would you object if I opened the roof of the sled, Elise?

"We'd die." She didn't sound worried.

"You'd die. I'm not sure I would. How do I know this body can't breathe methane?"

"It isn't likely." She stretched, voluptuously, languidly. "Where are you going?"

"Sight-seeing."

"It might not be safe here. You might break through the ice."

"Then we'd die. It would be restful, Elise."

The slid hit a crunching tongue of new ice. It bounced slightly, and so did Elise. Idly Burris watched the quiver ripple its way all through her abundant flesh. She had been with him a week now. Aoudad had produced her. There was much to be said for her voluptuousness, little for her soul. Burris wondered if poor Prolisse had known what sort of wife he had taken.

She touched his skin. She was always touching him, as if reveling in the wrongness of his texture. "Love me again," she said.

"Not now. Elise, what do you desire in me?"

"All of you."

"There's a universe full of men who can keep you happy in bed. What in particular do I have for you?"

"The Manipool changes."

"You love me for the way I look?"

"I love you because you're unusual."

"What about blind men? One-eyed men? Hunchbacks? Men with no noses?"

"There aren't any. Everyone gets a prosthetic now. Everyone's perfect."

"Except me."

"Yes. Except you." Her nails dug into his skin. "I can't scratch you. I can't make you sweat. I can't even look at you without feeling a little queasy. *That's* what I desire in you."

"Queasiness?"

"You're being silly."

"You're a masochist, Elise. You want to grovel. You pick the weirdest thing in the system and throw yourself at him and call it love, but it isn't love, it isn't even sex, it's just self-torture. Right?"

She looked at him queerly.

"You like to be hurt," he said. He put his hand over one of her breasts, spreading the fingers wide to encompass all the soft, warm bulk of it. Then he closed his hand. Elise winced. Her delicate nostrils flared and her eyes began to tear. But she said nothing as he squeezed. Her respiration grew more intense; it seemed to him that he could feel the thunder of her heart. She would absorb any quantity of this pain without a whimper, even if he tore the white globe of flesh from her body entirely. When he released her, there were six white imprints against the whiteness of her flesh. In a moment they began to turn red. She looked like a tigress about to spring. Above them, the Frozen Waterfall rushed downward in eternal stillness. Would it begin to flow? Would Saturn drop from the heavens and brush Titan with his whirling rings?

"I'm leaving for Earth tomorrow," he told her.

She lay back. Her body was receptive. "Make love to me, Minner."

"I'm going back alone. To look for Lona."

"You don't need her. Stop trying to annoy me." She tugged at him. "Lie down beside me. I want to look at Saturn again while you have me."

He ran his hand along the silkiness of her. Her eyes glittered. He whispered, "Let's get out of the sled. Let's run naked to that lake and swim in it."

Methane clouds puffed about them. The temperature outside would make Antarctica in winter seem tropical. Would they die first from freezing, or from the poison in their lungs? They'd never reach the lake. He saw them sprawled on the snowy dune, white on white, rigid as marble. He'd last longer than she would, holding his breath as she toppled and fell, as she flopped about, flesh caressed by the hydrocarbon bath. But he wouldn't last long.

"Yes!" she cried. "We'll swim! And afterward we'll make love beside the lake!"

She reached for the control that would lift the transparent roof of the sled. Burris admired the tension and play of her muscles as her arm stretched toward it, as her hand extended itself, as ligaments and tendons functioned beautifully under the smooth skin from wrist to ankle. One leg was folded up underneath her, the other nicely thrust forward to echo the line of her arm. Her breasts were drawn upward; her throat, which had a tendency toward loose flesh, was now taut. Altogether she was a handsome sight. She needed only to twist a lever and the roof would spring back, exposing them to the virulent atmosphere of Titan. Her slender fingers were on the lever. Burris ceased to contemplate her. He clamped his hand on her arm even as her muscles were tensing, pulled her away, hurled her back on the couch. She landed in a wanton way. As she sat up, he slapped her across the lips. Blood trickled to her chin and her eyes sparkled in pleasure. He hit her again, chopping blows that made the flesh of her leap about. She panted. She clutched at him. The odor of lust assailed his nostrils.

He hit her one more time. Then, realizing he was giving her only what she wanted, he moved away from her and tossed her her discarded breathing-suit.

"Put it on. We're going back to the dome."

She was the incarnation of raw hunger. She writhed in what could have been self-parody of desire. She called hoarsely to him.

"We're going back," he said. "And we aren't going back naked."

Reluctantly she dressed herself.

She would have opened the roof, he told himself. *She would have gone swimming with me in the methane lake.*

He started the sled and sped back to the hotel.

"Are you really leaving for Earth tomorrow?"

"Yes. I've booked passage."

"Without me?"

"Without you."

"What if I followed you again?"

"I can't stop you. But it won't do you any good."

The sled came to the airlock of the dome. He drove in and returned the sled at the rental desk. Elise looked rumpled and sweaty within her breathing-suit.

Burris, going to his room, closed the door quickly and locked it. Elise knocked a few times. He made no reply, and she went away. He rested his head in his hands. The fatigue was coming back, the utter weariness that he had not felt since the final quarrel with Lona. But it passed after a few minutes.

An hour later the hotel management came for him. Three men, grim-faced, saying very little. Burris donned the breathing-suit they gave him and went out into the open with them.

"She's under the blanket. We'd like you to identify her before we bring her in."

Subtle crystals of ammonia snow had fallen on the blanket. They blew aside as Burris peeled it back. Elise, naked, seemed to be hugging the ice. The spots on her breast where his fingertips had dug in had turned deep purple. He touched her. Like marble she was.

"She died instantly," said a voice at his elbow.

Burris looked up. "She had a great deal to drink this afternoon. Perhaps that explains it."

He stayed in his room the rest of that evening and through the morning that followed. At midday he was summoned for the ride to the spaceport, and within four hours he was aloft, bound for Earth via Ganymede. He said little to anyone all the while.

Twenty-Nine
Dona Nobis Pacem

She had come, washed up by the tides, to the Martlet Towers. There she lived in a single room, rarely going out, changing her clothes infrequently, speaking to no one. She knew the truth now, and the truth had imprisoned her.

...and then he found her.

She stood bird-like, ready for flight. "Who's there?"

"Minner."

"What do you want?"

"Let me in, Lona. Please."

"How did you find me here?"

"Some guesswork. Some bribery. Open the door, Lona."

She opened it for him. He looked unchanged over the weeks since she had last seen him. He stepped through, not smiling his equivalent of a smile, not touching her, not kissing. The room was almost in darkness. She moved to light it, but he cut her off with a brusque gesture.

"I'm sorry it's so shabby," she said.

"It looks fine. It looks just like the room I lived in. But that was two buildings over."

"When did you get back to Earth, Minner?"

"Several weeks ago. I've been searching hard."

"Have you seen Chalk?"

Burris nodded. "I didn't get much from him."

"Neither did I." Lona turned to the food conduit. "Something to drink?"

"Thanks, no."

He sat down. There was something blessedly familiar about the elaborate way he coiled himself into her chair, moving all his extra joints so carefully. Just the sight of it made her pulse-rate climb.

He said, "Elise is dead. She killed herself on Titan."

Lona made no response.

He said, "I didn't ask her to come to me. She was a very confused person. Now she's at rest."

"She's better at suicide than I am," Lona said.

"You haven't—"

"No. Not again. I've been living quietly, Minner. Should I admit the turth? I've been waiting for you to come to me."

"All you had to do was let somebody know where you were!"

"It was more complicated than that. I couldn't advertise myself. But I'm glad you're here. I have so much to tell you!"

"Such as?"

"Chalk isn't going to have any of my children transferred to me. I've been checking. He couldn't do it if he wanted to, and he doesn't want to. It was just a convenient lie to get me to work for him."

Burris's eyes flickered. "You mean, to get you to keep company with me?"

"That's it. I won't hide anything now, Minner. You already know, more or less. There had to be a price before I'd go with you. Getting the children was the price. I kept my end of the bargain, but Chalk isn't keeping his."

"I knew that you'd been bought, Lona. I was bought, too. Chalk found my price to come out of hiding and conduct an interplanetary romance with a certain girl."

"Transplant into a new body?"

"Yes," Burris said.

"You aren't going to get that, any more than I'm going to get my babies," she said flatly. "Am I killing any of your illusions? Chalk cheated you the way he cheated me."

"I've been discovering that," Burris said, "since my return. The body-transfer project is at least twenty years away. Not five years. They may never solve some of the problems. They can switch a brain into a new body and keep it alive, but the—what shall I say—*soul* goes. They get a zombi. Chalk knew all that when he offered me his deal."

"He got his romance out of us. And we got nothing out of him." Rising, Lona walked around the room. She came to the tiny potted cactus that she had once given to Burris and rubbed the tip of one finger idly over its bristly surface. Burris seemed to notice the cactus for the first time. He looked pleased.

Lona said, "Do you know why he brought us together, Minner?"

"To make money on the publicity. He picks two used-up people and tricks them into coming part way back to life, and tells the world about it, and—"

"No. Chalk has enough money. He didn't give a damn about the profit."

"Then what?" he asked.

"An idiot told me the real thing. An idiot named Melangio, who does a trick with calendars. Perhaps you've seen him on vid. Chalk used him in some shows."

"No."

"I met him at Chalk's place. Sometimes a fool speaks truth. He said Chalk's a drinker of emotion. He lives on fear, pain, envy, grief. Chalk sets up situations that he can exploit. Bring two people together who are so battered that they can't possibly allow happiness to take hold of them, and watch them suffer. And feed. And drain them."

Burris looked startled. "Even at long range? He could feed even when we were at Luna Tivoli? Or on Titan?"

"Each time we quarreled . . . we felt so tired afterward. As if we'd lost blood. As if we were hundreds of years old."

"Yes!"

"That was Chalk," she said. "Getting fatter on our suffering. He knew we'd hate each other, and that was what he wanted. Can there be a vampire of emotion?"

"So all the promises were false," he whispered. "We were puppets. If it's true."

"I know it's true."

"Because an idiot told you so?"

"A very wise idiot, Minner. Besides, work it all out for yourself. Think of everything Chalk ever said to you. Think of all that happened. Why was Elise always waiting in the wings

to throw her arms around you? Don't you think it was
deliberate, part of a campaign to infuriate me? We were tied
together by our strangeness... by our hatred. And Chalk
loved it."

Burris stared at her quietly a long moment. Then, without
a word, he went to the door, opened it, stepped out into the
hall, and pounced on something. Lona could not see what he
was doing until he returned with a struggling, squirming
Aoudad.

"I thought you'd be out there somewhere," Burris said.
"Come in. Come in. We'd like to talk with you."

"Minner, don't hurt him," Lona said. "He's only a tool."

"He can answer some questions. Won't you, Bart?"

Aoudad moistened his lips. His eyes flicked warily from
face to face.

Burris hit him.

The hand came up with blinding speed. Lona didn't see it,
and neither did Aoudad, but the man's head shot back and he
thumped heavily into the wall. Burris gave him no chance to
defend himself. Aoudad clung blearily to the wall as the
blows landed. Finally he sagged, eyes still open, face bloody.

"Talk to us," Burris said. "Talk to us about Duncan Chalk."

Later they left her room. Aoudad remained behind, sleeping peacefully. In the street below they found his car, waiting
on an uptake ramp. Burris started it and headed it toward
Chalk's office building.

"We were making a mistake," he said, "trying to change
ourselves back to what we once were. We are our own
essences. I am the mutilated starman. You are the girl with a
hundred babies. It's a mistake to try to flee."

"Even if we could flee."

"Even if we could. They could give me a different body
someday, yes, and where would that put me? I'd have lost
what I am now, and I'd have gained nothing. I'd lose myself.
And they could give you two of your babies, perhaps, but
what about the other ninety-eight? What's done is done. The
fact of your essence has absorbed you. And mine me. Is that
too cloudy for you?"

"You're saying that we have to face up squarely to what we
are, Minner."

"That's it. That's it. No more running away. No more
brooding. No more hatred."

"But the world—the normal people—"

"It's us against them. They want to devour us. They want to put us in the freak show. We have to fight back, Lona!"

The car halted. There was the low, windowless building. They entered, and, yes, Chalk would see them, if they would only wait awhile in an outer room. The waited. They sat side by side, scarcely looking at each other. In her hands Lona held the potted cactus. It was the only possession she had taken from her room. They were welcome to the rest.

Burris said quietly, "Turn the anguish outward. There's no other way we can fight."

Leontes d'Amore appeared. "Chalk will see you now," he said.

Up the crystal rungs. Toward the immense figure in the high throne.

"Lona? Burris? Together again?" Chalk asked. He laughed boomingly and tapped his belly. He clapped his hands on the columns of his thighs.

"You dined well on us, didn't you, Chalk?" Burris asked.

The laughter died away. Abruptly Chalk was sitting up, tense, wary. He seemed almost to be a thin man now, ready to take to his heels.

Lona said, "It's nearly evening. We've brought you your dinner, Duncan."

They stood facing him. Burris slipped his arm around her slender waist. Chalk's lips moved. No sounds came out, and his hand did not quite reach the alarm lever on his desk. The pudgy fingers fanned wide. Chalk contemplated them.

"For you," Burris said. "With our compliments. Our love."

Shared emotion flooded from them in shining waves.

It was a torrent Chalk could not withstand. He moved from side to side, buffeted by the furious stream, one side of his mouth quirking upward, then the other. A trail of spittle appeared on his chin. His head jerked sharply three times. Robot-like, he crossed and uncrossed his thick arms.

Burris clung so tightly to Lona that her ribs protested.

Did flames dance crackling along Chalk's desk? Did rivers of raw electrons become visible and glow green before him? He writhed, unable to move, as they gave him their souls in passionate intensity. He fed. But he could not digest. He grew more bloated. His face was bright with sweat.

No word was spoken.

Sink, white whale! Lash your mighty flukes and go down!

Retro me, Satanas!
Here's fire; come, Faustus, set it on.
Glad tidings from great Lucifer.
Chalk moved now. He spun in his chair, breaking from stasis, slamming his fleshy arms again and again onto the desk. He was bathed in the blood of the Albatross. He quivered, jerked, quivered again. The scream that left his lips was no more than a thin, feeble whine delivered by a gaping maw. Now he was strung taut, now he twanged with the rhythms of destruction. . . .

And then came slackness.

The eyeballs rolled. The lips dropped. The massive shoulders slumped. The cheeks sagged.

Consummatum est; this bill is ended.

All three figures were motionless: those who had hurled their souls, and he who had received them. One of the three would never move again.

Burris was the first to recover. It was an effort even to draw breath. To give power to his lips and tongue was a colossal task. He swung around, recovering the knowledge of his limbs, and put his hands on Lona. She was death-pale, frozen in her place. As he touched her, the strength seemed to flow swiftly back into her.

"We can't stay here any longer," he said gently.

They left, slowly, dwelling now in extreme old age, but growing younger as they descended the crystal rungs. Vitality returned. It would be many days before they had fully replenished themselves, but at least there would be no further drain.

No one interfered with them as they left the building.

Night had fallen. Winter was past, and the gray haze of a spring evening covered the city. The stars were barely visible. A faint chill still lingered, but neither of them shivered in the coolness.

"This world has no place for us," Burris said.

"It would only try to eat us. As he tried."

"We defeated him. But we can't defeat a whole world."

"Where will we go?"

Burris looked upward. "Come with me to Manipool. We'll visit the demons for Sunday tea."

"Are you serious?"

"Yes. Will you go there with me?"

"Yes."

They walked toward the car.

"How do you feel?" he asked.

"Very tired. So tired I can scarcely move. But I feel alive. More alive with every step. For the first time, Minner, I feel really alive."

"As do I."

"Your body—does it hurt you now?"

"I love my body," he said.

"Despite the pain?"

"Because of the pain," he said. "It shows that I live. That I feel." He turned to her and took the cactus from her hands. The clouds parted. The thorns gleamed by starlight. "To be alive—to feel, even to feel pain—how important that is, Lona!"

He broke a small limb from the plant and pressed it into the flesh of her hand. The thorns sank deep. She flinched only for a moment. Tiny droplets of blood appeared. From the cactus she took a second limb, and pressed it to him. It was difficult, breaking through that impervious skin of his, but the thorns did penetrate at last. He smiled as the blood began to flow. He touched her wounded hand to his lips, and she his hand to hers.

"We bleed," she said. "We feel. We live."

"Pain is instructive," said Burris, and they walked more quickly.

DOWNWARD TO THE EARTH

Who knoweth the spirit of man that goeth upward, and the spirit of the beast that goeth downward to the earth?

ECCLESIASTES 3:21

One

He had come back to Holman's World after all. He was not sure why. Call it irresistible attraction; call it sentimentality; call it foolishness. Gundersen had never planned to revisit this place. Yet here he was, waiting for the landing, and there it was in the vision screen, close enough to grasp and squeeze in one hand, a world slightly larger than Earth, a world that had claimed the prime decade of his life, a world where he had learned things about himself that he had not really wanted to know. Now the signal light in the lounge was flashing red. The ship would shortly land. Despite everything, he was coming back.

He saw the shroud of mist that covered the temperate zones, and the great sprawling icecaps, and the girdling blue-black band of the scorched tropics. He remembered riding through the Sea of Dust at blazing twilight, and he remembered a silent, bleak river-journey beneath bowers of twittering dagger-pointed leaves, and he remembered golden cocktails on the veranda of a jungle station on the Night of Five Moons, with Seena close by his side and a herd of nildoror mooing in the bush. That was a long time ago. Now the nildoror were masters of Holman's World again. Gundersen had a hard time accepting that. Perhaps that was the real reason why he had come back: to see what sort of job the nildoror could do.

"Attention, passengers in lounge," came a voice over the speaker. "We enter landing orbit for Belzagor in fifteen minutes. Please prepare to return to cradles."

Belzagor. That was what they called the planet now. The native name, the nildoror's own word. To Gundersen it seemed like something out of Assyrian mythology. Of course, it was a romanticized pronunciation; coming from a nildor it would really sound more like *Bllls'grr*. Belzagor it was, though. He would try to call the planet by the name it now wore, if that was what he was supposed to do. He attempted never to give needless offense to alien beings.

"Belzagor," he said. "It's a voluptuous sound, isn't it? Rolls nicely off the tongue."

The tourist couple beside him in the ship's lounge nodded. They agreed readily with whatever Gundersen said. The husband, plump, pale, overdressed, said, "They were still calling it Holman's World when you were last out here, weren't they?"

"Oh, yes," Gundersen said. "But that was back in the good old imperialist days, when an Earthman could call a planet whatever he damn pleased. That's all over now."

The tourist wife's lips tightened in that thin, pinched, dysmenorrheal way of hers. Gundersen drew a somber pleasure from annoying her. All during the voyage he had deliberately played a role out of Kipling for these tourists—posing as the former colonial administrator going out to see what a beastly botch the natives must be making out of the task of governing themselves. It was an exaggeration, a distortion, of his real attitude, but sometimes it pleased him to wear masks. The tourists—there were eight of them—looked upon him in mingled awe and contempt as he swaggered among them, a big fair-skinned man with the mark of outworld experience stamped on his features. They disapproved of him, of the image of himself that he gave them; and yet they knew he had suffered and labored and striven under a foreign sun, and there was romance in that.

"Will you be staying at the hotel?" the tourist husband asked.

"Oh, no. I'm going right out into the bush, toward the mist country. Look—there, you see? In the northern hemisphere, that band of clouds midway up. The temperature gradient's very steep: tropic and arctic practically side by side. Mist. Fog. They'll take you on a tour of it. I have some business in there."

"Business? I thought these new independent worlds were outside the zone of economic penetration that—"

"Not commercial business," Gundersen said. "Personal business. Unfinished business. Something I didn't manage to discover during my tour of duty here." The signal light flashed again, more insistently. "Will you excuse me? We really should cradle up now."

He went to his cabin and readied himself for landing. Webfoam spurted from the spinnerets and enfolded him. He closed his eyes. He felt deceleration thrust, that curiously archaic sensation hearkening back to space travel's earliest days. The ship dropped planetward as Gundersen swayed, suspended, insulated from the worst of the velocity change.

Belzagor's only spaceport was the one that Earthmen had built more than a hundred years before. It was in the tropics, at the mouth of the great river flowing into Belzagor's single ocean. Madden's River, Benjamini Ocean—Gundersen didn't know the nildoror names at all. The spaceport was self-maintaining, fortunately. Automatic high-redundancy devices operated the landing beacon; homeostatic surveillance kept the pad repaved and the bordering jungle cropped back. All, all by machine; it was unrealistic to expect the nildoror to operate a spaceport, and impossible to keep a crew of Earthmen stationed here to do it. Gundersen understood that there were still perhaps a hundred Earthmen living on Belzagor, even after the general withdrawal, but they were not such as would operate a spaceport. And there was a treaty, in any case. Administrative functions were to be performed by nildoror, or not at all.

They landed. The webfoam cradle dissolved upon signal. They went out of the ship.

The air had the tropical reek: rich loam, rotting leaves, the droppings of jungle beasts, the aroma of creamy flowers. It was early evening. A couple of the moons were out. As always, the threat of rain was in the air; the humidity was 99%, probably. But that threat almost never materialized. Rainstorms were rare in this tropical belt. The water simply precipitated out of the air in droplets all the time, imperceptibly coating you with fine wet beads. Gundersen saw lightning flicker beyond the tops of the hullygully trees at the edge of the pad. A stewardess marshaled the nine debarkees. "This way, please," she said crisply, and led them toward the one building.

On the left, three nildoror emerged from the bush and solemnly gazed at the newcomers. Tourists gasped and pointed. "Look! Do you see them? Like elephants, they are! Are those nili—nildoror?"

"Nildoror, yes," Gundersen said. The tang of the big beasts drifted across the clearing. A bull and two cows, he guessed, judging by the size of the tusks. They were all about the same height, three meters plus, with the deep green skins that marked them as western-hemisphere nildoror. Eyes as big as platters peered back at him in dim curiosity. The short-tusked

cow in front lifted her tail and placidly dropped an avalanche
of steaming purple dung. Gundersen heard deep blurred
sounds, but at this distance he could not make out what the
nildoror were saying. Imagine them running a spaceport, he
thought. Imagine them running a planet. But they do. But
they do.

There was no one in the spaceport building. Some robots,
part of the homeostasis net, were repairing the wall at the far
side, where the gray plastic sheeting had apparently succumbed
to spore implantation; sooner or later the jungle rot got
everything in this part of the planet. But that was the only
visible activity. There was no customs desk. The nildoror did
not have a bureaucracy of that sort. They did not care what
you brought with you to their world. The nine passengers
had undergone a customs inspection on Earth, just before
setting out; Earth did care, very much, what was taken to
undeveloped planets. There was also no spaceline office here,
nor were there money-changing booths, nor newsstands, nor
any of the other concessions one normally finds in a spaceport. There was only a big bare shed, which once had been
the nexus of a bustling colonial outpost, in the days when
Holman's World had been the property of Earth. It seemed
to Gundersen that he saw ghosts of those days all about him:
figures in tropical khaki carrying messages, supercargoes
waving inventory sheets, computer technicians draped in
festoons of memory beads, nildoror bearers laden with outgoing produce. Now all was still. The scrapings of the repair
robots echoed across the emptiness.

The spaceline stewardess was telling the eight passengers,
"Your guide should be here any minute. He'll take you to the
hotel, and—"

Gundersen was supposed to go to the hotel too, just for
tonight. In the morning he hoped to arrange for transport.
He had no formal plans for his northward journey; it was
going to be largely an improvisation, a reconnaissance into his
own pockmarked past.

He said to the stewardess, "Is the guide a nildor?"

"You mean, native? Oh, no, he's an Earthman, Mr.
Gundersen." She rummaged in a sheaf of printout slips. "His
name's Van Beneker, and he was supposed to be here at least
half an hour before the ship landed, so I don't understand
why—"

"Van Beneker was never strong on punctuality," Gundersen said. "But there he is."

A beetle, much rusted and stained by the climate, had pulled up at the open entrance to the building, and from it now was coming a short red-haired man, also much rusted and stained by the climate. He wore rumpled fatigues and a pair of knee-high jungle boots. His hair was thinning and his tanned bald skull showed through the slicked-down strands. He entered the building and peered around, blinking. His eyes were light blue and faintly hyperthyroid-looking.

"Van?" Gundersen said. "Over here, Van."

The little man came over. In a hurried, perfunctory way he said, while he was still far from them, "I want to welcome all you people to Belzagor, as Holman's World is now known. My name's Van Beneker, and I'm going to show you as much of this fascinating planet as is legally permissible to show you, and—"

"Hello, Van," Gundersen cut in.

The guide halted, obviously irritated, in mid-spiel. He blinked again and looked closely at Gundersen. Finally he said, clearly not believing it, "Mr. Gundersen?"

"Just Gundersen. I'm not your boss any more."

"Jesus, Mr. Gundersen. Jesus, are you here for the tour?"

"Not exactly. I'm here to take my own tour."

Van Beneker said to the others, "I want you to excuse me. Just for a minute." To the spaceline stewardess he said, "It's okay. You can officially convey them to me. I take responsibility. They are all here? One, two, three—eight. That's right. Okay, the luggage goes out there, next to the beetle. Tell them all to wait. I'll be right with them." He tugged at Gundersen's elbow. "Come on over here, Mr. Gundersen. You don't know how amazed I am. Jesus!"

"How have you been, Van?"

"Lousy. How else, on this planet? When did you leave, exactly?"

"2240. The year after relinquishment. Eight years ago."

"Eight years. And what have you been doing?"

"The home office found work for me." Gundersen said. "I keep busy. Now I've got a year's accumulated leave."

"To spend it *here*?"

"Why not?"

"What for?"

"I'm going up mist country," Gundersen said. "I want to visit the sulidoror."

"You don't want to do that," said Van Beneker. "What do you want to do that for?"

"To satisfy a curiosity."

"There's only trouble when a man goes up there. You know the stories, Mr. Gundersen. I don't need to remind you, how many guys went up there, how many didn't come back." Van Beneker laughed. "You didn't come all the way to this place just to rub noses with the sulidoror. I bet you got some other reason."

Gundersen let the point pass. "What do you do here now, Van?"

"Tourist guide, mostly. We get nine, ten batches a year. I take them up along the ocean, then show them a bit of the mist country, then we hop across the Sea of Dust. It's a nice little tour."

"Yes."

"The rest of the time I relax. I talk to the nildoror a lot, and sometimes I visit friends at the bush stations. You'll know everyone, Mr. Gundersen. It's all the old people, still out there."

"What about Seena Royce?" Gundersen asked.

"She's up by Shangri-la Falls."

"Still have her looks?"

"She thinks so," Van Beneker said. "You figure you'll go up that way?"

"Of course," Gundersen said. "I'm making a sentimental pilgrimage. I'll tour all the bush stations. See the old friends. Seena. Cullen. Kurtz. Salamone. Whoever's still there."

"Some of them are dead."

"Whoever's still there," Gundersen said. He looked down at the little man and smiled. "You'd better take care of your tourists, now. We can talk at the hotel tonight. I want you to fill me in on everything that's happened while I've been gone."

"Easy, Mr. Gundersen. I can do it right now in one word. Rot. Everything's rotting. Look at the spaceport wall over there."

"I see."

"Look at the repair robots, now. They don't shine much, do they? They're giving out too. If you get close, you can see the spots on their hulls."

"But homeostasis—"

"Sure. Everything gets repaired, even the repair robots. But the system's going to break down. Sooner or later, the rot will get into the basic programs, and then there won't be any more repairs, and this world will go straight back into the stone age. I mean *all* the way back. And then the nildoror will finally be happy. I understand those big bastards as much as anybody does. I know they can't wait to see the last trace of Earthmen rot right off this planet. They pretend they're friendly, but the hate's there all the time, real sick hate, and—"

"You ought to look after your tourists, Van," Gundersen said. "They're getting restless."

Two

A caravan of nildoror was going to transport them from the spaceport to the hotel—two Earthmen per alien, with Gundersen riding alone, and Van Beneker, with the luggage, leading the way in his beetle. The three nildoror grazing at the edge of the field ambled over to enroll in the caravan, and two others emerged from the bush. Gundersen was surprised that nildoror were still willing to act as beasts of burden for Earthmen. "They don't mind," Van Beneker explained. "They like to do us favors. It makes them feel superior. They can't hardly tell there's weight on them, anyhow. And they don't think there's anything shameful about letting people ride them."

"When I was here I had the impression they resented it," Gundersen said.

"Since relinquishment they take things like that easier. Anyway, how could you be sure what they thought? I mean, what they *really* thought."

The tourists were a little alarmed at riding nildoror. Van Beneker tried to calm them by telling them it was an important part of the Belzagor experience. Besides, he added, machinery did not thrive on this planet and there were hardly any functioning beetles left. Gundersen demonstrated how to mount, for the benefit of the apprehensive newcom-

ers. He tapped his nildor's left-hand tusk, and the alien knelt
in its elephantine way, ponderously coming down on its front
knees, then its back ones. The nildor wriggled its shoulders,
in effect dislocating them to create the deep swayback valley
in which a man could ride so comfortably, and Gundersen
climbed aboard, seizing the short backward-thrusting horns
as his pommels. The spiny crest down the middle of the
alien's broad skull began to twitch. Gundersen recognized it
as a gesture of welcome; the nildoror had a rich language of
gesture, employing not only the spines but also their long
ropy trunks and their many-pleated ears. "*Sssukh!*" Gundersen
said, and the nildor arose. "Do you sit well?" it asked him in
its own language. "Very well indeed," Gundersen said, feeling a surge of delight as the unforgotten vocabulary came to
his lips.

In their clumsy, hesitant way, the eight tourists did as he
had done, and the caravan set out down the river road toward
the hotel. Nightflies cast a dim glow under the canopy of
trees. A third moon was in the sky, and the mingled lights
came through the leaves, revealing the oily, fast-moving river
just to their left. Gundersen stationed himself at the rear of
the procession in case one of the tourists had a mishap. There
was only one uneasy moment, though, when a nildor paused
and left the rank. It rammed the triple prongs of its tusks into
the riverbank to grub up some morsel, and then resumed its
place in line. In the old days, Gundersen knew, that would
never have happened. Nildoror were not permitted then to
have whims.

He enjoyed the ride. The jouncing strides were agreeable,
and the pace was swift without being strenuous for the
passengers. What good beasts these nildoror are, Gundersen
thought. Strong, docile, intelligent. He almost reached forward to stroke his mount's spines, deciding at the last moment that it would seem patronizing. The nildoror are something other than funny-looking elephants, he reminded himself.
They are intelligent beings, the dominant life forms of their
planet, *people,* and don't you forget it.

Soon Gundersen could hear the crashing of the surf. They
were nearing the hotel.

The path widened to become a clearing. Up ahead, one of
the tourist women pointed into the bush; her husband shrugged
and shook his head. When Gundersen reached that place he
saw what was bothering them. Black shapes crouched be-

tween the trees, and dark figures were moving slowly to and fro. They were barely visible in the shadows. As Gundersen's nildor went past, two of the dim forms emerged and stood by the edge of the path. They were husky bipeds, close to three meters tall, covered with thick coats of dark red hair. Massive tails swished slowly through the greenish gloom. Hooded eyes, slit-wide even in this scant light, appraised the procession. Drooping rubbery snouts, tapir-long, sniffed audibly.

A woman turned gingerly and said to Gundersen, "What are they?"

"Sulidoror. The secondary species. They come from up mist country. These are northern ones."

"Are they dangerous?"

"I wouldn't call them that."

"If they're northern animals, why are they down here?" her husband wanted to know.

"I'm not sure," Gundersen said. He questioned his mount and received an answer. "They work at the hotel," Gundersen called ahead. "Bellhops. Kitchen hands." It seemed strange to him that the nildoror would have turned the sulidoror into domestic servants at an Earthman's hotel. Not even before relinquishment had sulidoror been used as servants. But of course there had been plenty of robots here then.

The hotel lay just ahead. It was on the coast, a glistening geodesic dome that showed no external signs of decay. Before relinquishment, it had been a posh resort run exclusively for the benefit of the top-level administrators of the Company. Gundersen had spent many happy hours in it. Now he dismounted, and he and Van Beneker helped the tourists down. Three sulidoror stood at the hotel entrance. Van Beneker gestured fiercely at them and they began to take the luggage from the beetle's storage hold.

Inside, Gundersen quickly detected symptoms of decline. A carpet of tiger-moss had begun to edge out of an ornamental garden strip along the lobby wall, and was starting to reach onto the fine black slabs of the main hall's floor; he saw the toothy little mouths hopefully snapping as he walked in. No doubt the hotel's maintenance robots once had been programmed to cut the ornamental moss back to the border of the garden bed, but the program must have subtly altered with the years so that now the moss was allowed to intrude on the interior of the building as well. Possibly the robots were gone altogether, and the sulidoror who had replaced them were lax in their pruning duties. And there were other hints that control was slipping away.

"The boys will show you to your rooms," Van Beneker said. "You can come down for cocktails whenever you're ready. Dinner will be served in about an hour and a half."

A towering sulidor conducted Gundersen to a third-floor room overlooking the sea. Reflex led him to offer the huge creature a coin; but the sulidor merely looked blankly at him and did not venture to take it. It seemed to Gundersen that there was a suppressed tension about the sulidor, an inward seething, but perhaps it existed only in his own imagination. In the old days sulidoror had rarely been seen outside the zone of mist, and Gundersen did not feel at ease with them.

In nildoror words he said, "How long have you been at the hotel?" But the sulidor did not respond. Gundersen did not know the language of the sulidoror, but he was aware that every sulidor was supposed to speak fluent nildororu as well as sulidororu. Enunciating more clearly, he repeated his question. The sulidor scratched its pelt with gleaming claws and said nothing. Moving past Gundersen, it deopaqued the window-wall, adjusted the atmospheric filters, and stalked solemnly out.

Gundersen frowned. Quickly he stripped and got under the cleanser. A quick whirr of vibration took from him the grime of his day's journey. He unpacked and donned evening clothes, a close gray tunic, polished boots, a mirror for his brow. He toned the color of his hair down the spectrum a short distance, dimming it from yellow almost to auburn.

Suddenly he felt very tired.

He was just into early middle years, only forty-eight, and travel ordinarily did not affect him. Why this fatigue, then? He realized that he had been holding himself unusually stiff these few hours he had been back on this planet. Rigid, inflexible, tense—uncertain of his motives in returning, unsure of his welcome, perhaps touched a bit by curdled guilts, and now the strain was telling. He touched a switch and made the wall a mirror. Yes, his face was drawn; the cheekbones, always prominent, now jutted like blades, and the lips were clamped and the forehead was furrowed. The thin slab of his nose was distended by tension-flared nostrils. Gundersen shut his eyes and went through one of the drills of a relaxation mode. He looked better thirty seconds later; but a drink might help, he decided. He went down to the lounge.

None of the tourists were there yet. The louvers were open, and he heard the roar and crash of the sea, smelled its saltiness. A white curdled line of accumulated salt had been allowed to form along the margin of the beach. The tide was in; only the tips of the jagged rocks that framed the bathing area were visible. Gundersen looked out over the moonslight-streaked water, staring into the blackness of the eastern horizon. Three moons had also been up on his last night here, when they gave the farewell party for him. And after the revelry was over, he and Seena had gone for a midnight swim, out to the tide-hidden shoal where they could barely stand, and when they returned to shore, naked and salt-encrusted, he had made love to her behind the rocks, embracing her for what he was sure would be the last time. And now he was back.

He felt a stab of nostalgia so powerful that he winced.

Gundersen had been thirty years old when he came out to Holman's World as an assistant station agent. He had been forty, and a sector administrator, when he left. In a sense the first thirty years of his life had been a pale prelude to that decade, and the last eight years of it had been a hollow epilogue. He had lived his life on this silent continent, bounded by mist and ice to the north, mist and ice to the south, the Benjamini Ocean to the east, the Sea of Dust to the west. For a while he had ruled half a world, at least in the absence of the chief resident; and this planet had shrugged him off as though he had never been. Gundersen turned away from the louvers and sat down.

Van Beneker appeared, still in his sweaty, rumpled fatigues. He winked cordially at Gundersen and began rummaging in a cabinet. "I'm the bartender too, Mr. G. What can I get you?"

"Alcohol," Gundersen said. "Any form you recommend."

"Snout or flask?"

"Flask. I like the taste."

"As you say. But snout for me. It's the effect, sir, the *effect*." He set an empty glass before Gundersen and handed him a flask containing three ounces of a dark red fluid. Highland rum, local product. Gundersen hadn't tasted it in eight years. The flask was equipped with its own condensation chiller; Gundersen thumbed it with a quick short push and quietly watched the flakes of ice beginning to form along the inside. When his drink was properly chilled he poured it and put it quickly to his lips.

"That's pre-relinquishment stock," Van Beneker said. "Not much of it left, but I knew you'd appreciate it." He was holding an ultrasonic tube to his left forearm. *Zzz!* and the snout spurted alcohol straight into his vein. Van Beneker grinned. "Works faster this way. The working-class man's boozer. Eh? Eh? Get you another rum, Mr. G?"

"Not just yet. Better look after your tourists, Van."

The tourist couples were beginning to enter the bar: first the Watsons, then the Mirafloreses, the Steins, finally the Christophers. Evidently they had expected to find the bar throbbing with life, full of other tourists giddily hailing one another from distant parts of the room, and red-jacketed waiters ferrying drinks. Instead there were peeling plastic walls, a sonic sculpture that no longer worked and was deeply cobwebbed, empty tables, and that unpleasant Mr. Gundersen moodily peering into a glass. The tourists exchanged cheated glances. Was this what they had spanned the light-years to see? Van Beneker went to them, offering drinks, weeds, whatever else the limited resources of the hotel might be able to supply. They settled in two groups near the windows and began to talk in low voices, plainly self-conscious in front of Gundersen. Surely they felt the foolishness of their roles, these soft well-to-do people whose boredom had driven them to peer at the remote reaches of the galaxy. Stein ran a helix parlor in California, Miraflores a chain of lunar casinos, Watson was a doctor, and Christopher—Gundersen could not remember what Christopher did. Something in the financial world.

Mrs. Stein said, "There are some of those animals on the beach. The green elephants."

Everyone looked. Gundersen signaled for another drink, and got it. Van Beneker, flushed, sweating, winked again and put a second snout to his arm. The tourists began to titter. Mrs. Christopher said, "Don't they have any shame at all?"

"Maybe they're simply playing, Ethel," Watson said.

"*Playing?* Well, if you call that playing—"

Gundersen leaned forward, glancing out the window without getting up. On the beach a pair of nildoror were coupling, the cow kneeling where the salt was thickest, the bull mounting her, gripping her shoulders, pressing his central tusk down firmly against the spiny crest of her skull, jockey-

ing his hindquarters about as he made ready for the consum-
mating thrust. The tourists, giggling, making heavy-handed
comments of appreciation, seemed both shocked and titillat-
ed. To his considerable surprise, Gundersen realized he was
shocked, too, although coupling nildoror were nothing new to
him; and when a ferocious orgasmic bellowing rose from
below he glanced away, embarrassed and not understanding
why.

"You look upset," Van Beneker said.

"They didn't have to do that *here*."

"Why not? They do it all over the place. You know how it
is."

"They deliberately went out there," Gundersen muttered.
"To show off for the tourists? Or to annoy the tourists? They
shouldn't be reacting to the tourists at all. What are they
trying to prove? That they're just animals, I suppose."

"You don't understand the nildoror, Gundy."

Gundersen looked up, startled as much by Van Beneker's
words as by the sudden descent from "Mr. Gundersen" to
"Gundy." Van Beneker seemed startled, too, blinking rapidly
and tugging at a stray sparse lock of fading hair.

"I don't?" Gundersen asked. "After spending ten years
here?"

"Begging pardon, but I never did think you understood
them, even when you were here. I used to go around with
you a lot to the villages when I was clerking for you. I
watched you."

"In what way do you think I failed to understand them,
Van?"

"You despised them. You thought of them as animals."

"That isn't so!"

"Sure it is, Gundy. You never once admitted they had any
intelligence at all."

"That's absolutely untrue," Gundersen said. He got up and
took a new flask of rum from the cabinet, and returned to the
table.

"I would have gotten that for you," Van Beneker said. "You
just had to ask me."

"It's all right." Gundersen chilled the drink and downed it
fast. "You're talking a load of nonsense, Van. I did everything
possible for those people. To improve them, to lift them
toward civilization. I requisitioned tapes for them, sound
pods, culture by the ton. I put through new regulations about

maximum labor. I insisted that my men respect their rights as the dominant indigenous culture. I—"

"You treated them like very intelligent animals. Not like intelligent alien *people*. Maybe you didn't even realize it yourself, Gundy, but I did, and God knows they did. You talked down to them. You were kind to them in the wrong way. All your interest in uplifting them, in improving them— crap, Gundy, they have their own culture. They didn't want yours!"

"It was my duty to guide them," Gundersen said stiffly. "Futile though it was to think that a bunch of animals who don't have a written language, who don't—" He stopped, horrified.

"Animals," Van Beneker said.

"I'm tired. Maybe I've had too much to drink. It just slipped out."

"Animals."

"Stop pushing me, Van. I did the best I could, and if what I was doing was wrong, I'm sorry. I tried to do what was right." Gundersen pushed his empty glass forward. "Get me another, will you?"

Van Beneker fetched the drink, and one more snout for himself. Gundersen welcomed the break in the conversation, and apparently Van Beneker did, too, for they both remained silent a long moment, avoiding each other's eyes. A sulidor entered the bar and began to gather the empties, crouching to keep from grazing the Earthman-scaled ceiling. The chatter of the tourists died away as the fierce-looking creature moved through the room. Gundersen looked toward the beach. The nildoror were gone. One of the moons was setting in the east, leaving a fiery track across the surging water. He realized that he had forgotten the names of the moons. No matter; the old Earthman-given names were dead history now. He said finally to Van Beneker, "How come you decided to stay here after relinquishment?"

"I felt at home here. I've been here twenty-five years. Why should I go anywhere else?"

"No family ties elsewhere?"

"No. And it's comfortable here. I get a company pension. I get tips from the tourists. There's a salary from the hotel. That's enough to keep me supplied with what I need. What I need, mostly, is snouts. Why should I leave?"

"Who owns the hotel?" Gundersen asked.

"The confederation of western-continent nildoror. The Company gave it to them."

"And the nildoror pay you a salary? I thought they were outside the galactic money economy."

"They are. They arranged something with the Company."

"What you're saying is the Company still runs this hotel."

"If anybody can be said to run it, the Company does, yes," Van Beneker agreed. "But that isn't much of a violation of the relinquishment law. There's only one employee. Me. I pocket my salary from what the tourists pay for accommodations. The rest I spend on imports from the money sphere. Don't you see, Gundy, it's all just a big joke? It's a routine designed to allow me to bring in liquor, that's all. This hotel isn't a commercial proposition. The Company is really out of this planet. Completely."

"All right. All right. I believe you."

Van Beneker said, "What are you looking for up mist country?"

"You really want to know?"

"It passes the time to ask things."

"I want to watch the rebirth ceremony. I never saw it, all the time I was here."

The bulging blue eyes seemed to bulge even more. "Why can't you be serious, Gundy?"

"I am."

"It's dangerous to fool with the rebirth thing."

"I'm prepared for the risks."

"You ought to talk to some people here about it, first. It's not a thing for us to meddle in."

Gundersen sighed. "Have you seen it?"

"No. Never. Never even been interested in seeing it. Whatever the hell the sulidoror do in the mountains, let them do it without me. I'll tell you who to talk to, though. Seena."

"She's watched the rebirth?"

"Her husband has."

Gundersen felt a spasm of dismay. "Who's her husband?"

"Jeff Kurtz. You didn't know?"

"I'll be damned," Gundersen murmured.

"You wonder what she saw in him, eh?"

"I wonder that she could bring herself to live with a man like that. You talk about *my* attitude toward the natives!

There's someone who treated them like his own property, and—"

"Talk to Seena, up at Shangri-la Falls. About the rebirth." Van Beneker laughed. "You're playing games with me, aren't you? You know I'm drunk and you're having a little fun."

"No. Not at all." Gundersen rose uneasily. "I ought to get some sleep now."

Van Beneker followed him to the door. Just as Gundersen went out, the little man leaned close to him and said, "You know, Gundy, what the nildoror were doing on the beach before—they weren't doing that for the tourists. They were doing it for you. It's the kind of sense of humor they have. Good night, Gundy."

Three

Gundersen woke early. His head was surprisingly clear. It was just a little after dawn, and the green-tinged sun was low in the sky. The eastern sky, out over the ocean: a welcome touch of Earthliness. He went down to the beach for a swim. A soft south wind was blowing, pushing a few clouds into view. The hullygully trees were heavy with fruit; the humidity was as high as ever; thunder boomed back from the mountains that ran in an arc paralleling the coast a day's drive inland. Mounds of nildoror dung were all over the beach. Gundersen stepped warily, zigzagging over the crunching sand and hurling himself flat into the surf. He went under the first curling row of breakers and with quick powerful strokes headed toward the shoals. The tide was low. He crossed the exposed sandbar and swam beyond it until he felt himself tiring. When he returned to the shore area, he found two of the tourist men had also come out for a swim, Christopher and Miraflores. They smiled tentatively at him. "Bracing," he said. "Nothing like salt water."

"Why can't they keep the beach clean, though?" Miraflores asked.

A sullen sulidor served breakfast. Native fruits, native fish. Gundersen's appetite was immense. He bolted down three golden-green bitterfruits for a start, then expertly boned a whole spiderfish and forked the sweet pink flesh into himself as though engaged in a speed contest. The sulidor brought him another fish and a bowl of phallic-looking forest candles. Gundersen still was working on these when Van Beneker entered, wearing clean though frayed clothes. He looked bloodshot and chastened. Instead of joining Gundersen at the table he merely smiled a perfunctory greeting and sailed past.

"Sit with me, Van," Gundersen said.

Uncomfortable, Van Beneker complied. "About last night—"

"Forget it."

"I was insufferable, Mr. Gundersen."

"You were in your cups. Forgiven. In vino veritas. You were calling me Gundy last night, too. You may as well do it this morning. Who catches the fish?"

"There's an automatic weir just north of the hotel. Catches them and pipes them right into the kitchen. God knows who'd prepare food here if we didn't have the machines."

"And who picks the fruit? Machines?"

"The sulidoror do that," Van Beneker said.

"When did sulidoror start working as menials on this planet?"

"About five years ago. Six, maybe. The nildoror got the idea from us, I suppose. If we could turn them into bearers and living bulldozers, they could turn the sulidoror into bellhops. After all, the sulidoror *are* the inferior species."

"But always their own masters. Why did they agree to serve? What's in it for them?"

"I don't know," Van Beneker said. "When did anybody ever understand the sulidoror?"

True enough, Gundersen thought. No one yet had succeeded in making sense out of the relationship between this planet's two intelligent species. The presence of two intelligent species, in the first place, went against the general evolutionary logic of the universe. Both nildoror and sulidoror qualified for autonomous ranking, with perception levels beyond those of the higher hominoid primates; a sulidor was considerably smarter than a chimpanzee, and a nildor was a good deal more clever than that. If there had been no nildoror here at all, the presence of the sulidoror alone would have been enough to force the Company to relinquish possession of the planet when the decolonization movement reached its peak. But why two species, and why the strange unspoken accommodation between them, the bipedal carnivorous sulidoror ruling over the mist country, the quadrupedal herbivorous nildoror dominating the tropics? How had they carved this world up so neatly? And why was the division of authority breaking down, if breaking down was really what was happening? Gundersen knew that there were ancient treaties between these creatures, that a system of claims and prerogatives existed, that every nildor went back to the mist country when the time for its rebirth arrived. But he did not know what role the sulidoror really played in the life and the rebirth of the nildoror. No one did. The pull of that mystery was, he admitted, one of the things that had brought him back to Holman's World, to Belzagor, now that he had shed his administrative responsibilities and was free to risk his life indulging private curiosities. The shift in the nildoror-sulidoror relationship that seemed to be taking place around this hotel troubled him, though; it had been hard enough to comprehend that relationship when it was static. Of course, the habits of alien beings were none of his business, really. Nothing was his business, these days. When a man had no business, he had to appoint himself to some. So he was here to do research, ostensibly, which is to say to snoop and spy. Putting it that way made his return to this planet seem more like an act of will, and less like the yielding to irresistible compulsion that he feared it had been.

"—more complicated than anybody ever thought," Van Beneker was saying.

"I'm sorry. I must have missed most of what you said."

"It isn't important. We theorize a lot, here. The last hundred of us. How soon do you start north?"

"In a hurry to be rid of me, Van?"

"Only trying to make plans, sir," the little man said, hurt. "If you're staying, we need provisions for you, and—"

"I'm leaving after breakfast. If you'll tell me how to get to the nearest nildoror encampment so I can apply for my travel permit."

"Twenty kilometers, southeast. I'd run you down there in the beetle, but you understand—the tourists—"

"Can you get me a ride with a nildor?" Gundersen suggested. "If it's too much bother, I suppose I can hike it, but—"

"I'll arrange things," Van Beneker said.

A young male nildor appeared an hour after breakfast to take Gundersen down to the encampment. In the old days

Gundersen would simply have climbed on his back, but now he felt the necessity of making introductions. One does not ask an autonomous intelligent being to carry you twenty kilometers through the jungle, he thought, without attempting to enter into elementary courtesies. "I am Edmund Gundersen of the first birth," he said, "and I wish you joy of many rebirths, friend of my journey."

"I am Srin'gahar of the first birth," replied the nildor evenly, "and I thank you for your wish, friend of my journey. I serve you of free choice and await your commands."

"I must speak with a many-born one and gain permission to travel north. The man here says you will take me to such a one."

"So it can be done. Now?"

"Now."

Gundersen had one suitcase. He rested it on the nildor's broad rump and Srin'gahar instantly curved his tail up and back to clamp the bag in place. Then the nildor knelt and Gundersen went through the ritual of mounting. Tons of powerful flesh rose and moved obediently toward the rim of the forest. It was almost as though nothing had ever changed.

They traveled the first kilometer in silence, through an ever-thickening series of bitterfruit glades. Gradually it occurred to Gundersen that the nildor was not going to speak unless spoken to, and he opened the conversation by remarking that he had lived for ten years on Belzagor. Srin'gahar said that he knew that; he remembered Gundersen from the era of Company rule. The nature of the nildoror vocal system drained overtones and implications from the statement. It came out flat, a mooing nasal grunt that did not reveal whether the nildor remembered Gundersen fondly, bitterly, or indifferently. Gundersen might have drawn a hint from the movements of Srin'gahar's cranial crest, but it was impossible for someone seated on a nildor's back to detect any but the broadest movements. The intricate nildoror system of non-verbal supplementary communication had not evolved for the convenience of passengers. In any event Gundersen had known only a few of the almost infinite number of supplementary gestures, and he had forgotten most of those. But the nildor seemed courteous enough.

Gundersen took advantage of the ride to practice his nildororu. So far he had done well, but in an interview with a many-born one he would need all the verbal skill he could muster. Again and again he said, "I spoke that the right way, didn't I? Correct me if I didn't."

"You speak very well," Srin'gahar insisted.

Actually the language was not difficult. It was narrow in range, simple in grammar. Nildororu words did not inflect; they agglutinated, piling syllable atop syllable so that a complex concept like "the former grazing-ground of my mate's clan" emerged as a long grumbled growl of sound unbroken even by a brief pause. Nildoror speech was slow and stolid, requiring broad rolling tones that an Earthman had to launch from the roots of his nostrils; when Gundersen shifted from nildororu to any Earth language, he felt sudden exhilaration, like a circus acrobat transported instantaneously from Jupiter to Mercury.

Srin'gahar was taking a nildoror path, not one of the old Company roads. Gundersen had to duck low-hanging branches now and then, and once a quivering nicalanga vine descended to catch him around the throat in a gentle, cool, quickly broken, and yet frightening embrace. When he looked back, he saw the vine tumescent with excitement, red and swollen from the thrill of caressing an Earthman's skin. Shortly the jungle humidity reached the top of the scale and the level of condensation became something close to that of rain; the air was so wet that Gundersen had trouble breathing, and streams of sweat poured down his body. The sticky moment passed. Minutes later they intersected a Company road. It was a narrow fading track in the jungle, nearly overgrown. In another year it would be gone.

The nildor's vast body demanded frequent feedings. Every half hour they halted and Gundersen dismounted while Srin'gahar munched shrubbery. The sight fed Gundersen's latent prejudices, troubling him so much that he tried not to look. In a wholly elephantine way the nildor uncoiled his trunk and ripped leafy branches from low trees; then the great mouth sagged open and in the bundle went. With his triple tusks Srin'gahar shredded slabs of bark for dessert. The big jaws moved back and forth tirelessly, grinding, milling. We are no prettier when we eat, Gundersen told himself, and the demon within him counterpointed his tolerance with a shrill insistence that his companion was a beast.

Srin'gahar was not an outgoing type. When Gundersen said nothing, the nildor said nothing; when Gundersen asked a question, the nildor replied politely but minimally. The strain of sustaining such a broken-backed conversation drained Gundersen, and he allowed long minutes to pass in silence. Caught up in the rhythm of the big creature's steady stride, he was content to be carried effortlessly along through the steamy jungle. He had no idea where he was and could not even tell if they were going in the right direction, for the trees far overhead met in a closed canopy, screening the sun. After the nildor had stopped for his third meal of the morning, though, he gave Gundersen an unexpected clue to their location. Cutting away from the path in a sudden diagonal, the nildor trotted a short distance into the most dense part of the forest, battering down the vegetation, and came to a halt in front of what once had been a Company building—a glassy dome now dimmed by time and swathed in vines.

"Do you know this house, Edmund of the first birth?" Srin'gahar asked.

"What was it?"

"The serpent station. Where you gathered the juices."

The past abruptly loomed like a toppling cliff above Gundersen. Jagged hallucinatory images plucked at his mind. Ancient scandals, long forgotten or suppressed, sprang to new life. This is the serpent station, this ruin? This the place of private sins, the scene of so many falls from grace? Gundersen felt his cheeks reddening. He slipped from the nildor's back and walked haltingly toward the building. He stood at the door a moment, looking in. Yes, there were the hanging tubes and pipes, the runnels through which the extracted venom had flowed, all the processing equipment still in place, half devoured by warmth and moisture and neglect. There was the entrance for the jungle serpents, drawn by alien music they could not resist, and there they were milked of their venom and there—and there—

Gundersen glanced back at Srin'gahar. The spines of the nildor's crest were distended: a mark of tension, a mark perhaps of shared shame. The nildoror, too, had memories of this building. Gundersen stepped into the station, pushing back the half-open door. It split loose from its moorings as he did so, and a musical tremor ran *whang whang whang* through the whole of the spherical building, dying away to a blurred feeble tinkle. *Whang* and Gundersen heard Jeff Kurtz's guitar again, and the years fell away and he was thirty-one years old once more, a newcomer on Holman's World and about to begin his first stint at the serpent station,

finally assigned to that place that was the focus of so much
gossip. Yes. Out of the shroud of memory came the image of
Kurtz. There he was standing just inside the station door,
impossibly tall, the tallest man Gundersen had ever seen,
with a great pale domed hairless head and enormous dark
eyes socketed in prehistoric-looking bony ridges, and a
bright-toothed smile that ran at least a kilometer's span from
cheek to cheek. The guitar went *whang* and Kurtz said,
"You'll find it interesting here, Gundy. This station is a
unique experience. We buried your predecessor last week."
Whang. "Of course, you must learn to establish a distance
between yourself and what happens here. That's the secret of
maintaining your identity on an alien world, Gundy. Comprehend the esthetics of distance: draw a boundary line about
yourself and say to the planet, thus far you can go in
consuming me, and no farther. Otherwise the planet will
eventually absorb you and make you part of it. Am I being
clear?"

"Not at all," said Gundersen.

"The meaning will manifest itself eventually." *Whang.* "Come
see our serpents."

Kurtz was five years older than Gundersen and had been
on Holman's World three years longer. Gundersen had known
him by reputation long before meeting him. Everyone seemed
to feel awe of Kurtz, and yet he was only an assistant station
agent, who had never been promoted beyond that lowly
rank. After five minutes of exposure to him, Gundersen
thought he knew why. Kurtz gave an impression of instability—
not quite a fallen angel but certainly a falling one, Lucifer on
his way down, descending from morn to noon, noon to dewy
eve, but now only in the morning of his drop. One could not
trust a man like that with serious responsibilities until he had
finished his transit and had settled into his ultimate state.

They went into the serpent station together. Kurtz reached
up as he passed the distilling apparatus, lightly caressing
tubing and petcocks. His fingers were like a spider's legs, and
the caress was astonishingly obscene. At the far end of the
room stood a short, stocky man, dark-haired, black-browed,
the station supervisor. Gio' Salamone. Kurtz made the introductions. Salamone grinned. "Lucky you," he said. "How did
you manage to get assigned here?"

"They just sent me," Gundersen said.

"As somebody's practical joke," Kurtz suggested.

"I believe it," said Gundersen. "Everyone thought I was fibbing when I said I was sent here without applying." "A test of innocence," Kurtz murmured.

Salamone said, "Well, now that you're here, you'd better learn our basic rule. The basic rule is that when you leave this station, you never discuss what happens here with anybody else. *Capisce?* Now say to me, 'I swear by the Father, Son, and Holy Ghost, and also by Abraham, Isaac, Jacob, and Moses—'"

Kurtz choked with laughter.

Bewildered, Gundersen said, "That's an oath I've never heard before."

"Salamone's an Italian Jew," said Kurtz. "He's trying to cover all possibilities. Don't bother swearing, but he's right: what happens here isn't anybody else's business. Whatever you may have heard about the serpent station is probably true, but nevertheless tell no tales when you leave here." *Whang. Whang.* "Watch us carefully, now. We're going to call up our demons. Loose the amplifiers, Gio'."

Salamone seized a plastic sack of what looked like golden flour and hauled it toward the station's rear door. He scooped out a handful. With a quick upward heave he sent it into the air; the breeze instantly caught the tiny glittering grains and carried them aloft. Kurtz said, "He's just scattered a thousand microamplifiers into the jungle. In ten minutes they'll cover a radius of ten kilometers. They're tuned to pick up the frequencies of my guitar and Gio's flute, and the resonances go bouncing back and forth all over the place." Kurtz began to play, picking up a melody in mid-course. Salamone produced a short transverse flute and wove a melody of his own through the spaces in Kurtz's tune. Their playing became a stately sarabande, delicate, hypnotic, two or three figures repeated endlessly without variations in volume or pitch. For ten minutes nothing unusual occurred. Then Kurtz nodded toward the edge of the jungle. "They're coming," he whispered. "We're the original and authentic snake charmers."

Gundersen watched the serpents emerging from the forest. They were four times as long as a man, and as thick as a big man's arm. Undulating fins ran down their backs from end to end. Their skins were glossy, pale green, and evidently sticky, for the detritus of the forest floor stuck to them in places, bits of leaves and soil and crumpled petals. Instead of eyes, they had rows of platter-sized sensor spots flanking their rippling dorsal fins. Their heads were blunt; their mouths only slits, suitable merely for nibbling on gobbets of soil. Where nostrils might be, there protruded two slender quills as long as a man's thumb; these extended to five times that length in moments of stress or when the serpent was under attack, and yielded a blue fluid, a venom. Despite the size of the creatures, despite the arrival of perhaps thirty of them at once, Gundersen did not find them frightening, although he would certainly have been uneasy at the arrival of a platoon of pythons. These were not pythons. They were not even reptiles at all, but low-phylum creatures, actually giant worms. They were sluggish and of no apparent intelligence. But clearly they responded powerfully to the music. It had drawn them to the station, and now they writhed in a ghastly ballet, seeking the source of the sound. The first few were already entering the building.

"Do you play the guitar?" Kurtz asked. "Here—just keep the sound going. The tune's not important now." He thrust the instrument at Gundersen, who struggled with the fingerings a moment, then brought forth a lame, stumbling imitation of Kurtz's melody. Kurtz, meanwhile, was slipping a tubular pink cap over the head of the nearest serpent. When it was in place, the cap began rhythmic contractions; the serpent's writhings became momentarily more intense, its fin moved convulsively, its tail lashed the ground. Then it grew calm. Kurtz removed the cap and slid it over the head of another serpent, and another, and another.

He was milking them of venom. These creatures were deadly to native metabolic systems, so it was said; they never attacked, but when provoked they struck, and the poison was universally effective. But what was poison on Holman's World was a blessing on Earth. The venom of the jungle serpents was one of the Company's most profitable exports. Properly distilled, diluted, crystallized, purified, the juice served as a catalyst in limb-regeneration work. A dose of it softened the resistance of the human cell to change, insidiously corrupting the cytoplasm, leading it to induce the nucleus to switch on its genetic material. And so it greatly encouraged the reawakening of cell division, the replication of bodily parts, when a new arm or leg or face had to be grown. How or why it worked, Gundersen knew not, but he had seen the stuff in action during his training period, when a fellow trainee had lost both legs below the knee in a soarer accident. The drug made the flesh flow. It liberated the guardians of the body's coded pattern, easing the task of the genetic surgeons tenfold by sensitizing and stimulating the zone of regeneration. Those legs had grown back in six months.

Gundersen continued to strum the guitar, Salamone to play his flute, Kurtz to collect the venom. Mooing sounds came suddenly from the bush; a herd of nildoror evidently had been drawn by the music as well. Gundersen saw them lumber out of the underbrush and stand almost shyly by the border of the clearing, nine of them. After a moment they entered into a clumsy, lurching, ponderous dance. Their trunks waved in time to the music; their tails swung; their spiny crests revolved. "All done." Kurtz announced. "Five liters—a good haul." The serpents, milked, drifted into the forest as soon as the music ceased. The nildoror stayed a while longer, peering intently at the men inside the station, but finally they left also. Kurtz and Salamone instructed Gundersen in the techniques of distilling the precious fluid, making it ready for shipment to Earth.

And that was all. He could see nothing scandalous in what had happened, and did not understand why there had been so much sly talk at headquarters about this place, nor why Salamone had tried to wring an oath of silence from him. He dared not ask. Three days later they again summoned the serpents, again collected their venom, and again the whole process seemed unexceptionable to Gundersen. But soon he came to realize that Kurtz and Salamone were testing his reliability before initiating him into their mysteries.

In the third week of his stint at the serpent station they finally admitted him to the inner knowledge. The collection was done: the serpents had gone; a few nildoror, out of more than dozen that had been attracted by that day's concert, still lingered outside the building. Gundersen realized that something unusual was about to happen when he saw Kurtz, after darting a sharp glance at Salamone, unhook a container of venom before it started on its route through the distilling apparatus. He poured it into a broad bowl that held at least a liter of fluid. On Earth, that much of the drug would be worth a year of Gundersen's salary as an assistant station agent. "Come with us," Kurtz said.

The three men stepped outside. At once three nildoror approached, behaving oddly, their spines upraised, their ears trembling. They seemed skittish and eager. Kurtz handed the

bowl of raw venom to Salamone, who sipped from it and
handed it back. Kurtz also drank. He gave the bowl to
Gundersen, saying, "Take communion with us?"

Gundersen hesitated. Salamone said, "It's safe. It can't
work on your nuclei when you take it internally."

Putting the bowl to his lips, Gundersen took a cautious
swig. The venom was sweet but watery.

"—only on your brain," Salamone added.

Kurtz gently took the bowl from him and set it down on the
ground. Now the largest nildor advanced and delicately dipped
his trunk into it. Then the second nildor drank, and the third.
The bowl now was empty.

Gundersen said, "If it's poisonous to native life—"

"Not when they drink it. Just when it's shot directly into
the bloodstream," Salamone said.

"What happens now?"

"Wait," Kurtz said, "and make your soul receptive to any
suggestions that arise."

Gundersen did not have to wait long. He felt a thickening
at the base of his neck and a roughness about his face, and his
arms seemed impossibly heavy. It seemed best to drop to his
knees as the effect intensified. He turned toward Kurtz,
seeking reassurance from those dark shining eyes, but Kurtz's
eyes had already begun to flatten and expand, and his green
and prehensile trunk nearly reached the ground. Salamone,
too, had entered the metamorphosis, capering comically,
jabbing the soil with his tusks. The thickening continued.
Now Gundersen knew that he weighed several tons, and he
tested his body's coordination, striding back and forth, learning how to move on four limbs. He went to the spring and
sucked up water in his trunk. He rubbed his leathery hide
against trees. He trumpeted bellowing sounds of joy in his
hugeness. He joined with Kurtz and Salamone in a wild
dance, making the ground quiver. The nildoror too were
transformed; one had become Kurtz, one had become Salamone,
one had become Gundersen, and the three former beasts
moved in wild pirouettes, tumbling and toppling in their
unfamiliarity with human ways. But Gundersen lost interest
in what the nildoror were doing. He concentrated solely on
his own experience. Somewhere at the core of his soul it
terrified him to know that this change had come over him and
he was doomed forever to live as a massive animal of the
jungle, shredding bark and ripping branches; yet it was

rewarding to have shifted bodies this way and to have access to an entirely new range of sensory data. His eyesight now was dimmed, and everything that he saw was engulfed in a furry halo, but there were compensations: he was able to sort odors by their directions and by their textures, and his hearing was immensely more sensitive. It was the equivalent of being able to see into the ultraviolet and the infrared. A dingy forest flower sent dizzying waves of sleek moist sweetness at him; the click of insect-claws in underground tunnels was like a symphony for percussion. And the bigness of him! The ecstasy of carrying such a body! His transformed consciousness soared, swooped, rose high again. He trampled trees and praised himself for it in booming tones. He grazed and gorged. Then he sat for a while, perfectly still, and meditated on the existence of evil in the universe, asking himself why there should be such a thing, and indeed whether evil in fact existed as an objective phenomenon. His answers surprised and delighted him, and he turned to Kurtz to communicate his insights, but just then the effect of the venom began to fade with quite startling suddenness, and in a short while Gundersen felt altogether normal again. He was weeping, though, and he felt an anguish of shame, as though he had been flagrantly detected molesting a child. The three nildoror were nowhere in sight. Salamone picked up the bowl and went into the station. "Come," Kurtz said. "Let's go in too."

They would not discuss any of it with him. They had let him share in it, but they would not explain a thing, cutting him off sternly when he asked. The rite was hermetically private. Gundersen was wholly unable to evaluate the experience. Had his body actually turned into that of a nildor for an hour? Hardly. Well, then, had his mind, his soul, somehow migrated into the nildor's body? And had the nildor's soul, if nildoror had souls, gone into his? What kind of sharing, what sort of union of innernesses, had occurred in that clearing?

Three days afterward, Gundersen applied for a transfer out of the serpent station. In those days he was easily upset by the unknown. Kurtz's only reaction, when Gundersen announced he was leaving, was a short brutal chuckle. The normal tour of duty at the station was eight weeks, of which Gundersen had done less than half. He never again served a stint there.

Later, he gathered what gossip he could about the doings at the serpent station. He was told vague tales of sexual

abominations in the grove, of couplings between Earthman
and nildor, between Earthman and Earthman; he heard
murmurs that those who habitually drank the venom underwent strange and terrible permanent changes of the body; he
heard stories of how the nildoror elders in their private
councils bitterly condemned the morbid practice of going to
the serpent station to drink the stuff the Earthmen offered.
But Gundersen did not know if any of these whispers were
true. He found it difficult, in later years, to look Kurtz in the
eye on the rare occasions when they met. Sometimes he
found it difficult even to live with himself. In some peripheral
way he had been tainted by his single hour of metamorphosis. He felt like a virgin who had stumbled into an orgy, and
who had come away deflowered but yet ignorant of what had
befallen her.

The phantoms faded. The sound of Kurtz's guitar diminished and was gone.

Srin'gahar said, "Shall we leave now?"

Gundersen slowly emerged from the ruined station. "Does
anyone gather the juices of the serpents today?"

"Not here," said the nildor. He knelt. The Earthman
mounted him, and in silence Srin'gahar carried him away,
back to the path they had followed earlier.

Four

In early afternoon they neared the nildoror encampment that
was Gundersen's immediate goal. For most of the day they
had been traveling across the broad coastal plain, but now the
back of the land dipped sharply, for this far inland there was a
long, narrow depression running from north to south, a deep
rift between the central plateau and the coast. At the approach to this rift Gundersen saw the immense devastation of
foliage that signaled the presence of a large nildoror herd
within a few kilometers. A jagged scar ran through the forest
from ground level to a point about twice a man's height.

Even the lunatic tropical fertility of this region could not
keep up with the nildoror appetite; it took a year or more for
such zones of defoliation to restore themselves after the herd

had moved on. Yet despite the impact of the herd, the forest
on all sides of the scar was even more close-knit here than on
the coastal plain to the east. This was a jungle raised to the
next higher power, damp, steamy, dark. The temperature was
considerably higher in the valley than at the coast, and
though the atmosphere could not possibly have been any
more humid here, there was an almost tangible wetness
about the air. The vegetation was different, too. On the plain
the trees tended to have sharp, sometimes dangerously sharp,
leaves. Here the foliage was rounded and fleshy, heavy sagging disks of dark blue that glistened voluptuously whenever
stray shafts of sunlight pierced the forest canopy overhead.

Gundersen and his mount continued to descend, following
the line of the grazing scar. Now they made their way along
the route of a stream that flowed perversely inland; the soil
was spongy and soft, and more often than not Srin'gahar
walked knee-deep in mud. They were entering a wide circular basin at what seemed to be the lowest point in the entire
region. Streams flowed into it on three or four sides, feeding
a dark weed-covered lake at the center; and around the
margin of the lake was Srin'gahar's herd. Gundersen saw
several hundred nildoror grazing, sleeping, coupling, strolling.

"Put me down," he said, taking himself by surprise. "I'll
walk beside you."

Wordlessly Srin'gahar allowed him to dismount.

Gundersen regretted his egalitarian impulse the moment
he stepped down. The nildor's broad-padded feet were able
to cope with the muddy floor; but Gundersen discovered that
he had a tendency to begin to sink in if he remained in one
place more than a moment. But he would not remount now.
Every step was a struggle, but he struggled. He was tense
and uncertain, too, of the reception he would get here, and
he was hungry as well, having eaten nothing on the long
journey but a few bitterfruits plucked from passing trees. The
closeness of the climate made each breath a battle for him.
He was greatly relieved when the footing became easier a
short distance down the slope. Here, a webwork of spongy
plants spreading out from the lake underwove the mud to
form a firm, if not altogether reassuring, platform a few
centimeters down.

Srin'gahar raised his trunk and sounded a trumpetblast of
greeting to the encampment. A few of the nildoror replied in
kind. To Gundersen, Srin'gahar said, "The many-born one

stands at the edge of the lake, friend of my journey. You see him, yes, in that group? Shall I lead you now to him?"

"Please," said Gundersen.

The lake was congested with drifting vegetation. Humped masses of it broke the surface everywhere: leaves like horns of plenty, cup-shaped spore-bodies, ropy tangled stems, everything dark blue against the lighter blue-green of the water. Through this maze of tight-packed flora there slowly moved huge semiaquatic mammals, half a dozen malidaror, whose tubular yellowish bodies were almost totally submerged. Only the rounded bulges of their backs and the jutting periscopes of their stalked eyes were in view, and now and then a pair of cavernous snorting nostrils. Gundersen could see the immense swaths that the malidaror had cut through the vegetation in this day's feeding, but at the far side of the lake the wounds were beginning to close as new growth hastened to fill the fresh gaps.

Gundersen and Srin'gahar went down toward the water. Suddenly the wind shifted, and Gundersen had a whiff of the lake's fragrance. He coughed; it was like breathing the fumes of a distillery vat. The lake was in ferment. Alcohol was a by-product of the respiration of these water-plants, and, having no outlet, the lake became one large tub of brandy. Both water and alcohol evaporated from it at a rapid pace, making the surrounding air not only steamy but potent; and during centuries when evaporation of water had exceeded the inflow from the streams, the proof of the residue had steadily risen. When the Company ruled this planet, such lakes had been the undoing of more than one agent, Gundersen knew.

The nildoror appeared to pay little heed to him as he came near them. Gundersen was aware that every member of the encampment was actually watching him closely, but they pretended to casualness and went about their business. He was puzzled to see a dozen brush shelters flanking one of the streams. Nildoror did not live in dwellings of any sort; the climate made it unnecessary, and besides they were incapable of constructing anything, having no organs of manipulation other than the three "fingers" at the tips of their trunks. He studied the crude lean-tos in bewilderment, and after a moment it dawned on him that he had seen structures of this sort before: they were the huts of sulidoror. The puzzle deepened. Such close association between the nildoror and the carnivorous bipeds of the mist country was unknown to him. Now he saw the sulidoror themselves, perhaps twenty of them, sitting crosslegged inside their huts. Slaves? Captives? Friends of the tribe? None of those ideas made sense.

"That is our many-born," Srin'gahar said, indicating with a wave of his trunk a seamed and venerable nildor in the midst of a group by the lakeshore.

Gundersen felt a surge of awe, inspired not only by the great age of the creature, but by the knowledge that this ancient beast, blue-gray with years, must have taken part several times in the unimaginable rites of the rebirth ceremony. The many-born one had journeyed beyond the barrier of spirit that held Earthmen back. Whatever nirvana the rebirth ceremony offered, this being had tasted it, and Gundersen had not, and that crucial distinction of experience made Gundersen's courage shrivel as he approached the leader of the herd.

A ring of courtiers surrounded the old one. They were gray-skinned and wrinkled, too: a congregation of seniors. Younger nildoror, of the generation of Srin'gahar, kept a respectful distance. There were no immature nildoror in the encampment at all. No Earthman had ever seen a young nildor. Gundersen had been told that the nildoror were always born in the mist country, in the home country of the sulidoror, and apparently they remained in close seclusion there until they had reached the nildoror equivalent of adolescence, when they migrated to the jungles of the tropics. He also had heard that every nildor hoped to go back to the mist country when its time had come to die. But he did not know if such things were true. No one did.

The ring opened, and Gundersen found himself facing the many-born one. Protocol demanded that Gundersen speak first; but he faltered, dizzied by tension perhaps, or perhaps by the fumes of the lake, and it was an endless moment before he pulled himself together.

He said at last, "I am Edmund Gundersen of the first birth, and I wish you joy of many rebirths, O wisest one."

Unhurriedly the nildor swung his vast head to one side, sucked up a snort of water from the lake, and squirted it into his mouth. Then he rumbled, "You are known to us, Edmundgundersen, from days past. You kept the big house of the Company at Fire Point in the Sea of Dust."

The nildor's sharpness of memory astonished and distressed him. If they remembered him so well, what chance did he have to win favors from these people? They owed him no kindnesses.

"I was there, yes, a long time ago," he said tightly.

"Not so long ago. Ten turnings is not a long time." The nildor's heavy-lidded eyes closed, and it appeared for some moments as though the many-born one had fallen asleep. Then the nildor said, eyes still closed, "I am Vol'himyor of the seventh birth. Will you come into the water with me? I grow tired easily on the land in this present birth of mine."

Without waiting, Vol'himyor strode into the lake, swimming slowly to a point some forty meters from shore and floating there, submerged up to the shoulders. A malidar that had been browsing on the weeds in that part of the lake went under with a bubbling murmur of discontent and reappeared far away. Gundersen knew that he had no choice but to follow the many-born one. He stripped off his clothing and walked forward.

The tepid water rose about him. Not far out, the spongy matting of fibrous stems below ground level gave way to soft warm mud beneath Gundersen's bare feet. He felt the occasional movement of small many-legged things under his soles. The roots of the water-plants swirled whip-like about his legs, and the black bubbles of alcohol that came up from the depths and burst on the surface almost stifled him with their release of vapor. He pushed plants aside, forcing his way through them with the greatest difficulty, and feeling a great relief when his feet lost contact with the mud. Quickly he paddled himself out to Vol'himyor. The surface of the water was clear there, thanks to the malidar. In the dark depths of the lake, though, unknown creatures moved to and fro, and every few moments something slippery and quick slithered along Gundersen's body. He forced himself to ignore such things.

Vol'himyor, still seemingly asleep, murmured, "You have been gone from this world for many turnings, have you not?"

"After the Company relinquished its rights here, I returned to my own world," said Gundersen.

Even before the nildor's eyelids parted, even before the round yellow eyes fixed coldly on him, Gundersen was aware that he had blundered.

"Your Company never had rights here to relinquish," said the nildor in the customary flat, neutral way. "Is this not so?"

"It is so," Gundersen conceded. He searched for a graceful

correction and finally said, "After the Company relinquished possession of this planet, I returned to my own world."

"Those words are more nearly true. Why, then, have you come back here?"

"Because I love this place and wish to see it again."

"Is it possible for an Earthman to feel love for Belzagor?"

"An Earthman can, yes."

"An Earthman can become *captured* by Belzagor," Vol'himyor said with more than usual slowness. "An Earthman may find that his soul has been seized by the forces of this planet and is held in thrall. But I doubt that an Earthman can feel love for this planet, as I understand your understanding of love."

"I yield the point, many-born one. My soul has become captured by Belzagor. I could not help but return."

"You are quick to yield such points."

"I have no wish to give offense."

"Commendable tact. And what will you do here on this world that has seized your soul?"

"Travel to many parts of your world," said Gundersen. "I wish particularly to go to the mist country."

"Why there?"

"It is the place that captures me most deeply."

"That is not an informative answer," the nildor said.

"I can give no other."

"What thing has captured you there?"

"The beauty of the mountains rising out of the mist. The sparkle of sunlight on a clear, cold, bright day. The splendor of the moons against a field of glittering snow."

"You are quite poetic," said Vol'himyor.

Gundersen could not tell if he were being praised or mocked.

He said, "Under present law, I must have the permission of a many-born one to enter the mist country. So I come to make application to you for such permission."

"You are fastidious in your respect for our law, my once-born friend. Once it was different with you."

Gundersen bit his lip. He felt something crawling up his calf, down in the depths of the lake, but he compelled himself to stare serenely at the many-born one. Choosing his words with care, he said, "Sometimes we are slow to understand the nature of others, and we give offense without knowing that we do so."

"It is so."

"But then understanding comes," Gundersen said, "and one feels remorse for the deeds of the past, and one hopes that one may be forgiven for his sins."

"Forgiveness depends on the quality of the remorse," said Vol'himyor, "and also on the quality of the sins."

"I believe my failings are known to you."

"They are not forgotten," said the nildor.

"I believe also that in your creed the possibility of personal redemption is not unknown."

"True. True."

"Will you allow me to make amends for my sins of the past against your people, both known and unknown?"

"Making amends for unknown sins is meaningless," said the nildor. "But in any case we seek no apologies. Your redemption from sin is your own concern, not ours. Perhaps you will find that redemption here, as you hope. I sense already a welcome change in your soul, and it will count heavily in your favor."

"I have your permission to go north, then?" Gundersen asked.

"Not so fast. Stay with us a while as our guest. We must think about this. You may go to shore, now."

The dismissal was clear. Gundersen thanked the many-born one for his patience, not without some self-satisfaction at the way he had handled the interview. He had always displayed proper deference toward many-born ones—even a really Kiplingesque imperialist knew enough to show respect for venerable tribal leaders—but in Company days it had never been more than a charade for him, a put-on show of humility, since ultimate power resided with the Company's sector agent, not with any nildor no matter how holy. Now, of course, the old nildor really did have the power to keep him out of the mist country, and might even see some poetic justice in banning him from it. But Gundersen felt that his deferential and apologetic attitude had been reasonably sincere just now, and that some of that sincerity had been communicated to Vol'himyor. He knew that he could not deceive the many-born one into thinking that an old Company hand like himself was suddenly eager to grovel before the former victims of Earth's expansionism; but unless some show of earnestness did come through, he stood no chance at all of gaining the permission he needed.

Abruptly, when Gundersen was still a good distance from

shore, something hit him a tremendous blow between the shoulders and flung him, stunned and gasping, face forward into the water.

As he went under, the thought crossed his mind that Vol'himyor had treacherously come up behind him and lashed him with his trunk. Such a blow could easily be fatal if aimed with real malice. Spluttering, his mouth full of the lake's liquor, his arms half numbed by the impact of the blow, Gundersen warily surfaced, expecting to find the old nildor looming above him ready to deliver the coup de grace.

He opened his eyes, with some momentary trouble focusing them. No, there was the many-born one far away across the water, looking in another direction. And then Gundersen felt a curious prickly premonition and got his head down just in time to avoid being decapitated by whatever it was that had hit him before. Huddling nose-deep in the water, he saw it swing by overhead, a thick yellowish rod like a broom out of control. Now he heard thunderous shrieks of pain and felt widening ripples sweeping across the lake. He glanced around.

A dozen sulidoror had entered the water and were killing a malidar. They had harpooned the colossal beast with sharpened sticks; now the malidar thrashed and coiled in its final agonies, and it was the mighty tail of the animal that had knocked Gundersen over. The hunters had fanned out in the shallows, waist-deep, their thick fur bedraggled and matted. Each group grasped the line of one harpoon, and they were gradually drawing the malidar toward shore. Gundersen was no longer in danger, but he continued to stay low in the water, catching his breath, rotating his shoulders to assure himself that no bones were broken. The malidar's tail must have given him the merest tip-flick the first time; he would surely have been destroyed the second time that tail came by, if he had not ducked. He was beginning to ache, and he felt half drowned by the water he had gulped. He wondered when he would start to get drunk.

Now the sulidoror had beached their prey. Only the malidar's tail and thick web-footed hind legs lay in the water, moving fitfully. The rest of the animal, tons of it, stretching five times the length of a man, was up on shore, and the sulidoror were methodically driving long stakes into it, one through each of the forelimbs and several into the broad wedge-shaped head. A few nildoror were watching the operation in mild curiosity.

Most ignored it. The remaining malidaror continued to browse in the woods as though nothing had happened.

A final thrust of a stake severed the malidar's spinal column. The beast quivered and lay still.

Gundersen hurried from the water, swimming quickly, then wading through the unpleasantly voluptuous mud, at last stumbling out onto the beach. His knees suddenly failed him and he toppled forward, trembling, choking, puking. A thin stream of fluid burst from his lips. Afterward he rolled to one side and watched the sulidoror cutting gigantic blocks of pale pink meat from the malidar's sides and passing them around. Other sulidoror were coming from the huts to share the feast. Gundersen shivered. He was in a kind of shock, and a few minutes passed before he realized that the cause of the shock was not only the blow he had received and the water he had swallowed, but also the knowledge that an act of violence had been committed in front of a herd of nildoror, and the nildoror did not seem at all disturbed. He had imagined that these peaceful, nonbelligerent creatures would react in horror to the slaughter of a malidar. But they simply did not care. The shock Gundersen felt was the shock of disillusionment.

A sulidor approached him and stood over him. Gundersen stared up uneasily at the towering shaggy figure. The sulidor held in its forepaws a gobbet of malidar meat the size of Gundersen's head.

"For you," said the sulidor in the nildoror language. "You eat with us?"

It did not wait for a reply. It tossed the slab of flesh to the ground next to Gundersen and rejoined its fellows. Gundersen's stomach writhed. He had no lust for raw meat just now.

The beach was suddenly very silent.

They were all watching him, sulidoror and nildoror both.

Five

Shakily Gundersen got to his feet. He sucked warm air into his lungs and bought a little time by crouching at the lake's edge to wash his face. He found his discarded clothing and consumed a few minutes by getting it on. Now he felt a little better; but the problem of the raw meat remained. The sulidoror, enjoying their feast, rending and tearing flesh and gnawing on bones, nevertheless frequently looked his way to see whether he would accept their hospitality. The nildoror, who of course had not touched the meat themselves, also seemed curious about his decision. If he refused the meat, would he offend the sulidoror? If he ate it, would he stamp himself as bestial in the eyes of the nildoror? He concluded that it was best to force some of the meat into him, as a gesture of good will toward the menacing-looking bipeds. The nildoror, after all, did not seem troubled that the sulidoror were eating meat; why should it bother them if an Earthman, a known carnivore, did the same?

He would eat the meat. But he would eat it as an Earthman would.

He ripped some leaves from the water-plant and spread them out to form a mat; he placed the meat on this. From his tunic he took his fusion torch, which he adjusted for wide aperture, low intensity, and played on the meat until its outer surface was charred and bubbling. With a narrower beam he cut the cooked meat into chunks he could manage. Then, squatting cross-legged, he picked up a chunk and bit into it.

The meat was soft and cheesy, interlaced by tough stringlike masses forming an intricate grid. By will alone Gundersen succeeded in getting three pieces down. When he decided he had had enough, he rose, called out his thanks to the sulidoror, and knelt by the side of the lake to scoop up some of the water. He needed a chaser.

During all this time no one spoke to him or approached him.

The nildoror had all left the water, for night was approaching. They had settled down in several groups well back from the shore. The feast of the sulidoror continued noisily, but was nearing its end; already several small scavenger-beasts had joined the party, and were at work at the lower half of the malidar's body while the sulidoror finished the other part.

Gundersen looked about for Srin'gahar. There were things he wished to ask.

It still troubled him that the nildoror had accepted the killing in the lake so coolly. He realized that he had somehow always regarded the nildoror as more noble than the other big beasts of this planet because they did not take life except

under supreme provocation, and sometimes not even then.
Here was an intelligent race exempt from the sin of Cain.
And Gundersen saw in that a corollary: that the nildoror,
because they did not kill, would look upon killing as a
detestable act. Now he knew that his reasoning was faulty
and even naïve. The nildoror did not kill simply because they
were not eaters of meat; but the moral superiority that he had
attributed to them on that score must in fact be a product of
his own guilty imagination.

The night came on with tropic swiftness. A single moon
glimmered. Gundersen saw a nildor he took to be Srin'gahar,
and went to him.

"I have a question, Srin'gahar, friend of my journey,"
Gundersen began. "When the sulidoror entered the water—"

The nildor said gravely, "You make a mistake. I am
Thali'vanoom of the third birth."

Gundersen mumbled an apology and turned away, aghast.
What a typically Earthman blunder, he thought. He remembered his old sector chief making the same blunder a dozen
dozen times, hopelessly confusing one nildor with another
and muttering angrily, "Can't tell one of these big bastards
from the next! Why don't they wear badges?" The ultimate
insult, the failure to recognize the natives as individuals.
Gundersen had always made it a point of honor to avoid such
gratuitous insults. And so, here, at this delicate time when he
depended wholly on winning the favor of the nildoror—

He approached a second nildor, and saw just at the last
moment that this one too was not Srin'gahar. He backed off as
gracefully as he could. On the third attempt he finally found
his traveling companion. Srin'gahar sat placidly against a
narrow tree, his thick legs folded beneath his body. Gundersen
put his question to him and Srin'gahar said, "Why should the
sight of violent death shock us? Malidaror have no *g'rakh*,
after all. And it is obvious that sulidoror must eat."

"No *g'rakh*?" Gundersen said. "This is a word I do not
know."

"The quality that separates the souled from the unsouled,"
Srin'gahar explained. "Without *g'rakh* a creature is but a
beast."

"Do sulidoror have *g'rakh*?"

"Of course."

"And nildoror also, naturally. But malidaror don't. What
about Earthmen?"

"It is amply clear that Earthmen have *g'rakh*."

"And one may freely kill a creature which lacks that quality?"

"If one has the need to do so, yes," said Srin'gahar. "These are elementary matters. Have you no such concepts on your own world?"

"On my world," said Gundersen, "there is only one species that has been granted *g'rakh*, and so perhaps we give such matters too little thought. We know that whatever is not of our own kind must be lacking in *g'rakh*."

"And so, when you come to another world, you have difficulty in accepting the presence of *g'rakh* in other beings?" Srin'gahar asked. "You need not answer. I understand."

"May I ask another question?" said Gundersen. "Why are there sulidoror here?"

"We allow them to be here."

"In the past, in the days when the Company ruled Belzagor, the sulidoror never went outside the mist country."

"We did not allow them to come here then."

"But now you do. Why?"

"Because now it is easier for us to do so. Difficulties stood in the way at earlier times."

"What kind of difficulties?" Gundersen persisted.

Softly Srin'gahar said, "You will have to ask that of someone who has been born more often than I. I am once-born, and many things are as strange to me as they are to you. Look, another moon is in the sky! At the third moon we shall dance."

Gundersen looked up and saw the tiny white disk moving rapidly, low in sky, seemingly skimming the fringe of the treetops. Belzagor's five moons were a random assortment, the closest one just outside Roche's Limit, the farthest so distant it was visible only to sharp eyes on a clear night. At any given time two or three moons were in the night sky, but the fourth and fifth moons had such eccentric orbits that they could never be seen at all from vast regions of the planet, and passed over most other zones no more than three or four times a year. One night each year all five moons could be seen at once, just along a band ten kilometers wide running at an angle of about forty degrees to the equator from northeast to southwest. Gundersen had experienced the Night of Five Moons only a single time.

The nildoror were starting to move toward the lakeshore now.

The third moon appeared, spinning retrograde into view from the south.

So he was going to see them dance again. He had witnessed their ceremonies once before, early in his career, when he was stationed at Shangri-la Falls in the northern tropics. That night the nildoror had massed just upstream of the falls, on both banks of Madden's River, and for hours after dark their blurred cries could be heard even above the roar of the water. And finally Kurtz, who was also stationed at Shangri-la then, said, "Come, let's watch the show!" and led Gundersen out into the night. This was six months before the episode at the serpent station, and Gundersen did not then realize how strange Kurtz was. But he realized it quickly enough after Kurtz joined the nildoror in their dance. The huge beasts were clustered in loose semicircles, stamping back and forth, trumpeting piercingly, shaking the ground, and suddenly there was Kurtz out there among them, arms upflung, bare chest beaded with sweat and shining in the moonlight, dancing as intensely as any of them, crying out in great booming roars, stamping his feet, tossing his head. And the nildoror were forming a group around him, giving him plenty of space, letting him enter fully into the frenzy, now running toward him, now backing away, a systole and diastole of ferocious power. Gundersen stood awed, and did not move when Kurtz called to him to join the dance. He watched for what seemed like hours, hypnotized by the boom boom *boom* boom of the dancing nildoror, until the end he broke from his trance, and searched for Kurtz and found him still in ceaseless motion, a gaunt bony skeletonic figure jerking puppet-like on invisible strings, looking fragile despite his extreme height as he moved within the circle of colossal nildoror. Kurtz could neither hear Gundersen's words nor take note of his presence, and finally Gundersen went back to the station alone. In the morning he found Kurtz, looking spent and worn, slumped on the bench overlooking the waterfall. Kurtz merely said, "You should have stayed. You should have danced."

Anthropologists had studied these rites. Gundersen had looked up the literature, learning what little there was to learn. Evidently the dance was preceded and surrounded by drama, a spoken episode akin to Earth's medieval mystery plays, a theatrical reenactment of some supremely important nildoror myth, serving both as mode of entertainment and as ecstatic religious experience. Unfortunately the language of the drama was an obsolete liturgical tongue, not a word of which could be understood by an Earthman, and the nildoror, who had not hesitated to instruct their first Earthborn visitors in their relatively simple modern language, had never offered any clue to the nature of the other one. The anthropological observers had noted one point which Gundersen now found cheering: invariably, within a few days after the performance of this particular rite, groups of nildoror from the herd performing it would set out for the mist country, presumably to undergo rebirth.

He wondered if the rite might be some ceremony of purification, some means of entering a state of grace before undergoing rebirth.

The nildoror all had gathered, now, beside the lake. Srin'gahar was one of the last to go. Gundersen sat alone on the slope above the basin, watching the massive forms assembling. The contrary motions of the moons fragmented the shadows of the nildoror, and the cold light from above turned their smooth green hides into furrowed black cloaks. Looking over to his left, Gundersen saw the sulidoror squatting before their huts, excluded from the ceremony but apparently not forbidden to view it.

In the silence came a low, clear, forceful flow of words. He strained to hear, hoping to catch some clue to the meaning, seeking a magical gateway that would let him burst through into an understanding of that secret language. But no understanding came. Vol'himyor was the speaker, the old many-born one, reciting words clearly familiar to everyone at the lake, an invocation, an introit. Then came a long interval of silence, and then came a response from a second nildor at the opposite end of the group, who exactly duplicated the rhythms and sinuosities of Vol'himyor's utterance. Silence again; and then a reply from Vol'himyor, spoken more crisply. Back and forth the center of the service moved, and the interplay between the two celebrants became what was for nildoror a surprisingly quick exchange of dialogue. About every tenth line the herd at large repeated what a celebrant had said, sending dark reverberations through the night.

After perhaps ten minutes of this the voice of a third solo nildor was heard. Vol'himyor made reply. A fourth speaker took up the recitation. Now isolated lines were coming in rapid bursts from many members of the congregation. No cue was missed; no nildor trampled on another's lines. Each seemed intuitively to know when to speak, when to stay silent. The tempo accelerated. The ceremony had become a mosaic of brief utterances blared forth from every part of the group in a random rotation. A few of the nildoror were up and moving slowly in place, lifting their feet, putting them down.

Lightning speared through the sky. Despite the closeness of the atmosphere, Gundersen felt a chill. He saw himself as a wanderer on a prehistoric Earth, spying on some grotesque conclave of mastodons. All the things of man seemed infinitely far away now. The drama was reaching some sort of climax. The nildoror were bellowing, stamping, calling to one another with tremendous snorts. They were taking up formations, assembling in aisled rows. Still there came utterances and responses, antiphonal amplifications of words heavy with strange significance. The air grew more steamy. Gundersen could no longer hear individual words, only rich deep chords of massed grunts, ah ah *ah* ah, ah ah *ah* ah, the old rhythm that he remembered from the night at Shangri-la Falls. It was a breathy, gasping sound now, ecstatic, an endless chuffing pattern of exhalations, ah ah *ah* ah, ah ah *ah* ah, ah ah *ah* ah, with scarcely a break between each group of four beats, and the whole jungle seemed to echo with it. The nildoror had no musical instruments whatever, yet to Gundersen it appeared that vast drums were pounding out that hypnotically intense rhythm. Ah ah *ah* ah. Ah ah *ah* ah. AH AH *AH* AH! AH AH *AH* AH!

And the nildoror were dancing.

Down below on the margin of the lake moved scores of great shadowy shapes, prancing like gazelles, two running steps forward, stamp down hard on the third step, regain the balance on the fourth. The universe trembled. Boom boom *boom* boom, boom boom *boom* boom. The earlier phase of the ceremony, the dramatic dialogue, which might have been some sort of subtle philosophical disquisition, had given way totally to this primeval pounding, this terrifying shuffling of gigantic elephantine bodies. Boom boom *boom* boom. Gundersen looked to his left and saw the sulidoror entranced, hairy heads switching back and forth in the rhythm of the dance; but not one of the bipeds had risen from the cross-legged posture. They were content to rock and nod, and now and then to pound their elbows on the ground.

Gundersen was cut off from his own past, even from a

sense of his own kinship to his species. Disjointed memories floated up. Again he was at the serpent station, a prisoner of the hallucinatory venom, feeling himself transformed into a nildor and capering thickly in the grove. Again he stood by the bank of the great river, seeing another performance of this very dance. And also he remembered nights spent in the safety of Company stations deep in the forest, among his own kind, when they had listened to the sound of stamping feet in the distance. All those other times Gundersen had drawn back from whatever strangeness this planet was offering him; he had transferred out of the serpent station rather than taste the venom a second time, he had refused Kurtz's invitation to join the dance, he had remained within the stations when the rhythmic poundings began in the forest. But tonight he felt little allegiance to mankind. He found himself longing to join that black and incomprehensible frenzy at the lakeshore. Something monstrous was running free within him, liberated by the incessant repetition of that boom boom *boom* boom. But what right had he to caper Kurtzlike in an alien ceremony? He did not intrude on their ritual.

Yet he discovered that he was walking down the spongy slope toward the place where the massed nildoror cavorted.

If he could think of them only as leaping, snorting elephants it would be all right. If he could think of them even as savages kicking up a row it would be all right. But the suspicion was unavoidable that this ceremony of words and dancing held intricate meanings for these people, and that was the worst of it. They might have thick legs and short necks and long dangling trunks, but that did not make them elephants, for their triple tusks and spiny crests and alien anatomies said otherwise; and they might be lacking in all technology, lacking even in a written language, but that did not make them savages, for the complexity of their minds said otherwise. They were creatures who possessed g'rakh. Gundersen remembered how he had innocently attempted to instruct the nildoror in the arts of terrestrial culture, in an effort to help them "improve" themselves; he had wanted to humanize them, to lift their spirits upward, but nothing had come of that, and now he found his own spirit being drawn—downward?—certainly to their level, wherever that might lie. Boom boom *boom* boom. His feet hesitantly traced out the four-step as he continued down the slope toward the lake. Did he dare? Would they crush him as blasphemous?

They had let Kurtz dance. They had let Kurtz dance.

It had been a different latitude, a long time ago, and other nildoror had been involved, but they had let Kurtz dance.

"Yes," a nildor called to him. "Come, dance with us!"

Was it Vol'himyor? Was it Srin'gahar? Was it Thali'vanoom of the third birth? Gundersen did not know which of them had spoken. In the darkness, in the sweaty haze, he could not see clearly, and all these giant shapes looked identical. He reached the bottom of the slope. Nildoror were everywhere about him, tracing out passages in their private journeys from point to point on the lakeshore. Their bodies emitted acrid odors, which, mixing with the fumes of the lake, choked and dizzied him. He heard several of them say to him, "Yes, yes, dance with us!"

And he danced.

He found an open patch of marshy soil and laid claim to it, moving forward, then backward, covering and recovering his one little tract in his fervor. No nildoror trespassed on him. His head tossed; his eyes rolled; his arms dangled; his body swayed and rocked; his feet carried him untiringly. Now he sucked in the thick air. Now he cried out in strange tongues. His skin was on fire; he stripped away his clothing, but it made no difference. Boom boom *boom* boom. Even now, a shred of his old detachment was left, enough so that he could marvel at the spectacle of himself dancing naked amid a herd of giant alien beasts. Would they, in their ultimate transports of passion, sweep in over his plot and crush him into the muck? Surely it was dangerous to stay here in the heart of the herd. But he stayed. Boom boom *boom* boom, again, again, yet again. As he whirled he looked out over the lake, and by sparkling refracted moonslight he saw the malidaror placidly munching the weeds, heedless of the frenzy on land. They are without *g'rakh*, he thought. They are beasts, and when they die their leaden spirits go downward to the earth. Boom. Boom. BOOM. Boom.

He became aware that glossy shapes were moving along the ground, weaving warily between the rows of dancing nildoror. The serpents! This music of pounding feet had summoned them from the dense glades where they lived.

The nildoror seemed wholly unperturbed that these deadly worms moved among them. A single stabbing thrust of the two spiny quills would bring even a mighty nildor toppling down; but no matter. The serpents were welcome, it appeared.

They glided toward Gundersen, who knew he was in no mortal danger from their venom, but who did not seek another encounter with it. He did not break the stride of his dance, though, as five of the thick pink creatures wriggled past him. They did not touch him.

The serpents passed through, and were gone. And still the uproar continued. And still the ground shook. Gundersen's heart hammered, but he did not pause. He gave himself up fully, blending with those about him, sharing as deeply as he was able to share it the intensity of the experience.

The moons set. Early streaks of dawn stained the sky.

Gundersen became aware that he no longer could hear the thunder of stamping feet. He danced alone. About him, the nildoror had settled down, and their voices again could be heard, in that strange unintelligible litany. They spoke quietly but with great passion. He could no longer follow the patterns of their words; everything merged into an echoing rumble of tones, without definition, without shape. Unable to halt, he jerked and twisted through his obsessive gyration until the moment that he felt the first heat of the morning sun.

Then he fell exhausted, and lay still, and slipped down easily into sleep.

Six

When he woke it was some time after midday. The normal life of the encampment had resumed; a good many of the nildoror were in the lake, a few were munching on the vegetation at the top of the slope, and most were resting in the shade. The only sign of last night's frenzy was in the spongy turf near the lakeshore, which was terribly scuffed and torn.

Gundersen felt stiff and numb. Also he was abashed, with the embarrassment of one who has thrown himself too eagerly into someone else's special amusement. He could hardly believe that he had done what he knew himself to have done. In his shame he felt an immediate impulse to leave the encampment at once, before the nildoror could show him their contempt for an Earthman capable of making himself a thrall to their festivity, capable of allowing himself to be beguiled by their incantations. But he shackled the thought, remembering that he had a purpose in coming here.

He limped down to the lake and waded out until its water came up to his breast. He soaked a while, and washed away the sweat of the night before. Emerging, he found his clothing and put it on.

A nildor came to him and said, "Vol'himyor will speak to you now."

The many-born one was halfway up the slope. Coming before him, Gundersen could not find the words of any of the greetings formulas, and simply stared raggedly at the old nildor until Vol'himyor said, "You dance well, my once-born friend. You dance with joy. You dance with love. You dance like a nildor, do you know that?"

"It is not easy for me to understand what happened to me last night," said Gundersen.

"You proved to us that our world has captured your spirit."

"Was it offensive to you that an Earthman danced among you?"

"If it had been offensive," said Vol'himyor slowly, "you would not have danced among us." There was a long silence. Then the nildor said, "We will make a treaty, we two. I will give you permission to go into the mist country. Stay there until you are ready to come out. But when you return, bring with you the Earthman known as Cullen, and offer him to the northernmost encampment of nildoror, the first of my people that you find. Is this agreed?"

"Cullen?" Gundersen asked. Across his mind flared the image of a short broad-faced man with fine golden hair and mild green eyes. "Cedric Cullen, who was here when I was here?"

"The same man."

"He worked with me when I was at the station in the Sea of Dust."

"He lives now in the mist country," Vol'himyor said, "having gone there without permission. We want him."

"What has he done?"

"He is guilty of a grave crime. Now he has taken sanctuary among the sulidoror, where we are unable to gain access to him. It would be a violation of our covenant with them if we removed this man ourselves. But we may ask you to do it."

Gundersen frowned. "You won't tell me the nature of his crime?"

"Does it matter? We want him. Our reasons are not trifling ones. We request you to bring him to us."

"You're asking one Earthman to seize another and turn him in for punishment," said Gundersen. "How am I to know where justice lies in this affair?"

"Under the treaty of relinquishment, are we not the arbiters of justice on this world?" asked one nildor.

Gundersen admitted that this was so.

"Then we hold the right to deal with Cullen as he deserves," Vol'himyor said.

That did not, of course, make it proper for Gundersen to act as catspaw in handing his old comrade over to the nildoror. But Vol'himyor's implied threat was clear: do as we wish, or we grant you no favors.

Gundersen said, "What punishment will Cullen get if he falls into your custody?"

"Punishment? Punishment? Who speaks of punishment?"

"If the man's a criminal—"

"We wish to purify him," said the many-born one. "We desire to cleanse his spirit. We do not regard that as punishment."

"Will you injure him physically in any way?"

"It is not to be thought."

"Will you end his life?"

"Can you mean such a thing? Of course not."

"Will you imprison him?"

"We will keep him in custody," said Vol'himyor, "for however long the rite of purification takes. I do not think it will take long. He will swiftly be freed, and he will be grateful to us."

"I ask you once more to tell me the nature of his crime."

"He will tell you that himself," the nildor said. "It is not necessary for me to make his confession for him."

Gundersen considered all aspects of the matter. Shortly he said, "I agree to our treaty, many-born one, but only if I may add several clauses."

"Go on."

"If Cullen will not tell me the nature of his crime, I am released from my obligation to hand him over."

"Agreed."

"If the sulidoror object to my taking Cullen out of the mist
country, I am released from my obligation also."

"They will not object. But agreed."

"If Cullen must be subdued by violence in order to bring
him forth, I am released."

The nildor hesitated a moment. "Agreed," he said finally.

"I have no other conditions to add."

"Then our treaty is made," Vol'himyor said. "you may
begin your northward journey today. Five of our once-born
ones must also travel to the mist country, for their time of
rebirth has come, and if you wish they will accompany you
and safeguard you along the way. Among them is Srin'gahar,
whom you already know."

"Will it be troublesome for them to have me with them?"

"Srin'gahar has particularly requested the privilege of serving as your guardian," said Vol'himyor. "But we would not
compel you to accept his aid, if you would rather make your
journey alone."

"It would be an honor to have his company," Gundersen
said.

"So be it, then."

A senior nildor summoned Srin'gahar and the four others
who would be going toward rebirth. Gundersen was gratified
at this confirmation of the existing data: once more the
frenzied dance of the nildoror had preceded the departure of
a group bound for rebirth.

It pleased him, too, to know that he would have a nildoror
escort on the way north. There was only one dark aspect to
the treaty, that which involved Cedric Cullen. He wished he
had not sworn to barter another Earthman's freedom for his
own safe-conduct pass. But perhaps Cullen had done something really loathsome, something that merited punishment—
or purification, as Vol'himyor put it. Gundersen did not
understand how that normally sunny man could have become
a criminal and a fugitive, but Cullen had lived on this world a
long time, and the strangeness of alien worlds ultimately
corroded even the brightest souls. In any case, Gundersen
felt that he had opened enough honorable exits for himself if
he needed to escape from his treaty with Vol'himyor.

Srin'gahar and Gundersen went aside to plan their route.
"Where in the mist country do you intend to go?" the nildor
asked.

"It does not matter. I just want to enter it. I suppose I'll have to go wherever Cullen is."

"Yes. But we do not know exactly where he is, so we will have to wait until we are there to learn it. Do you have special places to visit on the way north?"

"I want to stop at the Earthman stations," Gundersen said. "Particularly at Shangri-la Falls. So my idea is that we'll follow Madden's River northwestward, and—"

"These names are unknown to me."

"Sorry. I guess they've all reverted back to nildororu names. And I don't know those. But wait—" Seizing a stick, Gundersen scratched a hasty but serviceable map of Belzagor's western hemisphere in the mud. Across the waist of the disk he drew the thick swath of the tropics. At the right side he gouged out a curving bite to indicate the ocean; on the left he outlined the Sea of Dust. Above and below the band of the tropics he drew the thinner lines representing the northern and southern mist zones, and beyond them he indicated the gigantic icecaps. He marked the spaceport and the hotel at the coast with an X, and cut a wiggly line up from there, clear across the tropics into the northern mist country, to show Madden's River. At the midway point of the river he placed a dot to mark Shangri-la Falls. "Now," said Gundersen, "If you follow the tip of my stick—"

"What are those marks on the ground?" asked Srin'gahar.

A map of your planet, Gundersen wanted to say. But there was no nildororu word in his mind for "map." He found that he also lacked words for "image," "picture," and similar concepts. He said lamely, "This is your world. This is Belzagor, or at least half of it. See, this is the ocean, and the sun rises here, and—"

"How can this be my world, these marks, when my world is so large?"

"This is *like* your world. Each of these lines, here, stands for a place on your world. You see, here, the big river that runs out of the mist country and comes down to the coast, where the hotel is, yes? And this mark is the spaceport. These two lines are the top and the bottom of the northern mist country. The—"

"It takes a strong sulidor a march of many days to cross the northern mist country," said Srin'gahar. "I do not understand how you can point to such a small space and tell me it is the northern mist country. Forgive me, friend of my journey. I am very stupid."

Gundersen tried again, attempting to communicate the nature of the marks on the ground. But Srin'gahar simply could not comprehend the idea of a map, nor could he see how scratched lines could represent places. Gundersen considered asking Vol'himyor to help him, but rejected that plan when he realized that Vol'himyor, too, might not understand; it would be tactless to expose the many-born one's ignorance in any area. The map was a metaphor of place, an abstraction from reality. Evidently even beings possessing g'rakh might not have the capacity to grasp such abstractions.

He apologized to Srin'gahar for his own inability to express concepts clearly, and rubbed out the map with his boot. Without it, planning the route was somewhat more difficult, but they found ways to communicate. Gundersen learned that the great river at whose mouth the hotel was situated was called the Seran'nee in nildororu, and that the place where the river plunged out of the mountains into the coastal plain, which Earthmen knew as Shangri-la Falls, was Du'jayukh to nildoror. Then it was simple for them to agree to follow the Seran'nee to its source, with a stop at Du'jayukh and at any other settlement of Earthmen that happened to lie conveniently on the path north.

While this was being decided, several of the sulidoror brought a late breakfast of fruit and lake fish to Gundersen, exactly as though they recognized his authority under the Company. It was a curiously anachronistic gesture, almost servile, not at all like the way in which they had tossed him a raw slab of malidar meat the day before. Then they had been testing him, even taunting him; now they were waiting upon him. He was uncomfortable about that, but he was also quite hungry, and he made a point of asking Srin'gahar to tell him the sulidororu words of thanks. There was no sign that the powerful bipeds were pleased or flattered or amused by his use of their language, though.

They began their journey in late afternoon. The five nildoror moved in single file, Srin'gahar at the back of the group with Gundersen perched on his back; the Earthman did not appear to be the slightest burden for him. Their path led due north along the rim of the great rift, with the mountains that guarded the central plateau rising on their left. By the light of the sinking sun Gundersen stared toward that plateau. Down here in the valley, his surroundings had a certain familiarity; making the necessary allowances for the native plants and animals, he might almost be in some steamy jungle of South America. But the plateau appeared truly alien. Gundersen eyed the thick tangles of spiky purplish moss that festooned and nearly choked the trees along the top of the rift wall. The way the parasitic growth drowned its hosts the trees seemed grisly to him. The wall itself, of some soapy gray-green rock, dotted with angry blotches of crimson lichen and punctuated every few hundred meters by long ropy strands of a swollen blue fungus, cried out its other-worldliness: the soft mineral had never felt the impact of raindrops, but had been gently carved and shaped by the humidity alone, taking on weird knobbinesses and hollows over the millennia. Nowhere on Earth could one see a rock wall like that, serpentine and involute and greasy.

The forest beyond the wall looked impenetrable and vaguely sinister. The silence, the heavy and sluggish air, the sense of dark strangeness, the flexible limbs of the glossy trees bowed almost to the ground by moss, the occasional distant snort of some giant beast, made the central plateau seem forbidding and hostile. Few Earthmen had ever entered it, and it had never been surveyed in detail. The Company once had had some plans for stripping away large patches of jungle up there and putting in agricultural settlements, but nothing had come of the scheme, because of relinquishment. Gundersen had been in the plateau country only once, by accident, when his pilot had had to make a forced landing en route from coastal headquarters to the Sea of Dust. Seena had been with him. They spent a night and a day in that forest, Seena terrified from the moment of landing, Gundersen comforting her in a standard manly way but finding that her terror was somehow contagious. The girl trembled as one alien happening after another presented itself, and shortly Gundersen was on the verge of trembling too. They watched, fascinated and repelled, while an army of innumerable insects with irides-cent hexagonal bodies and long hairy legs strode with mania-cal persistence into a sprawling glade of tigermoss; for hours the savage mouths of the carnivorous plants bit the shining insects into pieces and devoured them, and still the horde marched on to destruction. At last the moss was so glutted that it went into sporulation, puffing up cancerously and sending milky clouds of reproductive bodies spewing into the air. By morning the whole field of moss lay deflated and helpless, and tiny green reptiles with broad rasping tongues

moved in to devour every strand, laying bare the soil for a
new generation of flora. And then there were the feathery
jelly-like things, streaked with blue and red, that hung in
billowing cascades from the tallest trees, trapping unwary
flying creatures. And bulky rough-skinned beasts as big as
rhinos, bearing mazes of blue antlers with interlocking tines,
grubbed for roots a dozen meters from their camp, glaring
sourly at the strangers from Earth. And long-necked browsers
with eyes like beacons munched on high leaves, squirting
barrelfuls of purple urine from openings at the bases of their
taut throats. And dark fat otter-like beings ran chattering
past the stranded Earthmen, stealing anything within quick grasp.
Other animals visited them also. This planet, which had
never known the hunter's hand, abounded in big mammals.
He and Seena and the pilot had seen more grotesqueness in a
day and a night than they had bargained for when they signed
up for outworld service.

"Have you ever been in there?" Gundersen asked Srin'gahar,
as night began to conceal the rift wall.

"Never. My people seldom enter that land."

"Occasionally, flying low over the plateau, I used to see
nildoror encampments in it. Not often, but sometimes. Do
you mean that your people no longer go there?"

"No," said Srin'gahar. "A few of us have need to go to the
plateau, but most do not. Sometimes the soul grows stale,
and one must change one's surroundings. If one is not ready
for rebirth, one goes to the plateau. It is easier to confront
one's own soul in there, and to examine it for flaws. Can you
understand what I say?"

"I think so," Gundersen said. "It's like a place of pilgrimage, then—a place of purification?"

"In a way."

"But why have the nildoror never settled permanently up
there? There's plenty of food—the climate is warm—"

"It is not a place where *g'rakh* rules" the nildor replied.

"Is it dangerous to nildoror? Wild animals, poisonous plants,
anything like that?"

"No, I would not say that. We have no fear of the plateau,
and there is no place on this world that is dangerous to us.
But the plateau does not interest us, except those who have
the special need of which I spoke. As I say, *g'rakh* is foreign
to it. Why should we go there? There is room enough for us
in the lowlands."

The plateau is too alien even for them, Gundersen thought. They prefer their nice little jungle. How curious!

He was not sorry when darkness hid the plateau from view. They made camp that night beside a hissing-hot stream. Evidently its waters issued from one of the underground cauldrons that were common in this sector of the continent; Srin'gahar said that the source lay not far to the north. Clouds of steam rose from the swift flow; the water, pink with high-temperature microorganisms, bubbled and boiled. Gundersen wondered if Srin'gahar had chosen this stopping place especially for his benefit, since nildoror had no use for hot water, but Earthmen notoriously did.

He scrubbed his face, taking extraordinary pleasure in it, and supplemented a dinner of food capsules and fresh fruit with a stew of greenberry roots—delectable when boiled, poisonous otherwise. For shelter while sleeping Gundersen used a monomolecular jungle blanket that he had stowed in his backpack, his one meager article of luggage on this journey. He draped the blanket over a tripod of boughs to keep away nightflies and other noxious insects, and crawled under it. The ground, thickly grassed, was a good enough mattress for him.

The nildoror did not seem disposed toward conversation. They left him alone. All but Srin'gahar moved several hundred meters upstream for the night. Srin'gahar settled down protectively a short distance from Gundersen and wished him a good sleep.

Gundersen said, "Do you mind talking a while? I want to know something about the process of rebirth. How do you know, for instance, that your time is upon you? Is it something you feel within yourself, or is it just a matter of reaching a certain age? Do you—" He became aware that Srin'gahar was paying no attention. The nildor had fallen into what might have been a deep trance, and lay perfectly still.

Shrugging, Gundersen rolled over and waited for sleep, but sleep was a long time coming.

He thought a good deal about the terms under which he had been permitted to make this northward journey. Perhaps another many-born one would have allowed him to go into the mist country without attaching the condition that he bring back Cedric Cullen; perhaps he would not have been granted safe-conduct at all. Gundersen suspected that the results would have been the same no matter which encampment of nildoror he had happened to go to for his travel permission. Though the nildoror had no means of long-distance communication, no governmental structure in an Earthly sense, no more coherence as a race than a population of jungle beasts, they nevertheless were remarkably well able to keep in touch with one another and to strike common policies.

What was it that Cullen had done, Gundersen wondered, to make him so eagerly sought?

In the old days Cullen had seemed overwhelmingly normal: a cheerful, amiable ruddy man who collected insects, spoke no harsh words, and held his liquor well. When Gundersen had been the chief agent out at Fire Point, in the Sea of Dust, a dozen years before, Cullen had been his assistant. Months on end there were only the two of them in the place, and Gundersen had come to know him quite well, he imagined. Cullen had no plans for making a career with the Company; he said he had signed a six-year contract, would not renew, and intended to take up a university appointment when he had done his time on Holman's World. He was here only for seasoning, and for the prestige that accrues to anyone who has a record of outworld service. But then the political situation of Earth grew complex, and the Company was forced to agree to relinquish a great many planets that it had colonized. Gundersen, like most of the fifteen thousand Company people here, had accepted a transfer to another assignment. Cullen, to Gundersen's amazement, was among the handful who opted to stay, even though that meant severing his ties with the home world. Gundersen had not asked him why; one did not discuss such things. But it seemed odd.

He saw Cullen clearly in memory, chasing bugs through the Sea of Dust, killing bottle jouncing against his hip as he ran from one rock outcropping to the next—an overgrown boy, really. The beauty of the Sea of Dust was altogether lost on him. No sector of the planet was more truly alien, nor more spectacular: a dry ocean bed, greater in size than the Atlantic, coated with a thick layer of fine crystalline mineral fragments as bright as mirrors when the sun was on them. From the station at Fire Point one could see the morning light advancing out of the east like a river of flame, spilling forth until the whole desert blazed. The crystals swallowed energy all day, and gave it forth all night, so that even at

twilight the eerie radiance rose brightly, and after dark a
throbbing purplish glow lingered for hours. In this almost
lifeless but wondrously beautiful desert the Company had
mined a dozen precious metals and thirty precious and
semiprecious stones. The mining machines set forth from the
station on far-ranging rounds, grinding up loveliness and
returning with treasure; there was not much for an agent to
do there except keep inventory of the mounting wealth and
play host to the tourist parties that came to see the splendor
of the countryside. Gundersen had grown terribly bored, and
even the glories of the scenery had become tiresome to him;
but Cullen, to whom the incandescent desert was merely a
flashy nuisance, fell back on his hobby for entertainment, and
filled bottle after bottle with his insects. Were the mining
machines still standing in the Sea of Dust, Gundersen wondered, waiting for the command to resume operations? If the
Company had not taken them away after relinquishment,
they would surely stand there throughout all eternity, unrusting,
useless, amidst the hideous gouges they had cut. The machines had scooped down through the crystalline layer to the
dull basalt below, and had spewed out vast heaps of tailings
and debris as they gnawed for wealth. Probably the Company
had left the things behind, too, as monuments to commerce.
Machinery was cheap, interstellar transport was costly; why
bother removing them? "In another thousand years," Gundersen
once had said, "the Sea of Dust will all be destroyed and
there'll be nothing but rubble here, if these machines continue to chew up the rock at the present rate." Cullen had
shrugged and smiled. "Well, one won't need to wear these
dark glasses, then, once the infernal glare is gone," he had
said. "Eh?" And now the rape of the desert was over and the
machines were still; and now Cullen was a fugitive in the mist
country, wanted for some crime so terrible the nildoror would
not even give it a name.

Seven

When they took to the road in the morning it was Srin'gahar,
uncharacteristically, who opened the conversation.

"Tell me of elephants, friend of my journey. What do they look like, and how do they live?"

"Where did you hear of elephants?"

"The Earthpeople at the hotel spoke of them. And also in the past, I have heard the word said. They are beings of Earth that look like nildoror, are they not?"

"There is a certain resemblance," Gundersen conceded.

"A close one?"

"There are many similarities." He wished Srin'gahar were able to comprehend a sketch. "They are long and high in the body, like you, and they have four legs, and tails, and trunks. They have tusks, but only two, one here, one here. Their eyes are smaller and placed in a poor position, here, here. And here—" He indicated Srin'gahar's skullcrest. "Here they have nothing. Also their bones do not move as your bones do."

"It sounds to me," said Srin'gahar, "as though these elephants look very much like nildoror."

"I suppose they do."

"Why is this, can you say? Do you believe that we and the elephants can be of the same race?"

"It isn't possible," said Gundersen. "It's simply a—a—" He groped for words; the nildororu vocabulary did not include the technical terms of genetics. "Simply a pattern in the development of life that occurs on many worlds. Certain basic designs of living creatures recur everywhere. The elephant design—the nildoror design—is one of them. The large body, the huge head, the short neck, the long trunk enabling the being to pick up objects and handle them without having to bend—these things will develop wherever the proper conditions are found."

"You have seen elephants, then, on many other worlds?"

"On some," Gundersen said. "Following the same general pattern of construction, or at least some aspects of it, although the closest resemblance of all is between elephants and nildoror. I could tell you of half a dozen other creatures that seem to belong to the same group. And this is also true of many other life-forms—insects, reptiles, small mammals, and so on. There are certain niches to be filled on every world. The thoughts of the Shaping Force travel the same path everywhere."

"Where, then, are Belzagor's equivalents of men?"

Gundersen faltered. "I didn't say that there were exact equivalents everywhere. The closest thing to the human pattern on your planet, I guess, is the sulidoror. And they aren't very close."

"On Earth, the men rule. Here the sulidoror are the secondary race."

"An accident of development. Your *g'rakh* is superior to that of the sulidoror; on our world we have no other species that possesses *g'rakh* at all. But the physical resemblances between men and sulidoror are many. They walk on two legs; so do we. They eat both flesh and fruit; so do we. They have hands which can grasp things; so do we. Their eyes are in front of their heads; so are ours. I know, they're bigger, stronger, hairier, and less intelligent than human beings, but I'm trying to show you how patterns can be similar on different planets, even though there's no real blood relationship between—"

Srin'gahar said quietly. "How do you know that elephants are without *g'rakh?*"

"We—they—it's clear that—" Gundersen stopped, uneasy. After a pause for thought he said carefully, "They've never demonstrated any of the qualities of *g'rakh*. They have no village life, no tribal structure, no technology, no religion, no continuing culture."

"We have no village life and no technology," the nildor said. "We wander through the jungles, stuffing ourselves with leaves and branches. I have heard this said of us, and it is true."

"But you're different. You—"

"How are we different? Elephants also wander through jungles, stuffing themselves with leaves and branches, do they not? They wear no skins over their own skins. They make no machines. They have no books. Yet you admit that we have *g'rakh*, and you insist that they do not."

"They can't communicate ideas," said Gundersen desperately. "They can tell each other simple things, I guess, about food and mating and danger, but that's all. If they have a true language, we can't detect it. We're aware of only a few basic sounds."

"Perhaps their language is so complex that you are *unable* to detect it," Srin'gahar suggested.

"I doubt that. We were able to tell as soon as we got here that the nildoror speak a language; and we were able to learn it. But in all the thousands of years that men and elephants have been sharing the same planet, we've never been able to see a sign that they can accumulate and transmit abstract concepts. And that's the essence of having *g'rakh*, isn't it?"

"I repeat my statement. What if you are so inferior to your elephants that you cannot comprehend their true depths?"

"A cleverly put point, Srin'gahar. but I won't accept it as any sort of description of the real world. If elephants have *g'rakh*, why haven't they managed to get anywhere in their whole time on Earth? Why does mankind dominate the planet, with the elephants crowded into a couple of small corners and practically wiped out?"

"You kill your elephants?"

"Not any more. But there was a time when men killed elephants for pleasure, or for food, or to use their tusks for ornaments. And there was a time when men used elephants for beasts of burden. If the elephants had *g'rakh*, they—"

He realized that he had fallen into Srin'gahar's trap.

The nildor said, "On this planet, too, the 'elephants' let themselves be exploited by mankind. You did not eat us and you rarely killed us, but often you made us work for you. And yet you admit we are beings of *g'rakh*."

"What we did here," said Gundersen, "was a gigantic mistake, and when we came to realize it, we relinquished your world and got off it. But that still doesn't mean that elephants are rational and sentient beings. They're animals, Srin'gahar, big simple animals, and nothing more."

"Cities and machines are not the only achievements of *g'rakh*."

"Where are their spiritual achievements, then? What does an elephant believe about the nature of the universe? What does he think about the Shaping Force? How does he regard his own place in his society?"

"I do not know," said Srin'gahar. "And neither do you, friend of my journey, because the language of the elephants is closed to you. But it is an error to assume the absence of *g'rakh* where you are incapable of seeing it."

"In that case, maybe the malidaror have *g'rakh* too. And the venom-serpents. And the trees, and the vines, and—"

"No," said Srin'gahar. "On this planet, only nildoror and sulidoror possess *g'rakh*. This we know beyond doubt. On your world it is not necessarily the case that humans alone have the quality of reason."

Gundersen saw the futility of pursuing the point. Was Srin'gahar a chauvinist defending the spiritual supremacy of elephants throughout the universe, or was he deliberately adopting an extreme position to expose the arrogances and moral vulnerabilities of Earth's imperialism? Gundersen did not know, but it hardly mattered. He thought of Gulliver discussing the intelligence of horses with the Houyhnhnms.

"I yield the point," he said curtly. "Perhaps someday I'll bring an elephant to Belzagor, and let you tell me whether or not it has g'rakh."

"I would greet it as a brother."

"You might be unhappy over the emptiness of your brother's mind," Gundersen said. "You would see a being fashioned in your shape, but you wouldn't succeed in reaching its soul."

"Bring me an elephant, friend of my journey, and I will be the judge of its emptiness," said Srin'gahar. "But tell me one last thing, and then I will not trouble you: when your people call us elephants, it is because they think of us as mere beasts, yes? Elephants are 'big simple animals,' those are your words. Is this how the visitors from Earth see us?"

"They're referring only to the resemblance in form between nildoror and elephants. It's a superficial thing. They say you are *like* elephants."

"I wish I could believe that," the nildor said, and fell silent, leaving Gundersen alone with his shame and guilt. In the old days it had never been his habit to argue the nature of intelligence with his mounts. It had not even occurred to him then that such a debate might be possible. Now he sensed the extent of Srin'gahar's suppressed resentment. Elephants—yes, that was how he too had seen the nildoror. Intelligent elephants, perhaps. But still elephants.

In silence they followed the boiling stream northward. Shortly before noon they came to its source, a broad bowshaped lake pinched between a double chain of steeply rising hills. Clouds of oily steam rose from the lake's surface. Thermophilic algae streaked its waters, the pink ones forming a thin scum on top and nearly screening the meshed tangles of the larger, thicker blue-gray plants a short distance underneath.

Gundersen felt some interest in stopping to examine the lake and its unusual life-forms. But he was strangely reluctant to ask Srin'gahar to halt. Srin'gahar was not only his carrier, he was his companion on a journey; and to say, tourist-fashion, "Let's stop here a while," might reinforce the nildor's belief that Earthmen still thought of his people merely as beasts of burden. So he resigned himself to passing up this bit of sightseeing. It was not right, he told himself, that he should delay Srin'gahar's journey toward rebirth merely to gratify a whim of idle curiosity.

But as they were nearing the lake's farther curve, there came such a crashing and smashing in the underbrush to the east that the entire procession of nildoror paused to see what was going on. To Gundersen it sounded as if some prowling dinosaur were about to come lurching out of the jungle, some huge clumsy tyrannosaur inexplicably displaced in time and space. Then, emerging from a break in the row of hills, there came slowly across the bare soil flanking the lake a little snub-snouted vehicle, which Gundersen recognized as the hotel's beetle, towing a crazy primitive-looking appendage of a trailer, fashioned from raw planks and large wheels. Atop this jouncing, clattering trailer four small tents had been pitched, covering most of its area; alongside the tents, over the wheels, luggage was mounted in several racks; and at the rear, clinging to a railing and peering nervously about, were the eight tourists whom Gundersen had last seen some days earlier in the hotel by the coast.

Srin'gahar said, "Here are some of your people. You will want to talk with them."

The tourists were, in fact, the last species whatever that Gundersen wanted to see at this point. He would have preferred locusts, scorpions, fanged serpents, tyrannosaurs, toads, anything at all. Here he was coming from some sort of mystical experience among the nildoror, the nature of which he barely understood; here, insulated from his own kind, he rode toward the land of rebirth struggling with basic questions of right and wrong, of the nature of intelligence, of the relationship of human to nonhuman and of himself to his own past; only a few moments before he had been forced into an uncomfortable, even painful confrontation with that past by Srin'gahar's casual, artful questions about the souls of elephants; and abruptly Gundersen found himself once more among these empty, trivial human beings, these archetypes of the ignorant and blind tourist, and whatever individuality he had earned in the eyes of his nildor companion vanished instantly as he dropped back into the undifferentiated class of Earthmen. These tourists, some part of his mind knew, were not nearly as vulgar and hollow as he saw them; they were merely ordinary people, friendly, a bit foolish, overprivileged, probably quite satisfactory human beings within the context of their lives on Earth, and only seeming to be cardboard figurines here because they were essentially irrelevant to the planet they had chosen to visit. But he was not yet ready to have Srin'gahar lose sight of him as a person separate from all the other Earthmen who came to Belzagor, and he feared that the tide of bland chatter welling out of these people would engulf him and make him one of them.

The beetle, obviously straining to haul the trailer, came to rest a dozen meters from the edge of the lake. Out of it came Van Beneker, looking sweatier and seedier than usual. "All right," he called to the tourists. "Everyone down! We're going to have a look at one of the famous hot lakes!" Gundersen, high atop Srin'gahar's broad back, considered telling the nildor to move along. The other four nildoror, having satisfied themselves about the cause of the commotion, had already done that and were nearly out of view at the far end of the lake. But he decided to stay a while; he knew that a display of snobbery toward his own species would win him no credit with Srin'gahar.

Van Beneker turned to Gundersen and called out, "Morning, sir! Glad to see you! Having a good trip?"

The four Earth couples clambered down from their trailer. They were fully in character, behaving exactly as Gundersen's harsh image of them would have them behave: they seemed bored and glazed, surfeited with the alien wonders they had already seen. Stein, the helix-parlor proprietor, dutifully checked the aperture of his camera, mounted it in his cap, and routinely took a 360-degree hologram of the scene; but when the printout emerged from the camera's output slot a moment later he did not even bother to glance at it. The act of picture-taking, not the picture itself, was significant. Watson, the doctor, muttered a joyless joke of some sort to Christopher, the financier, who responded with a mechanical chuckle. The women, bedraggled and junglestained, paid no attention to the lake. Two simply leaned against the beetle and waited to be told what it was they were being shown, while the other two, as they became aware of Gundersen's presence, pulled facial masks from their backpacks and hurriedly slipped the thin plastic films over their heads so that they could present at least the illusion of properly groomed features before the handsome stranger.

"I won't stay here long," Gundersen heard himself promising Srin'gahar, as he dismounted.

Van Beneker came up to him. "What a trip!" the little man blurted. "What a stinking trip! Well, I ought to be used to it by now. How's everything been going for you, Mr. G?"

"No complaints." Gundersen nodded at the trailer. "Where'd you get that noisy contraption?"

"We built it a couple of years ago when one of the old cargo haulers broke down. Now we use it to take tourists around when we can't get any nildoror bearers."

"It looks like something out of the eighteenth century."

"Well, you know, sir, out here we don't have much left in the way of modern equipment. We're short of servos and hydraulic walkers and all that. But you can always find wheels and some planks around. We make do."

"What happened to the nildoror we were riding coming from the spaceport to the hotel? I thought they were willing to work for you."

"Sometimes yes, sometimes no," Van Beneker said. "They're unpredictable. We can't force them to work, and we can't hire them to work. We can only ask them politely, and if they say they're not available, that's it. Couple of days back, they decided they weren't going to be available for a while, so we had to get out the trailer." He lowered his voice. "If you ask me, it's on account of these eight baboons here. They think the nildoror don't understand any English, and they keep telling each other how terrible it is that we had to hand a planet as valuable as this over to a bunch of elephants."

"On the voyage out here," said Gundersen, "some of them were voicing quite strong liberal views. At least two of them were big pro-relinquishment people."

"Sure. Back on Earth they bought relinquishment as a political theory. 'Give the colonized worlds back to their long-oppressed natives,' and all that. Now they're out here and suddenly they've decided that the nildoror aren't 'natives,' just animals, just funny-looking elephants, and maybe we should have kept the place after all." Van Beneker spat. "And the nildoror take it all in. They pretend they don't understand the language, but they do, they do. You think they feel like hauling people like that on their backs?"

"I see," said Gundersen. He glanced at the tourists. They were eyeing Srin'gahar, who had wandered off toward the bush and was energetically ripping soft boughs loose for his midday meal. Watson nudged Miraflores, who quirked his lips and shook his head as if in disapproval. Gundersen could not hear what they were saying, but he imagined that they were expressing scorn for Srin'gahar's enthusiastic foraging. Evidently civilized beings were not supposed to pull their meals off trees with their trunks.

Van Beneker said, "You'll stay and have lunch with us, won't you, Mr. G?"

"That's very kind of you," Gundersen said.

He squatted in the shade while Van Beneker rounded up his charges and led them down to the rim of the steaming lake. When they were all there Gundersen rose and quietly affiliated himself with the group. He listened to the guide's spiel, but managed to train only half his attention on what was being said. "High-temperature life-zone . . . better than 70°C . . . more in some places, even above boiling, yet things live in it . . . special genetic adaptation . . . thermophilic, we call it, that is, heat-loving . . . the DNA doesn't get cooked, no, but the rate of spontaneous mutation is pretty damned high, and the species change so fast you wouldn't believe it . . . enzymes resist the heat . . . put the lake organisms in cool water and they'll freeze in about a minute . . . life processes extraordinarily fast . . . unfolded and denatured proteins can also function when circumstances are such that . . . you get quite a range up to middle-phylum level . . . a pocket environment, no interaction with the rest of the planet . . . thermal gradients . . . quantitative studies . . . the famous kinetic biologist, Dr. Brock . . . continuous thermal destruction of sensitive molecules . . . unending resynthesis. . . ."

Srin'gahar was still stuffing himself with branches. It seemed to Gundersen that he was eating far more than he normally did at this time of day. The sounds of rending and chewing clashed with the jerky drone of Van Beneker's memorized scientific patter.

Now, unhooking a biosensitive net from his belt, Van Beneker began to dredge up samples of the lake's fauna for the edification of his group. He gripped the net's handle and made vernier adjustments governing the mass and length of the desired prey; the net, mounted at the end of an almost infinitely expandable length of fine flexible metal coil, swept back and forth beneath the surface of the lake, hunting for organisms of the programmed dimensions. When its sensors told it that it was in the presence of living matter, its mouth snapped open and quickly shut again. Van Beneker retracted it, bringing to shore some unhappy prisoner trapped within a sample of its own scalding environment.

Out came one lake creature after another, red-skinned, boiled-looking, but live and angry and flapping. An armored fish emerged, concealed in shining plates, embellished with fantastic excrescences and ornaments. A lobster-like thing came forth, lashing a long spiked tail, waving ferocious eye-stalks. Up from the lake came something that was a single immense claw with a tiny vestigial body. No two of Van Beneker's grotesque catches were alike. The heat of the lake, he repeated, induces frequent mutations. He rattled off the whole genetic explanation a second time, while dumping one little monster back into the hot bath and probing for the next.

The genetic aspects of the thermophilic creatures seemed to catch the interest of only one of the tourists—Stein, who, as a helix-parlor owner specializing in the cosmetic editing of human genes, would know more than a little about mutation himself. He asked a few intelligent-sounding questions, which Van Beneker naturally was unable to answer; the others simply stared, patiently waiting for their guide to finish showing them funny animals and take them somewhere else. Gundersen, who had never had a chance before to examine the contents of one of these high-temperature pockets, was grateful for the exhibition, although the sight of writhing captive lake-dwellers quickly palled on him. He became eager to move on.

He glanced around and discovered that Srin'gahar was nowhere in sight.

"What we've got this time," Van Beneker was saying, "is the most dangerous animal of the lake, what we call a razor shark. Only I've never see one like this before. You see those little horns? Absolutely new. And that lantern sort of thing on top of the head, blinking on and off?" Squirming in the net was a slender crimson creature about a meter in length. Its entire underbelly, from snout to gut, was hinged, forming what amounted to one gigantic mouth rimmed by hundreds of needle-like teeth. As the mouth opened and closed, it seemed as if the whole animal were splitting apart and healing itself. "This beast feeds on anything up to three times its own size," Van Beneker said. "As you can see, it's fierce and savage, and—"

Uneasy, Gundersen drifted away from the lake to look for Srin'gahar. He found the place where the nildor had been eating, where the lower branches of several trees were stripped bare. He saw what seemed to be the nildor's trail, leading away into the jungle. A painful white light of desolation flared in his skull at the awareness that Srin'gahar must quietly have abandoned him.

In that case his journey would have to be interrupted. He did not dare go alone and on foot into that pathless wilderness ahead. He would have to ask Van Beneker to take him back to some nildoror encampment where he might find another means of getting to the mist country.

The tour group was coming up from the lake now. Van Beneker's net was slung over his shoulder; Gundersen saw some lake creatures moving slowly about in it.

"Lunch," he said. "I got us some jelly-crabs. You hungry?"

Gundersen managed a thin smile. He watched, not at all hungry, as Van Beneker opened the net; a gush of hot water rushed from it, carrying along eight or ten oval purplish creatures, each different from the others in the number of legs, shell markings, and size of claws. They crawled in stumbling circles, obviously annoyed by the relative coolness of the air. Steam rose from their backs. Expertly Van Beneker pithed them with sharpened sticks, and cooked them with his fusion torch, and split open their shells to reveal the pale quivering jelly-like metabolic regulators within. Three of the women grimaced and turned away, but Mrs. Miraflores took her crab and ate it with delight. The men seemed to enjoy it. Gundersen, merely nibbling at the jelly, eyed the forest and worried about Srin'gahar.

Scraps of conversation drifted toward him.

"—enormous profit potential, just wasted, altogether wasted—"

"—even so, our obligation is to encourage self-determination on every planet that—"

"—but are they *people*?"

"—look for the soul, it's the only way to tell that—"

"—elephants, and nothing but elephants. Did you see him ripping up the trees and—"

"—relinquishment was the fault of a highly vocal minority of bleeding hearts who—"

"—no soul, no relinquishment—"

"—you're being too harsh, dear. There were definite abuses on some of the planets, and—"

"—stupid political expediency, I call it. The blind leading the blind—"

"—can they write? Can they think? Even in Africa we were dealing with human beings, and even there—"

"—the soul, the inner spirit—"

"—I don't need to tell you how much I favored relinquishment. You remember, I took the petitions around and everything. But even so, I have to admit that after seeing—"

"—piles of purple crap on the beach—"

"—victims of sentimental overreaction—"

"—I understand the annual profit was on the order of—"

"—no doubt that they have souls. No doubt at all." Gundersen realized that his own voice had entered the conversation. The others turned to him; there was a sudden vacuum to fill. He said, "They have a religion, and that implies the awareness of the existence of a spirit, a soul, doesn't it?"

"What kind of religion?" Miraflores asked.

"I'm not sure. One important part of it is ecstatic dancing—a kind of frenzied prancing around that leads to some sort of mystic experience. I know. I've danced with them. I've felt at least the edges of that experience. And they've got a thing called rebirth, which I suppose is central to their rituals. I don't understand it. They go north, into the mist country, and something happens to them there. They've always kept the details a secret. I think the sulidoror give them something, some drug, maybe, and it rejuvenates them in some inner way, and leads to a kind of illumination—am I at all clear?" Gundersen, as he spoke, was working his way almost unconsciously through the pile of uneaten jelly-crabs. "All I can tell you is that rebirth is vitally important to them, and they seem to derive their tribal status from the number of rebirths they've undergone. So you see they're not just animals. They have a society, they have a cultural structure—complex, difficult for us to grasp."

Watson asked, "Why don't they have a civilization, then?"

"I've just told you that they do."

"I mean cities, machines, books—"

"They're not physically equipped for writing, for building things, for any small manipulations," Gundersen said. "Don't you see, they have no *hands*? A race with hands makes one kind of society. A race built like elephants makes another." He was drenched in sweat and his appetite was suddenly insatiable. The women, he noticed, were staring at him strangely. He realized why: he was cleaning up all the food in sight, compulsively stuffing it into his mouth. Abruptly his patience shattered and he felt that his skull would explode if he did not instantly drop all barriers and admit the one great guilt that by stabbing his soul had spurred him into strange odysseys. It did not matter that these were not the right people from whom to seek absolution. The words rushed uncontrollably upward to his lips and he said, "When I came here I was just like you. I underestimated the nildoror. Which led me into a grievous sin that I have to explain to you. You know, I was a sector administrator for a while, and one of my jobs was arranging the efficient deployment of native labor. Since we didn't fully understand that the nildoror were intelligent autonomous beings, we *used* them, we put them to work on heavy construction jobs, lifting girders with their trunks, anything we thought' they were capable of handling on sheer muscle alone. We just ordered them around as if they were machines." Gundersen closed his eyes and felt the past roaring toward him, inexorably, a black cloud of memory that enveloped and overwhelmed him, "The nildoror let us use them, God knows why. I guess we were the crucible in which their race had to be purged. Well, one day a dam broke, out in Monroe District up in the north, not far from where the mist country begins, and a whole thorn-bush plantation was in danger of flooding, at a loss to the Company of who knows how many millions. And the main power plant of the district was endangered too, along with our station headquarters and—let's just say that if we didn't react fast, we'd lose our entire investment in the north. My responsibility. I began conscripting nildoror to build a secondary line of dikes. We threw every robot we had into the job, but we didn't have enough, so we got the nildoror too, long lines of them plodding in from every part of the jungle, and we worked day and night until we were all ready to fall down dead. We were beating the flood, but I couldn't be sure of it. And on the sixth morning I drove out to the dike site to see if the next crest would break through, and there were seven nildoror I hadn't ever seen before, marching along a path going north. I told them to follow me. They refused, very gently. They said, no, they were on their way to the mist country for the rebirth ceremony, and they couldn't stop. Rebirth? What did I care about rebirth? I wasn't going to take that excuse from them, not when it looked like I might lose

my whole district. Without thinking I ordered them to report
for dike duty or I'd execute them on the spot. Rebirth can
wait, I said. Get reborn some other time. This is serious
business. They put their heads down and pushed the tips of
their tusks into the ground. That's a sign of great sadness
among them. Their spines drooped. Sad. Sad. We pity you,
one of them said to me, and I got angry and told him what he
could do with his pity. Where did he get the right to pity me?
Then I pulled my fusion torch. Go on, get moving, there's a
work crew that needs you. Sad. Big eyes looking pity at me.
Tusks in the ground. Two or three of the nildoror said they
were very sorry, they couldn't do any work for me now, it was
impossible for them to break their journey. But they were
ready to die right there, if I insisted on it. They didn't want
to hurt my prestige by defying me, but they *had* to defy me,
and so they were willing to pay the price. I was about to fry one,
as an example to the others, and then I stopped and said to
myself, what the hell am I doing, and the nildoror waited,
and my aides were watching and so were some of our other
nildoror, and I lifted the fusion torch again, telling myself that
I'd kill one of them, the one who said he pitied me, and
hoping that then the others would come to their senses. They
just waited. Calling my bluff. How could I fry seven pilgrims
even if they were defying a sector chief's direct order? But
my authority was at stake. So I pushed the trigger. I just gave
him a slow burn, not deep, enough to scar the hide, that was
all, but the nildor stood there taking it, and in another few
minutes I would have burned right through to a vital organ.
And so I soiled myself in front of them by using force. It was
what they had been waiting for. Then a couple of the nildoror
who looked older than the others said, Stop it, we wish to
reconsider, and I turned off the torch, and they went aside for
a conference. The one I had burned was hobbling a little, and
looked hurt, but he wasn't badly wounded, not nearly as
badly as I was. The one who pushes the trigger can get hurt
worse than his target, do you know that? And in the end the
nildoror all agreed to do as I asked. So instead of going north
for rebirth they went to work on the dike, even the burned
one, and nine days later the flood crest subsided and the
plantation and the power plant and all the rest were saved
and we lived happily ever after." Gundersen's voice trailed
off. He had made his confession, and now he could not face
these people any longer. He picked up the shell of the one

remaining crab and explored it for some scrap of jelly, feeling depleted and drained. There was an endless span of silence.

Then Mrs. Christopher said, "So what happened then?"

Gundersen looked up, blinking. He thought he had told it all.

"Nothing happened then," he said. "The flood crest subsided."

"But what was the point of the story?"

He wanted to hurl the empty crab in her tensely smiling face. "The point?" he said. "The point? Why—" He was dizzy, now. He said, "Seven intelligent beings were journeying toward the holiest rite of their religion, and at gunpoint I requisitioned their services on a construction job to save property that meant nothing to them, and they came and hauled logs for me. Isn't the point obvious enough? Who was spiritually superior there? When you treat a rational autonomous creature as though he's a mere beast, what does that make you?"

"But it was an emergency," said Watson. "You needed all the help you could get. Surely other considerations could be laid aside at a time like that. So they were nine days late getting to their rebirth. Is that so bad?"

Gundersen said hollowly, "A nildor goes to rebirth only when the time is ripe, and I can't tell you how they know the time is ripe, but perhaps it's astrological, something to do with the conjunction of the moons. A nildor has to get to the place of rebirth at the propitious time, and if he doesn't make it in time, he isn't reborn just then. Those seven nildoror were already late, because the heavy rains had washed out the roads in the south. The nine days more that I tacked on made them *too* late. When they were finished building dikes for me, they simply went back south to rejoin their tribe. I didn't understand why. It wasn't until much later that I found out that I had cost them their chance at rebirth and they might have to wait ten or twenty years until they could go again. Or maybe never get another chance." Gundersen did not feel like talking any more. His throat was dry. His temples throbbed. How cleansing it would be, he thought, to dive into the steaming lake. He got stiffly to his feet, and as he did so he noticed that Srin'gahar had returned and was standing motionless a few hundred meters away, beneath a mighty swordflower tree.

He said to the tourists, "The point is that the nildoror have religion and souls, and that they are people, and that if you

can buy the concept of relinquishment at all, you can't object
to relinquishing this planet. The point is also that when
Earthmen collide with an alien species they usually do so
with maximum misunderstanding. The point is furthermore
that I'm not surprised you think of the nildoror the way you
do, because I did too, and learned a little better when it was
too late to matter, and even so I didn't learn enough to do me
any real good, which is one of the reasons why I came back to
this planet. And I'd like you to excuse me now, because this is
the propitious time for me to move on, and I have to go." He
walked quickly away from them.

Approaching Srin'gahar, he said, "I'm ready to leave now."
The nildor knelt. Gundersen remounted.

"Where did you go?" the Earthman asked. "I was worried
when you disappeared."

"I felt that I should leave you alone with your friends," said
Srin'gahar. "Why did you worry? There is an obligation on me
to bring you safely to the country of the mist."

Eight

The quality of the land was undoubtedly changing. They
were leaving the heart of the equatorial jungle behind, and
starting to enter the highlands that led into the mist zone.
The climate here was still tropical, but the humidity was not
so intense; the atmosphere, instead of holding everything in a
constant clammy embrace, released its moisture periodically
in rain, and after the rain the texture of the air was clear and
light until its wetness was renewed. There was different
vegetation in this region: harsh-looking angular stuff, with
stiff leaves sharp as blades. Many of the trees had luminous
foliage that cast a cold light over the forest by night. There
were fewer vines here, and the treetops no longer formed a
continuous canopy shutting out most of the sunlight; splashes
of brightness dappled the forest floor, in some places extending
across broad open plazas and meadows. The soil, leached by
the frequent rains, was a pale yellowish hue, not the rich
black of the jungle. Small animals frequently sped through
the underbrush. At a slower pace moved solemn slug-like

creatures, blue-green with ebony mantles, which Gundersen recognized as the mobil fungoids of the highlands—plants that crawled from place to place in quest of fallen boughs or a lightning-shattered tree-trunk. Both nildoror and men considered their taste a great delicacy.

On the evening of the third day northward from the place of the boiling lake Srin'gahar and Gundersen came upon the other four nildoror, who had marched on ahead. They were camped at the foot of a jagged crescent-shaped hill, and evidently had been there at least a day, judging by the destruction they had worked upon the foliage all around their resting-place. Their trunks and faces, smeared and stained with luminous juices, glowed brightly. With them was a sulidor, by far the largest one Gundersen had ever seen, almost twice Gundersen's own height, with a pendulous snout the length of a man's forearm. The sulidor stood erect beside a boulder encrusted with blue moss, his legs spread wide and his tail, tripod fashion, bracing his mighty weight. Narrowed eyes surveyed Gundersen from beneath shadowy hoods. His long arms, tipped with terrifying curved claws, hung at rest. The fur of the sulidor was the color of old bronze, and unusually thick.

One of the candidates for rebirth, a female nildor called Luu'khamin, said to Gundersen, "The sulidor's name is Na-sinisul. He wishes to speak with you."

"Let him speak, then."

"He prefers that you know, first, that he is not a sulidor of the ordinary kind. He is one of those who administers the ceremony of rebirth, and we will see him again when we approach the mist country. He is a sulidor of rank and merit, and his words are not to be taken lightly. Will you bear that in mind as you listen to him?"

"I will. I take no one's words lightly on this world, but I will give him a careful hearing beyond any doubt. Let him speak."

The sulidor strode a short distance forward and once again planted himself firmly, digging his great spurred feet deep into the resilient soil. When he spoke, it was in nildororu stamped with the accent of the north: thick-tongued, slow, positive.

"I have been on a journey," said Na-sinisul, "to the Sea of Dust, and now I am returning to my own land to aid in the preparations for the event of rebirth in which these five

travelers are to take part. My presence here is purely acci-
dental. Do you understand that I am not in this place for any
particular purpose involving you or your companions?"

"I understand," said Gundersen, astounded by the precise
and emphatic manner of the sulidor's speech. He had known
the sulidoror only as dark, savage, ferocious-looking figures
lurking in mysterious glades.

Na-sinisul continued, "As I passed near here yesterday, I
came by chance to the site of a former station of your
Company. Again by chance, I chose to look within, though it
was no business of mine to enter that place. Within I found
two Earthmen whose bodies had ceased to serve them. They
were unable to move and could barely talk. They requested
me to send them from this world, but I could not do such a
thing on my own authority. Therefore I ask you to follow me
to this station and to give me instructions. My time is short
here, so it must be done at once."

"How far is it?"

"We could be there before the rising of the third moon."

Gundersen said to Srin'gahar, "I don't remember a Company station here. There should be one a couple of days north
of here, but—"

"This is the place where the food that crawls was collected
and shipped downriver," said the nildor.

"Here?" Gundersen shrugged. "I guess I've lost my bearings again. All right, I'll go there." To Na-sinisul he said,
"Lead and I'll follow."

The sulidor moved swiftly through the glowing forest, and
Gundersen atop Srin'gahar, rode just to his rear. They seemed
to be descending, and the air grew warm and murky. The
landscape also changed, for the trees here had aerial roots
that looped up like immense scraggy elbows, and the fine
tendrils sprouting from the roots emitted a harsh green
radiance. The soil was loose and rocky; Gundersen could hear
it crunching under Srin'gahar's tread. Bird-like things were
perched on many of the roots. They were owlish creatures
that appeared to lack all color; some were black, some white,
some a mottled black and white. He could not tell if that was
their true hue or if the luminosity of the vegetation simply
robbed them of color. A sickly fragrance came from vast,
pallid parasitic flowers sprouting from the trunks of the trees.

By an outcropping of naked, weathered yellow rock lay the
remains of the Company station. It seemed even more

thoroughly ruined than the serpent station far to the south;
the dome of its roof had collapsed and coils of wiry-stemmed
saprophytes were clinging to its sides, perhaps feeding on the
decomposition products that the rain eroded from the abrasions
in the plastic walls. Srin'gahar allowed Gundersen to dismount. The Earthman hesitated outside the building, waiting
for the sulidor to take the lead. A fine warm rain began to fall;
the tang of the forest changed at once, becoming sweet where
it had been sour. But it was the sweetness of decay.

"The Earthmen are inside," said Na-sinisul. "You may go
in. I await your instructions."

Gundersen entered the building. The reek of rot was far
more intense here, concentrated, perhaps, by the curve of
the shattered dome. The dampness was all-pervasive. He
wondered what sort of virulent spores he sucked into his
nostrils with every breath. Something dripped in the darkness, making a loud tocking sound against the lighter patter
of the rain coming through the gaping roof. To give himself
light, Gundersen drew his fusion torch and kindled it at the
lowest beam. The warm white glow spread through the
station. At once he felt a flapping about his face as some
thermotropic creature, aroused and attracted by the heat of
the torch, rose up toward it. Gundersen brushed it away;
there was slime on his fingertips afterward.

Where were the Earthmen?

Cautiously he made a circuit of the building. He remembered it vaguely, now—one of the innumerable bush stations
the Company once had scattered across Holman's World. The
floor was split and warped, requiring him to climb over the
buckled, sundered sections. The mobile fungoids crawled
everywhere, devouring the scum that covered all interior
surfaces of the building and leaving narrow glistening tracks
behind. Gundersen had to step carefully to avoid putting his
feet on the creatures, and he was not always successful. Now
he came to a place where the building widened, puckering
outward; he flashed his torch around and caught sight of a
blackened wharf, overlooking the bank of a swift river. Yes, he
remembered. The fungoids were wrapped and baled here
and sent downriver on their voyage toward the market. But
the Company's barges no longer stopped here, and the tasty
pale slugs now wandered unmolested over the mossy relics of
furniture and equipment.

"Hello?" Gundersen called. "Hello, hello, hello?"

He received a moan by way of answer. Stumbling and slipping in the dimness, fighting a swelling nausea, he forced his way onward through a maze of unseen obstacles. He came to the source of the loud dripping sound. Something bright red and basket-shaped and about the size of a man's chest had established itself high on the wall, perpendicular to the floor. Through large pores in its spongy surface a thick black fluid exuded, falling in a continuous greasy splash. As the light of Gundersen's torch probed it, the exudation increased, becoming almost a cataract of tallowy liquid. When he moved the light away the flow became less copious, though still heavy.

The floor sloped here so that whatever dripped from the spongy basket flowed quickly down, collecting at the far side of the room in the angle between the floor and the wall. Here Gundersen found the Earthmen. They lay side by side on a low mattress; fluid from the dripping thing had formed a dark pool around them, completely covering the mattress and welling up over the bodies. One of the Earthmen, head lolling to the side, had his face totally immersed in the stuff. From the other one came the moans.

They both were naked. One was a man, one a woman, though Gundersen had some difficulty telling that at first; both were so shrunken and emaciated that the sexual characteristics were obscured. They had no hair, not even eyebrows. Bones protruded through parchment-like skin. The eyes of both were open, but were fixed in a rigid, seemingly sightless stare, unblinking, glassy. Lips were drawn back from teeth. Grayish algae sprouted in the furrows of their skins, and the mobile fungoids roamed their bodies, feeding on this growth. With a quick automatic gesture of revulsion Gundersen plucked two of the slug-like creatures from the woman's empty breasts. She stirred; she moaned again. In the language of the nildoror she murmured, "Is it over yet?" Her voice was like a flute played by a sullen desert breeze.

Speaking English, Gundersen said, "Who are you? How did this happen?"

He got no response from her. A fungoid crept across her mouth, and he flicked it aside. He touched her cheek. There was a rasping sound as his hand ran across her skin; it was like caressing stiff paper. Struggling to remember her, Gundersen imagined dark hair on her bare skull, gave her light arching brows, saw her cheeks full and her lips smiling. But nothing registered; either he had forgotten her, or he had never known her, or she was unrecognizable in her present condition.

"Is it over soon?" she asked, again in nildororu.

He turned to her companion. Gently, half afraid the fragile neck would snap, Gundersen lifted the man's head out of the pool of fluid. It appeared that he had been breathing it; it trickled from his nose and lips, and after a moment he showed signs of being unable to cope with ordinary air. Gundersen let his face slip back into the pool. In that brief moment he had recognized the man as a certain Harold—or was it Henry?—Dykstra, whom he had known distantly in the old days.

The unknown woman was trying to move one arm. She lacked the strength to lift it. These two were like living ghosts, like death-in-life, mired in their sticky fluid and totally helpless. In the language of the nildoror he said, "How long have you been this way?"

"Forever," she whispered.

"Who are you?"

"I don't . . . remember. I'm . . . waiting."

"For what?"

"For the end."

"Listen," he said, "I'm Edmund Gundersen, who used to be sector chief. I want to help you."

"Kill me first. Then him."

"We'll get you out of here and back to the spaceport. We can have you on the way to Earth in a week or ten days, and then—"

"No . . . please. . . . "

"What's wrong?" he asked.

"Finish it. Finish it." She found enough strength to arch her back, lifting her body halfway out of the fluid that nearly concealed her lower half. Something rippled and briefly bulged beneath her skin. Gundersen touched the taut belly and felt movement within, and that quick inward quiver was the most frightening sensation he had ever known. He touched the body of Dykstra, too: it also rippled inwardly.

Appalled, Gundersen scrambled to his feet and backed away from them. By faint torchlight he studied their shriveled bodies, naked but sexless, bone and ligament, shorn of flesh and spirit yet still alive. A terrible fear came over him. "Na-sinisul!" he called. "Come in here! Come in!"

The sulidor was at his side. Gundersen said, "Something's

inside their bodies. Some kind of parasite? It moves. What is it?"

"Look there," said Na-sinisul, indicating the spongy basket from which the dark fluid trickled. "They carry its young. They have become hosts. A year, two years, perhaps three, and the larvae will emerge."

"Why aren't they both dead?"

"They draw nourishment from this," said the sulidor, swishing his tail through the black flow. "It seeps into their skins. It feeds them, and it feeds that which is within them."

"If we took them out of here and sent them down to the hotel on rafts—?"

"They would die," Na-sinisul said, "moments after they were removed from the wetness about them. There is no hope of saving them."

"When does it end?" the woman asked.

Gundersen trembled. All his training told him never to accept the finality of death; any human in whom some shred of life remained could be saved, rebuilt from a few scraps of cells into a reasonable facsimile of the original. But there were no facilities for such things on this world. He confronted a swirl of choices. Leave them here to let alien things feed upon their guts; try to bring them back to the spaceport for shipment to the nearest tectogenetic hospital; put them out of their misery at once; seek to free their bodies himself of whatever held them in thrall. He knelt again. He forced himself to experience that inner quivering again. He touched the woman's stomach, her thighs, her bony haunches. Beneath the skin she was a mass of strangeness. Yet her mind still ticked, though she had forgotten her name and her native language. The man was luckier; though he was infested too, at least Dykstra did not have to lie here in the dark waiting for the death that could come only when the harbored larvae erupted from the enslaved human flesh. Was this what they had desired, when they refused repatriation from this world that they loved? An Earthman can become captured by Belzagor, the many-born nildor Vol'himyor had said. But this was too literal a capture.

The stink of bodily corruption made him retch.

"Kill them both," he said to Na-sinisul. "And be quick about it."

"This is what you instruct me to do?"

"Kill them. And rip down that thing on the wall and kill it too."

"It has given no offense," said the sulidor. "It has done only what is natural to its kind. By killing these two, I will deprive it of its young, but I am not willing to deprive it of life as well."

"All right," Gundersen said. "Just the Earthmen, then. Fast."

"I do this as an act of mercy, under your direct orders," said Na-sinisul. He leaned forward and lifted one powerful arm. The savage curved claws emerged fully from their sheath. The arm descended twice.

Gundersen compelled himself to watch. The bodies split like dried husks; the things within came spilling out, unformed, raw. Even now, in some inconceivable reflex, the two corpses twitched and jerked. Gundersen stared into their eroded depths. "Do you hear me?" he asked. "Are you alive or dead?" The woman's mouth gaped but no sound came forth, and he did not know whether this was an attempt to speak or merely a last convulsion of the ravaged nerves. He stepped his fusion torch up to high power and trained it on the dark pool. I am the resurrection and the life, he thought, reducing Dykstra to ashes, and the woman beside him, and the squirming unfinished larvae. Acrid, choking fumes rose; not even the torch could destroy the building's dampness. He turned the torch back to illumination level. "Come," he said to the sulidor, and they went out together.

"I feel like burning the entire building and purifying this place," Gundersen said to Na-sinisul.

"I know."

"But you would prevent me."

"You are wrong. No one on this world will prevent you from doing anything."

But what good would it do, Gundersen asked himself. The purification had already been accomplished. He had removed the only beings in this place that were foreign to it.

The rain had stopped. To the waiting Srin'gahar, Gundersen said, "Will you take me away from here?"

They rejoined the other four nildoror. Then, because they had lingered too long here and the land of rebirth was still far away, they resumed the march, even though it was night. By morning Gundersen could hear the thunder of Shangri-la Falls, which the nildoror called Du'jayukh.

Nine

It was as though a white wall of water descended from the sky. Nothing on Earth could match the triple plunge of this cataract, by which Madden's River, or the Seran'nee, dropped five hundred meters, and then six hundred, and then five hundred more, falling from ledge to ledge in its tumble toward the sea. Gundersen and the five nildoror stood at the foot of the falls, where the entire violent cascade crashed into a broad rock-flanged basin out of which the serpentine river continued its southeasterly course; the sulidor had taken his leave in the night and was proceeding northward by his own route. To Gundersen's rear lay the coastal plain, behind his right shoulder, and the central plateau, behind his left. Before him, up by the head of the falls, the northern plateau began, the highlands that controlled the approach to the mist country. Just as a titanic north-south rift cut the coastal plain off from the central plateau, so did another rift running east-west separate both the central plateau and the coastal plain from the highlands ahead.

He bathed in a crystalline pool just beyond the tumult of the cataract, and then they began their ascent. The Shangri-la Station, one of Company's most important outposts, was invisible from below; it was set back a short way from the head of the falls. Once there had been waystations at the foot of the falls and at the head of the middle cataract, but no trace of these structures remained; the jungle had swallowed them utterly in only eight years. A winding road, with an infinity of switchbacks, led to the top. When he first had seen it, Gundersen had imagined it was the work of Company engineers, but he had learned that it was a natural ridge in the face of the plateau, which the nildoror themselves had enlarged and deepened to make their journey toward rebirth more easy.

The swaying rhythm of his mount lulled him into a doze; he held tight to Srin'gahar's pommel-like horns and prayed that in his grogginess he would not fall off. Once he woke suddenly and found himself clinging only by his left hand, with his body half slung out over a sheer drop of at least two hundred meters. Another time, drowsy again, he felt cold spray and snapped to attention to see the entire cascade of the falling river rushing past him no more than a dozen meters away. At the head of the lowest cataract the nildoror paused to eat, and Gundersen dashed icy water in his face to shatter his sluggishness. They went on. He had less difficulty keeping awake now; the air was thinner, and the afternoon breeze was cool. In the hour before twilight they reached the head of the falls.

Shangri-la Station, seemingly unchanged, lay before him; three rectangular unequal blocks of dark shimmering plastic, a somber ziggurat rising on the western bank of the narrow gorge through which the river sped. The formal gardens of tropical planets, established by a forgotten sector chief at least forty years before, looked as though they were being carefully maintained. At each of the building's setbacks there was an outdoor veranda overlooking the river, and these, too, were bedecked with plants. Gundersen felt a dryness in his throat and a tightness in his loins. He said to Srin'gahar, "How long may we stay here?"

"How long do you wish to stay?"

"One day, two—I don't know yet. It depends on the welcome I get."

"We are not yet in a great hurry," said the nildor. "My friends and I will make camp in the bush. When it is time for you to go on, come to us."

The nildoror moved slowly into the shadows. Gundersen approached the station. At the entrance to the garden he paused. The trees here were gnarled and bowed, with long feathery gray fronds dangling down: highland flora was different from that to the south, although perpetual summer ruled here even as in the true tropics behind him. Lights glimmered within the station. Everything out here seemed surprisingly orderly; the contrast with the shambles of the serpent station and the nightmare decay of the fungoid station was sharp. Not even the hotel garden was this well tended. Four neat rows of fleshy, obscene-looking pink forest candles bordered the walkway that ran toward the building. Slender, stately globeflower trees, heavy with gigantic fruit, formed little groves to left and right. There were hullygully trees and bitterfruits—exotics here, imported from the steaming equatorial tropics—and the mighty swordflower trees in full bloom, lifting their long shiny stamens to the sky. Elegant glitterivy

and spiceburr vines writhed along the ground, but not in any
random way. Gundersen took a few steps farther in, and
heard the soft sad sigh of a sensifrons bush, whose gentle
hairy leaves coiled and shrank as he went by, opening warily
when he had gone past, shutting again when he whirled to
steal a quick glance. Two more steps, and he came to a low
tree whose name he could not recall, with glossy red winged
leaves that took flight, breaking free of their delicate stems
and soaring away; instantly their replacements began to sprout.
The garden was magical. Yet there were surprises here.
Beyond the glitterivy he discovered a crescent patch of
tiger-moss, the carnivorous ground cover native to the unfriendly central plateau. The moss had been transplanted to
other parts of the planet—there was a patch of it growing out
of control at the seacoast hotel—but Gundersen remembered
that Seena abhorred it, as she abhorred all the productions of
that forbidding plateau. Worse yet, looking upward so that he
could follow the path of the gracefully gliding leaves, Gundersen
saw great masses of quivering jelly, streaked with blue and
red neural fibers, hanging from several of the biggest trees:
more carnivores, also natives of the central plateau. What
were those sinister things doing in this enchanted garden? A
moment later he had a third proof that Seena's terror of the
plateau had faded: across his path there ran one of the plump,
thieving otter-like animals that had bedeviled them the time
they had been marooned there. It halted a moment, nose
twitching, cunning paws upraised, looking for something to
seize. Gundersen hissed at it and it scuttled into the shrubbery.

Now a massive two-legged figure emerged from a shadowed
corner and blocked his way. Gundersen thought at first it was a
sulidor, but he realized it was merely a robot, probably a
gardener. It said resonantly, "Man, why are you here?"

"As a visitor. I'm a traveler seeking lodging for the night."

"Does the woman expect you?"

"I'm sure she doesn't. But she'll be willing to see me. Tell
her Edmund Gundersen is here."

The robot scanned him carefully. "I will tell her. Remain
where you are and touch nothing."

Gundersen waited. What seemed like an unhealthily long
span of time went by. The twilight deepened, and one moon
appeared. Some of the trees in the garden became luminous.
A serpent, of the sort once used as a source of venom, slid
silently across the path just in front of Gundersen and vanished.

The wind shifted, stirring the trees and bringing him the faint sounds of a conversation of nildoror somewhere not far inland from the riverbank.

Then the robot returned and said, "The woman will see you. Follow the path and enter the station."

Gundersen went up the steps. On the porch he noticed unfamiliar-looking potted plants, scattered casually as though awaiting transplantation to the garden. Several of them waved tendrils at him or wistfully flashed lights intended to bring curious prey fatally close. He went in, and, seeing no one on the ground floor, caught hold of a dangling laddercoil and let himself be spun up to the first veranda. He observed that the station was as flawlessly maintained within as without, every surface clean and bright, the decorative murals unfaded, the artifacts from many worlds still mounted properly in their niches. This station had always been a showplace, but he was surprised to see it so attractive in these years of the decay of Earth's presence on Belzagor.

"Seena?" he called.

He found her alone on the veranda, leaning over the rail. By the light of two moons he saw the deep cleft of her buttocks and thought she had chosen to greet him in the nude; but as she turned toward him he realized that a strange garment covered the front of her body. It was a pale, gelatinous sprawl, shapeless, purple-tinged, with the texture and sheen that he imagined an immense amoeba might have. The central mass of it embraced her belly and loins, leaving her hips and haunches bare; her left breast also was bare, but one broad pseudopod extended upward over the right one. The stuff was translucent, and Gundersen plainly could see the red eye of her covered nipple, and the narrow socket of her navel. It was also alive, to some degree, for it began to flow, apparently of its own will, sending out slow new strands that encircled her left thigh and right hip.

The eeriness of this clinging garment left him taken aback. Except for it, she appeared to be the Seena of old; she had gained some weight, and her breasts were heavier, her hips broader, yet she was still a handsome woman in the last bloom of youth. But the Seena of old would never have allowed such a bizarreness to touch her skin.

She regarded him steadily. Her lustrous black hair tumbled to her shoulders, as in the past. Her face was unlined. She faced him squarely and without shame, her feet firmly planted, her arms at ease, her head held high. "I thought you were

never coming back here, Edmund," she said. Her voice had
deepened, indicating some inner deepening as well. When
he had last known her she had tended to speak too quickly,
nervously pitching her tone too high, but now, calm and
perfectly poised, she spoke with the resonance of a fine cello.
"Why are you back?" she asked.

"It's a long story, Seena. I can't even understand all of it
myself. May I stay here tonight?"

"Of course. How needless to ask!"

"You look so good, Seena. Somehow I expected—after
eight years—"

"A hag?"

"Well, not exactly." His eyes met hers, and he was shaken
abruptly by the rigidity he found there, a fixed and inflexible
gaze, a beadiness that reminded him terrifyingly of the
expression in the eyes of Dykstra and his woman at the last
jungle station. "I—I don't know what I expected," he said.

"Time's been good to you also, Edmund. You have that
stern, disciplined look, now—all the weakness burned away
by years, only the core of manhood left. You've never looked
better."

"Thank you."

"Won't you kiss me?" she asked.

"I understand you're a married woman."

She winced and tightened one fist. The thing she was
wearing reacted also, deepening in color and shooting a
pseudopod up to encircle, though not to conceal, her bare
breast. "Where did you hear that?" she asked.

"At the coast. Van Beneker told me you married Jeff
Kurtz."

"Yes. Not long after you left, as a matter of fact."

"I see. Is he here?"

She ignored his question. "Don't you *want* to kiss me? Or
do you have a policy about kissing other men's wives?"

He forced a laugh. Awkwardly, self-consciously, he reached
for her, taking her lightly by the shoulders and drawing her
toward him. She was a tall woman. He inclined his head,
trying to put his lips to hers without having any part of his
body come in contact with the amoeba. She pulled back
before the kiss.

"What are you afraid of?" she asked.

"What you're wearing makes me nervous."

"The slider?"

"If that's what it's called."

"It's what the sulidoror call it." Seena said. "It comes from the central plateau. It clings to one of the big mammals there and lives by metabolizing perspiration. Isn't it splendid?"

"I thought you hated the plateau."

"Oh, that was a long time ago. I've been there many times. I brought the slider back on the last trip. It's as much of a pet as it is something to wear. Look." She touched it lightly and it went through a series of color changes, expanding as it approached the blue end of the spectrum, contracting toward the red. At its greatest extension it formed a complete tunic covering Seena from throat to thighs. Gundersen became aware of something dark and pulsing at the heart of it, resting just above her loins, hiding the public triangle: its nerve-center, perhaps. "Why do you dislike it?" she asked. "Here. Put your hand on it." He made no move. She took his hand in hers and touched it to her side; he felt the slider's cool dry surface and was surprised that it was not slimy. Easily Seena moved his hand upward until it came to the heavy globe of a breast, and instantly the slider contracted, leaving the firm warm flesh bare to his fingers. He cupped it in a moment, and, uneasy, withdrew his hand. Her nipples had hardened; her nostrils had flared.

He said, "The slider's very interesting. But I don't like it on you."

"Very well." She touched herself at the base of her belly, just above the organism's core. It shrank inward and flowed down her leg in one swift rippling movement gliding away and collecting itself at the far side of the veranda. "Is that better?" Seena asked, naked, now, sweat-shiny, moist-lipped.

The coarseness of her approach startled him. Neither he nor she had ever worried much about nudity, but there was a deliberate sexual aggressiveness about this kind of self-display that seemed out of keeping with what he regarded as her character. They were old friends, yes; they had once been lovers for several years; they had been married in all but the name for many months of that time; but even so the ambiguity of their parting should have destroyed whatever intimacy once existed. And, leaving the question of her marriage to Kurtz out of it, the fact that they had not seen one another for eight years seemed to him to dictate the necessity of a more gradual return to physical closeness. He felt that by making herself pantingly available to him within minutes of his unexpected arrival she was committing a breach not of morals but of esthetics.

"Put something on," he said quietly. "And not the slider. I can't have a serious conversation with you while you're waving all those jiggling temptations in my face."

"Poor conventional Edmund. All right. Have you had dinner?"

"No."

"I'll have it served out here. And drinks. I'll be right back."

She entered the building. The slider remained behind on the veranda; it rolled tentatively toward Gundersen, as though offering to climb up and be worn by him for a while, but he glared at it and enough feeling got through to make the plateau creature move hurriedly away. A minute later a robot emerged, bearing a tray on which two golden cocktails sat. It offered one drink to Gundersen, set the other on the railing, and noiselessly departed. Then Seena returned, chastely clad in a soft gray shift that descended from her shoulders to her shins.

"Better?" she asked.

"For now." They touched glasses; she smiled; they put their drinks to their lips. "You remembered that I don't like sonic snouts," he said.

"I forget very little, Edmund."

"What's it like, living up here?"

"Serene. I never imagined that my life could be so calm. I read a good deal; I help the robots tend the garden; occasionally there are guests; sometimes I travel. Weeks often go by without my seeing another human being."

"What about your husband?"

"Weeks often go by without my seeing another human being," she said.

"You're alone here? You and the robots?"

"Quite alone."

"But the other Company people must come here fairly frequently."

"Some do. There aren't many of us left now," Seena said. "Less than a hundred, I imagine. About six at the Sea of Dust. Van Beneker down by the hotel. Four or five at the old rift station. And so on—little islands of Earthmen widely scattered. There's a sort of a social circuit, but it's a sparse one."

"Is this what you wanted when you chose to stay here?" Gundersen asked.

"I didn't know what I wanted, except that I wanted to stay. But I'd do it again. Knowing everything I know, I'd do it just the same way."

He said, "At the station just south of here, below the falls, I saw Harold Dykstra—"

"Henry Dykstra."

"Henry. And a woman I didn't know."

"Pauleen Mazor. She was one of the customs girls, in the time of the Company. Henry and Pauleen are my closest neighbors, I guess. But I haven't seen them in years. I never go south of the falls any more, and they haven't come here."

"They're dead, Seena."

"Oh?"

"It was like stepping into a nightmare. A sulidor led me to them. The station was a wreck, mold and fungoids everywhere, and something was hatching inside them, the larvae of some kind of basket-shaped red sponge that hung on a wall and dripped black oil—"

"Things like that happen," Seena said, not sounding disturbed. "Sooner or later this planet catches everyone, though always in a different way.'

"Dykstra was unconscious, and the woman was begging to be put out of her misery, and—"

"You said they were dead."

"Not when I got there. I told the sulidor to kill them. There was no hope of saving them. He split them open, and then I used my torch on them."

"We had to do that for Gio' Salamone, too," Seena said. "He was staying at Fire Point, and went out into the Sea of Dust and got some kind of crystalline parasite into a cut. When Kurtz and Ced Cullen found him, he was all cubes and prisms, outcroppings of the most beautiful iridescent minerals breaking through his skin everywhere. And he was still alive. For a while. Another drink?"

"Please. Yes."

She summoned the robot. It was quite dark, now. A third moon had appeared.

In a low voice Seena said, "I'm so happy you came tonight, Edmund. It was such a wonderful surprise."

"Kurtz isn't here now?"

"No," she said, "He's away, and I don't know when he'll be back."

"How has it been for him, living here?"

"I think he's been quite happy, generally speaking. Of course, he's a very strange man."

"He is," Gundersen said.

"He's got a quality of sainthood about him, I think."

"He would have been a dark and chilling saint, Seena."

"Some saints are. They don't all have to be St. Francis of Assisi."

"Is cruelty one of the desirable traits of a saint?"

"Kurtz saw cruelty as a dynamic force. He made himself an artist of cruelty."

"So did the Marquis de Sade. Nobody's canonized *him*."

"You know what I mean," she said. "You once spoke of Kurtz to me, and you called him a fallen angel. That's exactly right. I saw him out among the nildoror, dancing with hundreds of them, and they came to him and practically worshipped him. There he was, talking to them, caressing them. And yet also doing the most destructive things to them as well, but they loved it."

"What kind of destructive things?"

"They don't matter. I doubt that you'd approve. He—gave them drugs, sometimes."

"The serpent venom?"

"Sometimes."

"Where is he now? Out playing with the nildoror?"

"He's been ill for a while." The robot now was serving dinner. Gundersen frowned at the strange vegetables on his plate. "They're perfectly safe," Seena said "I grow them myself, in back. I'm quite the farmer."

"I don't remember any of these."

"They're from the plateau."

Gundersen shook his head. "When I think of how disgusted you were by the plateau, how strange and frightening it seemed to you that time we had to crash-land there—"

"I was a child then. When was it, eleven years ago? Soon after I met you. I was only twenty years old. But on Belzagor you must defeat what frightens you, or you will be defeated. I went back to the plateau. Again and again. It ceased to be strange to me, and so it ceased to frighten me, and so I came to love it. And brought many of its plants and animals back here to live with me. It's so very different from the rest of Belzagor—cut off from everything else, almost alien."

"You went there with Kurtz?"

"Sometimes. And sometimes with Ced Cullen. And most often alone."

"Cullen," Gundersen said. "Do you see him often?"

"Oh, yes. He and Kurtz and I have been a kind of triumvirate. My other husband, almost. I mean, in a spiritual way. Physical too, at times. But that's not as important."

"Where is Cullen now?" he asked, looking intently into her harsh and glossy eyes.

Her expression darkened. "In the north. The mist country."

"What's he doing there?"

"Why don't you go ask him?" she suggested.

"I'd like to do just that," Gundersen said. "I'm on my way up mist country, actually, and this is just a sentimental stop on the way. I'm traveling with five nildoror going for rebirth. They're camped in the bush out there somewhere."

She opened a flask of a musky gray-green wine and gave him some. "Why do you want to go to the mist country?" she asked tautly.

"Curiosity. The same motive that sent Cullen up there, I guess."

"I don't think his motive was curiosity."

"Will you amplify that?"

"I'd rather not," she said.

The conversation sputtered into silence. Talking to her led only in circles he thought. This new serenity of hers could be maddening. She told him only what she cared to tell him, playing with him, seemingly relishing the touch of her sweet contralto voice on the night air, communicating no information at all. This was not a Seena he had ever known. The girl he had loved had been resilient and strong, but not crafty or secretive; there had been an innocence about her that seemed totally lost now. Kurtz might not be the only fallen angel on this planet.

He said suddenly, "The fourth moon has risen!"

"Yes. Of course. Is that so amazing?"

"One rarely see four, even in this latitude."

"It happens at least ten times a year. Why waste your awe? In a little while the fifth one will be up, and—"

Gundersen gasped. "Is that what tonight is?"

"The Night of Five Moons, yes."

"No one told me!"

"Perhaps you never asked."

"Twice I missed it because I was at Fire Point. One year I was at sea, and once I was in the southern mist country, the time that the copter went down. And so on and on. I managed to see it only once, Seena, right here, ten years ago, with you. When things were at their best for us. And now, to come in by accident and have it happen!"

"I thought you had arranged to be here deliberately. To commemorate that other time."

"No. No. Pure coincidence."

"Happy coincidence, then."

"When does it rise?"

"Perhaps an hour."

He watched the four bright dots swimming through the sky. It was so long ago that he had forgotten where the fifth moon should be coming from. Its orbit was retrograde, he thought. It was the most brilliant of the moons, too, with a high-albedo surface of ice, smooth as a mirror.

Seena filled his glass again. They had finished eating. "Excuse me," she said. "I'll be back soon."

Alone, he studied the sky and tried to comprehend this strangely altered Seena, this mysterious woman whose body had grown more voluptuous and whose soul, it seemed, had turned to stone. He saw now that the stone had been in her all along: at their breakup, for example, when he had put in for her transfer to Earth, and she had absolutely refused to leave Holman's World. I love you, she had said, and I'll always love you, but this is where I stay. Why? Why? Because I want to stay, she told him. And she stayed; and he was just as stubborn, and left without her; and they slept together on the beach beneath the hotel on his last night, so that the warmth of her body was still on his skin when he boarded the ship that took him away. She loved him and he loved her, but they broke apart, for he saw no future on this world, and she saw all her future on it. And she had married Kurtz. And she had explored the unknown plateau. And she spoke in a rich deep new voice, and let alien amoebas clasp her loins, and shrugged at the news that two nearby Earthmen had died a horrible death. Was she still Seena, or some subtle counterfeit?

Nildoror sounds drifted out of the darkness. Gundersen heard another sound, too, closer by, a kind of stifled snorting grunt that was wholly unfamiliar to him. It seemed like a cry of pain, though perhaps that was his imagination. Probably it was one of Seena's plateau beasts, snuffling around searching for tasty roots in the garden. He heard it twice more, and then not again.

Time went by and Seena did not return.

Then he saw the fifth moon float placidly into the sky, the size of a large silver coin, and so bright that it dazzled the eye. About it the other four danced, two of them mere tiny dots, two of them more imposing, and the shadows of the moonslight shattered and shattered again as planes of brilliance intersected. The heavens poured light upon the land in icy cascades. He gripped the rail of the veranda and silently begged the moons to hold their pattern; like Faust he longed to cry out to the fleeting moment, stay, stay forever, stay, you are beautiful! But the moons shifted, driven by the unseen Newtonian machinery; he knew that in another hour two of them would be gone and the magic would ebb. Where was Seena?

"Edmund?" she said, from behind him.

She was bare, again, and once more the slider was on her body, covering her loins, sending a long thin projection up to encompass only the nipple of each ripe breast. The light of the five moons made her tawny skin glitter and shine. Now she did not seem coarse to him, nor overly aggressive; she was perfect in her nudity, and the moment was perfect, and unhesitatingly he went to her. Quickly he dropped his clothing. He put his hands to her hips, touching the slider, and the strange creature understood, flowing obediently from her body, a chastity belt faithless to its task. She leaned toward him, her breasts swaying like fleshy bells, and he kissed her, here, here, here, there, and they sank to the veranda floor, to the cold smooth stone.

Her eyes remained open, and colder than the floor, colder than the shifting light of the moons, even at the moment when he entered her.

But there was nothing cold about her embrace. Their bodies thrashed and tangled, and her skin was soft and her kiss was hungry, and the years rolled away until it was the old time again, the happy time. At the highest moment he was dimly aware of that strange grunting sound once more. He clasped her fiercely and let his eyes close.

Afterward they lay side by side, wordless in the moonslight, until the brilliant fifth moon had completed its voyage across

the sky and the Night of the Five Moons had become as any
other night.

Ten

He slept by himself in one of the guest rooms on the topmost
level of the station. Awakening unexpectedly early, he watched
the sunrise coming over the gorge, and went down to walk
through the gardens, which still were glistening with dew.
He strolled as far as the edge of the river, looking for his
nildoror companions; but they were not to be seen. For a
long time he stood beside the river watching the irresistible
downward sweep of that immense volume of water. Were
there fish in the river here, he wondered? How did they
avoid being carried over the brink? Surely anything once
caught up in that mighty flow would have no choice but to
follow the route dictated for it, and be swept toward the
terrible drop.

He went back finally to the station. By the light of morning
Seena's garden seemed less sinister to him. Even the plants
and animals of the plateau appeared merely strange, not
menacing; each geographical district of this world had its own
typical fauna and flora, that was all, and it was not the fault of
the plateau's creatures that man had not chosen to make
himself at ease among them. A robot met him on the first
veranda and offered him breakfast.

"I'll wait for the woman," Gundersen said.

"She will not appear until much later in the morning."

"That's odd. She never used to sleep that much."

"She is with the man," the robot volunteered. "She stays
with him and comforts him at this hour."

"What man?"

"The man Kurtz, her husband."

Gundersen said, amazed, "Kurtz is here at the station?"

"He lies ill in his room."

She said he was away somewhere, Gundersen thought. She
didn't know when he'd be coming back.

Gundersen said, "Was he in his room last night?"

"He was."

"How long has he been back from his last journey away from here?"

"One year at the solstice," the robot said. "Perhaps you should consult the woman on these matters. She will be with you after a while. Shall I bring breakfast?"

"Yes," Gundersen said.

But Seena was not long in arriving. Ten minutes after he had finished the juices, fruits, and fried fish that the robot had brought him, she appeared on the veranda, wearing a filmy white wrap through which the contours of her body were evident. She seemed to have slept well. Her skin was clear and glowing, her stride was vigorous, her dark hair streamed buoyantly in the morning breeze; but yet the curiously rigid and haunted expression of her eyes was unchanged, and clashed with the innocence of the new day.

He said, "The robot told me not to wait breakfast for you. It said you wouldn't be down for a long while."

"That's all right. I'm not usually down this early, it's true. Come for a swim?"

"In the river?"

"No, silly!" She stripped away her wrap and ran down the steps into the garden. He sat frozen a moment, caught up in the rhythms of her swinging arms, her jouncing buttocks; then he followed her. At a twist in the path that he had not noticed before, she turned to the left and halted at a circular pool that appeared to have been punched out of the living rock on the river's flank. As he reached it, she launched herself in a fine arching dive, and appeared to hang suspended a moment, floating above the dark water, her breasts drawn into a startling roundness by gravity's pull. Then she went under. Before she came up for breath, Gundersen was naked and in the pool beside her. Even in this mild climate the water was bitterly cold.

"It comes from an underground spring," she told him. "Isn't it wonderful? Like a rite of purification."

A gray tendril rose from the water behind her, tipped with rubbery claws. Gundersen could find no words to warn her. He pointed with short stabbing motions of two fingers and made hollow chittering noises of horror. A second tendril spiraled out of the depths and hovered over her. Smiling, Seena turned, and seemed to fondle some large creature; there was a thrashing in the water and then the tendrils slipped out of view.

"What was *that*?"

"The monster of the pool," she said. "Ced Cullen brought it for me as a birthday present two years ago. It's a plateau medusa. They live in lakes and sting things."

"How big is it?"

"Oh, the size of a big octopus, I'd say. Very affectionate. I wanted Ced to catch me a mate for it, but he didn't get around to it before he went north, and I suppose I'll have to do it myself before long. The monster's lonely." She pulled herself out of the pool and sprawled out on a slab of smooth black rock to dry in the sun. Gundersen followed her. From this side of the pool, with the light penetrating the water at just the right angle, he was able to see a massive many-limbed shape far below. Seena's birthday present.

He said, "Can you tell me where I can find Ced now?"

"In the mist country."

"I know. That's a big place. Any particular part?"

She rolled over onto her back and flexed her knees. Sunlight made prisms of the droplets of water on her breasts. After a long silence she said, "Why do you want to find him so badly?"

"I'm making a sentimental journey to see old friends. Ced and I were very close, once. Isn't that reason enough for me to go looking for him?"

"It's no reason to betray him, is it?"

He stared at her. The fierce eyes now were closed; the heavy mounds of her breasts rose and fell slowly, serenely. "What do you mean by that?" he asked.

"Didn't the nildoror put you up to going after him?"

"What kind of crazy talk is that?" he blurted, not sounding convincingly indignant even to himself.

"Why must you pretend?" she said, still speaking from within that impregnable core of total assurance. "The nildoror want him brought back from there. By treaty they're prevented from going up there and getting him themselves. The sulidoror don't feel like extraditing him. Certainly none of the Earthmen living on this planet will fetch him. Now, as an outsider you need nildoror permission to enter the mist country, and since you're a stickler for the rules you probably applied for such permission, and there's no special reason why the nildoror should grant favors to you unless you agree to do something for them in return. Eh? Q.E.D."

"Who told you all this?"

"Believe me, I worked it all out for myself."

He propped his head on his hand and reached out admiringly with the other hand to touch her thigh. Her skin was dry and warm now. He let his hand rest lightly, and then not so lightly, on the firm flesh. Seena showed no reaction. Softly he said, "Is it too late for us to make a treaty?"

"What kind?"

"A nonaggression pact. We've been fencing since I got here. Let's end the hostilities. I've been hiding things from you, and you've been hiding things from me, and what good is it? Why can't we simply help one another? We're two human beings on a world that's much stranger and more dangerous than most people suspect, and if we can't supply a little mutual aid and comfort, what are the ties of humanity worth?"

She said quietly,

"Ah, love, let us be true

To one another: for the world, which seems

To lie before us like a land of dreams,

So various, so beautiful, so new—"

The words of the old poem flowed up from the well of his memory. His voice cut in: ·

"—Hath really neither joy, nor love, nor light,

Nor certitude, nor peace, nor help for pain;

And we are here as on a darkling plain

Swept with confused alarms of struggle and flight

Where—where—"

"'Where ignorant armies clash by night,'" she finished for him. "Yes. How like you it is, Edmund, to fumble your lines just at the crucial moment, just at the final climax."

"Then there's to be no nonaggression pact?"

"I'm sorry. I shouldn't have said that." She turned toward him, took his hand from her thigh, pressed it tenderly between her breasts, brushed her lips against it. "All right, we've been playing little games. They're over, and now we'll speak only truth, but you go first. Did the nildoror ask you to bring Ced Cullen out of the mist country?"

"Yes," Gundersen said. "It was the condition of my entry."

"And you promised you'd do it?"

"I made certain reservations and qualifications, Seena. If he won't go willingly, I'm not bound by honor to force him.

But I do have to find him, at least. That much I've pledged.
So I ask you again to tell me where I should look."

"I don't know," she said. "I have no idea. He could be
anywhere at all up there."

"Is this the truth?"

"The truth," she said, and for a moment the harshness was
gone from her eyes, and her voice was the voice of a woman
and not that of a cello.

"Can you tell me, at least, why he fled, why they want him
so eagerly?"

She was slow in replying. Finally she said, "About a year
ago, he went down into the central plateau on one of his
regular collecting trips. He was planning to get me another
medusa, he said. Most of the time I went with him into the
plateau, but this time Kurtz was ill and I had to stay behind.
Ced went to a part of the plateau we had never visited
before, and there he found a group of nildoror taking part in
some kind of religious ceremony. He stumbled right into
them and evidently he profaned the ritual."

"Rebirth?" Gundersen asked.

"No, they do rebirth only in the mist country. This was
something else, something almost as serious, it seems. The
nildoror were furious. Ced barely escaped alive. He came
back here and said he was in great trouble, that the nildoror
wanted him, that he had committed some sort of sacrilege
and had to take sanctuary. Then he went north, with a posse
of nildoror chasing him right to the border. I haven't heard
anything since. I have no contact with the mist country. And
that's all I can tell you."

"You haven't told me what sort of sacrilege he committed,"
Gundersen pointed out.

"I don't know it. I don't know what kind of ritual it was, or
what he did to interrupt it. I've told you only as much as he
told me. Will you believe that?"

"I'll believe it," he said. He smiled. "Now let's play
another game, and this time I'll take the lead. Last night you
told me that Kurtz was off on a trip, that you hadn't seen him
for a long time and didn't know when he'd be back. You also
said he'd been sick, but you brushed over that pretty quickly.
This morning, the robot who brought me breakfast said that
you'd be late coming down, because Kurtz was ill and you
were with him in his room, as you were every morning at this
time. Robots don't ordinarily lie."

"The robot wasn't lying. I was."

"Why?"

"To shield him from you," Seena said. "He's in very bad shape, and I don't want him to be disturbed. And I knew that if I told you he was here, you'd want to see him. He isn't strong enough for visitors. It was an innocent lie, Edmund."

"What's wrong with him?"

"We aren't sure. You know, there isn't much of a medical service left on this planet. I've got a diagnostat, but it gave me no useful data when I put him through it. I suppose I could describe his disease as a kind of cancer. Only cancer isn't what he has."

"Can you describe the symptoms?"

"What's the use? His body began to change. He became something strange and ugly and frightening, and you don't need to know the details. If you thought that what had happened to Dykstra and Pauleen was horrible, you'd be rocked to your roots by Kurtz. But I won't let you see him. It's as much to shield you from him as the other way around. You'll be better off not seeing him." Seena sat up, cross-legged on the rock, and began to untangle the wet snarled strands of her hair. Gundersen thought he had never seen her looking as beautiful as she looked right at this moment, clothed only in alien sunlight, her flesh taut and ripe and glowing, her body supple, full-blown, mature. And the fierceness of her eyes, the one jarring discordancy? Had that come from viewing, each morning, the horror that Kurtz now was? She said after a long while, "Kurtz is being punished for his sins."

"Do you really believe that?"

"I do," she said. "I believe that there are such things as sins, and that there is retribution for sin."

"And that an old man with a white beard is up there in the sky, keeping score on everyone, running the show, tallying up an adultery here, a lie there, a spot of gluttony, a little pride?"

"I have no idea who runs the show," said Seena. "I'm not even sure that anyone does. Don't mislead yourself, Edmund: I'm not trying to import medieval theology to Belzagor. I won't give you the Father, the Son, and the Holy Ghost, and say that all over the universe certain fundamental principles hold true. I simply say that here on Belzagor we live in the presence of certain moral absolutes, native to this planet, and if a stranger comes to Belzagor and transgresses against those absolutes, he'll regret it. This world is not ours, never was, never will be, and we who live here are in a constant state of peril, because we don't understand the basic rules."

"What sins did Kurtz commit?"

"It would take me all morning to name them," she said. "Some were sins against the nildoror, and some were sins against his own spirit."

"We all committed sins against the nildoror," Gundersen said.

"In a sense, yes. We were proud and foolish, and we failed to see them for what they were, and we used them unkindly. That's a sin, yes, of course, a sin that our ancestors committed all over Earth long before we went into space. But Kurtz had a greater capacity for sin than the rest of us, because he was a greater man. Angels have farther to fall, once they fall."

"What did Kurtz do to the nildoror? Kill them? Dissect them? Whip them?"

"Those are sins against their bodies," said Seena. "He did worse."

"Tell me."

"Do you know what used to go on at the serpent station, south of the spaceport?"

"I was there for a few weeks with Kurtz and Salamone," Gundersen said. "Long ago, when I was very new here, when you were still a child on Earth. I watched the two of them call serpents out of the jungle, and milk the raw venom from them, and give the venom to nildoror to drink. And drink the venom themselves."

"And what happened then?"

He shook his head. "I've never been able to understand it. When I tried it with them, I had the illusion that the three of us were turning into nildoror. And that three nildoror had turned into us. I had a trunk, four legs, tusks, spines. Everything looked different; I was seeing through nildoror eyes. Then it ended, and I was in my own body again, and I felt a terrible rush of guilt, of shame. I had no way of knowing whether it had been a real bodily metamorphosis or just hallucination."

"It was hallucination," Seena told him. "The venom opened your mind, your soul, and enabled you to enter the nildor consciousness, at the same time that the nildor was entering

yours. For a little while that nildor thought he was Edmund
Gundersen. Such a dream is great ecstasy to a nildor."

"Is this Kurtz's sin, then? To give ecstasy to nildoror?"

"The serpent venom," Seena said, "is also used in the
rebirth ceremony. What you and Kurtz and Salamone were
doing down there in the jungle was going through a very
mild—*very* mild—version of rebirth. And so were the nildoror.
But it was blasphemous rebirth for them, for many reasons.
First, because it was held in the wrong place. Second,
because it was done without the proper rituals. Third, because the celebrants who guided the nildoror were men, not
sulidoror, and so the entire thing became a wicked parody of
the most sacred act this planet has. By giving those nildoror
the venom, Kurtz was tempting them to dabble in something
diabolical, literally diabolical. Few nildoror can resist that
temptation. He found pleasure in the act—both in the hallucinations that the venom gave him, and in the tempting of
the nildoror. I think that he enjoyed the tempting even more
than the hallucinations, and that was his worst sin, for
through it he led innocent nildoror into what passes for
damnation on this planet. In twenty years on Belzagor he
inveigled hundreds, perhaps thousands, of nildoror into sharing a bowl of venom with him. Finally his presence became
intolerable, and his own hunger for evil became the source of
his destruction. And now he lies upstairs, neither living nor
dead, no longer a danger to anything on Belzagor."

"You think that staging the local equivalent of a Black Mass
is what brought Kurtz to whatever destiny it is that you're
hiding from me?"

"I know it," Seena replied. She got to her feet, stretched
voluptuously, and beckoned to him. "Let's go back to the
station now."

As though this were time's first dawn they walked naked
through the garden, close together, the warmth of the sun
and the warmth of her body stirring him and raising a fever in
him. Twice he considered pulling her to the ground and
taking her amidst these alien shrubs, and twice he held back,
not knowing why. When they were a dozen meters from the
house he felt desire climb again, and he turned to her and
put his hand on her breast. But she said, "Tell me one more
thing, first."

"If I can."

"Why have you come back to Belzagor? Really. What draws you to the mist country?"

He said, "If you believe in sin, you must believe in the possibility of redemption from sin."

"Yes."

"Well, then, I have a sin on my conscience, too. Perhaps not as grave a sin as the sins of Kurtz, but enough to trouble me, and I've come back here as an act of expiation."

"How have you sinned?" she asked.

"I sinned against the nildoror in the ordinary Earthman way, by collaborating in their enslavement, by patronizing them, by failing to credit their intelligence and their complexity. In particular I sinned by preventing seven nildoror from reaching rebirth on time. Do you remember, when the Monroe dam broke, and I commandeered those pilgrims for a labor detail? I used a fusion torch to make them obey, and on my account they missed rebirth. I didn't know that if they were late for rebirth they'd lose their turn, and if I had known I wouldn't have thought it mattered. Sin within sin within sin. I left here feeling stained. Those seven nildoror bothered me in my dreams. I realized that I had to come back and try to cleanse my soul."

"What kind of expiation do you have in mind?" she asked.

His eyes had difficulty meeting hers. He lowered them, but that was worse, for the nakedness of her unnerved him even more, as they stood together in the sunlight outside the station. He forced his glance upward again.

He said, "I've determined to find out what rebirth is, and to take part in it. I'm going to offer myself to the sulidoror as a candidate."

"No."

"Seena, what's wrong? You—"

She trembled. Her cheeks were blazing, and the rush of scarlet spread even to her breasts. She bit her lip, spun away from him, and turned back. "It's insanity," she said. "Rebirth isn't something to Earthmen. Why do you think you can possible expiate anything by getting yourself mixed up in an alien religion, by surrendering yourself to a process none of us knows anything about, by—"

"I have to, Seena."

"Don't be crazy."

"It's an obsession. You're the first person I've ever spoken to about it. The nildoror I'm traveling with aren't aware of it.

I can't stop. I owe this planet a life, and I'm here to pay. I have to go, regardless of the consequences."

She said, "Come inside the station with me." Her voice was flat, mechanical, empty.

"Why?"

"Come inside."

He followed her silently in. She led him to the middle level of the building, and into a corridor blocked by one of her robot guardians. At a nod from her the robot stepped aside. Outside a room at the rear she paused and put her hand to the door's scanner. The door rolled back. Seena gestured to him to walk in with her.

He heard the grunting, snorting sound that he had heard the night before, and now there was no doubt in his mind that it had been a cry of terrible throttled pain.

"This is the room where Kurtz spends his time," Seena said. She drew a curtain that had divided the room. "And this is Kurtz," she said.

"It isn't possible," Gundersen murmured. "How—how—"

"How did he get that way?"

"Yes."

"As he grew older he began to feel remorse for the crimes he had committed. He suffered greatly in his guilt, and last year he resolved to undertake an act of expiation. He decided to travel to the mist country and undergo rebirth. This is what they brought back to me. This is what a human being looks like, Edmund, when he's undergone rebirth."

Eleven

What Gundersen beheld was apparently human, and probably it had once even been Jeff Kurtz. The absurd length of the body was surely Kurtzlike, for the figure in the bed seemed to be a man and a half long, as if an extra section of vertebrae and perhaps a second pair of femurs had been spliced in. The skull was plainly Kurtz's too: mighty white dome, jutting brow-ridges. The ridges were even more prominent that Gundersen remembered. They rose above Kurtz's closed eyes like barricades guarding against some invasion from the north. But the thick black brows that had covered those ridges were gone. So were the lush, almost feminine eyelashes.

Below the forehead the face was unrecognizable.

It was as if everything had been heated in a crucible and allowed to melt and run. Kurtz's fine high-bridged nose was now a rubbery smear, so snoutlike that Gundersen was jolted by its resemblance to a sulidor's. His wide mouth now had slack, pendulous lips that drooped open, revealing toothless gums. His chin sloped backward in pithecanthropoid style. Kurtz's cheekbones were flat and broad, wholly altering the planes of his face.

Seena drew the coverlet down to display the rest. The body in the bed was utterly hairless, a long boiled-looking pink thing like a giant slug. All superfluous flesh was gone, and the skin lay like a shroud over plainly visible ribs and muscles. The proportions of the body were wrong. Kurtz's waist was an impossibly great distance from his chest, and his legs, though long, were not nearly as long as they should have been; his ankles seemed to crowd his knees. His toes had fused, so that his feet terminated in bestial pads. Perhaps by compensation, his fingers had added extra joints and were great spidery things that flexed and clenched in irregular rhythms. The attachment of his arms to his torso appeared strange, though it was not until Gundersen saw Kurtz slowly rotate his left arm through a 360-degree twist that he realized the armpit must have been reconstructed into some kind of versatile ball-and-socket arrangement.

Kurtz struggled desperately to speak, blurting words in a language Gundersen had never heard. His eyeballs visibly stirred beneath his lids. His tongue slipped forth to moisten his lips. Something like a three-lobed Adam's apple bobbed in his throat. Briefly he humped his body, drawing the skin tight over curiously broadened bones. He continued to speak. Occasionally an intelligible word in English or nildororu emerged, embedded in a flow of gibberish: "River...death...lost... horror...river...cave...warm...lost...warm...smash... black...go...god...horror...born...lost...born...."

"What is he saying?" Gundersen asked.

"No one knows. Even when we can understand the words, he doesn't make sense. And mostly we can't even understand the words. He speaks the language of the world where he must live now. It's a very private language."

"Has he been conscious at all since he's been here?"

"Not really," Seena said. "Sometimes his eyes are open, but he never responds to anything around him. Come. Look." She went to the bed and drew Kurtz's eyelids open. Gundersen saw eyes that had no whites at all. From rim to rim their shining surfaces were a deep, lustrous black, dappled by random spots of light blue. He held three fingers up before those eyes and waved his hand from side to side. Kurtz took no notice. Seena released the lids, and the eyes remained open, even when the tips of Gundersen's fingers approached quite closely. But as Gundersen withdrew his hand, Kurtz lifted his right hand and seized Gundersen's wrist. The grotesquely elongated fingers encircled the wrist completely, met, and coiled halfway around it again. Slowly and with tremendous strength Kurtz pulled Gundersen down until he was kneeling beside the bed.

Now Kurtz spoke only in English. As before he seemed to be in desperate anguish, forcing the words out of some nightmare recess, with no perceptible accenting or punctuation: "Water sleep death save sleep sleep fire love water dream cold sleep plan rise fall rise fall rise rise rise." After a moment he added, "Fall." Then the flow of nonsense syllables returned and the fingers relinquished their fierce grip on Gundersen's wrist.

Seena said, "He seemed to be telling us something. I never heard him speak so many consecutive intelligible words."

"But what was he saying?"

"I can't tell you that. But a meaning was there."

Gundersen nodded. The tormented Kurtz had delivered his testament, his blessing: *Sleep plan rise fall rise fall rise rise rise. Fall.* Perhaps it even made sense.

"And he reacted to your presence," Seena went on. "He saw you, he took your arm! Say something to him. See if you can get his attention again."

"Jeff?" Gundersen whispered, kneeling. "Jeff, do you remember me? Edmund Gundersen. I've come back, Jeff. Can you hear anything I'm saying? If you understand me, Jeff, raise your right hand again."

Kurtz did not raise his hand. He uttered a strangled moan, low and appalling; then his eyes slowly closed and he lapsed into a rigid silence. Muscles rippled beneath his altered skin. Beads of acrid sweat broke from his pores. Gundersen got to his feet shortly and walked away.

"How long was he up there?" he asked.

"Close to half a year. I thought he was dead. Then two sulidoror brought him back, on a kind of stretcher."

"Changed like this?"

"Changed. And here he lies. He's changed much more than you imagine," Seena said. "Inside, everything's new and different. He's got almost no digestive tract at all. Solid food is impossible for him; I give him fruit juices. His heart has extra chambers. His lungs are twice as big as they should be. The diagnostat couldn't tell me a thing, because he didn't correspond to any of the parameters for a human body."

"And this happened to him in rebirth?"

"In rebirth, yes. They take a drug, and it changes them. And it works on humans too. It's the same drug they use on Earth for organ regeneration, the venom, but here they use a stronger dose and the body runs wild. If you go up there, Edmund, this is what'll happen to you."

"How do you *know* it was rebirth that did this to him?"

"I know."

"How?"

"That's what he said he was going up there for. And the sulidoror who brought him back said he had undergone rebirth."

"Maybe they were lying. Maybe rebirth is one thing, a beneficial thing, and there's another thing, a harmful thing, which they gave to Kurtz because he had been so evil."

"You're deceiving yourself," Seena said. "There's only one process, and this is its result."

"Possibly different people respond differently to the process, then. If there is only one process. But I still say you can't be sure that it was rebirth that actually did this to him."

"Don't talk nonsense!"

"I mean it. Maybe something within Kurtz made him turn out like this, and I'd turn out another way. A better way."

"Do you *want* to be changed, Edmund?"

"I'd risk it."

"You'd cease to be human!"

"I've tried being human for quite a while. Maybe it's time to try something else."

"I won't let you go," Seena said.

"You won't? What claim do you have on me?"

"I've already lost Jeff to them. If you go up there too—"

"Yes?"

She faltered. "All right. I've got no way to threaten you. But don't go."

"I have to."

"You're just like him! Puffed up with the importance of your own supposed sins. Imagining the need for some kind of ghastly redemption. It's sick, don't you see? You just want to hurt yourself, in the worst possible way." Her eyes glittered even more brightly. "Listen to me. If you need to suffer, I'll help you. You want me to whip you? Stamp on you? If you've got to play masochist, I'll play sadist for you. I'll give you all the torment you want. You can wallow in it. But don't go up mist country. That's carrying a game too far, Edmund."

"You don't understand, Seena."

"Do you?"

"Perhaps I will, when I come back from there."

"You'll come back like *him*!" she screamed. She rushed toward Kurtz's bed. "Look at him! Look at those feet! Look at his eyes! His mouth, his nose, his fingers, his everything! He isn't human any more. Do you want to lie there like him—muttering nonsense, living in some weird dream all day and all night?"

Gundersen wavered. Kurtz *was* appalling; was the obsession so strong in him that he wanted to undergo the same transformation?

"I have to go," he said, less firmly than before.

"He's living in hell," Seena said. "You'll be there too."

She came to Gundersen and pressed herself against him. He felt the hot tips of her breasts grazing his skin; her hands clawed his back desperately; her thighs touched his. A great sadness came over him, for all that Seena once had meant to him, for all that she had been, for what she had become, for what her life must be like with this monster to care for. He was shaken by a vision of the lost and irrecoverable past, of the dark and uncertain present, of the bleak, frightening future. Again he wavered. Then he gently pushed her away from him. "I'm sorry," he said. "I'm going."

"Why? Why? What a *waste*!" Tears trickled down her cheeks. "If you need a religion," she said, "pick an Earth religion. There's no reason why you have to—"

"There is a reason," Gundersen said. He drew her close to him again and very lightly kissed her eyelids, and then her lips. Then he kissed her between the breasts and released her. He walked over to Kurtz and stood for a moment looking

down, trying to come to terms with the man's bizarre metamorphosis. Now he noticed something he had not observed
earlier: the thickened texture of the skin of Kurtz's back, as if
dark little plaques were sprouting on both sides of his spine.
No doubt there were many other changes as well, apparent
only on a close inspection. Kurtz's eyes opened once again,
and the black glossy orbs moved, as if seeking to meet
Gundersen's eyes. He stared down at them, at the pattern of
blue speckles against the shining solid background. Kurtz
said, amidst many sounds Gundersen could not comprehend,
"Dance...live...seek...die...die."

It was time to leave.

Walking past the motionless, rigid Seena, Gundersen went
out of the room. He stepped onto the veranda and saw that
his five nildoror were gathered outside the station, in the
garden, with a robot uneasily watching lest they begin ripping up the rarities for fodder. Gundersen called out, and
Srin'gahar looked up.

"I'm ready," Gundersen said. "We can leave as soon as I
have my things."

He found his clothes and prepared to depart. Seena came
to him again: she was dressed in a clinging black robe, and
her slider was wound around her left arm. Her face was
bleak. He said, "Do you have any messages for Ced Cullen, if
I find him?"

"I have no messages for anyone."

"All right. Thanks for the hospitality, Seena. It was good to
see you again."

"The next time I see you," she said, "you won't know who I
am. Or who you are."

"Perhaps."

He left her and went to the nildoror. Srin'gahar silently
accepted the burden of him. Seena stood on the veranda of
the station, watching them move away. She did not wave, nor
did he. In a little while he could no longer see her. The
procession moved out along the bank of the river, past the
place where Kurtz had danced all night with the nildoror so
many years ago.

Kurtz. Closing his eyes, Gundersen saw the glassy blind
stare, the lofty forehead, the flattened face, the wasted flesh,
the twisted legs, the deformed feet. Against that he placed
his memories of the old Kurtz, that graceful and extraordinary-
looking man, so tall and slender, so self-contained. What

demons had driven Kurtz, in the end, to surrender his body and his soul to the priests of rebirth? How long had the reshaping of Kurtz taken, and had he felt any pain during the process, and how much awareness did he now have of his own condition? What had Kurtz said? I am Kurtz who toyed with your souls, and now I offer you my own? Gundersen had never heard Kurtz speak in any tone but that of sardonic detachment; how could Kurtz have displayed real emotion, fear, remorse, guilt? I am Kurtz the sinner, take me and deal with me as you wish. I am Kurtz the fallen. I am Kurtz the damned. I am Kurtz, and I am yours. Gundersen imagined Kurtz lying in some misty northern valley, his bones softened by the elixirs of the sulidoror, his body dissolving, becoming a pink jellied lump which now was free to seek a new form, to strive toward an altered kurtzness that would be cleansed of its old satanic impurities. Was it presumptuous to place himself in the same class as Kurtz, to claim the same spiritual shortcomings, to go forward to meet that same terrible destiny? Was Seena not right, that this was a game, that he was merely playing at masochistic self-dramatization, electing himself the hero of a tragic myth, burdened by the obsession to undertake an alien pilgrimage? But the compulsion seemed real enough to him, and not at all a pretense. I will go, Gundersen told himself. I am not Kurtz, but I will go, because I must go. In the distance, receding but yet powerful, the roar and throb of the waterfall still sounded, and as the rushing water hurtled down the face of the cliff it seemed to drum forth the words of Kurtz, the warning, the blessing, the threat, the prophecy, the curse: *water sleep death save sleep sleep fire love water dream cold sleep plan rise fall rise fall rise rise rise.*

Fall.

Twelve

For administrative purposes, the Earthmen during their years of occupation of Holman's World had marked off boundaries arbitrarily here and here and here, choosing this parallel of latitude, that meridian of longitude, to encompass a district or sector. Since Belzagor itself knew nothing of parallels of latitude nor of other human measures and boundaries, those demarcations by now existed only in the archives of the Company and in the memories of the dwindling human population of the planet. But one boundary was far from arbitrary, and its power still held: the natural line dividing the tropics from the mist country. On one side of that line lay the tropical highlands, sunbathed, fertile, forming the upper limit of the central band of lush vegetation that stretched down to the torrid equatorial jungle. On the other side of that line, only a few kilometers away, the clouds of the north came rolling in, creating the white world of the mists. The transition was sharp and, for a newcomer, even terrifying. One could explain it prosaically enough in terms of Belzagor's axial tilt and the effect that had on the melting of polar snows; one could speak learnedly of the huge icecaps in which so much moisture was locked, icecaps that extended so far into the temperate zones of the planet that the warmth of the tropics was able to nibble at them, liberating great masses of water-vapor that swirled upward, curved pole-ward, and returned to the icecaps as regenerating snow; one could talk of the clash of climates and of the resulting marginal zones that were neither hot nor cold, and forever shrouded in the dense clouds born of that clash. But even these explanations did not prepare one for the initial shock of crossing the divide. One had a few hints: stray tufts of fog that drifted across the boundary and blotted out broad patches of the tropical high-lands until the midday sun burned them away. Yet the actual change, when it came, was so profound, so absolute, that it stunned the spirit. On other worlds one grew accustomed to an easy transition from climate to climate, or else to an unvarying global climate; one could not easily accept the swiftness of the descent from warmth and ease to chill and bleakness that came here.

Gundersen and his nildoror companions were still some kilometers short of that point of change when a party of sulidoror came out of the bush and stopped them. They were border guards, he knew. There was no formal guard system, nor any other kind of governmental or quasi-governmental organization; but sulidoror nevertheless patrolled the border and interrogated those who wished to cross it. Even in the time of the Company the jurisdiction of the sulidoror had been respected, after a fashion: it might have cost too much effort to override it, and so the few Earthmen bound for the mist-country stations obligingly halted and stated their destinations before going on.

Gundersen took no part in the discussion. The nildoror and the sulidoror drew to one side, leaving him alone to contemplate the lofty banks of white mist on the northern horizon. There seemed to be trouble. One tall, sleek young sulidor pointed several times at Gundersen and spoke at length; Srin'gahar replied in a few syllables, and the sulidor appeared to grow angry, striding back and forth and vehemently knocking bark from trees with swipes of his huge claws. Srin'gahar spoke again, and then some agreement was reached; the angry sulidor stalked off into the forest and Srin'gahar beckoned to Gundersen to remount. Guided by the two sulidoror who remained, they resumed the northward march.

"What was the argument about?" Gundersen asked.

"Nothing."

"But he seemed very angry."

"It did not matter," said Srin'gahar.

"Was he trying to keep me from crossing the boundary?"

"He felt you should not go across," Srin'gahar admitted.

"Why? I have a many-born's permission."

"This was a personal grudge, friend of my journey. The sulidor claimed that you had offended him in time past. He knew you from the old days."

"That's impossible," Gundersen said. "I had hardly any contact at all with sulidoror back then. They never came out of the mist country and I scarcely ever went into it. I doubt that I spoke a dozen words to sulidoror in eight years on this world."

"The sulidor was not wrong in remembering that he had had contact with you," said Srin'gahar gently. "I must tell you that there are reliable witnesses to the event."

"When? Where?"

"It was a long time ago," Srin'gahar said. The nildor appeared content with that vague answer, for he offered no other details. After a few moments of silence he added, "The sulidor had good reason to be unhappy with you, I think. But we told him that you meant to atone for all of your past deeds, and in the end he yielded. The sulidoror often are a stubborn and vindictive race."

"What did I *do* to him?" Gundersen demanded.

"We do not need to talk of such things," replied Srin'gahar.

Since the nildor then retreated into impermeable silence, Gundersen had ample time to ponder the grammatical ambiguities of that last sentence. On the basis of its verbal content alone, it might have meant "It is useless to talk of such things," or "It would be embarrassing to me to talk of such things," or "It is improper to talk of such things," or "It is tasteless to talk of such things." Only with the aid of the supplementary gestures, the movements of the crestspines, the trunk, the ears, could the precise meaning be fathomed, and Gundersen had neither the skill nor the right position for detecting those gestures. He was puzzled, for he had no recollection of ever having given offense to a sulidor, and could not comprehend how he might have done it even indirectly or unknowingly; but after a while he concluded that Srin'gahar was deliberately being cryptic, and might be speaking in parables too subtle or too alien for an Earthman's mind to catch. In any case the sulidor had withdrawn his mysterious objections to Gundersen's journey, and the mist country was only a short distance away. Already the foliage of the jungle trees was more sparse than it had been a kilometer or two back, and the trees themselves were smaller and more widely spaced. Pockets of heavy fog now were more frequent. In many places the sandy yellow soil was wholly exposed. Yet the air was warm and clear and the underbrush profuse, and the bright golden sun was reassuringly visible; this was still unmistakably a place of benign and even commonplace climate.

Abruptly Gundersen felt a cold wind out of the north, signaling change. The path wound down a slight incline, and when it rose on the far side he looked over a hummock into a broad field of complete desolation, a no-thing's-land between the jungle and the mist country. No tree, no shrub, no moss grew here; there was only the yellow soil, covered with a sprinkling of pebbles. Beyond this sterile zone Gundersen was confronted by a white palisade fiercely glittering with reflected sunlight; seemingly it was a cliff of ice hundreds of meters high that barred the way as far as he could see. In the extreme distance, behind and above this white wall, soared the tip of a high-looming mountain, pale red in color, whose rugged spires and peaks and parapets stood forth sharply and strangely against an iron-gray sky. Everything appeared larger than life, massive, monstrous, excessive.

"Here you must walk by yourself," said Srin'gahar. "I

regret this, but it is the custom. I can carry you no farther."

Gundersen clambered down. He was not unhappy about the change; he felt that he should go to rebirth under his own power, and he had grown abashed at sitting astride Srin'gahar for so many hundreds of kilometers. But unexpectedly he found himself panting after no more than fifty meters of walking beside the five nildoror. Their pace was slow and stately, but the air here, evidently, was thinner than he knew. He forced himself to hide his distress. He would go on. He felt light-headed, oddly buoyant, and he would master the pounding in his chest and the throbbing in his temples. The new chill in the air was invigorating in its austerity. They were halfway across the zone of emptiness, and Gundersen now could clearly tell that what had appeared to be a solid white barrier stretching across the world was in fact a dense wall of mist at ground level. Outlying strands of that mist kissed his face. At its clammy touch images of death stirred in his mind, skulls and tombs and coffins and veils, but they did not dismay him. He looked toward the rose-red mountain dominating the land far to the north, and as he did so the clouds that lay over the mist country parted, permitting the sun to strike the mountain's highest peak, a snowy dome of great expanse, and it seemed to him then that the face of Kurtz, transfigured, serene, looked down at him out of that smooth rounded peak.

From the whiteness ahead emerged the figure of a giant old sulidor: Na-sinisul, keeping the promise he had made to be their guide. The sulidoror who had accompanied them this far exchanged a few words with Na-sinisul and trudged off back toward the jungle belt. Na-sinisul gestured. Walking alongside Srin'gahar, Gundersen went forward.

In a few minutes the procession entered the mist.

He did not find the mist so solid once he was within it. Much of the time he could see for twenty or thirty or even fifty meters in any direction. There were occasional inexplicable vortices of fog that were much thicker in texture, and in which he could barely make out the green bulk of Srin'gahar beside him, but these were few and quickly traversed. The sky was gray and sunless; at moments the solar ball could be discerned as a vague glow behind the clouds. The landscape was one of raw rock, bare soil, and low trees—practically a tundra, although the air was merely chilly and not really cold.

Many of the trees were of species also found in the south, but here they were dwarfed and distorted, sometimes not having the form of trees at all, but running along the ground like woody vines. Those trees that stood upright were no taller than Gundersen, and gray moss draped every branch. Beads of moisture dotted their leaves, their stems, the outcroppings of rock, and everything else.

No one spoke. They marched for perhaps an hour, until Gundersen's back was bowed and his feet were numb. The ground sloped imperceptibly upward; the air seemed to grow steadily thinner; the temperature dropped quite sharply as the day neared its end. The dreary envelope of low-lying fog, endless and all-engulfing, exacted a toll on Gundersen's spirit. When he had seen that band of mist from outside, glittering brilliantly in the sunlight, it had stirred and excited him, but now that he was inside it he felt small cheer. All color and warmth had drained from the universe. He could not even see the glorious rose-red mountain from here.

Like a mechanical man, he went onward, sometimes even forcing himself into a trot to keep up with the others. Na-sinisul set a formidable pace, which the nildoror had no difficulty in meeting, but which pushed Gundersen to his limits. He was shamed by the loudness of his own gasps and grunts, though no one else took notice of them. His breath hung before his face, fog within fog. He wanted desperately to rest. He could not bring himself to ask the others to halt a while and wait for him, though. This was their pilgrimage; he was merely the self-invited guest.

A dismal dusk began to descend. The grayness grew more gray, and the faint hint of sunlight that had been evident now diminished. Visibility lessened immensely. The air became quite cold. Gundersen, dressed for jungle country, shivered. Something that had never seemed important to him before now suddenly perturbed him: the alienness of the atmosphere. Belzagor's air, not only in the mist country but in all regions, was not quite the Earthnorm mix, for there was a trifle too much nitrogen and just a slight deficiency in oxygen; and the residual impurities were different as well. But only a highly sensitive olfactory system would notice anything amiss. Gundersen, conditioned to Belzagor's air by his years of service here, had had no awareness of a difference. Now he did. His nostrils reported a sinister metallic tang; the back of his throat, he believed, was coated with some dark grime. He knew it was a foolish illusion born of fatigue. Yet for a few minutes he found himself trying to reduce his intake of breath, as though it was safest to let as little of dangerous stuff as possible into his lungs.

He did not stop fretting over the atmosphere and other discomforts until the moment when he realized he was alone.

The nildoror were nowhere to be seen. Neither was Nasinisul. Mist engulfed everything. Stunned, Gundersen rolled back the screen of his memory and saw that he must have been separated from his companions for several minutes, without regarding it as in any way remarkable. By now they might be far ahead of him on some other road.

He did not call out.

He yielded first to the irresistible and dropped to his knees to rest. Squatting, he pressed his hands to his face, then put his knuckles to the cold ground and let his head loll forward while he sucked in air. It would have been easy to sprawl forward altogether and lose consciousness. They might find him sleeping in the morning. Or frozen in the morning. He struggled to rise, and succeeded on the third attempt.

"Srin'gahar?" he said. He whispered it, making only a private appeal for help.

Dizzy with exhaustion, he rushed forward, stumbling, sliding, colliding with trees, catching his feet in the undergrowth. He saw what was surely a nildor to his left and ran toward it, but when he clutched its flank he found it wet and icy, and he realized that he was grasping a boulder. He flung himself away from it. Just beyond, a file of massive shapes presented themselves: the nildoror marching past him? "Wait?" he called, and ran, and felt the shock at his ankles as he plunged blindly into a shallow frigid rivulet. He fell, landing on hands and knees in the water. Grimly he crawled to the far bank and lay there, recognizing the dark blurred shapes now as those of low, broad trees whipped by a rising wind. All right, he thought. I'm lost. I'll wait right here until morning. He huddled into himself, trying to wring the cold water from his clothes.

The night came, blackness in place of grayness. He sought moons overhead and found none. A terrible thirst consumed him, and he tried to creep back to the brook, but he could not even find that. His fingers were numb; his lips were cracking. But he discovered an island of calm within his discomfort and fear, and clung to it, telling himself that none of what was happening was truly perilous and that all of it was somehow necessary.

Unknown hours later, Srin'gahar and Na-sinisul came to him.

First Gundersen felt the soft probing touch of Srin'gahar's trunk against his cheek. He recoiled and flattened himself on the ground, relaxing slowly as he realized what it was that had brushed his skin. Far above, the nildor said, "Here he is."

"Alive?" Na-sinisul asked, dark voice coming from worlds away, swaddled in layers of fog.

"Alive. Wet and cold. Edmundgundersen, can you stand up?"

"Yes. I'm all right, I think." Shame flooded his spirit. "Have you been looking for me all this time?"

"No," said Na-sinisul blandly. "We continued on to the village. There we discussed your absence. We could not be sure if you were lost or had separated yourself from us with a purpose. And then Srin'gahar and I returned. Did you intend to leave us?"

"I got lost," Gundersen said miserably.

Even now he was not permitted to ride the nildor. He staggered along between Srin'gahar and Na-sinisul, now and then clutching the sulidor's thick fur or grasping the nildor's smooth haunch, steadying himself whenever he felt his strength leaving him or whenever the unseen footing grew difficult. In time lights glimmered in the dark, a pale lantern glow coming milkily through the fogbound blackness. Dimly Gundersen saw the shabby huts of a sulidor village. Without waiting for an invitation he lurched into the nearest of the ramshackle log structures. It was steep-walled, musty-smelling, with strings of dried flowers and the bunched skins of animals suspended from the rafters. Several seated sulidoror looked at him with no show of interest. Gundersen warmed himself and dried his clothing; someone brought him a bowl of sweet, thick broth, and little while afterward he was offered some strips of dried meat, which were difficult to bite and chew but extraordinarily well flavored. Dozens of sulidoror came and went. Once, when the flap of hide covering the door was left open, he caught sight of his nildoror sitting just outside the hut. A tiny fierce-faced animal, fog-white and wizened, skittered up to him and inspected him with disdain: some northern beast, he supposed, that the sulidoror favored as pets. The creature plucked at Gundersen's still soggy clothing and made a cackling sound. Its tufted ears twitched; its sharp little fingers probed his sleeve; its long prehensile tail curled and uncurled. Then it leaped into Gundersen's lap, seized his arm with quick claws, and nipped his flesh. The bite was no more painful than the pricking of a mosquito, but Gundersen wondered what hideous alien infection he would now contract. He made no move to push the little animal away, however. Suddenly a great sulidor paw descended, claws retracted, and knocked the beast across the room with a sweeping swing. The massive form of Na-sinisul lowered itself into a crouch next to Gundersen; the ejected animal chattered its rage from a far corner.

Na-sinisul said, "Did the munzor bite you?"

"Not deeply. Is it dangerous?"

"No harm will come to you," said the sulidor. "We will punish the animal."

"I hope you won't. It was only playing."

"It must learn that guests are sacred," said Na-sinisul firmly. He leaned close. Gundersen was aware of the sulidor's fishy breath. Huge fangs gaped in the deep-muzzled mouth. Quietly Na-sinisul said, "This village will house you until you are ready to go on. I must leave with the nildoror, and continue to the mountain of rebirth."

"Is that the big red mountain north of here?"

"Yes. Their time is very close, and so is mine. I will see them through their rebirths, and then my turn will come."

"Sulidoror undergo rebirth too, then?"

Na-sinisul seemed surprised. "How else could it be?"

"I don't know. I know so little about all of this."

"If sulidoror were not reborn," said Na-sinisul, "then nildoror could not be reborn. One is inseparable from the other."

"In what way?"

"If there were no day, could there be night?"

That was too cryptic. Gundersen attempted to press for an explanation, but Na-sinisul had come to speak of other matters. Avoiding the Earthman's questions, the sulidor said, "They tell me that you have come to our country to speak with a man of your own people, the man Cullen. Is that so?"

"It is. It's one of the reasons I'm here, anyway."

"The man Cullen lives three villages north of here, and one village to the west. He has been informed that you have arrived, and he summons you. Sulidoror of this village will conduct you to him when you wish to leave."

"I'll leave in the morning," Gundersen said.

"I must declare one thing to you first. The man Cullen has taken refuge among us, and so he is sacred. There can be no hope of removing him from our country and delivering him to the nildoror."

"I ask only to speak with him."

"That may be done. But your treaty with the nildoror is known to us. You must remember that you can fulfill that treaty only by a breach of our hospitality."

Gundersen made no reply. He did not see how he could promise anything of this nature to Na-sinisul without at the same time forswearing his promise to the many-born Vol'himyor. So he clung to his original inner treaty: he would speak with Cedric Cullen, and then he would decide how to act. But it disturbed him that the sulidoror were already aware of his true purpose in seeking Cullen.

Na-sinisul left him. Gundersen attempted to sleep, and for a while he achieved an uneasy doze. But the lamps flickered all night in the sulidor hut, and lofty sulidoror strode back and forth noisily around and about him, and the nildoror just outside the building engaged in a long debate of which Gundersen could catch only a few meaningless syllables. Once Gundersen awoke to find the little long-eared munzor sitting on his chest and cackling. Later in the night three sulidoror hacked up a bloody carcass just next to the place where Gundersen huddled. The sounds of the rending of flesh awakened him briefly, but he slipped back into his troubled sleep, only to wake again when a savage quarrel erupted over the division of the meat. When the bleak gray dawn came, Gundersen felt more tired than if he had not slept at all.

He was given breakfast. Two young sulidoror, Se-holomir and Yi-gartigok, announced that they had been chosen to escort him to the village where Cullen was staying. Na-sinisul and the five nildoror prepared to leave for the mountain of rebirth. Gundersen made his farewells to his traveling companions.

"I wish you joy of your rebirth," he said, and watched as the huge shapes moved off into the mist.

Not long afterward he resumed his own journey. His new guides were taciturn and aloof: just as well, for he wanted no

conversation as he struggled through this hostile country. He
needed to think. He was not sure at all what he would do
after he had seen Cullen; his original plan of undergoing
rebirth, which had seemed so noble in the abstract, now
struck him as the highest folly—not only because of what
Kurtz had become, but because he saw it as a trespass, an
unspontaneous and self-conscious venture into the rites of
an alien species. Go to the rebirth mountain, yes. Satisfy
your curiosity. But submit to rebirth? For the first time
he was genuinely unsure whether he would, and more than
half suspicious that in the end he would draw back,
unreborn.

The tundra of the border zone was giving way now to forest
country which seemed a curious inversion to him: trees
growing larger here in higher latitudes. But these were
different trees. The dwarfed and twisted shrubs to his rear
were natives of the jungle, making an unhappy adaptation to
the mist; here, deeper in the mist country, true northern
trees grew. They were thick-boled and lofty, with dark corrugated bark and tiny sprays of needle-like leaves. Fog shrouded
their upper branches. Through this cold and misty forest too
there ran lean, straggly animals, long-nosed and bony, which
erupted from holes in the ground and sped up the sides of
trees, evidently in quest of bough-dwelling rodents and birds.
Broad patches of ground were covered with snow here,
although summer was supposedly approaching in this hemisphere. On the second night northward there came a hail-
storm when a dense and tossing cloud of ice rode toward
them on a thin whining wind. Mute and glum, Gundersen's
companions marched on through it, and so did he, not
enjoying it.

Generally now the mist was light at ground level, and often
there was none at all for an hour or more, but it congealed far
overhead as an unbroken veil, hiding the sky. Gundersen
became accustomed to the barren soil, the angular branches
of so many bare trees, the chilly penetrating dampness that
was so different from the jungle's humidity. He came to find
beauty in the starkness. When fleecy coils of mist drifted like
ghosts across a wide gray stream, when furry beasts sprinted
over glazed fields of ice, when some hoarse ragged cry broke
the incredible stillness, when the marchers turned an angle
in the path and came upon a white tableau of harsh wintry

emptiness, Gundersen responded with a strange kind of delight. In the mist country, he thought, the hour is always the hour just after dawn, when everything is clean and new.

On the fourth day Se-holomir said, "The village you seek lies behind the next hill."

Thirteen

It was a substantial settlement, forty huts or more arranged in two rows, flanked on one side by a grove of soaring trees and on the other by a broad silvery-surfaced lake. Gundersen approached the village through the trees, with the lake shining beyond. A light fall of snowflakes wandered through the quiet air. The mists were high just now, thickening to an impenetrable ceiling perhaps five hundred meters overhead.

"The man Cullen—?" Gundersen asked.

Cullen lay in a hut beside the lake. Two sulidoror guarded the entrance, stepping aside at a word from Yi-gartigok; two sulidoror more stood at the foot of the pallet of twigs and hides on which Cullen rested. They too stepped aside, revealing a burned-out husk of a man, a remnant, a cinder.

"Are you here to fetch me?" Cullen asked. "Well, Gundy, you're too late."

Cullen's golden hair had turned white and gone coarse; it was a tangled snowy mat through which patches of pale blotched scalp showed. His eyes, once a gentle liquid green, now were muddy and dull, with angry bloodshot streaks in the yellowed whites. His face was a mask of skin over bones, and the skin was flaky and rough. A blanket covered him from the chest down, but the severe emaciation of his arms indicated that the rest of his body probably was similarly eroded. Of the old Cullen little seemed to remain except the mild, pleasant voice and the cheerful smile, now grotesque emerging from the ravaged face. He looked like a man of a hundred years.

"How long have you been this way?" Gundersen demanded.

"Two months. Three, I don't know. Time melts here,

Gundy. But there's no going back for me now. This is where I stop. Terminal. Terminal."

Gundersen knelt by the sick man's pallet. "Are you in pain? Can I give you something?"

"No pain," Cullen said. "No drugs. Terminal."

"What do you have?" Gundersen asked, thinking of Dykstra and his woman lying gnawed by alien larvae in a pool of muck, thinking of Kurtz anguished and transformed at Shangri-la Falls, thinking of Seena's tale of Gio' Salamone turned to crystal. "A native disease? Something you picked up around here?"

"Nothing exotic," said Cullen. "I'd guess it's the old inward rot, the ancient enemy. The crab, Gundy. The crab. In the gut. The crab's pincers are in my gut."

"Then you *are* in pain?"

"No," Cullen said. "The crab moves slowly. A nip here, a nip there. Each day there's a little less of me. Some days I feel that there's nothing left of me at all. This is one of the better days."

"Listen," Gundersen said, "I could get you downriver to Seena's place in a week. She's bound to have a medical kit, a space tube of anticarcin for you. You aren't so far gone that we couldn't manage a remission if we act fast, and then we could ship you to Earth for template renewal, and—"

"No. Forget it."

"Don't be absurd! We aren't living in the Middle Ages, Ced. A case of cancer is no reason for a man to lie down in a filthy hut and wait to die. The sulidoror will set up a litter for you. I can arrange it in five minutes. And then—"

"I wouldn't ever reach Seena's, and you know it," Cullen said softly. "The nildoror would pick me up the moment I came out of the mist country. You know that, Gundy. You *have* to know that."

"Well—"

"I don't have the energy to play these games. You're aware, aren't you, that I'm the most wanted man on this planet?"

"I suppose so."

"Were you sent here to fetch me?"

"The nildoror asked me to bring you back," Gundersen admitted. "I had to agree to it in order to get permission to come up here."

"Of course." Bitterly.

"But I stipulated that I wouldn't bring you out unless you'd come willingly," Gundersen said. "Along with certain other stipulations. Look, Ced, I'm not here as Judas. I'm traveling for reasons of my own, and seeing you is strictly a side-venture. But I want to help you. Let me bring you down to Seena's so you can get the treatment that you have to—"

"I told you," Cullen said, "the nildoror would grab me as soon as they had a chance."

"Even if they knew you were mortally ill and being taken down to the falls for medical care?"

"Especially so. They'd love to save my soul as I lay dying. I won't give them the satisfaction, Gundy. I'm going to stay here, safe, beyond their reach, and wait for the crab to finish with me. It won't be long now. Two days, three, a week, perhaps even tonight. I appreciate your desire to rescue me. But I won't go."

"If I got a promise from the nildoror to let you alone until you were able to undergo treat—"

"I won't go. You'd have to force me. And that's outside the scope of your promise to the nildoror, isn't it?" Cullen smiled for the first time in some minutes. "There's a flask of wine in the corner there. Be a good fellow."

Gundersen went to get it. He had to walk around several sulidoror. His colloquy with Cullen had been so intense, so private, that he had quite forgotten that the hut was full of sulidoror: his two guides, Cullen's guards, and at least half a dozen others. He picked up the wine and carried it to the pallet. Cullen, his hand trembling, nevertheless managed not to spill any. When he had had his fill, he offered the flask to Gundersen, asking him so insistently to drink that Gundersen could not help but accept. The wine was warm and sweet.

"Is it agreed," Cullen said, "that you won't make any attempt to take me out of this village? I know you wouldn't seriously consider handing me over to the nildoror. But you might decide to get me out of here for the sake of saving my life. Don't do that either, because the effect would be the same: the nildoror would get me. I stay here. Agreed?"

Gundersen was silent a while. "Agreed," he said finally.

Cullen looked relieved. He lay back, face toward the wall,

and said, "I wish you hadn't wasted so much of my energy on that one point. We have so much more to talk about. And now I don't have the strength."

"I'll come back later. Rest, now."

"No. Stay here. Talk to me. Tell me where you've been all these years, why you came back here, who you've seen, what you've done. Give me the whole story. I'll rest while I'm listening. And afterward—and afterward—"

Cullen's voice faded. It seemed to Gundersen that he had slipped into unconsciousness, or perhaps merely sleep. Cullen's eyes were closed; his breath was slow and labored. Gundersen remained silent. He paced the hut uneasily, studying the hides tacked to the walls, the crude furniture, the debris of old meals. The sulidoror ignored him. Now there were eight in the hut, keeping their distance from the dying man and yet focusing all their attention on him. Momentarily Gundersen was unnerved by the presence of these giant two-legged beasts, these nightmare creatures with fangs and claws and thick tails and drooping snouts, who came and went and moved about as though he were less than nothing to them. He gulped more wine, though he found the texture and flavor of it unpleasant.

Cullen said, eyes still shut, "I'm waiting. Tell me things."

Gundersen began to speak. He spoke of his eight years on Earth, collapsing them into six curt sentences. He spoke of the restlessness that had come over him on Earth, of his cloudy and mystifying compulsion to return to Belzagor, of the sense of a need to find a new structure for his life now that he had lost the scaffolding that the Company had been for him. He spoke of his journey through the forest to the lakeside encampment, and of how he had danced among the nildoror, and how they had wrung from him the qualified promise to bring them Cullen. He spoke of Dykstra and his woman in their forest ruin, editing the tale somewhat in respect for Cullen's own condition, though he suspected that such charity was unnecessary. He spoke of being with Seena again on the Night of the Five Moons. He spoke of Kurtz and how he had been changed through rebirth. He spoke of his pilgrimage into the mist country.

He was certain at least three times that Cullen had fallen asleep, and once he thought that the sick man's breathing had ceased altogether. Each time Gundersen paused, though, Cullen gave some faint indication—a twitch of the mouth, a flick of the fingertips—that he should go on. At the end, when Gundersen had nothing left to say, he stood in silence a long while waiting for some new sign from Cullen, and at last, faintly, Cullen said, "Then?"

"Then I came here."

"And where do you go after here?"

"To the mountain of rebirth," said Gundersen quietly.

Cullen's eyes opened. With a nod he asked that his pillows be propped up, and he sat forward, locking his fingers into his coverlet. "Why do you want to go there?" he asked.

"To find out what kind of thing rebirth is."

"You saw Kurtz?"

"Yes."

"He also wanted to learn more about rebirth," Cullen said. "He already understood the mechanics of it, but he had to know its inwardness as well. To try it for himself. It wasn't just curiosity, of course. Kurtz had spiritual troubles. He was courting self-immolation because he'd persuaded himself he needed to atone for his whole life. Quite true, too. Quite true. So he went for rebirth. The sulidoror obliged him. Well, behold the man. I saw him just before I came north."

"For a while I thought I might try rebirth also," said Gundersen, caught unawares by the words surfacing in his mind. "For the same reasons. The mixture of curiosity and guilt. But I think I've given the idea up now. I'll go to the mountain to see what they do, but I doubt that I'll ask them to do it to me."

"Because of the way Kurtz looks?"

"Partly. And also because my original plan looks too—well, too *willed*. Too unspontaneous. An intellectual choice, not an act of faith. You can't just go up there and volunteer for rebirth in a coldly scientific way. You have to be driven to it."

"As Kurtz was?" Cullen asked.

"Exactly."

"And as you aren't?"

"I don't know any longer," Gundersen said. "I thought I was driven, too. I told Seena I was. But somehow, now that I'm so close to the mountain, the whole quest has started to seem artificial to me."

"You're sure you aren't just afraid to go through with it?"

Gundersen shrugged. "Kurtz wasn't a pretty sight."

"There are good rebirths and bad rebirths," Cullen said. "He had a bad rebirth. How it turns out depends on the quality of one's soul, I gather, and on a lot of other things. Give us some more wine, will you?"

Gundersen extended the flask. Cullen, who appeared to be gaining strength, drank deeply.

"Have you been through rebirth?" Gundersen asked.

"Me? Never. Never even tempted. But I know a good deal about it. Kurtz wasn't the first of us to try it, of course. At least a dozen went before him."

"Who?"

Cullen mentioned some names. They were Company men, all of them from the list of those who had died while on field duty. Gundersen had known some of them; others were figures out of the far past, before he or Cullen had ever come to Holman's World.

Cullen said, "And there were others. Kurtz looked them up in the records, and the nildoror gave him the rest of the story. None of them ever returned from the mist country. Four or five of them turned out like Kurtz—transformed into monsters."

"And the others?"

"Into archangels, I suppose. The nildoror were vague about it. Some sort of transcendental merging with the universe, an evolution to the next bodily level, a sublime ascent—that kind of thing. All that's certain is that they never came back to Company territory. Kurtz was hoping on an outcome like that. But unfortunately Kurtz was Kurtz, half angel and half demon, and that's how he was reborn. And that's what Seena nurses. In a way it's a pity you've lost your urge, Gundy. You might just turn out to have one of the good rebirths. Can you call Hor-tenebor over? I think I should have some fresh air, if we're going to talk so much. He's the sulidor leaning against the wall there. The one who looks after me, who hauls my old bones around. He'll carry me outside."

"It was snowing a little while ago, Ced."

"So much the better. Shouldn't a dying man see some snow? This is the most beautiful place in the universe," Cullen said. "Right here, in front of this hut. I want to see it. Get me Hor-tenebor."

Gundersen summoned the sulidor. At a word from Cullen, Hor-tenebor scooped the fragile, shrunken invalid into his immense arms and bore him through the door-flap of the hut, setting him down on a cradle-like framework overlooking the

lake. Gundersen followed. A heavy mist had descended on
the village, concealing even the huts closest at hand, but the
lake itself was clearly visible under the gray sky. Fugitive
wisps of mist hung just above the lake's dull surface. A bitter
chill was in the air, but Cullen, wrapped only in a thin hide,
showed no discomfort, He held forth his hand, palm upraised,
and watched with the wonder of a child as snowflakes struck
it.

At length Gundersen said, "Will you answer a question?"
"If I can."
"What was it you did that got the nildoror so upset?"
"They didn't tell you when they sent you after me?"
"No," Gundersen said. "They said that you would, and that
in any case it didn't really matter to them whether I knew or
not. Seena didn't know either. And I can't begin to guess. You
were never the kind who went in for killing or torturing
intelligent species. You couldn't have been playing around
with the serpent venom the way Kurtz was—he was doing
that for years and they never tried to grab him. So what could
you possibly have done that caused so much—"
"The sin of Actaeon," said Cullen.
"Pardon?"
"The sin of Actaeon, which was no sin at all, but really just
an accident. In Greek myth he was a huntsman who blundered
upon Diana bathing, and saw what he shouldn't have seen.
She changed him into a stag and he was torn to pieces by his
own hounds."
"I don't understand what that has to do with—"
Cullen drew a long breath. "Did you ever go up on the
central plateau?" he asked, his voice low but firm. "Yes. Yes,
of course you did. I remember, you crash-landed there, you
and Seena, on your way back to Fire Point after a holiday on
the coast, and you were stranded a little while and weird
animals bothered you and that was when Seena first started
to hate the plateau. Right? Then you know what a strange
and somehow mysterious place it is, a place apart from the
rest of this planet, where not even the nildoror like to go. All
right. I started to go there, a year or two after relinquishment.
It became my private retreat. The animals of the plateau
interested me, the insects, the plants, everything. Even the
air had a special taste—sweet, clean. Before relinquishment,
you know, it would have been considered a little eccentric for
anybody to visit the plateau on his free time, or at any other

time. Afterward nothing mattered to anyone. The world was mine. I made a few plateau trips. I collected specimens. I brought some little oddities to Seena, and she got to be fond of them before she realized they were from the plateau, and little by little I helped her overcome her irrational fear of the plateau. Seena and I went there often together, sometimes with Kurtz also. There's a lot of flora and fauna from the plateau at Shangri-la Station; maybe you noticed it. Right? We collected all that. The plateau came to seem like any other place to me, nothing supernatural, nothing eerie, merely a neglected backwoods region. And it was my special place, where I went whenever I felt myself growing empty or bored or stale. A year ago, maybe a little less than a year, I went into the plateau. Kurtz had just come back from his rebirth, and Seena was terribly depressed by what had happened to him, and I wanted to get her a gift, some animal, to cheer her up. This time I came down a little to the southwest of my usual landing zone, over in a part of the plateau I had never seen before, where two rivers meet. One of the first things I noticed was how ripped up the shrubbery was. Nildoror! Plenty nildoror! An immense area had been grazed, and you know how nildoror graze. It made me curious. Once in a while I had seen an isolated nildor on the plateau, always at a distance, but never a whole herd. So I followed the line of devastation. On and on it went, this scar through the forest, with broken branches and trampled underbrush, all the usual signs. Night came, and I camped, and it seemed to me I heard drums in the night. Which was foolish, since nildoror don't use drums; I realized after a while that I heard them dancing, pounding the ground, and these were reverberations carried through the soil. There were other sounds, too: screams, bellows, the cries of frightened animals. I had to know what was happening. So I broke camp in the middle of the night and crept through the jungle, hearing the noise grow louder and louder, until finally I reached the edge of the trees, where the jungle gave way to a kind of broad savanna running down to the river, and there in the open were maybe five hundred nildoror. Three moons were up, and I had no trouble seeing. Gundy, would you believe that they had *painted* themselves? Like savages, like something out of a nightmare. There were three deep pits in the middle of the clearing. One of the pits was filled with a kind of wet red mud, and the other two contained branches and berries and leaves that the nildoror had trampled to release dark pigments, one black, one blue. And I watched the nildoror going down to these pits, and first they'd roll in the pit of red mud and come up plastered with it, absolutely scarlet; and then they'd go to the adjoining pits and give each other dark stripes over the red, hosing it on with their trunks. A barbaric sight: all that color, all that flesh. When they were properly decorated, they'd go running—not strolling, *running*— across the field to the place of dancing, and they'd begin that four-step routine. You know it: boom boom *boom* boom. But infinitely more fierce and frightening now, on account of the war-paint. An army of wild-looking nildoror, stamping their feet, nodding their tremendous heads, lifting their trunks, bellowing, stabbing their tusks into the ground, capering, singing, flapping their ears. Frightening, Gundy, frightening. And the moonslight on their painted bodies—

"Keeping well back in the forest, I circled around to the west to get a better view. And saw something on the far side of the dancers that was even stranger than the paint. I saw a corral with log walls, huge, three or four times the size of this village. The nildoror couldn't have build it alone; they might have uprooted trees and hauled them with their trunks, but they must have needed sulidoror to help pile them up and shape them. Inside the corral were plateau animals, hundreds of them, all sizes and shapes. The big leaf-eating ones with giraffe necks, and the kind like rhinos with antlers, and timid ones like gazelles, and dozens that I'd never even seen before, all crowded together as if in a stockyard. There must have been sulidoror hunters out beating the bush for days, driving that menagerie together. The animals were restless and scared. So was I. I crouched in the darkness, waiting, and finally all the nildoror were properly painted, and then a ritual started in the midst of the dancing group. They began to cry out, mostly in their ancient language, the one we can't understand, but also they were talking in ordinary nildororu, and eventually I understood what was going on. Do you know who these painted beasts were? They were sinning nildoror, nildoror who were in disgrace! This was the place of atonement and the festival of purification. Any nildor who had been tinged with corruption in the past year had to come here and be cleansed. Gundy, do you know what sin they had committed? They had taken the venom from Kurtz. The old game, the one everybody used to play down at the serpent station, give the nildoror a swig, take one yourself, let the hallucinations come? These painted prancing nildoror here had all been led astray by Kurtz. Their souls were stained. The Earthman-devil had found their one vulnerable place, the one area of temptation they couldn't resist. So here they were, trying to cleanse themselves. The central plateau is the nildoror purgatory. They don't live there because they need it for their rites, and obviously you don't set up an ordinary encampment in a holy place.

"They danced, Gundy, for hours. But that wasn't the rite of atonement. It was only the prelude to the rite. They danced until I was dizzy from watching them, the red bodies, the dark stripes, the boom of their feet, and then, when no moons were left in the sky, when dawn was near, the real ceremony started. I watched it, and I looked right down into the darkness of the race, into the real nildoror soul. Two old nildoror approached the corral and started kicking down the gate. They broke an opening maybe ten meters wide, and stepped back, and the penned-up animals came rushing out onto the plain. The animals were terrified from all the noise and dancing, and from being imprisoned, and they ran in circles, not knowing what to do or where to go. And the rest of the nildoror charged into them. The peaceful, noble, nonviolent nildoror, you know? Snorting. Trampling. Spearing with their tusks. Lifting animals with their trunks and hurling them into trees. An orgy of slaughter. I became sick, just watching. A nildor can be a terrible machine of death. All that weight, those tusks, the trunk, the big feet—everything berserk, all restraints off. Some of the animals escaped, of course. But most bodies were trapped right in the middle of the chaos. Crushed bodies everywhere, rivers of blood, scavengers coming out of the forest to have dinner while the killing was still going on. That's how the nildoror atone: sin for sin. That's how they purge themselves. The plateau is where they loose their violence, Gundy. They put aside all their restraints and let out the beast that's within them. I've never felt such horror as when I watched how they cleansed their souls. You know how much respect I had for the nildoror. Still have. But to see a thing like that, a massacre, a vision of hell—Gundy, I was numb with despair. The nildoror didn't seem to enjoy the killing, but they weren't hesitant about it, either; they just went on and on, because it had to be done, because this was the form of the ceremony, and they thought nothing more of it than Socrates would think of sacrificing a lamb to Zeus, a cock to Aesculapius. That was the real horror, I think. I watched the nildoror destroying life for the sake of their souls, and it was like dropping through a trapdoor, entering a new world whose existence I had never even suspected, a dark new world beneath the old. Then dawn came. The sun rose, lovely, golden, light glistening on the trampled corpses, and the nildoror were sitting calmly in the midst of the devastation, resting calm, purged, all their inner storms over. It was amazingly peaceful. They had wrestled with their demons, and they had won. They had come through all the night's horror, all the the ghastliness, and—I don't know how—they really *were* purged and purified. I can't tell you how to find salvation through violence and destruction. It's alien to me and probably to you. Kurtz knew, though. He took the same road as the nildoror. He fell and fell and fell, through level after level of evil enjoying his corruption, glorying in depravity, and then in the end he was still able to judge himself and find himself wanting, and recoil at the darkness he found inside himself, and so he went and sought rebirth, and showed that the angel within him wasn't altogether dead. This finding of purity by passing through evil—you'll have to come to terms with it by yourself, Gundy. I can't help you. All I can do is tell you of the vision I had at sunrise that morning beside the field of blood. I looked into an abyss. I peered over the edge, and saw where Kurtz had gone, where these nildoror had gone. Where perhaps you'll go. I couldn't follow.

"And then they almost caught me.

"They picked up my scent. While the frenzy was on them, I guess they hadn't noticed—especially with hundreds of animals giving off fear-smells in the corral. But they began to sniff. Trunks started to rise and move around like periscopes. The odor of sacrilege was on the air. The reek of a blaspheming spying Earthman. Five, ten minutes they sniffed, and I stood in the bushes still wrapped in my vision, not even remotely realizing they were sniffing *me*, and suddenly it dawned on me that they knew I was there, and I turned and began to slip away through the forest, and they came after me. Dozens. Can you imagine what it's like to be chased through the jungle by a herd of angry nildoror? But I could fit through places too small for them. I gave them the slip. I ran and ran and ran, until I fell down dizzy in a thicket and vomited, and

I rested, and then I heard them bashing along on my trail, and I ran some more. And came to a swamp, and jumped in, hoping they'd lose my scent. And hid in the reeds and marshes, while things I couldn't see nipped at me from below. And the nildoror ringed the entire region. We know you're in there, they called to me. Come out. Come out. We forgive you and we wish to purify you. They explained it quite reasonably to me. I had inadvertently—oh, of course, inadvertently, they were diplomatic!—seen a ceremony that no one but a nildor was allowed to see, and now it would be necessary to wipe what I had seen from my mind, which could be managed by means of a simple technique that they didn't bother to describe to me. A drug, I guess. They invited me to come have part of my mind blotted out. I didn't accept. I didn't say anything. They went right on talking, telling me that they held no malice, that they realized it obviously hadn't been my intention to watch their secret ceremony, but nevertheless since I had seen it they must now take steps, et cetera, et cetera. I began to crawl downstream, breathing through a hollow reed. When I surfaced the nildoror were still calling to me, and now they sounded more angry, as far as it's possible to tell such a thing. They seemed annoyed that I had refused to come out. They didn't blame me for spying on them, but they did object that I wouldn't let them purify me. That was my real crime: not that I hid in the bushes and watched them, but declining afterward to undergo the treatment. That's what they still want me for. I stayed in the creek all day, and when it got dark I slithered out and picked up the vector-beep of my beetle, which turned out to be about half a kilometer away. I expected to find it guarded by nildoror, but it wasn't, and I got in and cleared out fast and landed at Seena's place by midnight. I knew I didn't have much time. The nildoror would be after me from one side of the continent to the other. I told her what had happened, more or less, and I collected some supplies, and I took off for the mist country. The sulidoror would give me sanctuary. They're jealous of their sovereignty; blasphemy or not, I'd be safe here. I came to this village. I explored the mist country a good bit. Then one day I felt the crab in my gut and I knew it was all over. Since then I've been waiting for the end, and the end isn't far away."

He fell silent.

Gundersen, after a pause, said, "But why not risk going

back? Whatever the nildoror want to do to you can't be as bad as sitting on the porch of a sulidor hut and dying of cancer."

Cullen made no reply.

"What if they give you a memory-wiping drug?" Gundersen asked. "Isn't it better to lose a bit of your past than to lose your whole future? If you'll only come back, Ced, and let us treat your disease—"

"The trouble with you, Gundy, is that you're too logical," Cullen said. "Such a sensible, reasonable, rational chap! There's another flask of wine inside. Would you bring it out?"

Gundersen walked past the crouching sulidoror into the hut, and prowled the musty darkness a few moments, looking for the wine. As he searched, the solution to the Cullen situation presented itself: instead of bringing Cullen to the medicine, he would bring the medicine to Cullen. He would abandon his journey toward the rebirth mountain at least temporarily and go down to Shangri-la Falls to get a dose of anticarcin for him. It might not be too late to check the cancer. Afterward, restored to health, Cullen could face the nildoror or not, as he pleased. What happens between him and the nildoror, Gundersen told himself, will not be a matter that concerns me. I regard my treaty with Vol'himyor as nullified. I said I would bring Cullen forth only with his consent, and clearly he won't go willingly. So my task now is just to save his life. Then I can go to the mountain.

He located the wine and went outside with it.

Cullen leaned backward on the cradle, his chin on his chest, his eyes closed, his breath slow, as if his lengthy monologue had exhausted him. Gundersen did not disturb him. He put the wine down and walked away, strolling for more than an hour, thinking, reaching no conclusion. Then he returned. Cullen had not moved. "Still asleep?" Gundersen asked the sulidoror.

"It is the long sleep," one of them replied.

Fourteen

The mist came in close, bringing jewels of frost that hung from every tree, every hut; and by the brink of the leaden lake Gundersen cremated Cullen's wasted body with one long fiery burst of the fusion torch, while sulidoror looked on, silent, solemn. The soil sizzled a while when he was done, and the mist whirled wildly as cold air rushed in to fill the zone of warmth his torch had made. Within the hut were a few unimportant possessions. Gundersen searched through them, hoping to find a journal, a memoir, anything with the imprint of Cedric Cullen's soul and personality. But he found only some rusted tools, and a box of dried insects and lizards, and faded clothing. He left these things where he found them.

The sulidoror brought him a cold dinner. They let him eat undisturbed, sitting on the wooden cradle outside Cullen's hut. Darkness came, and he retreated into the hut to sleep. Se-holomir and Y-gartigok posted themselves as guards before the entrance, although he had not asked them to stay there. He said nothing to them. Early in the evening he fell asleep.

He dreamed, oddly, not of the newly dead Cullen but of the still living Kurtz. He saw Kurtz trekking through the mist country, the old Kurtz, not yet metamorphosed to his present state: infinitely tall, pale, eyes burning in the domed skull, glowing with strange intelligence. Kurtz carried a pilgrim's staff and strode tirelessly forward into the mist. Accompanying him, yet not really with him, was a procession of nildoror, their green bodies stained bright red by pigmented mud; they halted whenever Kurtz halted, and knelt beside him, and from time to time he let them drink from a tubular canteen he was carrying. Whenever Kurtz offered his canteen to the nildoror, he and not they underwent a transformation. His lips joined in a smooth sealing; his nose lengthened; his eyes, his fingers, his toes, his legs changed and changed again. Fluid, mobile, Kurtz kept no form for long. At one stage in the journey he became a sulidor in all respects but one: his own high-vaulted bald head surmounted the massive hairy body. Then the fur melted from him, the claws shrank, and he took on another form, a lean loping thing, rapacious and swift with double-jointed elbows and long spindly legs. More changes followed. The nildoror sang hymns of adoration, chanting in thick monotonous skeins of gray sound. Kurtz was gracious. He bowed, he smiled, he waved. He passed around his canteen, which never needed replenishing. He rippled through cycle upon cycle of dizzy metamorphosis. From his backpack he drew gifts that he distributed among

the nildoror: torches, knives, books, message cubes, computers, statues, color organs, butterflies, flasks of wine, sensors,
transport modules, musical instruments, beads, old etchings,
holy medallions, baskets of flowers, bombs, flares, shoes,
keys, toys, spears. Each gift fetched ecstatic sighs and snorts
and moos of gratitude from the nildoror; they frolicked about
him, lifting their new treasures in their trunks, excitedly
displaying them to one another. "You see?" Kurtz cried. "I am
your benefactor. I am your friend. I am the resurrection and
the life." They came now to the place of rebirth, not a
mountain in Gundersen's dream but rather an abyss, dark
and deep, at the rim of which the nildoror gathered and
waited. And Kurtz, undergoing so many transformations that
his body flickered and shifted from moment to moment, now
wearing horns, now covered with scales, now clad in shimmering
flame, walked forward while the nildoror cheered him, saying
to him, "This is the place, rebirth will be yours," and he
stepped into the abyss, which enfolded him in absolute night.
And then from the depths of the pit came a single prolonged
cry, a shrill wail of terror and dismay so awful that it awakened
Gundersen, who lay sweating and shivering for hours waiting
for dawn.

In the morning he shouldered his pack and made signs of
departing. Se-holomir and Yi-gartigok came to him; and one
of the sulidoror said, "Where will you go now?"

"North."

"Shall we go with you?"

"I'll go alone," Gundersen said.

It would be a difficult journey, perhaps a dangerous one,
but not impossible. He had direction-finding equipment,
food concentrates, a power supply, and other such things. He
had the necessary stamina. He knew that the sulidoror villages along the way would extend hospitality to him if he
needed it. But he hoped not to need it. He had been
escorted long enough, first by Srin'gahar, then by various
sulidoror; he felt he should finish this pilgrimage without a
guide.

Two hours after sunrise he set out.

It was a good day for beginning such an endeavor. The air
was crisp and cool and clear and the mist was high; he could
see surprisingly far in all directions. He went through the
forest back of the village and emerged on a fair-sized hill from
the top of which he was able to gauge the landscape ahead.

He saw rugged, heavily forested country, much broken by rivers and streams and lakes; and he succeeded in glimpsing the tip of the mountain of rebirth, a jagged sentinel in the north. That rosy peak on the horizon seemed close enough to grasp. Just reach out; just extend the fingers. And the fissures and hillocks and slopes that separated him from his goal were no challenge; they could be traversed in a few quick bounds. His body was eager for the attempt: heartbeat steady, vision exceptionally keen, legs moving smoothly and tirelessly. He sensed an inward soaring of the soul, a restrained but ecstatic upsweep toward life and power; the phantoms that had veiled him for so many years were dropping away; in this chill zone of mist and snow he felt annealed, purified, tempered, ready to accept whatever must be accepted. A strange energy surged through him. He did not mind the thinness of the air, nor the cold, nor the bleakness of the land. It was a morning of unusual clarity, with bright sunlight cascading through the lofty covering of fog and imparting a dreamlike brilliance to the trees and the bare soil. He walked steadily onward.

The mist closed in at midday. Visibility dwindled until Gundersen could see only eight or ten meters ahead. The giant trees became serious obstacles; their gnarled roots and writhing buttresses now were traps for unwary feet. He picked his way with care. Then he entered a region where large flat-topped boulders jutted at shallow angles from the ground, one after another, slick mist-slippery slabs forming stepping-stones to the land beyond. He had to crawl over them, blindly feeling along, not knowing how much of a drop he was likely to encounter at the far end of each boulder. Jumping off was an act of faith; one of the drops turned out to be about four meters, and he landed hard, so that his ankles tingled for fifteen minutes afterward. Now he felt the first fatigue of the day spreading through his thighs and knees. But yet the mood of controlled ecstasy, sober and nevertheless jubilant, remained with him.

He made a late lunch beside a small, flawlessly circular pond, mirror-bright, rimmed by tall narrow-trunked trees and hemmed in by a tight band of mist. He relished the privacy, the solitude of the place; it was like a spherical room with walls of cotton, within which he was perfectly isolated from a perplexing universe. Here he could shed the tensions of his journey, after so many weeks of traveling with nildoror and sulidoror, worrying all the while that he would give offense in some unknown but unforgivable way. He was reluctant to leave.

As he was gathering his belongings, an unwelcome sound punctured his seclusion: the drone of an engine not far overhead. Shading his eyes against the glare of the mist, he looked up, and after a moment caught a glimpse of an airborne beetle flying just below the cloud-ceiling. The little snubnosed vehicle moved in a tight circle, as if looking for something. For me, he wondered? Automatically he shrank back against a tree to hide, though he knew it was impossible for the pilot to see him here even in the open. A moment later the beetle was gone, vanishing in a bank of fog just to the west. But the magic of the afternoon was shattered. That ugly mechanical droning noise in the sky still reverberated in Gundersen's mind, shattering his newfound peace.

An hour's march onward, passing through a forest of slender trees with red gummy-looking bark, Gundersen encountered three sulidoror, the first he had seen since parting from Yi-gartigok and Se-holomir that morning. Gundersen was uneasy about the meeting. Would they permit him free access here? These three evidently were a hunting party returning to a nearby village; two of them carried, lashed to a pole slung from shoulder to shoulder, the trussed-up carcass of some large four-legged grazing animal with velvety black skin and long recurved horns. He felt a quick instinctive jolt of fear at the sight of the three gigantic creatures coming toward him among the trees; but to his surprise the fear faded almost as rapidly as it came. The sulidoror, for all their ferocious mien, simply did not hold a threat. True, they could kill him with a slap, but what of that? They had no more reason to attack him than he did to burn them with his torch. And here in their natural surroundings, they did not even seem bestial or savage. Large, yes. Powerful. Mighty of fang and claw. But natural, fitting, proper, and so not terrifying.

"Does the traveler journey well?" asked the lead sulidor, the one who bore no part of the burden of the kill. He spoke in a soft and civil tone, using the language of the nildoror.

"The traveler journeys well," said Gundersen. He improvised a return salutation: "Is the forest kind to the huntsmen?"

"As you see, the huntsmen have fared well. If your path goes toward our village, you are welcome to share our kill this night."

"I go toward the mountain of rebirth."

"Our village lies in that direction. Will you come?"

He accepted the offer, for night was coming on, and a harsh wind was slicing through the trees now. The sulidoror village was a small one, at the foot of a sheer cliff half an hour's walk to the northeast. Gundersen passed a pleasant night there. The villagers were courteous though aloof, in a manner wholly free of any hostility; they gave him a corner of a hut, supplied him with food and drink, and left him alone. He had no sense of being a member of a despised race of ejected conquerors, alien and unwanted. They appeared to look upon him merely as a wayfarer in need of shelter, and showed no concern over his species. He found that refreshing. Of course, the sulidoror did not have the same reasons for resentment as the nildoror, since these forest folk had never actually been turned into slaves by the Company; but he had always imagined a seething, sizzling rage within the sulidoror, and their easygoing kindness now was an agreeable departure from that image, which Gundersen now suspected might merely have been a projection of his own guilts. In the morning they brought him fruits and fish, and then he took his leave.

The second day of his journey alone was not as rewarding as the first. The weather was bad, cold and damp and frequently snowy, with dense mist hanging low nearly all the time. He wasted much of the morning by trapping himself in a cul-de-sac, with a long ridge of hills to his right, another to his left, and, unexpectedly, a broad and uncrossable lake appearing in front of him. Swimming it was unthinkable; he might have to pass several hours in its frigid water, and he would not survive the exposure. So he had to go on a wearying eastward detour over the lesser ridge of hills, which swung him about so that by midday he was in no higher a latitude than he had been the night before. The sight of the fog-wreathed rebirth mountain drew him on, though, and for two hours of the afternoon he had the illusion that he was making up for the morning's delay, only to discover that he was cut off by a swift and vast river flowing from west to east, evidently the one that fed the lake that had blocked him earlier. He did not dare to swim this, either; the current would sweep him into the distant deeps before he had reached the farther bank. Instead he consumed more than an hour following the river upstream, until he came to a place where he might ford it. It was even wider here than below, but its bed looked much more shallow, and some geological upheaval had strewn a line of boulders across it like a necklace, from bank to bank. A dozen of the boulders jutted up, with white water swirling around them; the others, though submerged, were visible just below the surface. Gundersen started across. He was able to hop from the top of one boulder to the next, keeping dry until he had gone nearly a third of the way. Then he had to scramble in the water, wading shin-deep, slipping and groping. The mist enveloped him. He might have been alone in the universe, with nothing ahead but billows of whiteness, nothing to the rear but the same. He could see no trees, no shore, not even the boulders awaiting him. He concentrated rigidly on keeping his footing and staying to his path. Putting one foot down awry, he slid and toppled, landing in a half-crouch in the river, drenched to the armpits, buffeted by the current, and so dizzied for a moment that he could not rise. All his energy was devoted to clinging to the angular mass of rock beneath him. After a few minutes he found the strength to get to his feet again, and tottered forward, gasping, until he reached a boulder whose upper face stood half a meter above the water; he knelt on it, chilled, soaked, shivering, trying to shake himself dry. Perhaps five minutes passed. With the mist clinging close, he got no drier, but at least he had his breath again, and he resumed his crossing. Experimentally reaching out the tip of a boot, he found another dry-topped boulder just ahead. He went to it. There was still another beyond it. Then came another. It was easy, now: he would make it to the far side without another soaking. His pace quickened, and he traversed another pair of boulders. Then, through a rift in the mist, he was granted a glimpse of the shore.

Something seemed wrong.

This mist sealed itself; but Gundersen hesitated to go on without some assurance that all was as it should be. Carefully he bent low and dipped his left hand in the water. He felt the thrust of the current coming from the right and striking his open palm. Wearily, wondering if cold and fatigue had affected his mind, he worked out the topography of his situation several times and each time came to the same dismaying conclusion: if I am making a northward crossing of a river that flows from west to east, I should feel the current coming from my *left*. Somehow, he realized, he had turned himself around while scrambling for purchase in the water, and since then he had with great diligence been heading back toward the southern bank of the river.

His faith in his own judgment was destroyed. He was tempted to wait here, huddled on this rock, for the mist to clear before going on; but then it occurred to him that he might have to wait through the night, or even longer. He also realized belatedly that he was carrying gear designed to cope with just such problems. Fumbling in his backpack, he pulled out the small cool shaft of his compass and aimed it at the horizon, sweeping his arm in an arc that terminated where the compass emitted its north-indicating beep. It confirmed his conclusions about the current, and he started across the river again, shortly coming to the place of the submerged stepping-stones where he had fallen. This time he had no difficulties.

On the far shore he stripped and dried his clothing and himself with the lowest-power beam of his fusion torch. Night now was upon him. He would not have regretted another invitation to a sulidoror village, but today no hospitable sulidoror appeared. He spent an uncomfortable night huddled under a bush.

The next day was warmer and less misty. Gundersen went warily forward, forever fearing that his hours of hard hiking might be wasted when he came up against some unforeseen new obstacle, but all went well, and he was able to cope with the occasional streams or rivulets that crossed his path. The land here was ridged and folded as though giant hands, one to the north and one to the south, had pushed the globe together; but as Gundersen was going down one slope and up the next, he was also gaining altitude constantly, for the entire continent sloped upward toward the mighty plateau upon which the rebirth mountain was reared.

In early afternoon the prevailing pattern of east-west folds in the land subsided; here the landscape was skewed around so that he found himself walking parallel to a series of gentle north-south furrows, which opened into a wide circular meadow, grassy but treeless. The large animals of the north, whose names Gundersen did not know, grazed here in great numbers, nuzzling in the lightly snow-covered ground. There seemed to be only four or five species—something heavy-legged and humpbacked, like a badly designed cow, and something in the style of an oversize gazelle, and several others—but there were hundreds or even thousands of each kind. Far to the east, at the very border of the plain,

Gundersen saw what appeared to be a small sulidoror hunting-party rounding up some of the animals.

He heard the drone of the engine again.

The beetle he had seen the other day now returned, passing quite low overhead. Instinctively Gundersen threw himself to the ground, hoping to go unnoticed. About him the animals milled uneasily, perplexed at the noise, but they did not bolt. The beetle drifted to a landing about a thousand meters north of him. He decided that Seena must have come after him, hoping to intercept him before he could submit himself to the sulidoror of the mountain of rebirth. But he was wrong. The hatch of the beetle opened, and Van Beneker and his tourists began to emerge.

Gundersen wriggled forward until he was concealed behind a tall stand of thistle-like plants on a low hummock. He could not abide the thought of meeting that crew again, not at this stage in his pilgrimage, when he had been purged of so many vestiges of the Gundersen who had been.

He watched them.

They were walking up to the animals, photographing them, even daring to touch some of the more sluggish beasts. Gundersen heard their voices and their laughter cracking the congealed silence; isolated words drifted randomly toward him, as meaningless as Kurtz's flow of dream-fogged gibberish. He heard, too, Van Beneker's voice cutting through the chatter, describing and explaining and expounding. These nine humans before him on the meadow seemed as alien to Gundersen as the sulidoror. More so, perhaps. He was aware that these last few days of mist and chill, this solitary odyssey through a world of whiteness and quiet, had worked a change in him that he barely comprehended. He felt lean of soul, stripped of the excess baggage of the spirit, a simpler man in all respects, and yet more complex.

He waited an hour or more, still hidden, while the tourist party finished touring the meadow. Then everyone returned to the beetle. Where now? Would Van take them north to spy on the mountain of rebirth? No. No. It wasn't possible. Van Beneker himself dreaded the whole business of rebirth, like any good Earthman; he wouldn't dare to trespass on that mysterious precinct.

When the beetle took off, though, it headed toward the north.

Gundersen, in his distress, shouted to it to turn back. As though heeding him, the gleaming little vehicle veered round as it gained altitude. Van Beneker must have been trying to catch a tailwind, nothing more. Now the beetle made for the south. The tour was over, then. Gundersen saw it pass directly above him and disappear into a lofty bank of fog. Choking with relief, he rushed forward, scattering the puzzled herds with wild loud whoops.

Now all obstacles seemed to be behind him. Gundersen crossed the valley, negotiated a snowy divide without effort, forded a shallow brook, pushed his way through a forest of short, thick, tightly packed trees with narrow pointed crowns. He slipped into an easy rhythm of travel, paying no heed any longer to cold, mist, damp, altitude, or fatigue. He was tuned to his task. When he slept, he slept soundly and well; when he foraged for food to supplement his concentrates, he found that which was good; when he sought to cover distance, he covered it. The peace of the misty forest inspired him to do prodigies. He tested himself, searching for the limits of his endurance, finding them, exceeding them at the next opportunity.

Through this phase of the journey he was wholly alone. Sometimes he saw sulidoror tracks in the thin crust of snow that covered much of the land, but he met no one. The beetle did not return. Even his dreams were empty; the Kurtz phantom that had plagued him earlier was absent now, and he dreamed only blank abstractions, forgotten by the time of awakening.

He did not know how many days had elapsed since the death of Cedric Cullen. Time had flowed and melted in upon itself. He felt no impatience, no weariness, no sense of wanting it all to be over. And so it came as a mild surprise to him when, as he began to ascend a wide, smooth, shelving ledge of stone, about thirty meters wide, bordered by a wall of icicles and decorated in places by tufts of grass and scraggly trees, he looked up and realized that he had commenced the scaling of the mountain of rebirth.

Fifteen

From afar, the mountain had seemed to rise dramatically from the misty plain in a single sweeping thrust. But now that

Gundersen was actually upon its lower slopes, he saw that at close range the mountain dissolved into a series of ramps of pink stone, one atop another. The totality of the mountain was the sum of that series, yet from here he had no sense of a unified bulk. He could not even see the lofty peaks and turrets and domes that he knew must hover thousands of meters above him. A layer of clinging mist severed the mountain less than halfway up, allowing him to see only the broad, incomprehensible base. The rest, which had guided him across hundreds of kilometers, might well have never been.

The ascent was easy. To the right and to the left Gundersen saw sheer faces, impossible spires, fragile bridges of stone linking ledge to ledge; but there was also a switchback path, evidently of natural origin, that gave the patient climber access to the higher reaches. The dung of innumerable nildoror littered this long stone ramp, telling him that he must be on the right route. He could not imagine the huge creatures going up the mountain any other way. Even a sulidor would be taxed by those precipices and gullies.

Chattering munzoror leaped from ledge to ledge, or walked with soft, shuffling steps across terrifying abysses spanned by strands of vines. Goat-like beasts, white with diamond-shaped black markings, capered in graveled pockets of unreachable slopes, and launched booming halloos that echoed through the afternoon. Gundersen climbed steadily. The air was cold but invigorating; the mists were wispy at this level, giving him a clear view before and behind. He looked back and saw the fog-shrouded lowlands suddenly quite far below him. He imagined that he was able to see all the way to the open meadow where the beetle had landed.

He wondered when some sulidor would intercept him.

This was, after all, the most sacred spot on this planet. Were there no guardians? No one to stop him, to question him, to turn him back?

He came to a place about two hours' climb up the mountainside where the upward slope diminished and the ramp became a long horizontal promenade, curving off to the right and vanishing beyond the mass of the mountain. As Gundersen followed it, three sulidoror appeared, coming around the bend. They glanced briefly at him and went past, taking no other notice, as though it were quite ordinary that an Earthman should be going up the mountain of rebirth.

Or, Gundersen thought strangely, as though he were *expected*.

After a while the ramp turned upward again. Now an overhanging stone ledge formed a partial roof for the path, but it was no shelter, for the little cackling wizen-faced munzoror nested up there, dropping pebbles and bits of chaff and worse things down. Monkeys? Rodents? Whatever they were, they introduced a sacrilegious note to the solemnity of this great peak, mocking those who went up. They dangled by their prehensile tails; they twitched their long tufted ears; they spat; they laughed. What were they saying? "Go away, Earthman, this is no shrine of yours!" Was that it? How about, "Abandon hope, all ye who enter here!"

He camped for the night beneath that ledge. Munzoror several times scrambled across his face. Once he woke to what sounded like the sobbing of a woman, deep and intense, in the abyss below. He went to the edge and found a bitter snowstorm raging. Soaring through the storm, rising and sinking, rising and sinking, were sleek bat-like things of the upper reaches, with tubular black bodies and great rubbery yellow wings; they went down until they were lost to his sight, and sped upward again toward their eyries clasping chunks of raw meat in their sharp red beaks. He did not hear the sobbing again. When sleep returned, he lay as if drugged until a brilliant dawn crashed like thunder against the side of the mountain.

He bathed in an ice-rimmed stream that sped down a smooth gully and intersected the path. Then he went upward, and in the third hour of his morning's stint he overtook a party of nildoror plodding toward rebirth. They were not green but pinkish-gray, marking them as members of the kindred race, the nildoror of the eastern hemisphere. Gundersen had never known whether these nildoror enjoyed rebirth facilities in their own continent, or came to undergo the process here. That was answered now. There were five of them, moving slowly and with extreme effort. Their hides were cracked and ridged, and their trunks—thicker and longer than those of western nildoror—drooped limply. It wearied him just to look at them. They had good reason to be tired, though: since nildoror had no way of crossing the ocean, they must have taken the land route, the terrible northeastward journey across the dry bed of the Sea of Dust. Occasionally, during his tour of duty there, Gundersen had seen eastern nildoror dragging themselves through that crystalline wasteland, and at last he understood what their destination had been.

"Joy of your rebirth!" he called to them as he passed, using the terse eastern inflection.

"Peace be on your journey," one of the nildoror replied calmly.

They, too, saw nothing amiss in his presence here. But he did. He could not avoid thinking of himself as an intruder, an interloper. Instinctively he began to lurk and skulk, keeping to the inside of the path as though that made him less conspicuous. He anticipated his rejection at any moment by some custodian of the mountain, stepping forth suddenly to block his climb.

Above him, another two or three spirals of the path overhead, he spied a scene of activity.

Two nildoror and perhaps a dozen sulidoror were in view up there, standing at the entrance to some dark chasm in the mountainside. He could see them only by taking up a precarious position at the rim of the path. A third nildor emerged from the cavern; several sulidoror went in. Some way-station, maybe, on the road to rebirth? He craned his neck to see, but as he continued along his path he reached a point from which that upper level was no longer visible.

It took him longer than he expected to reach it. The switchback path looped out far to one side in order to encircle a narrow jutting spiky tower of rock sprouting from the great mountain's flank, and the detour proved to be lengthy. It carried Gundersen well around to the northeastern face. By the time he·was able to see the level of the chasm again, a sullen twilight was falling, and the place he sought was still somewhere above him.

Full darkness came before he was on its level. A heavy blanket of fog sat close upon things now. He was perhaps midway up the peak. Here the path spread into the mountain's face, creating a wide plaza covered with brittle flakes of pale stone, and against the vaulting wall of the mountain Gundersen saw a black slash, a huge inverted V, the opening of what must be a mighty cavern. Three nildoror lay sleeping to the left of this entrance, and five sulidoror, to its right, seemed to be conferring.

He hung back, posting himself behind a convenient boulder and allowing himself wary peeps at the mouth of the cavern. The sulidoror went within, and for more than an hour nothing happened. Then he saw them emerge, awaken one of the nildoror, and lead it inside. Another hour passed before they came back for the second. After a while they fetched the third. Now the night was well advanced. The mist, the constant companion here, approached and clung. The big-beaked bat-creatures, like marionettes on strings, swooped down from higher zones of the mountain, shrieking past and vanishing in the drifting fog below, returning moments later in equally swift ascent. Gundersen was alone. This was his moment to peer into the cavern, but he could not bring himself to make the inspection. He hesitated, shivering, unable to go forward. His lungs were choked with mist. He could see nothing in any direction now; even the bat-beasts were invisible, mere dopplering blurts of sound as they rose and fell. He struggled to recapture some of the jauntiness he had felt on that first day after Cullen's death, setting out unaccompanied through this wintry land. With a conscious effort he found a shred of that vigor at last.

He went to the mouth of the cavern.

He saw only darkness within. Neither sulidoror nor nildoror were evident at the entrance. He took a cautious step inward. The cavern was cool, but it was a dry coolness far more agreeable than the mist-sodden chill outside. Drawing his fusion torch, he risked a quick flash of light and discovered that he stood in the center of an immense chamber, the lofty ceiling of which was lost in the shadows overhead. The walls of the chamber were a baroque fantasy of folds and billows and buttresses and fringes and towers, all of stone, polished and translucent, gleaming like convoluted glass during the instant that the light was upon them. Straight ahead, flanked by two rippling wings of stone that were parted like frozen curtains, lay a passageway, wide enough for Gundersen but probably something of a trial for the bulky nildoror who had earlier come this way.

He went toward it.

Two more brief flashes from the torch got him to it. Then he proceeded by touch, gripping one side of the opening and feeling his way into its depths. The corridor bent sharply to the left and, about twenty paces farther on, angled just as sharply the other way. As Gundersen came around the second bend a dim light greeted him. Here a pale green fungoid growth lining the ceiling afforded a minimal sort of illumination. He felt relieved and yet suddenly vulnerable, for, while he now could see, he could also be seen.

The corridor was about twice a nildor's width and three times a nildor's height, rising to the peaked vault in which the fungoids dwelled. It stretched for what seemed an infinite distance into the mountain. Branching off it on both sides, Gundersen saw, were secondary chambers and passages.

He advanced and peered into the nearest of these chambers.

It held something that was large and strange and apparently alive. On the floor of a bare stone cell lay a mass of pink flesh, shapeless and still. Gundersen made out short thick limbs and a tail curled tightly over broad flanks; he could not see its head, nor any distinguishing marks by which he could associate it with a species he knew. It might have been a nildor, but it did not seem quite large enough. As he watched, it swelled with the intake of a breath, and slowly subsided. Many minutes passed before it took another breath. Gundersen moved on.

In the next cell he found a similar sleeping mound of unidentifiable flesh. In the third cell lay another. The fourth cell, on the opposite side of the corridor, contained a nildor of the western species, also in deep slumber. The cell beside it was occupied by a sulidor lying oddly on its back with its limbs poking rigidly upward. The next cell held a sulidor in the same position, but otherwise quite startlingly different, for it had shed its whole thick coat of fur and lay naked, revealing awesome muscles beneath a gray, slick-looking skin. Continuing, Gundersen came to a chamber that housed something even more bizarre: a figure that had a nildor's spines and tusks and trunk but a sulidor's powerful arms and legs and a sulidor's frame. What nightmare composite was this? Gundersen stood awed before it for a long while, trying to comprehend how the head of a nildor might have been joined to the body of a sulidor. He realized that no such joining could have occurred; the sleeper here simply partook of the characteristics of both races in a single body. A hybrid? A genetic mingling?

He did not know. But he knew now that this was no mere way-station on the road toward rebirth. This was the place of rebirth itself.

Far ahead, figures emerged from one of the subsidiary corridors and crossed the main chamber: two sulidoror and a nildor. Gundersen pressed himself against the wall and remained motionless until they were out of sight, disappearing into some distant room. Then he continued inward.

He saw nothing but miracles. He was in a garden of fantasies where no natural barriers held.

Here was a round spongy mass of soft pink flesh with just one recognizable feature sprouting from it: a sulidor's huge tail.

Here was a sulidor, bereft of fur, whose arms were foreshortened and pillar-like, like the limbs of a nildor, and whose body had grown round and heavy and thick.

Here was a sulidor in full fur with a nildor's trunk and ears.

Here was raw meat that was neither nildor nor sulidor, but alive and passive, a mere thing awaiting a sculptor's shaping hand.

Here was another thing that resembled a sulidor whose bones had melted.

Here was still another thing that resembled a nildor who had never had bones.

Here were trunks, spines, tusks, fangs, claws, tails, paws. Here was fur, and here was smooth hide. Here was flesh flowing at will and seeking new shapes. Here were dark chambers, lit only by flickering fungoid-glow, in which no firm distinction of species existed.

Biology's laws seemed suspended here. This was no trifling gene-tickling that he saw, Gundersen knew. On Earth, any skilled helix-parlor technician could redesign an organism's gene-plasm with some cunning thrusts of a needle and a few short spurts of drugs; he could make a camel bring forth a hippopotamus, a cat bring forth a chipmunk, or, for that matter, a woman bring forth a sulidor. One merely enhanced the desired characteristics within sperm and ovum, and suppressed other characteristics, until one had a reasonable facsimile of the creature to be reproduced. The basic genetic building-blocks were the same for every life-form; by rearranging them, one could create any kind of strange and monstrous progeny. But that was not what was being done here.

On Earth, Gundersen knew, it was also possible to persuade any living cell to play the part of a fertilized egg, and divide, and grow, and yield a full organism. The venom from Belzagor was one catalyst for that process; there were others. And so one could induce the stump of a man's arm to regrow that arm; one could scrape a bit of skin from a frog and generate an army of frogs with it; one could even rebuild an

entire human being from the shards of his own ruined body.
But that was not what was being done here.

What was being done here, Gundersen realized, was a
transmutation of species, a change worked not upon ova but
upon adult organisms. Now he understood Na-sinisul's re-
mark, when asked if sulidoror also underwent rebirth: "If
there were no day, could there be night?" Yes. Nildor into
sulidor. Sulidor into nildor. Gundersen shivered in shock. He
reeled, clutching at a wall. He was plunged into a universe
without fixed points. What was real? What was enduring?

He comprehended now what had happened to Kurtz in
this mountain.

Gundersen stumbled into a cell in which a creature lay
midway in its metamorphosis. Smaller than a nildor, larger
than a sulidor; fangs, not tusks; trunk, not snout; fur, not
hide; flat footpads, not claws; body shaped for walking upright.

"Who are you?" Gundersen whispered. "What are you?
What were you? Which way are you heading?"

Rebirth. Cycle upon cycle upon cycle. Nildoror bound
upon a northward pilgrimage, entering these caves, becoming
. . . sulidoror? Was it possible?

If this is true, Gundersen thought, then we have never
really known anything about this planet. And this is true.

He ran wildly from cell to cell, no longer caring whether
he might be discovered. Each cell confirmed his guess. He
saw nildoror and sulidoror in every stage of metamorphosis,
some almost wholly nildoror, some unmistakably sulidoror,
but most of them occupying intermediate positions along that
journey from pole to pole; more than half were so deep in
transformation that it was impossible for him to tell which way
they were heading. All slept. Before his eyes flesh flowed,
but nothing moved. In these cool shadowy chambers change
came as a dream.

Gundersen reached the end of the corridor. He pressed his
palms against cold, unyielding stone. Breathless, sweat-
drenched, he turned toward the last chamber in the series
and plunged into it.

Within was a sulidor not yet asleep, standing over three of
the sluggish serpents of the tropics, which moved in gentle
coils about him. The sulidor was huge, age-grizzled, a being
of unusual presence and dignity.

"Na-sinisul?" Gundersen asked.

"We knew that in time you must come here, Edmund-gundersen."

"I never imagined—I didn't understand—" Gundersen paused, struggling to regain control. More quietly he said, "Forgive me if I have intruded. Have I interrupted your rebirth's beginning?"

"I have several days yet," the sulidor said. "I merely prepare the chamber now."

"And you'll come forth from it as a nildor."

"Yes. Over and over, rebirth after rebirth."

"Life goes in a cycle here, then? Sulidor to nildor to sulidor to nildor to—"

"Yes. Over and over, rebirth after rebirth."

"All nildoror spend part of their lives as sulidoror? All sulidoror spend part of their lives as nildoror?"

"Yes. All."

How had it began, Gundersen wondered? How had the destinies of these two so different races become entangled? How had an entire species consented to undergo such a metamorphosis? He could not begin to understand it. But he knew now why he had never seen an infant nildor or sulidor. He said, "Are young ones of either race ever born on this world?"

"Only when needed as replacements for those who can be reborn no more. It is not often. Our population is stable."

"Stable, yet constantly changing."

"Through a predictable pattern of change," said Na-sinisul. "When I emerge, I will be Fi'gontor of the ninth birth. My people have waited for thirty turnings for me to rejoin them; but circumstances required me to remain this long in the forest of the mists."

"Is nine rebirths unusual?"

"There are those among us who have been here fifteen times. There are some who wait a hundred turnings to be called once. The summons comes when the summons comes. And for those who merit it, life will have no end."

"No—end—"

"Why should it?" Na-sinisul asked. "In this mountain we are purged of the poisons of age, and elsewhere we purge ourselves of the poisons of sin."

"On the central plateau, that is."

"I see you have spoken with the man Cullen."

"Yes," Gundersen said. "Just before his—death."

"I knew also that his life was over," said Na-sinisul. "We learn things swiftly here."

Gundersen said, "Where are Srin'gahar and Luu'khamin and the others I traveled with?"

"They are here, in cells not far away."

"Already in rebirth?"

"For some days now. They will be sulidoror soon, and will live in the north until they are summoned to assume the nildor form again. Thus we refresh our souls by undertaking new lives."

"During the sulidor phase, you keep a memory of your past life as a nildor?"

"Certainly. How can experience be valuable if it is not retained? We accumulate wisdom. Our grasp of truth is heightened by seeing the universe now through a nildor's eyes, now through a sulidor's. Not in body alone are the two forms different. To undergo rebirth is to enter a new world, not merely a new life."

Hesitantly Gundersen said, "And when someone who is not of this planet undergoes rebirth? What effect is there? What kind of changes happen?"

"You saw Kurtz?"

"I saw Kurtz," said Gundersen. "But I have no idea what Kurtz has become."

"Kurtz has become Kurtz," the sulidor said. "For your kind there can be no true transformation, because you have no complementary species. You change, yes, but you become only what you have the potential to become. You liberate such forces as already exist within you. While he slept, Kurtz chose his new form himself. No one else designed it for him. It is not easy to explain this with words, Edmundgundersen."

"If I underwent rebirth, then, I wouldn't necessarily turn into something like Kurtz?"

"Not unless your soul is as Kurtz's soul, and that is not possible."

"What *would* I become?"

"No one may know these things before the fact. If you wish to discover what rebirth will do to you, you must accept rebirth."

"If I asked for rebirth, would I be permitted to have it?"

"I told you when we first met," said Na-sinisul, "that no one on this world will prevent you from doing anything. You were not stopped as you ascended the mountain of rebirth.

You were not stopped when you explored these chambers. Rebirth will not be denied you if you feel you need to experience it."

Easily, serenely, instantly, Gundersen said, "Then I ask for rebirth."

Sixteen

Silently, unsurprised, Na-sinisul leads him to a vacant cell and gestures to him to remove his clothing. Gundersen strips. His fingers fumble only slightly with the snaps and catches. At the sulidor's direction, Gundersen lies on the floor, as all other candidates for rebirth have done. The stone is so cold that he hisses when his bare skin touches it. Na-sinisul goes out. Gundersen looks up at the glowing fungoids in the distant vault of the ceiling. The chamber is large enough to hold a nildor comfortably; to Gundersen, on the floor, it seems immense.

Na-sinisul returns, bearing a bowl made from a hollow log. He offers it to Gundersen. The bowl contains a pale blue fluid. "Drink," says the sulidor softly.

Gundersen drinks.

The taste is sweet, like sugar-water. This is something he has tasted before, and he knows when it was: at the serpent station, years ago. It is the forbidden venom. He drains the bowl, and Na-sinisul leaves him.

Two sulidoror whom Gundersen does not know enter the cell. They kneel on either side of him and begin a low mumbling chant, some sort of ritual. He cannot understand any of it. They knead and stroke his body; their hands, with the fearful claws retracted, are strangely soft, like the pads of a cat. He is tense, but the tension ebbs. He feels the drug taking effect now: a thickness at the back of his head, a tightness in his chest, a blurring of his vision. Na-sinisul is in the room again, although Gundersen did not see him enter. He carries a bowl.

"Drink," he says, and Gundersen drinks.

It is another fluid entirely, or perhaps a different distillate of the venom. Its flavor is bitter, with undertastes of smoke

and ash. He has to force himself to get to the bottom of the
bowl, but Na-sinisul waits, silently insistent, for him to finish
it. Again the old sulidor leaves. At the mouth of the cell he
turns and says something to Gundersen, but the words are
overgrown with heavy blue fur, and will not enter Gundersen's
ears. "What did you say?" the Earthman asks. "What? What?"
His own words sprout leaden weights, teardrop-shaped, somber. They fall at once to the floor and shatter. One of the
chanting sulidoror sweeps the broken words into a corner
with a quick motion of his tail.

Gundersen hears a trickling sound, a glittering spiral of
noise, as of water running into his cell. His eyes are closed,
but he feels the wetness swirling about him. It is not water,
though. It has a more solid texture. A sort of gelatin, perhaps. Lying on his back, he is several centimeters deep in it,
and the level is rising. It is cool but not cold, and it insulates
him nicely from the chill rock of the floor. He is aware of the
faint pink odor of the inflowing gelatin, and of its firm
consistency, like the tones of a bassoon in its deepest register.
The sulidoror continue to chant. He feels a tube sliding into
his mouth, a sleek piccolo-shriek of a tube, and through its
narrow core there drips yet another substance, thick, oily,
emitting the sound of muted kettledrums as it hits his palate.
Now the gelatin has reached the lower curve of his jaw. He
welcomes its advance. It laps gently at his chin. The tube is
withdrawn from his mouth just as the flow of gelatin covers
his lips. "Will I be able to breath?" he asks. A sulidor answers
him in cryptic Sumerian phrases, and Gundersen is reassured.

He is wholly sealed in the gelatin. It covers the floor of the
chamber to a depth of one meter. Light dimly penetrates it.
Gundersen knows that its upper surface is smooth and flawless, forming a perfect seal where it touches the walls of the
cell. Now he has become a chrysalis. He will be given
nothing more to drink. He will lie here, and he will be
reborn.

One must die in order that one may be reborn, he knows.

Death comes to him and enfolds him. Gently he slides into
a dark abyss. The embrace of death is tender. Gundersen
floats through a realm of trembling emptiness. He hovers
suspended in the black void. Bands of scarlet and purple light
transfix him, buffeting him like bars of metal. He tumbles.
He spins. He soars.

He encounters death once more, and they wrestle, and he

is defeated by death, and his body is shivered into splinters, and a shower of bright Gundersen-fragments scatters through space.

The fragments seek one another. They solemnly circle one another. They dance. They unite. They take on the form of Edmund Gundersen, but this new Gundersen glows like pure, transparent glass. He is glistening, a transparent man through whom the light of the great sun at the core of the universe passes without resistance. A spectrum spreads forth from his chest. The brilliance of his body illuminates the galaxies.

Strands of color emanate from him and link him to all who possess g'rakh in the universe.

He partakes of the biological wisdom of the cosmos.

He tunes his soul to the essence of what is and what must be.

He is without limits. He can reach out and touch any soul. He reaches toward the soul of Na-sinisul, and the sulidor greets him and admits him. He reaches toward Srin'gahar, toward Vol'himyor the many-born, toward Luu'khamin, Seholomir, Yi-gartigok, toward the nildoror and sulidoror who lie in the caves of metamorphosis, and toward the dwellers in the misty forests, and toward the dwellers in the steaming jungles, and toward those who dance and rage in the forlorn plateau, and to all others of Belzagor who share in g'rakh.

And he comes now to one that is neither nildor nor sulidor, a sleeping soul, a veiled soul, a soul of a color and a timbre and a texture unlike the others. It is an Earthborn soul, the soul of Seena, and he calls softly to her, saying, Awaken, awaken, I love you, I have come for you. She does not awaken. He calls to her, I am new, I am reborn, I overflow with love. Join me. Become part of me. Seena? Seena? Seena? And she does not respond.

He sees the souls of the other Earthmen now. They have g'rakh, but rationality is not enough; their souls are blind and silent. Here is Van Beneker; here are the tourists; here are the lonely keepers of solitary outposts in the jungle. Here is the charred gray emptiness where the soul of Cedric Cullen belongs.

He cannot reach any of them.

He moves on, and a new soul gleams beyond the mist. It is the soul of Kurtz. Kurtz comes to him, or he to Kurtz, and Kurtz is not asleep.

Now you are among us, Kurtz says, and Gundersen says, Yes, here I am at last. Soul opens to soul and Gundersen looks down into the darkness that is Kurtz, past the pearl-gray curtain that shrouds his spirit, into a place of terror where black figures shuttle with many legs along ridged webs. Chaotic forms cohere, expand, dissolve within Kurtz. Gundersen looks beyond this dark and dismal zone, and beyond it he finds a cold hard bright light shining whitely out of the deepest place, and then Kurtz says, See? Do you see? Am I a monster? I have goodness within me.

You are not a monster, Gundersen says.

But I have suffered, says Kurtz.

For your sins, Gundersen says.

I have paid for my sins with my suffering, and I should now be released.

You have suffered, Gundersen agrees.

When will my suffering end, then?

Gundersen replies that he does not know, that it is not he who sets the limits of such things.

Kurtz says, I knew you. Nice young fellow, a little slow. Seena speaks highly of you. Sometimes she wishes things had worked out better for you and her. Instead she got me. Here I lie. Here lie we. Why won't you release me?

What can I do, asks Gundersen?

Let me come back to the mountain. Let me finish my rebirth.

Gundersen does not know how to respond, and he seeks along the circuit of g'rakh, consulting Na-sinisul, consulting Vol'himyor, consulting all the many-born ones, and they join, they join, they speak with one voice, they tell Gundersen in a voice of thunder that Kurtz is finished, his rebirth is over, he may not come back to the mountain.

Gundersen repeats this to Kurtz, but Kurtz has already heard. Kurtz shrivels. Kurtz shrinks back into darkness. He becomes enmeshed in his own webs.

Pity me, he calls out to Gundersen across a vast gulf. Pity me, for this is hell, and I am in it.

Gundersen says, I pity you. I pity you. I pity you. I pity you.

The echo of his own voice diminishes to infinity. All is silent. Out of the void, suddenly, comes Kurtz's wordless reply, a shrill and deafening crescendo blast of rage and malevolence, the scream of a flawed Prometheus flailing at the beak that pierces him. The shriek reaches a climax of shattering intensity. It dies away. The shivering fabric of the universe grows still again. A soft violet light appears, absorbing the lingering disharmonies of that one terrible outcry.

Gundersen weeps for Kurtz.

The cosmos streams with shining tears, and on that salty river Gundersen floats, traveling without will, visiting this world and that, drifting among the nebulae, passing through clouds of cosmic dust, soaring over strange suns.

He is not alone. Na-sinisul is with him, and Srin'gahar, and Vol'himyor, and all the others.

He becomes aware of the harmony of all things *g'rakh*. He sees, for the first time, the bonds that bind *g'rakh* to *g'rakh*. He, who lies in rebirth, is in contact with them all, but also they are each in contact with one another, at any time, at every time, every soul on the planet joined in wordless communication.

He sees the unity of all *g'rakh*, and it awes and humbles him.

He perceives the complexity of this double people, the rhythm of its existence, the unending and infinite swing of cycle upon cycle of rebirth and new creation, above all the union, the oneness. He perceives his own monstrous isolation, the walls that cut him off from other men, that cut off man from man, each a prisoner in his own skull. He sees what it is like to live among people who have learned to liberate the prisoner in the skull.

That knowledge dwindles and crushes him. He thinks, We made them slaves, we called them beasts, and all the time they were linked, they spoke in their minds without words, they transmitted the music of the soul one to one to one. We were alone, and they were not, and instead of kneeling before them and begging to share the miracle, we gave them work to do.

Gundersen weeps for Gundersen.

Na-sinisul says, This is no time for sorrow, and Srin'gahar says, The past is past, and Vol'himyor says, Through remorse you are redeemed, and all of them speak with one voice and at one time, and he understands. He understands.

Now Gundersen understands all.

He knows that nildor and sulidor are not two separate species but merely forms of the same creature, no more different than caterpillar and butterfly, though he cannot tell which is the caterpillar, which the butterfly. He is aware of how it was for the nildoror when they were still in their primeval state, when they were born as nildoror and died helplessly as nildoror, perishing when the inevitable decay of their souls came upon them. And he knows the fear and the ecstasy of those first few nildoror who accepted the serpent's temptation and drank the drug of liberation, and became things with fur and claws, misshapen, malformed, transmuted. And he knows their pain as they were driven out, even into the plateau where no being possessing g'rakh would venture.

And he knows their sufferings in that plateau.

And he knows the triumph of those first sulidoror, who, surmounting their isolation, returned from the wilderness bearing a new creed. Come and be changed, come and be changed! Give up this flesh for another! Graze no more, but hunt and eat flesh! Be reborn, and live again, and conquer the brooding body that drags the spirit to destruction!

And he sees the nildoror accepting their destiny and giving themselves up joyfully to rebirth, a few, and then more, and then more, and then whole encampments, entire populations, going forth, not to hide in the plateau of purification, but to live in the new way, in the land where mist rules. They cannot resist, because with the change of body comes the blessed liberation of soul, the unity, the bond of g'rakh to g'rakh.

He understands now how it was for these people when the Earthmen came, the eager, busy, ignorant, pitiful, short-lived Earthmen, who were beings of g'rakh yet who could not or would not enter into the oneness, who dabbled with the drug of liberation and did not taste it to the fullest, whose minds were sealed one against the other, whose roads and buildings and pavements spread like pockmarks over the tender land. He sees how little the Earthmen knew, and how little they were capable of learning, and how much was kept from them since they would misunderstand it, and why it was necessary for the sulidoror to hide in the mists of all these years of occupation, giving no clue to the strangers that they might be related to the nildoror, that they were the sons of the nildoror and the fathers of the nildoror as well. For if the Earthmen had known even half the truth they would have recoiled in fright, since their minds are sealed one against the other, and they would not have it any other way, except for the few who dared to learn, and too many of those were dark and demon-ridden, like Kurtz.

He feels vast relief that the time of pretending is over on this world and that nothing need be hidden any longer, that the sulidoror may go down into the lands of the nildoror and move freely about, without fear that the secret and the mystery of rebirth may accidentally be revealed to those who could not withstand such knowledge.

He knows joy that he has come here and survived the test and endured his liberation. His mind is open now, and he has been reborn.

He descends, rejoining his body. He is aware once more that he lies embedded in congealed gelatin on the cold floor of a dark cell abutting a lengthy corridor within a rose-red mountain wreathed in white mist on a strange world. He does not rise. His time is not yet come.

He yields to the tones and colors and odors and textures that flood the universe. He allows them to carry him back, and he floats easily along the time-line, so that now he is a child peering at the shield of night and trying to count the stars, and now he is timidly sipping raw venom with Kurtz and Salamone, and now he enrolls in the Company and tells a personnel computer that his strongest wish is to foster the expansion of the human empire, and now he grasps Seena on a tropic beach under the light of several moons, and now he meets her for the first time, and now he sifts crystals in the Sea of Dust, and now he mounts a nildor, and now he turns his torch on Cedric Cullen, and now he climbs the rebirth mountain, and now he trembles as Kurtz walks into a room, and now he takes the wafer on his tongue, and now he stares at the wonder of a white breast filling his cupped hand, and now he steps forth into mottled alien sunlight, and now he crouches over Hendry Dykstra's swollen body, and now, and now, and now, and now. . . .

He hears the tolling of mighty bells.

He feels the planet shuddering and shifting on its axis.

He smells dancing tongues of flame.

He touches the roots of the rebirth mountain.

He feels the souls of nildoror and sulidoror all about him.

He recognizes the words of the hymn the sulidoror sing, and he sings with them.

He grows. He shrinks. He burns. He shivers. He changes.

He awakens.

"Yes," says a thick, low voice. "Come out of it now. The time is here. Sit up. Sit up."

Gundersen's eyes open. Colors surge through his dazzled brain. It is a moment before he is able to see.

A sulidor stands at the entrance to his cell.

"I am Ti-munilee," the sulidor says. "You are born again."

"I know you," Gundersen says. "But not by that name. Who are you?"

"Reach out to me and see," says the sulidor.

Gundersen reaches out.

"I knew you as the nildor Srin'gahar," Gundersen says.

Seventeen

Leaning on the sulidor's arm, Gundersen walked unsteadily out of the chamber of rebirth. In the dark corridor he asked, "Have I been changed?"

"Yes, very much," Ti-munilee said.

"How? In what way?"

"You do not know?"

Gundersen held a hand before his eyes. Five fingers, yes, as before. He looked down at his naked body and saw no difference in it. Obscurely he experienced disappointment; perhaps nothing had really happened in that chamber. His legs, his feet, his loins, his belly—everything as it had been.

"I haven't changed at all," he said.

"You have changed greatly," the sulidor replied.

"I see myself, and I see the same body as before."

"Look again," advised Ti-munilee.

In the main corridor Gundersen caught sight of himself dimly reflected in the sleek glassy walls by the light of the glowing fungoids. He drew back, startled. He had changed, yes; he had outkurtzed Kurtz in his rebirth. What peered back at him from the rippling sheen of the walls was scarcely human. Gundersen stared at the mask-like face with hooded slots for eyes, at the slitted nose, the gill-pouches trailing to his shoulders, the many-jointed arms, the row of sensors on the chest, the grasping organs at the hips, the cratered skin, the glow-organs in the cheeks. He looked down again at himself and saw none of those things. Which was the illusion?

He hurried toward daylight.

"Have I changed, or have I not changed?" he asked the sulidor.

"You have changed."

"Where?"

"The changes are within," said the former Srin'gahar.

"And the reflection?"

"Reflections sometimes lie. Look at yourself through my eyes, and see what you are."

Gundersen reached forth again. He saw himself, and it was his old body he saw, and then he flickered and underwent a phase shift and he beheld the being with sensors and slots, and then he was himself again.

"Are you satisfied?" Ti-munilee asked.

"Yes," said Gundersen. He walked slowly toward the lip of the plaza outside the mouth of the cavern. The seasons had changed since he had entered that cavern; now an iron winter was on the land, and the mist was piled deep in the valley, and where it broke he saw the heavy mounds of snow and ice. He felt the presence of nildoror and sulidoror about him, though he saw only Ti-munilee. He was aware of the soul of old Na-sinisul within the mountain, passing through the final phases of a rebirth. He touched the soul of Vol'himyor far to the south. He brushed lightly over the soul of tortured Kurtz. He sensed suddenly, startlingly, other Earthborn souls, as free as his, open to him, hovering nearby.

"Who are you?" he asked.

And they answered, "You are not the first of your kind to come through rebirth intact."

Yes. He remembered. Cullen had said that there had been others, some transformed into monsters, others simply never heard from again.

"Where are you?" he asked them.

They told him, but he did not understand, for what they said was that they had left their bodies behind. "Have I also left my body behind?" he asked. And they said, no, he was still wearing his flesh, for so he had chosen, and they had chosen otherwise. Then they withdrew from him.

"Do you feel the changes?" Ti-munilee asked.

"The changes are within me," said Gundersen.

"Yes. Now you are at peace."

And, surprised by joy, he realized that that was so. The

fears, the tensions, were gone. Guilt was gone. Sorrow was gone. Loneliness was gone.

Ti-munilee said, "Do you know who I was, when I was Srin'gahar? Reach toward me."

Gundersen reached. He said, in a moment, "You were one of those seven nildoror whom I would not allow to go to their rebirth, many years ago."

"Yes."

"And yet you carried me on your back all the way to the mist country."

"My time had come again." said Ti-munilee, "and I was happy. I forgave you. Do you remember, when we crossed into the mist country, there was an angry sulidor at the border?"

"Yes," Gundersen said.

"He was another of the seven. He was the one you touched with your torch. He had had his rebirth finally, and still he hated you. Now he no longer does. Tomorrow, when you are ready, reach toward him, and he will forgive you. Will you do that?"

"I will," said Gundersen. "But will he really forgive?"

"You are reborn. Why should he not forgive?" Ti-munilee said. Then the sulidor asked, "Where will you go now?"

"South. To help my people. First to help Kurtz, to guide him through a new rebirth. Then the others. Those who are willing to be opened."

"May I share your journey?"

"You know that answer."

Far off, the dark soul of Kurtz stirred and throbbed. Wait, Gundersen told it. Wait. You will not suffer much longer.

A blast of cold wind struck the mountainside. Sparkling flakes of snow whirled into Gundersen's face. He smiled. He had never felt so free, so light, so young. A vision of a mankind transformed blazed within him. I am the emissary, he thought. I am the bridge over which they shall cross. I am the resurrection and the life. I am the light of the world: he that followeth me shall not walk in darkness, but shall have the light of life. A new commandment I give unto you, that ye love one another.

He said to Ti-munilee, "Shall we go now?"

"I am ready when you are ready."

"Now."

"Now," said the sulidor, and together they began to descend the windswept mountain.

THE WORLD INSIDE

For Ejler Jakobsson

We were born to unite with our fellow-men and to join in community with the human race.
Cicero: *De finibus, IV*

Of all animals, men are the least fitted to live in herds. If they were crowded together as sheep are they would all perish in a short time. The breath of man is fatal to his fellows.
Jean-Jacques Rousseau: *Emile, I*

One

Here begins a happy day in 2381. The morning sun is high enough to touch the uppermost fifty stories of Urban Monad 116. Soon the building's entire eastern face will glitter like the bosom of the sea at daybreak. Charles Mattern's window, activated by the dawn's early photons, deopaques. He stirs. God bless, he thinks. His wife yawns and stretches. His four children, who have been awake for hours, now can officially start their day. They rise and parade around the bedroom, singing:

God bless, god bless, god bless!
God bless us every one!
God bless Daddo, god bless Mommo, god bless you and me!
God bless us all, the short and tall,
Give us fer-til-i-tee!

They rush toward their parents' sleeping platform. Mattern rises and embraces them. Indra is eight, Sandor is seven, Marx is five, Cleo is three. It is Charles Mattern's secret shame that his family is so small. Can a man with only four children truly be said to have reverence for life? But Principessa's womb no longer flowers. The medics have declared that she will not bear again. At twenty-seven she is sterile. Mattern is thinking of taking in a second woman. He longs to hear the yowls of an infant again; in any case, a man must do his duty to god.

Sandor says, "Daddo, Siegmund is still here."

The child points. Mattern sees. On Principessa's side of the sleeping platform, curled against the inflation pedal, lies fourteen-year-old Siegmund Kluver, who had entered the Mattern home several hours after midnight to exercise his rights of propinquity. Siegmund is fond of older women. He has become quite notorious in the past few months. Now he snores; he has had a good workout. Mattern nudges him. "Siegmund? Siegmund, it's morning!" The young man's eyes open. He smiles at Mattern, sits up, reaches for his wrap. He is quite handsome. He lives on the 787th floor and already has one child and another on the way.

"Sorry," says Siegmund. "I overslept. Principessa really drains me. A savage, she is!"

"Yes, she's quite passionate," Mattern agrees. So is Siegmund's wife, Mamelon, according to what Mattern has heard. When she is a little older, Mattern plans to try her. Next spring, perhaps.

Siegmund sticks his head under the molecular cleanser. Principessa now has left the bed. Nodding faintly to her husband, she kicks the pedal and the platform deflates swiftly. She begins to program breakfast. Indra, reaching forth a pale, almost transparent little hand, switches on the screen. The wall blossoms with light and color. "Good morning," says the screen heartily. "The external temperature, if anybody's interested, is 28⁰. Today's population figure at Urbmon 116 is 881,115, which is +102 since yesterday and +14,187 since the first of the year. God bless, but we're slowing down! Across the way at Urbmon 117 they've added 131 since yesterday, including quads for Mrs. Hula Jabotinsky. She's eighteen and has had seven previous. A servant of god, isn't she? The time is now 0620. In exactly forty minutes Urbmon 116 will be honored by the presence of Nicanor Gortman, the visiting sociocomputator from Hell, who can be recognized by his distinctive outbuilding costume in crimson and ultraviolet. Dr. Gortman will be the guest of the Charles Matterns of the 799th floor. Of course we'll treat him with the same friendly blessmanship we show one another. God bless Nicanor Gortman! Turning now to news from the lower levels of Urbmon 116—"

Principessa says, "Hear that, children? We'll have a guest, and we must be blessworthy toward him. Come and eat."

When he has cleansed himself, dressed, and breakfasted, Charles Mattern goes to the thousandth-floor landing stage to meet Nicanor Gortman. As he rises through the building to the summit, Mattern passes the floors on which his brothers and sisters and their families live. Three brothers, three sisters. Four of them younger than he, two older. All quite successful. One brother died, unpleasantly, young. Jeffrey. Mattern rarely thinks of Jeffrey. Now he is passing through the floors that make up Louisville, the administrative sector. In a moment he will meet his guest. Gortman has been touring the tropics and is about to visit a typical urban monad in the temperate zone. Mattern is honored to have been named the official host. He steps out on the landing stage, which is at the very tip of Urbmon 116. A force-field shields him from the fierce winds that sweep the lofty spire. He looks to his left and sees the western face of Urban Monad 115 still in darkness. To his right, Urbmon 117's eastern windows sparkle. Bless Mrs. Hula Jabotinsky and her eleven littles, Mattern thinks. Mattern can see other urbmons in the row, stretching on and on toward the horizon, towers of super-stressed concrete three kilometers high, tapering ever so gracefully. It is a thrilling sight. God bless, he thinks. God bless, god bless, god bless!

He hears a cheerful hum of rotors. A quickboat is landing. Out steps a tall, sturdy man dressed in high-spectrum garb. He must surely be the visiting sociocomputator from Hell.

"Nicanor Gortman?" Mattern asks.

"Bless god. Charles Mattern?"

"God bless, yes. Come."

Hell is one of the eleven cities of Venus, which man has reshaped to suit himself. Gortman has never been on Earth before. He speaks in a slow, stolid way, no lilt in his voice at all; the inflection reminds Mattern of the way they talk in Urbmon 84, which Mattern once visited on a field trip. He has read Gortman's papers: solid stuff, closely reasoned. "I particularly liked 'Dynamics of the Hunting Ethic,'" Mattern tells him while they are in the dropshaft. "Remarkable. A revelation."

"You really mean that?" Gortman asks, flattered.

"Of course. I try to keep up with the better Venusian journals. It's so fascinating to read about alien customs. Such as hunting wild animals."

"There are none on Earth?"

"God bless, no," Mattern says. "We couldn't allow that! But I love gaining insight into different ways of life."

"My essays are escape literature for you?" asks Gortman.

Mattern looks at him strangely. "I don't understand the reference."

"Escape literature. What you read to make life on Earth more bearable for yourself."

"Oh, no. Life on Earth is quite bearable, let me assure you. There's no need for escape literature. I study offworld journals for *amusement*. And to obtain a necessary parallax,

you know, for my own work," says Mattern. They have
reached the 799th level. "Let me show you my home first."
He steps from the dropshaft and beckons to Gortman. "This
is Shanghai. I mean, that's what we call this block of forty
floors, from 761 to 800. I'm in the next-to-top level of
Shanghai, which is a mark of my professional status. We've
got twenty-five cities altogether in Urbmon 116. Reykjavik's
on the bottom and Louisville's on the top."

"What determines the names?"

"Citizen vote. Shanghai used to be Calcutta, which I
personally prefer, but a little bunch of malcontents on the
778th floor rammed through a referendum in '75."

"I thought you had no malcontents in the urban monads,"
Gortman said.

Mattern smiles. "Not in the usual sense. But we allow
certain conflicts to exist. Man wouldn't be man without
conflicts, eh? Even here. Eh?"

They are walking down the eastbound corridor toward
Mattern's home. It is now 0710, and children are streaming
from their apartments in groups of three and four, rushing to
get to school. Mattern waves to them. They sing as they run
along. Mattern says, "We average 6.2 children per family on
this floor. It's one of the lowest figures in the building, I have
to admit. High-status people don't seem to breed well.
They've got a floor in Prague—I think it's 117—that averages
9.9 per family! Isn't that glorious?"

"You are speaking with irony?" Gortman asks.

"Not at all." Mattern feels an uptake of tension. "We *like*
children. We *approve* of breeding. Surely you realized that
before you set out on this tour of—"

"Yes, yes," says Gortman, hastily. "I was aware of the
general cultural dynamic. But I thought perhaps your own
attitude—"

"Ran counter to norm? Just because I have a scholar's
detachment, you shouldn't assume that I disapprove in any
way of my cultural matrix. Perhaps you're guilty of projecting
your own disapproval, eh?"

"I regret the implication. And please don't think I feel the
slightest negative attitudes in relation to your matrix, although I admit your world seems quite strange to me. Bless
god, let us not have strife, Charles."

"God bless, Nicanor. I didn't mean to seem touchy."

They smile. Mattern is dismayed by his show of irritability.

Gortman says, "What is the population of the 799th floor?"

"805, last I heard."

"And of Shanghai?"

"About 33,000."

"And of Urbmon 116?"

"881,000."

"And there are fifty urban monads in this constellation of houses?"

"Yes."

"Making some 40,000,000 people," Gortman says. "Or somewhat more than the entire human population of Venus. Remarkable!"

"And this isn't the biggest constellation, not by any means!" Mattern's voice rings with pride. "Sansan is bigger, and so is Boshwash! And there are several larger ones in Europe—Berpar, Wienbud, I think two others. With more being planned!"

"A global population of—"

"—75,000,000,000," Mattern cries. "God bless! There's never been anything like it! No one goes hungry! Everybody happy! Plenty of open space! God's been good to us, Nicanor!" He pauses before a door labeled 79915. "Here's my home. What I have is yours, dear guest." They go in.

Mattern's home is quite adequate. He has nearly ninety square meters of floor space. The sleeping platform deflates; the children's cots retract; the furniture can easily be moved to provide play area. Most of the room, in fact, is empty. The screen and the data terminal occupy two-dimensional areas of wall that in an earlier era had to be taken up by bulky television sets, bookcases, desks, file drawers, and other encumbrances. It is an airy, spacious environment, particularly for a family of just six.

The children have not yet left for school; Principessa has held them back, to meet the guest, and so they are restless. As Mattern enters, Sandor and Indra are struggling over a cherished toy, the dream-stirrer. Mattern is astounded. Conflict in the home? Silently, so their mother will not notice, they fight. Sandor hammers his shoes into his sister's shins. Indra, wincing, claws her brother's cheek. "God *bless*," Mattern says sharply. "Somebody wants to go down the chute, eh?" The children gasp. The toy drops. Everyone stands at attention. Principessa looks up, brushing a lock of dark hair from her eyes; she has been busy with the youngest child and has not even heard them come in.

Mattern says, "Conflict sterilizes. Apologize to each other."

Indra and Sandor kiss and smile. Meekly Indra picks up the toy and hands it to Mattern, who gives it to his younger son, Marx. They are all staring now at the guest. Mattern says to Gortman, "What I have is yours, friend." He makes introductions. Wife, children. The scene of conflict has unnerved him a little, but he is relieved when Gortman produces four small boxes and distributes them to the children. Toys. A blessful gesture. Mattern points to the deflated sleeping platform. "This is where we sleep," he explains. "There's ample room for three. We wash at the cleanser, here. Do you like privacy when voiding waste matter?"

"Please, yes."

"You press this button for the privacy shield. We excrete in this. Urine here, feces there. Everything is reprocessed, you understand. We're a thrifty folk in the urbmons."

"Of course," Gortman says.

Principessa says, "Do you prefer that we use the shield when we excrete? I understand some outbuilding people do."

"I would not want to impose my customs on you," says Gortman.

Smiling, Mattern says, "We're a post-privacy culture, naturally. But it wouldn't be any trouble for us to press the button, if—" He falters. A troublesome new thought. "There's no general nudity taboo on Venus, is there? I mean, we have only this one room, and—"

"I am adaptable," Gortman insists. "A trained sociocomputator must be a cultural relativist, of course!"

"Of course," Mattern agrees, and he laughs nervously.

Principessa excuses herself from the conversation and sends the children, still clutching their new toys, off to school.

Mattern says, "Forgive me for being overobvious, but I must bring up the matter of your sexual prerogatives. We three will share a single platform. My wife is available to you, as am I. Within the urbmon it is improper to refuse any reasonable request, so long as no injury is involved. Avoidance of frustration, you see, is the primary rule of a society such as ours, where even minor frictions could lead to uncontrollable oscillations of disharmony. And do you know our custom of nightwalking?"

"I'm afraid I—"

"Doors are not locked in Urbmon 116. We have no personal property worth guarding, and we all are socially adjusted. At night it is quite proper to enter other homes. We exchange partners in this way all the time; usually wives stay home and husbands migrate, though not necessarily. Each of us has access at any time to any other adult member of our community."

"Strange," says Gortman. "I'd think that in a society where there are so many people living so close together, an exaggerated respect for privacy would develop, rather than a communal freedom."

"In the beginning we had many notions of privacy. God bless, they were allowed to erode! Avoidance of frustration must be our goal, otherwise impossible tensions develop. And privacy is frustration."

"So you can go into any room in this whole gigantic building and sleep with—"

"Not the whole building," Mattern says, interrupting. "Only Shanghai. We frown on nightwalking beyond one's own city." He chuckles. "We do impose a few little restrictions on ourselves, you see, so that our freedoms don't pall."

Gortman turns toward Principessa. She wears a loinband and metallic cup over her left breast. She is slender but voluptuously constructed, and even though her childbearing days are over she has not lost the sensual glow of young womanhood. Mattern is proud of her, despite everything.

Mattern says, "Shall we begin our tour of the building?"

They go toward the door. Gortman bows gracefully to Principessa as he and Mattern leave. In the corridor, the visitor says, "Your family is smaller than the norm, I see."

It is an excruciatingly impolite statement, but Mattern is able to be tolerant of his guest's faux pas. Mildly he replies, "We would have had more children, but my wife's fertility had to be terminated surgically. It was a great tragedy for us."

"You have always valued large families here?"

"We value life. To create new life is the highest virtue. To prevent life from coming into being is the darkest sin. We all love our big bustling world. Does it seem unendurable to you? Do we seem unhappy?"

"You seem surprisingly well adjusted," Gortman says. "Considering that—" He stops.

"Go on."

"Considering that there are so many of you. And that you

spend your whole lives inside a single colossal building. You never do go out, do you?"

"Most of us never do," Mattern admits. "I have traveled, of course—a sociocomputator needs perspective, obviously. But Principessa has never left the building. I believe she has never been below the 350th floor, except when she was taken to see the lower levels while she was in school. Why should she go anywhere? The secret of our happiness is to create self-contained villages of five or six floors within the cities of forty floors within the urbmons of a thousand floors. We have no sensation of being overcrowded or cramped. We know our neighbors; we have hundreds of dear friends; we are kind and loyal and blessworthy to one another."

"And everybody remains happy forever?"

"Nearly everybody."

"Who are the exceptions?" Gortman asks.

"The flippos," says Mattern. "We endeavor to minimize the frictions of living in such an environment; as you see, we never deny one another anything, we never thwart a reasonable desire. But sometimes there are those who abruptly decide they can no longer abide by our principles. They flip; they thwart others; they rebel. It is quite sad."

"What do you do with flippos?"

"We remove them, of course," Mattern says. He smiles, and they enter the dropshaft once again.

Mattern has been authorized to show Gortman the entire urbmon, a tour that will take several days. He is a little apprehensive; he is not as familiar with some parts of the structure as a guide should be. But he will do his best.

"The building," he says, "is made of superstressed concrete. It is constructed about a central service core two hundred meters square. Originally, the plan was to have fifty families per floor, but we average about 120 today, and the old apartments have all been subdivided into single-room occupancies. We are wholly self-sufficient, with our own schools, hospitals, sports arenas, houses of worship, and theaters."

"Food?"

"We produce none, of course. But we have contractual access to the agricultural communes. I'm sure you've seen that nearly nine tenths of the land area of this continent is used for food production; and then there are the marine farms. Oh, we have plenty of food on this planet, now that we no longer waste space by spreading out horizontally over good land."

"But aren't you at the mercy of the food-producing communes?"

"When were city-dwellers not at the mercy of farmers?" Mattern asks. "But you seem to regard life on Earth as an affair of fang and claw. Actually the ecology of our world is neatly in mesh. We are vital to the farmers—their only market, their only source of manufactured goods. They are vital to us—our only source of food. Reciprocal indispensabilities, eh? And the system works. We could support many billions of additional people. Someday, god blessing, we will."

The dropshaft, coasting downward through the building, glides into its anvil at the very bottom. Mattern feels the oppressive bulk of the whole urbmon over him, and is vaguely surprised by the intensity of his distress; he tries not to show that he is uneasy. He says, "The foundation of the structure is four hundred meters deep. We are now at the lowest level. Here we generate our power." They cross a catwalk and peer into an immense generating room, forty meters from floor to ceiling, in which sleek green turbines whirl. "Most of our power is obtained," he points out, "through combustion of compacted solid refuse. We burn everything we don't need, and sell the residue as fertilizer. We have auxiliary generators that work on accumulated body heat, also."

"I was wondering about that," Gortman murmurs. "What you do with the heat."

Cheerily Mattern says, "Obviously 800,000 people within one sealed enclosure will produce an immense thermal surplus. Some of this heat is directly radiated from the building through cooling fins along the outer surface. Some is piped down here and used to run the generator. In winter, of course, we pump it evenly through the building to maintain temperature. The rest of the excess heat is used in water purification and similar things."

They peer at the electrical system for a while. Then Mattern leads the way to the reprocessing plant. Several hundred school-children are touring it; silently the two men join the tour.

The teacher says, "Here's where the urine comes down, see?" She points to gigantic plastic pipes. "It passes through the flash chamber to be distilled, and the pure water is drawn off here—follow me, now—you remember from the flow chart, the part about how we recover the chemicals and sell them to the farming communes—"

Mattern and his guest inspect the fertilizer plant, too, where fecal reconversion is taking place. Gortman asks a number of questions. He seems deeply interested. Mattern is pleased; there is nothing more significant to him than the details of the urbmon way of life, and he had feared that this stranger from Venus, from a place where men live in private houses and walk around in the open, would regard the urbmon way as repugnant or hideous.

They go onward. Mattern speaks of air-conditioning, the system of dropshafts and liftshafts, and other such topics.

"It's all wonderful," Gortman says. "I couldn't imagine how one little planet with 75,000,000,000 people could even survive, but you've turned it into—into—"

"Utopia?"

"I meant to say that, yes," says Gortman.

Power production and waste disposal are not really Mattern's specialties. He knows how such things are handled here, but only because the workings of the urbmon are so enthralling to him. His real field of study is sociocomputation, after all, and he has been asked to show the visitor how the social structure of the giant building is organized. Now they go up, into the residential levels.

"This is Reykjavik," Mattern announces. "Populated chiefly by maintenance workers. We try not to have too much status stratification, but each city does have its predominant populations—engineers, academics, entertainers, you know. My Shanghai is mostly academic. Each profession is clannish." They walk down the hall. Mattern feels edgy in this low level, and he keeps talking to cover his nervousness. He describes how each city within the urbmon develops its characteristic slang, its way of dressing, its folklore, and heroes.

"Is there much contact between cities?" Gortman asks.

"We try to encourage it. Sports, exchange students, regular mixer evenings. Within reason, that is. We don't have people from the working-class levels mixing with those from the academic levels, much. It would make everyone unhappy, eh? But we attempt to get a decent flow between cities of roughly similar intellectual level. We think it's healthy."

"Wouldn't it help the mixing process if you encouraged intercity nightwalking?"

Mattern frowns. "We prefer to stick to our propinquity groups for that. Casual sex with people from other cities is a mark of a sloppy soul."

"I see."

They enter a large room. Mattern says, "This is a newly-wed dorm. We have them every five or six levels. When adolescents mate, they leave their family homes and move in here. After they have their first child they are assigned to homes of their own."

Puzzled, Gortman asks, "But where do you find room for them all? I assume that every room in the building is full, and you can't possibly have as many deaths as births, so—how—?"

"Deaths do create vacancies, of course. If your mate dies and your children are grown, you go to a senior citizen dorm, creating room for the establishment of a new family unit. But you're correct that most of our young people don't get accommodations in the building, since we form new families at about two percent a year and deaths are far below that. As new urbmons are built, the overflow from the newlywed dorms is sent to them. By lot. It's hard to adjust to being expelled, they say, but there are compensations in being among the first group into a new building. You acquire automatic status. And so we're constantly overflowing, casting out our young, creating new combinations of social units—utterly fascinating, eh? Have you read my paper, 'Structural Metamorphosis in the Urbmon Population'?"

"I'm afraid I haven't encountered it," Gortman replied. "I'll be eager to look it up." He glances around the dorm. A dozen couples are having intercourse on a nearby platform. "They seem so young," he says.

"Puberty comes early among us. Girls generally marry at twelve, boys at thirteen. First child about a year later, god blessing."

"And nobody tries to control fertility at all?"

"*Control fertility?*" Mattern clutches his genitals in shock at the unexpected obscenity. Several copulating couples look up, amazed. Someone giggles. Mattern says, "Please don't use that phrase again. Particularly if you're near children. We don't—ah—think in terms of control."

"But—"

"We hold that life is sacred. Making new life is blessed.

One does one's duty to god by reproducing." Mattern smiles, feeling that he sounds too earnest. "To be human is to meet challenges through the exercise of intelligence, right? And one challenge is the multiplication of inhabitants in a world that has seen the conquest of disease and the elimination of war. We could limit births, I suppose, but that would be sick, a cheap, anti-human way out. Instead we've met the challenge of overpopulation triumphantly, wouldn't you say? And so we go on and on, multiplying joyously, our numbers increasing by three billion a year, and we find room for everyone, and food for everyone. Few die, and many are born, and the world fills up, and god is blessed, and life is rich and pleasant, and as you see we are all quite happy. We have matured beyond the infantile need to place layers of insulation between man and man. Why go outdoors? Why yearn for forests and deserts? Urbmon 116 holds universes enough for us. The warnings of the prophets of doom have proved hollow. Can you deny that we are happy here? Come with me. We will see a school now."

The school Mattern has chosen is in a working-class district of Prague, on the 108th floor. He thinks Gortman will find it especially interesting, since the Prague people have the highest reproductive rate in Urban Monad 116, and families of twelve or fifteen are not at all uncommon. Approaching the school door, Mattern and Gortman hear the clear treble voices singing of the blessedness of god. Mattern joins the singing; it is a hymn he sang too, when he was their age, dreaming of the big family he would have:

> And now he plants the holy seed.
> That grows in Mommo's womb,
> And now a little sibling comes—

There is an unpleasant and unscheduled interruption. A woman rushes toward Mattern and Gortman in the corridor. She is young, untidy, wearing only a flimsy gray wrap; her hair is loose; she is well along in pregnancy. "Help!" she shrieks. "My husband's gone flippo!" She hurls herself, trembling, into Gortman's arms. The visitor looks bewildered.

Toward her there runs a man in his early twenties, haggard, eyes bloodshot. He carries a fabricator torch; its tip glows with heat. "Goddamn bitch," he mumbles. "Allatime babies! Seven babies already and now number eight and I gonna go off my *head!*" Mattern is appalled. He pulls the woman away from Gortman and shoves the dismayed visitor through the door of the school.

"Tell them there's a flippo out here," Mattern says. "Get help, fast!" He is furious that Gortman should witness so atypical a scene, and wishes to take him away from it.

The trembling girl cowers behind Mattern. Quietly, Mattern says, "Let's be reasonable, young man. You've spent your whole life in urbmons, haven't you? You understand that its blessed to create. Why do you suddenly repudiate the principles on which—"

"Get the hell away from her or I gonna burn you too!"

The young man feints with the torch, jabbing it straight at Mattern's face. Mattern feels the heat and flinches. The young man swipes past him at the woman. She leaps away, but she is clumsy with girth, and the torch slices her garment. Pale white distended flesh is exposed, with a brilliant burn-streak slashed across it. She cups her jutting belly and falls, screaming. The young man jostles Mattern out of the way and prepares to thrust the torch into her side. Mattern tries to seize his arm. He deflects the torch; it chars the floor. The young man, cursing, drops it and throws himself on Mattern, pounding frenziedly with his fists. "Help me!" Mattern calls. "Help!"

Into the corridor erupt dozens of schoolchildren. They are between eight and eleven years of age. They continue to sing their hymn as they pour forth. They pull Mattern's assailant from him. Swiftly, smoothly, they cover him with their bodies. He can dimly be seen beneath the flailing, thrashing mass. Dozens more rush from the schoolroom and join the heap. A siren wails. A whistle blows. The teacher's amplified voice booms, "The police are here! Everyone off!"

Four men in uniform have arrived. They survey the situation. The injured woman lies groaning, rubbing her burn. The insane man is unconscious; his face is bloody and one eye appears to be destroyed. "What happened?" a policeman asks. "Who are you?"

"Charles Mattern, sociocomputator, 799th level, Shanghai. The man's a flippo. Attacked his pregnant wife with the torch. Attempted to attack me."

The policemen haul the flippo to his feet. He sags, dazed, battered, in their midst. The police leader says, rattling the

words into one another, "Guilty of atrocious assault on woman
of childbearing years currently carrying unborn life, dangerous countersocial tendencies, menace to harmony and stability, by virtue of authority vested in me I pronounce sentence
of erasure, carry out immediately. Down the chute with the
bastard, boys!" They haul the flippo away. Medics appear and
cluster about the fallen woman. The children, once again gaily
singing, return to the classroom. Nicanor Gortman looks
stunned and shaken. Mattern seizes his arm and whispers
fiercely, "All right, so those things happen sometimes. I don't
deny it. But it was a billion to one against having it happen
where you'd see it! It isn't typical! It isn't typical!"

They enter the classroom.

* * *

The sun is setting. The Western face of the neighboring
urban monad is streaked with red. Nicanor Gortman sits
quietly at dinner with the members of the Mattern family.
The children, voices tumbling in chaotic interplay, chatter of
their day at school. The evening news comes on the screen; the
announcer mentions the unfortunate event on the 108th floor.
"The mother was not seriously injured," he says, "and no
harm came to her unborn child. Sentence on the assailant has
been carried out and a threat to the security of the whole
urbmon has thus been eliminated." Principessa murmurs,
"Bless god." After dinner Mattern requests copies of his most
recent technical papers from the data terminal and gives the
whole sheaf to Gortman to read at his leisure. Gortman
thanks him energetically.

"You look tired," Mattern says.

"It was a busy day. And a rewarding one."

"Yes. We really covered ground, didn't we?"

Mattern is tired too. They have visited nearly three dozen
levels already; he has shown Gortman town meetings, fertility
clinics, religious services, business offices, all on this first day.
Tomorrow there will be much more to see. Urban Monad 116
is a varied, complex community. And a happy one, Mattern
tells himself firmly. We have a few little incidents from time
to time, but we're *happy*.

The children, one by one, go to sleep, charmingly kissing
Daddo and Mommo and the visitor good night and running
across the room, sweet nude little pixies, to their cots. The
lights automatically dim. Mattern feels faintly depressed; the
unpleasantness on 108 has spoiled what was otherwise an

excellent day. Yet he still thinks that he has succeeded in helping Gortman see past the superficialities to the innate harmony and serenity of the urbmon way. And now he will allow the guest to experience for himself one of their most useful techniques for minimizing the interpersonal conflicts that could be so destructive to their kind of society. Mattern arises.

"It's nightwalking time," he says. "I'll go. You stay here- ...with Principessa." He suspects that the visitor would appreciate some privacy.

Gortman looks uneasy.

"Go on," Mattern says. "Enjoy yourself. People don't deny pleasure to people, here. We weed the selfish ones out early. Please. What I have is yours. Isn't that so, Principessa?"

"Certainly," she says.

Mattern steps out of the room, walks quickly down the corridor, enters the dropshaft, and descends to the 770th floor. As he gets out he hears sudden angry shouts, and he stiffens, fearing that he will become involved in another nasty episode, but no one appears. He walks on. He passes the black door of a chute access and shivers a little, and he cannot avoid thinking of the young man with the fabricator torch, and what has become of him. And then, without warning, there swims up from memory the face of the brother he had once had who had gone down that same chute, the brother one year his senior, Jeffrey, the whiner, the stealer, Jeffrey the selfish, Jeffrey the unadaptable, Jeffrey who had had to be given to a chute. For an instant Mattern is sickened and dizzied. He starts to fall, and wildly seizes a doorknob to steady himself.

The door opens. He goes in. He has never been a night-walker on this floor before. Five children lie asleep in their cots, and on the sleeping platform are a man and a woman, both younger than he is, both asleep. Mattern removes his clothing and lies down by the woman's left side. He touches her thigh, then her small cool breast. She opens her eyes and he says, "Hello. Charles Mattern, 799."

"Gina Burke," she says. "My husband Lenny."

Lenny awakens. He sees Mattern, nods, turns over, and returns to sleep. Mattern kisses Gina Burke lightly on the lips. She opens her arms to him. He trembles in his need, and sighs as she receives him. God bless, he thinks. It has been a happy day in 2381, and now it is over.

Two

The city of Chicago is bounded on the north by Shanghai and on the south by Edinburgh. Chicago currently has 37,402 people, and is undergoing a mild crisis of population that will have to be alleviated in the customary manner. Its dominant profession is engineering. Above, in Shanghai, they are mostly scholars; below, in Edinburgh, computer men cluster.

Aurea Holston was born in Chicago in 2368 and has lived there all of her life. Aurea is now fourteen years old. Her husband, Memnon, is nearly fifteen. They have been married almost two years. God has not blessed them with children. Memnon has traveled through the entire building, but Aurea has scarcely ever been out of Chicago. Once she went to visit a fertility expert, an old midwife down in Prague, and once she went up to Louisville, where her powerful uncle, an urban administrator, lives. Many times she and Memnon have been to their friend Siegmund Kluver's apartment in Shanghai. Other than that she has not seen much of the building. Aurea does not really care to travel. She loves her own city very much.

Chicago is the city that occupies the 721st through the 760th floors of Urban Monad 116. Memnon and Aurea Holston live in a dormitory for childless couples on the 735th floor. The dorm is currently shared by thirty-one couples, eight above optimum.

"There's got to be a thinning soon," Memnon says. "We're starting to bulge at the seams. People will have to go."

"Many?" Aurea asks.

"Three couples here, five there—a slice from each dorm. I suppose Urbmon 116 will lose about two thousand couples. That's how many went the last time they thinned."

Aurea trembles. "Where will they go?"

"They tell me that the new urbmon is almost ready. Number 158."

Her soul floods with pity and terror. "How horrid to be sent somewhere else! Memnon, they *wouldn't* make us leave here!"

"Of course not. God bless, we're valuable people! I have a skill rating of—"

"But we have no children. That kind goes first, doesn't it?"

"God will bless us soon." Memnon takes her in his arms. He is strong and tall and lean, with rippling scarlet hair and a taut, solemn expression. Aurea feels weak and fragile beside him, although in fact she is sturdy and supple. Her crown of golden hair is deepening in tone. Her eyes are pale green. Her breasts are full and her hips are broad. Siegmund Kluver says she looks like a goddess of motherhood. Most men desire her and night-walkers come frequently to share her sleeping platform. Yet she remains barren. Lately she has become quite sensitive about that. The irony of her wasted voluptuousness is not lost on her.

Memnon releases her and she walks wearily through the dormitory. It is a long, narrow room that makes a right-angle bend around the central service core of the urbmon. Its walls glow with changing inlaid patterns of blue and gold and green. Rows of sleeping platforms, some deflated, some in use, cover the floor. The furniture is stark and simple and the lighting, though indirectly suffused from the entire area of the floor and the ceiling, is bright almost to harshness. Several viewscreens and three data terminals are mounted on the room's eastern wall. There are five excretion areas, three communal recreation areas, two cleanser stations, and two privacy areas.

By unspoken custom the privacy shields are never turned on in this dormitory. What one does, one does before the others. The total accessibility of all persons to all other persons is the only rule by which the civilization of the urbmon can survive, and in a mass residence hall such as this the rule is all the more vital.

Aurea halts by the majestic window at the dormitory's western end, and stares out. The sunset is beginning. Across the way, the magnificent bulk of Urban Monad 117 seems stained with golden red. Aurea follows the shaft of the great tower with her eyes, down from the landing stage at its thousandth-floor tip, down to the building's broad waist. She cannot see, at this angle, very far below the 400th floor of the adjoining structure. What is it like, she wonders, to live in Urbmon 117? Or 115, or 110, or 140? She has never left the urbmon of her birth. All about her, to the horizon, sprawl the towers of the Chipitts constellation, fifty mighty concrete piles, each three kilometers high, each a self-contained entity housing some 800,000 human beings. In Urbmon 117, Aurea tells herself, there are people who look just like us. They walk, talk, dress, think, love, just like ourselves. Urbmon 117 is not another world. It is only the building next door. We are not unique. We are not unique. We are not unique.

Fear engulfs her.

"Memnon," she says raggedly, "when the thinning time comes, they're going to send us to Urbmon 158."

Siegmund Kluver is one of the lucky ones. His fertility has won him an unimpeachable place in Urbmon 116. His status is secure.

Though he is just past fourteen, Siegmund has fathered two children. His son is called Janus and his newborn daughter has been named Persephone. Siegmund lives in a handsome fifty-square-meter home on the 787th floor, slightly more than midway up in Shanghai. His specialty is the theory of urban administration, and despite his youth he already spends much of his time as a consultant to the administration in Louisville. He is short, finely made, quite strong, with a large head and thick curling hair. In boyhood he lived in Chicago and was one of Memnon's closest friends. They still see each other quite often; the fact that they now live in different cities is no bar to their friendship.

Social encounters between the Holstons and the Kluvers always take place at Siegmund's apartment. The Kluvers never come down to Chicago to visit Aurea and Memnon. Siegmund claims there is no snobbery in this. "Why should the four of us sit around a noisy dorm," he asks, "when we can get together comfortably in the privacy of my apartment?" Aurea is suspicious of this attitude. Urbmon people are not supposed to place such a premium on privacy. Is the dorm not a good enough place for Siegmund Kluver?

Siegmund once lived in the same dorm as Aurea and Memnon. That was two years ago, when they all were newly married. Several times, in those long-ago days, Aurea yielded her body to Siegmund. She was flattered by his attentions. But very swiftly Siegmund's wife became pregnant, qualifying the Kluvers to apply for an apartment of their own, and the progress he was making in his profession permitted him to find room in the city of Shanghai. Aurea has not shared her sleeping platform with Siegmund since he left the dormitory. She is distressed by this, for she enjoyed Siegmund's embraces, but there is little she can do about it. The chance that he will come to her as a nightwalker is slight. Sexual relationships between people of different cities are currently considered improper, and Siegmund abides by custom. He may nightwalk in cities above his own, but he is not likely to go lower.

Siegmund now is evidently bound for higher things. Memnon says that by the time he is seventeen he will be, not a specialist in the theory of urban administration, but an actual administrator, and will live in lofty Louisville. Already Siegmund spends much time with the leaders of the urbmon. And with their wives as well, Aurea has heard.

He is an excellent host. His apartment is warm and agreeable, and two of its walls glisten with panels of one of the new decorative materials, which emits a soft hum keyed to the spectral pattern its owner has chosen. Tonight Siegmund has turned the panels almost into the ultraviolet and the audio emission is pitched close to the supersonic; the effect is to strain the senses, pushing them toward their maximum receptivity, a stimulating challenge. He has exquisite taste in handling the room's scent apertures too: jasmine and hyacinth flavor the air. "Care for some tingle?" he asks. "Just in from Venus. Quite blessworthy." Aurea and Memnon smile and nod. Siegmund fills a large fluted silver bowl with the costly scintillant fluid and places it on the pedestal-table. A touch of the floor pedal and the table rises to a height of 150 centimeters.

"Mamelon?" he says. "Will you join us?"

Siegmund's wife slides her baby into the maintenance slot near the sleeping platform and crosses the room to her guests. Mamelon Kluver is quite tall, dark of complexion and hair, elegantly beautiful in a haggard way. Her forehead is high, her cheekbones prominent, her chin sharp; her eyes, alert and glossy and wide-set, seem almost too big, too dominant, in her pale and tapering face. The delicacy of Mamelon's beauty makes Aurea feel defensive about her own soft features: her snub nose, her rounded cheeks, her full lips, the light dusting of freckles over tawny skin. Mamelon is the oldest person in the room, almost sixteen. Her breasts are swollen with milk; she is only eleven days up from childbed, and she is nursing. Aurea has never known anyone else who chose to nurse. Mamelon has always been different, though. Aurea is still somewhat frightened of Siegmund's wife, who is so cool, so self-possessed, so mature. So passionate too. At twelve, a new bride, Aurea found her sleep broken again and again by Mamelon's cries of ecstasy, echoing through the dormitory.

Now Mamelon bends forward and puts her lips to the tingle bowl. The four of them drink at the same moment. Tiny bubbles dance on Aurea's lips. The bouquet dizzies her. She peers into the depths of the bowl and sees abstract patterns forming and sundering. Tingle is faintly intoxicating, faintly hallucinogenic, an enhancer of vision, a suppressant of inner disturbance. It comes from certain musky swamps in the lowlands of Venus; the serving Siegmund has offered contains billions of alien microorganisms, fermenting and fissioning even as they are digested and absorbed. Aurea feels them spreading out through her, taking possession of her lungs, her ovaries, her liver. They make her lips slippery. They detach her from her sorrows. But the high is also a low; she gets through the early visionary moments and emerges tranquil and resigned. A spurious happiness possesses her as the last coils of color slide behind her eyelids and disappear.

After the ritual of drinking, they talk. Siegmund and Memnon discuss world events: the new urbmons, the agricultural statistics, the rumor of a spreading zone of disurbanized life outside the communes, and so forth. Mamelon shows Aurea her baby. The little girls lies within the maintenance slot, drooling, gurgling, cooing. Aurea says, "What a relief it must be not to be carrying her any longer!"

"One enjoys being able to see one's feet again, yes," Mamelon says.

"Is it very uncomfortable, being pregnant?"

"There are annoyances."

"The stretching? How can you puff up that way and stand it? The skin like going to burst any minute." Aurea shudders. "And everything getting pushed around inside your body. Your kidneys rammed up into your lungs, that's how I always think of it. Pardon me. I guess I'm exaggerating. I mean, I don't really know."

"It's not that bad," says Mamelon. "Though of course it's strange and a little bothersome. Yet there are positive aspects. The moment of birth itself—"

"Does it hurt terribly?" Aurea asks. "I imagine it would. Something that big, ripping through your body, popping right out of your—"

"Gloriously blessful. One's entire nervous system awakens. A baby coming out is like a man going in, only twenty times as thrilling. It's impossible to describe the sensation. You must experience it for yourself."

"I wish I could," says Aurea, downcast, groping for the last shreds of her high. She slips a hand into the maintenance slot to touch Mamelon's child. A quick burst of ions purifies her skin before she makes contact with little Persephone's downy cheek. Aurea says, "God bless, I want to do my duty! The medics say there's nothing wrong with either of us. But—"

"You must be patient, love." Mamelon embraces Aurea lightly. "Bless god, your moment will come."

Aurea is skeptical. For twenty months she has surveyed her flat belly, waiting for it to begin to bulge. It is blessed to create life, she knows. If everyone were as sterile as she, who would fill the urbmons? She has a sudden terrifying vision of the colossal towers nearly empty, whole cities sealed off, power failing, walls cracking, just a few shriveled old women shuffling through halls once thronged with happy multitudes.

Her one obsession has led her to the other one, and she turns to Siegmund, breaking into the conversation of the men to say, "Siegmund, is it true that they'll be opening Urbmon 158 soon?"

"So I hear, yes."

"What will it be like?"

"Very much like 116, I imagine. A thousand floors, the usual services. I suppose seventy families per floor, at first, maybe 250,000 people altogether, but it won't take long to bring it up to par."

Aurea clamps her palms together. "How many people will be sent there from here, Siegmund?"

"I'm sure I don't know that."

"There'll be some, won't there?"

Memnon says mildly, "Aurea, why don't we talk about something pleasant."

"Some people will be sent there from here," she persists. "Come on, Siegmund. You're up in Louisville with the bosses all the time. *How many?*"

Siegmund laughs. "You've really got an exaggerated idea of my significance in this place, Aurea. Nobody's said a word to me about how Urbmon 158 will be stocked."

"You know the theory of these things, though. You can project the data."

"Well, yes," Siegmund is quite cool; this subject has a purely impersonal interest for him. He seems unaware of the source of Aurea's agitation. "Naturally, if we're going to do our duty to god by creating life, we've also got to be sure that there's a place for everyone to live," he says. Hand flicks a vagrant lock of hair into place. Eyes glow; Siegmund loves to lecture. "So we go on building urban monads, and, naturally, whenever a new urbmon is added to the Chipitts constellation, it has to be stocked from the other Chipitts buildings. That makes good genetic sense. Even though each urbmon is big enough to provide an adequate gene-mix, our tendency to stratify into cities and villages within the building leads to a good deal of inbreeding, which they say isn't healthy for the species on a long-term basis. But if we take five thousand people from each of fifty urbmons, say, and toss them together into a new urbmon, it gives us a pooled gene-mix of 250,000 individuals that we didn't have before. Actually, though, easing population pressure is the most urgent reason for erecting new buildings."

"Keep it clean, Siegmund," Memnon warns.

Siegmund grins. "No, I mean it. Oh, sure, there's a cultural imperative telling us to breed and breed and breed. That's natural, after the agonies of the pre-urbmon days, when everybody went around wondering where we were going to put all the people. But even in a world of urban monads we have to plan in an orderly way. The excess of births over deaths is pretty consistent. Each urbmon is designed to hold 800,000 people comfortably, with room to pack in maybe 100,000 more, but that's the top. At the moment, you know, every urbmon more than twenty years old in the Chipitts constellation is at least 10,000 people above maximum, and a couple are pushing maximum. Things aren't too bad yet in 116, but you know yourselves that there are trouble spots. Why, Chicago has 38,000—"

"37,402 this morning," Aurea says.

"Whatever. That's close to a thousand people a floor. The programed optimum density for Chicago is only 32,000, though. That means that the waiting list in your city for a private apartment is getting close to a full generation long. The dorms are packed, and people aren't dying fast enough to make room for the new families, which is why Chicago is offloading some of its best people to places like Edinburgh and Boston and—well, Shanghai. Once the new building is open—"

Aurea says, steely-voiced, "How many from 116 are going to be sent there?"

"The theory is 5,000 from each monad, at current levels," Siegmund says. "It'll be adjusted slightly to compensate for population variations in different buildings, but figure on 5,000. Now there'll be about a thousand people in 116 who'll volunteer to go—"

"*Volunteer?*" Aurea gasps. It is inconceivable to her that anyone will *want* to leave his native urbmon.

Siegmund smiles. "Older people, love. In their twenties and thirties. Bored, maybe stalemated in their careers, tired of their neighbors, who knows? It sounds obscene, yes. But there'll be a thousand volunteers. That means that about 4,000 more will have to be picked by lot."

"I told you so this morning," Memnon says.

"Will these 4,000 be taken at random throughout the whole urbmon?" Aurea asks.

Gently Siegmund says, "At random, yes. From the newly-wed dorms. From the childless."

At last. The truth revealed.

"Why from us?" Aurea wails.

"Kindest and most blessworthy way," says Siegmund. "We can't uproot small children from their urbmon matrix. Dorm couples haven't the same kind of community ties that we— that others—that—" He falters, as if recognizing for the first time that he is not speaking of hypothetical individuals, but of Aurea and her own calamity. Aurea starts to sob. He says, "Love, I'm sorry. It's the system, and it's a good system. Ideal, in fact."

"Memnon, we're going to be *expelled!*"

Siegmund tries to reassure her. She and Memnon have only a slim chance of being chosen, he insists. In this urbmon thousands upon thousands of people are eligible for transfer. And so many variable factors exist, he maintains—but she will not be consoled. Unashamed, she lets geysers of raw emotion spew into the room, and then she feels shame. She knows she has spoiled the evening for everyone. But Siegmund and Mamelon are kind about it, and Memnon does not chide her as he hurries her out, into the dropshaft, down fifty-two floors to their home in Chicago.

* * *

That night, although she wants him intensely, she turns her back on Memnon when he reaches for her. She lies awake listening a long time to the gasps and happy groans of the couples sprawled on the sleeping platforms about her, and then sleep comes. Aurea dreams of being born. She is down in the power plant of Urban Monad 116, 400 meters underground, and they are sealing her into a liftshaft capsule. The building throbs. She is close to the heat-sink and the urine-reprocessing plant and the refuse compactors and all the rest of the service gear that keeps the structure alive, all those dark, hidden sectors of the urbmon that she had to tour when she was a schoolgirl. Now the liftshaft carries her up, up through Reykjavik where the maintenance people live, up through brawling Prague where everyone has ten babies, up through Rome, Boston, Edinburgh, Chicago, Shanghai, even through Louisville where the administrators dwell in unimaginable luxury, and now she is at the summit of the building, at the landing stage where the quickboats fly in from distant towers, and a hatch opens in the landing stage and Aurea is ejected. She soars into the sky, safe within her snug capsule while the cold winds of the upper atmosphere buffet it. She is six kilometers above the ground, looking down for the first time on the entire urbmon world. So this is how it is, she thinks. So many buildings. And yet so much open space!

She drifts across the constellation of towers. It is early spring, and Chipitts is greening. Below her are the tapered structures that hold the 40,000,000 + people of this urban cluster. She is awed by the neatness of the constellation, the geometrical placement of the buildings to form a series of hexagons within the larger area. Green plazas separate the buildings. No one enters the plazas, ever, but their well-manicured lawns are a delight to behold from the windows of the urbmon, and at this height they seem wondrously smooth, as if painted against the ground. The lower-class people on the lower floors have the best views of the gardens and pools, which is a compensation of sorts. From her vantage point high above, Aurea does not expect to see the details of the plazas well, but her dreaming mind suddenly gives her an intense clarity of vision and she discerns small golden floral heads; she smells the tang of floral fragrance.

Her brain whirls as she engorges herself on the complexities of Chipitts. How many cities at twenty-five to an urban monad? 1,250. How many villages at seven or eight to a city?

More than 10,000. How many families? How many night-walkers now prowling, now slipping into available beds? How many births a day? How many deaths? How many joys? How many sorrows?

She rises effortlessly to a height of ten kilometers. She wishes to behold the agricultural communes that lie beyond the urban constellation.

She sees them now, stretching to the horizon, neat flat bands of green bordered in brown. Seven eighths of the land area of the continent, she has been told endlessly, is used for the production of food. Or is it nine tenths? Five eighths? Twelve thirteenths? Busy little men and women oversee the machines that till the fertile fields. Aurea has heard tales of the terrible rites of the farming folk, the bizarre and primitive customs of those who must live outside the civilized urban world. Perhaps that is all fantasy; no one she knows has ever visited the communes. No one she knows has ever set foot outside Urban Monad 116. The courier pods trundle endlessly and without supervision toward the urbmons, carrying produce through subterranean channels. Food in; machinery and other manufactured goods out. A balanced economy. Aurea is borne upward on a transport of joy. How miraculous it is that there can be 75,000,000,000 people living harmoniously on one small world! God bless, she thinks. A full room for every family. A meaningful and enriching city life. Friends, lovers, mates, children.

Children. Dismay seizes her and she begins to spin.

In her dizziness she seems to vault to the edge of space, so that she sees the entire planet; all of its urban constellations are jutting toward her like spikes. She sees not only Chipitts but also Sansan and Boswash, and Berpar, Wienbud, Shankong, Bocarac, every gathering of mighty towers. And also she sees the plains teeming with food, the former deserts, the former savannas, the former forests. It is all quite wonderful, but it is terrifying as well, and she is uncertain for a moment whether the way man has reshaped his environment is the best of all possible ways. Yes, she tells herself, yes; we are servants of god this way, we avoid strife and greed and turmoil, we bring new life into the world, we thrive, we multiply. We multiply. We multiply. And doubt smites her and she begins to fall, and the capsule splits and releases her, leaving her bare body unprotected as it tumbles through the cold air. And she sees the spiky tips of Chipitts' fifty towers below her, but now there is a new tower, a fifty-first, and she drops toward it, toward a gleaming bronzed needle-sharp summit, and she cries out as it penetrates her and she is impaled. And she wakes, sweating and shaking, her tongue dry, her mind dazed by a vision beyond her grasp, and she clutches Memnon, who murmurs sleepily and sleepily enters her.

They are beginning now to tell the people of Urban Monad 116 about the new building. Aurea hears it from the wallscreen as she does her morning chores in the dormitory. Out of the patterns of light and color on the wall there congeals a view of an unfinished tower. Construction machines swarm over it, metal arms moving frantically, welding arcs glimmering off octagonal steel-paneled torsos. The familiar voice of the screen says, "Friends, what you see is Urbmon 158, one month eleven days from completion. God willing, it'll shortly be the home of a great many happy Chipittsians who will have the honor of establishing first-generation status there. The news from Louisville is that 802 residents of your own Urbmon 116 have already signed up for transfer to the new building, as soon as—"

Next, a day later, comes an interview with Mr. and Mrs. Dismas Cullinan of Boston, who, with their nine littles, were the very first people in 116 to request transfer. Mr. Cullinan, a meaty, red-faced man, is a specialist in sanitary engineering. He explains, "I see a real opportunity for me to move up to the planning level over in 158. I figure I can jump eighty, ninety floors in status in one hell of a hurry." Mrs. Cullinan complacently pats her middle. Number ten is on the way. She purrs over the immense social advantages the move will confer on her children Her eyes are too bright; her upper lip is thicker than the lower one and her nose is sharp. "She looks like a bird of prey," someone in the dorm comments. Someone else says, "She's obviously miserable here. Hoping to grab rungs fast over there." The Cullinan children range from two to thirteen years of age. Unfortunately, they resemble their parents. A runny-nosed girl claws at her brother while on screen. Aurea says firmly, "The building's better off without the lot of them."

Interviews with other transferees follow. On the fourth day of the campaign, the screen offers an extensive tour of the interior of 158, showing the ultramodern conveniences it will offer. Thermal irrigation for everybody, superspeed liftshafts and dropshafts, three-wall screens, a novel programing system for delivery of meals from the central kitchens, and many other wonders, representing the finest examples of urban progress. The number of volunteers for transfer is up now to 914.

Perhaps, Aurea thinks giddily, they will fill the entire quota with volunteers.

Memnon says, "The figure is fake. Siegmund tells me they've got only ninety-one volunteers so far."

"Then why—"

"To encourage the others."

In the second week, the transmissions dealing with the new building now indicate that the number of volunteers has leveled off at 1,060. Siegmund admits privately that the actual figure is somewhat less than this, although surprisingly not much less. Few additional volunteers are expected. The screen begins gently to introduce the possibility that conscription of transferees will be necessary. Two management men from Louisville and a pair of helix adjusters from Chicago are shown discussing the need for a proper genetic mix at the new building. A moral engineer from Shanghai speaks about the importance of being blessworthy under all circumstances. It is blessworthy to obey the divine plan and its representatives on Earth, he says. God is your friend and will not harm you. God loves the blessworthy. The quality of life in Urbmon 158 will be diminished if its initial population does not reach planned levels. This would be a crime against those who have volunteered to go to 158. A crime against your fellow man is a crime against god, and who wants to injure *him*? Therefore it is each man's duty to society to accept transfer if transfer is offered.

Next there is an interview with Kimon and Freya Kurtz, ages fourteen and thirteen, from a dorm in Bombay. Recently married. They are not about to volunteer, they admit, but they wouldn't mind being conscripted. "The way we look at it," Kimon Kurtz declares, "it could be a great opportunity. I mean, once we have some children, we'd be able to find top status for them right away. It's a brand new world over there—no limits on how fast you can rise, no one in the way. The readjustment of going over would be a little nudgy at first, but we'd be jumping soon enough. And we'd know that our littles wouldn't have to enter a dorm when they got old enough to marry. They could get rooms of their own without waiting, even before they had littles too. So even though

we're not eager to leave our friends and all, we're ready to go
if the wheel points to us." Freya Kurtz, ecstatic, breathless,
says, "Yes. That's right."

The softening-up process continues with an account of how
the conscriptees will be chosen: 3,878 in all, no more than
200 from any one city or thirty from any one dorm. The pool
of eligibles consists of married men and women between the
ages of twelve and seventeen who have no children, a current
pregnancy not being counted as a child. Selection will be by
random lot.

At last the names of the conscripts are released.

The screen's cheerful voice announces, "From Chicago's
735th floor dormitory the following blessworthy ones have
been chosen, and may god give them fertility in their new
life;

"Brock, Aylward and Alison.

"Feuermann, Sterling and Natasha.

"Holston, Memnon and Aurea—"

She will be wrenched from her matrix. She will be torn
from the pattern of memories and affections that defines her
identity. She is terrified of going.

She will fight the order.

"Memnon, file an appeal! Do something, fast!" She kneads
the gleaming wall of the dormitory. He looks at her blankly;
he is about to leave for work. He has already said there is
nothing they can do. He goes out.

Aurea follows him into the corridor. The morning rush has
begun; the citizens of 735th-floor Chicago stream past. Aurea
sobs. The eyes of others are averted from her. She knows
nearly all of these people. She has spent her life among them.
She tugs at Memnon's hand. "Don't just walk out on me!"
she whispers harshly. "How can we let them throw us out of
116?"

"It's the law, Aurea. People who don't obey the law go
down the chute. Is that what you want? To end up contributing combustion mass to the generators?"

"I won't go! Memnon, I've always lived here! I—"

"You're talking like a flippo," he says, keeping his voice
low. He pulls her back inside the dormitory. Staring up, she
sees only cavernous dark nostrils. "Pop a pill, Aurea. Talk to
the floor consoler, why don't you? Stay calm and let's adjust."

"I want you to file an appeal."

"There is no appeal."

"I refuse to go."

He seizes her shoulders. "Look at it rationally, Aurea. One building isn't that different from another. We'll have some of our friends there. We'll make new friends. We—"

"No."

"There's no alternative," he says. "Except down the chute."

"I'd rather go down the chute, then!"

For the first time since they were married, she sees him regarding her contemptuously. He cannot abide irrationality. "Don't heave nonsense," he tells her. "See the consoler, pop a pill, think it through. I've got to leave now."

He departs again, and this time she does not go after him. She slumps on the floor, feeling cold plastic against her bare skin. The others in the room tactfully ignore her. She sees fiery images: her schoolroom, her first lover, her parents, her sisters and brothers, all melting, flowing across the room, a blazing trickle of acrid fluid. She presses her thumbs to her eyes. She will not be cast out. Gradually she calms. I have influence, she tells herself. If Memnon will not act, I will act for us. She wonders if she can ever forgive Memnon for his cowardice. For his transparent opportunism. She will visit her uncle.

She strips off her morning robe and dons a chaste gray girlish cloak. From the hormone chest she selects a capsule that will cause her to emanate the odor that inspires men to act protectively toward her. She looks sweet, demure, virginal; but for the ripeness of her body she could pass for ten or eleven years of age.

The liftshaft takes her to the 975th floor, the throbbing heart of Louisville.

All is steel and spongeglass here. The corridors are spacious and lofty. There is no rush of people through the halls; the occasional human figure seems incongruous and superfluous, though silent machines glide on unfathomable errands. This is the abode of those who administer the plans. Designed to awe; calculated to overwhelm; the permissible *mana* of the ruling class. How comfortable here. How sleek. How self-contained. Rip away the lower 90 percent of the building and Louisville would drift in serene orbit, never missing a thing.

Aurea halts outside a glistening door inlaid with moiré-generating stripes of bright white metal. She is scanned by

hidden sensors, asked to name her business, evaluated, shunted
into a waiting room. At length her mother's brother consents
to see her.

His office is nearly as large as a private residential suite. He
sits behind a broad polygonal desk from which protrudes a
bank of shimmering monitor dials. He wears formal top-level
clothes, a cascading gray tunic tipped with epaulets radiating
in the infrared. Aurea feels the crisp blast of heat from where
she stands. He is cool, distant, polite. His handsome face
appears to have been fashioned from burnished copper.

"It's been many months, hasn't it, Aurea?" he says. A
patronizing smile escapes him. "How have you been?"

"Fine, Uncle Lewis."

"Your husband?"

"Fine."

"Any littles yet?"

Blurting. "Uncle Lewis, we've been picked to go to 158!"

His plastic smile does not waver. "How fortunate! God
bless, you can start a new life right at the top!"

"I don't want to go. Get me out of it. Somehow. Anyhow."
She rushes toward him, a frightened child, tears flowing,
knees melting. A force-field captures her when she is two
meters from the outer rim of his desk. Her breasts feel it
first, and as they flatten painfully against the invisible barrier
she averts her head and injures her cheek. She drops to her
knees and whimpers.

He comes to her. He lifts her. He tells her to be brave, to
do her duty to god. He is kind and calm at first, but as she
goes on protesting, his voice turns cold, with a hard edge of
irritation, and abruptly Aurea begins to feel unworthy of his
attention. He reminds her of her obligations to society. He
hints delicately that the chute awaits those who persist in
abrading the smooth texture of community life. Then he
smiles again, and his icy blue eyes meet hers and engulf
them, and he tells her to be brave and go. She creeps away.
She feels disgraced by her weakness.

As she plunges downward from Louisville, her uncle's spell
ebbs and her indignation revives. Perhaps she can get help
elsewhere. The future is crashing around her, falling towers
burying her in clouds of brick-black dust. A harsh wind blows
out of tomorrow and the great building sways. She returns to
the dorm and hastily changes her clothing. She alters her
hormone balance too. A drop or two of golden fluid, sliding

down to the mysterious coils of the female machinery. Now she is clad in iridescent mesh through which her breasts, thighs, and buttocks are intermittently visible, and she exudes an odor of distilled lust. She notifies the data terminal that she requests a private meeting with Siegmund Kluver of Shanghai. She paces the dorm, waiting. One of the young husbands comes to her, eyes gleaming. He grasps her haunch and gestures toward his sleeping platform. "Sorry," she murmurs. "I'll be going out." Some refusals are allowed. He shrugs and goes away, pausing to glance back at her in a wistful way. Eight minutes later word comes that Siegmund has consented to meet with her in one of the rendezvous cubicles on the 790th floor. She goes up.

His face is smudged and memoranda bulge in his breast pocket. He seems cross and impatient. "Why did you pull me away from my work?" he asks.

"You know Memnon and I have been—"

"Yes, of course." Brusquely. "Mamelon and I will be sorry to lose your friendship."

Aurea attempts to assume a provocative stance. She knows she cannot win Siegmund's aid merely by making herself available; he is hardly that easily swayed. Bodies are easily possessed here, career opportunities are few and not lightly jeopardized. Her aims are trivial. She feels rejection flowing out of the minutes just ahead. But perhaps she can recruit Siegmund's influence. Perhaps she can lead him to feel such regret at her departure that he will aid her. She whispers, "Help us get out of going, Siegmund."

"How can I—"

"You have connections. Amend the program somehow. Support our appeal. You're a rising man in the building. You have high friends. You can do it."

"No one can do such a thing."

"Please, Siegmund.'" She approaches him, pulls her shoulders back, unsubtly lets her nipples come thrusting through her garment of mesh. Hopeless. How can she magic him with two pink nubs of stiff flesh? She moistens her lips, narrows her eyes to slits. Too stagy. He will laugh. Huskily she says, "Don't you want me to stay? Wouldn't you like to take a turn or two with me? You know I'd do anything if you'd help us get off that list. *Anything!*" Face eager. Nostrils flaring, offering promise of unimaginable erotic delights. She will do things not yet invented.

She sees his flickering momentary smile and knows that she has oversold herself; he is amused, not tempted, by her forwardness. Her face crumples. She turns away.

"You don't want me," she mutters.

"Aurea, please! You're asking the impossible." He catches her shoulders and pulls her toward him. His hands slip within the mesh and caress her flesh. She knows that he is merely consoling her with a counterfeit of desire. He says, "If there was any way I could fix things for you, I would. But we'd all get tossed down the chute." His fingers find her body's core. Moist, slippery, despite herself. She does not want him now, not this way. With a wriggle of her hips she tries to free herself. His embrace is mere kindness; he will take her out of pity. She pivots and stiffens.

"No," she says, and then she realizes how hopeless everything is, and she yields to him only because she knows that there will never be another chance.

Memnon says, "I've heard from Siegmund about what happened today. And from your uncle. You've got to stop this, Aurea."

"Let's go down the chute, Memnon."

"Come with me to the consoler. I've never seen you acting this way before."

"I've never felt so threatened."

"Why can't you adjust to it?" he asks. "It's really a grand chance for us."

"I can't. I can't." She slumps forward, defeated, broken.

"Stop it," he tells her. "Brooding sterilizes. Won't you cheer up a bit?"

She will not give way to chiding, however reasonable the tone. He summons the machines; they take her to the consoler. Soft rubbery orange pads gently grasping her arms all the way through the halls. In the consoler's office she is examined and her metabolism is probed. He draws the story from her. He is an elderly man, kind, gentle, somewhat bored, with a cloud of white hair rimming a pink face. She wonders whether he hates her behind his sweetness. At the end he tells her, "Conflict sterilizes. You must learn to comply with the demands of society, for society will not nurture you unless you play the game." He recommends treatment.

"I don't want treatment," she says thickly, but Memnon

authorizes it, and they take her away. "Where am I going?" she asks. "For how long?"

"To the 780th floor, for about a week."

"To the moral engineers?"

"Yes," they tell her.

"Not there. Please, not there."

"They are gentle. They heal the troubles."

"They'll change me."

"They'll improve you. Come. Come. Come."

For a week she lives in a sealed chamber filled with warm, sparkling fluids. She floats idly in a pulsing tide, thinking of the huge urbmon as a wondrous pedestal on which she sits. Images soak from her mind and everything becomes deliciously cloudy. They speak to her over audio channels embedded in the walls of the chamber. Occasionally she glimpses an eye peering through an optical fiber dangling above her. They drain the tensions and resistances from her. On the eighth day Memnon comes for her. They open the chamber and she is lifted forth, nude, dripping, her skin puckered, little beads of glittering fluid clinging to her. The room is full of strange men. Everyone else is clothed; it is dreamlike to be bare in front of them, but she does not really mind. Her breasts are full, her belly is flat, why then be ashamed? Machines towel her dry and clothe her. Memnon leads her by the hand. Aurea smiles quite often. "I love you," she tells Memnon softly.

"God bless," he says. "I've missed you so much."

The day is at hand, and she has paid her farewells. She has had two months to say good-bye, first to her blood kin, then to her friends in her village, then to others whom she has known within Chicago, and at last to Siegmund and Mamelon Kluver, her only acquaintances outside her native city. She has rewound her past into a tight coil. She has revisited the home of her parents and her old schoolroom, and she has even taken a tour of the urbmon, like a visitor from outbuilding, so that she may see the power plant and the service core and the conversion stations one final time.

Meanwhile Memnon has been busy too. Each night he reports to her on that day's accomplishments. The 5,202 citizens of Urban Monad 116 who are destined to transfer to the new structure have elected twelve delegates to the steering committee of Urbmon 158, and Memnon is one of

the twelve. It is a great honor. Night after night the delegates
take part in a multiscreen linkage embracing all of Chipitts,
so that they can plan the social framework of the building
they are going to share. It has been decided, Memnon tells
her, to have fifty cities of twenty floors apiece, and to name
the cities not after the vanished cities of old Earth, as has
been the general custom, but rather after distinguished men
of the past: Newton, Einstein, Plato, Galileo, and so forth.
Memnon will be given responsibility for an entire sector of
heat-diffusion engineers. It will be administrative rather than
technical work, and so he and Aurea will live in Newton, the
highest city.

Memnon expands and throbs with increased importance.
He cannot wait for the hour of transfer to arrive. "We'll be
really influential people," he tells Aurea exultantly. "And in
ten or fifteen years we'll be legendary figures in 158. The first
settlers. The founders, the pioneers. They'll be making up
ballads about us in another century or so."

"And I was unwilling to go," Aurea says mildly. "How
strange to think of myself acting like that!"

"It's an error to react with fear until you perceive the true
shape of things," Memnon replies. "The ancients thought it
would be a calamity to have as many as 5,000,000,000 people
in the world. Yet we have fifteen times as much and look how
happy we are!"

"Yes. Very happy. And we'll always be happy, Memnon."

The signal comes. The machines are at the door to fetch
them. Memnon indicates the box that contains their few
possessions. Aurea glows. She glances about the dorm,
astonished by the crowdedness of it, the crush of couples in
so little space. We will have our own room in 158, she
reminds herself.

Those members of the dorm who are not leaving form a
line, and offer Memnon and Aurea one final embrace.

Memnon follows the machines out, and Aurea follows
Memnon. They go up to the landing stage on the thousandth
floor. It is an hour past dawn and summer sunlight gleams in
shining splotches on the tips of Chipitts' towers. The transfer
operation has already begun; quickboats capable of carrying
100 passengers each will be moving back and forth between
Urbmons 116 and 158 all day.

"And so we leave this place," Memnon says. "We begin a
new life. Bless god!"

"God bless!" cries Aurea.

They enter the quickboat and it soars aloft. The pioneers bound for Urbmon 158 gasp as they see, for the first time, how their world really looks from above. The towers are beautiful, Aurea realizes. They glisten. On and on they stretch, fifty-one of them, like a ring of upraised spears in a broad green carpet. She is very happy. Memnon folds his hand over hers. She wonders how she could ever have feared this day. She wishes she could apologize to the universe for her foolishness.

She lets her free hand rest lightly on the curve of her belly. New life now sprouts within her. Each moment the cells divide and the little one grows. They have dated the hour of conception to the evening of the day when she was discharged by the consoler's office. Conflict indeed sterilizes, Aurea has realized. Now the poison of negativeness has been drained from her; she is able to fulfill a woman's proper destiny.

"It'll be so different," she says to Memnon, "living in such an empty building. Only 250,000! How long will it take for us to fill it?"

"Twelve or thirteen years," he answers. "We'll have few deaths, because we're all young. And lots of births."

She laughs. "Good. I hate an empty house."

The quickboat's voice says, "We now will turn to the southeast, and on the left to the rear you can catch a last glimpse of Urbmon 116."

Her fellow passengers strain to see. Aurea does not make the effort. Urbmon 116 has ceased to concern her.

Three

They are playing tonight in Rome, in the spishy new sonic center on the 530th level. Dillon Chrimes hasn't been that far up in the building in weeks. Lately he and the group have been doing the grime stint: Reykjavik, Prague, Warsaw, down among the grubbos. Well, they're entitled to some entertainment too. Dillon lives in San Francisco, not so lofty himself. The 370th floor; the heart of the cultural ghetto. But he doesn't mind that. He isn't deprived of variety. He gets around, everywhere from the bottom to the top in the course of a year, and it's only a statistical anomaly that it's been nothing but bottoms up for a while. The odds are he'll be blowing Shanghai, Chicago, Edinburgh, that crowd, in the month to come. With all those clean long-limbed lovelies to spread for him after the show.

Dillon is seventeen. More than middle height, with silken blond hair to his shoulders. Traditional, the old Orpheus bit. Crystalline blue eyes. He loves staring at them in a round of polymirrors, seeing the icy spheres intersect. Happily married, and three littles already, god bless! His wife's name is Electra. She paints psychedelic tapestries. Sometimes she accompanies him when he's touring with the group, but not often. Not now. He has met only one woman who lights him nearly as much. A Shanghai slicko, wife of some Louisville-bound headknocker. Mamelon Kluver, her name. The other girls of the urbmon are just so many slots, Dillon often thinks, but Mamelon connects. He has never told Electra about her. Jealousy sterilizes.

He plays the vibrastar in a cosmos group. That makes him valuable personnel. "I'm unique, like a flow-sculpture," he sometimes boasts. Actually there's another vibrastar man in the building, but to be one out of merely two is still a decent accomplishment. There are only two cosmos groups in Urbmon 116; the building can't really afford much redundancy in its entertainers. Dillon doesn't think highly of the rival group, though his opinion is based more on prejudice than familiarity—he's heard them three times, is all. There's been talk of getting both groups together for an all-out headblaster of a joint concert, perhaps in Louisville, but no one takes such teasers seriously. Meanwhile they go their separately programed ways, moving up and down through the urbmon as the spiritual weather dictates. The usual gig is five nights in a city. That allows everybody in, say, Bombay, who stones on cosmos groups to see them the same week, thereby providing conversation fodder for the general sharing. Then they move along, and, counting nights off, they theoretically can make the circuit of the whole building every six months. But sometimes gigs are extended. Do the lower levels need excesses of bread and circuses? The group may be handed fourteen nights running in Warsaw, then. Do the upper levels need psychic deconstipation in a big way? A twelve-night run in Chicago, maybe. Or the group itself may go sour and have to get its filters reamed, necessitating a layoff of two weeks or more. Allowing for all of these factors, there have to be two groups roaming the urbmon if every city is going to get a crack at a cosmos show at least once a year. Right now, Dillon thinks, the other operation is playing Boston for the third week. Some kind of problem with sexual turnoffs there, of all wildnesses!

He wakes at noon. Electra loyally beside him; the littles long gone to school, except for the baby, gurgling in its maintenance slot. Artists and performers keep their own hours. Her lips touch his. A torrent of fiery hair across his face. Her hand at his loins, wandering, grasping. Fingertips playfully rimming him. "Love me?" she sings. "Love me not? Love me? Love me not?"

"You medieval witch."

"You look so pretty when you sleep, Dill. The long hair. The sweet skin. Like a girl, even. You bring out the sappho in me."

"Do I?" he laughs and crams his genitals out of sight between his lean thighs. Clamps his legs. "Then do me!" He gouges his palms against his chest, trying to push up ersatz breasts. "Come on," he says hoarsely. "Here's your chance. Get on board. Flick that tongue."

"Silly. Stop that!"

"I think I'd be very pretty as a girl."

"Your hips are all wrong," she says, and pulls his locked feet apart. Up pops penis, half-erect. She whangs it with the backs of two fingertips, gently. Further stiffening. But there will be no sex between them now. He rarely indulges at this time of day, with a performance coming up. And in any case the mood is wrong, too skittish, too brittle. She vaults off the sleeping platform and deflates it with a kick of the pedal while he is still on it. An airy whooshing. That sort of mood; presexual, childish. He watches her waltz to the cleanser. What a fine butt she has, he thinks. So pale. So full. The splendid deep cleft. The elegant dimples. He creeps toward her and stoops to nip a hinder cheek, carefully, not wanting to leave a blemish. They share the cleanser. The baby begins to yowl. Dillon glances over his shoulder. "God bless, god bless, god bless!" he sings, beginning basso, ending falsetto. What a good life, he thinks. How neat existence can be. Electra, pulling on her clothes, says, "Can I get you some fumes?" A transparent band over her breasts. Rosy nipples

360   **Robert Silverberg**

like little blind eyes. He is pleased that she has stopped
nursing; biology is tremendously moving, yes, but the drib-
bles of bluish-white milk over everything annoyed him. Doubtless a failing to eradicate. Why be so fastidious? Electra
enjoyed nursing. She still lets the little suck, saying it's for
the child's pleasure, but there can hardly be much kick in a
dry tit, so Dillon knows the locus of the joy in that particular
transaction. He hunts for his clothing.

"Will you paint today?" he asks.

"Tonight. While you're performing."

"You haven't worked much lately."

"I haven't felt the strings pulling."

It is her special idiom. To practice her art she must feel
rooted to the earth. Strings rising from the planet's core,
entering her body, snaking into her slot, slipping through the
openings of her nipples. And then tugging. As the world
turns, the imagery is wrenched from her blazing distended
body. Or so she says; Dillon never questions the claims of a
fellow artist, especially when she is his wife. He admires her
accomplishments. It would have been madness to marry
another cosmos-grouper, although when he was eleven he
had just such a thing in mind. To share his destinies with the
comet-harp girl. He'd be a widower now if he had. Down the
chute, down the chute! What a flippy filther that one had
been. And had wrecked a perfectly wonderful incantator, too,
Peregrun Connelly. Could have been me. Could have been
me. Marry outside your art, boys; avoid unblessworthy
invidiousness.

"*No fumar¿*" Electra asks. She has been studying ancient
languages lately. "*¿Por qué¿*"

"Working tonight. It spills the galactic juices if I indulge
this early."

"Mind if I?"

"Suit yourself."

She takes a fume, nipping the cap neatly with a daggered
forefingernail. Quickly her face flushes, her eyes dilate. A
lovable quality about her: she is such an easy turnon. She puffs
vapors at the baby, who chortles, while the maintenance slot's
field buzzes in a solemn attempt to purify the child's atmosphere. "*Grazie mille, mama!*" Electra says, mimicking ven-
triloquy. "*È molto bello! È delicioso! Was für shhönes Wetter!
Quella gioia!*" She dances around the room, chanting fragments of exclamations in strange tongues, and tumbles, laugh-

ing, into the deflated sleeping platform. Her frilly frock blows up; he sees an auburn pubic glow and is tempted to top her despite his resolutions, but he regains his austerity and merely blows her a kiss. As if perceiving the phases of his mental processes, she piously closes her thighs and covers herself. He switches on the screen, selecting the abstract channel, and patterns blaze on the wall. "I love you," he tells her. "Can I have something to eat?"

She breakfasts him. Afterward she goes out, saying that she is scheduled to visit the blessman this afternoon. He is privately glad to see her go, for just now her vitality is too much for him. He must slide into the mood of the concert, which requires some spartan denials from him. Once she has gone, he programs the terminal for a reverberant oscillation, and, as the resonant tones march across his skull, he slips lightly into the proper frame of mind. The baby, meanwhile, remains in its slot, enjoying the best of care. He thinks nothing of leaving it alone when, at 1600 hours, he must go off to Rome to set up for the evening's performance.

The liftshaft shoots him 160 levels heavenward. When he gets off, he is in Rome. Crowded halls, tight faces. The people here are mostly minor bureaucrats, a middle echelon of failed functionaries, those who would never get to Louisville except to deliver a report. They are not smart enough to hope for Chicago or Shanghai of Edinburgh. Here they will stay in this good gray city, frozen in hallowed stasis, doing dehumanized jobs that any computer could handle forty times as well. Dillon feels a cosmic pity for everyone who is not an artist, but he pities the people of Rome most of all, sometimes. Because they are nothing. Because they can use neither their brains nor their muscles. Crippled souls; walking zeros; better off down the chute. A Roman slams right into him as he stands outside the liftshaft bank, considering these things. Male, maybe forty, all the spirit drained from his eyes. The walking dead. The running dead. "Sorry," the man mumbles, and speeds on. "Truth!" Dillon cries after him. "Love! Loosen up! Fuck a lot!" He laughs. But what good does it do; the Roman will not laugh with him. Others of his kind come rushing down the corridor, their leaden bodies absorbing the last vibrations of Dillon's exclamations. *"Truth! Love!"* Blurred sounds, fading, graying, going. Gone. I will entertain you tonight, he tells them silently. I will drive you out of your

wretched minds and you will love me for it. If I could only
burn your brains! If I could only singe your souls!

He thinks of Orpheus. They would tear me apart, he
realizes, if I ever really reached them.

He saunters toward the sonic center.

Pausing by the elbow bend of the corridor, still halfway
around the building from the auditorium, Dillon feels a
sudden ecstatic awareness of the splendor of the urbmon. A
frenzied epiphany: he sees it as a spike suspended between
heaven and earth. And he is almost at the midway point right
now with a little more than five hundred floors over his head,
a little less than five hundred floors under his feet. People
moving around, copulating, eating, giving birth, doing a
million blessworthy things, each one out of 800-how-many-
thousand traveling on his own orbit. Dillon loves the building.
Right now he feels he could almost soar on its multiplicity the
way others might soar on a drug. To be at the equator, to
drink the divine equilibrium—oh, yes, yes! But of course
there is a way to experience the whole complexity of the
urbmon in one wild rush of information. He has never tried
it; he is not really heavy on groovers, and has stayed away
from the more elaborate drugs, the ones that open your mind
so wide that anything can wander in. Nevertheless, here in
the middle of the urbmon, he knows that this is the night to
try the multiplexer. After the performance. To pop the pill
that will allow him to drop the mental barriers, to let the full
immensity of Urban Monad 116 interpenetrate his consciousness. Yes. He will go to the 500th floor to do it. If the
performance goes well. Nightwalking in Bombay. He really
should turn on in the city where tonight's concert will be
held, but Rome goes no farther down than the 521st floor,
and he must go the 500th. For the mystic symmetry of the
thing. Even though it is still inexact. Where is the true
midpoint in a building of a thousand floors? Somewhere
between 499 and 500, no? But the 500th floor will have to do.
We learn to live with approximations.

He enters the sonic center.

A fine new auditorium, three stories high, with a toadstool
of a stage in the center and audience webs strung concentri-
cally around it. Lightglow drifts in the air. The mouths of
speakers, set into the domed rich-textured ceilings, pucker
and gape. A warm room, a good room, placed here by the
divine mercy of Louisville to bring a little joy into the lives of

these bleak juiceless Romans. There is no better hall for a
cosmos group in the entire urbmon. The other members of
the group are here already, tuning in. The comet-harp, the
incantator, the orbital diver, the gravity-drinker, the doppler-
inverter, the spectrum-rider. Already the room trembles with
shimmering plinks of sound and jolly blurts of color, and a
shaft of pure no-referent texture, abstract and immanent, is
rising from the doppler-inverter's central cone. Everyone
waves to him. "Late, man," they say, and "Where you been?"
and "We thought you were skimming out," and he says, "I've
been in the halls, peddling love to the Romans," which
shatters them into strands of screeching laughter. He clambers onto the stage. His instrument sits untended near the
perimeter, its lattices dangling, its lovely gaudy skin
unilluminated. A lifting machine stands by, waiting to help
him put it in its proper place. The machine brought the
vibrastar to the auditorium; it would also tune it in for him, if
he asked it to, but of course he will not do that. Musicians
have a mystique about tuning in their own instruments. Even
though it will take him at least two hours to do it, and the
machine could do it in ten minutes. Maintenance workers
and other humbles of the grubbo class have the same mystique. Not strange: one must battle constantly against one's
own obsolescence if one is going to go on thinking of oneself
as having a purpose in life.

"Over here," Dillon tells the machine.

Delicately it brings his vibrastar to the output node and
makes the connection. Dillon could not possibly have moved
the immense instrument. He does not mind letting machines
do the things humans were never meant to do, like lifting
three-ton loads. Dillon puts his hands on the manipulatrix
and feels the power thrumming through the keyboard. Good.
"Go," he tells the machine, and silently it slides away. He
kneads and squeezes the projectrons of the manipulatrix. As
if milking them. Sensual pleasure in making contact with the
machine. A little orgasm with every crescendo. Yeah. Yeah.
Yeah.

"Tuning in!" he warns the other musicians.

They make feedback adjustments in their own instruments;
otherwise the sudden surge of his entrance might damage
both instruments and players. One by one they nod their
readiness to him, with the gravity-drinker lad chiming in last,
and finally Dillon can let out the clutch. Yeah! The hall fills

with light. Stars stream from the walls. He coats the ceiling with dripping nebulae. He is the basic instrument of the group, the all-important continuo, providing the foundation against which the others will do their things. With a practiced eye he checks the focus. Everything sharp. Nat the spectrum-rider says, "Mars is a little off-color, Dill." Dillon hunts for Mars. Yes. Yes. He feeds it an extra jolt of orange. And Jupiter? A shining globe of white fire. Venus. Saturn. And all the stars. He is satisfied with the visuals.

"Bringing up the sound, now," he says.

The heels of his hands hit the control panel. From the gaping speakers comes a tender blade of white noise. The music of the spheres. He colors it now, bringing up the gain on the galactic side, letting the stellar drift impart plangent hues to the tone. Then, with a quick downward stab on the projectrons, he kicks in the planetary sounds. Saturn whirls like a belt of knives. Jupiter booms. "Are you getting it?" he calls out. "How's the clarity?" Sophro the orbital diver says, "Fat up the asteroids, Dill," and he does it, and Sophro nods, happy, his chins trembling in pleasure.

After an hour of preliminary maneuvers Dillon has his primary tuning finished. So far, though, he has done only the solo work. Now to coordinate with the others. Slow, delicate work: to reach reciprocity with them one by one, building a web of interrelationship, a seven-way union. Plagued all the way by heisenberging effects, so that a whole new cluster of adjustments has to be made each time another instrument is added to the set. Change one factor, you change everything; you can't just hold your own while keying in more and more and more output. He takes on the spectrum-rider first. Easy. Dillon gives forth a shower of comets and Nat modulates them pleasantly into suns. Then they add the incantator. A slight stridency at first, quickly corrected. Good going. Then the gravity-drinker. No problem. The comet-harp, now. Rasp! Rasp! The receptors go bleary and the entire thing falls apart. He and the incantator have to return separately, rejoin, bring the comet-harp into the net again. This time all right. Great plumey curves of tone go lalloping through the hall. Then the orbital diver. Fifteen sweaty minutes; the balances keep souring. Dillon expects a system collapse any second, but no, they hang on and finally get the levels even. And now the really tough one, the doppler-inverter, which threatens always to clash with his own instrument because both rely as much on visuals as audio, and both are generators, not just modulators of someone else's playing. He almost gets it. But they lose the comet-harp. It makes a thin edgy whining sound and drops out. So they go back two steps and try again. Precarious balance, constantly falling off. Up till five years ago, there had been only five instruments in cosmos groups; it was simply too difficult to hold more than that together. Like adding a fourth actor in Greek tragedy: an impossible technical feat, or so it must have seemed to Aeschylus. Now they were able to coordinate six instruments reasonably well, and a seventh with some effort, by sending the circuit bouncing up to a computer nexus in Edinburgh, but it is still a filther to put them all in synch. Dillon gestures madly with his left shoulder, encouraging the doppler-inverter to get with it. "Come on, come on, come on, come *on*!" and this time they make it. The time is 1840. Everything sticks together.

"Let's run it through now," Nat sings out. "Give us an A for tuning, maestro."

Dillon hunches forward and clutches the projections. Feeds power. Gets a sensory shift; the knobs abruptly feel like the cheeks of Electra's buttocks in his hands. Smiles at the sensation. Firm, bouncy, cool. Up we go! And he gives them the universe in one sizzling blare of light and sound. The hall swims with images. The stars leap and cross and mate. The incantator man picks up his sonics and does his trick, enhancing, multiplying, intensifying, until the whole urbmon shakes. The comet-harp makes bleeping blurting loops of dizzying counterpoint and starts to rearrange Dillon's constellations. The orbital diver, hanging back, makes a sudden plunge at an unexpected moment, and dials spin on everybody's control panel, but it is such a devastating entry that Dillon inwardly applauds it. The gravity-drinker smoothly sucks tone. Now the doppler-inverter goes at it, shooting up its own shaft of light, which sizzles and steams for perhaps thirty seconds before the spectrum-rider grabs it and runs with it, and now all seven of them are jamming madly, each trying to put the others on, shooting forth such a welter of signals that the sight must surely be visible from Boshwash to Sansan.

"Hold it! Hold it! Hold it!" Nat screams. "Don't waste it! Man, *don't waste it!*"

And they cut out of phase and go down, and sit there

idling, sweaty, nerves twinkling. Withdrawal pains; it hurts to step away from such beauty. But Nat is right: they mustn't use themselves up before the audience gets here.

Dinner break, right on stage. No one eats much. They leave the instruments tuned and running, of course. Lunacy to disrupt the synch after working so hard to get it right. Now and then one of the idling instruments flares past its threshold and emits a blob of light or a squeak of sound. They'd play themselves if we'd only let them, Dillon thinks. It might just be a wild soar to turn everything on and sit back, doing nothing, while the instruments themselves give the concert, self-programed. You'd get some strange percepts then. The mind of the machine. On the other hand it might be a hell of a dropper to find out you were superfluous. How frail is our prestige. Celebrated artists today, but let the secret sneak out and we'll all be pushing junk-buckets in Reykjavik tomorrow.

The audience begins to show up at 1945. An older crowd; since this is the first night of the Rome run, the rules of seniority have governed the distribution of tickets and the undertwenties have been left out. Dillon, midstage, does not trouble to hide his scorn for the gray, baggy people settling into the audience webs all around him. Will the music reach them? Can anything reach them? Or will they sit passively, not even going halfway out to the performance? Dreaming of making more littles. Ignoring the sweating artists; taking up a good seat and getting nothing from the fireworks about them. We throw you the whole universe, and you don't catch. Is it because you're old? How much can a plumpish many-mother, thirty-three years old, pull from a cosmos show? No, it isn't age. In the more sophisticated cities there's no problem of audience response, young or old. No, it's a matter of your basic attitude toward the world of art. At the bottom of the building, the grubbos respond with their eyes, their guts, their balls. Either they're fascinated by the colored lights and the wild sounds, or else they're baffled and hostile, but they aren't indifferent. In the top levels, where the use of the mind is not only permitted but desired, they reach out for the show, knowing that the more they bring to it the more they get from it. And isn't that what life is all about, to wring all the sensory percepts you can out of the outputs drifting past your head? What else is there? But here, here in the middle levels, all the responses are dulled. The walking dead. The important thing is *being present in the auditorium,* grabbing that ticket away from someone else, showing off. The performance itself doesn't matter. That's just noise and light, some crazy kids from San Francisco having a workout. So there they sit, these Romans, disconnected from skull to crotch. What a joke. Romans? The real Rome wasn't like that, you bet. Calling their city Rome is a crime against history. Dillon glares at them. Then, overfocusing his eyes, he deliberately blurs them out; he does not want to see their flabby gray faces, for fear the sight of them will color his performance. He is here to give. If they aren't capable of taking, tough.

"Let's go up now," Nat murmurs. "Ready, Dill?"

He is ready. He brings his hands up for a virtuoso pounce and slams them down on the projectrons. The old headblaster! Moon and sun and planets and stars come roaring out of his instrument. The whole glittering universe erupts in the hall. He doesn't dare look at the audience. Did he rock them? Are they gasping and tugging at their droopy lower lips? Come on, come on, come on! The others, as if sensing that he's into something special, let him take an introductory solo. Furies fly through his brain. He jabs the manipulatrix. Pluto! Saturn! Betelgeuse! Deneb! Here sit people who spend their whole lives locked inside a single building; give them the stars in one skullblowing rush. Who says you can't start with your climax? The power drain must be immense; lights must be dimming all the way to Chicago. What of it? Did Beethoven give a fart about the power drain? There. There. There. Throw stars around. Make them shimmer and shake. An eclipse of the sun—why not? Let the corona crackle and fry. Make the moon dance. And bring up the sound, too, a great heaving pedal-point that sneaks up the webbing at them, a spear of fifty-cycle vibration nailing them in their assholes. Help them digest their dinner. Shake up all the old shit clogging the colon. Dillon laughs. He wishes he could see his face now; something demonic, maybe. How long is the solo going to last? Why don't they pick up on him, now? He's going to burn out. He doesn't mind, throwing himself into the machine like that, except for the faint paranoid feeling that the others are deliberately allowing him to strain past his limits so he'll injure himself. The rest of his life sitting like a slug, going booble-booble-booble. Not me! He pulls out all the stops. Fantastic! He's never done things like this before. It must be his rage at these dull Romans that is inspiring him.

And all of it wasted on them. Slot that, though: what counts is what's happening inside him, his own artistic fulfillment. If he can blow their skulls, that's a bonus. But this is ecstasy. The whole universe is vibrating around him. A gigantic solo. God himself must have felt this way when he got to work on the first day. Needles of sound descending from the speakers. A mighty crescendo of light and tone. He feels the power surging through him; he is so happy with what he is doing that he grows hard below, and tips himself back in his seat to make it ram more visibly against his clothes. Has anyone ever done something like this before, this improvised symphony for solo vibrastar? Hello, Bach! Hello, Mick! Hello, Wagner! Shoot your skulls! Let it all fly! He is past the crest, starting to come down now, no longer relying on raw energy but dabbling in subtler things, splashing Jupiter with golden splotches, turning the stars into icy white points, bringing up little noodling ostinatos. \He makes Saturn trill: a signal to the others. Who ever heard of opening a concert with a cadenza? But they pick up on it.

Ah, now. Here they come. Gently the doppler-inverter noodles in with a theme of its own, catching something of the descending fervor of Dillon's stellar patterns. At once the comet-harp overlays this with a more sensational series of twanging tones that immediately transmute themselves into looping blares of green light. These are seized by the spectrum-rider, who climbs up on top of them and, grinning broadly, skis off toward the ultraviolet in a shower of hissing crispness. Old Sophro now does his orbital dives, a swoop and a pickup followed by a swoop and a pickup again, playing against the spectrum-rider in the kind of cunning way that only someone right inside the meshing group can appreciate. Then the incantator enters, portentous, booming, sending reverberations shivering through the walls, heightening the significance of the tonal and astronomical patterns until the convergences become almost unbearably beautiful. It is the cue for the gravity-drinker, who disrupts everybody's stability with wonderful, wild liberating bursts of force. By this time Dillon has retreated to his proper place as the coordinater and unifier of the group, tossing a skein of melody to this one, a loop of light to that one, embellishing everything that passes near him. He fades into the undertones. His manic excitement passes; playing in a purely mechanical way, he is as much listener as performer, quietly appreciating the variations and divagations his partners are producing. He does not need to draw attention now. He can simply go *oomp oomp oomp* the rest of the night. Not that he will; the construct will tumble if he doesn't feed new data every ten or fifteen minutes. But this is his time to coast.

Each of the others takes a solo in turn. Dillon can no longer see the audience. He rocks, he pivots, he sweats, he sobs; he caresses the projectrons furiously; he seals himself in a cocoon of blazing light; he juggles alternations of light and darkness. The rod in his pants has softened. He is calm at the eye of the storm, fully professional, quietly doing his work. That moment of ecstasy seems to belong to some other day, even to some other man. How long had the solo lasted, anyway? He has lost track of the time. But the performance is going well, and he leaves it to methodical Nat to keep watch of the hour.

After its frenzied opening the concert had settled into routine. The center of the action has shifted to the doppler-inverter man, who is spinning off a series of formula flashes. Quite nice, but stale stuff, over-rehearsed, unspontaneous. His offhandedness infects the others and the whole group vamps for perhaps twenty minutes, going through a set of changes that numb the ganglia and abort the soul, until finally Nat spectacularly shrieks through the whole spectrum from someplace south of infrared into what, as far as anyone can tell, may be the X-ray frequencies, and this wild takeoff not only stimulates a rebirth of inventiveness but also signals the end of the show. Everybody picks up on him and they blast free, swirling and floating and coming together, forming one entity with seven heads as they bombard the flaccid data-stoned audience with mountains of overload. Yes yes yes yes yes. Wow wow wow wow wow. Flash flash flash flash flash. Oh oh oh oh oh. Come come come come come. Dillon is at the heart of it, tossing off bright purple sparks, pulling down suns and chewing them up, and he feels even more plugged in than during his big solo, for this is a joint thing, a blending, a merging, and he knows that what he is feeling now explains everything: this is the purpose of life, this is the reason for it all. To tune in on beauty, to plunge right to the hot source of creation, to open your soul and let it all in and let it all out again, to give to give to give to give
    to give
    to give

and it ends. Pull the plug. They let him have the final
chord and he cuts off with a skullblower, a five-way planetary
conjunction and a triple fugue, the whole showoff burst
lasting no more than ten seconds. Then down with the hands
and off with the switch and a wall of silence rises ninety
kilometers high. This time he's done it. He's emptied everybody's skull. He sits there shivering, biting his lip, dazed by
the house lights, wanting to cry. He dares not look at the
others in the group. How much time is passing? Five minutes, five months, five centuries, five megayears? And at last
the reaction. A stampede of applause. All of Rome on its feet,
yelling slapping cheeks—the ultimate tribute, 4,000 people
struggling out of their comfortable webs to pound their palms
against their faces—and Dillon laughs, throwing back his
head, getting up himself, bowing, holding his hands out to
Nat, to Sophro, to all six of them. Somehow it was better
tonight. Even these Romans know it. What did they do to
deserve it? By being such lumps, Dillon tells himself, they
drew forth the best we had in us. To turn them on. And we
did. We knocked them out of their miserable soggy skulls.

The cheering continues.

Fine. Fine. We are great artists. Now I've got to get out of
here, before I come down from it all.

He never socializes with the rest of the group after a
performance. They have all discovered that the less they see
of each other in leisure hours, the more intimate their
professional collaboration will be; there is no intragroup
friendship, not even intragroup sex. They all feel that would
be death, any kind of coupling, hetero, homo, triple-up—
save that for outsiders. They have their music to unite them.
So he goes off by himself. The audience starts to flow toward
the exits, and, without saying good night to anybody, Dillon
steps into the artists' trap door and makes his escape one
level down. His clothes are stiff and wet with perspiration,
clammy, uncomfortable. He must do something about that
quickly. Prowling along the 529th floor for a dropshaft, he
opens the first apartment door he comes to and finds a
couple, sixteen, seventeen years old, squatting before the
screen. He naked, she wearing only breastcoils, both of them
plainly soaring on one of the harder ones, but not so high
that they can't recognize him. "Dillon Chrimes!" the girl
gasps, her squeal waking two or three littles.

"Hey, hello," he says. "I just have to use the cleanser,

okay? Don't let me disturb you. I don't even want to talk, you know? I'm still way up." He strips off his sodden clothes and gets under the cleanser. It hums and rumbles and peels his grime from him. He lets it work on his clothes next. The girl is creeping toward him. She has the breastcoils off; the white imprints of the metal on her pink dangling flesh are turning rapidly red. Kneeling before him. Hand goes to his thighs. Her lips heading for his loins. "No," he says. "Don't."

"No?"

"I can't do it here."

"But why?"

"Just wanted to use the cleanser. Couldn't stand my own stink. I've got to do my nightwalking on 500 tonight." Her fingers sliding between his legs. Gently he pries them. Back into his clothing; the girl looks on, astonished, as he covers himself.

"You aren't going to?" she asks.

"Not here. Not here." She continues to blink at him as he goes out. Her look of shock saddens him. Tonight he must go to the middle of the building, but tomorrow, for sure, he will come to her, and he'll explain everything then. He makes a note of the room number. 52908. Nightwalking is supposed to be random, but to hell with that; he owes her a thrill. Tomorrow.

In the hall he finds a groover dispenser and requisitions his pill, tapping his metabolic coefficient out on the console. The machine performs the necessary calculations and delivers a five-hour dose, timed to go off in twelve minutes. He swallows it and steps into the dropshaft.

Floor 500.

As close to halfway as he can get. A metaphysical fancy, but why not? He has not lost the capacity to play games. We artists remain happy because we remain as children. Eleven minutes to his high. He goes down the corridor, opening doors. In the first room he finds a man, a woman, another man. "Sorry," he calls. In the second room three girls. Momentarily tempting, but only momentarily. Anyway, they look fully busied with each other. "Sorry, sorry, sorry." In the third room a middle-aged couple; they give him a hopeful stare, but he backs out.

Fourth time lucky. A dark-haired girl, alone, pouting a little. Obviously her husband is out nightwalking and no one has come to her, a statistical fluke that distresses her. Early

twenties, Dillon guesses, with fine tapering nose, glossy
eyes, elegant breasts, olive skin. The flesh over her eyelids is
puffy, which may become a flaw of appearance ten years from
now but which gives her a sultry, sensual look at the moment.
She has been brooding for hours, he guesses, because her
sullenness does not evaporate until he has actually been in
the room fifteen seconds or so; she is slow to realize that she
is being nightwalked with. "Hello," he says. "Smile? Won't
you smile a little?"

"I know you. The cosmos group?"

"Dillon Chrimes, yes. On the vibrastar. We're playing
Rome tonight."

"Playing Rome and nightwalking Bombay?"

"What the hell. I have philosophical reasons. To be in the
middle of the building, you know? Or as close as I can come.
Don't ask me to explain." He looks around the room. Six
littles. One of them, awake, is at least nine years old, a
skinny girl with her mother's olive skin. Mother isn't as
young as she looks, then. At least twenty-five, maybe. Dillon
doesn't mind. In a little while he'll be groping the whole
urbmon, anyway, all the ages, sexes, shapes. He says, "I have
to tell you about my trip. I'm on a multiplexer. It'll hit me in
six minutes."

She puts her hand to her lips. "We don't have much time,
then. You ought to be inside me before you go up."

"Is that the way they work?"

"Don't you know?"

"I've never gone that way before," he confesses. "Never
got around to it."

"Neither have I. I didn't think anybody actually did take
multiplexers, really. But I've heard of what you're supposed
to do." She is disrobing as she talks. Heavy breasts, big dark
circles around the nipples. Her legs strangely thin; when she
stands straight the insides of her thighs are far apart. There is
a folkmyth of some sort about girls built that way, but Dillon
cannot remember it. He drops his clothes. The drug has
started to get to him, several minutes ahead of schedule—the
walls are shimmering, the lights look fuzzy. Odd. Unless the
fact that he was already way up from performing should have
been calculated into the dosage request. The metabolism
turned to high, maybe, on nothing but sound and light. Well,
no harm done. He moves toward the sleeping platform.
"What's your name?" he asks.

"Alma Clune."

"I like the sound of that. Alma." She takes him into her arms. This will not be an extraordinary erotic experience for her, he fears. Once the multiplexer takes hold, he doubts that he can concentrate properly on her needs, and in any case the time element has made it necessary to skip all foreplay. But she seems to be understanding. She will not spoil his trip. "Get in," she says. "It's all right. I get wet fast there." He enters her. Her tongue against his; her sinewy thighs encircling him. He covers her body with his. "Are you grooving yet?" she asks.

He is silent a moment. In and out, in and out. "I feel it starting," he tells her. "It's like having two girls at once. I'm getting echoes." Tension. He doesn't want to wreck everything by coming before the effect hits him. On the other hand, if she's the quick-coming type, he'd be happy to let her have a spasm or two; the multiplexing must still be ninety seconds away. All these calculations chill him. And then they become pointless. "It's happening," he whispers. "Oh, god, here I go up!"

"Easy," Alma murmurs. "Don't rush anything. Slow... slow. ... You're doing fine. You want this one to last. Don't worry about me. Just go on up."

In and out. In and out. And multiplexing now. His spirit is spreading out. The drug makes him psychosensitive; it breaks down his brain's chemical defenses against direct telepathic input, so that he can perceive the sensory intake of those around him. Reaching wider and wider, moment by moment. At the full high, they say, everyone's eyes and ears become your own; you pick up an infinity of responses, you are everywhere in the building at once. Is it true? Are other minds pouring their intake through his? It does seem so. He watches the fluttering fiery mantle of his soul engulf and absorb Alma, so that now he is face up as well as face down, and each time he thrusts deep into her hot cavern he can also feel the blunt sword sliding into his own vitals. That's just the beginning. He is spreading over Alma's littles now. The unfleeced nine-year-old. The gurgling baby. He is six children and their mother. How easy this is! He is the family next door. Eight littles, mother, nightwalker from the 495th floor. He extends his reach upward one level. And downward. And along the corridors. In dreamy multiplexication he is taking possession of the whole building. Layers of drifting images

enshroud him: 500 floors above his head, 499 below, and he
sees all 999 of them as a column of horizontal striations, tiny
notches on a tall shaft. With ants. And he is all the ants at
once. Why has he never done this before? To become an
entire urbmon!

He must reach at least twenty floors in each direction now.
And still spreading out. Tendrils of him going everywhere.
Just the beginning. Intermingling his substance with the
totality of the building.

With Alma rocking beneath him. Pelvis grinding against
pelvis; he is dimly aware of her as she softly moans her
pleasure. But only one atom of himself is occupied with her.
The rest is roaming the halls of the cities that make up Urban
Monad 116. Entering every room. Part of him up in Boston,
part of him down in London, and all of him in Rome and
Bombay as well. Hundreds of rooms. Thousands. The swarm
of biped bees. He is fifty squalling littles crammed into three
London rooms. He is two doddering Bostonians entering
upon their 5,000th sexual congress. He is a hot-blooded
thirteen-year-old nightwalker prowling the 483rd floor. He is
six swapping couples in a London dorm. Now he is into a
wider range, reaching down to San Francisco, up to Nairobi.
The farther he goes, the easier it gets. The hive. The mighty
hive. He embraces Tokyo. He embraces Chicago. He embraces Prague. He touches Shanghai. He touches Vienna. He
touches Warsaw. He touches Toledo. Paris! Reykjavik! Louisville!
Louisville! Top to bottom, top to bottom! Now he is all
881,000 people on all thousand floors. His soul is stretched to
its fullest. His skull is snapping. The images come and go
across the screen of his mind, drifting films of reality, oily
wisps of smoke bearing faces, eyes, fingers, genitals, smiles,
tongues, elbows, profiles, sounds, textures. Gently they mesh
and lock and drift apart. He is everywhere and everyone at
once. God bless! For the first time he understands the nature
of the delicate organism that is society; he sees the checks
and balances, the quiet conspiracies of compromise that paste
it all together. And it is wondrously beautiful. Tuning this vast
city of many cities is just like tuning the cosmos group:
everything must relate, everything must belong to everything
else. The poet in San Francisco is part of the grubbo stoker in
Reykjavik. The little snotty ambition-monger in Shanghai is
part of the placid defeated Roman. How much of this, Dillon

wonders, will stay with him when he comes down? His spirit whirls. He grooves on thousands of souls at once.

And the sexual thing. The hundred thousand copulatory transactions taking place behind his forehead. The spread thighs, the offered rumps, the parted lips. He loses his virginity; he takes a virginity; he surrenders to men, women, boys, girls; he is agressor and aggressed; he spurts ecstasy, he narrowly misses orgasm, he triumphantly impales, he shamefully suffers loss of erection, he enters, he is entered, he takes pleasure, he gives pleasure, he retreats from pleasure, he denies pleasure.

He rides the liftshafts of his mind. Going up! 501, 502, 503, 504, 505! 600! 700! 800! 900! He stands on the landing stage at the summit of the urbmon, staring out into the night. Towers all around him, the neighboring monads, 115, 117, 118, the whole crowd of them. Occasionally he has wondered what life is like in the other buildings that make up the Chipitts constellation. Now he does not care. There is wonder enough in 116. More than 800,000 intersecting lives. He has heard some of his friends say, in San Francisco, that it was an evil deed to change the world this way, to pile up thousands of people in a single colossal building, to create this beehive life. But how wrong those mutterers are! If they could only multiplex and get true perspective. Taste the rich complexity of our vertical existence. Going down! 480, 479, 476, 475! City upon city. Each floor holding a thousand puzzleboxes of pure delight. Hello, I'm Dillon Chrimes, can I be you for a while? And you? And you? And you? Are you happy? Why not? Have you *seen* this gorgeous world you live in?

What? You'd like a bigger room? You want to travel? You don't like your littles? You're bored with your work? You're full of vague unfocused discontent? idiot. Come up here with me, fly from floor to floor, *see*! And groove on it. And love it.

"Is it good?" Alma asks. "Your eyes are shining!"

"I can't describe it," Dillon murmurs, soaring, threading himself down the service core to the levels below Reykjavik, then floating up to Louisville again, and simultaneously intersecting every point between root and tip. An ocean of broiling minds. A sizzle of snarled identities. He wonders what time it is. The trip is supposed to last five hours. His body is still joined to Alma's, which leads him to think he has not been up more than ten or fifteen minutes, but perhaps it

is more than that. Things are becoming very tactile now. As
he drifts through the building he touches walls, floors, screens,
faces, fabrics. He suspects he may be coming down. But no.
No. Still on his way up. The simultaneity increases. He is
flooded with percepts. People moving, talking, sleeping, coupling, bending, reaching, eating, reading. I am all of you. You
are all parts of me. He can focus sharply on individual
identities. Here is Electra, here is Nat the spectrum-rider,
here is Mamelon Kluver, here is a tight-souled sociocomputator
named Charles Mattern, here is a Louisville administrator,
here is a Warsaw grubbo, here is. Here is. Here are. Here
am I. The whole blessing building.

Oh what a beautiful place. Oh how I love it here. Oh this is
the real thing. Oh!

When he comes down, he sees the dark-haired woman
curled in a corner of the sleeping platform, asleep. He cannot
remember her name. He touches her thigh and she awakes
quickly, eyes fluttering. "Hello," she says. "Welcome back."

"What's your name?"

"Alma. Clune. Your eyes are all red."

He nods. He feels the weight of the whole building on
him. 500 floors jamming down on his head, 499 floors pressing up against his feet. The meeting place of the two forces is
somewhere close to his pancreas. If he does not leave here
quickly, his internal organs must surely pop. Only shreds of
his trip remain. Straggly streamers of debris clutter his mind.
Vaguely he feels columns of ants trekking from level to level
behind his eyes.

Alma reaches for him. To comfort him. He shakes her off
and hunts for his clothing. A cone of silence surrounds him.
He will go back to Electra, he thinks, and try to tell her
where he has been and what has been happening to him, and
then perhaps he will cry and feel better. He leaves without
thanking Alma for her hospitality and looks for a dropshaft.
Instead he finds a liftshaft, and somehow, pretending it is an
accident, he gets off at 530. Heading for Rome's sonic center.
Dark there. The instruments still on stage. Quietly he slips
down in front of the vibrastar. Switches it on. His eyes are
wet. He dredges up some phantom images of his trip. The
faces, the thousand floors. The ecstasy. Oh what a beautiful
place. Oh how I love it here. Oh this is the real thing. Oh!
Certainly he felt that way. But no longer. A thin sediment of

doubt is all that remains. Asking himself: Is this how it was meant to be? Is this how it has to be? Is this the best we can do? This building. This mighty hive. Dillon's hands caress the projectrons, which feel prickly and hot; he depresses them at random and sour colors drift out of the instrument. He cuts in the audio and gets sounds that remind him of the shifting of old bones within flabby flesh. What went wrong? He should have expected it. You go all the way up, then you come all the way down. But why does down have to be so far down? He cannot bear to play. After ten minutes he switches the vibrastar off and goes out. He will walk to San Francisco. 160 floors down. That's not too many levels; he'll be there before dawn.

Four

Jason Quevedo lives in Shanghai, though just barely: his apartment is on the 761st floor, and if he lived only one level lower he would be in Chicago, which is no place for a scholar. His wife Micaela frequently tells him that their lowly status in Shanghai is a direct reflection of the quality of his work. Micaela is the sort of wife who often says things like that to her husband.

Jason spends most of his working time down in Pittsburgh, where the archives are. He is a historian and needs to consult the documents, the records of how it used to be. He does his research in a clammy little cubicle on the urbmon's 185th floor, almost in the middle of Pittsburgh. He does not really have to work down there, since anything in the archives can easily be piped up to the data terminal in his own apartment. But he feels it is a matter of professional pride to have an office where he can file and arrange and handle the source materials. He said as much when he was pulling strings to have the office assigned to him: "The task of recreating previous eras is a delicate and complex one, which must be performed under optimal circumstances, or—"

The truth is that if he didn't escape from Micaela and their five littles every day, he'd go flippo. That is, accumulated frustration and humiliation would cause him to commit nonsocial acts, perhaps violent ones. He is aware that there is no room for the nonsocial person in an urban monad. He knows that if he loses his temper and behaves in a seriously unblessworthy way they will simply throw him down the chute and turn his mass into energy. So he is careful.

He is a short, soft-spoken man with mild green eyes and thinning sandy hair. "Your meek exterior is deceptive," lovely Mamelon Kluver told him throatily at a party last summer. "Your type is like a sleeping volcano. You explode suddenly, astonishingly, passionately." He thinks she may be right. He fears the possibilities.

He has been desperately in love with Mamelon Kluver for perhaps the last three years, and certainly since the night of that party. He has never dared to touch her. Mamelon's husband is the celebrated Siegmund Kluver, who though not yet fifteen is universally recognized as one of the urbmon's future leaders. Jason is not afraid that Siegmund would object. In an urban monad, naturally, no man has a right to withhold his wife from anyone who desires her. Nor is Jason afraid of what Micaela would say. He knows his privileges. He is simply afraid of Mamelon. And perhaps of himself.

> *For ref. only. Urbmon sex mores.*
> *Univ. sex. accessibility. Trace decline of proprietary marriage, end of adultery concept. Nightwalkers: when first socially acceptable? Limit of allowable frustration: how determined? Sex as panacea. Sex as compensation for lessened quality of life under urbmon conditions. Query: was quality of life really lessened by triumph or urbmon system? (Careful— beware the chute!) Separation of sex & procreation. Value of max. interchange of partners in high-density culture. Problem: what is still forbidden (any thing?) Examine taboo on extracity nightwalking. How powerful? How widely observed? Check effects of univ. permiss. on contempt. fiction. Loss of dramatic tension? Erosion of raw material of narr. conflict? Query: is urbmon moral struc. amoral, postmoral, per-, im-?*

Jason dictates such memoranda whenever and wherever some new structural hypothesis enters his mind. These are thoughts that come to him during a nightwalking excursion on the 155th floor, in Tokyo. He is with a thickset young brunette named Gretl when the sequence of ideas arrives.

He has been fondling her for some minutes and she is panting, ready, her hips pumping, her eyes narrowed to steamy slits.

"Excuse me," he says, and reaches across her heavy quivering breasts for a stylus. "I have to write something down." He activates the date terminal's input screen and punches the button that will relay a printout of his memorandum to his desk at his research cubicle in Pittsburgh. Then, quickly pursing his lips and scowling, he begins to make his notations.

He frequently goes nightwalking, but never in his own city of Shanghai. Jason's one audacity: boldly he flouts the tradition that one should stay close to home during one's nocturnal prowls. No one will punish him for his unconventional behavior, since it is merely a violation of accepted custom, not of urban law. No one will even criticize him to his face for doing it. Yet his wanderings give him the mild thrill of doing the forbidden. Jason explains his habit to himself by saying that he prefers the crosscultural enrichment that comes from sleeping with women of other cities. Privately he suspects he is just uneasy about getting mixed up with women he knows, such as Mamelon Kluver. Especially Mamelon Kluver.

So on his nightwalking nights he takes the dropshafts far into the depths of the building, to such cities as Pittsburgh or Tokyo, even to squalid Prague or grubby Reykjavik. He pushes open strange doors, lockless by statute, and takes his place on the sleeping platforms of unknown women smelling of mysterious lower-class vegetables. By law they must embrace him willingly. "I am from Shanghai," he tells them, and they go "Ooooh!" in awe, and he mounts them tigerishly, contemptuously, swollen with status.

Breasty Gretl waits patiently while Jason records his latest notions. Then he turns toward her again. Her husband, bloated on whatever the local equivalent of tingle or mindblot may be, lies belly-up at the far side of the sleeping platform, ignoring them. Gretl's large dark eyes glow with admiration. "You Shanghai boys sure got brains," she says, as Jason pounces and takes her in a single fierce thrust.

Later he returns to the 761st floor. Wraiths flit through the dim corridors: other citizens of Shanghai, back from their own nightwalking rounds. He enters his apartment. Jason has forty-five square meters of floor space, not really enough for a man with a wife and five littles, but he does not complain. God bless, you take what you get: others have less. Micaela is asleep, or pretends to be. She is a long-legged, tawny-skinned woman of twenty-three, still quite attractive, though quirky lines are beginning to appear in her face. She frowns too much. She lies half uncovered, her long black glossy hair spread out wildly around her. Her breasts are small but perfect; Jason compares them favorably to the udders of Tokyo's Gretl. He and Micaela have been married nine years. Once he loved her a great deal, before he discovered the gritty residue of bitter shrewishness at the bottom of her soul.

She smiles an inward smile, stirs, still sleeping, brushes her hair back from her eyes. She has the look of a woman who has just had a thoroughly satisfactory sexual experience. Jason has no way of knowing whether some nightwalker visited Micaela tonight while he was gone, and, of course, he cannot ask. (Search for evidence? Stains on the sleeping platform? Stickiness on her thigh? Don't be barbaric!) He suspects that even if no one had come to her tonight, she would try to make him think that someone had; and if someone had come and had given her only modest pleasure, she would nevertheless smile for her husband's benefit as though she had been embraced by Zeus. He knows his wife's style.

The children seem peaceful. They range in age from two to eight. Soon he and Micaela will have to think about having another. Five littles is a fair-sized family, but Jason understands his duty to serve life by creating life. When one ceases to grow, one begins to die; it is true of a human being and also of the population of an urban monad, of an urbmon constellation, of a continent, of a world. God is life and life is god.

He lies down beside his wife.

He sleeps.

He dreams that Micaela has been sentenced to the chute for countersocial behavior.

Down she goes! Mamelon Kluver makes a condolence call. "Poor Jason," she murmurs. Her pale skin is cool against him. The musky fragrance of her. The elegance of her features. The look of total mastery of self. Not even seventeen; how can she be so imperiously complete? "Help me dispose of Siegmund and we'll belong to each other," Mamelon says. Eyes bright, mischievous, goading him to be her creature. "Jason," she whispers. "Jason, Jason, Jason." Her tone a caress. Her hand on his manhood. He wakes, trembling, sweating, horrified, half an inch from messy ecstasy. He sits up and goes through one of the forgiveness modes for improper thoughts. God bless, he thinks, god bless, god bless, god bless. I did not mean such things. It was my mind. My monstrous mind free of shackles. He completes the spiritual exercise and lies down once more. He sleeps and dreams more harmless dreams.

In the morning the littles run madly off to school and Jason prepares to go to his office. Micaela says suddenly, "Isn't it interesting that you go 600 floors *down* when you go to work, and Siegmund Kluver goes up on top, to Louisville?"

"What the god bless do you mean by that?"

"I see symbolic meaning in it."

"Symbolic garbage. Siegmund's in urban administration; he goes up where the administrators are. I'm in history; I go down where the history is. So?"

"Wouldn't you like to live in Louisville someday?"

"No."

"Why don't you have any ambition?"

"Is your life so miserable here?" he asks, holding himself in check.

"Why has Siegmund made so much of himself at the age of fourteen or fifteen, and here you are at twenty-six and you're still just an input-pusher?"

"Siegmund is ambitious," Jason replies evenly, "and I'm merely a time-server. I don't deny it. Maybe it's genetic. Siegmund strives and gets away with it. Most men don't. Striving sterilizes, Micaela. Striving is primitive. God bless, what's wrong with my career? What's wrong with living in Shanghai?"

"One floor lower and we'd be living in—"

"—Chicago," he says. "I know. But we aren't. May I go to my office now?"

He leaves. He wonders whether he ought to send Micaela to the consoler's office for a reality adjustment. Her threshold of thwarting-acceptance has dipped alarmingly of late; her expectations-level has risen just as disturbingly. Jason is well aware that such things should be dealt with at once, before they become uncontrollable and lead to countersocial behavior and the chute. Probably Micaela needs the services of the moral engineers. But he puts aside the idea of calling the consoler. It is because I dislike the idea of having anyone

tamper with my wife's mind, he tells himself piously, and a
mocking inner voice tells him that he is taking no action
because he secretly wishes to see Micaela become so
countersocial that she must be thrown down the chute.

He enters the dropshaft and programs for the 185th floor.
Down he goes to Pittsburgh. He sinks, inertia-free, through the
cities that make up Urbmon 116. Down he goes through
Chicago, through Edinburgh, through Nairobi, through Colombo.

He feels the comforting solidity of the building about him
as he descends. The urbmon is his world. He has never been
outside it. Why should he go out? His friends, his family, his
whole life are here. His urbmon is adequately supplied with
theaters, sports arenas, schools, hospitals, houses of worship.
His data terminal gives him access to any work of art that is
considered blessworthy for human consumption. No one he
knows has ever left the building, except for the people who
were chosen by lot to settle in the newly opened Urbmon 158
a few months ago, and they, of course, will never come back.
There are rumors that urban administrators sometimes go
from building to building on business, but Jason is not sure
that this is true, and he does not see why such travel would
be necessary or desirable. Are there not systems of instantaneous communication linking the urbmons, capable of trans-
mitting all relevant data?

It is a splendid system. As a historian, privileged to explore
the records of the pre-urbmon world, he knows more fully than
most people how splendid it is. He understands the awful
chaos of the past. The terrifying freedoms; the hideous necessity of making choices. The insecurity. The confusion. The
lack of plan. The formlessness of contexts.

He reaches the 185th floor. He makes his way through the
sleepy corridors of Pittsburgh to his office. A modest room,
but he loves it. Glistening walls. A wet mural over his desk.
The necessary terminals and screens.

Five small glistening cubes lie on his desk. Each holds the
contents of several libraries. He has been working with these
cubes for two years, now. His theme is *The Urban Monad as
Social Evolution: Parameters of the Spirit Defined by Community Structure*. He is attempting to show that the transition to an urbmon society has brought about a fundamental
transformation of the human soul. Of the soul of Western
man, at any rate. An orientalization of the Occidentals, as
formerly aggressive people accept the yoke of the new envi-

ronment. A more pliant, more acquiescent mode of response to events, a turning away from the old expansionist-individualist philosophy, as marked by territorial ambition, the *conquistador* mentality, and the pioneering way, toward a kind of communal expansion centered in the orderly and unlimited growth of the human race. Definitely a psychic evolution of some sort, a shift toward graceful acceptance of hive-life. The malcontents bred out of the system generations ago. We who have not gone down the chute accept the inexorabilities. Yes. Yes. Jason believes that he has struck upon a significant subject. Micaela disparaged the theme when he announced it: "You mean you're going to write a book showing that people who live in different kinds of cities are different? That urbmon people have a different attitude than jungle people? Some scholar. I could prove your point in six sentences." Nor was there much enthusiasm for the subject when he proposed it at a staff meeting, although he did manage to get clearance for it. His technique so far has been to steep himself in the images of the past, to turn himself, so far as is possible, into a citizen of the pre-urbmon society. He hopes that that will give him the essential parallax, the perspective on his own society, that he will need when he begins to write his study. He expects to start writing in another two or three years.

He consults a memorandum, chooses a cube, plugs it into a playback slot. His screen brightens.

A kind of ecstasy comes over him as scenes out of the ancient world materialize. He leans close to his input speaker and begins to dictate. Frantically, frenziedly, Jason Quevedo sets down notes on the way it used to be.

Houses and streets. A horizontal world. Individual family shelter units: this is my house, this is my castle. Fantastic! Three people, taking up maybe a thousand square meters of surface. Roads. Concept of road hard for us to understand. Like a hallway going on and on. Private vehicles. Where are they all going? Why so fast? Why not stay home? Crash! Blood. Head goes through glass. Crash again! In the rear. Dark combustible fluid flows in street. Middle of day, spring-time, major city. Street scene. Which city? Chicago, New York, Istanbul, Cairo. People walking about IN THE OPEN. Paved streets. This for walkers, this for drivers. Filth. Esti-mated grid reading: 10,000 pedestrians this sector alone, in strip eight meters wide and eighty meters long. Is that figure

*right? Check it. Elbow to elbow. And they'd think our world
was overcrowded? At least we don't impinge on each other
like that. We know how to keep our distances within the
overall structure of urbmon life. Vehicles move down middle
of street. The good old chaos. Chief activity: the purchase of
goods. Private consumption. Cube 11Ab8 shows interior vec-
tor of a shop. Exchanging of money for merchandise. Not
much different there except random nature of transaction. Do
they need what they buy? Where do they PUT it all?*

This cube holds nothing new for him. Jason has seen such
city scenes many times before. Yet the fascination is ever
fresh. He is tense, with sweat flowing freely, as he strains to
comprehend a world in which people may live where they
please, where they move about on foot or in vehicles in the
open, where there is no planning, no order, no restraint. He
must perform a double act of imagination: it is necessary for
him to see that vanished world from within, as though he
lived in it, and then he must try to see the urbmon society as
it might seem to someone wafted forward from the twentieth
century. The magnitude of the task dismays him. He knows
roughly how an ancient would feel about Urbmon 116: it is a
hellish place, the ancient would say, in which people live
hideously cramped and brutal lives, in which every civilized
philosophy is turned on its head, in which uncontrolled
breeding is nightmarishly encouraged to serve some incredible concept of a deity eternally demanding more worshipers, in which dissent is ruthlessly stifled and dissenters are
peremptorily destroyed. Jason knows the right phrases, the
sort of words an intelligent liberal American of, say, 1958
would use. But the inner spirit is missing. He tries to see his
own world as a species of hell, and fails. To him it is not
hellish. He is a logical man; he knows why the vertical society
had to evolve out of the old horizontal one, and why it then
became obligatory to eliminate—preferably before they were
old enough to reproduce—all those who would not adapt or
could not be adapted to the fabric of society. How could
troublemakers be allowed to remain in the tight, intimate,
carefully balanced structure of an urbmon? He knows that the
probable result of tossing flippos down the chute has been,
over a couple of centuries, the creation of a new style of
human being through selective breeding. Is there now a
Homo urbmonensis, placid, adjusted, fully content? These

are topics he means to explore intensively when he writes his book. But it is so hard, so absurdly hard, to grasp them from the viewpoint of ancient man!

Jason struggles to understand the uproar over overpopulation in the ancient world. He has drawn from the archives scores of tracts directed against indiscriminate human spawning—angry polemics composed at a time when less than 4,000,000,000 people inhabited the world. He is aware, of course, that humans can choke a whole planet quickly when they live spread out horizontally the way they did; but why were they so worried about the future? Surely they could have forseen the beauties of the vertical society!

No. No. That's just the point, he tells himself unhappily. They did *not* foresee any such thing. Instead they talked about limiting fertility, if necessary by imposing a governmental authority to hold population down. Jason shivers. "Don't you see," he asks his cubes, "that only a totalitarian regime could enforce such limits? You say that *we're* a repressive society. But what kind of society would you have built, if the urbmons hadn't developed?"

The voice of ancient man replies, "I'd rather take my chances on limiting births and allowing complete freedom otherwise. You've accepted the freedom to multiply, but it's cost you all the other freedoms. Don't you see—"

"You're the one who doesn't see," Jason blurts. "A society must sustain its momentum through the exploitation of god-given fertility. We've found a way to make room for everybody on Earth, to support a population ten or twenty times greater than what you imagined was the absolute maximum. You see it merely as suppression and authoritarianism. But what about the billions of lives that could never have come into being at all under your system? Isn't that the ultimate suppression—forbidding humans to exist in the first place?"

"But what good is letting them exist, if the best they can hope for is a box inside a box inside a box? What about the quality of life?"

"I see no defects in the quality of our life. We find fulfillment in the interplay of human relationships. Do I need to go to China or Africa for my pleasures, when I can find them within a single building? Isn't it a sign of inner dislocation to feel compelled to roam all over the world? In your day everybody traveled, I know, and in mine no one does. Which is a more stable society? Which is happier?"

"Which is more human? Which exploits man's potential
more fully? Isn't it our nature to seek, to strive, to reach
out—?"

"What about seeking within? Exploring the inner life?"

"But don't you see—?"

"But don't you see—?"

"If you only would listen—"

"If you only would listen—"

Jason does not see. Ancient man's spokesman does not see.
Neither will listen. There is no communication. Jason wastes
another dismal day wrestling with his intractable material.
Only as he is about to leave does he remember last night's
memorandum. He will study ancient sexual mores in a new
attempt to gain insight into that vanished society. He punches
out his requisition. The cubes will be on his desk when he
returns to his office tomorrow.

He goes home to Shanghai, home to Micaela.

That evening the Quevedos have dinner guests: Michael,
Micaela's twin brother, and his wife Stacion. Michael is a
computer-primer; he and Stacion live in Edinburgh, on the
704th floor. Jason finds his company challenging and rewarding,
although the physical resemblance between his brother-in-
law and his wife, which he once found amusing, now alarms
and disturbs him. Michael affects shoulder-length hair, and is
barely a centimeter taller than his tall, slender sister. They
are, of course, only fraternal twins, yet their facial features
are virtually identical. They have even settled into the same
pattern of tense, querulous smirks and scowls. From the rear
Jason has difficulties in telling them apart unless he sees
them side by side; they stand the same way, arms akimbo,
heads tilted backward. Since Micaela is small-breasted, the
possibility of confusion exists also in profile, and sometimes,
looking at one of them in front view, Jason has momentarily
wondered whether he beholds Michael or Micaela. If only
Michael would grow a beard! But his cheeks are smooth.

Now and again Jason feels sexually drawn to his brother-in-
law. It is a natural attraction, considering the physical pull
Micaela has always exerted on him. Seeing her across the
room, angled away from him, her smooth back bare, the little
globe of one breast visible under her arms as she reaches
toward the data terminal, he feels the urge to go to her and
caress her. And if she were Michael? And if he slid his hand

to her bosom and found it flat and hard? And if they tumbled down together in a passionate tangle? His hand going to Micaela's thighs and finding not the hot hidden slot but the dangling flesh of maleness? And turning her over. Him? Parting the pallid muscular buttocks. The sudden strange thrust. No. Jason flushes the fantasy from his mind. Once again. Not since the rough easy days of boyhood has he had any kind of sexual contact with his own sex. He will not permit it. There are no penalties for such things, naturally, in the society of the urbmon, where all adults are equally accessible. Many of them do it. For all he knows, Michael himself. If Jason wants Michael, he has only to ask. Refusal a sin. He does not ask. He fights the temptation. It is not fair, a man who looks so much like my wife. The devil's snare. Why do I resist, though? If I want him, why not take? But no. I don't really want. It's just a sneaky urge, a sidewise way of desiring Micaela. And yet the fantasy surges again. Himself and Michael, spoon-fashion, mouths gaping and stuffed. The image glows so brightly that Jason rises in a brusque tense motion, knocking over the flask of wine that Stacion has brought tonight, and, as Stacion dives for and rescues it, he crosses the room, aghast at the erection prodding his taut gold and green shorts. He goes to Micaela and cups one of her breasts. The nipple is soft. He snuggles against her, nibbles the nape of her neck. She tolerates these attentions in a remote way, not interrupting the programing of dinner. But when, still distraught, he slips his left hand into the open side of her sarong and runs it across her belly to her loins, she wriggles her hips in displeasure and whispers harshly, "*Stop* it! Not with *them* sitting there!"

Wildly he finds the fumes and offers them around. Stacion refuses; she is pregnant. A plump pleasant red-haired girl, complacent, easy. Out of place in this congregation of hypertense. Jason sucks the smoke deep and feels the knots loosen slightly inside. Now he can look at Michael and not fall prey to unnatural urges. Yet he still speculates. Does Michael suspect? Would he laugh if I told him? Take offense? Angry at me for wanting to? Angry at me for not trying to? Suppose he asked *me* to, what would I do? Jason takes a second fume and the swarm of buzzing questions leaves his mind. "When is the little due?" he asks, in counterfeit geniality.

"God bless, fourteen weeks," Michael says. "Number five. A girl, this time."

"We'll name her Celeste," Stacion puts in, patting her
middle. Her maternity costume is a short yellow bolero and a
loose brown waist sash. leaving the bulging belly bare. The
everted navel like the stem of the swollen fruit. Milky breasts
swaying in and out of visibility under the open jacket. "We're
talking about requesting twins for next year," she adds. "A
boy and a girl. Michael's always telling me about the good
times he and Micaela used to have together when they were
young. Like a special world for twins."

Jason is caught unawares by the bringdown, and is plunged
abruptly into feverish fantasy once more. He sees Micaela's
spread legs sticking out from under Michael's lean pumping
body, sees her childish ecstatic face looking up over his busy
shoulder. The good times they used to have. Michael the first
one into her. At nine, ten, maybe? Even younger? Their
awkward experiments. Let me get on top of you this time,
Michael. Oh, it's deeper this way. Do you think we're doing
anything wrong? No, silly, didn't we sleep together for nine
whole months? Put your hand here. And your mouth on me
again. Yes. You're hurting my breasts, Michael. Oh. Oh.
that's nice. But wait, just another few seconds. The good
times they used to have. "Is something the matter, Jason?"
Michael's voice. "You look so tight." Jason forces himself to
pull out of it. Hands trembling. Another fume. He rarely
takes three before dinner.

Stacion has gone to help Micaela unload the food from the
delivery slot. Michael says to Jason, "I hear you've started a
new research project. What's the basic theme?"

Kind of him. Senses that I'm ill at ease. Draw me out of my
morbid brooding. All these sick thoughts.

Jason replies, "I'm investigating the notion that urbmon life
is breeding a new kind of human being. A type that adapts
readily to relatively little living space and a low privacy
quotient."

"You mean a genetic mutation?" Michael asks, frowning.
"Literally, an inherited social characteristic?"

"So I believe."

"Are such things possible, though? Can you call it a genetic
trait, really, if people voluntarily decide to band together in a
society like ours and—"

"Voluntarily?"

"Isn't it?"

Jason smiles. "I doubt that it ever was. In the beginning,

you know, it was a matter of necessity. Because of the chaos in the world. Seal yourself up in your building or be exposed to the food bandits. I'm talking about the famine years, now. And since then, since everything stabilized, has it been so voluntary? Do we have any choice about where we live?"

"I suppose we could go outside if we really wanted to," Michael says, "and live in whatever they've got out there."

"But we don't. Because we recognize that that's a hopeless fantasy. We stay here, whether we like it or not. And those who don't like it, those who eventually can't take it—well, you know what happens to them."

"But—"

"Wait. Two centuries of selective breeding, Michael. Down the chute for the flippos. And no doubt some population loss through leaving the buildings, at least at the beginning. Those who remain adapt to circumstances. They *like* the urbmon way. It seems altogether natural to them."

"Is this really genetic, though? Couldn't you simply call it psychological conditioning? I mean, in the Asian countries, didn't people always live jammed together the way we do, only much worse, no sanitation, no regulation—and didn't they accept it as the natural order of things?"

"Of course," Jason says. "Because rebellion against the natural order of things had been bred out of them thousands of years ago. The ones who stayed, the ones who reproduced, were the ones who accepted things as they were. The same here."

Doubtfully Michael says, "How can you draw the line between psychological conditioning and long-term selective breeding? How do you know what to attribute to which?"

"I haven't faced that problem yet," Jason admits.

"Shouldn't you be working with a geneticist?"

"Perhaps later I will. After I've established my parameters of inquiry. You know, I'm not ready to *defend* this thesis, yet. I'm just collecting data to discover if it can be defended. The scientific method. We don't make a priori assumptions and look around for supporting evidence; we examine the evidence first and—"

"Yes, yes, I know. Just between us, though, you do think it's really happening, don't you? An urbmon species."

"I do. Yes. Two centuries of selective breeding, pretty ruthlessly enforced. And all of us so well adapted now to this kind of life."

"Ah. Yes. All of us so well adapted."

"With some exceptions," Jason says, retreating a bit. He and Michael exchange wary glances. Jason wonders what thoughts lie behind his brother-in-law's cool eyes. "General acceptance, though. Where has the old Western expansionist philosophy gone? Bred out of the race, I say. The urge to power? The love of conquest? The hunger for land and property? Gone. Gone. Gone. I don't think that's just a conditioning process. I suspect it's a matter of stripping the race of certain genes that lead to—"

"Dinner, professor," Micaela calls.

A costly meal. Proteoid steaks; root salad, bubble pudding, relishes, fish soup. Nothing reconstituted and hardly anything synthetic. For the next two weeks he and Micaela will have to go on short rations until they've made up the deficit in their luxury allotment. He conceals his annoyance. Michael always eats lavishly when he comes here; Jason wonders why, since Micaela is not nearly so solicitous of her seven other brothers and sisters. Scarcely ever invites two or three of them. But Michael here at least five times a year, always getting a feast. Jason's suspicions reawaken. Something ugly going on between those two? The childhood passions still smoldering? Perhaps it is cute for twelve-year-old twins to couple, but should they still be at it when twenty-three and married? Michael a nightwalker in my sleeping platform? Jason is annoyed at himself. Not bad enough that he has to fret over his idiotic homosexual fixation on Michael; now he has to torment himself with fears of an incestuous affair behind his back. Poisoning his hours of relaxation. What if they are? Nothing socially objectionable in it. Seek pleasure where you will. In your sister's slot if you be so moved. Shall all the men of Urban Monad 116 have access to Micaela Quevedo, save only the unfortunate Michael? Must his status as her wombmate deny her to him? Be realistic, Jason tells himself. Incest taboos make sense only where breeding is involved. Anyway, they probably aren't doing it, probably never have. He wonders why so much nastiness has sprouted in his soul lately. The frictions of living with Micaela, he decides. Her coldness is driving me into all kinds of unblessworthy attitudes, the bitch. If she doesn't stop goading me I'll—

—I'll what? Seduce Michael away from her? He laughs at the intricacy of his own edifice of schemes.

"Something funny?" Micaela asks. "Share it with us, Jason."

He looks up, helpless. What shall he say? "A silly thought," he improvises. "About you and Michael, how much you look like each other. I was thinking, perhaps some night you and he could switch rooms, and then a nightwalker would come here, looking for you, but when he actually got under the covers with you he'd discover that he was in bed with a man, and—and—" Jason is smitten with the overwhelming fatuity of what he is saying and descends into a feeble silence.

"What a peculiar thing to imagine," Micaela says.

"Besides, so what?" Stacion asks. "The nightwalker might be a little surprised for a minute, maybe, but then he'd just go ahead and make it with Michael, wouldn't he? Rather than make a big scene or bother to go someplace else. So I don't see what's funny."

"Forget it," Jason growls. "I told you it was silly. Micaela insisted on knowing what was crossing my mind, and I told you, but I'm not responsible if it doesn't make any sense, am I? Am I?" He grabs the flask of wine and pours most of what remains into his cup. "This is good stuff," he mutters.

After dinner they share an expander, all but Stacion. They groove in silence for a couple of hours. Shortly before midnight, Michael and Stacion leave. Jason does not watch as his wife and her brother make their farewell embraces. As soon as the guests are gone, Micaela strips away her sarong and gives him a bright, fierce stare, almost defying him to have her tonight. But though he knows it is unkind to ignore her wordless invitation, he is so depressed by his own inner performance this evening that he feels he must flee. "Sorry," he says. "I'm restless." Her expression changes: desire fades and is replaced by bewilderment, and then by rage. He does not wait. Hastily he goes out, rushing to the dropshaft and plummeting to the 59th floor. Warsaw. He enters an apartment and finds a woman of about thirty, with fuzzy blond hair and a soft fleshy body, asleep alone on an unkempt sleeping platform. At least eight littles stacked up on cots in the corners. He wakes her. "Jason Quevedo," he says. "I'm from Shanghai."

She blinks. Having trouble focusing her eyes. "Shanghai? But are you supposed to be here?"

"Who says I can't?"

She ponders that. "Nobody says. But Shanghai never comes here. Really, Shanghai? You?"

"Do I have to show you my identiplate?" he asks harshly.

His educated inflections destroy her resistance. She begins to primp, arranging her hair, reaching for some kind of cosmetic spray for her face, while he drops his clothing. He mounts the platform. She draws her knees up almost to her breasts, presenting herself. Crudely, impatiently, he takes her. Michael, he thinks. Micaela. Michael. Micaela. Grunting, he floods her with his fluid.

In the morning, at his office, he begins his newest line of inquiry, summoning up data on the sexual mores of ancient times. As usual, he concentrates on the twentieth century, which he regards as the climax of the ancient era, and therefore most significant, revealing as it does the entire cluster of attitudes and responses that had accumulated in the pre-urbmon industrial era. The twenty-first century is less useful for his purposes, being, like all transitional periods, essentially chaotic and unschematic, and the twenty-second century brings him into modern times with the beginning of the urbmon age. So the twentieth is his favorite area of study. Seeds of the collapse, portents of doom running through it like bad-trip threads in a psychedelic tapestry.

Jason is careful not to fall victim to the historian's fallacy of diminished perspective. Though the twentieth century, seen from this distance, seems to be a single seamless entity, he knows that this is an error of evaluation caused by overfacile abstracting; there may be certain apparent patterns that ride one unbroken curve across the ten decades, but he realizes that he must allow for certain qualitative changes in society that have created major historical discontinuities between decade and decade. The unleashing of atomic energy created one such discontinuity. The development of swift intercontinental transportation formed another. In the moral sphere, the availability of simple and reliable contraception caused a fundamental change in sexual attitudes, a revolution not to be ascribed to mere rebelliousness. The arrival of the psychedelic age, with its special problems and joys, marked one more great gulf, setting off part of the century from all that went before. So 1910 and 1930 and 1950 and 1970 and 1990 occupy individual summits in Jason's jagged image of the century, and in any sampling of its mentality that he takes, he draws evidence from each of its discrete subepochs.

Plenty of evidence is available to him. Despite the dislocations caused by the collapse, an enormous weight of data on the eras of pre-urbmon time exists, stored in some subterranean vault, Jason knows not where. Certainly the central data bank (if there is indeed only one, and not a redundant series of them scattered through the world) is not anywhere in Urbmon 116, and he doubts that it is even in the Chipitts constellation. It does not matter. He can draw from that vast deposit any information that he requires, and it will come instantaneously. The trick lies in knowing what to ask for.

He is familiar enough with the sources to be able to make intelligent data requisitions. He thumbs the keys and the new cubes arrive. Novels. Films. Television programs. Leaflets. Handbills. He knows that for more than half the century popular attitudes toward sexual matters were recorded both in licit and illicit channels: the ordinary novels and motion pictures of the day, and an underground stream of clandestine, "forbidden" erotic works. Jason draws from both groups. He must weigh the distortions of the erotica against the distortions of the legitmate material: only out of this Newtonian interplay of forces can the objective truth be mined. Then, too, he surveys the legal codes, making the appropriate allowances for laws observed only in the breach. What is this in the laws of New York: "A person who willfully and lewdly exposes his person or the private parts thereof, in any public place, or in any place where others are present, or procures another to so expose himself shall be guilty of..."? In the state of Georgia, he reads, any sleeping car passenger who remains in a compartment other than the one to which he is assigned is guilty of a misdemeanor and is subject to a maximum fine of $1000 or twelve months' imprisonment. The laws of the state of Michigan tell him: "Any person who shall undertake to medically treat any female person, and while so treating her shall represent to such female that it is, or will be necessary, or beneficial to her health that she shall have sexual intercourse with a man, and any man, not being the husband of such female, who shall have sexual intercourse with her by reason of such representation, shall be guilty of a felony, and be punished by a maximum term of ten years." Strange. Stranger still: "Every person who shall carnally know, or shall have sexual intercourse in any manner with any animal or bird, is guilty of sodomy. ..." No wonder everything's extinct! And this? "Whoever shall carnally know any male or female by the anus (rectum) or with the mouth or

tongue, or who shall attempt intercourse with a dead
body... $2000 and/or five years' imprisonment...." Most
chilling of all: in Connecticut the use of contraceptive articles
is forbidden, under penalty of a minimum fine of $50 or sixty
days to one year in prison, and in Massachusetts "whoever
sells, lends, gives, exhibits (or offers to) any instrument or
drug, or medicine, or any article whatever for the prevention
of conception, shall be subject to a maximum term of five
years in prison or a maximum fine of $1000." What? What?
Send a man to prison for decades for cunnilingualizing his
wife, and impose so trifling a sentence on the spreaders of
contraception? Where was Connecticut, anyway? Where was
Massachusetts? Historian that he is, he is not sure. God
bless, he thinks, but the doom that came upon them was well
merited. A bizarre folk to deal so lightly with those who
would limit births!

He skims a few novels and dips into several films. Even
though it is only the first day of his research, he perceives
patterns, a fitful loosening of taboos throughout the century,
accelerating greatly between 1920 and 1930 and again after
1960. Timid experiments in revealing the ankle lead, shortly,
to bared breasts. The curious custom of prostitution erodes as
liberties become more commonly obtained. The disappearance of taboos on the popular sexual vocabulary. He can
barely believe some of what he learns. So compressed were
their souls! So thwarted were their urges! And why? And
why? Of course, they did grow looser. Yet terrible restraints
prevail throughout that dark century, except toward the end,
when the collapse was near and all limits burst. But even
then there was something askew in their liberation. He sees a
forced, self-conscious mode of amorality coming into being.
The shy nudists. The guilt-wracked orgiasts. The apologetic
adulterers. Strange, strange, strange. He is endlessly fascinated by the twentieth century's sexual concepts. The wife as
husband's property. The premium on virginity: well, they
seemed to get rid of *that*! Attempts by the state to dictate
positions of sexual intercourse and to forbid certain supplementary acts. The restrictions even on words! A phrase leaps
out of a supposedly serious twentieth-century work of social
criticism: "Among the most significant developments of the
decade was the attainment of the freedom, at last, for the
responsible writer to use such words as *fuck* and *cunt* where
necessary in his work." Can that have been so? Such impor-

tance placed on mere words? Jason pronounces the odd monosyllables aloud in his research cubicle. "Fuck. Cunt. Fuck. Cunt. Fuck." They sound merely antiquated. Harmless, certainly. He tries the modern equivalents. "Top. Slot. Top. Slot. Top." No impact. How can words ever have held such inflammatory content that an apparently penetrating scholar would feel it worthwhile to celebrate their free public use? Jason is aware of his limitations as a historian when he runs into such things. He simply cannot comprehend the twentieth century's obsession with words. To insist on giving God a capital letter, as though He might be displeased to be called a god! To suppress books for printing words like c-t and f-k and s-t!

By the close of his day's work he is more convinced than ever of the validity of his thesis. There has been a monumental change in sexual morality in the past three hundred years, and it cannot be explained only on cultural grounds. We are different, he tells himself. We have changed, and it is a cellular change, a transformation of the body as well as the soul. They could not have permitted, let alone encouraged, our total-accessibility society. Our nightwalking, our nudity, our freedom from taboos, our lack of irrational jealousies, all of this would have been wholly alien to them, distasteful, abominable. Even those who lived in a way approaching ours, and there were a few, did so for the wrong reasons. They were responding not to a positive societal need but to an existing system of repression. We are different. We are fundamentally different.

Weary, satisfied with what he has found, he leaves his office an hour ahead of time. When he returns to his apartment, Micaela is not there.

This puzzles him. Always here at this hour. The littles left alone, playing with their toys. Of course it is a bit early, not much. Just stepped out for a chat? I don't understand. She hasn't left a message. He says to his eldest son, "Where's Mommo?"

"Went out."

"Where?"

A shrug. "Visiting."

"How long ago?"

"An hour. Maybe two."

Some help. Fidgety, perturbed, Jason calls a couple of women on the floor, Micaela's friends. They haven't seen her.

The boy looks up and says brightly, "She was going to visit a man." Jason stares sharply at him. "A man? Is that what she said? What man?" But the boy has exhausted his information. Fearful that she has gone off for a rendezvous with Michael, he debates phoning Edinburgh. Just to see if she's there. A lengthy inner debate. Furious images racing in his skull. Micaela and Michael entangled, indistinguishable, united, inflamed. Locked together in incestuous passion. As perhaps every afternoon. How long has this been going on? And she comes to me at dinnertime every evening hot and wet from *him*. He calls Edinburgh and gets Stacion on the screen. Calm, bulgy. "Micaela? no, of course she isn't here. Is she supposed to be?"

"I thought maybe—dropping in—"

"I haven't heard from her since we were at your place."

He hesitates. Just as she moves to break the connection he blurts, "Do you happen to know where Michael is right now?"

"Michael? He's at work. Interface Crew Nine."

"Are you sure?"

Stacion looks at him in obvious surprise. "Of course I'm sure. Where else would he be? His crew doesn't break till 1730." Laughs. "You aren't suggesting that Michael—that Micaela—"

"Of course not. What kind of fool do you think I am? I just wondered—that perhaps—if—" He is adrift. "Forget it, Stacion. Give him my love when he comes home." Jason cuts the contact. Head bowed, eyes full of unwanted visions. Michael's long fingers encircling his sister's breasts. Rosy nipples poking through. Mirror-image faces nose to nose. Tonguetips touching. No. Where is she, then? He is tempted to try to reach him in Interface Crew Nine. Find out if he really is on duty. Or maybe off in some dark cubbyhole topping his sister. Jason throws himself face down on the sleeping platform to consider his position. He tells himself that it is not important that Micaela is letting her brother top her. Not at all. He will not let himself be trapped into primeval twentieth-century attitudes of morality. On the other hand, it is a considerable violation of custom for Micaela to go off in midafternoon to be topped. If she wants Michael, Jason thinks, let him come here decently after midnight, as a nightwalker. Instead of this skulking and sneaking. Does she think I'd be shocked to know who her lover is? Does she have to hide it from me this way? It's a hundred times as bad to steal away like this. It introduces a note of deceit. Old-fashioned adultery; the secret rendezvous. How ugly! I'd like to tell her—

The door opens and Micaela comes in. She is naked under a translucent flutter-robe and has a flushed, rumpled look. She smirks at Jason. He perceives the loathing behind the smirk.

"Well?" he says.

"Well?"

"I was surprised not to find you here when I got home."

Coolly Micaela disrobes. She gets under the cleanser. From the way she scrubs herself there can be no doubt that she has just been topped. After a moment she says, "I got back a little late, didn't I? Sorry."

"Got back from where?"

"Siegmund Kluver's."

He is astounded and relieved all at once. What is this? *Daywalking?* And a woman taking the sexual initiative? But at least it wasn't Michael. At least it wasn't Michael. If he can believe her. "Siegmund?" he says. "What do you mean, Siegmund?"

"I visited him. Didn't the littles tell you? He had some free time today and I went up to his place. Quite blessworthy, I must say. An expert slotman. Not my first time with him of course, but by far the best."

She steps out from the cleanser, seizes two of the littles, strips them, thrusts them under for their afternoon bath. Paying almost no attention to Jason. He contemplates her lithe bare body in dismay. A lecture on urbmon sexual ethics almost spills from him, but he dams his lips, baffled and agog. Having laboriously adjusted himself to accept the unacceptable notion of her incestuous love, he cannot easily come to terms with this other business of Siegmund. Chasing after him?: Daywalking. *Daywalking.* Has she no shame? Why has she done this? Purely for spite, he tells himself. To mock me. To anger me. To show me how little she cares for me. Using sex as a weapon against me. Flaunting her illicit hour with Siegmund. But Siegmund should have had more sense. A man with his ambitions, violating custom? Perhaps Micaela overwhelmed him. She can do that. Even to Siegmund. The bitch! The bitch! He sees her looking at him now, eyes sparkling, mouth quirked in a hostile smile. Daring him to start a fight. Begging him to try to make trouble. No,

Micaela, I won't play your game. As she bathes the littles he says quite serenely, "What are you programing for dinner tonight?"

At work the next day he decubes a motion picture of 1969—ostensibly a comedy, he imagines, about two California couples who decide to exchange mates for a night, then find themselves without the courage to go through with it. Jason is wholly drawn into the film, enthralled not only by the scenes of private houses and open countryside but by the sheer alienness of the characters' psychology—their transparent bravado, their intense anguish over a matter as trivial as who will poke what into whom, their ultimate cowardice. It is easier for him to understand the nervous hilarity with which they experiment with what he takes to be cannabis, since the film, after all, dates from the dawn of the psychedelic era. But their sexual attitudes are wondrously grotesque. He watches the film twice, taking copious notes. Why are these people so timid? Do they fear an unwanted pregnancy? A social disease? No, the time of the film is after the venereal era, he believes. Is it pleasure itself that they fear? Tribal punishment for violation of the monopolistic concept of twentieth-century marriage? Even if the violation is conducted with absolute secrecy? That must be it, Jason concludes. They dread the laws against extramarital intercourse. The rack and the thumbscrew, the stocks and the ducking stool, so to speak. Hidden eyes watching. The shameful truth destined to out. So they draw back; so they remain locked in the cells of their individual marriages.

Watching their antics, he suddenly sees Micaela in the context of twentieth-century bourgeois morality. Not a timid fool like the four people in the film, of course. Brazen, defiant—bragging about her visit to Siegmund, using sex as a way of diminishing her husband. A very twentieth-century attitude, far removed from the easy acceptance characteristic of the urbmon world. Only someone whose view of sex is tied to its nature as a commodity could have done what Micaela has done. She has reinvented adultery in a society where the concept has no meaning! His anger rises. Out of 800,000 people in Urban Monad 116, why must he be married to the one sick one? Flirting with her brother because she knows it annoys me, not because she's really interested in topping him. Going to Siegmund instead of waiting for Siegmund to come to her. The slotty barbarian! I'll show her, though. I know how to play her silly sadistic game!

At midday he leaves his cubicle, having done less than five hours' work. The liftshaft takes him to the 787th floor. Outside the apartment of Siegmund and Mamelon Kluver he succumbs to sudden terrible vertigo and nearly falls. He recovers his balance; but his fear is still great, and he is tempted to leave. He argues with himself, trying to purge his timidity. Thinking of the people in the motion picture. Why is he afraid? Mamelon's just another slot. He's had a hundred as attractive as she. But she's clever. Might cut me down with a couple of quick quips. Still, I want her. Denied myself all these years. While Micaela blithely marches off to Siegmund in the afternoon. The bitch. The bitch. Why should I suffer? We aren't supposed to have to feel frustration in the urbmon environment. I want Mamelon, therefore. He pushes open the door.

The Kluver apartment is empty. A baby in the maintenance slot, no other sign of life.

"Mamelon?" he asks. Voice almost cracking.

The screen glows and Mamelon's pre-programed image appears. How beautiful, he thinks. How radiant she is. Smiling. She says, "Hello. I have gone to my afternoon polyrhythm class and will be home at 1500 hours. Urgent messages may be relayed to me in Shanghai Somatic Fulfillment Hall, or to my husband Siegmund at Louisville Access Nexus. Thank you." The image fades.

1500 hours. Nearly a two-hour wait. Shall he go?

He craves another glimpse of her loveliness. "Mamelon?" he says.

She reappears on screen. He studies her. The aristocratic features, the dark mysterious eyes. A self-contained woman, undriven by demons. A personality in her own right, not, like Micaela, a frayed neurotic whipped by the psychic winds. "Hello. I have gone to my afternoon polyrhythm class and will be home at 1500 hours. Urgent messages may be relayed—"

He waits.

The apartment, which he has seen before, impresses him anew with its elegance. Rich textures of hangings and draperies, sleek objects of art. Marks of status; soon Siegmund will move up to Louisville, no doubt, and these private possessions are harbingers of his coming elevation to the ruling caste. To ease his impatience Jason toys with the wall panels, inspects the furniture, programs all the scent apertures. He peers at the baby, cooing in its maintenance slot. He paces. The other Kluver child must be two years old by now. Will it come home from the creche soon? He is not eager to entertain a little all afternoon while waiting tautly for Mamelon.

He tunes the screen and watches one of the afternoon abstractions. The flow of forms and colors carries him through another impatient hour. Mamelon will be here soon.

1450. She comes in, holding her little's hand. Jason rises, athrob, dry-throated. She is dressed simply and unglamorously in a cascading blue tunic, knee-length, and gives an unusually disheveled impression. Why not? She has spent the afternoon in physical exercise; he cannot expect her to be the impeccable, glistening Mamelon of the evenings.

"Jason? Is something wrong? Why—"

"Just a visit," he says, barely able to recognize his own voice.

"You look half flippo, Jason! Are you ill? Can I get you anything?" She discards her tunic and tosses it, crumpled, under the cleanser. Now she wears only a filmy wrap; he averts his eyes form her blazing nudity. And stares out of the corners as she drops the wrap also, washes, and dons a light housecoat. Turning to him again, she says, "You're acting very strangely."

Out with it in a rush.

"Let me top you, Mamelon!"

A surprised laugh from her. "Now? Middle of the afternoon?"

"Is that so wicked?"

"It's unusual," she says. "Especially coming from a man who hasn't ever been to me as a nightwalker. But I suppose there's no harm in it. All right: come on."

As simple as that. She takes off the housecoat and inflates the sleeping platform. Of course; she will not frustrate him, for that would be unblessworthy. The hour is strange, but Mamelon understands the code by which they live, and does not hold him strictly to the rules. She is his. The white skin, the high full breasts. Deep-set navel. Black matted thatch curling lavishly onto her thighs. She beckons to him from the platform, smiles, rubs her knees together to ready herself. He removes his clothing, carefully folding everything. He lies down beside her, takes one of her breasts nervously in his hand, lightly nips her earlobe. He wants desperately to tell her that he loves her. But that would be a breach of custom far more serious than any he has committed thus far. In a sense, not the twentieth-century sense, she belongs to Siegmund, and he has no right to intrude his emotions between them, only his rigid organ. With a quick tense leap he climbs her. As usual, panic makes him hurry. He goes into her and they begin to move. I'm topping Mamelon Kluver. Actually. At last. He gains control of himself and slows it down. He dares to open his eyes and is gratified to find that hers are closed. The nostrils flared, the lips drawn back. Such perfect white teeth. She seems to be purring. He moves a little faster. Clasping her in his arms; the mounds of her breasts flattening against him. Abruptly, amazingly, something extraordinary is kindled within her, and she shrieks and pumps her hips and makes hoarse animal noises as she claws at him. He is so astonished by the fury of her coming that he forgets to notice his own. So it ends. Exhausted, he clings to her a little while after, and she strokes his sweaty shoulders. Analyzing it in the afterward coolness, he realizes that it was not so very different from what he has experienced elsewhere. One wilder-than-usual moment, perhaps. But otherwise only the familiar process. Even with Mamelon Kluver, the object of his incandescent imaginings for three years, it was only the old two-backed beast: I thrust and she thrusts and up we go. So much for romanticism. In the dark all cats are gray: old twentieth-century proverb. So now I've topped her. He withdraws and they go to the cleanser together.

She says, "Better, now?"

"I think so."

"You were terribly tight when I came in."

"I'm sorry," he says.

"Can I get you anything?"

"No."

"Would you like to talk about it?"

"No. No." He is averting his eyes from her body again. He searches for his clothing. She does not bother to dress. "I guess I'll go," he says.

"Come back some time. Perhaps during regular nightwalking hours. I don't mean that I really mind your coming in the afternoon, Jason, but it might be more relaxed at night. Do you follow what I'm saying?"

She is frighteningly casual. Does she realize that this is the first time he has topped a woman of his own city? What if he told her that all his other adventures had been in Warsaw and

Reykjavik and Prague and the other grubbo levels? He wonders now what he had feared. He will come back to her, he is sure. He makes his exit amid a flurry of grins, nods, half winks, and furtive direct glances. Mamelon blows him a kiss.

In the corridor. Still early afternoon. The whole point of this excursion will be lost if he comes home on time. He takes the dropshaft to his office and consumes two futile hours there. Even so, too early. Returning to Shanghai a little past 1800, he enters the Somatic Fulfillment Hall and dumps himself into an imagebath; the warm undulating currents are soothing, but he responds badly to the psychedelic vibrations from below and his mind fills with visions of shattered, blackened urbmons, all girders and skewed concrete. When he comes up it is 1920 and the screen in the dressing room, picking up his emanations, says, "Jason Quevedo, your wife is trying to trace you." Fine. Late for dinner. Let her squirm. He nods to the screen and goes out. After walking the halls for close to an hour, beginning at the 770th floor and snaking his way up to 792, he drops to his own level and heads for home. A screen in the hall outside the shaft tells him again that tracers are out for him. "I'm coming. I'm coming," he mutters, irritated.

Micaela looks rewardingly worried. "Where have you been?" she asks the instant he appears.

"Oh, around. Around."

"You weren't working late. I called you there. I had tracers on you."

"As if I were a lost boy."

"It wasn't like you. You don't just disappear in the middle of the afternoon."

"Have you had dinner yet?"

"I've been waiting," she says sourly.

"Let's eat, then. I'm starved."

"You won't explain?"

"Later." Working hard at an air of mystery.

He scarcely notices his food. Afterward, he spends the usual time with the littles. They go off to sleep. He rehearses what he will say to Micaela, arranging the words in various patterns. He tries inwardly to practice a self-satisfied smirk. For once he will be the aggressor. For once he will hurt *her*.

She has become absorbed in the screen transmission. Her earlier anxiety about his disappearance seems to have vanished.

Finally he is forced to say. "Do you want to discuss what I did today?"

She looks up. "What you did? Oh, you mean this afternoon?" She no longer cares, it appears. "Well?"

"I went to Mamelon Kluver."

"Daywalking? You?"

"Me."

"Was she good?"

"She was superb," he says, puzzled by Micaela's air of unconcern. "She was everything I imagined she'd be."

Micaela laughs.

"Is it funny?" he asks.

"It isn't. *You* are."

"Tell me what you mean by that."

"All these years you deny yourself nightwalking in Shanghai, and go off to the grubbos. Now, for the stupidest possible reason, you finally allow yourself Mamelon—"

"You knew I never nightwalked here?"

"Of course I knew," she says. "Women talk. I ask my friends. You never topped any of them. So I started to wonder. I had some checking done on you. Warsaw. Prague. Why did you have to do down *there*, Jason?"

"That doesn't matter now."

"What does?"

"That I spent the afternoon on Mamelon's sleeping platform."

"You idiot."

"Bitch."

"Failure."

"Sterilizer!"

"Grubbo!"

"Wait," he says. "Wait. Why did you go to Siegmund?"

"To annoy you," she admits. "Because he's a rung-grabber, and you aren't. I wanted to get you excited. To make you move."

"So you violated all custom and aggressively daywalked with the man of your choice. Not pretty, Micaela. Not at all feminine, I might add."

"That keeps things even, then. A female husband and a mannish wife."

"You're quick with the insults, aren't you?"

"Why did you go to Mamelon?"

"To get you angry. To pay you back for Siegmund. Not that I give a damn about your letting him top you. We can take that stuff for granted, I think. But your *motives*. Using sex as a weapon. Deliberately playing the wrong role. Trying to stir me up. It was ugly, Micaela."

"And *your* motives? Sex as revenge? Nightwalking is supposed to reduce tensions, not create them. Regardless of the time of day you do it. You want Mamelon, fine; she's a lovely girl. But to come here and *brag* about it, as if you think I care whose slot you plow—"

"Don't be a filther, Micaela."

"Listen to him! Listen to him! Puritan! Moralist!"

The littles begin to cry. They have never heard shouting before. Micaela makes a hushing gesture at them behind her back.

"At least I *have* morals," he says. "What about you and your brother Michael?"

"What about us?"

"Do you deny you've let him top you?"

"When we were kids, yes, a couple of times," she says, flushing. "So? You never put it up your sisters, I suppose?"

"Not only when you were kids. You're still making it with him."

"I think you're insane, Jason."

"You deny it?"

"Michael hasn't touched me in ten years. Not that I see anything wrong with his doing it, except that it hasn't happened. Oh, Jason, Jason, Jason! You've spent so much time mucking around in your archives that you've turned yourself into a twentieth-century man. You're jealous, Jason. Worried about incest, no less. And whether I obey the rules about female initiative. What about you and your Warsaw nightwalking? Don't we have a propinquity custom? Are you imposing a double standard, Jason? You do what you like and I observe custom? And upset about Siegmund. Michael. You're jealous, Jason. *Jealous*. We abolished jealousy a hundred fifty years ago!"

"And you're a social climber. A would-be slicko. You aren't satisfied with Shanghai, you want Louisville. Well, ambition is obsolete too, Micaela. Besides, you were the one who started this whole business of using sex to score debating points. By going to Siegmund and making sure I knew it. You think *I'm* a puritan? You're a throwback, Micaela. You're full of pre-urbmon morality."

"If I am, I got that way from you," she cries.

"No. I got that way from you. You carry the poison around in you! When you—"

The door opens. A man looks in. Charles Mattern, from 799. The sleek, fast-talking sociocomputator; Jason has worked with him on several research projects. Evidently he has overheard the unblessworthy furor going on in here, for he is frowning in embarrassment. "God bless," he says softly, "I'm just out nightwalking, and I thought I'd—"

"No," Micaela screams. "Not now! Go away!"

Mattern shows his shock. He starts to say something, then shakes his head and ducks out of the room, muttering an apology for his intrusion.

Jason is appalled. To turn away a legitimate nightwalker? To order him out of the room?

"Savage!" he cries, and slaps her across the face. "How could you have done that?"

She recoils, rubbing her cheek. "Savage? Me? And you hitting? I could have you thrown down the chute for—"

"I could have *you* thrown down the chute for—"

He stops. They both are silent.

"You shouldn't have sent Mattern away," he says quietly, a little later.

"You shouldn't have hit me."

"I was worked up. Some rules just mustn't be broken. If he reports you—"

"He won't. He could see we were having an argument. That I wasn't exactly available for him right then."

"Even having an argument," he says. "Screaming like that. Both of us. At the very least it could get us sent to the moral engineers."

"I'll fix things with Mattern, Jason. Leave it to me. I'll get him back here and explain, and I'll give him the topping of his life." She laughs gently. "You dumb flippo." There is affection in her voice. "We probably sterilized half the floor with out screeching. What was the sense, Jason?"

"I was trying to make you understand something about yourself. Your essentially archaic psychological makeup, Micaela. If you could only see yourself objectively, the pettiness of a lot of your motivations lately—I don't want to start another fight, I'm just trying to explain things now—"

"And your motivations, Jason? You're just as archaic as I

am. We're both throwbacks. Our heads are both full of
primitive moralistic reflexes. Isn't that so? Can't you see it?"

He walks away from her. Standing with his back to her, he
fingers the rubbing-node set into the wall near the cleanser,
and lets some of the tensions flow from him into it. "Yes," he
says after a long while. "Yes, I see it. We have a veneer of
urbmonism. But underneath—jealousy, envy, possessiveness—"

"Yes. Yes."

"And you see what discovering this does to my work, of
course?" He manages a chuckle. "My thesis that selective
breeding has produced a new species of human in the urbmons?
Maybe so, but *I* don't belong to the species. *You* don't belong.
Maybe *they* do, some of them. But how many? How many,
really?"

She comes up behind him and leans close. He feels her
nipples against his back. Hard, tickling him. "Most of them,
perhaps," she says. "Your thesis may still be right. But we're
wrong. We're out of place."

"Yes."

"Throwbacks to an uglier age."

"Yes."

"So we've got to stop torturing each other, Jason. We have
to wear better camouflage. Do you see?"

"Yes. Otherwise we'll end up going down the chute. We're
unblessworthy, Micaela."

"Both of us."

"Both of us."

He turns. His arms surround her. He winks. She winks.

"Vengeful barbarian," she says tenderly.

"Spiteful savage," he whispers, kissing her earlobe.

They slip together onto the sleeping platform. The night-
walkers will simply have to wait.

He has never loved her as much as he does this minute.

Five

In Louisville, Siegmund Kluver still feels like a very small
boy. He cannot persuade himself that he has any rightful
business up there. A prowling stranger. An illicit intruder.

When, he goes up to the city of the urbmon's masters a strange boyish shyness settles over him that he must consciously strive to hide. He finds himself forever wanting to peer nervously over his shoulder. Looking for the patrols that he fears will intercept him. The stern brawny figure blocking the wide corridor. What are you doing here, son? You shouldn't be wandering around on these floors. Louisville is for the administrators, don't you know that? And Siegmund will babble excuses, his face blazing. And rush for the dropshaft.

He tries to keep this silly sense of embarrassment a secret. He knows it doesn't fit with the image of himself that everyone else sees. Siegmund the cool customer. Siegmund the man of destiny. Siegmund who was obviously Louisville-bound from childhood. Siegmund the swaggering cocksman, plowing his way lustily through the finest womanhood Urban Monad 116 has to offer.

If they only knew. Underneath it all a vulnerable boy. Underneath it a shy, insecure Siegmund. Worried that he's climbing too fast. Apologizing to himself for his success. Siegmund the humble, Siegmund the uncertain.

Or is that just an image too? Sometimes he thinks that this hidden Siegmund, this private Siegmund, is merely a façade that he has erected so that he can go on liking himself, and that beneath this subterranean veneer of shyness, somewhere beyond the range of his insight, lies the real Siegmund, every bit as ruthless and cocky and rung-grabbing as the Siegmund that the outer world sees.

He goes up to Louisville nearly every morning, now. They requisition him as a consultant. Some of the top men there have made a pet of him—Lewis Holston, Nissim Shawke, Kipling Freehouse, men at the very highest levels of authority. He knows they are exploiting him, dumping on him all the dreary, tedious jobs they don't feel like handling themselves. Taking advantage of his ambitions. Siegmund, prepare a report on working-class mobility patterns. Siegmund, run a tabulation of adrenal balances in the middle cities. Siegmund, what's the waste-recycling ratio this month? Siegmund. Siegmund. Siegmund. But he exploits them too. He is rapidly making himself indispensable, as they slide into the habit of using him to do their thinking. In another year or two, beyond much doubt, they will have to ask him to move up in the building. Perhaps they'll jump him from Shanghai to Toledo or Paris; more likely they'll take him right into Louisville

at the next vacancy. Louisville before he's twenty! Has anyone ever done that before?

By that time, maybe, he'll feel comfortable among the
members of the ruling class.

He can see them laughing at him behind their eyes. They
made it to the top so long ago that they've forgotten that
others still have to strive. To them, Siegmund knows, he
must seem comical—an earnest, pushy little rung-grabber,
his gut afire with the upward urge. They tolerate him because he's capable—more capable, maybe, than most of them.
But they don't respect him. They think he's a fool for wanting
so badly something that they've had time to grow bored with.

Nissim Shawke, for instance. Possibly one of the two or
three most important men of the urbmon. (Who is the *most*
important? Not even Siegmund knows. At the top level,
power becomes a blurry abstraction; in one sense everybody
in Louisville has absolute authority over the entire building,
and in another sense no one has.) Shawke is about sixty,
Siegmund supposes. Looks much younger. A lean, athletic,
olive-skinned man, cool-eyed, physically powerful. Alert, wary,
a man of great tensile strength. He gives the illusion of being
enormously dynamic. A teeming reservoir of potential. Yet so
far as Siegmund can see, Shawke does nothing at all. He
refers all governmental matters to his subordinates; he glides
through his offices at the crest of the urbmon as though the
building's problems are mere phantoms. Why should Shawke
strive? He's at the summit. He has everybody fooled, everyone but Siegmund, perhaps. Shawke need not *do* but only
be. Now he marks time and enjoys the comforts of his
position. Sitting there like a Renaissance prince. One word
from Nissim Shawke could send almost anybody down the
chute. A single memorandum from him might be able to
reverse some of the urbmon's most deeply cherished policies.
Yet he originates no programs, he vetoes no proposals, he
ducks all challenges. To have such power, and to refuse to
exercise it, strikes Siegmund as making a joke out of the
whole idea of power. Shawke's passivity carries implied contempt for Siegmund's values. His sardonic smile mocks all
ambition. It denies that there is merit in serving society. I am
here, Shawke says with every gesture, and that is sufficient
for me; let the urbmon look after itself; anyone who voluntarily assumes its burdens is an idiot. Siegmund, who yearns to
govern, finds that Shawke blights his soul with doubt. What if

Shawke is right? What if I get to his place fifteen years from now and discover that it's all meaningless? But no. Shawke is sick, that's all. His soul is empty. Life *does* have a purpose, and service to the community fulfills that purpose. I am well qualified to govern my fellow man; therefore I betray mankind and myself as well if I refuse to do my duty. Nissim Shawke is wrong. I pity him.

But why do I shrivel when I look into his eyes?

Then there is Shawke's daughter, Rhea. She lives in Toledo, on the 900th floor, and is married to Kipling Freehouse's son Paolo. There is a great deal of intermarriage among the families of Louisville. The children of the administrators do not generally get to live in Louisville themselves; Louisville is reserved for those who actually govern. Their children, unless they happen to find places of their own in the ranks of the administrators, live mostly in Paris and Toledo, the cities immediately below Louisville. They form a privileged enclave there, the offspring of the great. Siegmund does much of his nightwalking in Paris and Toledo. And Rhea Shawke Freehouse is one of his favorites.

She is ten years older than Siegmund. She has her father's wiry, supple form: a lean, somewhat masculine body, with small breasts and flat buttocks and long solid muscles. Dark complexion; eyes that glitter with private amusement; a sharp elegant nose. She has only three littles. Siegmund does not know why her family is so small. She is quick-witted, knowing, well-informed. She is more nearly bisexual than anyone Siegmund knows; he finds her tigerishly passionate, but she has told him also of the joy she takes in loving other women. Among her conquests has been Siegmund's wife Mamelon, who, he thinks, is in may ways a younger version of Rhea. Perhaps that's why he finds Rhea so attractive: she combines all that he finds most interesting about Mamelon and Nissim Shawke.

Siegmund was sexually precocious. He made his first erotic experiments in his seventh year, two years ahead of the urbmon norm. By the time he was nine he was familiar with the mechanics of intercourse, and consistently drew the highest marks in his physical relations class, doing so well that he was allowed to enroll with the eleven-year-olds. Puberty began for him at ten; at twelve he married Mamelon, who was more than a year his senior; shortly he had her

pregnant and the Kluvers were on their way out of the
Chicago newlywed dorm and off to an apartment of their own
in Shanghai. Sex always has seemed agreeable to him for its
own sake, but lately he has come to realize its value in
building character.

He nightwalks assiduously. Young women bore him; he
prefers those who are past twenty, like Principessa Mattern
and Micaela Quevedo of Shanghai. Or Rhea Freehouse.
Women of their experience tend to be better in bed than
most adolescents, of course. Not that that is his prime
concern. One slot isn't ever that much better than another,
and the pursuit of slot for its own sake is no longer very
important to him; Mamelon can give him all the physical
pleasure he needs. But he feels that these older women teach
him a great deal about the world, sharing their experience
with him in an implicit way. From them he draws subtle
insights into the dynamics of adult life, the crises, conflicts,
rewards, depths of character. He loves to learn. His own
maturity, he is convinced, stems from his extensive sexual
encounters with women of the older generation.

Mamelon tells him that he is generally believed to nightwalk
even in Louisville. This is in fact not so. He had never dared.
There are women up there who tempt him, women in their
thirties and forties, even some younger ones, such as Nissim
Shawke's second wife, who is hardly older than Rhea. But the
self-confidence that makes him seem so awesome to his peers
vanishes at the thought of topping the wives of the administrators. It is bold enough for him to venture out of Shanghai
to use women of Toledo or Paris. But Louisville? To slip into
bed with Shawke's wife, and then have Shawke himself
arrive, smiling coldly, saluting, offering him a bowl of tingle—
hello, Siegmund, are you having a good time? No. Maybe
five years from now, when he's living in Louisville himself.
Not yet. But he does have Rhea Shawke Freehouse and some
others of her stature. Not bad for a start.

In Nissim Shawke's lavishly furnished office. There's space
to waste in Louisville. Shawke has no desk; he conducts his
business, such that it is, from a gravity-web slung hammock-
fashion near the broad gleaming window. It is midmorning.
The sun is high. From here one has a stunning view of the
neighboring urbmons. Siegmund enters, having received a
summons from Shawke five minutes before. Uneasily he

meets Shawke's cold gaze. Trying not to look too humble, too obsequious, too defensive, too hostile. "Closer," Shawke orders. Playing his usual game. Siegmund crosses the immense room. He must stand virtually nose-to-nose with Shawke. A mockery of intimacy; instead of forcing Siegmund to remain at a distance, as one usually requires of subordinates, he brings him so close that it is impossible for Siegmund to keep his eyes locked on both of Shawke's. The image wanders; the strain is painful. Sharp focus is lost and the features of the older man seem distorted. In a casual, barely audible voice, Shawke says, "Will you take care of this?" and flips a message cube to Siegmund. It is, Shawke explains, a petition from the civic council of Chicago requesting a liberalization of the urbmon's sex-ratio restrictions. "They want more freedom to pick the sex of their children," Shawke says. "Claiming that the present rules unnecessarily violate individual liberties and are generally unblessworthy. You can play it later for the details. What do you think, Siegmund?"

Siegmund examines his mind for whatever theoretical information it may contain on sex-ratio questions. Not much there. Work intuitively. What kind of advice does Shawke want? He usually wants to be told to leave things just as they are. All right. How, now, to justify the sex-ratio rules without seeming intellectually lazy? Siegmund improvises swiftly. His gift is an easy penetration into the logic of administration.

He says, "My impulse is to tell you to refuse the request."

"Good. Why?"

"The basic dynamic thrust of an urban monad has to be toward stability and predictability, and away from randomness. The urbmon can't expand physically, and our facilities for offloading surplus population aren't all that flexible. So we need to program orderly growth, above all else."

Shawke squints at him chillingly and says, "If you don't mind the obscenity, let me tell you that you sound exactly like a propagandist for limiting births."

"No!" Siegmund blurts. "God bless, no! Of *course* there's got to be universal fertility!" Shawke is silently laughing at him again. Goading, baiting. A streak sadism his main diversion in life. "What I was getting at," Siegmund continues doggedly, "is that within the framework of a society that encourages unlimited reproduction, we've got to impose certain checks and balances to prevent disruptive destabilizing processes. If we allow people to pick the sex of their children themselves, we could very possibly get a generation that's 65 percent male and 35 percent female. Or vice versa, depending on whims and fads of the moment. If that happened, how would we deal with the uncoupled surplus? Where would the extras go? Say, 15,000 males of the same age, all with no available mates. Not only would we have extraordinarily unblessworthy social tensions—imagine an epidemic of rape!—but those bachelors would be lost to the genetic pool. An unhealthy competitive aspect would establish itself. And such ancient customs as prostitution might have to be revived to meet the sexual needs of the unmated. The obvious consequences of an unbalanced sex ratio among a newborn generation are so serious that—"

"Obviously," Shawke drawls, not hiding his boredom.

But Siegmund, wound up in an exposition of theory, cannot easily stop. "Freedom to choose your child's sex would therefore be worse than having no sex-determination processes at all. In medieval times the ratios were governed by random biological events, and naturally tended to gravitate toward a 50-50 split, not taking into account such special factors as war or emigration, which of course would not concern us. But since we *are* able to control our society's sex ratio, we must be careful not to allow the citizens to bring about an arbitrarily gross imbalance. We cannot afford the risk that in a given year an entire city may opt for female children, let's say—and stranger phenomena of mass fancy than that have been known. On compassionate grounds we may allow a particular couple to request and receive permission for, say, a daughter as their next little, but such requests must be compensated for elsewhere in the city in order to ensure the desired overall 50-50 division, even if this causes some distress or inconvenience to certain citizens. Therefore I would recommend a continuation of our present policy of loose control over sex ratios, maintaining the established parameters for free choice but always working within an understood assumption that the good of the urbmon as a whole must be—"

"God bless, Siegmund, that's enough."

"Sir?"

"You've made your point. Over and over. I wasn't asking for a dissertation, just an opinion."

Siegmund feels mashed. He steps back, unable to face Shawke's stony, contemptuous eyes at such close range. "Yes, sir," he murmurs. "What shall I do about this cube, then?"

"Prepare a reply to go out in my name. Covering basically what you've told me, only embellishing it a little, dragging in some scholarly authority. Talk to a sociocomputator and get him to give you a dozen impressive-sounding reasons why free choice of sex would probably lead to an imbalance. Get hold of some historian and ask for figures on what actually happened to society the last time sex-ratio freedom was allowed. Wrap it all up with an appeal to their loyalty to the larger community. Clear?"

"Yes, sir."

"And tell them, without quite putting it in those words, that the request is refused."

"I'll say we're referring it to the high council for further study."

"Exactly," Shawke says. "How much time will you need for all this?"

"I could have it done by tomorrow afternoon."

"Take three days. Don't hurry it." Shawke makes a gesture of dismissal. As Siegmund leaves, Shawke winks cruelly and says, "Rhea sends her love."

"I don't understand why he has to treat me that way," Siegmund says, fighting to keep the whine out of his voice. "Is he like that with everyone?"

He lies beside Rhea Freehouse. Both of them naked; they have not yet made love tonight. Above them a pattern of lights twines and shifts. Rhea's new sculpture, purchased during the day from one of the San Francisco artists. Siegmund's hand on her left breast. Hard little lump of flesh, all pectoral muscle and mammary tissue, practically no fat in it. His thumb to her nipple.

She says, "Father has a very high regard for you."

"He shows it in a strange way. Toying with me, almost sneering at me. He finds me funny."

"You're imagining it, Siegmund."

"No. Not really. Well, I suppose I can't blame him. I must seem ridiculous to him. Taking the problems of urbmon life so seriously. Spouting long theoretical lectures. Those things don't matter to him any more, and I can't expect a man to remain as committed to his career at the age of sixty as he was at thirty, but he makes me feel like such an idiot for being committed myself. As if there's something inherently stupid about anyone who's involved with administrative challenges."

"I never realized you thought so little of him," Rhea says.

"Only because he falls so far short of realizing his abilities. He could be such a great leader. And instead he sits up there and laughs at everything."

Rhea turns toward him. Her expression is grave. "You're misjudging him, Siegmund. He's as committed to the community welfare as you are. You're so put off by his manner that you don't see what a dedicated administrator he is."

"Can you give me one example of—"

"Very often," she continues, "we project onto other people our own secret, repressed attitudes. If *we* think, down deep, that something is trivial or worthless, we indignantly accuse other people of thinking so. If we wonder privately if we're as conscientious and devoted to duty as we say we are, we complain that others are slackers. It might just happen that your passionate involvement with administrative affairs, Siegmund, represents more of a desire for mere rung-grabbing than it does a strong humanitarian concern, and you feel so guilty about your intense ambitions that you believe others are thinking about you in the same terms that yourself—"

"Wait! I absolutely deny—"

"Stop it, Siegmund. I'm not trying to pull you down. I'm just offering some possible explanations of your troubles in Louisville. If you'd rather I kept quiet—"

"Go on."

"I'll say just one more thing, and you can hate me afterward, if you like. You're terribly young, Siegmund, to be where you are. Everybody knows you have tremendous ability, that you *deserve* to be on the brink of going to Louisville, but you're uneasy yourself over how fast you've risen. You try to hide it, but you can't hide it from me. You're afraid that people resent your climb—even some people who are still above you may resent you, you sometimes think. So you're self-conscious. You're extra-sensitive. You read all sorts of terrible things into people's innocent expressions. If I were you, Siegmund, I'd relax and try to enjoy myself more. Don't worry about what people think, or seem to think, about you. Don't fret about grabbing rungs—you're headed for the top, you can't miss, you can afford to slack off and not always worry about the theory of urban administration. Try to be cooler. Less businesslike, less obviously dedicated to your career. Cultivate friendships among people your own age—value people for their own sake, not for where they can help you get. Soak up human nature, work at being more human yourself. Go around the building; do some nightwalking in Warsaw or Prague, maybe. It's irregular, but not illegal, and it'll knock some of the tightness out of you. See how simpler people live. Does any of this make sense to you?"

Siegmund is silent.

"Some," he says finally. "More than some."

"Good."

"It's sinking in. Nobody's ever spoken to me like that before."

"Are you angry with me?"

"No. Of course not."

Rhea runs her fingertips lightly along the line of his jaw. "Do you mind topping me now, then? I'd rather not have to be a moral engineer when I have company on my platform."

His mind is full of her words. He is humiliated but not offended, for much of what she has said rings true. Lost in self-analysis, he turns mechanically to her, caressing her breasts, taking his place between her thighs. His belly against hers. Trying to do combat with a limp sword; he is so preoccupied with the intricacies of her entry into his character that he scarcely notices that he is unable to enter her. She finally makes him aware of the failure of his virility. Playfully dangling him. "Not interested tonight?" she asks.

"Tired," he lies. "All slot and no sleep makes Siegmund a feeble topper."

Rhea laughs. She puts her lips to him and he rises; it was lack of attention, not fatigue, that held him down, and the stimulus of her warm wet mouth returns him to the proper business of the moment. He is ready. Her lithe legs encircle him. With a quick eager thrust he plugs her slot. The only coin with which he can repay her for her wisdom. Now she ceases to be the perceptive, mature arbiter of personality; she is just another writhing woman. She snorts. She bucks. She quivers. Siegmund gives value for value, pumping her full of ecstasy. While he waits for her he thinks about how he must reshape his public image. Not to look ridiculous before the men of Louisville. Much he must do. She trembles now at the abyss of completion, and he pushes her over and follows her, and subsides, sweaty, depressed, when the climax has swept by.

* * *

Home again; not long after midnight. Two heads on his sleeping platform. Mamelon is entertaining a nightwalker. Nothing unusual about that; Siegmund knows that his wife is one of the most desired women in the urbmon. For good reason. Standing by the door, he idly watches the humping bodies under the sheet. Mamelon is making sounds of passion, but to Siegmund they sound false and forced, as though she is courteously flattering an incompetent partner. The man grunts hoarsely in his final frenzies. Siegmund feels vague resentment. If you're going to have my wife, man, at least give her a decent time. He strips and cleanses himself, and when he steps out from under the ultrasonic field the pair on the platform lie still, finished. The man gasping. Mamelon barely breathing hard, confirming Siegmund's suspicion that she was pretending. Politely Siegmund coughs. Mamelon's visitor looks up, blinking, red-faced, alarmed. He's Jason Quevedo, the innocuous little historian, Micaela's man. Mamelon is rather fond of him, though Siegmund can't see why. Nor does Siegmund understand how Quevedo manages to cope with that tempestuous woman Micaela. Mine not to reason why. The sight of Quevedo reminds him that he must visit Micaela again soon. Also that he has work for Jason. "Hello, Siegmund," Jason says, not meeting his eyes. Getting off the platform, looking for his scattered clothes. Mamelon winks at her husband. Siegmund blows her a kiss.

He says, "Before you go, Jason. I was going to call you tomorrow, but this'll do. A project. Historical research."

Quevedo looks eager to get out of the Kluver apartment.

Siegmund continues, "Nissim Shawke is preparing a response to a petition from Chicago concerning possible abandonment of sex-ratio regulations. He wants me to get together some background on how it was in the early days of ratio determination, when people were picking their children's sexes without regard to what anyone else was doing. Since your specialty is the twentieth century, I wondered if you could—"

"Yes, certainly. Tomorrow, first thing. Call me." Quevedo edging doorwards. Eager to flee.

Siegmund says, "What I need is some fairly detailed documentation covering first the medieval period of random births, what the sex distribution was, you see, and then going into the early period of control. While you're getting that, I'll talk to Mattern, I guess, get some sociocomputation on the political implications of—"

"It's so late, Siegmund!" Mamelon complains. "Jason said you can talk to him about it in the morning." Quevedo nods. Afraid to walk out while Siegmund is speaking, yet obviously unwilling to stay. Siegmund realizes he is being too diligent again. Change the image, change the image; business can wait. "All right," he says. "God bless, Jason, I'll call you tomorrow." Grateful, Quevedo escapes, and Siegmund lies down beside his wife. She says, "Couldn't you see he wanted to run? He's so hideously shy."

"Poor Jason," Siegmund says. Stroking Mamelon's sleek flank.

"Where were you tonight?"

"Rhea."

"Interesting?"

"Very. In unexpected ways. She was telling me that I'm too earnest, that I have to try to be more relaxed."

"She's wise," Mamelon says. "Do you agree with her?"

"I suppose so." He dims the lights. "Meet frivolity with frivolity, that's the secret. Take my work casually. I'll try. I'll try. But I can't help getting involved in what I do. This petition from Chicago, for example. Of *course* we can't allow free choice of children's sexes! The consequences would be—"

"Siegmund." She takes his hand and slides it to the base of her belly. "I'd rather not hear all that now. I need you. Rhea didn't use you all up, did she? Because Jason certainly wasn't much good tonight."

"The vigor of youth remains. I hope." Yes. He can manage it. He kisses Mamelon and slips into her. "I love you," he whispers. My wife. My only true. I must remember to talk to Mattern in the morning. And Quevedo. Get the report on Shawke's desk by the afternoon, anyway. If only Shawke *had* a desk. Statistics, quotations, footnotes. Siegmund visualizes every detail of it. Simultaneously he moves atop Mamelon, carrying her to her quick explosive coming.

Siegmund ascends to the 975th floor. Most of the key administrators have their offices here—Shawke, Freehouse, Holston, Donnelly, Stevis. Siegmund carries the Chicago cube and his draft of Shawke's reply, loaded with quotes and data supplied by Charles Mattern and Jason Quevedo. He pauses in the hallway. So peaceful here, so opulent; no littles barging past you, no crowds of working folk. Someday mine. He sees a vision of a sumptuous suite on one of Louisville's residential levels, three or even four rooms, Mamelon reigning like a queen over it all; Kipling Freehouse and Monroe Stevis dropping by with their wives for dinner; an occasional awed visitor coming up from Chicago or Shanghai, an old friend; power and comfort, responsibility and luxury. Yes.

"Siegmund?" A voice from an overhead speaker. "In here. We're in Kipling's place." Shawke's voice. They have picked him up on the scanners. Instantly he rearranges his face, knowing that it must have worn a vacuous, dreaming look. All business now. Angry with himself for forgetting that they might have been watching. He turns left and presents himself outside the office of Kipling Freehouse. The door slides back.

A grand, curving room lined with windows. The glittering face of Urbmon 117 revealed outside, tapering stunningly to its landing-stage summit. Siegmund is startled by the number of top-rank people gathered here. Their potent faces dazzle him. Kipling Freehouse, the head of the data-projection secretariat, a big plump-cheeked man with shaggy eyebrows. Nissim Shawke. The suave, frosty Lewis Holston, dressed as always in incandescently elegant costume. Wry little Monroe Stevis. Donnelly. Kinsella. Vaughan. A sea of greatness. Everyone who counts is here, except only a few; a flippo with a psych-bomb, loose in this room, could cripple the urbmon's government. What terrible crisis has brought them together like this? Frozen in awe, Siegmund can barely manage to step forward. A cherub among the archangels. Stumbling into the making of history. Perhaps they want him here, as if unwilling to take whatever step it is that they're considering without a representative of the coming generation of leaders to give his approval. Siegmund is dizzingly flattered by his own inter- pretation. I will be part of it. Whatever it is. His self- importance expands and the glare of their aura diminishes, and he moves in something close to a swagger as he approaches them. Then he realizes that there are some others present who might not be thought to belong at any high-powered policy session. Rhea Freehouse? Paolo, her indolent hus- band? And these girls, no more than fifteen or sixteen, in gossamerwebs or even less: mistresses of the great ones, handmaidens. Everyone knows that Louisville administrators keep extra girls. But here? Now? Giggling on the brink of history? Nissim Shawke salutes Siegmund without rising and says, "Join the party. You name the groover, we've probably got some. Tingle, mindblot, millispans, multiplexers, anything."

Party? Party?

"I've got the sex-ratio report here. Historical data—the sociocomputator—"

"Crot that, Siegmund. Don't spoil the fun."

Fun?

Rhea comes toward him. Lurching, blurred, obviously grooving. Yet her keen intelligence showing through the haze of druggedness. "You forgot what I told you. Loosen up, Siegmund." Whispering. Kisses the tip of his nose. Takes his report from him, puts it on Freehouse's desk. Draws her hands across his cheeks; fingers wet. Wouldn't be surprised if she's leaving stains on me. Wine. Blood. Anything. Rhea says, "Happy Somatic Fulfillment Day. We're celebrating. You can have me, if you like, or one of the girls, or Paolo, or anybody else you want." She giggles. "My father, too. Have you ever dreamed of topping Nissim Shawke? Just don't be a spoiler."

"I came up here because I had to give an important document to your father and—"

"Oh, shove it up the access nexus," Rhea says, and turns away from him, her disgust unhidden.

Somatic Fulfillment Day. He had forgotten. The festival will start in a few hours; he should be with Mamelon. But he is here. Shall he leave? They are looking at him. A place to hide. Sink into the undulating psychosensitive carpet. Don't spoil the fun. His mind is still full of the business of the morning. *Whereas the random, or purely biological, determination of the sex of unborn infants normally results by expectable statistical distribution in a relatively symmetrical division of. Removal of the element of chance introduces the danger that. It was the experience of the former city of Tokyo, between 1987 and 1996, that the incidence of birth of female offspring declined by a factor of almost. Risks are not counterbalanced by. Therefore it is recommended that.* The party, he sees, looking more closely, is essentially an orgy. He has been to orgies before, but not with people of this level. Fumes rising. The nakedness of Monroe Stevis. A huddled heap of fleshy girls. "Come on," Kipling Freehouse bellows, "enjoy yourself, Siegmund! Pick a girl, any girl!" Laughter. A wanton child pushes a capsule into his hand. He is trembling, and it drops. Seized and gobbled by one of the other girls. People are still coming in. Dignified, elegant Lewis Holston has a girl on each knee. And one kneeling before him. "Nothing, Siegmund?" Nissim Shawke asks. "You won't have a *thing*? Poor Siegmund. If you're going to live in Louisville, you've got to know how to play as well as work."

Judging him. Testing his compatibility: will he fit in with the elite, or must he be relegated to the ranks of the drudges, the middle-level bureaucracy? Siegmund sees himself demoted to Rome. His ambitions take over. If knowing how to play is the criterion for admission, he'll play. Grins. "I'd like some tingle," he says. Stick to what you know you can handle.

"Tingle, coming up!"

He makes the effort. A golden-hair nymph offers him the tingle bowl; he gulps, pinches her, gulps again. The sparkling fluid popping in his throat. A third gulp. Swill it down; you aren't paying! They cheer him. Rhea nods approval. Clothes are coming off around the room. The amusements of the masters. There must be fifty people in here now. A clap on the back. Kipling Freehouse. Shouting, deafeningly hearty: "You're all right, boy! Worried about you, you know! So serious, so dedicated! Not bad virtues to have, eh, but there's got to be more, you follow? A playful spirit. Eh? Eh?"

"Yes, sir. I know what you mean, sir."

Siegmund dives into the heap. Breasts, thighs, buttocks, tongues. Musky womansmells. A fountain of sensation. Someone pops something into his mouth. He swallows, and moments later feels the back of his skull lift. Laughter. He is being kissed. Forced down against the carpet by his assailant. Gropes and feels small hard breasts. Rhea? Yes. And her husband Paolo closing in on the other side of him. Music blaring from above. In the tangle he discovers himself sharing a girl with Nissim Shawke. A cold wink from him; an icy grin. Shawke testing his capacity for pleasure. Everyone watching him, seeing he's decadent enough to deserve promotion to their midst. Let yourself go! Let everything go!

Urgently he compels himself to revel. Much depends on this. Below him 974 wondrous floors of urbmon and if he wants to stay up here he must know how to play. Disillusioned that the administrators are like this. So common, so vulgar, the cheap hedonism of a ruling class. They could be Florentine dukes, Parisian grandees, Borgias, drunken boyars. Unable to accept this image of them, Siegmund constructs a

fantasy: they have staged this revel solely to test his character, to determine whether he is indeed merely a dreary
drudge or if he has the breadth of spirit a Louisville man
needs. Folly to think they spend their priceless time swilling
and topping like this; but they are flexible, they can enjoy
life, they turn from work to play with equal gusto. And if he
wants to live among them he must demonstrate equal many-
sidedness. He will. He will.

His furry brain swirls with conflicting chemical messages.
"Let's sing!" he yells desperately. "Everybody sing!"
Bellowing:

> *"If you come to me by the dark of night*
> *With your blessman all aglow*
> *And you slip down beside me*
> *And try to get inside me—"*

They sing with him. He cannot hear his own voice. Dark
eyes peer into his. "God bless," a long rippling lass murmurs.
"You're cute. The famous Siegmund Kluver." She belches
tingle-bubbles.

"We've met before, haven't we?"

"Once, I think, in Nissim's office. Scylla Shawke."

The great man's wife. Startling in her beauty. Young.
Young. No more than twenty-five. He had heard a rumor that
the first Mrs. Shawke, Rhea's mother, went down the chute,
flippo. Someday he must check on the truth of that. Scylla
Shawke wriggles close to him. Her soft black hair dangling in
his face. He is almost paralyzed with fear. The consequences;
can this be going too far? Recklessly he grabs her and plunges
his hand into her tunic. She cooperates. Full warm breasts.
Soft moist lips. Can he fail this test by an excess of
shamelessness? Never mind. Never mind. Happy Somatic
Fulfillment Day! Her body grinds against his, and he realizes, in shock, that it would be no problem to top her right
now, here, in this heaving mass of high-level humanity on the
floor of Kipling Freehouse's sprawling office. Too far, too fast.
He slides free of her grasp. Catching the single flicker of
disappointment and reproach in her eyes at his withdrawal.
Rolls over: Rhea. "Why didn't you?" she whispers. And
Siegmund says, "I couldn't," just before another girl, strad-
dling him, kneels and pours something sweet and sticky into
his mouth. He whirls within his skull. "It was a mistake,"

Rhea tells him. "She was being set up for you." Her words fracture and the pieces rebound, soaring high and drifting about the room. Something strange has happened to the lights; everything has become prismatic, and from all plane surfaces an eerie radiance is streaming. Siegmund crawls through the tumult, searching for Scylla Shawke. Instead he finds Nissim.

"I'd like to discuss the business of the Chicago sex-ratio petition with you now," the administrator tells him.

When Siegmund returns to his apartment hours later, he finds Mamelon pacing grimly about. "Where have you been?" she demands. "Somatic Fulfillment Day's almost over. I've called the access nexus, I've had tracers all over the building, I've—"

"I was in Louisville," Siegmund says. "Kipling Freehouse had a party." Stumbles past her. Drops face-down on the sleeping platform. First come the dry sobs, then the tears, and by the time they stop flowing Somatic Fulfillment Day might just as well be over.

Six

Interface Crew Nine works in a flat, high strip of gloomy space stretching along the outside of the service core of Urban Monad 116 from the 700th to the 730th floors. Though the work area is lofty, it is scarcely more than five meters deep, a skimpy envelope through which dust motes dance toward sucking filters. Standing within it, the ten men of Interface Crew Nine are sandwiched between the urbmon's outlayer of residential and commercial sectors and its hidden heart, the service core, in which the computers are housed.

The crewmen rarely enter the core itself. They function on its periphery, keeping watch over the looming wall that bears the access nodes of the building's master computer nexus. Soft green and yellow lights gleam on the nodes, constantly relaying information about the health of the unseen mechanisms. The men of Interface Crew Nine serve as the ultimate backup for the platoons of self-regulating devices that monitor the workings of the computers. Whenever heavy load causes some facet of the control system to sag, the crewmen quickly prime it so that it can go on bearing its burden. It is not difficult work, but it is vital to the life of the entire gigantic building.

Each day at 1230, when their shift-time begins, Michael Statler and his nine crewmates crawl through the Edinburgh irishatch on 700 and make their way into the perpetual dusk of the interface to take up their primer stations. Pushchairs carry them to their assigned levels—Michael starts by monitoring the nodes spanning floors 709 to 712—and as the day progresses they slide up and down the interface to the changing zones of trouble.

Michael is twenty-three years old. He has been a computer-primer in this interface crew for eleven years. By now the work is purely automatic for him; he has become simply an extension of the machinery. Drifting along the interface, he boosts or drains, shunts or couples, blends or splits, meeting every need of the computer he serves, and does it all in cool mindless efficiency, operating on reflex alone. There is nothing reprehensible about this. It is not desirable for a primer to think, merely to act correctly; even here in the fifth century of computer technology the human brain is still given a high rating for its information-handling capacity per cubic centimeter, and a properly trained interface crew is in effect a group of ten of these excellent little organically grown computers jacked into the main unit. So Michael follows the shifting patterns of lights, making all necessary adjustments, and the cerebral centers of his mind are left free for other things.

He dreams a great deal as he works.

He dreams of all the strange places outside Urban Monad 116, places that he has seen on the screen. He and his wife Stacion are devoted screen-viewers, and they rarely miss one of the travelog shows. The portrayals of the old pre-urbmon world, of the relicts, the dusty remnants. Jerusalem. Istanbul. Rome. The Taj Mahal. The stumps of New York. The tips of London's buildings above the waves. All the bizarre, romantic, alien places beyond the urbmon's skin. Mount Vesuvius. The geysers of Yellowstone. The African plains. The isles of the South Pacific. The Sahara. The North Pole. Vienna. Copenhagen. Moscow. Angkor Wat. The Great Pyramid and the Sphinx. The Grand Canyon. Chichén Itzá. The Amazon jungle. The Great Wall of China.

Do any of these places still exist?

Michael has no idea. A lot of what they show on the screen is a hundred years old or older. He knows that the spread of urbmon civilization has required the demolition of much that is ancient. The wiping away of the cultured past. Everything carefully recorded in three dimensions first, of course. But gone. A puff of white smoke; the smell of pulverized stone, dry on the nostrils, bitter. Gone. Doubtless they've saved the famous monuments. No need to chew up the Pyramids just to make room for more urbmons. But the big sprawls must have been cleaned away. The former cities. After all, here we are in the Chipitts constellation, and he has heard his brother-in-law Jason Quevedo, the historian, say that once there were two cities called Chicago and Pittsburgh that marked the polar ends of the constellation, with a continuous strip of urban settlement between them. Where are Chicago and Pittsburgh now? Not a trace left, Michael knows; the fifty-one towers of the Chipitts constellation rise along that strip. Everything neat and well-organized. We eat our past and excrete urbmons. Poor Jason; he must miss the ancient world. As do I. As do I.

Michael dreams of adventure outside Urban Monad 116.

Why not go outside? Must he spend all his remaining years hanging here in a pushchair on the interface, tickling access nodes? To go out. To breathe the strange unfiltered air with the smell of green plants on it. To see a river. To fly, somehow, around this barbered planet, looking for the shaggy places. Climb the Great Pyramid! Swim in an ocean, any ocean! *Salt water. How curious*. Stand under the naked sky, exposing his skin to the dread solar blaze, letting the chilly moonlight bathe him. The orange glow of Mars. At dawn to blink at Venus.

"Look, I could do it," he tells his wife. Placid bulgy Stacion. Carrying their fifth little, a girl, coming a few months hence. "It wouldn't be any trouble at all to reprime a node so it would give me an egress pass. And down the shaft and out the building before anybody's the wiser. Running in the grass. Traveling cross-country. I'd go east, I'd go to New York, right by the edge of the sea. They didn't tear New York down, Jason says so. They just went right around it. A monument to the troubles."

"How would you get food?" Stacion asks. A practical girl.

"I'd live off the land. Wild seeds and nuts, like the Indians did. Hunt! The herds of bison. Big, slow brown things; I'd come up behind one and jump on its back, right up there on the smelly greasy hump, and my hands into its throat, *yank*! It wouldn't understand. No one hunts any more. Fall down dead, and I'd have meat for weeks. Even eat it raw."

"There aren't any bison, Michael. There aren't any wild animals at all. You know that."

"Wasn't serious. Do you think I'd really kill? *Kill?* God bless, I may be peculiar, but I'm not crazy! No. Listen, I'd raid the communes. Sneak in at night, grab off vegetables, a load of proteoid steak, anything that's loose. Those places aren't guarded. They don't *expect* urbmon folk to come sneaking around. I'd eat. And I'd see New York, Stacion, I'd see New York! Maybe even find a whole society of wild men there. With boats, planes, something to take me across the ocean. To Jerusalem! To London! To Africa!"

Stacion laughs. "I love you when you start going flippo like this," she says, and pulls him down next to her. Rests his throbbing head on the smooth taut curve of her gravidity. "Do you hear the little yet?" Stacion asks. "Is she singing in there? God bless, Michael, how I love you."

She doesn't take him seriously. Who would? But he'll go. Hanging there on the interface, flipping switches and palming shunt-plates, he envisions himself as a world traveler. A project: to visit all the real cities for which the cities of Urbmon 116 were named. As many as are left. Warsaw, Reykjavik, Louisville, Colombo, Boston, Rome, Tokyo, Toledo, Paris, Shanghai, Edinburgh, Nairobi. London. Madrid. San Francisco. Birmingham. Leningrad. Vienna, Seattle, Bombay, Prague. Even Chicago and Pittsburgh, unless they really are gone. And the others. Did I name them all? He tries to count up. Warsaw, Reykjavik, Vienna, Colombo. He loses track. But anyway, I'll go out. Even if I can't cover the world. Maybe it's bigger than I imagine it is. But I'll see something. I'll feel rain on my face. Listen to the surf. My toes wriggling in cold wet sand. And the sun! The sun, the sun! Tanning my skin!

Supposedly, scholars still travel around, visiting the ancient places, but Michael doesn't know of anyone who has. Jason, though he specializes in the twentieth century, certainly hasn't gone. He could visit the ruins of New York, couldn't he? Get a more vivid feel of what it was like. Of course, Jason

is Jason, he wouldn't go even if he could. But he ought to. I'd
go in his place. Were we meant to spend all our lives inside a
single building? He has seen some of Jason's cubes of the old
days, the open streets, the moving cars, the little buildings
housing only a single family, three or four people. Incredibly
strange. Irresistibly fascinating. Of course, it didn't work; the
whole scrambled society fell apart. We have to have something
that's better organized. But Michael understands the pull of
that kind of life. He feels the centrifugal yank toward freedom,
and wants to taste a bit of it. We don't have to live the way
they did, but we don't have to live this way, either. Not all
the time. To go out. To experience horizontality. Instead of up
and down. Our thousand floors, our Somatic Fulfillment Halls,
our sonic centers, our blessmen, our moral engineers, our
consolers, our everything. There must be more. A short visit
outside: the supreme sensation of my life. I'll do it. Hanging
on the interface, serenely nudging his nodes downspectrum
as the priming impulses impinge on his reflexes, he promises
himself that he won't die with his dream unfulfilled. He'll
go out. Someday.

His brother-in-law Jason has unknowingly fed the fires of
Michael's secret yearning. His theories about a special race of
urbmon people, expressed one night when Michael and
Stacion were visiting the Quevedos. What had Jason said? *I'm
investigating the notion that urbmon life is breeding a new
kind of human being. A type that adapts readily to relatively
little living space and a low privacy quotient.* Michael had
had his doubts about that. It didn't seem like so much of a
genetic thing to him, that people were cooping themselves
up in urban monads. More like psychological conditioning.
Or even voluntary acceptance of the situation in general.
But the more Jason spoke, the more sense his ideas made.
Explaining why we don't go outside the urbmons, even
though there's no real reason why we can't. *Because we
recognize that that's a hopeless fantasy. We stay here, whether we like it or not. And those who don't like it, those who
eventually can't take it—well, you know what happens to
them.* Michael knows. *Down the chute for the flippos. Those
who remain adapt to circumstances. Two centuries of selective breeding, pretty ruthlessly enforced. And all of us so well
adapted now to this kind of life.*

And Michael saying, *Ah, yes. All of us so well adapted*. Not believing it was true about all of us.

With some exceptions. Jasons' mild concession.

Michael thinks about that, hanging on the interface. No doubt selective breeding accounts for a lot of it. The universal acceptance of urbmon life. Almost universal. Everybody takes it for granted that this is what life is like, 885,000 people under the same roof, a thousand floors, have lots of littles, cuddle up close. Everybody accepts. With some exceptions. A few of us who look through the windows, out at the naked world, and rage and sweat inside our guts. Wanting to get out there. Are we missing the gene for acceptance?

If Jason is right, if the urbmon population's been bred to enjoy the life it has to lead, then there must be a few recessives in the stack. Laws of genetics. You can't eradicate a gene. You just bury it somewhere, but it pops up to haunt you eight generations along the track. Me. In me. I carry the filthy thing. And so I suffer.

Michael decides to confer with his sister about these matters.

He goes to her one morning, 1100 hours, when he's fairly sure of finding her at home. She is, busy with the littles. His luscious twin, only looking a bit harried just now. Her dark hair askew. Her only garment a dirty towel slung over her shoulder. A smudge on her cheek. Looking around, suspicious, as he enters. "Oh. You." She smiles at him. How lovely she looks, all lean and flat like that. Stacion's breasts are full of milk; they swing and joggle, big juicy bags. He prefers supple women. "Just visiting," he tells Micaela. "Mind if I stay awhile?"

"God bless, whatever you like. Don't mind me. The littles are running me up the wall."

"Can I help you?" But she shakes him no. He sits crosslegged, watching her run around the room. Pop this one under the cleanser, that one into the maintenance slot. The others off at school, thank god. Her legs long and lean, her buttocks tight, unpuckered by excess flesh. He is half tempted to top her, right now, only she's too tense from her morning chores. Somehow he hasn't ever done it, at least not in years and years. Not since they were children. He put it into her then, sure, everybody topped his sister. Especially that they were twins; it was natural to get together. A very special closeness, like having an extra self, only female. Asking each other things. She touching him, when they were maybe nine. "What does it feel like, having all that growing between your legs? Dangling. Don't they get in your way when you walk?" And he trying to explain. Later, when she grew her breasts, he asked her the same sort of question. Actually she developed ahead of him. Hair on hers long before he had any on his. And she was bleeding early. That was a kind of gulf between them for a while, she adult, he still a child, and them womb-fellows despite it all. Michael smiles. "If I ask you some things," he says, "will you promise not to tell anyone? Even Jason?"

"Have I ever been a blabber?"

"All right. Just making sure."

She finishes with the littles and sinks down, exhausted, facing him. Lets the towel drape itself on her thighs. Chastely. He wonders what she would think if he asked her to. Oh, yes, she'd do it, she'd have to, but would she want to? Or be uncomfortable about opening it for her brother. She wasn't, once. But that was long ago.

He says, "Have you ever wanted to leave the urbmon, Micaela?"

"To go to another one, you mean?"

"Just to go out. To the Grand Canyon. The Pyramids. Outside. Do you ever feel restless inside the building?"

Her dark eyes glitter. "God bless, yes! Restless. I never thought much about the Pyramids, but there are days when I feel the walls on me like a bunch of hands. Pressing in."

"You too, then!"

"What are you talking about, Michael?"

"Jason's theory. People who've been bred generation after generation to tolerate urbmon existence. And I was thinking, some of us aren't like that. We're recessives. The wrong genes."

"Throwbacks."

"Throwbacks, yes! Like we're out of place in time. We shouldn't have been born now. But when people were free to move around. I know I feel that way. Micaela, I want to leave the building. Just roam around outside."

"You aren't serious."

"I think I am. Not that I'll necessarily do it. But I want to. And that means I'm a, well, a throwback. I don't fit into Jason's peaceful population. The way Stacion does. She loves it here. An ideal world. But not me. And if it's a genetic thing, if I'm really not fit for this civilization, you ought to be the same way. You having all my genes and me all yours. So I thought I'd check. To understand myself better. Finding out how well adjusted *you* are."

"I'm not."

"I knew it!"

"Not that I want to leave the building," Micaela says. "But other things. Emotional attitudes. Jealousy, ambition. I have a lot of unblessworthy stuff in my head, Michael. So does Jason. We had a fight over it only last week." She chuckles. "And we decided that we *were* throwbacks, the two of us. Like savages out of ancient times. I don't want to go into all the details, but yes, yes, basically I think you're right, you and I aren't really urbmon people inside. It's just a veneer. We pretend."

"Exactly! A veneer!" Michael slaps his hands together. "All right. It's what I wanted to know."

"You won't go out of the building, will you?"

"If I do, it'll just be a short while. To see what it's like. But forget I said it." He detects distress in her eyes. Going to her, pulling her up into his arms, he says, "Don't mess me up, Micaela. If I do it, it'll be because I *have* to. You know me. You understand that. So keep quiet until I'm back. If I go."

He has no doubts at all now, except about some of the peripheral problems, like saying good-bye. Shall he slip out without saying a word to Stacion? He'd better; she'd never understand, and she might cause complications. And Micaela. He is tempted to visit her just before he goes. A special farewell. There's no one he's closer to in the entire building, and he might just not return from his outbuilding jaunt. He thinks he'd like to top her, and he suspects she wants him. A loving farewell, just in case. But can he risk it? He mustn't place too much faith in this genetic thing; if she finds out that he's actually planning to leave the urbmon, she might just have him picked up and sent to the moral engineers. For his own sake. No doubt she considers his project a flippo idea. Weighing everything, Michael decides not to say anything to her. He will top her in his mind. Her lips to his, her tongue busy, his hands stroking her springy firmness. The thrust. Their bodies moving in perfect coordination. We are only the sundered halves of a single entity, now joined once more. For this brief moment. It becomes so vivid in his imagination that he nearly abandons his resolution. Nearly.

But in the end he goes without telling anyone.

Done rather easily. He knows how to make the great machine serve his needs. On his regular shift that day he stays a little wider awake than usual, dreams a little less. Monitoring his nodes, riding again on all the fugitive impulses floating through the giant building's mighty ganglia: food requisitions, birth and death statisitics, atmospheric reports, a sonic center's amplification level, the replenishment of groovers in the mechanical dispensers, the urine-recycling figures, communications links, et cetera cetera cetera. And as he makes his adjustments he casually fingers a node and obtains a plug-in to the data reservoir. Now he is in direct contact with the central brain, the big machine. It flashes him a string of brassy spurts of golden light: telling him that it is ready to accept repriming. Very well. He instructs it to issue one egress pass for Michael Statler of apartment 70411, obtainable by the said Statler on demand at any terminal and valid until used. Seeing the possibilities for cowardice in that, he amends the order immediately: valid only for twelve hours after issuance. Plus ingress privileges whenever requested. The node flashes him an acceptance symbol. Good. Now he records two messages, noting them down for delivery fifteen hours after the issuance of the egress pass. To Mrs. Micaela Quevedo, apartment 76124. Dear Sister, I did it, wish me luck. I'll bring you some sand from the seashore. And the other message to Mrs. Stacion Statler, apartment 70411. Explaining briefly where he has gone and why. Telling her he'll be back soon, not to worry, this is something he has to do. So much for farewells.

He finishes his shift. Now it is 1730. It makes no sense to leave the building with night coming on. He returns to Stacion; they have dinner, he plays with the littles, they watch the screen awhile, they make love. Maybe the last time. She says, "You seem very withdrawn tonight, Michael."

"Tired. A lot of shunting on the wall today."

She dozes. He cuddles her in his arms. Soft and warm and big, getting bigger every second. The cells dividing in her belly, the magical mitosis. God bless! He is almost unable to bear the idea of going away from her. But then the screen blazes with images of lands afar. The isle of Capri at sunset, gray sky, gray sea, horizon meeting the zenith, roads winding along a cliff overgrown with lush greenery. Here the villa of the Emperor Tiberius. Farmers and shepherds here, living as they did ten thousand years ago. untouched by the changes in the mainland world. No urbmons here. Lovers rolling in the grass, if they want. Pull up her skirt. Laughter; the thorns of berry-laden vines scratching the pink acreage of her buttocks as she pumps beneath you, but she doesn't mind. Hearty hot-slotted peasant wench. An example of obsolete barbarism. You and she get dirty together, soil between your toes and ground into the skin of your knees. And look here, these men in ragged grimy clothes, they're passing a flask of golden wine around, right in the fields where the grapes are grown. How dark their skins are! Like leather, if that's what leather really looked like—how can you be sure? Brown, tough. Tanned by the authentic sun. Far below, the waves roll gently in. Grottoes and fantastic sculptured rocks by the edge of the sea. The sun is gone behind the clouds, and the grayness of sky and shore deepens. A fine mist of rain comes. Night. Birds singing their hymns to the coming of darkness. Goats settling down. He walks the leafy paths, avoiding the hot shining turds, pausing to touch the rough bark of this tree, to taste the sweetness of this swollen berry. He can almost smell the salt spray from below. Sees himself running along the beach at dawn with Micaela, both of them naked, the nightfog lifting, the first crimson light splashing their pale skins. The water all golden. They leap in, swim, float, the salty water giving them buoyancy. They dive and paddle underwater, eyes open, studying each other. Her hair streaming out behind her. A trail of bubbles pursuing her kicking feet. He catches up with her and they embrace far from shore. Friendly dolphins watching them. They engender an incestuous little while coupling in the famous Mediterranean. Where Apolla nailed his sister, didn't he? Or was that another god. Classical echoes all around. Textures, tastes, the chilly bite of the dawn breeze as they drag themselves up on shore, the sand sticking to their wet skins, a bit of seaweed tangled in her hair. A boy with a baby goat coming toward them. *Vino? Vino?* Holding out a flask. Smiling. Micaela petting the goat. The boy admiring her slender naked body. *Si*, you say, *vino*, but of course you have no money, and you try to explain, but the boy doesn't care about that. He gives you the flask. You drink deep. Cold wine, alive, tingling. The boy looks at Micaela. *Un bacio?* Why not, you think. No harm in it. *Si, si, un bacio*, you say, and the boy goes to Micaela, puts his lips shyly to hers, reaches up as though to touch her breasts, then does not dare to, and just kisses. And pulls away, grinning, and goes to you and kisses you too, quickly, and then runs, he and his goat, madly down the beach, leaving you with the flask of wine. You pass it to Micaela. The wine dribbling past her chin, leaving bright beads in the brightening sunlight. When the wine is gone you hurl the flask far out to sea. A gift for the mermaids. You take Micaela's hand. Up the cliff, through the brambles, pebbles turning beneath your bare feet. Textures, changes of temperature, scents, sounds. Birds. Laughter. The glorious isle of Capri. The boy with the goat is just ahead, waving to you from beyond a ravine, telling you to hurry, hurry, come and see. The screen goes dark. You are lying on the sleeping platform beside your drowsy pregnant wife on the 704th floor of Urban Monad 116.

He must leave. He *must* leave.

He gets up. Stacion stirs. "Shh," he says. "Sleep."

"Going nightwalking?"

"I think so," he says. Strips, stands under the cleanser. Then puts on a fresh tunic, sandals, his most durable clothes. What else shall he take? He has nothing. He will go like this.

Kisses Stacion. *Un bacio. Ancora un bacio.* The last one, perhaps. Hand resting lightly on her belly a moment. She'll get his message in the morning. Good-bye, good-bye. To the sleeping littles. He goes out. Looks upward as if seeing through the intervening fifty-odd floors. Good-bye, Micaela. Love. It is 0230 hours. Still long before dawn. He will move slowly. Pausing, he studies the walls about him, the metallic-looking dark plastic with the warmth of burnished bronze. A sturdy building, well-designed. Rivers of unseen cables snaking through the service core. And that huge watchful man-made mind in the middle of everything. So easily deceived. Michael finds a terminal in the corridor and identifies himself. Michael Statler, 70411. One egress pass, please. Of course, sir. Here you are. From the slot a gleaming blue circlet for his wrist. Slips it on. Takes the dropshaft down. Gets off at 580 for no particular reason. Boston. Well, he has time to kill. Like a visitor from Venus he wanders the hall, occasionally meeting a sleepy nightwalker on his way home. As is his privilege, he opens a few doors, peers in at the people within, some awake, most not. A girl invites him to share her platform. He shakes his head. "Just passing through," he says, and goes to the dropshaft. Down to 375. San Francisco. The artists live here. He can hear music. Michael has always envied the San Franciscans. They have purpose in life. They have their art. He opens doors here too.

"Come on," he wants to say, "I have an egress pass, I'm going outside! Come with me, all of you!" Sculptors, poets, musicians, dramatists. He will be the pied piper. But he is not sure his pass will get more than one out of the building, and he says nothing. Down, instead. Birmingham. Pittsburgh, where Jason toils to rescue the past, which is beyond rescue. Tokyo. Prague. Warsaw. Reykjavik. The whole vast building is sitting on his back now. A thousand floors, 885,000 people. A dozen littles are being born as he stands here. A dozen more are being conceived. Maybe someone is dying. And one man is escaping. Shall he say good-bye to the computer? Its tubes and coils, its liquid-filled guts, its tons of skeleton. A million eyes everywhere in the city. Eyes watching him, but it's all right, he has a pass.

First floor. All out.

This is so easy. But where is the exit? *This?* Just a tiny hatch. But he was expecting a grand lobby, onyx floors, alabaster pillars, bright lights, polished brass, a shining swinging glass door. Of course no one important ever uses this exit. High dignitaries travel by quickboat, arriving and departing at the landing stage on the thousandth floor. And the courier pods of farm produce from the communes enter the urbmon far below-ground. Perhaps years at a time go by between each traversal of the first-floor opening. Yet he will. How shall he do it? Holds his egress pass up, hoping there are scanners nearby. Yes. A red light blazes above the hatch. And it opens. And it opens. He goes forward, finding himself in a long, cool tunnel, poorly lit. The hatch door closing behind him. Yes, well, preventing contamination by outside air, he supposes. He waits, and a second door opens in front of him, creaking a little. Michael sees nothing beyond, only darkness, but he goes through the door, and feels steps, seven or eight of them, and descends them, coming unexpectedly to the last. Bump. And then the ground. Strangely spongy, strangely yielding. Earth. Soil. Dirt. He is outside.

He is outside.

* * *

He feels somewhat like the first man to walk on the moon. A faltering step, not knowing what to expect. So many unfamiliar sensations to absorb at once. The hatch closing behind him. On his own, then. But unafraid. I must concentrate on one thing at a time. The air, first. He pulls it deep into his throat. Yes, it has a different taste, sweeter, more alive, a natural taste; the air seems to expand as he breathes it, seeking out the folds and byways of his lungs. In a minute, though, he can no longer isolate the factors of novelty in it. It is simply air, neutral, familiar. As if he has breathed it all his life. Will it fill him with deadly bacteria? He comes from an aseptic, sealed environment, after all. Lying puffed and discolored on the ground in final agonies an hour from now, maybe. Or strange pollen borne by the breeze, sprouting in his nostrils. Choked by massing fungi. Forget the air. He looks up.

Dawn is still more than an hour away. The sky is blue-black; there are stars everywhere, and a crescent moon is high. From the windows of the urbmon he has seen the heavens, but never like this. Head back, legs flung wide, arms outstretched. Embracing the starlight. A billion icy lances striking his body. He is tempted to strip and lie naked in the night until he is starburned, moonburned. Smiling, he takes another ten steps away from the urbmon. Glancing back then. A pillar of salt. Three kilometers high. It hangs in the air like a toppling mass, terrifying him; he begins to count the floors, but the effort dizzies him and he gives up before the fiftieth. At this angle most of the building is invisible to him, rising so steeply over his head, yet what he sees is enough. Its bulk threatens to crush him. He moves away, into the gardened plaza. The frightening mass of a nearby urbmon looms in front of him, at a distance sufficient to give him a truer picture of its size. Jabbing the stars, almost. So much, so much! All those windows. And behind them 850,000 people, or more, whom he has never met. Littles, nightwalkers, computer-primers, consolers, wives, mothers, a whole world up there. Dead. Dead. He looks to his left. Another urbmon, shrouded in the mists of coming day. To his right. Another. He brings his gaze down, closer to earth. The garden. Formal pathways. This is grass. Kneels, breaks off a blade, feels instant remorse as he cradles the green shaft in his cupped hands. *Killer*. He puts the grass in his mouth; not much taste. He had thought it might be sweet. This is soil. Digs his fingertips in. Blackness under his nails. Draws a grooved row through a flower bed. Sniffs a yellow globe of petals. Looks up at a tree. Hand against the bark.

A robot gardener is moving through the plaza, pruning things, fertilizing things. It swings around on its heavy black base and peers at him. Interrogative. Michael holds up his wrist and lets the gardener scan his egress pass. It loses interest in him.

Now he is far from Urbmon 116. Again he turns and studies it, seeing its full height at last. Indistinguishable from 117 and 115. He shrugs and follows a path that takes him out of the line in which the row of urbmons is set. A pool: he crouches beside it, dipping his hand in. Then puts his face to its surface and drinks. Splashes the water gaily. Dawn has begun to stain the sky. The stars are gone, the moon is going. Hastily he strips. Slowly into the pool, hissing when the water reaches his loins. Swims carefully, putting his feet down now and then to feel the cold muddy floor, at last coming to a place where he no longer can touch bottom. Birds singing. This is the first morning of the world. Pale light slides across the silent sky. After a while he comes out of the water and stands dripping and naked by the edge of the pool, shivering a little, listening to the birds, watching the red disk of the sun climbing out of the east. Gradually he becomes aware that he is crying. The beauty of it. The solitude. He is alone at time's first dawn. To be naked is right; I am Adam. He touches his genitals. Looking off afar, he sees three urbmons glowing with pearly light, and wonders which is 116. Stacion in there, and Micaela. If only she was with me now. Both of us naked by this pool. And turning to her, and sinking myself into her. While the snake watches from the tree. He laughs. God bless! He is alone, and not frightened at all by it, no one within sight and he loves it, though he misses Micaela, Stacion, both, each. Trembling. Hard with desire. Dropping to the moist black earth beside the pool. Still crying a little, hot teardrops trickling down his face occasionally, and he watches the sky turn blue, and puts his hand on himself, and bites his lip, and summons his vision of the beach at Capri, the wine, the boy, the boat, the kisses, Micaela, the two of them bare at dawn, and he gasps as his seed spurts. Fertilizing the naked earth. Two hundred million unborn littles in that sticky puddle. He swims again; then he begins to walk once more, carrying his clothes over his arm, and after perhaps an hour he puts them on, fearing the kiss of the soaring sun on his tender indoor hide.

By noon, plazas and pools and formal gardens are far behind, and he has entered the outlying territory of one of the agricultural communes. The world is wide and flat here, and the distant urbmons are glossy brown spikes on the horizon, receding to east and west. There are no trees. No unruly wild vegetation at all, in fact, none of the chaotic tumble of greenery that was so appealing in that tour of Capri. Michael sees long aisles of low plants, separated by strips of bare dark soil, and here and there an entire tremendous field totally empty, as if awaiting seed. These must be the vegetable fields. He inspects the plants: thousands of something spherical and coiled, clutching itself to itself, and thousands of something vertical and grassy, with dangling tassels, and thousands of another kind, and another, and another. As he walks along the crops keep changing. Is this corn? Beans? Squash? Carrots? Wheat? He has no way of matching the product to its source. His childhood geography lessons have faded and run; all he can do is guess, and probably to guess badly. He breaks leaves from this and this and this. He tastes shoots and pods. Sandals in hand, he walks barefoot through the voluptuous turned-up clods of earth.

He thinks he is heading east. Going toward the place where the sun came from. But now that the sun is high overhead it is hard to determine directions. The dwindling row of urbmons is no help. How far is it to the sea? At the thought of a beach his eyes grown damp again. The heaving surf. The taste of salt. A thousand kilometers? How far is that? He works out an analogy. Lay an urbmon on end, then put another one at its tip, and another one beyond that. It will take 333 urbmons, end to end, to reach from here to the sea, if I am a thousand kilometers from the sea now. His heart sinks. And he has no real idea of distances. It might be ten thousand kilometers. He imagines what it would be like to walk from Reykjavik to Louisville 333 times, even horizontally. But with patience he can do it. If only he can find something to eat. These leaves, these stalks, these pods do him no good. Which part of the plant is edible, anyway? Must he cook it? How? This journey will be more complex than he imagined. But his alternative is to scurry back to the urbmon, and he will not do that. It would be like dying, never having lived. He goes on.

Tiring. A little lightheaded from hunger, since he's been on the trek six or seven hours now. Physical fatigue, too. This horizontal walking must use different muscles. Going up and down stairs is easy; riding dropshafts and liftshafts is easier still; and the short horizontal walks along the corridors have not prepared him for this. The ache in the backs of the thighs. The rawness in the ankles, as of bone grating against bone. The shoulders struggling to keep the head held high. Scrambling over this irregular earthy surface multiplies the problem. He rests awhile. Soon afterward he comes to a stream, a sort of ditch, cutting across the fields; he drinks, then strips and bathes. The cool water refreshes him. He goes on, stopping three times to sample the unripened crops. Suppose you get too far from the urbmon to get back, if you begin starving? Struggling through these fields as strength leaves you, trying to drag yourself across the kilometers toward the far-off tower. Dying of hunger amidst all this green plenty. No. He'll manage.

Being alone starts to upset him, too. Something of a surprise, that. In the urbmon he frequently was irritated by the sheer surging multiplicitous masses. Littles underfoot everywhere, clots of women in the halls, that kind of thing. Relishing, in a distinctly unblessworthy way, the daily hours on the interface, in the dimness, no one around him except his nine crewmates and they far away, minding their own nodes. For years cherishing this vision of escaping into privacy, his cruel retrogressive fantasy of solitude. Now he has it, and at the beginning he wept for sheer joy of it, but by afternoon it does not seem so charming. He finds himself darting little hopeful glances to the periphery of his sight, as if he might pick up the aura of a passing human being. Perhaps if Micaela had come with him it would be better. Adam, Eve. But of course she wouldn't have. Only his fraternal twin; not precisely the same genes; she's restless but she'd never have done anything as wild as this. He pictures her trudging beside him. Yes. Stopping now and then to top her in the green crops. But the aloneness is getting him.

He shouts. Calls his name, Micaela's, Stacion's. Cries out the names of his littles. "I am a citizen of Edinburgh!" he bellows. "Urban Monad 116! The 704th floor!" The sounds float away toward the fleecy clouds. How lovely the sky is now, blue and gold and white.

A sudden droning sound out of the—north?—growing louder moment by moment. Harsh, throbbing, raucous. Has he brought some monster upon himself by his noise? Shading his eyes. There it is: a long black tube soaring slowly toward him at a height of, oh, maybe a hundred meters at most. Throws himself to the ground, huddles between the rows of cabbages or turnips or whatever. The black thing has a dozen stubby nozzles protruding along its sides, and from each nozzle spurts a cloudy green mist. Michael understands. Spraying the crops, probably. A poison to kill insects and other pests. What will it to do me? He coils, knees to his chest, hands to his face, eyes closed, mouth buried in palm. That terrible roaring overhead; kill me with decibels if not with your filthy spray. The intensity of the sound diminishes. The thing is past him. The pesticide drifting down, he supposes, trying not to breathe. Lips clamped. Fiery petals dropping from heaven. Flowers of death. There it is, now, a faint dampness on his cheeks, a clinging moist veil. How soon will it kill him? He counts the passing minutes. Still alive. The flying thing no longer in earshot. Cautiously, he opens his eyes and stands up. Perhaps no danger, then; but he runs through the fields toward the glittering ribbon of a nearby creek, and plunges in, peeling in panic, to scrub himself. And only coming out realizes the creek must have been sprayed too. Well, not dead yet, anyway.

How far is it to the nearest commune?

Somehow, in their infinite wisdom, the planners of this farm have allowed one low hill to survive. Mounting it in midafternoon, Michael takes stock. There are the urbmons, curiously dwindled. There are the cultivated fields. He sees machines, now, moving in some of the rows, things with many arms, possibly pulling up weeds. No sign of a settlement, though. He descends the hill and shortly encounters one of the agricultural machines. The first company he's had all day. "Hello. Michael Statler, from Urbmon 116. What's you name, machine? What kind of work do you do?"

Baleful yellow eyes study him and turn away. The machine is loosening the soil at the base of each plant in the row. Squirting something milky over the roots. Unfriendly filther, aren't you? Or just not programed to talk. "I don't mind," he says. "Silence is golden. If you could just tell me where I could get a little to eat, though. Or find some people."

Droning sound again. Crot! Another stinking crop-sprayer! He gets down, ready to curl up again, but no, this flying thing is not spraying, nor does it go past. Hovering overhead, it swings into a tight circle, making an infernal holocaust of noise, and a hatch opens in its belly. Out drops a double strand of find golden fiber, reaching to the ground. Down it, riding a clip-pod, slides a human being, a woman, followed by a man. They land deftly and come toward him. Grim faces. Beady eyes. Weapons at their waists. Their only garments are glossy red wraps covering them from thigh to belly. Their skins are tanned; their bodies are lean. The man has a stiff, bushy black beard: incredible, grotesque facial hair! The woman's breasts are small and hard. Both of them drawing their weapons now. "Hello!" Michael calls hoarsely. "I'm from an urbmon! Just visiting your country. Friend! Friend! Friend!"

The woman says something unintelligible.

He shrugs. "Sorry, I don't under—"

The weapon poking in his ribs. How cold her face is! The eyes like icy buttons. Will they kill him? Now the man speaks. Slowly and clearly, very loud, as one would speak to a three-year-old. Every syllable an alien one. Accusing him of trespassing in the fields, probably. One of the farming machines must have reported him to the commune. Michael points; the urbmons can still be seen from here. Indicates them, taps his chest. For whatever good that will do. They must know where he's from. His captors nod, unsmiling. A frosty pair. Arrested. Intruder menacing the sanctity of the fields. Woman takes him by the elbow. Well, at least they aren't going to kill him outright. The devilish noisy flying thing still racketing overhead in its narrow orbit. They guide him toward the dangling fiber strands. The woman is in the clip-pod, now. Goes up. Then the man tells Michael something which he suspects means "Now you." Michael smiles. Cooperation his only hope. Figures out how to get into the clip-pod; the man makes the adjustments, locking him in, and up he goes. The woman, waiting above, depods him and pushes him into a webwork cradle. Keeps her weapon ready. A moment later the man is aboard too; the hatch closes and the flying machine goes roaring off. During the flight both of them interrogate him, hurling little jabbing bursts of words at him, but he can only reply apologetically, "I don't speak your language. How can I tell you what you want to know?"

Minutes later the machine lands. They jostle him out onto a bare reddish-brown field. Along its rim he sees low flat-roofed brick buildings, curious snub-fronted gray vehicles, several many-armed farming machines, and dozens of men and women wearing the glossy red loincloths. Not many children; perhaps they're at school, although it's getting late in the day. Everyone pointing at him. Speaking rapidly. Harsh unintelligible comments. Some laughter. He is frightened somewhat, not by the possibility that he is in peril so much as by the strangeness of everything. He knows this must be an agricultural commune. All this day's walking was prelude; he now has truly passed over from one world to another.

The man and woman who captured him push him across the bare field and through the crowd of farming folk into one of the buildings nearby. As he passes, the farmers finger his clothing, touch his bare arms and face, murmur softly. Wonderstruck. Like a man from Mars in their midst. The building is poorly lit, roughly constructed, with crooked walls, low ceilings, warped floors of some pale pocked plastic material. Dumped into a bare, dismal room. A sour smell pervading it: vomit? Before she leaves him, the woman points out the facilities with a few brusque gestures. From this he can get water; it is a basin of some white artificial substance with the texture of smooth stone, yellowing and cracked in places. There is no sleeping platform, but probably he is meant to use the heap of rumpled blankets against one wall. No sign of a cleanser. For excretion he has a single unit, nothing more than a kind of plastic funnel going into the floor, with a button to push when he wishes to clear it. Evidently it is for urine and feces both. An odd arrangement; but then he realizes they wouldn't need to recycle wastes here. The room has no source of artificial light. Through its one window there streams the last feeble sun of the afternoon. The window faces the plaza where the farmers still are gathered, discussing him; he sees them pointing, nodding, nudging each other. There are metal bars on the window, set too close together to permit a man to slip through. A prison cell, then. He checks the door. Locked. How friendly of them. He'll never reach the seacoast this way.

"Listen," he calls to those in the plaza, "I don't mean any harm! You don't need to lock me up!"

They laugh. Two young men stroll over and stare solemnly at him. One of them puts his hand to his mouth and painstakingly covers his entire palm with saliva; when this is done he offers the palm to his companion, who presses his hand against it, and both break into wild laughter. Michael watches, mystified. He has heard about the barbaric customs in the communes. Primitive, incomprehensible. The young men say something contemptuous-sounding to him and walk away. A girl takes their place by his window. Fifteen, sixteen years old, he guesses. Her breasts are large and deeply tanned, and between them hangs an explicit phallic amulet. She fondles it in what strikes him as lascivious invitation. "I'd love to," he says. "If you can only get me out of here." He puts his hands through the bars as if to caress her. She leaps back, wild-eyed, and makes a fierce gesture, jabbing her left hand at him with the thumb clenched under the other four fingers aimed at his face. Clearly an obscenity. As she goes, some older people come to stare. A woman taps her chin in slow, steady, apparently meaningful rhythm; a withered man soberly presses his left palm to his right elbow three times; another man stoops, puts his hands on the ground, and rises, lifting them far above his head, perhaps pantomiming the growth of a lofty plant, perhaps the construction of an urban monad. Whatever, he breaks into shrill laughter and stumbles off. Night is coming, now. Through the dusk Michael sees a succession of crop-spraying machines landing in the plaza like birds returning tó the nest at sundown, and dozens of many-legged mobile farming units come striding out of the fields. The onlookers vanish; he watches them going into the other buildings around the plaza. Despite the uncertainties of being a prisoner, he is captivated by the alien nature of this place. To live so close to the ground, to walk about all day long under the naked sun, to know nothing of an urbmon's crowded richness—

An armed girl brings him dinner, popping his door open, setting down a tray, leaving without a word. Stewed vegetables, a clear broth, some unfamiliar red fruits, and a capsule of cold wine: the fruits are bruised and, to his taste, overripe, but everything else is excellent. He eats greedily, cleaning the tray. Then he goes to the window. The center of the plaza is still empty, although at the far side eight or ten men, evidently a maintenance crew, have gone to work on the farming machines by the light of three floating luminous globes. His cell now is in complete darkness. Since there is nothing else to do, he removes his clothes and sprawls out on the blankets. Though he is exhausted by the long day's trek, sleep will not come at first: his mind ticks furiously, contemplating options. Doubtless they will interrogate him tomorrow. Someone around here must know the language of the urbmons. With luck he can demonstrate that he means no harm. Smile a lot, act friendly, an air of innocence. Perhaps even get them to escort him out of their territory. Fly him eastward, dump him in some other commune's land, let him make his way to the sea. Will he be arrested at commune after commune? A dreary prospect. Maybe he can find a route that bypasses the agricultural zone—through the ruins of some former cities, possibly. Unless there are wild men living there. At least the farmers are civilized, in their fashion. He envisions himself cooked by cannibals in some blasted rubbleheap, the former Pittsburgh, say. Or just eaten raw. Why are the farmers so suspicious? What can one lone wanderer do to them? The natural xenophobia of an isolated culture, he decides. Just as we wouldn't want a farmer loose in an urbmon. But of course urbmons are closed systems. Everybody numbered, inoculated, assigned to a proper place. These folk have a less rigid system, don't they? They don't need to fear strangers. Try convincing them of that.

He drifts into an uneasy sleep.

He is awakened, not more than an hour or two later, by discordant music, raw and disturbing. Sits up: red shadows flickering on the wall of his cell. Some kind of visual projections? Or a fire outside? Rushes to the window. Yes. An immense mound of dried stems, branches, vegetable debris of all sorts, is ablaze in the middle of the plaza. He has never seen fire before, except sometimes on the screen, and the sight of it terrifies and delights him. Those wavering bursts of redness rising and vanishing—where do they go? And he can feel the surging heat even from where he stands. The constant flux, the shifting shape of the dancing flames—how incredibly beautiful! And menacing. Aren't they afraid, letting fire loose like this? But of course there's that zone of bare dirt around it. Fire can't cross that. The earth doesn't burn.

He forces his eyes away from the hypnotic frenzy of the fire. A dozen musicians sit close together to the left of the blaze. The instruments weirdly medieval: everything operated by blowing or pounding or scraping or pressing keys, and the sounds are uneven and imprecise, flickering around the proper pitches but missing by a fraction of a tone. The human element; Michael, whose sense of pitch is unusually good, cringes at these tiny but perceptible variations from the absolute. Yet the farmers don't seem to mind. Unspoiled by the mechanical perfection of modern scientific music. Hundreds of them, perhaps the entire population of the village, sit in ragged rows along the perimeter of the plaza, nodding in time to the wailing, screeching melodies, pounding their heels against the ground, rhythmically clapping their hands to their elbows. The light of the fire transforms them into an assemblage of demons; the red glow ripples eerily over their half-nude bodies. He sees children among them, but still not very many. Two here, three there, many adult couples with one or none. Stunned by the realization: *they limit births here.* His skin crawls. He is amused by his own involuntary reaction of horror; it tells him that no matter what configuration his genes may have, he is by conditioning a man of the urbmons.

The music grows even wilder. The fire soars. The farmers begin to dance. Michael expects the dancing to be amorphous and frantic, a helter-skelter flinging-out of arms and legs, but no: surprisingly, it is tight and disciplined, a controlled and formal series of movements. Men in this row, women in that; forward, back, interchange partners, elbows high, head thrown back, knees pumping, now hop, turn around, form lines again, link hands. The pace constantly accelerating, but the rhythms always distinct and coherent. A ritualized progression of patterns. Eyes glazed, lips tight. This is no revel, he is suddenly aware; it is a religious festival. The rites of the commune people. What are they building toward? Is he the sacrificial lamb? Providence has sent them an urbmon man, eh? Panicky, he looks about for signs of a caldron, a spit, a stake, anything on which they might cook him. Tales of the communes circulate gaudily in the urbmon; he has always dismissed them as ignorant myths. But possibly not.

When they come for him, he decides, he will lunge and attack them. Better to be shot down quickly than to die on the village altar.

Yet half an hour passes, and no one has even looked in the direction of his cell. The dancing has continued without a break. Oiled with sweat, the farmers seem like dream figures, glittering, grotesque. Bare breasts bobbling; nostrils distended, eyes aglow. New boughs on the fire. The musicians goading one another into fresh frenzies. And now, what's this? Masked figures parading solemnly into the plaza: three men, three women. Faces hidden by intricate spherical constructions, nightmarish, bestial, garish. The women carry oval baskets in which can be seen products of the commune: seeds, dried ears of corn, ground meal. The men encircle a seventh person, a woman, two of them tugging at her arms and one pushing her from behind. She is pregnant, well along, into her sixth or even seventh month. She wears no mask, and her face is tense and rigid, the lips clamped, the eyes wide and frightened. They fling her down before the fire, and stand flanking her. She kneels, head drooping, long hair almost touching the ground, swollen breasts swaying with each ragged intake of breath. One of the masked men—it is impossible not to think of them as priests—intones a resonant invocation. One of the masked women places an ear of corn in each hand of the pregnant one. Another sprinkles her back with meal; it sticks to her sweaty skin. The third scatters seeds in her hair. The other two men join the chant. Michael, gripping the bars of his cell, feels as though he has been hurled thousands of years back in time, to some Neolithic festival; it is almost impossible for him to believe that one day's march from here there rises the thousand-story bulk of Urban Monad 116.

They have finished anointing the pregnant woman with produce. Now two of the priests lift her, shaking, to a standing position, and one of the priestesses rips away her single garment. A howl from the villagers. They spin her around. Displaying her nakedness to all. The heavy protruding belly, drum-tight, glistening in the firelight. The broad hips and solid thighs, the meaty buttocks. Sensing something sinister just ahead, Michael presses his face against the bars, fighting off terror. Is she and not he the sacrificial victim? A flashing knife, the unborn fetus ripped from the womb, a devilish propitiation of the harvest gods? Please, no. Maybe he is to be the chosen executioner. His feverish imagination, unbidden, supplies the scenario: he sees himself taken from the cell, thrust into the plaza, a sickle pushed into his hand, the woman lying spread-eagled near the fire, belly upturned, the priests chanting, the priestesses leaping, and in pantomime they tell him what he must do, they indicate the taut curve of her body, draw their fingers across the preferred place of incision, while the music climbs toward insanity and the fire flares ever higher, and. No. No. He turns away, flinging one arm over his eyes. Shivering, nauseated. When he can bring himself to look again, he sees that the villagers are getting up and dancing toward the fire, toward the pregnant woman. She stands flatfooted, bewildered, clutching the ears of corn, pressing her thighs together, wriggling her shoulders in a way that somehow indicates she is shamed by her nudity. And they caper around her. Shouting raucous abuse. Making the four-fingered jab of contempt. Pointing, mocking, accusing. A condemned witch? An adulteress? The woman shrinks into herself. Suddenly the mob closes in on her. He sees them slapping her, pushing her, spitting at her. God bless, no! "Let her alone!" he screams. "You filthy grubbos, get your hands off her!" His wails are drowned by the music. A dozen or so farmers now ring the woman and they are shoving her back and forth. A double-handed push; she staggers, barely managing to stay upright, and stumbles across the ring, only to be seized by her breasts and slammed back the other way. She is panting, wild with terror, searching for escape, but the ring is tight, and they fling her around. When at last she drops, they tug her upright and toss her some more, grabbing her arms and whirling her from hand to hand around the ring. Then the circle opens. Other villagers sweep toward her. More abuse. The blows all are open-handed ones, and no one seems to hit her belly, yet they are delivered with great force; a trickle of blood stains her chin and throat, and one knee and one buttock are scraped raw from when she has been knocked to the ground. She is limping, too; she must have turned an ankle. Vulnerable as she is in her nakedness, she makes no attempt to defend herself or even to protect her pregnancy. Clutching the ears of corn, she simply accepts her torment, letting herself be hurled about, allowing the vindictive hands to poke and pinch and slap her. The mob surges about her, everyone having a turn. How much more can she take? Is the idea to beat her to death? To make her drop her baby while they watch? He has never imagined anything so chilling. He feels the blows as if they are landing on his own body. If he could, he would strike these people dead with thunderbolts. Where is their respect for life? That woman should be sacred, and instead they torture her.

She vanishes under a horde of screaming attackers.

When they clear away, a minute or two later, she is kneeling, half-conscious, close to collapse. Her lips writhe in hysterical choking sobs. Her entire body is trembling. Her head hands forward. Someone's clawed hand has left a series of parallel bloody tracks across the globe of her right breast. She is smudged everywhere with dirt.

The music grows oddly soft, as if some climax is approaching and momentum must be gained. Now they come for me, Michael thinks. Now I'm supposed to kill her, or top her, or kick her in the belly, or god knows what. But no one even looks toward the building in which he is jailed. The three priests are chanting in unison; the music gains gradually in intensity; the villagers fall back, clustering along the perimeter of the plaza. And the woman rises, shakily, uncertainly. Looks down at her bloodied and battered self. Face wholly blank; she is beyond pain, beyond shame, beyond terror. Slowly walks toward the fire. Stumbles once. Recovers, stays upright. Now she stands by the edge of the fire, almost within reach of the licking tongues of flame. Her back to him. Plump heavy rump, deeply dimpled. Scratches on her back. Wide pelvis, the bone's spreading out as the little's time approaches. The music is deafening now. The priests silent, frozen. Obviously the great moment. Does she leap into the flames?

No. Raises her arms. The ears of corn outlined against the brightness of the fire. Throws them in: two quick flares and they vanish. An immense roar from the villagers, a tremendous crashing discord from the musicians. The naked woman stumbles away from the fire, tottering, exhausted. Falls, landing with a thump on her left haunch, lies there sobbing. Priests and priestesses march into the darkness with stiff, pompous strides. The villagers simply fade away, leaving only the woman crumpled in the plaza. And a man coming toward her, a tall, bearded figure; Michael remembers seeing him in the midst of the mob when they were beating her. Lifts her now. Cradles her tenderly against him. Kisses her scratched breast. Runs his hand lightly over her belly, as though assuring himself that the child is unharmed. She clings close. He talks softly to her; the strange words drift across to

Michael's cell. She replies, stammering, her voice thick with
shock. Unbothered by her weight, the man slowly carries her
away, toward one of the buildings on the opposite side of the
plaza. All is still, now. Only the fire remains, crackling
harshly, crumbling in upon itself. When after a long while no
one appears, Michael turns away from his window and,
stunned, baffled, throws himself on his blankets. Silence.
Darkness. Images of the bizarre ceremony churn in his mind.
He shivers; he trembles; he feels almost at the edge of tears.
Finally he sleeps.

The arrival of breakfast awakens him. He studies the tray a
few minutes before forcing himself to get up. Stiff and sore
from yesterday's walking; every muscle protesting. Doubled
up, he hobbles to the window: a heap of ashes where the fire
had been, villagers moving about on their morning chores,
the farming machines already heading toward the fields. He
splashes water in his face, voids his wastes, looks automatically for the cleanser, and, not finding it, begins to wonder how
he will tolerate the crust of grime that has accumulated on his
skin. He had not realized before how ingrained a habit it was
for him to get under the ultrasonic wave at the beginning of
each day. He goes then to the tray: juice, bread, cold fruit,
wine. It will do. Before he is finished eating, his cell door
opens and a woman enters, clad in the usual brief commune
costume. He knows instinctively that she is someone of
importance; her eyes have the clear cold light of authority,
and her expression is an intelligent, perceptive one. She is
perhaps thirty years old, and like most of these farming
women her body is lean and taut, with supple muscles, long
limbs, small breasts. She reminds him in some ways of
Micaela, although her hair is auburn and close-cropped, not
long and black. A weapon is strapped to her left thigh.

"Cover yourself," she says briskly. "I don't welcome the
sight of your nakedness. Cover yourself, and then we can
talk."

She speaks the urbmon tongue! A strange accent, true,
with every word cut short as if her sharp shining teeth have
clipped its tail as it passes her lips. The vowels blurred and
distorted. But unmistakably the language of his native building. Immense relief. Communication at last.

He pulls his clothing hastily on. She watches him, stony-
faced. A tough one, she is. He says, "In the urbmons we

don't worry much above covering our bodies. We live in what
we call a post-privacy culture. I didn't realize—"

"You don't happen to be in an urbmon just now."

"I realize that. I'm sorry if I've given offense through my
ignorance of your customs."

He is fully dressed. She seems to soften a bit, perhaps at
his apology, perhaps merely because he has concealed his
nudity. Taking a few steps farther into the room, she says,
"It's a long time since we've had a spy from your people
among us."

"I'm not a spy."

A cool, skeptical smile. "No? Then why are you here?"

"I didn't intend to trespass on your commune's land. I was
just passing through, heading eastward. On my way toward
the sea."

"Really?" As though he had said he had set out to walk to
Pluto. "Traveling alone, are you?"

"I am."

"When did this marvelous journey begin?"

"Yesterday morning, very early," Michael says. "I'm from
Urban Monad 116. A computer-primer, if that means anything to you. Suddenly I felt I couldn't stay inside that
building any more, that I had to find out what the outside
world was like, and so I arranged to get an egress pass and
slipped out just before dawn, and started walking, and then
I came to your fields and your machines saw me, I guess, and I
was picked up, and because of the language problem I couldn't
explain to anyone who I—"

"What do you hope to gain by spying on us?"

His shoulders slump. "I told you," he says wearily. "I'm
not a spy."

"Urbmon people don't slip out of their buildings. I've dealt
with your kind for years; I know how your minds work." Her
eyes level with his. Cold, cold. "You'd be paralyzed with
terror five minutes after you set out," she assures him.
"Obviously you've been trained for this mission, or you'd
never have been able to keep your sanity for a full day in the
fields. What I don't understand is why they'd send you. You
have your world and we have ours; there's no conflict, no
overlapping; there's no need for espionage."

"I agree," Michael says. "And that's why I'm not a spy." He
finds himself drawn to her despite the severity of her attitude. Her competence and self-confidence attract him. And if

she would only smile she would be quite beautiful. He says, "Look, how can I get you to believe this? I just wanted to see the world outside the urbmon. All my life indoors. Never smelling fresh air, never feeling the sun on my skin. Thousands of people living on top of me. I'm not really well adjusted to urbmon society, I discovered. So I went outside. Not a spy. All I want to do is travel. To the sea, particularly. Have you ever seen the sea? . . . No? That's my dream—to walk along the shore, to hear the waves rolling in, to feel the wet sand under my feet—"

Possibly the fervor in his tone is beginning to convince her. She shrugs, looks less flinty, and says, "What's your name?"

"Michael Statler."

"Age?"

"Twenty-three."

"We could put you aboard the next courier pod, with the fungus shipment. You'd be back at your urbmon in half an hour."

"No," he says softly. "Don't do that. Just let me keep going east. I'm not ready to go back so soon."

"Haven't gathered enough information, you mean?"

"I told you, I'm not—" He stops, realizing she is teasing him.

"All right. Maybe you aren't a spy. Just a madman, perhaps." She smiles, for the first time, and slides down until she is squatting against the wall, facing him. In an easy conversational tone she says, "What do you think of our village, Statler?"

"I don't even know where to begin answering that."

"How do we strike you? Simple? Complicated? Evil? Frightening? Unusual?"

"Strange," he says.

"Strange in comparison to the kind of people you've lived among, or just strange, absolutely?"

"I'm not sure I know the distinction. It's like another world out here, anyway. I—I—what's your name, by the way?"

"Artha."

"Arthur? Among us that's a man's name."

"A-R-T-H-A."

"Oh. Artha. How interesting. How beautiful." He knots his fingers tightly. "The way you live so close to the soil here, Artha. There's something dreamlike about that for me. These little houses. The plaza. Seeing you walking around in the

open. The sun. Building fires. Not having any upstairs or
downstairs. And that business last night, the music, the
pregnant woman. What was that all about?"

"You mean the unbirth dance?"

"Is *that* what it was? Some kind of"—he falters—"sterility
rite?"

"To ensure a good harvest," Artha says. "To keep the crops
healthy and childbirths low. We have rules about breeding,
you understand."

"And the woman everybody was hitting—she got pregnant
illegally, is that it?"

"Oh, no." Artha laughs. "Milcha's child is quite legal."

"Then why—tormenting her like that—she could have lost
the child—"

"Someone had to do it," Artha tells him. "The commune
has eleven pregnants, just now. They drew lots and Milcha
lost. Or won. It isn't punishment, Statler. It's a religious
thing: she's the celebrant, the holy scapegoat, the—the—I
don't have the words in your language. Through her suffering
she brings health and prosperity upon the commune. Ensuring
that no unwanted children will come into our women, that all
will remain in perfect balance. Of course, it's painful for her.
And there's the shame, being naked in front of everyone. But
it has to be done. It's a great honor. Milcha will never have to
do it again, and she'll have certain privileges for the rest of
her life, and of course everyone is grateful to her for accepting
our blows. Now we're protected for another year."

"Protected?"

"Against the anger of the gods."

"Gods," he says quietly. Swallowing the word and trying to
comprehend it. After a moment he asks, "Why do you try to
avoid having children?"

"Do you think we own the world?" she replies, her eyes
abruptly fiery. "We have our commune. Our alloted zone of
land. We must make food for ourselves and also for the
urbmons, right? What would happen to you if we simply bred
and bred and bred, until our village sprawled out over half of
the present fields, and such remaining food as we produced
was merely enough for our own needs? With nothing to spare
for you. Children must be housed. Houses occupy land. How
can we farm land covered by a house? We must set limits."

"But you don't need to sprawl your village out into the
fields. You could build upward. As we do. And increase your

numbers tenfold without taking up any more land area. Well, of course, you'd need more food and there'd be less to ship to us, that's true, but—"

"You absolutely don't understand," Artha snaps. "Should we turn our commune into an urbmon? You have your way of life; we have ours. Ours requires us to be few in number and live in the midst of fertile fields. Why should we become like you? We pride ourselves on *not* being like you. So if we expand, we must expand horizontally, right? Which would in time cover the surface of the world with a dead crust of paved streets and roads, as in the former days. No. We are beyond such things. We impose limits on ourselves, and live in the proper rhythm of our way, and we are happy. And so it shall be forever with us. Does this seem so wicked? We think the urbmon folk are wicked, for they will not control their breeding. And even *encourage* breeding."

"There's no need for us to control it," he tells her. "It's been mathematically proven that we haven't begun to exhaust the possibilities of the planet. Our population could double or even triple, and as long as we continued to live in vertical cities, in urban monads, there'd be room for everyone. Without encroaching on productive farmland. We build a new urbmon every few years, and even so the food supplies aren't diminishing, the rhythm of *our* way holds up, and—"

"Do you think this can continue infinitely?"

"Well, no, not infinitely," Michael concedes. "But for a long time. Five hundred years, maybe, at the present rate of increase, before we'd feel any squeeze."

"And then?"

"They can solve that problem when the time comes."

Artha shakes her head furiously. "No! No! How can you say such a thing? To go on breeding, letting the future worry about it—"

"Look," he says, "I've talked to my brother-in-law, who's a historian. Specializes in the twentieth century. Back then it was believed that everybody would starve if the world's population got past five or six billion. Much talk of a population crisis, etc., etc. Well, then came the collapse, and afterward things were reorganized, the first urbmons went up, the old horizontal pattern of land use was prohibited, and guess what? We found there was room for *ten* billion people. And then twenty. And then fifty. And now seventy-five. Taller buildings, more efficient food production, greater concentra-

tion of people on the unproductive land. So who are we to
say that our descendants won't continue to cope with expanding
population, on up to five hundred billion, a thousand billion,
who knows? The twentieth century wouldn't have believed it
was possible to support this many people on Earth. So if we
worry in advance about a problem that may in fact never
cause any trouble, if we unblessworthily thwart god by
limiting births, we sin against life without any assurance
that—"

"Pah!" Artha snorts. "You will never understand us. And I
suppose we will never understand you." Rising, she strides
toward the door. "Tell me this, then. If the urbmon way is so
wonderful, why did you slip away, and go out wandering in
our fields?" And she does not stay for an answer. The door
clicks behind her; he goes to it and finds that she has locked
it. He is alone. And still a prisoner.

A long drab day. No one comes to him, except the girl
bringing lunch: in and out. The stench of the cell oppresses
him. The lack of a cleanser becomes unbearable; he imagines
that the filth gathering on his skin is pitting and corroding it.
From his narrow window he watches the life of the commune,
craning his neck to see it all. The farming machines coming
and going. The husky peasants loading sacks of produce aboard
a conveyor belt disappearing into the ground—going, no doubt,
to the courier-pod system that carries food to the urbmons
and industrial goods to the communes. Last night's scapegoat, Milcha, passes by, limping, bruised, apparently exempt
from work today; villagers hail her with obvious reverence.
She smiles and pats her belly. He does not see Artha at all.
Why do they not release him? He is fairly certain that he has
convinced her he is no spy. And in any case can hardly harm
the commune. Yet here he remains as the afternoon fades.
The busy people outside, sweating, sun-tanned, purposeful.
He sees only a speck of the commune: outside the scope of
his vision there must be schools, a theater, a governmental
building, warehouses, repair shops. Images of last night's
unbirth dance glow morbidly in his memory. The barbarism;
the wild music; the agony of the woman. But he knows that it
is an error to think of these farmers as primitive, simple
folk, despite such things. They seem bizarre to him, but
their savagery is only superficial, a mask they don to set
themselves apart from the urban people. This is a complex

society held in a delicate balance. As complex as is his own. Sophisticated machinery to care for. Doubtless a computer center somewhere, controlling the planting and tending and harvesting of the crops, that requires a staff of skilled technicians. Biological needs to consider: pesticides, weed suppression, all the ecological intricacies. And the problems of the barter system that ties the commune to the urbmons. He perceives only the surface of this place, he realizes.

In late afternoon Artha returns to his cell.

"Will they let me go soon?" he asks immediately.

She shakes her head. "It's under discussion. I've recommended your release. But some of them are very suspicious people."

"What do you mean?"

"The chiefs. You know, they're old men, most of them, with a natural mistrust of strangers. A couple of them want to sacrifice you to the harvest god."

"Sacrifice?"

Artha grins. There is nothing stony about her now; she is relaxed, clearly friendly. On his side. "It sounds horrid, doesn't it? But it's been known to happen. Our gods occasionally demand lives. Don't you ever take life in the urbmon?"

"When someone threatens the stability of our society, yes," he admits. "Lawbreakers go down the chute. In the combustion chambers at the bottom of the building. Contributing their body mass to our energy output. But—"

"So you kill for the sake of keeping everything running smoothly. Well, sometimes so do we. Not often. I don't really think they'll kill you. But it isn't decided yet."

"When will it be?"

"Perhaps tonight. Or tomorrow."

"How can I represent any threat to the commune?"

"No one says you do," Artha tells him. "Even so, to offer the life of an urbmon man may have positive values here. Increasing our blessings. It's a philosophical thing, not easy to explain: the urbmons are the ultimate consumers, and if our harvest god symbolically consumed an urbmon instead— in a metaphorical way, taking you to stand for the whole society you come from—it would be a mystic affirmation of the unity of the two societies, the link that binds commune to urbmon and urbmon to commune, and—oh, never mind. Maybe they'll forget about it. It's only the day after the unbirth dance; we don't need any more sacred protection so

soon. I've told them that. I'd say your chances of going free
are fairly good."

"Fairly good," he repeats gloomily. "Wonderful." The distant sea. The ashy cone of Vesuvius. Jerusalem. The Taj
Mahal. As far away as the stars, now. The sea. The sea. This
stinking cell. He chokes on despair.

Artha tries to cheer him. Squatting close beside him on the
tipsy floor. Her eyes warm, affectionate. Her earlier military
brusqueness gone. She seems fond of him. Getting to know
him better, as though she has surmounted the barrier of
cultural differences that made him seem so alien to her
before. And he the same with her. The separations dwindling. Her world is not his, but he thinks he could adjust to
some of its unfamiliar assumptions. Strike up a closeness.
He's a man, she's a woman, right? The basics. All the rest is
façade. But as they talk, he is plunged again and again into
new awarenesses of how different she is from him, he from
her. He asks her about herself and she says she is unmarried.
Stunned, he tells her that there are no unmarried people in
the urbmons past the age of twelve or thirteen. She says she
is thirty-one. Why has someone so attractive never married?
"We have enough married women here," she replies. "I had
no reason to marry." Does she not want to bear children? No,
not at all. The commune has its alloted number of mothers.
She has other responsibilities to occupy her. "Such as?" She
explains that she is part of the liaison staff handling urbmon
commerce. Which is why she can speak the language so well;
she deals frequently with the urbmons, arranging for ex-
changes of produce for manufactured goods, setting up servic-
ing arrangements whenever the commune's machinery suffers
a breakdown beyond the skills of the village technicians, and
so forth. "I may have monitored your calls occasionally," he
says. "Some of the nodes I prime run through the procure-
ment level. If I ever get back home, I'll listen for you, Artha."
Her smile is dazzling. He begins to suspect that love is
blossoming in this cell.

She asks him about the urbmon.

She has never been inside one; all her contacts with the
urban monads come via communications channels. A vast
curiosity is evident in her. She wants him to describe the
residential apartments, the transport system, liftshafts and
dropshafts, the schools, the recreational facilities. Who prepares the food? Who decides what professions the children

will follow? Can you move from one city to another? Where do you keep all the new people? How do you manage not to hate each other, when you must live so close together? Don't you feel like prisoners? Thousands of you milling about like bees in a hive—how do you stand it? And the stale air, the pale artificial light, the separation from the natural world. Incomprehensible to her: such a narrow, compressed life. And he tries to tell her about the urbmon, how even he, who chose to flee from it, really loves it. The subtle balance of need and want in it, the elaborate social system designed for minimal friction and frustration, the sense of community within one's own city and village, the glorification of parenthood, the colossal mechanical minds in the service core that keep the delicate interplay of urban rhythms coordinated—he makes the building seem a poem of human relationships, a miracle of civilized harmonies. His words soar. Artha seems captivated. He goes on and on, in a kind of rapture of narrative, describing toilet facilities, sleeping arrangements, screens and data terminals, the recycling and reprocessing of urine and feces, the combustion of solid refuse, the auxiliary generators that produce electrical power from accumulated surplus body heat, the air vents and circulation system, the social complexity of the building's different levels, maintenance people here, industrial workers there, scholars, entertainers, engineers, computer technicians, administrators. The senior citizen dorms, the newlywed dorms, the marriage customs, the sweet tolerance of others, the sternly enforced commandment against selfishness. And Artha nods, and fills in words for him when he leaves a sentence half finished to hurry on to the next, and her face grows flushed with excitement, as if she too is caught up in the lyricism of his account of the building. Seeing for the first time in her life that it is not necessarily brutal and antihuman to pack hundreds of thousands of people into a single structure in which they spend their entire lives. As he speaks he wonders whether he is not letting himself be carried away by his own rhetoric; the words rushing from him must make him sound like an impassioned propagandist for a way of life about which, after all, he had come to have serious doubts. But yet he goes on describing, and by implication praising, the urbmon. He will not condemn. There was no other way for humanity to develop. The necessity of the vertical city. The beauty of the urbmon. It's wondrous complexity, its intricate texture. Yes, of course, there is beauty outside it, he admits that, he has gone in search of it, but it is folly to think that the urbmon itself is something loathsome, something to be deplored. In its own way magnificent. The unique solution to the population crisis. Heroic response to immense challenge. And he thinks he is getting through to her. This shrewd, cool commune woman, raised under the hot sun. His verbal intoxication transforms itself into something explicitly sexual, now: he is communicating with Artha, he is reaching her mind, they are coming together in a way that neither of them would have thought possible yesterday, and he interprets this new closeness as a physical thing. The natural eroticism of the urbmondweller: everyone accessible to everyone else at all times. Confirm their closeness by the direct embrace. It seems like the most reasonable extension of their communion, from the conversational to the copulatory. So close already. Her eyes shining. Her small breasts. Reminding him of Micaela. He leans toward her. Left hand slipping around her shoulders, fingers groping for and finding her nearer breast. Cupping it. Nuzzles the line of her jaw with his lips, going toward her earlobe. His other hand at her waist, seeking the secret of her one garment. In a moment she'll be naked. His body against hers, approaching congruency. Cunning experienced fingers opening the way for his thrust. And then.

"No. Stop."

"You don't mean that, Artha." Loosening the glossy red wrap now. Clutching the hard little breast. Hunting for her mouth. "You're all tensed up. Why not relax? Loving is blessworthy. Loving is—"

"*Stop it!*"

Flinty again. A sharp-edged command. Suddenly struggling in his arms.

Is this the commune mode of lovemaking? The pretense of resistance? She grasps at her wrap, pushes him with her elbow, tries to bring up her knee. He surrounds her with his arms and attempts to press her to the floor. Still caressing. Kissing. Murmuring her name.

"Get *off*."

This is a wholly new experience for him. A reluctant woman, all sinews and bone, fighting his advances. In the urbmon she could be put to death for this. Unblessworthy thwarting of a fellow citizen. But this is not the urbmon. This is not the urbmon. Her struggles inflame him; as it is he has gone several days without a woman, the longest span of abstinence he can remember, and he is stiff, agonizingly erect, carrying a blazing sword. No finesse possible; he wants in, as quickly as it can be managed. "Artha. Artha. Artha." Primordial grunts. Her body pinned beneath him. The wrap off; as they fight he catches a glimpse of slender thighs, matted auburn delta. The flat girlish belly of the unchilded. If he can only get his own clothes off somehow, while holding her down. Fighting like a demon. Good thing she wasn't wearing her weapon when she came in. Watch out, the eyes! Panting and gasping. A wild flurry of hammering fists. The salty taste of blood on his split lip. He looks into her eyes and is appalled. Her rigid, murderous gaze. The harder she fights, the more he wants her. A savage! If this is how she fights, how will she love? His knee between her legs, slowly forcing them apart. She starts to scream; he gets his mouth down on her lips; her teeth hunt for his flesh. Fingernails clawing his back. She is surprisingly strong. "Artha," he begs, "don't fight me. This is insanity. If you'll only—"

"Animal!"

"Let me show you how much I love—"

"Lunatic!"

Her knee suddenly in his crotch. He pivots, avoiding the worst of her attack, but she hurts him anyway. This is no coy game. If he wants to have her, he must break her strength. Immobilize her. Raping an unconscious woman? No. No. It has all gone wrong. Sadness overwhelms him. His lust suddenly subsides. He rolls free of her and kneels near the window, looking at the floor, breathing hard. Go on, tell the old men what I did. Feed me to your god. Naked, standing above him, she sullenly dons her wrap. The harsh sound of her breathing. He says, "In an urbmon, when someone makes sexual advances, it's considered highly improper to refuse him." His voice hollow with shame. "I was attracted to you, Artha. I thought you were to me. And then it was too late for me to stop myself. The whole idea that someone might refuse me—I just didn't understand—"

"What animals you all must be!"

Unable to meet her eyes. "In context, it makes sense. We can't allow explosive frustration-situations. No room for conflicts in an urbmon. But here—it's different, is it?"

"Very."

"Can you forgive me?"

"We couple with those we deeply love," she says. "We don't open for anyone at all who asks. Nor is it a simple thing. There are rituals of approach. Intermediaries must be employed. Great complications. But how could you have known all that?"

"Exactly. How could I?"

Her voice whiplashing with irritation and exasperation. "We were getting along so well! Why did you have to touch me?"

"You said it yourself. I didn't know. I didn't know. The two of us together—I could feel the attraction growing—it was so natural for me to reach out toward you—"

"And it was so natural for you to rape me when you felt me resisting."

"I stopped in time, didn't I?"

A bitter laugh. "So to speak. If you call that stopping. If you call that in time."

"Resistance isn't an easy thing for me to understand, Artha. I thought you were playing a game with me. I didn't realize at first that you were refusing me." Looking up at her now. Her eyes holding mingled contempt and sorrow. "It was all a misunderstanding, Artha. Can't we turn time back half an hour? Can't we try to put things together again?"

"I will remember your hands on my body. I will remember your making me naked."

"Don't carry a grudge. Try to look at it from my point of view. The cultural gulf between us. A different set of assumptions in operation. I—"

She shakes her head slowly. No hope of forgiveness.

"Artha—"

She goes out. He sits alone in the dusk. An hour later, his dinner comes for him. Night descends; he eats with no interest in his food, nursing his bitterness. Engulfed by shame. Although he insists he was not entirely at fault. A clash of irreconcilable cultures. It was so natural for him. It was so natural. And the sadness. Thinking of how close they had come to be before it happened. How close.

Several hours after sundown they begin building a new bonfire in the plaza. He watches gloomily. She has gone to the village elders, then, to tell them of his attack on her. An outrage; they console her and promise vengeance. Now they will surely sacrifice him to their god. His last night of life. All the turmoil of his existence converging on this day. No one to grant a final wish. He'll die miserably, his body unclean. Far from home. So young. Jangling with unfulfilled desires. Never to see the sea.

And what's this, now? A farming machine being trundled up close to the fire, a giant upright thing, five meters high, with eight long, jointed arms, six many-kneed legs, a vast mouth. Some kind of harvester, maybe. Its polished brown metallic skin reflecting the fire's leaping red fingers. Like a mighty idol. Moloch. Baal. He sees his body swept aloft in the great clutching fingers. His head nearing the metal mouth. The villagers capering about him in rhythmic frenzy. Bruised swollen Milcha chanting ecstatically as he goes to his doom. Icy Artha rejoicing in her triumph. Her purity restored by his sacrifice. The priests droning. Please, no. No. Perhaps he's all wrong. Last night, the sterility rite, he thought they were punishing the pregnant one. And she was really the most honored one. But how vicious that machine looks! How deadly!

The plaza is full of villagers now. A major event.

Listen, Artha, it was merely a misunderstanding. I thought you desired me, I was acting within the context of my society's mores, can't you see that? Sex isn't a big complicated operatic thing with us. It's like exchanging smiles. Like touching hands. When two people are together and there's an attraction, they do it, because why not? I only wanted to give you pleasure, really. We were getting along so well together. Really.

The sound of drums. The awful skirling screeches of out-of-tune wind instruments. Orgiastic dancing is starting. God bless, I want to live! Here are the priests and priestesses in their nightmare masks. No doubt of it, the full routine. And I'm the central spectacle tonight.

An hour passes, and more, and the scene in the plaza grows more frenzied, but no one comes to fetch him. Has he misunderstood again? Does tonight's ritual actually concern him as little as did the one last night?

A sound at his door. He hears the lock turning. The door opens. The priest must be coming for him. So now the end is near, eh? He braces himself, hoping for a painless finish. To die for metaphorical reasons, to become a mystic link binding commune to urbmon—such a fate seems improbable and unreal to him. But it is about to befall him all the same.

Artha enters the cell.

She closes the door quickly and presses her back against it. The only illumination is the streaming firelight glaring through his window; it shows her to him with her face tense and stern, her body rigid. This time she wears her weapon. Taking no chances.

"Artha! I—"

"Quiet. If you want to live, keep your voice down."

"What's happening out there?"

"They prepare the harvest god."

"For me?"

"For you."

He nods. "You told them I tried to rape you, I suppose. And now my punishment. All right. All right. It isn't fair, but who expects fairness?"

"I told them nothing," she says. "It was their decision, taken at sundown. I did not cause this."

She sounds sincere. He wonders.

She goes on. "They will take you before the god at midnight. Just now they are praying that he will receive you gracefully. It is a lengthy prayer." She walks cautiously past him, as though expecting him to pounce on her again, and looks out the window. Nods to herself. Turns. "Very well. No one will notice. Come with me, and make no sound whatever. If I'm caught with you, I'll have to kill you and say you were trying to escape. Otherwise it'll be my life too. Come. Come."

"Where?"

"*Come!*" A fierce impatient whispered gust.

She leads him from the cell. In wonder he follows her through a labyrinth of passages, through dank subterranean chambers, through tunnels barely wider than himself, and they emerge finally at the back of the building. He shivers: a chill in the night air. Music and chanting floating toward him from the plaza. Artha gestures, runs out between two houses, looks in all directions, gestures again. He runs after her. By quick nervous stages they reach the other edge of the commune. He glances back; from here he can see the fire, the idol, the tiny dancing figures, like images on a screen. Ahead of him are the fields. Above him the crescent sliver of the moon, the shining sprawl of the stars. A sudden sound. Artha clutches at him and tugs him down, under a clump of shrubs. Her body against his; the tips of her breasts like points of fire. He does not dare to move or speak. Someone goes by: a sentry, maybe. Broad back, thick neck. Out of sight. Artha, trembling, holds his wrists, keeping him down. Then at last getting up. Nodding. Silently saying the way is clear. She slips into the fields, between the burgeoning rows of tall, leafy plants. For perhaps ten minutes they trot away from the village, until his untrained body is gasping for breath. When she halts, the bonfire is only a stain on the distant horizon and the singing is drowned out by the chirping of insects. "From here you go by yourself," she tells him. "I have to return. If anyone misses me for long, they might suspect."

"Why did you do this?"

"Because I was unjust to you," she says, and for the first time since coming to him this evening she manages to smile. A ghost-smile, a quick flicker, the merest specter of the warmth of the afternoon. "You were drawn to me. There was no way for you to know our attitudes about such things. I was cruel, I was hateful—and you were only trying to show love. I'm sorry, Statler. So this is my atonement. Go."

"If I could tell you how grateful—"

His hand lightly touches her arm. He feels her quiver—in desire, in disgust, what?—and on a sudden insane impulse he pulls her into an embrace. She is taut at first, then melting. Lips to lips. His fingers on her bare muscular back. Do I dare touch her breasts? Her belly pressed to his. He has a quick wild vision of this afternoon's breach healed: Artha sinking gladly to the sweet earth here, drawing him down on her and into her, the union of their bodies creating that metaphorical link between urbmon and commune that the elders would have forged with his blood. But no. It is an unrealistic vision, however satisfying artistically. There will be no coupling in the moonlit field. Artha lives by her code. Obviously these thoughts have passed through her mind in these few seconds, and she has considered and rejected the possibilities of a passionate farewell, for now she slides free of him, severing the contact moments before he can capitalize on her partial surrender. Her eyes bright and loving in the darkness. Her smile awkward and divided. "Go, now," she whispers. Turning. Running back a dozen paces toward the commune. Turning again, gesticulating with the flats of her hands, trying to push him into motion. "Go. Go. What are you standing there for?"

Hurriedly through the moonsilvered night. Stumbling, lurching, tripping. He does not bother to pick a cautious route between the rows of growing things; in his haste he tramples plants, pushes them aside, leaves a swath of destruction by which, come dawn, he could readily be traced. He knows he must get out of the commune's territory before morning. Once the crop sprayers are aloft they can easily find him and bring him back to feed him to thwarted Moloch. Possibly they will send the sprayers out by night to hunt for him, as soon as they find that he has escaped. Do those yellow eyes see in the dark? He halts and listens for the horrid droning sound, but all is still. And the farming machines—will they go forth to track him down? He has to hurry. Presumably if he gets beyond the commune's domain he will be safe from the worshipers of the harvest god.

Where shall he go?

There is only one destination conceivable now. Looking toward the horizon, he sees the awesome columns of the Chipitts urbmons, eight or ten of them visible from here as brilliant beacons, thousands of windows ablaze. He cannot pick out individual windows, but he is aware of constant shiftings and flowings in the patterns of light as switches go on and off. The middle of the evening there. Concerts, somatic contests, glow-duels, all the nightly amusements in full swing. Stacion sitting home, fearful, wondering about him. How long has he been gone? Two days, three? All blurred. The littles crying. Micaela distraught, probably quarreling mercilessly with Jason to ease her tension. While here he is, many kilometers away, newly fled from a world of idols and rites, of pagan dancing, of unyielding and infertile women. Mud on his shoes, stubble on his cheeks. He must look awful and smell worse. No access to a cleanser. What bacteria now breed in his flesh? He must go back. His muscles ache so desperately that he has passed into a discomfort beyond mere fatigue. The reek of the cell clings to his nostrils. His tongue feels furry and puffed. He imagines that his skin is cracking from exposure to sun, moon, air.

What of the sea? What of Vesuvius and the Taj Mahal?

Not this time. He is willing to admit defeat. He has gone as far as he dares, and for as much time as he can permit himself; now with all his soul he longs for home. His conditioning asserting itself after all. Environment conquering genetics. He has had his adventure; someday, god willing, he will have another; but his fantasy of crossing the continent, slipping from commune to commune, must be abandoned. Too many idols wait with polished jaws, and he may not be lucky enough to find an Artha in the next village. Home, then.

His fear ebbs as the hours pass. No one and nothing pursues him. He slips into a steady, mechanical rhythm of march, step and step and step and step, hauling himself robotlike toward the vast towers of the urban monads. He has no idea what time it is, but he supposes it must be past midnight; the moon has swung far across the sky, and the urbmons have grown dimmer as people go to sleep. Night-walkers now prowl there. Siegmund Kluver of Shanghai dropping in to see Micaela, maybe. Jason on his way to his grubbo sweethearts in Warsaw or Prague. Another few hours, Michael supposes, and he will be home. It took him only from sunrise to late afternoon to reach the commune, and that was with much circuitous rambling; with the towers rising before him at all times he will have no difficulty going straight to his goal.

All is silence. The starry night has a magical beauty. He almost regrets his decision to return to the urbmon. Under the crystalline sky he feels the pull of nature. After perhaps four hours walking he stops to bathe in an irrigation canal, and emerges naked and refreshed; washing with water is not as satisfying as getting under the ultrasonic cleanser, but at least he no longer need be obsessed with the layers of grime and corruption clinging to his skin. More springily, now, he strides along. His adventure already is receding into history: he encapsulates it and retrospectively relives it. How good to have done this. Tasting the fresh air, the dawn's mist, dirt under his fingernails. Even his imprisonment now seems a high excitement rather than an imposition. Watching the unbirth dance. His fitful, unconsummated love for Artha. Their struggle and their dreamlike reconciliation. The gaping jaws of the idol. The fear of death. His escape. What man of Urbmon 116 has done such things?

This access of self-congratulation gives him strength that sends him plunging on, across the commune's unending fields, in renewed vigor. Only the urbmons seem to be getting no closer. A trick of perspective. His weary eyes. Is he heading, he wonders, towards 116? It would be a sad prank of topography to get turned about and come into the urban constellation at 140 or 145 or so. If, say, he is moving at an angle to his true course, the divergence could be immense by the end of his march, leaving him with a dreadful numbing hypotenuse to traverse. He has no way of knowing which of the urbmons ahead of him is his own. He simply goes onward.

The moon vanishes. The stars fade. Dawn is creeping in.

He has reached the zone of unused land between the commune's rim and the Chipitts constellation. His legs are ablaze, but he forces himself on. So close to the buildings that they seem to hang, unsupported, in midair. The formal gardens in view. Robot gardeners serenely going about their trade. Blossoms opening to the first light of day. Perfume drifting on the soft breeze. Home. Home. Stacion. Micaela. Get some rest before going back on the interface. Find a plausible excuse.

Which is Urbmon 116?

The towers bear no numbers. Those who live inside them know where they live. Half staggering, Michael approaches the nearest building. Its flanks illuminated with radiant dawnlight. Looking up a thousand floors. The delicacy, the complexity, of its myriad tiny chambers. Beneath him the mysterious underground roots, the power plants, the waste-processing plants, the hidden computers, all the concealed wonders that give the urbmon its life. And above, rising like some immense vegetable growth, its sides marvelously intricate, a hatchwork of textures, the urbmon. Within the hundreds of thousands of interwoven lives, artists and scholars, musicians and sculptors, welders and janitors. His eyes are moist. Home. Home. But is it? He goes to the hatch. Holds up his wrist, shows the egress pass. The computer authorized to admit him on demand. "If this is Urbmon 116, open up! I'm Michael Statler." Nothing happening. Scanners scanning him, but all stays sealed. "What building is this?" he asks. Silence. "Come on," he says. "Tell me where I am!"

A voice from an invisible speaker says, "This is Urban Monad 123 of the Chipitts constellation."

123! So many kilometers from home!

But he can only continue. Now the sun is above the horizon and turning quickly from red to gold. If that is the east, then where is Urbmon 116? He calculates with a numbed mind. He must go east. Yes? No? He plods through the interminable series of gardens separating 123 from its eastern neighbor, and interrogates the speaker at the hatch.

Yes: this is Urbmon 122. He proceeds. The buildings are set at long diagonals, so that one will not shade the next, and he moves down the center of the constellation, keeping careful count, while the sun climbs and swarms over him. Dizzy, now, with hunger and exhaustion. Is this 116? No, he must have lost count; it will not open for him. Then this?

Yes. The hatch slides back as he offers his pass. Michael clambers in. Waiting as the door rolls shut behind him. Now the inner door to open. Waiting. Well? "Why don't you open?" he asks. "Here. Here. Scan this." Holding up his pass. Perhaps some kind of decontamination procedure. No telling what he's brought in from outside. And now the door opens.

Lights in his eyes. A dazzling glare. "Remain where you are. Make no attempt to leave the entryway." The cold metallic voice nailing him where he stands. Blinking, Michael takes half a step forward, then realizes it might be unwise and stops. A sweetsmelling cloud engulfs him. They have sprayed him with something. Congealing fast, forming a security cocoon. The lights now go down. Figures blocking his path: four, five of them. Police. "Michael Statler?" one of them asks.

"I have a pass," he says uncertainly. "It's all quite legitimate. You can check the records. I—"

"Under arrest. Alteration of program, illicit departure from building, undesirable harboring of countersocial tendencies. Orders to immobilize you immediately upon your return to building. Now carried out. Mandatory sentence of erasure to follow."

"Wait a minute. I have the right of appeal, don't I? I demand to see—"

"Case has already been considered and referred to us for final disposition." A note of inexorability in the policeman's tone. They are at his sides, now. He cannot move. Sealed within the hardening spray. Whatever alien microorganisms he has collected are sealed in it with him. To the chute? No. No. Please. But what else did he expect? What other outcome could there be? Did he think he had fooled the urbmon? Can you repudiate an entire civilization and hope to slip yourself smoothly back into it? They have loaded him aboard some kind of dolly. Dim shapes outside the cocoon. "Let's get a detailed print of this on the record, boys. Move him toward the scanners. Yes. That's it."

"Can't I see my wife, at least? My sister? I mean, what harm will it do if I just talk to them one last time—"

"Menace to harmony and stability, dangerous countersocial tendencies, immediate removal from environment to prevent spreading of reactive pattern." As though he carries a plague of rebelliousness. He has seen this before: the summary judgment, the instant execution. And never really understood. And never imagined.

Micaela. Stacion. Artha.

Now the cocoon is fully hardened. He sees nothing outside it.

"Listen to me," he says, "whatever you're going to do, I want you to know that *I've been there*. I've seen the sun and the moon and the stars. It wasn't Jerusalem, it wasn't the Taj Mahal, but it was something. That you never saw. That you never will. The possibilities out there. The hope of enlarging your soul. What would you understand about that?"

Droning sounds from the far side of the milky web that contains him. They are reading him the relevant sections of the legal code. Explaining how he threatens the structure of society. Necessary to eradicate the source of peril. The words blend and mingle and are lost to him. The dolly begins to roll forward again.

Micaela. Stacion. Artha.

I love you.

"Okay, open the chute." Clear, unmistakable, unambiguous.

He hears the rushing of the tide. He feels the crash of the waves against the sleek shining sands. He tastes salt water. The sun is high; the sky is aglow, a flawless blue. He has no regrets. It would have been impossible ever to leave the building again; if they had let him live, it would be only under conditions of constant surveillance. The urbmon's million million watching eyes. A lifetime hanging on the interface. What for? This is better. To have lived a little bit, just once. To have seen. The dancing, the bonfire, the smell of growing things. And now he is so tired, anyway. Rest will be welcome. He feels a sense of movement. Pushing the dolly again. In and then down. Good-bye. Good-bye. Good-bye. Calmly descending. In his mind the leafy cliffs of Capri, the boy, the goat, the flask of cool golden wine. Fog and dolphins, thorns and pebbles. God bless! He laughs within his cocoon. Going down. Good-bye. Micaela. Stacion. Artha. A final vision of the building comes to him, its 885,000 people moving blankfaced

through the crowded corridors, floating upward or downward
in the transportation shafts, jamming themselves into the
sonic centers and the Somatic Fulfillment Halls, sending a
myriad of messages along the communications nexus as they
ask for their meals, talk with one another, make assignations,
negotiate. Breeding. Fruitful and multiply. Hundreds of thousands of people on interlocking orbits, each traveling his own
little circuit within the mighty tower. How beautiful the
world is, and all that is in it. The urbmons at sunrise. The
farmers' fields. Good-bye.

Darkness.

The journey is over. The source of peril has been eradicat-
ed. The urbmon has taken the necessary protective steps,
and an enemy of civilization has been removed.

Seven

This is the bottom. Siegmund Kluver prowls uneasily among
the generators. The weight of the building presses crushingly
on him. The whining song of the turbines troubles him. He
feels disoriented, a wanderer in the depths. How huge this
room is: an immense box far below the ground, so big that
the globes of light in its ceiling are barely able to illuminate
the distant concrete floor. Siegmund creeps along a catwalk
midway between floor and ceiling. Palatial Louisville three
kilometers above his head. Carpets and draperies, inlays of
rare woods, the trappings of power, very far away now. He
hadn't meant to come here, not this far down. Warsaw was his
intended destination tonight. But somehow first here. Stalling
for time. Siegmund is frightened. Searching for an excuse not
to do it. If they only knew. The cowardice within. Un-
Siegmundlike.

He rubs his hands along the catwalk railing. Cold metal,
shaky fingers. A constant throbbing boom running through
the building here. He is not far from the terminus of the
chutes that convey solid wastes to the power plant: discards
of all kinds, old clothes, used date cubes, wrappers and
packages, the bodies of the dead, occasionally the bodies of
the living, coursing down the spiraling slideways and tum-

bling into the compactors. And moving thence on gliding belts into the combustion chambers. The liberation of heat for electrical generation: waste not, want not. The electrical load is heavy at this hour. Every apartment is lit. Siegmund closes his eyes and receives a vision of urban Monad 116's 885,000 people linked by an enormous tangle of wiring. A giant human switchboard. And I am no longer plugged into it. Why am I no longer plugged into it? What has happened to me? What is happening to me? What is about to happen to me?

Sluggishly he moves along the catwalk and passes out of the generating room. Entering a sleek-walled tunnel; behind its glossy paneled sides, he knows, run the transmission lines along which power flows toward the debooster circuitry. And here the reprocessing plant—urine pipes, fecal reconversion chambers. All the wondrous stuff by which the urbmon lives. No other human being in sight. The heavy weight of the solitude. Siegmund shivers. He must go up to Warsaw soon. Yet he continues to drift like a touring schoolchild through the utility center at the urbmon's lowest level. Hiding here from himself. The cold eyes of electronic scanners staring at him out of hundreds of shielded openings in floors and walls and ceilings. I am Siegmund Kluver of Shanghai, 787th floor. I am fifteen years and five months old. My wife's name is Mamelon, my son is Janus, my daughter is Persephone. I am assigned to work duty as a consultant in Louisville Access Nexus and within the next twelve months I will undoubtedly receive notice of my promotion to the highest administrative levels of this urban monad. Therefore shall I rejoice. I am Siegmund Kluver of Shanghai, 787th floor. He bows to the scanners. All hail. All hail. The future leader. Passing his hand nervously through his coarse bushy hair. For an hour now he has wandered about down here. You should go up. What are you afraid of? To Warsaw. To Warsaw.

He hears the voice of Rhea Shawke Freehouse, coming as though from a recording mounted at the core of his brain. *If I were you, Siegmund, I'd relax and try to enjoy myself more. Don't worry about what people think, or seem to think, about you. Soak up human nature, work at being more human yourself. Go around the building; do some nightwalking in Warsaw or Prague, maybe. See how simpler people live.* Shrewd words. Wise woman. Why be afraid? Go up. Go up. It's getting late.

Standing outside a NO ADMITTANCE hatch leading to one of the computer ganglia, Siegmund spends several minutes steadying the tremor of his right hand. Then he hurries to the liftshaft and tells it to take him to the sixtieth floor. The middle of Warsaw.

Narrow corridors, here. Many doors. A compressed quality to the atmosphere. This is a city of extraordinarily high population density, not only because the inhabitants are so blessworthy in their fecundity, but also because much of the city's area is given over to industrial plants. Even though the building is much broader here than in its upper reaches, the citizens of Warsaw are pushed together into a relatively small residential zone. Here are the machines that stamp out machines. Dies, lathes, templates, reciprocators, positioners, fabrication plaques. Much of the work is computerized and automated, but there is plenty for human beings to do: feeding the conveyors, guiding and positioning, driving the fork-lifts, tagging the finished work for its destination. Late last year Siegmund pointed out to Nissim Shawke and Kipling Freehouse that nearly everything being done by human labor in the industrial levels could be handled by machines; instead of employing thousands of people in Warsaw, Prague, and Birmingham, they could set up a totally automated output program, with a few supervisors to keep watch over inventory homeostasis, and a few maintenance men to handle emergencies, such as repairing the repair machines. Shawke gave him a patronizing smile. "But if they had no work, what would all those poor people do with their lives?" he asked. "Do you think we can turn them into poets, Siegmund? Professors of urban history? We deliberately devise labor for them, don't you see?" And Siegmund embarrassed by his naïveté. A rare failure, for him, of insight into the methodology of government. He still feels uncomfortable about that conversation. In an ideal commonwealth, he believes, every person should have meaningful work to do. He wishes the urban monad to be an ideal commonwealth. But yet certain practical considerations of human limitations interpose themselves. But yet. But yet. The makework in Warsaw is a blot on the theory.

Pick a door. Say, 6021. 6023. 6025. Strange to see the apartments bearing four-digit numbers. 6027. 6029. Siegmund puts his hand to the knob. Hesitates. A rush of sudden timidity. Imagining, within, a brawny hairy growling sullen working-class husband, a shapeless weary working-class wife. And he must intrude on their intimacies. Their resentful glare upon seeing his upper-level clothing. What is this Shanghai dandy doing here? Doesn't he have any regard for decency? And so forth. And so forth. Siegmund almost flees. Then he takes hold of himself. They dare not refuse. They dare not be sullen. He opens the door.

The room is dark. Only the nightglow on; his eyes adjust and he sees a couple on the sleeping platform and five or six littles on cots. He approaches the platform. Stands over the sleepers. His imagined portrait of the room's occupants altogether inaccurate. They could be any young married pair of Shanghai, Chicago, Edinburgh. Strip away the clothes, let sleep eradicate the facial expressions denoting position in the social matrix, and distinctions of class and city perhaps disappear. The naked sleepers are only a few years older than Siegmund—he maybe nineteen, she possibly eighteen. The man slender, narrow shoulders, unspectacular muscles. The woman trim, standard, agreeable body, soft yellow hair. Siegmund lightly touches her shoulder. A ride of bone lying close beneath the skin. Blue eyes flickering open. Fear giving way to understanding: oh, a nightwalker. And understanding giving way to confusion: the nightwalker wears upper-building clothes. Etiquette demands an introduction. "Siegmund Kluver," he says. "Shanghai."

The girl's tongue passes hurriedly over her lips. "Shanghai? Really?" The husband awakes. Blinking, puzzled. "Shanghai?" he says. "What for, down here, huh?" Not hostile, just wondering. Siegmund shrugs, as if to say a whim, a fancy. The husband gets off the platform. Siegmund assures him that it isn't necessary for him to leave, that it'll be quite all right to have him here, but that kind of thing evidently isn't practiced in Warsaw: the arrival of the nightwalker is the signal for the husband to clear out. Loose cotton wrap already over his pale, almost hairless body. A nervous smile: see you later, love. And out. Siegmund alone with the woman. "I never met anybody from Shanghai before," she says.

"You haven't told me your name."

"Ellen."

He lies down beside her. Stroking her smooth skin. Rhea's words echo. *Soak up human nature. See how simpler people live.* He is so tightly drawn. His flesh mysteriously invaded by a spreading network of fine golden wires. Penetrating the lobes of his brain. "What does your husband do, Ellen?"

"He's on fork-lift now. Used to be a cabler, but he got hurt sheathing. The whiplash."

"He works hard, doesn't he?"

"The sector boss says he's one of the best. I think he's okay, too." A sniggering little giggle. "What floors are Shanghai, anyway? That's someplace around 700, isn't it?"

"761 to 800." Caressing her haunches. Her body quivers—fear or desire? Shyly her hand goes to his clothing. Maybe just eager to get him in and out and gone. The frightening stranger from the upper levels. Or else not accustomed to foreplay. A different milieu. He'd rather talk awhile first. *See how simpler people live.* He's here to learn, not merely to top. Looking around the room: the furnishings drab and crude, no grace, no style. Yet designed by the same craftsmen who furnish Louisville and Toledo. Obviously aiming for a low taste. A prevailing film of grayness over everything. Even the girl. I could be with Micaela Quevedo now. I could be with Principessa. Or with. Or perhaps with. But I am here. He searches for probing questions to ask. To bring out the essential humanity of this obscure person over whom he one day will help to rule. Do you read much? What are your favorite screen shows? What sort of foods do you like? Are you doing what you can to help your littles rise in the building? What do you think of the people down in Reykjavik? And those in Prague? But he says nothing. What's the use? What can he learn? Impassable barriers between person and person. Touching her here and here and here. Her fingers on him. He is still soft.

"You don't like me," she says sadly.

He wonders how often she uses the cleanser. "Maybe I'm a little tired," he says. "So busy these days." Pressing his body against hers. The warmth of her possibly will resurrect him. Her eyes staring into his. Blue lenses over inner emptiness. He kisses the hollow of her throat. "Hey, that tickles!" she says, wriggling. He trails his fingers down her belly. To the core of her. Hot and moist and ready. But he isn't. Can't. "Is there anything special?" she asks. "If it isn't too complicated maybe I could." He shakes his head. He isn't interested in whips and chains and thongs. Just the usual. But he can't. His fatigue only a pretense; what cripples him is his sense of isolation. Alone among 885,000 people. And I can't reach her.

Not even with this. Pushing the limp rod against her gate.
The Shanghai swell, incapable, unmanned. Now she is no
longer afraid of him and not very sympathetic. She takes his
failure as a sign of his contempt for her. He wants to tell her
how many hundreds of women he has topped in Shanghai and
Chicago, and even Toledo. Where he is regarded as devilishly
virile. Desperately he turns her over. His sweaty belly against
her cool buttocks. "Listen, I don't know what you think
you're doing, but—" Even this won't help. She squirms indignantly. He releases her. Rises, adjusts himself. Face blazing.
As he goes to the door he looks back. She is sitting up wan-
tonly, looking mockery at him. Makes a gesture with three
fingers, no doubt a scabrous obscenity here. He says, "I just
want you to know. The name I gave you when I came in—it
isn't mine. That's not me at all." And goes hastily out. So
much for soaking up human nature. So much for Warsaw.

He takes the liftshaft randomly to 118, Prague, gets out,
walks halfway around the building without entering any
apartment or speaking to anyone he meets; gets into a
different liftshaft; goes up to 173 in Pittsburgh; stands for
awhile in a corridor, listening to the pounding of the blood in
the capillaries of his temples. Then he steps into a Somatic
Fulfillment Hall. Even at this late hour there are people
making use of its facilities: a dozen or so in the whirl-pool
tumbler, five or six prancing on the treadmill, a few couples
in the copulatorium. His Shanghai clothes earn him some
curious stares but no one approaches him. Feeling desire
return, Siegmund moves vaguely toward the copulatorium,
but at its entrance he loses heart and turns aside. Shoulders
slumping, he goes slowly out of the Somatic Fulfillment Hall.
Now he takes to the stairs, plodding up the great coil that
runs the whole thousand-floor height of Urban Monad 116.
He looks up the mighty helix and sees the levels stretching
toward infinity, with banks of lights glittering above him to
denote each landing. Birmingham, San Francisco, Colombo,
Madrid. He grasps the rail and looks down. Eyes spiraling
along the descending path. Prague, Warsaw, Reykjavik. A
dizzying vortex; a monstrous well through which the light of a
million globes drifts from above like snowflakes. He clambers
doggedly up the myriad steps. Hypnotized by his own mechanical movements. Before he realizes it, he has climbed
forty floors. Sweat drenches him and the muscles of his calves

are bunching and knotting. He yanks open the doorway and lurches out into the main corridor. This is the 213th floor. Birmingham. Two men with the smirking look of nightwalkers on their way home stop him and offer him some kind of groover, a small translucent capsule containing a dark, oily orange fluid. Siegmund accepts the capsule without a word and swallows it unquestioningly. They tap his biceps in a show of good fellowship and go on their way. Almost at once he feels nausea. Then blurred red and blue lights sway before his eyes. He wonders dimly what they have given him. He waits for the ecstasy. He waits. He waits.

The next thing he knows, the thin light of dawn is in his eyes and he is sitting in an unfamiliar room, sprawled out in a web of oscillating, twanging metal mesh. A tall young man with long golden hair stands over him, and Siegmund can hear his own voice saying, "Now I know why they go flippo. One day it just gets to be too much for you. The people right up against your skin. You can feel them. And—"

"Easy. Back it up a little. You're overloading."

"My head is about to explode." Siegmund sees an attractive red-haired woman moving around in the far corner of the room. He is having difficulty focusing his eyes. "I'm not sure I know where I am," he says.

"370th. That's San Francisco. You're really sectioned off, aren't you?"

"My head. As if it needs to be pumped out."

"I'm Dillon Chrimes. My wife, Electra. She found you wandering in the halls." His host's friendly face smiling into his. Strange blue eyes, like plaques of polished stone. "About the building," Chrimes says. "You know, one night not too long ago I took a multiplexer and I *became* the whole crotting building. And really flew on it. You know, seeing it as one big organism, a mosaic of thousands of minds. Beautiful. Until I started to come down, and on the downside it struck me as just an awful hideous beehive of a place. You lose your perspective when you mess your mind with chemicals. But then you regain it."

"I can't regain it."

"What's the good of hating the building? I mean, the urbmon's a real solution to real problems, isn't it?"

"I know."

"And most of the time it works. So it's a sterilizer to waste your time hating it."

"I don't hate it," Siegmund says. "I've always admired the theory of verticality in urban thrust. My specialty is urbmon administration. Was. Is. But suddenly everything's all wrong, and I don't know where the wrongness is. In me or in the whole system? And maybe not so suddenly."

"There's no real alternative to the urbmon," Dillon Chrimes says. "I mean, you can jump down the chute, I guess, or run off to the communes, but those aren't sensible alternatives. So we stay here. And groove on the richness of it all. You must just have been working too hard. Look, you want something cold to drink?"

"Please. Yes," Siegmund says.

The red-haired woman puts a flask in his hand. As she leans toward him, her breasts sway out. tolling like fleshy bells. She is quite beautiful. A tiny spurt of hormones within him. Reminding him of how this night had begun. Nightwalking in Warsaw. A girl. He has forgotten her name. His failure to top her.

Dillon Chrimes says, "The screen's been broadcasting an alarm for Siegmund Kluver of Shanghai. Tracers out for him since 0400. Is that you?"

Siegmund nods.

"I know your wife. Mamelon, right?" Chrimes shoots a glance at his own wife. As if there is a jealousy problem here. In a lower tone he says to Siegmund, "Once when I was doing a performance in Shanghai I met her on a nightwalk. Lovely. That cool grace of hers. A statue full of passion. Probably very worried about you right now, Siegmund."

"Performance?"

"I play the vibrastar in one of the cosmos groups." Chrimes makes ecstatic keyboard gestures with his fingers. "You've probably seen me. How about letting me put through a call to your wife, all right?"

Siegmund says, "A purely personal thing. A sense of coming apart. Or breaking loose from my roots."

"What?"

"A kind of rootlessness. As though not belonging in Shanghai, not belonging in Louisville, not belonging in Warsaw, not belonging anywhere. Just a cluster of ambitions and inhibitions, no real self. And I'm lost inside."

"Inside what?"

"Inside myself. Inside the building. A sense of coming apart. Leaving pieces of me all over the place. Films of self peeling away, drifting off." Siegmund realizes that Electra Chrimes is staring at him. Appalled. He struggles for self-control. Sees himself stripped down to the bone. Spinal column exposed, the comb of vertebrae, the oddly angular cranium. Siegmund. Siegmund. Dillon Chrimes' earnest, troubled face. A handsome apartment. Polymirrors, psychedelic tapestries. These happy people. Fulfilled in their art. Plugged into the switchboard. "Lost," Siegmund says.

"Transfer to San Francisco," Chrimes suggests. "We don't push hard here. We can make room. Maybe you'll discover artistic talent. You could write programs for the screen shows, maybe. Or—"

Siegmund laughs harshly. His throat is furry. "I'll write this show about the hungry rung-grabber who gets almost to the top and decides he doesn't want it. I'll—no, I won't. I don't mean any of this. It's the groover talking out of my mouth. Those two slipped me a filther, that's all. You'd better call Mamelon." Getting to his feet. Trembling. A sensation of being at least ninety years old. He starts to fall. Chrimes and his wife catch him. His cheek against Electra's swaying breasts. Siegmund manages a smile. "It's the groover talking out of my mouth," he says again.

"It's a long dull story," he tells Mamelon. "I got into a place where I didn't want to be, and somehow I took a capsule without knowing what I was taking, and everything got confused after that. But I'm all right now. I'm all right."

After a day's medical absence he returns to his desk in Louisville Access Nexus. A pile of memoranda awaits him. Much need of his services by the great men of the administrative class. Nissim Shawke wants him to do a follow-up reply to the petitioners from Chicago, on that business of asking for freedom to determine the sex of one's offspring. Kipling Freehouse requests an intuitive interpretation of certain figures in the next quarter's production-balance estimates. Monroe Stevis is after a double flow-chart showing attendance at sonic centers plotted against visits to blessmen and consolers: a psychological profile of the populations of six cities. And so on. Picking his brains. How blessworthy to be useful. How wearying to be used.

He does his best, laboring under his handicap. A sense of coming apart. A dislocation of the soul.

Midnight. Sleep will not come. He lies beside Mamelon, tossing. He has topped her, and still his nerves rustle in the darkness. She knows he is awake. Her soothing hand roams him.

"Can't you relax?" she asks.

"It gets harder."

"Would you like some tingle? Or even mindblot."

"No. Nothing."

"Go nightwalking then," she suggests. "Burn up some of that energy. You're all wired up, Siegmund."

Held together by golden thread. Coming apart. Coming apart.

Go up to Toledo, maybe? Seek consolation in Rhea's arms. She always is helpful. Or even nightwalk in Louisville. Drop in on Nissim Shawke's wife Scylla. The audacity of it. But they were trying to push me onto her at that party, Somatic Fulfillment Day. Seeing whether I had the blessmanship to deserve promotion to Louisville. Siegmund knows he failed a test that day. But maybe it is not too late to undo that. He will go to Scylla. Even if Nissim's there. See, I have the requisite amorality! See, I defy all bounds. Why should a Louisville wife not be accessible to me? We all live under the same code of law, regardless of the inhibitions of custom that we have lately imposed upon ourselves. So he will say if he finds Nissim. And Nissim will applaud his bravado.

"Yes," he tells Mamelon. "I think I'll nightwalk."

But he remains on the sleeping platform. Some minutes go by. A failure of impulse. He does not want to go; he pretends to be asleep, hoping Mamelon will doze. Some minutes more. Cautiously he opens one eye, slit-wide. Yes, she sleeps. How beautiful she is, how noble even while asleep. The fine bones, the pale skin, the jet-black hair. My Mamelon. My treasure. Lately he has felt little desire even for her. Boredom born of fatigue? Fatigue born of boredom?

The door opens and Charles Mattern comes in.

Siegmund watches the sociocomputator tiptoe toward the platform and silently undress. Mattern's lips are tightly compressed, his nostrils flaring. Signs of yearning. His penis already half erect. Mattern hungers for Mamelon; something has been developing between them over the past two months,

Siegmund suspects, something more than mere nightwalking. Siegmund hardly cares. Just so she is happy. Mattern's harsh breathing loud in the room. He starts to awaken Mamelon.

"Hello, Charles," Siegmund says.

Mattern, caught by surprise, flinches and laughs nervously. "I was trying not to wake you, Siegmund."

"I've been up. Watching you."

"You might have said something, then. To save me all this stealthing around."

"I'm sorry. It didn't occur to me."

Mamelon is awake now too. Sitting up, bare to the waist. A stray coil of ebony hair passing deliciously across her pink left nipple. The whiteness of her skin illuminated by the faint glow of the nightlight. Smiling chastely at Mattern: the dutiful female citizen, ready to accept her nocturnal visitor.

Siegmund says, "Charles, as long as you're here, I can tell you that I've got an assignment to do that'll involve working with you. For Stevis. He wants to see if people are spending more time than usual with blessmen and consolers, and less in sonic centers. A double flow-chart that—"

"It's late, Siegmund." Curtly. "Why don't you tell me about it in the morning."

"Yes. All right. All right." Flushing, Siegmund rises from the sleeping platform. He does not have to leave, even with a nightwalker here for Mamelon, but he does not want to stay. Like a Warsaw husband, granting a superfluous and unasked privacy to the other two. He hurriedly finds some clothing. Mattern reminds him that he's free to remain. But no. Siegmund leaves, a little wildly. Almost running down the hall. I will go up to Louisville, to Scylla Shawke. However, instead of asking the liftshaft to take him to the level where the Shawkes live, he calls out a Shanghai floor, 799. Charles and Principessa Mattern live there. He does not dare risk attempting Scylla while he is in this jangled state. Failure could be costly. Principessa will do. A tigress, she is. A savage. Her sheer animal vigor may restore his well-being. She is the most passionate woman he knows, short of Mamelon. And a good age, ripe but not overripe. Siegmund halts outside Principessa's door. It strikes him that it is somewhat bourgeois, something of a pre-urbmon thing, for him to be seeking the wife of the man who is now with his own wife. Nightwalking should be more random, less structured, merely a way of extending the rang of one's life-experiences.

Nevertheless. He nudges the door open. Relieve and dismayed to hear sounds of ecstasy from within. Two people on the platform: he sees arms and legs that must be Principessa's, and, covering her, emitting earnest grunts, is Jason Quevedo, thrusting and pumping. Siegmund quickly ducks out. Alone in the corridor. Where to, now? The world is too complicated for him tonight. The obvious next destination is Quevedo's apartment. For Micaela. But no doubt she will have a visitor too. Siegmund's forehead begins to throb. He does not want to roam the urbmon endlessly. He wants only to go to sleep. Nightwalking suddenly seems an abomination to him: forced, unnatural, compulsive. The slavery of absolute freedom. At this moment thousands of men roam the titanic building. Each determined to do the blessworthy thing. Siegmund, scuffing at the floor, strolls along the corridor and halts by a window. Outside, a moonless night. The sky ablaze with stars. The neighboring urbmons seeming farther away than usual. Their windows bright, thousands of them. He wonders if it is possible to see a commune, far to the north. The crazy farmers. Micaela Quevedo's brother Michael, the one who went flippo, supposedly visited a commune. At least so the story goes. Micaela still brooding about her brother's fate. Down the chute with him as soon as he stuck his head back inside the urbmon. But of course a man like that can't be permitted to resume his former life here. An obvious malcontent, spreading poisons of dissatisfaction and unblessworthiness. A hard thing for Micaela, though. Very close to her brother, she says. Her twin. Thinks he should have had a formal hearing in Louisville. He did, though. She won't believe it, but he did. Siegmund remembers when the papers came through. Nissim Shawke issuing the decree: if this man ever returns to 116, dispose of him at once. Poor Micaela. Something unhealthy going on, maybe, between her and her brother. I might ask Jason. I might.

Where shall I go now?

He realizes that he has been standing by the window for more than an hour. He stumbles toward the stairs and jogs down twelve levels to his own. Mattern and Mamelon lie sleeping side by side. Siegmund drops his clothing and joins them on the platform. Coming apart. Dislocation. Finally he sleeps too.

The solace of religion. Siegmund has gone to see a blessman. The chapel is on the 770th floor: a small room off a commercial arcade, decorated with fertility symbols and incrustations of captive light. Entering, he feels like an intruder. Never any religious impulses before. His mother's grandfather was a Christer, but everyone in the family assumed it was because the old man had antiquarian instincts. The ancient religions have few followers, and even the cult of god's blessing, which is officially supported by Louisville, can claim no more than a third of the building's adult population, according to the last figures Siegmund has seen. Though perhaps things are changing lately.

"God bless," the blessman says, "what is your pain?"

He is plump, smooth-skinned, with a round complacent face and cheerily shining eyes. At least forty years old. What does he know of pain?

"I have begun not to belong," Siegmund says. "My future is unraveling. I am coming unplugged. Everything has lost its meaning and my soul is hollow."

"Ah. Angst. Anomie. Dissociation. Identity drain. Familiar complaints, my son. How old are you?"

"Past fifteen."

"Career profile?"

"Shanghai going on Louisville. Perhaps you know of me. Siegmund Kluver."

The blessman's lips go taut. The eyes veil themselves. He toys with sacred emblems on his tunic's collar. He has heard of Siegmund, yes.

He says, "Are you fulfilled in your marriage?"

"I have the most blessworthy wife imaginable."

"Littles?"

"A boy and a girl. We will have a second girl next year."

"Friends?"

"Sufficient," Siegmund says. "And yet this feeling of decomposition. Sometimes my skin itchy all over. Films of decay drifting through the building and wrapping themselves about me. A great restlessness. What's happening to me?"

"Sometimes," the blessman says, "those of us who live in the urban monads experience what is called the crisis of spiritual confinement. The boundaries of our world, that is to say our building, seem too narrow. Our inner resources become inadequate. We are grievously disappointed in our relationships with those we have always loved and admired. The result of such a crisis is often violent: hence the flippo

phenomenon. Others may actually leave the urbmon and
seek a new life in the communes, which, of course, is a form
of suicide, since we are incapable of adapting to that harsh
environment. Now, those who neither go berserk nor separate themselves physically from the urbmon occasionally undertake an internal migration, drawing into their own souls
and, in effect, contracting as a response to the impingement
of adjacent individuals on their psychic space. Does this have
any meaning for you?" As Siegmund nods doubtfully, the
blessman goes smoothly on, saying, "Among the leaders of
this building, the executive class, those who have been
propelled upward by the blessworthy drive to serve their
fellow men, this process is particularly painful, bringing
about as it does a collapse of values and a loss of motivation.
But it can be easily cured."

"Easily?"

"I assure you."

"Cured? How?"

"We will do it at once, and you will go out of here healthy
and whole, Siegmund. The way to health is through kinship
with god, you see, god being considered in our view the
integrative force giving wholeness to the universe. And I will
show you god."

"You will show me god," Siegmund repeats, uncompre-
hending.

"Yes. Yes." The blessman, bustling around, is busy darkening
the chapel, switching off lights and cutting in opaquers. From
the floor sprouts a cup-shaped web-seat into which Siegmund
is gently nudged. Lying there looking up. The chapel's
ceiling, he discovers, is a single broad screen. In its glassy
green depths an image of the heavens appears. Stars strewn
like sand. A billion billion points of light. Music issues from
concealed speakers: the plashy plinks of a cosmos group. He
makes out the magical sounds of a vibrastar, the dark twangs
of a comet-harp, the wild lurches of an orbital diver. Then the
whole group going at once. Perhaps Dillon Chrimes is playing.
His friend of that dismal night. Overhead the depth of the
perceptive field is deepening; Siegmund sees the orange glint
of Mars, the pearly blaze of Jupiter. So god is a light-show
plus a cosmos group? How shallow. How empty.

The blessman, speaking over the music, says, "What you
see is a direct relay from the thousandth floor. This is the sky
over our urbmon at our present moment. Look into the black

cone of night. Accept the cool light of the stars. Open yourself to the immensity. What you see is god. What you see is god."

"Where?"

"Everywhere. Immanent and all-enduing."

"I don't see."

The music is turned up. Siegmund now is surrounded by a cage of heavy sound. The astronomical scene takes on a greater intensity. The blessman directs Siegmund's attention to this group of stars and to that, urging him to merge with the galaxy. The urbmon is not the universe, he murmurs. Beyond these shining walls lies an awesome vastness that is god. Let him take you into himself and heal you. Yield. Yield. Yield. But Siegmund cannot yield. He wonders if the blessman should have given him some sort of drug, a multiplexer of some kind that would make it easier for him to open himself to the universe. But the blessman scoffs at the idea. One can reach god without chemical assistance. Simply stare. Contemplate. Peer into infinity. Search for the divine pattern. Meditate on the forces in balance, the beauties of celestial mechanics. God is within and without us. Yield. Yield. Yield. "I still don't feel it," Siegmund says. "I'm locked up inside my own head." A note of impatience enters the blessman's tone. What's wrong with you, he seems to be saying. Why can't you? It's a perfectly good religious experience. But it is no use. After half an hour Siegmund sits up, shaking his head. His eyes hurt from staring at the stars. He cannot make the mystical leap. He authorizes a credit transfer to the blessman's account, thanks him, and goes out of the chapel. Perhaps god was somewhere else today.

The solace of the consoler. A purely secular therapist, relying heavily on metabolic adjustments. Siegmund is apprehensive about seeing him; he has always regarded those who have to go to a consoler as somehow defective, and it pains him to be joining that group. Yet he must end this inner turmoil. And Mamelon insists. The consoler he visits is surprisingly young, perhaps thirty-three, with a pinched, bleak face and frosty, ungenerous eyes. He knows the nature of Siegmund's complaint almost before it is described to him. "And when you attended this party in Louisville," he asks, "what effect did it have on you to learn that your idols weren't quite the men you thought they were?"

"It emptied me out," Siegmund says. "My ideals, my values, my guiding images. To see them cavorting like that. Never having imagined they did. I think that's where all the trouble started."

"No," says the consoler, "that's merely where the trouble surfaced. It was there before. In you, deep, waiting for something to push it up into view."

"How can I learn to cope with it?"

"You can't. You'll have to be sent into therapy. I'm going to turn you over to the moral engineers. You can use a reality adjustment."

He is afraid of being changed. They will put him into a tank and let him drift there for days or weeks, while they cloud his mind with their mysterious substance and whisper things to him and massage his aching body and alter the imprinting of his brain. And he will come forth healthy and stable and different. Another person. All his Siegmundness lost along with his anguish. He remembers Aurea Holson, whose number came up in the lottery for the stocking of the new Urbmon 158, and who did not want to go, and who was persuaded by the moral engineers that it would not be so bad to leave her native urbmon. And came forth from her tank docile and placid, a vegetable in place of a neurotic. Not for me, Siegmund thinks.

It will be the end of his career, too. Louisville does not want men who have had crises. They will find some middle-rung post for him in Boston or Seattle, some tepid minor administrative job, and forget about him. A formerly promising young man. Full reports on reality adjustments are placed each week before Monroe Stevis. Stevis will tell Shawke and Freehouse. Have you heard about poor Siegmund? Two weeks in the tank. Some sort of breakdown. Yes, sad. Very sad. We'll drop him, of course.

No.

What can he do? The consoler has already made up the adjustment request and filed it with one of the computer nodes. Sparkling impulses of neural energy are traveling through the information system, bearing his name. Time is being cleared for him on the 780th floor, among the moral engineers. Soon his screen will tell him the hour of his appointment. And if he does not go to them, they will come for him. The machines with soft rubbery pads on their arms, gathering him up, pushing him along.

No.

He tells Rhea of his predicament. Not even Mamelon knows yet, but Rhea. He can trust her. His best interests at heart. "Don't go to the engineers," she advises.

"Don't go? How? The order's already in."

"Have it countermanded."

He looks at her as though she has recommended demolition of the Chipitts urbmon constellation.

"Pull it out of the computer," she tells him. "Get one of the interface men to do it for you. Use your influence. Nobody'll find out."

"I couldn't do that."

'You'll go to the moral engineers, then. And you know what that means."

The urbmon is toppling. Clouds of debris swirl in his brain. Who would arrange such a thing for him?

Micaela Quevedo's brother worked in an interface crew, didn't he? But he's gone now. There must be others within his grasp, though. When he leaves Rhea, Siegmund consults the records in the access nexus. The virus of unblessworthiness already at work in his soul. Then he realizes he doesn't even need to use his influence. Merely make it a matter of professional routine. In his office he taps out a data requisition: status of Siegmund Kluver, remanded for therapy on 780th floor. Instantly comes the information that Kluver is due for therapy in seventeen days. The computer does not withhold data from Louisville Access Nexus. The presumption exists that anyone who asks, using the equipment in the nexus, has the right to do so. Very well. The vital next step. Siegmund instructs the computer to yank the therapy assignment for Siegmund Kluver. This time there is a bit of resistance: the computer wants to know who authorizes the yanking. Siegmund meditates on that for a moment. Then inspiration comes. The therapy of Siegmund Kluver, he informs the machine, is being canceled by order of Siegmund Kluver of the Louisville Access Nexus. Will it work? "No," the machine may say, "you can't cancel your own therapy appointment. Do you think I'm stupid?" But the mighty computer *is* stupid. Thinking with the speed of light but unable to cross the gaps of intuition. Does Siegmund Kluver of Louisville Access Nexus have the right to cancel a therapy appointment? Yes, certainly; he must be acting on behalf of Louisville itself. Therefore let it be canceled. The instructions flicker through the proper node. No matter whose appointment it is, as long as authority to cancel can be attributed properly. It is done. Siegmund taps out a data requisition: status of Siegmund Kluver, remanded for therapy on 780th floor. Instantly comes the information that Kluver's appointment for therapy has been canceled. His career is safe, then. But he is left with his anguish. There is that to consider.

This is the bottom. Siegmund Kluver prowls uneasily among the generators. The weight of the building presses crushingly on him. The whining song of the turbines troubles him. He feels disoriented, a wanderer in the depths. How huge this room is.

He enters apartment 6029, Warsaw. "Ellen?" he says. "Listen, I've come back. I want to apologize for the last time. It was all a tremendous mistake." She shakes her head. She has already forgotten him. But she is willing to accept him, naturally. The universal custom. Her legs parted, her knees flexed. Instead he kisses her hand. "I love you," he whispers, and flees.

This is the office of Jason Quevedo, historian, on the 185th floor, Pittsburgh. Where the archives are. Jason sits before his desk, manipulating data cubes, as Siegmund enters. "It's all here, isn't it?" Siegmund asks. "The story of the collapse of civilization. And how we rebuilt it again .Verticality as the central philosophical thrust of human congruence patterns. Tell me the story, Jason. Tell me." Jason looking at him strangely. "Are you ill, Siegmund?" And Siegmund: "No, not at all. How perfectly healthy I am. Micaela's been explaining your thesis to me. The genetic adaptation of humanity to urbmon life. I'd like more details. How we've been bred to be what we are. We happy many." Siegmund picks up two of Jason's cubes and fondles them, almost sexually, leaving fingerprints on their sensitive surfaces. Tactfully Jason takes them from him. "Show me the ancient world," Siegmund says, but as Jason slips a cube into the playback slot, Siegmund goes out.

* * *

This is the great industrial city of Birmingham. Pale, sweating, Siegmund Kluver watches machines stamping out machines. While slumped and sullen human handlers supervise the work. This thing with arms will help in next autumn's harvest at a commune. This dark glossy tube will fly above the fields, spraying insects with poison. Siegmund finds himself weeping. He will never see the communes. He will never dig his fingers into the rich brown soil. The beautiful meshing ecology of the modern world. The poetic interplay of commune and urbmon for the benefit of all. How lovely. How lovely. Then why am I weeping?

San Francisco is where the musicians and artists and writers live. The cultural ghetto. Dillon Chrimes is rehearsing with his cosmos group. The thunderous web of sounds. An intruder. "Siegmund?" Chrimes says, breaking his concentration. "How are you getting along, Siegmund? Good to see you." Siegmund laughs. He gestures at the vibrastar, the comet-harp, the incantator, and the other instruments. "Please," he murmurs, "keep on playing. I'm simply looking for god. You don't mind if I listen? Maybe he's here. Play some more."

On the 761st floor, Shanghai's bottom level, he finds Micaéla Quevedo. She does not look well. Her black hair is dull and stringy, her eyes are bitter, her lips are clamped. Seeing Siegmund in midday startles her. He says quickly, "Can we talk awhile? I want to ask you some things about your brother Michael. Why he left the building. What he hoped to find out there. Can you give me any information?" Micaéla's expression grows even harder. Coldly she says, "I don't know a thing. Michael went flippo, that's all that matters. He didn't explain himself to me." Siegmund knows that this is untrue. Micaéla is concealing vital data. "Don't be unblessworthy," he urges. "I need to know. Not for Louisville. Just for myself." His hand on her thin wrist. "I'm thinking of leaving the building, too," Siegmund confides.

He halts at his own apartment on the 787th floor. Mamelon is not there. As usual, she is at the Somatic Fulfillment Hall, enhancing her supple body. Siegmund records a brief message for her. "I loved you," he says. "I loved you. I loved you."

*   *   *

He meets Charles Mattern in a Shanghai hallway. "Come have dinner with us," the sociocomputator says. "Principessa's always happy to see you. And the children. Indra and Sandor talk about you. Even Marx. When's Siegmund coming again, they say? We like Siegmund so much." Siegmund shakes his head. "I'm sorry, Charles. Not tonight. But thanks for asking." Mattern shrugs. "God bless, we'll get together soon, eh?" he says, and strolls away, leaving Siegmund in the midst of the flow of pedestrian traffic.

This is Toledo, where the pampered children of the administrative caste make their homes. Rhea Shawke Freehouse lives here. Siegmund does not dare pay a call on her. She is too perceptive; she will understand at once that he is in a terminal phase of collapse, and undoubtedly will take preventive action. But yet he must make some move in her direction. Siegmund pauses outside her apartment and tenderly presses his lips to the door. Rhea. Rhea. Rhea. I loved you too. He goes up.

Nor does he make any visits in Louisville, though it would please him to see some of the masters of the urbmon tonight, Nissim Shawke or Monroe Stevis or Kipling Freehouse. Magical names, names that resonate in his soul. Best to bypass them. He goes directly to the landing stage on the thousandth floor. Stepping out on the flat breeze-swept platform. Night, now. The stars glittering fiercely. Up there is god, immanent and all-enduing, floating serenely amidst the celestial mechanics. Below Siegmund's feet is the totality of Urban Monad 116. What is today's population? 888,904. Or some such. +131 since yesterday and +9,902 since the first of the year, adjusted for the departure of those who went to stock the new Urbmon 158. Maybe he has the figures all wrong. It hardly matters. The building is athrob with life, at any rate. Fruitful and multiplying. God bless! So many servants of god. Shanghai's 34,000 souls. Warsaw. Prague. Tokyo. The ecstasy of verticality. In this single slender tower we compress so many thousands of lives. Plugged into the same switchboard. Homeostasis, and the defeat of entrophy. We are well organized here. All thanks to our dedicated administrators.

And look, look there! The neighboring urbmons! The wondrous row of them! Urbmon 117, 118, 119, 120. The fifty-one towers of the Chipitts constellation. Total population now 41,516,883. Or some such. And east of Chipitts lies Boshwash. And west of Chipitts is Sansan. And across the sea is Berpar and Wienbud and Shankong and Bocarac. And more. Each cluster of towers with its millions of encapsulated souls. What is the population of our world now? Has it reached 76,000,000,000 yet? They project 100,000,000,000 for the not too distant future. Many new urbmons must be built to house those added billions. Plenty of land left though. And they can put platforms on the sea.

To the north, on the horizon, he imagines he can see the blaze of a commune's bonfires. Like the flash of a diamond in sunlight. The farmers dancing. Their grotesque rites. Bringing fertility to the fields. God bless! It is all for the best. Siegmund smiles. He stretches forth his arms. If he could only embrace the stars, he might find god. He walks to the very edge of the landing stage. A railing and a force-field protect him against the vagrant gusts of wind that might hurl him to his death. It is very windy here. Three kilometers high, after all. A needle sticking into god's eye. If he could only spring into the heavens. Looking down as he floats past, seeing Chipitts below, the rows of towers, the farmland surrounding them, the miraculous urban rhythm of verticality plotted against the miraculous commune rhythm of horizontality. How beautiful the world is tonight. Siegmund throws his head back. Eyes shining. And there is god. The blessman was right. There! There! Wait, I'm coming! Siegmund mounts the railing. Teeters a little. Currents of wind buffeting him. He has risen above the protective forcefield. It seems almost as though the whole building is swaying. Think of the body heat that 888,904 human beings under the same roof must generate. Think of the waste products they daily send down the chute. All these linked lives. The switchboard. And god watching over us. I'm coming! I'm coming. Siegmund flexes his knees, gathers his strength, sucks air deep into his lungs. And sails toward god in a splendid leap.

Now the morning sun is high enough to touch the uppermost fifty stories of Urban Monad 116. Soon the building's entire eastern face will glitter like the bosom of the sea at daybreak. Thousands of windows, activated by the dawn's early photons, deopaque. Sleepers stir. Life goes on. God bless! Here begins another happy day.

ABOUT THE AUTHOR

ROBERT SILVERBERG was born in New York and makes his home in the San Francisco area. He has written several hundred science fiction stories and over seventy science fiction novels, including *Lord Valentine's Castle*, *Majipoor Chronicles*, *Valentine Pontifex*, *Dying Inside*, *Thorns*, *The Book of Skulls*, *Star of Gypsies* and *At Winter's End*. He has won three Hugo awards and five Nebula awards. He is a past president of the Science Fiction Writers of America.